Auschwitz Rose

A novel by Father Edward B. Gabriel

Inspired by the true story of Helena Citrónová and Franz Wunsch

PART ONE

1

Rimavská Sobota, Czechoslovakia
October 1942

The ground rumbled, and the boy froze.

It was strictly *verboten* to be outside after dark, but that silly kitten of his had slipped out the window again and he needed to find it before someone else caught and ate it. He was being careful, making sure nobody saw him, but still... He was quite nervous. Some of the other kids he sometimes played with during the day spoke of creatures that roamed the streets at night, snatching naughty children and taking them to a horrible, horrible place from whence they never returned.

He wasn't sure he quite believed them, but some kids *had* simply vanished without a trace. Like that boy who always cheated at marbles. And that girl who had once offered to teach him what else he could do with his little man before it was too late, whatever *that* meant. And not only children either. Adults too. One day they were there, and the next... poof, they were not, taken away never to be seen again.

The rumble came once more, but this time the boy also saw a flash of light in the distance. He felt his little knees weaken and he backed into an alley, hiding in the darkness and in his haste tripping over an abandoned bicycle. The boy and the bike in turn fell into a pile of empty trashcans, causing such a ruckus that his heart just about leaped out of his chest. Somewhere above him someone, an old woman by the sound of the voice, yelled something he didn't understand. He paid her no attention. He had much more pressing matters to attend, such as returning home as quickly as he could and to hell with that damn kitten. It was so skinny he couldn't imagine anyone wanting to stew it anyway.

But to return home, he'd have to get away from those creatures he now knew did haunt the streets at night.

The creatures were now so close that he could hear their growl. He had to get out of here before they got any closer and found him; the only problem was that he had nowhere to go. On each side of him rose tall buildings and the alley dead ended after about 100 feet, stoppered by a brick wall he had no hope of climbing. The wall hadn't always been there, the men in the gray uniforms had erected it the year before, but that didn't matter. It was there today, and today it marked the boundaries of his world, and today it meant that he was trapped like a rat.

His only hope was to run straight ahead, as fast as he could, but that meant risking detection and possibly capture by the creatures. His bowels constricted and he noticed that his bladder was burning. Tears welled in his eyes. He wiped them away with closed fists and fought to control his quivering lips as he resolved to go out with a fight. If the creatures wanted to take him away, well... let them try. He'd give them all he had. He'd been in fights before, nothing new there, and he'd always held his own.

The boy bent down and righted the bicycle. He had no idea if it belonged to someone, but if it did, well maybe that someone should have taken better care of it. And besides. He had no intention of actually keeping it, he was just borrowing it. He'd return it the next day... if he still lived, of course.

The bike was much too big for him and the tires felt a little soft, but that couldn't be helped. Somewhere in the distance a dog began barking in alarm – or perhaps it had smelled his kitten, who knew? - but then came the sound of a slap and a whine and then silence. The rumble was getting closer, louder, nastier. The boy briefly considered staying put, or perhaps hiding at the very back of the alley, flattening himself against the wall where the darkness was deepest in the hope that the creatures would simply pass him by... but no. He knew that'd never do. The creatures were almost right on top of him and any minute now they'd smell him, smell his fear, smell his sweat, smell his blood, smell his unwashed body, and they'd hone right in on him. Nowhere on Earth was there a hole deep enough to hide from them.

He had to get out of here. Now. His life depended on it. Hesitating any longer meant certain death.

The boy stepped back about fifteen steps, holding the bicycle with trembling hands. He took a deep breath and silently wished for his father to miraculously appear and whisk him to safety. But knowing that he was on his own, he began running as fast as he could, pumping his short legs as rapidly as possible, mindless of the pebbles and shards of broken glass that cut at his feet. The bike felt a little wobbly and one of the wheels was clearly bent, but he had reached the mouth of the alley and it was time to go.

He launched himself on the seat at the last possible moment and emerged into the deserted street just as the convoy of trucks came around the corner. The boy looked to his right and was momentarily blinded by the headlights of the lead vehicle. The truck was less than twenty feet away and headed straight for him. The driver, a convicted murderer who'd been granted his release when he'd accepted to join the army, jumped in surprise and his first reflex was to hit the brakes, but he caught himself just in time. If he braked suddenly, he risked being rear-ended by the truck behind him and causing a chain-reaction of collisions that would probably land him back in jail.

The driver also remembered, in a flash, who lived here, who these people were, what they represented, and mostly what he was here to do. Running one of them over would simply mean one less to transport. Nobody would care. So he grinned and instead of braking, he floored the accelerator, knowing that he would barely feel the impact of running over such a puny creature. His headlights sliced through the darkness like a sharp blade through putrid flesh and he burst out laughing at the boy frozen in the middle of the road, the urge to kill that ran in his blood as demented as ever.

The boy's entire world was now filled by the light of those headlamps and by the roar of the engine. The creature had clearly seen him – how could it have not, with such huge, luminous eyes? – and it howled as it readied to devour him. In a moment it would open its maw and swallow him whole, and the next day his friends would wonder, but only briefly, what had become of him before returning to their play.

The boy sent up a silent apology to his parents for having been so naughty, for the anguish his disappearance would certainly cause them, and he prepared to fight and die. He'd try punching the creature in the eye, a tactic he'd used with some success in the past, in the hope that the pain would distract it long enough for him to get away. But really... what chance did he stand against such a nightmarish monster?

Acting on their own, independently of his paralyzed mind, his feet instinctively found the pedals. They barely touched, but barely would be enough. This night, barely would have to do. The tip of his toes against the cold metal jolted the boy into action and, without really realizing it, he began pedaling. He had to stand up and get off the seat to propel himself, and even then the bike's horizontal bar banged painfully against his crotch, but at least he was moving forward.

The truck, the creature, was less than six feet behind him. In less than a second it would be too late. The boy bent over the handlebars and pushed down one last time with all his might; the bike swerved to the right and the truck roared angrily by, so close that the blast of wind in its wake destabilized him. He fell off the bicycle, tumbling head over heels and disappearing from the view of the truck driver, who cursed and slapped the dashboard with both hands.

The boy disentangled himself from the wrecked bike and stood up. He'd banged his left knee hard and his right shoulder hurt, but he wasn't seriously injured. He watched as the trucks vanished around the corner, their red lights trailing behind them, and he finally saw them for what they really were: mechanized contraptions, not demons out to devour little children. And with that realization, his fear suddenly vanished.

Trucks, not monsters. Trucks. Mere trucks.

Chastising himself for a fool, the boy dusted the grit and dirt from his clothes and wondered how much trouble he'd be in when he got home. Surely his absence would have been noticed by now. He didn't doubt that his father would...

Home. That single thought made him look up and after the trucks again. They'd turned left, which meant that... that... which meant that there was only one place they could possibly be going.

The boy ran after them with every last ounce of strength he had left, hoping he wouldn't be too late but knowing that he likely would be.

Adriana couldn't sleep. She had gone to bed almost an hour ago but sleep eluded her; the thin, scratchy sheet itched and her empty stomach wouldn't quiet down.

She had heard her little brother slip out earlier. She hadn't said anything. She had no idea if her parents also knew of his nightly escapades, but she'd have to tell them eventually if he kept this up. First though, she'd talk to him about it the next morning. Again. The boy was restless, something she understood only too well, but this needed to stop. They had all done their best to shield him from the madness that had descended on them all, but that had proved to be a double-edged sword since the child clearly didn't fully appreciate the danger they were in. Maybe she'd have to scare him straight with the truth.

God knew, the truth was scary enough.

God. Now there was Someone she'd like to have a word with. The first question she'd ask him would be, where are You? Then, why are You allowing this to happen? If You truly are all-powerful and all-knowing, why aren't You stopping this insanity? Why not simply wipe those animals off the face of the Earth? What purpose could their continued existence possibly serve? She knew rabbi Rubenstein would sternly disapprove of such questions, but what did she care what that old fool thought?

So many questions, so few answers. She snickered in the dark. Who could go on believing in God when the Devil clearly ruled the Earth? Certainly not her. Her parents still prayed, and she prayed along with them so as not to make things even worse, but the truth was that her heart had turned as dark and as cold as the night outside. She no longer believed. Not in God, not in hope, not in love, and certainly not in her fellow man. Not in anything. Tonight, alone and hungry in her bed, all she believed in was the despair she felt.

She had almost drifted off to sleep when she heard a noise outside. Immediately, in the room next to hers, there was a thump as her father jumped out of his own bed and ran to the window. She heard her mother murmur something urgently to him, the fear in her tone chilling Adriana's soul through the walls, and his reply was just as urgent and as tainted with worry.

Adriana threw the covers away and found her slippers. Her heart was racing and her mind had gone blank. She stood in the middle of her room, incapable of thought or movement, her hands clasped to her chest, staring at her closed door as though expecting it to burst open at any moment. You always think these things happened solely to others, she thought, until such a day came as they happened to you. That day was today. Today she and her family had become someone else's *others*.

She heard her parents open their door but she didn't move. To her, it was as though leaving her own door closed kept whatever was happening on the other side from becoming real. As long as she kept it closed, she could pretend that this wasn't happening, that this was nothing but a nightmare, but as soon as she opened it... As soon as she opened it, she knew, reality would engulf her in a torrent of flames and her life would never again be the same.

But reality wouldn't be denied her prey. She let out a cry of fright and covered her mouth with her hands when her door suddenly flew open, apparently of its own volition.

"Adriana, we must go, quickly," her father whispered to her, apparently not surprised to find her standing motionless in the middle of her room. "They're here. They're coming for us. Where is your brother?"

Why had the warning not come? He didn't wait for her reply before returning to his own room, where he kept a suitcase packed at all times for just such an emergency.

Adriana's paralysis finally broke and she stepped into the dimly-lit hallway, her arms still wrapped around her chest as though to shield herself from whatever was about to happen. Her parents emerged from their own room fully dressed mere moments later, and Adriana wondered if they hadn't been sleeping with their clothes on all along. Her mother stopped and stared at her in dismay.

"Adriana! Go get dressed! Now!" she snapped at her.

But they were too late. There wasn't enough time. The light of powerful headlamps filtered through the drawn curtains as the trucks pulled up in front of their apartment complex and stopped. Then came the sound of slamming doors and of boots hitting the ground, and they understood that it was all over. Their network had failed them and the warning they had been counting on to escape in time had never come.

There was a loud crash downstairs as someone broke down the entrance door. Then men, many of them, were coming up the stairs, like rolling thunder on a warm summer night, and Adriana's father grabbed her mother with one hand. With the other, he straightened his raggedy clothes and smoothed out his long, gray beard. He then went to stand in the middle of the hallway, directly in front of the door, prepared to meet the invaders with all the pride and dignity he could muster, and Adriana loved him for it. He readjusted his coat one last time, nervously, as though looking his best might bring about a different outcome.

The noise in the stairway had barely stopped that someone was banging on their door. Adriana gasped and took a step back. This really was happening. To them. Tonight.

"Herr Zöbel, open this door immediately," someone called loudly and with authority from the other side of the door.

Her father hesitated only a moment before motioning at her mother to comply. He pulled himself up to his full height of five feet and five inches, trying to make himself appear as tall and as self-assured as possible, but to Adriana never before had he looked more scared and more helpless. Her father was a quiet, genteel, bookish owl of a man who had never known anger in his entire life, the most ill-equipped man in the world to face down the gargoyles about to invade their home.

Her father always believed that things would turn out for the best, and he was usually right. But tonight, he was about to be proved wrong. Very wrong.

"Herr Zöbel, I won't ask you again! Open this door immediately," the lead gargoyle barked.

Adriana's mother unfastened the security chain with a trembling, deliberate hand. She then wrapped her fingers around the door handle and turned it slowly. That was all the gargoyles needed.

The door flew open violently, the solid oak edge striking Adriana's mother in the forehead. The woman fell backward with a scream, her face already covered in blood, as a dozen men rushed into their small apartment. Her father raised a hand to halt them but the first man simply batted it away before grabbing the old man by his lengthy beard and pulling his head down.

"Herr Zöbel," the man began, "you and your family have been ordered deported. You are to come with us immediately."

"Please", her father began. He was still bent forward, his two hands wrapped around that of the man who had now twisted his fingers into his beard. "Please. We have money. Take it, but leave us. Please... the money."

Adriana had retreated several steps into her room and she didn't think the men had noticed her. Not yet. From where she stood, she saw their eyes light up at the mention of money. Her father was motioning with his free hand at the suitcase that lay forgotten on the floor, next to her stunned and bloodied mother.

"The money, it's all there," her father repeated desperately, his voice shaking with fear and pain. "Take it, take it all, but leave us... I beg of you."

Adriana didn't quite understand. What was this about money? She had always assumed, perhaps incorrectly, that the suitcase contained clothes and papers and such. But money? How could her father possibly have enough to buy their freedom? They lived modestly and her last "new dress" had been a hand-me-down from her sister Tatiyana, who had married and moved away a few years earlier. Her father always pleaded poverty and the need to be ready when the day came. Could that day be today?

The scharführer who held her father by the beard looked over his shoulder and nodded at the man who stood behind him. Words weren't needed. The man walked rapidly to the suitcase and when, in her confusion, Adriana's mother tried to grab it from him, he booted her violently in the face, smashing her nose and throwing her against the wall. Adriana's gasped in fright and ran to her mother. She dropped to her knees next to the old woman and cradled the limp body in her arms, the blood soaking her thin nightdress.

The SS staff sergeant was accompanied not by other SS men but by members of the Hlinka Guard, that militia of goons and thugs formed by the country's pro-Nazi regime. Paying the two women no mind, the guardsman dragged the suitcase to the middle of the room and put a knee down. Adriana saw him licking his lips as he placed his thumbs against the two latches and prepared to flip them. The was a small *click* when he did and he hesitated for a moment before raising the lid, knowing that all eyes were on him. Adriana knew that her future depended on what that suitcase contained.

The guardsman stared at the contents as though struck dumb with disbelief. Adriana thought she might collapse on the spot when she heard the scharführer curse under his breath. Now they would die. She was certain of it. If not here, tonight, with a bullet in their brain, then later, in circumstances she dared not imagine. No other outcome was possible.

The guardsman raised the suitcase with both hands and tipped out the contents. A bunch of rumpled clothes plummeted out and scattered on the floor. And through her mother's old socks and her father's stained undergarments, here and there could be seen the odd crumpled bill. A few pieces of ugly jewelry, the only ones her mother possessed, also tumbled out, thunking hard against the floor and glowing weakly in the dim light of a single light bulb. The guardsman picked up a ring Adriana's mother had inherited from her own grandmother and stared at it in disgust before handing in to the scharführer.

The officer examined it with equal disgust before shoving it against Adriana's father face.

"With this you think to buy your freedom herr Zöbel? With this *ramsch*?" The cruel sound of the man's mirthless laughter chilled Adriana to the bone. He threw the ring aside. "I think not". Then, to his men he said: "Take them all."

Pushing the others aside and never relinquishing his painful hold on Adriana's father's beard, he mercilessly dragged the old man down the stairs. The other soldiers filed out behind him, two of them roughly ripping Adriana's half-conscious mother out of her arms and carrying her to the waiting canvas-sided trucks. Adriana instinctively stood up to hang on to her mother but the soldiers simply pushed her back.

Adriana was now alone in the empty apartment with the last two guardsmen. She expected them to grab her arms and pull her outside as well, but instead, the two men looked at one another briefly. One of them then peeked out the door rapidly and nodded to his comrade before closing it slowly.

Adriana felt her knees buckle.

She had turned 21 a few weeks earlier and she was a strikingly beautiful young woman. Her long black hair had remained full and luxurious even through these times of hardship and deprivation, and her generous figure had brought more than one hopeful suitor to the Zöbel household. All had gone home empty-handed, having been judged unworthy by her father.

Adriana took a few steps back until her shoulders came to rest against the wall. She wrapped her arms around her and only then did she notice that her blood-soaked nightdress clung revealingly to her body. The men, she knew, *had* noticed and a horrible night was just about to turn into a real nightmare.

"No, please," she said feebly as the men closed in on her.

They grabbed her by the arms and pulled her into her bedroom. She fought and she cried and she screamed, knowing those outside could hear her, but to no avail. The men were too strong and the door to their apartment remained closed.

A punch to the stomach winded her and made her want to puke, and Adriana fell silent. Her attackers let her collapse to the floor as she tried to summon one last ounce of energy to resist. One of the men knelt above her head and pulled her arms up as the other knelt between her legs, hastily unfastening his britches. Adriana wanted to kick him but it was though her whole body had gone limp. She felt as feeble as a newborn. She twisted her head from side to side, hoping to find something to bite, but the man's hands were safely out of reach.

She managed one howl of absolute despair, but then she could scream no more.

The man between her legs pushed her nightdress up before ripping off her undergarments with a practiced move. Adriana's mind went blank, flying her away from this hell she was in, and then the man was lying on top of her, lustily trying to plow her virgin garden with his swollen member.

Adriana could feel his hot, fetid breath against her neck. His fingers were digging painfully into the soft, tender flesh of her left breast. She could hear him panting and groaning but the noise came to her from a great distance, like a conversation heard from across the street. The other man was telling him to hurry up, to be done with it already before the scharführer returned.

He also said other, nastier things, but those her mind locked away and would only set free much, much later, in another time and place.

Time stood still. Her body was here, enduring the man's clumsy assault, but her mind was elsewhere. Maybe it lasted a minute, maybe it lasted an hour. To her seconds had become weeks and weeks had become seconds. She had completely detached herself from whatever was being done to her, from whatever violations were being visited upon her body. Whatever was happening to her wasn't *really* happening to her, but rather to the corporeal vessel that usually housed her essence. Her true self was somewhere else, safely far away.

But then a shaft of light tore through the stygian darkness and the curtains that had enshrouded her soul parted, if ever so slightly. Her hands were free and the man was now longer crushing her under his weight. There were new sounds in the room. Screams. Curses. Punches. Someone, she saw, was waving a gun wildly, trying to find someone, something to shoot at.

Adriana got to her feet. The guardsman who had held her wrists was the one with the gun. His back was turned to her. His accomplice was spinning around wildly, circling from left to right and from right to left, all the while wailing like a banshee. His pants were still around his knees, which seriously limited his range of motion, and he kept tripping and falling and getting back up. He would have looked quite comical under any other circumstances. The gun was pointed in his general direction but his companion didn't dare fire.

The rapist seemed to have grown a huge hump on his back, something like that on a buffalo, and that hump was what the second guardsman was trying to aim at through his partner's wild gyrations. Except that it wasn't a hump. There was someone else in the room with them, Adriana now realized. And she had a dreadful feeling that she knew who that person was.

The guardsman tripped once again and this time, he and his hump fell out of the bedroom's darkness and into the relative light of the hallway.

"Aaron?" Adriana shouted at the top of her lungs.

Her little brother had returned just in time to see his bloodied mother being loaded onto one of the trucks and to hear his sister's screams of terror emanating from their apartment. Emerging from the night he had slipped, ghostlike, through a whole platoon of Hlinka Guards and raced upstairs at full speed, where he had found Adriana wrestling on the ground with one of the monsters in the gray uniforms.

Aaron, courageous little Aaron who had come to their family late in life, past when such things were said to be possible, had launched himself on the man's back and wrapped his hands around his face, plunging his tiny fingers into any orifice he found. Two fingers had encountered the man's eyes and twin rivulets of blood now ran from both sockets.

"Aaron! No!" she screamed again, but nobody was paying her any mind.

The guardsman, the same former convict who moments earlier had tried to run Aaron over, once again found his feet. He looked like a man trying to fend off a swarm of angry wasps as he tried, simultaneously, to remove the boy's fingers from his eyes and to fling him off his back. But Aaron was hanging on with all his might, his fear and anger endowing him with the unimaginable strength of the drowning man who leaves fingerprints in solid rock.

The guardsman reached behind him, over his head, and finally managed to grab Aaron's shoulders. He then bent forward rapidly as he yanked, catapulting the boy off his back. Aaron thumped against the floor, hard, and let out a single, deep gasp. Finally relieved, the howling man stumbled back with both palms pressed against his ruined eyes as Aaron lay, stunned, on the ground.

Adriana saw what was about to happen but she was too slow to stop it. The other guardsman was less than a meter away from her, but he might as well have been standing on the other side of the city. She saw him raise the pistol and she moved to shove him, to push his arm down, to throw herself in front of the muzzle, to cover Aaron with her own body, to do anything that she possibly could to save her little brother's life, but again, as before, her body refused to obey her. Her feet wouldn't move and her arms were frozen. All she could do was watch.

The guardsman fired a single shot. At such short range he couldn't, wouldn't, miss. And he didn't. The bullet struck Aaron square in the chest and the little body immediately went limp. An instant later, Adriana saw – she *saw* – Aaron's soul leaving his body. The ethereal form floated in place for a moment and to Adriana it looked as though it was staring straight at her, perhaps bidding her goodbye one last time. And then it was gone, as though it had never been there at all.

That scene she would remember many times over the rest of her life but never, not for one moment, would she doubt what she had seen.

The last thing Adriana heard before passing out was the sound of the wooden staircase creaking and rattling under the assault of dozens of boots, bringing this nightmare to a close in the same manner as that in which it had begun.

Rudolf Höss collapsed into his favorite leather chair, the one right next to the hearth, and sighed with exhaustion as he slipped off his boots.

This had been an impossible task. When he thought back to what had greeted him upon his arrival just over two years ago, right after his posting at Sachsenhausen, and he compared it to what he could see out his window today, well, it was nothing short of amazing. He knew Berlin had noticed, for the Reichsführer himself had expressed his satisfaction at the results. And since the Reichsführer was not a man easily pleased, Höss knew he could be proud of himself.

He had taken abandoned and dilapidated Polish army barracks and turned them into an institution that, he believed, History would remember as having made a crucial contribution to the Reich's victory. When historians wrote of the Reich's birth a thousand years from now, he knew his name would be mentioned alongside those of Hitler and Himmler and Eichmann, visionaries who had dared dream of a better, stronger, purer world, and had then fought to create it. Let those idiotic Americans worship their Founding Fathers; the Reich's citizens, the rulers of the world, would worship their own.

Lulled by his dreams of eternal glory, Höss closed his eyes groggily as the flames roared in the fireplace next to him. He had almost fallen asleep when a knock at the door startled him.

"Come", he barked after hurriedly putting his boots back on.

He stood up and straightened out his uniform as an hauptsturmführer whose name he had yet to learn entered the room.

"Heil Hitler", the young man said proudly, snapping his right arm and clicking his heels together in a perfect Nazi salute.

"Heil Hitler", Höss replied a bit more sloppily.

"Forgive the interruption, herr obersturmbannführer, but a dozen new guards arrived about an hour ago, and I thought perhaps you would like to greet them personally."

Höss sighed silently and dropped his head.

The new guards. Of course. He had forgotten about them. Obtaining new personnel wasn't difficult, all he had to do was ask and more were sent, but he feared how his repeated requests might eventually be perceived in Berlin. It was the sorest point of his new command to have witnessed firsthand that not all were willing to do what was necessary, no matter how unpleasant, to ensure the Reich's victory. Granted, theirs was a very special task and one not suited to all, and even *he* had his moments of weakness when faced with screaming and pleading children, but he still managed to acquit himself more than honorably of his duty.

The same couldn't be said of everyone. The number of reports of self-inflicted gunshot wounds - *accidents* all, of course - that came across his desk in a single week was sometimes baffling, as was the fact that most victims managed to shoot themselves in the foot and rarely somewhere that might actually endanger their lives. Were the SS' ranks really encumbered with such blundering *täuschen*? And if they were, why were these imbeciles apparently all drawn to him like flies to a rotten corpse?

I'll put the word out that whoever is discharged from here will immediately be sent to convalesce on the Russian front, he thought to himself with a smile. *That should teach them to handle their sidearms more carefully.*

"Apologies, herr obersturmbannführer, but did I say something amusing?" the hauptsturmführer asked worriedly.

Höss realized he was smirking and coughed in his fist. "No, not at all. Is there... is there anything special about these new guards? Something I need to know?"

The hauptsturmführer shook his head. "Nein, herr obersturmbannführer", he said a bit too hastily before thinking better of it. "Well, there is this one individual who seems particularly eager. He's already asking for more responsibilities."

That's a nice change, Höss reflected. "Really? What's his name?"

"Mattias Traugott, herr obersturmbannführer."

Höss shrugged. The name didn't mean anything to him. "Very well. Make sure you point him out to me later. I could use someone trustworthy."

"As you wish, herr obersturmbannführer", the young officer acquiesced with a nod.

Höss didn't relish leaving the warm comfort of his home to venture outside in the cold. Still, he took pride in leading by example, so he concealed his displeasure as he grabbed his overcoat and wrapped it around his shoulders. "Lead the way, hauptsturmführer", he said, gesturing at the open door. "Let's go and give our new recruits a proper Auschwitz welcome."

"I am very so sorry about your son, my friend. I feel it is my fault. If I had been able to warn you in time, maybe you could have got away", a man she only knew as Mr Dobrin told Adriana's father. "But they arrived in the night, like thieves, and caught us by surprise. I didn't even have time to get dressed."

Simeon Zöbel hadn't said a word since learning of his son's death. He had tried to jump off the truck upon hearing the shot fired, but the Hinka guardsmen had beat him back mercilessly. Then three thugs had emerged from the building, two dragging an unconscious Adriana between them and the third carrying little Aaron's lifeless body slung over his shoulder, and the truth had become undeniable. Adriana's mother had let out a heart-piercing shriek and collapsed while her father had sat back down heavily and buried his face in his hands.

But now he looked up at his friend of 30 years, half-dressed and like him dispossessed of every last shred of dignity, and his gentle nature wouldn't be denied.

"Do not blame yourself, old friend", he said quietly as the truck rumbled through the vacant streets. "There was nothing you could have done. It was God's will."

Adriana wondered how it could possibly be "God's will" for an 11-year-old boy to be shot dead in cold blood by his sister's rapist, but her father had once again lowered his head and fallen quiet so she kept her anger in check. For now.

The Jews of Rimavská Sobota had heard the stories. They knew what was going on outside their insulated little world. They knew the Slovak government had agreed to paid the Germans 500 Reichsmarks per head for the right to deport its Jews to the Nazi death camps. They had known their day would come, just like it had for countless others, and they had prepared. A network had been set up, each member tasked with warning at least three others, in the hope that information might travel faster than death. The second you heard, you were meant to warn others who in turn would warn others, and perhaps a few would get to live a while longer. But the system had failed. Dobrin had never been able to warn the Zöbel household, probably because he himself hadn't been warned in time. And those who had relied on Simeon Zöbel to warn them had also, in all likelihood, been woken up in the night by a pounding on their door.

But it was pointless to seek to assign blame. The system had simply failed and now hundreds, thousands, would die.

The truck hit a pothole and they were all jolted roughly. Adriana lost her balance and was only saved from falling when the man standing next to her grabbed her elbow. Her flesh crawled at his touch and she pulled away from him more rudely than she'd meant. She still managed to thank him and to smile briefly, knowing he meant well and had no idea what she'd just gone through, before lowering her head again and staring self-consciously at her blood-soaked nightdress. A woman had lent her a shawl that she'd graciously wrapped around her shoulders, but it did little to hide the fact that she was essentially naked underneath.

Still. That kind gesture had raised her spirits, just as had the fact that the elderly among them, including her parents, had been given space on the truck's two wooden benches, while the younger ones stood and held on as best they could. Somehow, through all this, most people still managed to retain a sense of decency.

Adriana looked at her parents and wondered what would become of them. Her mother had rested her head against her father's shoulder and seemed to have dozed off. Her nose and lips had swollen to almost half their normal size and her left eye was partially shut. The gash on her forehead had mostly stopped bleeding, but it still oozed a thin, bloody liquid that ran down her face. She swiped the back of her hand absentmindedly across her cheek, smearing it a sickly pink. The old woman then let out a deep, ragged sigh, as though crushed by the weight of the night, and seemed to fall back asleep. Adriana's father reached over and grabbed one of his wife's hands in his. Their fingers instinctively intertwined, each drawing comfort from the other's proximity.

Adriana didn't fear for herself as much as she feared for them. She was young and healthy and good-looking, and she didn't doubt the Nazis would have some use for her. No matter what they asked of her, no matter how degrading, now matter how vile, she resolved to triumph by keeping her head held high and, ultimately, emerging alive on the other side. Changed and perhaps even damaged, but alive.

Her parents were another story altogether. The weak and the old represented nothing more than useless mouths to feed. Unless the Nazis needed a skilled seamstress or a decent accountant whose only know luxury was a cologne that smelled of pine needles, something Adriana doubted very much, Simeon and Raanah Zöbel were in all likelihood doomed, just as were most of those crammed on the truck together with them. Ashamed, she wondered whether the quick death that probably awaited them wasn't preferable to the years of torment that lay before her.

She was jolted out of her somber thoughts by the sound of the truck braking. She estimated they had been on the road for maybe an hour, perhaps a little longer. Those who had fallen asleep immediately woke up and a quiet chatter began, each person hoping others might know what was happening, where they were, why they had stopped. Why this would be known to anyone Adriana couldn't understand, but you couldn't blame a condemned man for seeking the certitude and safety of knowledge. They heard other trucks stopping around them, which only served to heighten their anxiety by indicating that they had all indeed reached their final destination.

Loud voices assaulted them through the thin canvas. Orders were being barked. Children began crying and a few wailing voices, whether those of men or women it was impossible to ascertain, fed into the cacophony. Adriana's truck rocked when all those sitting stood up almost simultaneously and she grabbed her father's hand, knowing he was still holding on to her mother and hoping this might keep them from being separated. His pudgy fingers closed around hers and she was shocked by the coldness of his skin.

Someone lowered the rear door of the truck and then two SS soldiers – not Hlinka goons as before, but this time true SS men - were waving at them with their automatic weapons and ordering them to get out.

"*RAUS! RAUS!*" the soldiers screamed, grabbing and roughly pulling out those who had the misfortune of finding themselves nearest them.

Having been among the last to board, Adriana and her parents were among the first to disembark. One of the SS tried to grab Adriana's nightdress to pull her out, probably hoping to rip it off her at the same time, but she somehow managed to avoid his hand and she landed on her feet.

She then turned around to help her parents as the soldiers shouted at her to move faster. One of them shoved her from behind and Adriana lost her grip on her mother's hand. The old woman lost her balance and fell out of the truck, crashing on her shoulder with a cry of pain.

Without thinking, Adriana spun around and backhanded the soldier who had shoved her hard across the face.

"Have you no shame?" she screamed at him, without knowing if he even understood her. "Even a monster like you has parents, doesn't he?"

The soldier stared at her in disbelief. His eyes widened in anger and he raised his weapon over his shoulder to brain her with the butt. Remembering her earlier resolve never again to be cowed by a Nazi, Adriana lifted her chin and met the SS' angry stare, hoping her eyes betrayed none of the fear that made her soul tremble. Unsettled by her defiance, the soldier raised his weapon even higher and Adriana needed every last bit of her dwindling courage to keep from flinching. The SS hesitated. Had this Jewish *hure* been either younger or older, he would have killed her on the spot. But the Reichsführer's orders couldn't have been more explicit: workers were in desperately short supply and those who could be of any use to the Reich were to be treated with extra care. Killing her could mean the end of his own life at the hands of officers eager to please their own superiors.

The soldier lowered his weapon and barked something Adriana didn't understand. It didn't matter. She had backed down and wouldn't harm her now. Her entire being shaking, she turned her back to him and, slowly and deliberately, crouched down to help her mother get back up. She linked her right arm through her mother's left while her father did the same thing on the other side and together, they walked by the SS without sparing him a single glance.

Adriana was shocked by the scene that greeted them. Hundreds of Jews huddled in the darkness, the yellow stars on their clothes gleaming in the moonlight, under the hateful watch of a mixture of SS men and Hlinka guardsmen. Her convoy had apparently been the last to arrive and the newcomers were being made to merge with those already here. Snarling dogs were barking wildly, straining at their leashes, and men were shouting unintelligible orders. Adriana tightened her grip on her mother's arm as they burrowed deeper into the crowd, relentlessly pushed forward by those behind them.

"Zöbel?" Someone was calling after them.

She stopped and looked to her right. A man was walking rapidly in their direction, waving at them, but she couldn't make out his features in the night. "Zöbel?" he called again.

She sensed her father perk up. "Sándor?" he said softly before letting go of his wife's arm to embrace the other man. They kissed each other on the cheek.

"They brought you all the way here?" the newcomer asked. Adriana's father nodded. "Yes. At least now I know where we are."

It was the other man's turn to nod. He then bowed theatrically. "Welcome to Spišská Nová Ves, my hometown. Though I can't say I'm very proud of it at the moment. Neighbor turning on neighbor, friend on friend, colleague on colleague... Bah! Who can believe such a thing!"

Simeon Zöbel turned to his wife and daughter. "This is my friend Sándor Pfircsik", he began. "He owns a small furniture company here. I have been keeping his books for..."

"Don't say it", Pfircsik interrupted him amicably. "If you do, they'll guess how old we *really* are." Adriana smiled despite herself. Even in the midst of this madness, some retained their sense of humor.

"Sándor was one of my very first clients", Simeon explained. "He trusted me."

"But Simeon, you must introduce me", Pfircsik said. "I know these ladies are your wife and daughter but tell me who is who, for I certainly can't tell!" There was a sparkle of mirth in his eyes that made Adriana smile again. "And what of your son, Aaron? He must be almost a man by now!"

Adriana's mother would have collapsed had she not caught her and her father dropped a heavy hand on his friend's shoulder. The man's good humor was instantly vaporised. "Oh my friend no", he said gently. "Tell me he's not... tell me they didn't..."

He didn't have to explain who he meant by *they*. *They* were here, all around them, demons in the guise of men.

"I'm so, so sorry", Pfircsik said, placing his own hand over Simeon's.

"It was God's will", Simeon Zöbel again answered, and it was all Adriana could do to keep from exploding at her father's unshakable faith in a God that had clearly deserted them.

A moment of heavy silence engulfed them. Adriana's mother was sobbing softly while the two men stared at the ground, as though it might provide the answers they sought. A cold breeze made Adriana shiver and she wrapped the shawl around her shoulders as tightly as she could, but the thin fabric provided little protection against the chill of the night.

Sándor Pfircsik broke the spell with a deep sigh.

"Sometimes I wonder if there's any good left in the world", he said, shaking his head. "There was this woman, a young mother with three children whose husband died just after she became pregnant with the fourth... She came to me after the baby was born, asking for my help. I took pity on her and I had my best man make her a nice crib for her baby. I could have sold it for 40 dollars but I just gave it to her for free. She was so grateful!"

"What happened to her?" Adriana asked.

"I don't know, but I last saw her a few hours ago", he answered coldly. "She was standing across the street as I was being led away by two Hlinka *psi*. She just... watched me, without saying a word. For all I know she's the one who led them to me! *There's a Jew, arrest him!* But then when she felt it was safe, she ran across the street and into my house. Right through the front door without any hesitation! No shame! She knew I lived alone and there wouldn't be anyone there. She's probably tearing my little place apart with her bare hands, looking for all that *gold* I've hoarded under the floorboards!"

He paused for a moment before adding, almost to himself, "Bah! Who can believe such a thing?" which seemed to be something he said frequently.

"Why would she think there is gold under your floor?" Adriana asked.

Pfircsik shrugged, as though amused by her naivety. "Because that's what she heard and she wants it so desperately to be true", he explained. "But methinks she'll be disappointed", he continued, this time with a touch of his old mischievousness. "I heard rats scurrying under there last week, so I pried a few floorboards to set down traps. So let me tell you... not only will she not find any gold, but she'll also be cursing this crazy old Jew before the night is out."

Adriana smiled and was about to reply something about there being some justice after all when a noise to her left claimed her attention. She stood on tiptoes and craned her neck and in the distance saw a speck of light coming in their direction. The speck grew bigger and bigger, and the noise louder and louder, until the ground began to shake.

Had Aaron still been alive and there with them, he would have warned Adriana that when the ground begins to rumble, it's time to flee.

"What is this place?" Simeon Zöbel asked his friend, raising his voice to cover the deafening sound.

"An old foundry", Pfircsik replied. "They used to need tons and tons of coal, but... trains haven't come here in years. Those tracks are disaffected."

"Not anymore", Adriana whispered.

Hundreds of people watched, silenced by awe and fear, as the train rolled slowly to a stop. The brakes whistled and squealed, sparks flew in the darkness and steam hissed white against the night, and the monster finally came to a halt about 50 yards from Adriana. Still, no one spoke. An eerie quiet had descended upon the courtyard, and it lured them with a false sense of comfort and security. As long as they remained as they were, frozen in time, they could fool themselves into believing they were still relatively safe. At least they were still with their loved ones. Torn from their homes, perhaps, but least not alone, and that was better than nothing.

So don't anyone move. Don't talk. Don't disturb the silence. Don't do anything to provoke it. Maybe the train wasn't meant for them. Maybe it was simply bringing more Jews to join them. Maybe it would go as it had come. Maybe...

Maybe they were all fools and they would all die.

The doors slid open and all Hell broke loose. Behind them, all at once, men began shouting and dogs resumed their demented barking. Shots were fired in the air. A shiver of surprise and fear rippled across the crowd, spreading from one person to the next, as though the assembled Jews now formed a single, living organism. Adriana looked behind her and, in the dim light, saw clubs raise and fall, heard them thud against flesh and bone, she heard the crack of whips, and then screams of pain added to the madness.

The crowd surged forward, toward the train, as people tried to get away from the violence. Shoved by those behind them, the Jews closer to the train began climbing aboard. They really had no choice in the matter. It was either that or get trampled to death or crushed against the boxcars.

More shots were fired and the crowd panicked. Thinking they were being fired upon, people began running in all directions. The way forward being blocked by the train, left and right they fled only to slam into those coming in the opposite direction. People collided in the darkness, fights broke out, those who fell and couldn't get back up quickly enough were crushed by hundreds of feet. All rational thought lost, some also began running toward the back, where the armed guards were hitting and kicking and shoving all those unfortunate enough to find themselves within their reach.

Fangs bared, the blood-thirsty dogs snapped and snarled at everything that moved. Having either slipped its collar or snapped its leash, one beast found itself free and bounded around madly until it clamped its jaws down on the arm of a little girl of no more than three. It yanked the child away from her mother and began shaking her like a rag doll. The child's mother howled in fear and managed to grab her daughter's other arm. The woman began pulling, trying to rip her daughter away from the dog, and the ungodly tug of war ended only when the child's sleeve finally ripped from her coat. The woman quickly gathered the terrified child into her arms while the dog set about shredding its bloody trophy.

Adriana was momentarily paralyzed and disoriented by the madness unfolding around her. She had no idea what they should do. She only knew that they couldn't remain where they were.

"Quickly!" she shouted at her parents. She looked for Sándor Pfircsik but he was nowhere to be found. What had become of him? Had he also succumbed to panic and fled? She had no time to worry about him now. "We must get to the train! It's our only safety!"

They all linked hands and began moving toward the train. They were constantly being jostled by those coming up behind them and by those trying to get around them. The closer they got to the train, the denser the crowd got and the harder it was to make progress, until it became impossible to move at all. Those in front had nowhere to go and those behind were still trying to get to safety. Adriana and her parents were relentlessly being squeezed, to the point that they could hardly breathe.

"Stop! Please stop pushing!" she screamed, but her words were lost to the night.

They were less than twenty yards from the train and ahead she could see people climbing aboard, but no more than two or three at a time. Those already on board were doing their best to help, frenetically handling luggage and children, grabbing proffered hands and pulling, but it was nowhere near enough to relieve the increasing pressure. Adriana began to wonder what they would do if they reached the train and the boxcar was full. Would they simply die here, crushed by hoards of desperate souls?

Adriana's free hand was pressed, elbow bent, against the back of the man in front of her. He had on a thick wool coat and she almost welcomed the warmth that radiated from him. She had to push against him constantly to resist those pushing against her from behind, just as the man surely pushed against someone else in front of him to resist her. To her right, her mother stood between her and her father, holding on to both of them as best she could.

Adriana's muscles, her shoulders, her calves, her thighs, were beginning to burn.

The man must have got tangled in his own feet and fallen. Or perhaps he was tripped. Maybe Adriana herself tripped him, though she had no recollection of their feet ever touching. Maybe whatever demon haunted this place decided to add a new layer to their torment. Maybe God, seeing what the demon was up to, gave him a conspiratorial wink and smirked, turning His face away from them and pretending not to have noticed.

One second the man was propping Adriana up against those shoving her forward, the next he was gone. He simply fell away from her. The warmth of the wool against her hands gave way to a cold emptiness and Adriana lurched forward. Her heart dropped in her chest and a single thought flashed across her mind.

If I fall, I die. I must... not... fall.

She instinctively raised her foot and the tip of her naked toes brushed against something, someone that, had the demon had its way, would certainly have tripped her and spelled her doom. Still off balance, her foot came down hard on something soft and warm... *the man's back, under his wool coat, I just stomped on him*... then her other foot also did and she almost fell when the human being she was standing on tried to heave himself up, like a wild mustang bucking off a cowboy. She jumped off him just in time to keep from being toppled over but her heel then crushed human flesh. She felt small bones snap and a shout of pain arose from beneath her.

Only then did Adriana realize that several had fallen and not solely the man in front of her, the domino effect of falling bodies having abruptly created an empty space through which she was being propelled against her will. Like the ocean that suddenly floods an inlet at high tide, the crazed refugees around her had instantly filled this void, mindless of the bodies they were trampling. This human tide carried her forward just as it threatened to drown her should she trip and fall. She couldn't resist its power and had no other choice but to let it take her where it would. Trying to stand against it would have guaranteed rapid death.

Adriana took longer strides, trying to avoid as many bodies as she could, but to no avail. The more people fell, the more others tripped and fell in turn, until it became almost impossible to put a foot down without stepping on another human being. The ground was carpeted with tangled bodies that threatened to bring her down at any moment. Cries of despair and calls for help and shouts of anger exploded all around her. One of these cries was silenced when her foot stamped down on something wet that gave way with a sickening crack, and Adriana knew she had just smashed someone's jaw and teeth.

The mad rush forward stopped just as suddenly as it had begun. Adriana was once again standing on solid ground and the pressure to move forward had essentially vanished. She had gone almost twenty-five yards in the space of a few seconds and now stood at the front of the crowd. Only a few people separated her from the boxcar and already these were being pulled aboard. Her turn would come shortly.

Then her mind snapped back to the present. Adriana looked around her and her heart sank.

"Mother? Father?" she shrieked. "Mother! Father!"

She spun around and fought to make her way back through the crowd, swimming against the incoming tide, having no idea where her parents might be but determined to find them. She couldn't lose them, not tonight, not after seeing Aaron shot dead just a few hours earlier.

"Let me through! Let me through!" she shouted at the top her lungs, but her distress was but a drop in this ocean of despair and no one paid her the least attention.

She found her way blocked by a mountain of a man who, to boot, carried a leather suitcase under each arm, making him almost as wide as he was tall. Adriana tried going around him on the right and then on the left, she even tried ducking under his luggage, but it was pointless. Not only was the man huge, but he was also hemmed in on all sides by other refugees trying to reach the train. She might as well have been an insect trying to fly around the Himalayas.

She banged her puny fists against his chest, trying to get his attention, but he never even noticed her. She screamed at him and even slapped his bearded face, but he had the vacant, terrified stare of a man who knows his life is in jeopardy and who won't be denied his only chance of survival. His eyes never wavered away from the train that was his goal.

Adriana had to find a way around him if she were to have any chance of finding her parents. She hoped against hope they were still standing somewhere and not dead on the cold ground, being trampled by countless feet; her soul knew better, but her mind wouldn't yet acknowledge the harsh reality. Finding herself suddenly capable of acts she would have considered unthinkable the day before, Adriana grabbed two handfuls of the giant's clothes and extended her right leg behind her as far as she could. Then, as she pulled him toward her, she raised it in a single motion, kneeing him between the legs with all the strength she had left.

That, at long last, got his attention.

His eyes bulged, his face turned red and he deflated with a loud *ooomph* before dropping his suitcases. His knees buckled inwards as he placed both hands against his crotch and Adriana saw her chance if not to go around him then perhaps to climb *over* him and keep going. She placed both hands on top of his head and pushed down as she prepared to leap.

A pair of strong hands seized her hair from behind and she had already taken five steps backward, going in the wrong direction, before she fully realized what was happening to her. She grabbed the hands in her hair and tried fighting back, but she slipped and lost her footing. Her heels dragged painfully against the ground as she was pulled mercilessly toward the train.

Revenge was at hand. The SS she had slapped earlier had tracked her progress through the crowd, looking for any reason to pay her back. He had watched with savage glee as she had almost been swamped and trampled to death by the other refugees, but she had kept her balance and he had been denied his vengeance. Overcome with rage and seeing her about to board the train and slip out of his reach forever, he had raced around the crowd and come to stand directly in her path, hoping she might give him the slightest excuse for retribution. There was much that might happen, unnoticed, in this mayhem.

She had almost reached the front of the crowd when she froze, spun around and charged crazily back through the masses behind her. He thought for a moment perhaps she had seen him and was trying to get away, but no... Their eyes had not met and her mind had clearly been somewhere else. Then he watched in amazement as she began striking a man twice her size, just as she had struck him earlier. Had this woman no fear? He fully expected the giant to swat her aside like a fly, perhaps even to knock her to the ground to be trampled like the bitch that she was, but the man simply ignored her. His amazement turned to shock when she kneed the giant in the balls, doubling him over.

A vicious snarl distorted the SS' upper lip. The Reichsführer's orders about preserving valuable workers, the same orders that had kept him from braining her an hour ago, would now protect him as he exacted revenge upon this whore. Clearly this man, with his size and strength, would prove invaluable to the Reich. He couldn't very well stand idly by as she assaulted and perhaps even maimed him, could he? No, he could not. So he uncoiled his whip and quickly cleared a path through the crowd, leaving behind him a trail of bleeding bodies. He reached the woman just as she was about to leapfrog over her victim.

"Remember me?" he growled in her ear as he dragged her backward.

He threw her to the ground at the foot of the train and raised his whip high above his head. He brought it down once, twice, and Adriana howled in pain when the leather ripped her flesh through her bloody nightdress. The SS was about to strike her again when someone grabbed his arm from behind, stopping it in mid-air. He spun around in a fury, tearing away from whoever had dared interfere, and his jaw dropped open when he found himself face to face with a short, pudgy, elderly Jew.

"Stop this right now! Beating a woman! Who can believe such a thing?" Sándor Pfircsik berated him fearlessly with a raised finger.

The SS opened and closed his mouth like a fish out water. Then his anger abated just enough for him to realize that this was a problem easily solved.

"The Reich may need her, but it certainly doesn't need an old bastard like you", he snarled. He pulled out his sidearm, a 9mm Pistole 35(p), placed it against Pfircsik's forehead and fired a single shot. The bullet tore through the man's brain and the back of his skull exploded in a shower of bone and blood.

Half a dozen hands pulled Adriana to her feet and steadied her when she wobbled. Then more hands grabbed her and her feet left the ground as she was hoisted on board the train. The sound of a gunshot had somehow registered through the burning pain that made her whole body throb, but she had no idea what had just transpired. One moment the SS had been beating her to death, the next... And now a man lay dead, though she did not know it, having gladly traded his life for hers.

Adriana found herself sitting at the back of the boxcar. She closed her eyes, trying to block out the pain, and silent tears rolled down her dirty cheeks. She wanted to get up, to jump off the wagon, to go find her parents or die trying, but she couldn't have lifted a single finger to save her life. She was as weak and defenseless as a kitten. Twice in the past few hours she had been assaulted, and once almost killed, all her loved ones were dead, and she simply could not fight anymore.

She rested her head against the wall of the boxcar and opened her eyes just as the sun broke over the horizon, bathing them in a soft, golden light whose promise of renewal and hope made her cry even harder.

Then the boxcar was plunged into complete darkness as someone slammed and locked the sliding door, condemning them all to death.

Auschwitz Concentration Camp
Kanada sector

Each jacket, each dress, each pair of pants represented one dead person. This the woman knew, though she rarely stopped to think about it for fear of collapsing under the weight of the inhuman task set to her.

These clothes had all once been those of Jews like her, ripped from their homes and brought here to die a horrible, suffocating death. Each garment had once been carefully packed away by someone who had dared hope that perhaps the rumors weren't true, that perhaps the Nazis' lies of *deportation* and *relocation* were in fact the truth. Had they had the courage to truly face what awaited them, they wouldn't have packed. The simple act of taking a suitcase along is testament to one's belief in still living the next day. No one cares about clean underwear or a warm jacket if one knows that Death awaits in a few hours.

The worst were the children's shoes. There was a mountain of them in the next room and that had been the woman's first task upon being assigned here, the sector the inmates had taken to calling Kanada due to the fabled riches of that faraway land. Day after day she had sorted these tiny shoes, throwing some away and putting others aside, all the while thinking of the little, innocent feet that had carried them here. The feet of trusting and carefree children who had confidently grabbed an adult's hand and blindly followed them to Hell's very doorstep.

Children who had been gassed to death within an hour of their arrival here.

Then one day, as she dug through the endless pile, a pair of pink leather shoes tumbled from the top and right into her lap. She caught them instinctively, a little girl's shoes, almost new, with a big yellow flower on the front, right above the big toe. The shoes were in her hands almost before she realized it and in her mind emerged the cherubic face of the curly-haired 7-year-old who had probably insisted on wearing them after being assured by her parents that they were going "on vacation" for a few days. She could imagine the child skipping merrily next to her mother in her new shoes, never tiring of looking down to admire them, as they walked to the nearest train station.

The woman's hands had begun to tremble and her eyes filled with tears, but she knew she could show no weakness. If she did, it would be her who'd be sent to the gas chambers the next day, of that she had no doubt. There were a hundred other women out there who wanted nothing more than to take her place. Being assigned to Kanada was the best you could hope for in a place such as this and the looks of envy some of the other inmates fired in her direction sometimes made her fear for her life. So she'd quickly put the shoes aside, as though they burned her skin, and resumed her work. The next day, she discretely offered another woman a small chunk of hard, rancid bread to switch tasks with her and never again had she entered the room with the shoes.

From that day the woman learned to detach herself from the clothes she was sorting, to block from her mind the faceless people who once wore them. To her, the clothes ceased to be mementos of lives lived and wasted and merely became means of ensuring her own survival for a while longer.

So now she reached into the towering pile in front of her and pulled out a pair of slacks that she set about examining for any hidden valuables. There was much work to be done.

Mattias Traugott was both surprised and slightly worried when he was summoned to the camp commander's office the day after his arrival.

Rudolf Höss tried his best to make him feel at ease, asking him about his family and which region of Germany he came from and so on, but it was clear from the start that the obersturmbannführer's mind was preoccupied.

Traugott wondered if, perhaps, his reputation had preceded him here and he would now, again, have to defend some of his past actions.

After a moment Höss fell silent and walked around his desk, where he sat in a swivel chair that squeaked every time he moved.

"I need someone I can trust, Traugott", the obersturmbannführer said. "I am hoping you are that someone."

Traugott was caught short and didn't quite know what to answer. "Yes, herr obersturmbannführer. I mean... thank you, herr obersturmbannführer."

Höss opened a drawer and pulled out a sheet he stared at for an instant before handing it over to Traugott, who took it with a hand that trembled imperceptibly. "I received these directives from the SS-Wirtschafts-Verwaltungshauptamt last month", Höss began slowly. "I trust you know who they are?"

"Yes, of course, herr obersturmbannführer", Traugott nodded. The SS-WHVA, the Economic and Administrative Main Office of the Nazi SS, managed several aspects of the Allgemeine-SS, including its finances, supply systems and various business projects. It also ran the concentration camps.

Traugott scanned the document rapidly. It was signed by the head of the SS-WHVA, SS-Obergruppeführer Oswald Pohl, and it stipulated, in the minutest of details, how the goods seized from the Jews were to be handled. Cash, rare metals, jewelry and precious stones, for example, were to be handed over to the SS-WHVA, who would then transfer them to the Reichsbank. Sunglasses and umbrellas, on the other hand, were to be sent to the Hauptamt Volksdeutsche Mittelstelle (the Main Welfare Office for Ethnic Germans), who might pay for them later on.

Traugott's mind was reeling. Why was Höss showing him this? What did he want with him? He read the document over to give himself some time to think, but in the end, there was only one thing he knew for sure: the obersturmbannführer sure as hell hadn't called him into his office to discuss sunglasses and umbrellas.

"I'm not sure what to say, herr obersturmbannführer", he finally said. "How does this concern me?"

Höss let out a deep, irritated sigh. "I'll be very frank with you, Traugott", the camp commander replied, his tone as hard as steel and as cold as ice. "The Reich's victory and survival are my only concern. I'm sure they're yours as well."

"Of course, herr obersturmbannführer", Traugott answered immediately. What else was he supposed to say?

"Unfortunately, it seems that not all share our loyalty to the Führer", Höss explained. "I have serious reasons to believe that some are taking advantage of their position here to enrich themselves to the detriment of the Reich."

Traugott's heart quickened as he sensed opportunity rearing its greedy head. His eyes then narrowed when Höss' words coalesced the notion that had begun to take shape in his mind.

"All valuables confiscated from the inmates are to be transferred to Berlin, without exception", the camp commander said. "But the yield coming out of our Aufräumungskommando - what some are calling Kanada - isn't satisfactory. Not satisfactory at all."

He hammered his last four words to make sure Traugott didn't miss his point.

"Herr obersturmbannführer... Are you saying some guards are keeping those valuables for themselves? That they are, in fact, stealing from the Reich?" he asked, almost managing to sound indignant.

"That's exactly what I'm saying", Höss replied with rage in his eyes.

Traugott almost smiled. In a flash, he understood what would be asked of him and how he would profit from it. It was all so very simple.

"I'm assigning you to this so-called Kanada", Höss said. "This will make you somewhat unpopular. You have just arrived and this is a very sought-after posting."

"I can handle it, herr obersturmbannführer", Traugott assured him eagerly, hoping Höss wouldn't notice the gleam of greed in his eyes.

"I'm sure you can. Beyond that... I'll let your loyalty to the Reich and your faith in our Führer, not to mention your own honor, dictate your behavior. Am I making myself clear?" the camp commander asked.

"Very much so, herr obersturmbannführer."

"Don't let me down, Traugott. You're dismissed."

It took less than a week for Mattias Traugott to witness firsthand the behavior the obersturmbannführer suspected. A guard simply pocketed a gold watch that had been deposited in a box, in full view of all those present, and walked away without a second thought.

Less than a month after Traugott's arrival, the worst offenders had mysteriously been transferred out of Auschwitz and replaced by newcomers whose sole true allegiance was to the man who had got them this plum assignment and, by the same token, to the man who could take it away with a single word, a man who clearly had the obersturmbannführer's ear: Mattias Traugott.

The yield out of the Aufräumungskommando increased dramatically, to Höss' immense pleasure. Those assigned to the warehouses where the Jews' goods were sorted now lived by one very simple cardinal rule: a smaller cut of the loot is better than no cut at all. Höss was satisfied, they still grew rich – Traugott more than anyone else – and everybody was happy.

Insulated by the undying loyalty of his men and made untouchable by Rudolf Höss' blind faith in him, Mattias Traugott had in the space of just a few weeks turned himself into the uncontested king and ruler of the golden goose that was Auschwitz's Kanada.

Life was good.

Somewhere in Eastern Poland
October 1942

The bucket was filled to the brim. Its foul contents flopped over the side every time the boxcar rattled, filling the death chamber with a stench that made many gag and vomit, which only added to the rancid reek.

Still, every once in a while a brave, desperate soul would approach it reluctantly, all the while futilely trying to avoid stepping in the waste that covered the floor, and crouch or stand with legs spread wide and try to be done as rapidly and cleanly and decently as possible, prevented by whatever little human dignity they still retained from simply shitting on the floor or pissing their pants, as so many others had done.

Once, a woman relieving herself lost her balance when the boxcar suddenly lurched. She fell into the bucket and remained stuck, the filthy slop soaking into her clothes, her feet slipping and not finding any purchase as she madly tried to get up, until her husband came to her rescue and led her away as she cried hysterically.

Day had turned into night and night into day. Time was no longer relevant. There was only before, and now. There was no later, no tomorrow, no next week. Hunger and thirst and pain no longer existed, nor did hope or fear or despair. Children no longer cried, men no longer fought and women no longer loved. Those who had thought to escape had long since given up hope. Even the younger men, those who had defiantly pledged to fight back should they be given the chance, or who had come up with plan after plan for breaking out of the boxcar, had fallen silent, beaten into submission by the oppressive weight of the deep, heavy stupor that had descended upon them.

A rabbi among them still attempted to lead them into prayer, but the ranks of his flock grew ever thinner.

Another man, his mind completely gone, kept asking, *Do you know where they're taking us? Do you know where they're taking us? Do you know where they're taking us?* Nobody answered him anymore. Having heard rumors that those taken to Germany never returned, the man would then say, *I hope they're not taking us to Germany. I hope they're not taking us to Germany. I hope they're not taking us to Germany.* Then he'd start all over again.

It seemed as though the train would roll on forever. Sometimes it sped up, sometimes it slowed down, and sometimes even it stopped, but always, sooner or later, it resumed its infernal trek.

The heat inside the boxcar was unbearable. A few shouted for some water during an early stop. *Five gold watches!*, came back the disembodied answer from outside. The watches were hurriedly collected and handed through a small window at the top of the boxcar. A bucket of water was then thrown through the same opening. Those standing right next to it were drenched, but no one got a single drop to drink.

The same stratagem was repeated at the next stop, and then at the next, and then they stopped asking. They'd run out of gold watches anyway.

So now the stops no longer raised any hope, as they had before, that perhaps they had finally arrived. Those on board hardly even noticed anymore. Once, perhaps an hour ago, perhaps the day before, they'd heard cries and shouts as more of their brethren had been loaded onto the accursed wagons. That roused some to get up to peer through the planks, but what good would that do? Most simply remained where they were, raising themselves above the filth that covered the floor on the suitcases and bundles they had brought.

Adriana had lost all feeling in her legs and buttocks. She had been sitting in the same position for an eternity, squeezed in so tightly between those on each side of her that she couldn't move, and after a while her lower limbs had simply gone to sleep. She didn't even dare bend her knees, for fear that whatever space she vacated would instantly be claimed by someone else. She had tried massaging her legs, rubbing them down with open hands, but to no avail; now she wished, she hoped, for the numbness to spread to the rest of her body and put her to sleep.

She was about to piss herself. Again. At first she resisted her body's urgent demands, refusing to either humiliate herself further by using the bucket or to sacrifice her spot by getting up to do so, until her bladder had been filled to the point of rupture. Her dilemma was solved when the man next to her flopped onto his side before releasing a powerful stream of hot, pungent urine that struck her in the hip, soaking her battered, bloody nightdress. Adriana's first reaction was one of disgust and indignation and she wanted to scream at the man and claw his eyes out, but then her body betrayed her by relieving itself of the unbearable pressure in her abdomen. She stared down at herself in disbelief, her anger dissolving in the warm puddle that spread beneath her, struck dumb both by shame and by incomprehension until the moment passed and nothing changed. Those around her didn't complain - some didn't notice, but most were by now so far removed from their former selves that a stranger's warm urine was no longer something that roused their anger - and with that she lost a little bit more of her dignity.

That first time was the hardest. After that, she simply relieved herself on the spot without giving it a second thought, a bit less human and a bit more of an animal. But that only solved part of the problem. Already, she dreaded what would happen when the increasingly painful abdominal cramps that seized her periodically became simply intolerable.

Adriana turned her face to the right. She had discovered, immediately next to her head, a tiny space between two planks that let in a thin whistle of cool, fresh air. She didn't think anyone else had noticed, and it became her own private way of escaping reality. If she put her nose right next to it, she got some relief from the inhuman stench and heat that pervaded every nook and cranny of the boxcar. Every once in a while she caught a whiff of the outside world, either of belching smokestacks or of manured fields or – the worst, for the smell reminded her of childhood summer evenings spent by the lake with her brother and sister - of fresh water, and she wondered what the workers and peasants who saw this train made of it. Did they think it loaded with war supplies? With soldiers headed to the front? How could they even guess of the cargo of human misery it truly contained?

Perhaps they knew and simply chose not to care, burdened as they had to be by their own troubles.

A droplet of cool freshness fell against Adriana's upper lip, startling her. Her eyes snapped open but there was nothing for her to see; it was the middle of the night and darkness reigned uncontested. Another droplet came, and then she became aware of a faraway drumming sound superimposed over the background noise of the rolling train, to which she had grown habituated. It was raining, and an almost inexistent rivulet of water was sneaking into the wagon through what she now thought of as "her" aperture. Concealed by the night, she stuck out her tongue and the next droplet fell into her parched mouth, almost making her sob with surprise and happiness.

Thank you Aaron for sending me this water, she thought. *You're a good boy. Take good care of Mother and Father. Save me a good seat. I'll be joining you shortly.*

She then closed her eyes again and waited eagerly for the relief the next droplet would bring.

Auschwitz Concentration Camp
October 1942

Mattias Traugott narrowed his eyes and pulled deeply on his cigarette as he observed the woman sorting through the pile of clothes in front of her.

Filthy Jewess.

He'd had his doubts about her for a while now, but he'd never been able to catch her in the act. Either he was mistaken and nothing was amiss, or she was exceedingly crafty and she'd been getting away with *something* for far too long. Whatever was going on had to end and he was determined to get to the bottom of it today.

He watched as she grabbed a pair of pants from the pile. She turned out the pockets, but they were empty. She then ran her fingers along the waist and all the seams, looking for any valuables that might have been sown in the garment. Having found nothing, she conducted a second, cursory inspection before throwing the pants on top of a separate pile and reaching for another item to examine.

So far so good. She was following instructions to the letter.

Traugott sneered as he crushed the butt of his cigarette with his boot. He knew she was up to something. He could feel it in his bones. The woman looked too honest to be trustworthy. She was too good a worker – one of his best in fact – and maybe that was what set off his alarm bells. No Jew he'd ever heard of was that honest, that hardworking, that subservient. It was simply not possible. It had to be an act. The woman was playing him for a fool and she'd pay for it.

Traugott could quite conveniently come down with a bout of temporary blindness whenever one of his guards pocketed a few coins on the side. He had nothing to fear from them. They were *his* guards. They were here because of him. They knew their place, they knew there was a line not to be crossed, and most of all they understood the pecking order. They knew who the alpha male was and they sure as hell knew better than to try and rise above their station. But an inmate trying to pull a fast one on him? Trying to dupe him? That was something else entirely, something that had to be crushed in blood.

He would make an example out of her.

Traugott could have simply sent to woman to her death. He had the power to do so. A simple word from him, a look, a nod, and she'd be dead within the hour, no questions asked, problem solved. He had a power of life and death over all the women who worked under him. He was their God, since theirs had clearly forsaken them. Goodbye Yahwe, hello Mattias Traugott.

The idea was appealing and he smiled. He would grab her by the hair and drag her, screaming and pleading, to the gas chambers and he'd shove her in inside himself. He hoped she resisted with all her strength and fought with all her might, he hoped she prayed him to spare her life, he hoped she cried out in despair and fear as he beat her down mercilessly, crushing her fingers with savage kicks as she tried to hang on to the jambs before the door inevitably slammed shut, sealing her fate. Then he'd stand outside and listen with a delight of almost sexual intensity as she suffocated with hundreds of other swine like her.

But no. Simply killing her would solve nothing. The woman had found a way to trick him and if he wanted to keep others from fooling him in the same manner in the future, he first had to pierce her secret. *Then* he'd kill her.

His attention had wandered but he still caught a movement out of the corner of his eye that made his heart jump. What the hell...? In less time than it takes a snake to strike, her hand had dipped into one of the pockets of the jacket she was inspecting, she had brought it back to her, and now the hand was back inspecting the garment, as though nothing had happened. And now...

Traugott almost howled in triumph as he rushed the woman. She never even saw him coming. He didn't slow down before kicking her in the kidneys, putting all his weight behind the strike and catapulting her into the pile of clothes in front of her. The woman let out a mixed scream of surprise and pain that came out strangely muffled. Traugott grabbed her by the back of her dress and pulled her out, collapsing the pile. Around him, shouts were heard as other guards ordered the inmates to ignore the disturbance and keep working. No one would interfere.

The woman was lying on her stomach at his feet, crying. He reared back and kicked her in the ribs with the toe of his boot several times, until she twisted onto her side. He then kicked her in the stomach and she immediately spat out a whitish, slimy glob. Traugott stopped and stared at it, puzzled. Instead of the gold coin or diamond he'd been expecting, the woman had spit out a half-chewed chunk of bread. Instantly, his surprise morphed into rage at having wasted so much time worrying about a woman whose only crime had been to gobble the odd crumb. He reared back again and aimed for her face. He'd kick all her teeth in and watch as she drowned in her own blood.

Sin by the mouth, die by the mouth, bitch.

He was about to stomp her to death when he was interrupted.

"Traugott! The obersturmbannführer is requesting your presence", a voice barked.

Traugott looked up, ready to kill whoever had dared interfere. His rage abated just enough for him to recognize Höss' junior adjutant, a young man who wielded an influence comparable to his own with the camp commander. The newcomer also outranked him, but barely. Otto Ludwig Möckel was an SS-Obersturmführer (the equivalent of an American 1st lieutenant) while Höss had elevated Traugott to the rank of SS-Untersturmführer (2nd lieutenant) to grant him some official authority over his men. Technically, Traugott should have stood to attention and saluted a superior officer, but he purposefully did no such thing, letting his contempt show clearly.

The two men had grown up in neighboring villages and inherited a decades-long feud between the Traugott and Möckel clans, a quarrel that had arisen between their respective grandfathers over a wayward billygoat. Fifty years later, after numerous members of both extended families had been beaten senseless, after barns had been incinerated and cattle maimed and fields poisoned with salt, after countless acts of petty retribution, the feud was still alive and well. There was no love lost between the two men, and each looked for any occasion to get rid of the other.

The obersturmführer fought to keep his rage under control. He was clearly boiling inside at Traugott's defiance and his upper lip twitched almost inconspicuously. Traugott smiled thinly as a few guards came to stand behind him, showing the other man whose yard he was in.

Möckel finally recovered his composure and an evil glint showed in his eye. "Immediately", he added with a hint of an impertinent smirk when Traugott didn't reply.

It was Traugott's turn to fight his emotions. To be ordered around by such an upstart of a mangy pup. The man wasn't even old enough to shave, and *he* was ordering *him* around? Traugott was still hot from beating the woman and he could easily have vented what remained of his rage on his rival. After all, this was *his* kingdom and these were *his* men. The obersturmführer had no idea the danger he had placed himself in by coming here. If a fight were to break out between the two of them, and if Traugott were to kill him in the process, who did Möckel think the guards' testimony would favor? The man who was making them richer by the day or the officer who would snatch it all away?

All work had stopped as the inmates watched the unfolding confrontation between the two men. Then the woman at Traugott's feet moaned, breaking the spell. Knowing in his heart that he had won the day, Traugott dropped his eyes and delivered one last, savage kick to the woman's midsection. She immediately coughed up a fine spray of blood and saliva that covered his jackboots in slime.

"Take her away, she's done here", Traugott told his men, knowing the woman would be dead before he returned. He straightened his uniform and took a moment both to compose himself and to keep his rival waiting a moment longer. "Lead the way, herr obersturmführer", he then told the younger man with an icy smile.

The two men emerged into the cold sunlight and Traugott was instantly assaulted by the foul stench emanating from the ovens. He looked to his left and saw a column of thick, black smoke belching from the huge smokestack that towered over the crematorium. The smell was bad most of the time but on days like today, when the wind blew in the wrong direction and pushed the acrid smoke over the camp instead of away from it, it became simply intolerable. His eyes watered and bile rose in the back of his throat, and he forced himself to take very shallow breaths. He knew Möckel was also incommodated, and it became a silent contest between the two of them as to who would show the least discomfort, as to who would remain the most stoic, ever the ideal Prüssian soldier.

Still, unconsciously, they both quickened their step and moved away from the section where the smell was worst. Traugott began to breathe a bit more normally and realized the other man hadn't specified *why* the obersturmbannführer wanted to see him. He knew he had nothing to worry about, but he liked to go into any situation as prepared and as informed as he possibly could. But asking Möckel for details would have granted the other man a position of superiority and to Traugott, such a humiliation would have been worst than his current ignorance.

In any case, his questions were answered shortly thereafter when he saw that they were heading for the camp's main entrance. Höss was already standing on the ramp, along with a few other officers, when they arrived. Traugott and Möckel stopped short and fired salutes of rivaling crispness and intensity in his direction.

"Heil, herr obersturmbannführer", they said in unison.

"Heil", the camp commander replied. He seemed about to say something else but a whistle sounded in the distance, delivering a shot of adrenaline to all those present. An officer barked an unintelligible order, conjuring out of thin air armed men that lined up from one end of the ramp to the other.

The whistle blew again and this time it was accompanied by a faint but clear tremor. The tremor grew more powerful as the train approached, emerging from behind the woods that hid it from sight until the last moment. It then seemed to pick up speed, which was hardly logical, as it covered the last mile that still separated it from the camp. The men's eyes were fixated on its headlamp, the sole luminous eye of a dragon of steel come to regurgitate its human cargo. The dragon's roar grew louder as it neared, until the men couldn't hear themselves think.

Traugott was shaking with excitement. This was only the second such transport he had witnessed. The first, three days earlier, had left him stunned and speechless with its fury, its intensity - and its efficiency. Never before had he felt prouder to be German, never before had he had felt more at peace with the world, never before had he felt such a sense of purpose. All his senses overwhelmed by what unfolded before his eyes, Traugott had stood back and watched as the Jews had been unloaded and sorted. The unexpected mayhem had left him somewhat paralyzed, uncertain of what was expected of him, and he had felt a certain shame later on at having been so passive.

That wouldn't happen today.

The train pulled up alongside the ramp and stopped with a final sigh. It had barely come to a halt that men rushed to unlock the sliding doors while others stood several feet away with their rifles shouldered. Anyone stupid enough to jump out would instantly be shot dead. Then, as if of a common accord, the men opened all of the sliding doors at once. Bodies immediately tumbled out; one guard stepped aside just in time to avoid being crushed by the bloated, blackened body of an old woman who had clearly been dead for several days. The woman landed on her back and a stinking, slimy geyser erupted with surprising force from her mouth and directly into the guard's face. The man recoiled in horror and he fled blindly as he tried to clear his eyes, until he fell to his knees and began retching.

Traugott watched as the bodies were dragged away. Those who were already dead would be taken directly to the ovens; those who still lived were destined to the gas chambers and would soon wish they had died along the way. If you were too weak to stand on your two feet at Auschwitz, you had better already be dead or you would soon be.

The relative quiet that had prevailed until then was shattered by an infernal chorus of shouting men and barking dogs. "*Alles raus! Alles raus!*" the men began screaming as soon as the surviving Jews began to show themselves in the enclosure of the open doors. After days of unending darkness, they were dazed and disoriented by the sudden light, and their confusion was only increased by the violence and madness of the world in which they now found themselves. Most simply stood there, shielding their eyes with a raised forearm, unable to comprehend where they were, let alone what was happening to them.

The Nazis had understood very early on that a scared, disoriented and confused prisoner is also a docile prisoner. They weren't about to give the newcomers a single moment of respite to get their bearings. Most of them would be on their way to the gas chambers or to a new life of Hell on Earth that would make them wish for death before they finally began to understand what, exactly, had just happened.

The guards moved with a speed and efficiency borne of long practice, a technique designed to keep the inmates destabilized and disorganized for as long as possible. Those nearest the boxcars began grabbing the inmates by their clothes, pulling them off balance and onto the ramp, where they were roughly lined up in rows of five. Some managed to land on their feet, but most did not; after days of enforced immobility, their muscles had turned to stone and they could barely stand erect. Not that it mattered. All were immediately seized by other guards who shoved them left and right, roughly separating the men from the women and children, mercilessly beating and whipping those who didn't comply rapidly enough.

Traugott smiled at what happened next. The same thing had happened three days earlier and to him, it defied all logic. In his mind, it also demonstrated beyond any possible doubt the Jews' inner idiocy and cowardice.

After the first few inmates - those who had been the first to show themselves in the doors - had been physically pulled out of the boxcars, all the others began jumping out of their own accord, even though they could clearly see what was happening, like sheep that stupidly leap off a cliff one behind the other. And the more Jews jumped out, the more others followed, figuring it had to be the right thing to do. Not one seemed to stop and think about what was happening, which served the Nazis' evil purposes perfectly. The process almost became orderly as the Jews helped one another onto the ramp, the young helping the old, the strong helping the weak, and Traugott could have wept with despair at their docility.

A few prisoners working nearby shouted at the children to pretend to be 15 or 16, but their voices barely pierced the cacophony and their warnings mostly went unnoticed.

Traugott spotted Otto Möckel in the thick of things. A man was lying on the ground at the officer's feet and seemed to be indicating that he couldn't get up, that he had twisted his ankle leaping out of the boxcar. The obersturmführer was shouting at him to stand up immediately, to go join the other men, but the Jew kept pointing at his ankle and grimacing. As Traugott watched, Möckel grabbed the fallen man by the front of his clothes and, in an impressive feat of strength, pulled him up onto his feet. He then spun him around and shoved him forward with a vicious kick to the rear. His pain and injury apparently forgotten, the man turned around arrogantly to face the obersturmführer, but the officer was ready for him. He slashed the inmate across the face with his whip, leaving an angry red welt on the man's cheek. The Jew let out a howl of pain that no one heard, his hands flew to his face and, his earlier defiance crushed, he obeyed Möckel's orders.

His rival's ruthless efficiency shocked Traugott into action. He realized, again with some shame, that he had been standing idly by since the train's arrival and he worried who might have noticed. Unsure what he should do, but determined to do *something*, he ventured into the milling crowd of Jews, randomly grabbing and shoving, shouting orders to move faster, delivering the odd punch and kick here and there, but overall feeling a bit lost and not really contributing anything neither truly essential nor really useful.

All around him people screamed and cried, their wails mixing into a single song of despair and fear. Husbands looked for their wives, mothers shouted for their children, families were split apart only to be reunited and divided again, and through this unimaginable insanity Mattias Traugott waded like a man possessed, blood roaring in his ears, all senses on high alert, feeling himself to be truly a member of a superior race, one chosen to rule the world.

"Excuse me, herr offizier, but could you help me with my luggage, bitte? My suitcase is quite heavy".

Traugott stopped dead in his tracks and stared at the short man who stood before him; a man who, it appeared, had mistaken him for the bellboy of some fancy hotel. When Traugott didn't reply, the man sighed and dug a hand in his pocket before pressing something round and hard into Traugott's hand.

Traugott glanced down and smiled when he caught a glint of gold.

"Certainly. Where is your bag?" he asked, eager to get his hands on it now that he guessed what it contained that made it so heavy.

The man led him to it and, an instant later, Traugott had handed it off to one of his trusted acolytes for safekeeping and later inspection. The Jew protested but Traugott simply grabbed him by his clothes and took him to one of the fake Red Cross lorries parked nearby. The familiar emblem reassured the man who, mistaking the vehicle for an ambulance, boarded it calmly.

"*Dieses ist krank, ihn zu töten*", Traugott said as he slammed the door, condemning the man to a swift but hardly painless death.

It had all taken less than five minutes but by the time he made his way back to the ramp, a relative calm and order had been restored. Men stood in one group, women and children in another, and while the odd cry could still be heard here and there, it was as nothing when compared to the earlier mayhem.

A crying child came up to a guard and asked where his parents were. The guard laughed and pointed to the smoke swirling from a chimney.

"Do you see that? That's where your parents are", he said.

The women and the children, useless mouths that need not be fed, would now be taken directly to the gas chambers. Men would be taken to a separate section for further inspection; the strong would be allowed to live for as long as they remained productive while the weak would shortly be joining the women and children.

Orders were barked and Traugott stepped aside as the two groups began moving, each headed in a different direction. Loved ones shouted last goodbyes, destined never again to be together, and almost by magic Traugott found himself alone on the deserted ramp. Disturbed only by the soft whistling of the wind the silence felt strange, almost alien, in the wake of the earlier cacophony.

The ramp was littered with lost and discarded items: mostly shoes and hats, but also toys and food and even, over there, a broken crutch, flotsam left behind by the ebbing human tide. Traugott threaded his way carefully, kicking a few objects aside as he slowly walked the length of the train, trying to imagine what it must have been like to have been trapped in those cages for days. The stench alone, while quite different from the one produced by the ovens, was enough to make him gag and he stopped to cover his nose and mouth with his handkerchief.

That simple act, he later reflected, probably saved his life thirty years later.

At first he thought it was only the wind whistling in the empty silence. But then the noise came again, startling him. He looked around the ramp but as before, it was deserted. He was entirely alone – or so he thought.

Thinking his mind must be playing tricks on him and cursing himself for a foolish old woman spooked by ghouls and ghosts, Traugott snickered as he shook a cigarette out of his pack with a hand that still trembled slightly. He lit it and inhaled the smoke deeply into his lungs, grateful for the warmth that flooded his body. He rested his back against the boxcar, enjoying a rare moment of peace and quiet, and closed his eyes as his mind slowly settled down.

Traugott almost jumped out of his skin when the silence was again broken by a sinister moaning sound. He threw his cigarette away and pulled out his sidearm.

"Who's there? Show yourself immediately!" he said loudly.

But there was no one there who could have answered him. The ramp was empty. He was there alone. And he knew he must look like a fool standing there talking to himself and threatening to shoot imaginary voices. He holstered his sidearm after a moment and tried to regain some composure.

The moaning was coming from inside the boxcar, behind him. This time he heard it clearly, a bit louder, and he spun around as though someone had poked him with a red-hot branding iron. His heart was racing and he was sweating despite the chill in the air. He took a step closer, trying to peer through the darkness inside, but the boxcar seemed to be completely deserted. And yet...

Traugott took another step as the sound came again, his earlier fright having given way to a strangely compelling curiosity.

"Is someone in there? Come out immediately!" he ordered.

The moaning voice's reply was unintelligible. Traugott looked around, hoping for a couple of guards he could order inside the boxcar to investigate, but again, as before, he was by himself. All the others had left. He tried to convince himself that he wasn't scared to enter the boxcar as much as he was disgusted, for he could easily guess what awaited him inside, but he wasn't entirely successful.

Traugott pulled on his leather gloves, took a deep breath and climbed into the boxcar. He immediately stepped into something that squished and slipped under his foot, and he almost lost his balance. The stench inside, if such a thing was possible, was a million times worse than it had been standing just outside the door. Traugott's throat constricted and he felt on the verge of vomiting. He placed a hand over his mouth and nose and fought a sudden, primal urge to escape this place before it dissolved what little soul he retained.

His eyes adjusted to the lack of light after a few seconds and he saw that the floor of the boxcar was covered with excrement. *Swine*, he thought. *Filthy swine*. There were also various discarded items, similar to those he had seen on the ramp, and he dared not take another step for fear that he might trip and fall into this horrifying slime.

Traugott almost missed the shape huddled against the far wall of the boxcar. The hump was of a dark color, which made it almost invisible in this environment, and he might not have seen it had it not moved slightly. But now that he *had* seen it, he could look at nothing else and he began to make out a few details, such as long, matted, dark-colored hair that fell over a face, hiding it, and a garment – a dress of some sort – that had once been light in color but was now almost entirely dark brown.

The shape moaned and Traugott, startled, took an involuntary step back.

"You! I see you! Come here immediately!" he ordered, his voice sounding a bit muffled in the close confines of the boxcar.

The shape moved but it gave no indication it had heard Traugott or that it intended to obey his command.

Traugott was rapidly regaining control of himself and the situation, now that he understood what he was dealing with: not a ghost, not a ghoul, not even a figment of his imagination – nothing more threatening than a lowly, stinking Jew on the verge of death. He cursed and turned around to jump out, intending to summon those inmates charged with cleaning the boxcars after each arrival, when the shape uttered its first discernible sentence.

"Aaron? Is that you, Aaron? Please... please help me."

Traugott froze and stared at the shape. The voice, now that he heard it, was unmistakably that of a woman. He hesitated, even though he knew he should just ignore it. This wasn't his business. He should just walk away. A Jewess dying in her own filth was no concern of his. Let others deal with it.

"Get up and come here", he barked instead. "I am giving you an order, you bitch!"

The woman simply moaned again. Traugott could sense his anger bubbling up inside him. No Jew had ever defied him and lived to tell about it. This one would certainly not be the first. He whipped out his sidearm and let off a single round that pierced a neat, round hole less than two inches from the woman's head. She didn't even flinch.

I really meant to kill her, Traugott would later confess. *I was that angry, that hateful. But I missed, even though I never miss. Maybe that's what fate is all about. Had I killed her, would we all be here today?*

His anger now uncontrollable, Traugott simply dropped his gun into the muck and reached the prostrated woman in a couple of quick steps, oblivious of the swill of human waste that splashed up to his knees. He grabbed her by a handful of hair and dragged her rapidly out of the boxcar and onto the ramp.

Traugott was breathing hard. The woman was lying at his feet, face against the ground, her long, black hair falling all around her in tangled clumps.

"Get up", Traugott snarled. "GET UP", he yelled again when the woman neither moved nor replied. He instinctively reached for his sidearm, forgetting that he had abandoned it in the boxcar, and he swore when he encountered the tepid leather of an empty holster. His rage now boiling over, he bent down and grabbed the broken crutch he had spotted before. He was about to club the woman to death when someone coughed discretely behind him.

"I must say, your uniform has seen better days", a man said with a barely concealed hint of amusement and contempt.

Traugott recognized the voice instantly and he vowed to kill the Jewish bitch responsible for the humiliation he was about to endure. He dropped the crutch, removed his gloves one finger at a time and turned around.

"Herr obersturmführer", Traugott said icily. "What an unexpected pleasure."

"Indeed", Otto Möckel replied, chuckling.

Traugott looked down at his jackboots and saw that they were covered in an indescribable mixture of mud and filth and excrement. There were also numerous large dark splotches on his pants, almost up to his crotch, and he even spotted a few spots on his jacket and sleeves. He sighed.

"I... I must apologize for my appearance, herr obersturmführer", he said, almost choking on the words. "I caught this whore hiding in the boxcar and..."

The officer dismissed his explanation with an arrogant wave of the hand that infuriated Traugott. It was only then that Traugott noticed the three cleaning crews standing behind Möckel, which explained his presence here. The emaciated men looked barely conscious, as though the slightest breeze might topple them over. They just stood there, ghostlike with their sunken eyes and hollow cheeks and translucent skin, inhabitants of the haunted badlands that are the realm of those damned souls making the perilous crossing from life to death - of those damned souls who have forgotten how to live but have yet to learn how to die.

Otto Möckel glanced at the unconscious woman at their feet.

"Leave her to me", he said after a moment. "I believe I may have a... *use* for her."

Traugott was stunned. He knew perfectly well what *use* the obersturmführer might have for such a reasonably healthy young woman. He also knew that any SS caught having intercourse with a Jewess would receive an automatic death sentence. But if Möckel wanted to defile himself – not to mention risk his life - by copulating with a Jewish *säen*, well, let him. And who knew? The information might even, somehow, reach the obersturmbannführer's ears.

"As you wish", Traugott simply replied before walking away rapidly.

He smiled and knew he had scored a direct hit when he heard Möckel's sharp, involuntary intake of breath when he again failed to salute him.

Adriana was remotely aware of someone peeling off her nightdress. The air felt cool against her skin, although her entire body had essentially gone numb.

"Why is she here?" she heard a woman ask imperceptibly. "Why didn't they kill her?"

"You know why", another woman replied. "She's young and good-looking, not a dried-up old hag like us. Even animals have needs. But look at her... I don't think she has much longer left to live anyway."

The two women were whispering, as though they feared being overheard. They began washing the grime and filth from her skin. One of them was singing and the other seemed to be praying under her breath. They both fell simultaneously silent when their cleaning uncovered the large welts inflicted by the SS guard earlier, the whipping Sándor Pfircsik had stopped with his death.

"Poor child", one of the women said. "We should just let you die. Life here isn't worth living."

Then one woman was painfully pulling at her hair with a comb while the other began washing her private parts. Adriana feebly tried to protest but the woman just batted her hand away and shushed her.

"We should just shear it off", the woman working on her hair said. "It's an impossible mess. And she'll get lice like she won't believe."

"No, that'll come later", the other woman rebuked her sharply. "Obersturmführer Möckel was very explicit: for now she's to keep as much of it as possible, like those others he brought us. Cut out the worst clumps but don't do too much damage, or we'll answer for it."

Adriana drifted in and out as the women worked on her body. In her moments of clearer lucidity she kept her eyes closed, feigning unconsciousness, listening to their conversation and trying to understand where she had been taken; but all the women seemed interested in was who had died and watery rations and when the next transport was expected and whether anyone had news from home and other such mundane considerations. She still found their touch and care strangely comforting, even though they were complete strangers.

But Adriana was exhausted and those moments of lucidity never lasted for very long. She always plunged back into a deep, black sleep that refused, despite her best efforts, to keep her in its grip forever, always eventually releasing her to surface in a world of which she understood nothing.

It was during one of those trips to the surface that Adriana became aware of a burning, stinging sensation against the inside of her left forearm. She jerked and her muscles tensed, but many hands held her down and someone – perhaps one of the women who had washed her – whispered in her ear to be still, that it would only last a second, and it did. The pain abated and Adriana plunged under once again.

8

One week later

Otto Mockël rubbed his gloved hands together in satisfaction as he surveyed the room. Everything had to be perfect, and everything appeared to be.

The hardest part had been hiding everything from Rudolf Höss. The obersturmbannführer's vigilance was well-known, and there was little that occurred at Auschwitz that escaped his notice. If he didn't know about *it* firsthand, then he likely knew someone who had knowledge of *it* and would be informing him of *it* very shortly. But even though the need for secrecy had been obvious, and even though he had been entrusted with this mission by the second-most feared person at Auschwitz, Mockël still felt ill at ease lying to one of the most powerful men in a 100-mile radius.

He had agreed to the task nonetheless, knowing that great risk is more often than not accompanied by great reward. Success, he hoped, would significantly heighten his standing in the camp commander's eyes, while failure... well, failure was something he preferred not to think about.

The whole thing had been orchestrated by Höss' wife, Hedwig, a woman not exactly known for her understanding and eagerness to forgive. After convincing Mockël to take up this mission, the *frau* Höss had seemingly begun to consider him her personal valet and servant; instead of the collaboration Mockël had foolishly expected, her contribution had been one of escalating demands, watchfulness that bordered on harassment and hardly-subtle reminders of what happened to those who displeased her.

So invitations had been sent out, food ordered, staff recruited – sometimes forcibly, sometimes not – and a few prayers discretely offered.

Mockël was both impressed and pleased by the dignitaries who had trekked all the way to Auschwitz for the occasion. Several high-ranking Nazis had traveled from Germany, notable among them the former chief of Heinrich Himmler's personal staff, obergruppenführer Karl Wolff – a presence that lost some of its luster when one knew that Wolff was essentially passing through on his way to a posting with Benito Mussolini in Italy after falling out of favor with the Reichsführer in the wake of Stellvertretender Reichsprotektor Reinhard Heydrich's assassination earlier that year by Jan Kubiš and Jozef Gabčík.

The government of the province of Upper Silesia, which encompassed the camp, was represented by Gauleiter Fritz Bracht and by Artur Stegner, the mayor of Katowice, the nearest town of any significance. The two politicians had been seated at a table with representatives from corporations such as Messerschmitt, Junkers, Siemens and IG Farben, companies that increasingly relied on forced laborers to sustain their war effort.

Half a dozen inmates streamed in from the kitchens, bearing trays overloaded with steaming bowls of *kartoffelsuppe,* a type of potato soup closely associated with the German region of Baden-Württemberg from which obersturmbannführer Höss originated. The soup would be served with three different types of sausages and hot rolls. The rich aroma filled the room and the assembled men spontaneously interrupted their conversations to applaud.

Mockël could have burst with pride.

The inmates carefully placed a bowl in front of each guest as Mockël watched. He could see that some of them were trembling slightly, either from exhaustion or from terror. Or maybe the temptation of food was proving harder to resist than he had anticipated. Mockël had personally selected them for this very special night; they had been washed and shaved and dressed in clean uniforms, but they had also been warned: one single mistake, one dropped crumb, one spilled glass, one single bite stolen would cost them their lives.

He had given no thought whatsoever to the torture it might represent for starving men to find themselves in the presence of so much food.

In a rare gesture of magnanimity, but also because he so desperately wanted the evening to be a resounding success, he had promised to let them lick the empty plates at the end of the night. It wouldn't be as simple as the inmates imagined, obviously. Mockël thought it might be more entertaining to place the plates on the floor and bind the inmates' hands behind their backs, so they'd have to kneel and eat like dogs, but he was also toying with the idea of offering them a single plate and watching them fight over it. He chuckled silently at the image that formed in his mind.

The Nazi officials dug in with enthusiasm. The walls soon reverberated with the hum of resumed conversations and a cloud of blue smoke formed against the ceiling as men lit cigarettes to accompany their food. A three-piece orchestra, also composed of inmates, struck up the first chords to Richard Wagner's *Siegfried-Idyll*.

"A nice success so far", someone said behind Mockël, startling him.

The young man looked over his shoulder and saluted clumsily when he recognized hauptsturmführer Robert Mulka, Höss' adjutant and his immediate superior.

"Yes, sir... Thank you, sir. I'm glad you feel that way", Mockël managed to say.

Mulka was a hard, merciless man who lived his life under a cloud of perpetual anger. His gaze, when fueled by wrath, was enough to make the toughest of men tremble in their boots. Mockël often thought it would be preferable to face a Russian artillery barrage - during a blizzard, in the middle of the night - than to run afoul of Mulka's fury.

The hauptsturmführer grinned humorlessly. "At ease, Mockël, at ease. This is the obersturmbannführer's evening. Let's not stand on ceremony." Mulka then nodded in the direction of the inmates. "Your... *staff* is performing admirably so far", he said, his bald head gleaming with sweat in the dim light.

Mockël smiled coldly. "They better, sir", he answered slowly. "Their lives depend on it."

Mulka nodded. "I thought that might be the case", he said approvingly. "And that special event *frau* Höss requested?"

"All taken care of, sir", Mockël replied, proudly standing up a bit straighter. "They're waiting in an adjacent room, under guard. They'll be here right before dessert is served, as planned."

Mulka gave a curt nod and left without saluting to rejoin Höss' table. Mockël breathed an internal sigh of relief and wondered whether this conversation had been fortuitous or whether his boss had been purposely checking up on him.

China clinked as the inmates began collecting the dishes and piling them on trays. Mockël observed them carefully as they worked, almost hoping to catch one desperate enough to lick a finger discretely dipped into an empty bowl; that one would be sent directly to the gas chambers, a sentence that would ensure an irreproachable performance from the others for the rest of the night. But he didn't see anything amiss and less than a minute elapsed before the waiters returned with bottles of Reisling he'd manage to procure directly from Germany. They began filling glasses and the chatter was propelled to a new level of excitement by this unexpected taste from home.

The inmates returned to the kitchens to fetch the main course, an assortment of rolls of meat, fish and cabbage leaves known as *rouladen*. These seasoned rolls were filled with bacon and onions and would be served with potatoes, dumplings and red cabbage.

Dessert, Mockël expected, would be a triumph since he had located and brought to Auschwitz – at significant personal expense – a pastry chef who specialized in *dampfnudel*, a treat Höss' mother had prepared for him and which, Mockël had learned, was the obersturmbannführer's absolute favorite. This night they would be topped with vanilla sauce and stewed fruit.

If this birthday party doesn't impress Höss and put me permanently in his good graces, Mockël thought, *I don't know what will.*

Mockël now had one final detail to see to, one last variable to control to ensure the night's success. He swung through the kitchens to keep all those working there on their toes, to remind them of his presence and unwavering watchfulness, and headed straight for the staircase that led to the second floor. The guard posted in front of the third door on the right snapped to attention when he appeared at the top of the stairs.

Mockël paid him no mind.

"Open the door", he ordered.

The guard saluted and pulled from his pocket a key with which he unlocked the door. He then opened it and stepped aside as Mockël almost barged into the room.

The young officer smiled at the scene before him. It was all absolutely perfect.

"Very well", he told the guard after a moment. "I'll send for them shortly. Do *not* keep me waiting when I do."

"*Natürlich*, herr obersturmführer", the man replied.

But Mockël wasn't listening. In his mind, it was already twenty minutes later, the guests had already been floored by his surprise and obersturmbannführer Rudolf Höss himself had already come to shake his hand and congratulate him publicly for the best birthday party of his life.

Adriana was feeling a bit dizzy.

She rubbed absentmindedly at her left forearm and looked down at the reddened skin that still highlighted the number that had been tattooed into her flesh. Nineteen hundred and seventy-one. That's all she'd been called this past week. *Neunzehn... hundert... ein... und... siebzig.*

Traumatized and bruised, she had slowly slipped into a state of semi-consciousness on board the train. Both her mind and her body had progressively shut down, until she had lost all sense of who and where she was. She had vague memories of Aaron coming for her, of Aaron calling her name, but then Aaron had grabbed her by the hair and pulled her into the sunlight, where she had passed out again. Then there had been two women, one singing, one praying, and they had said something about her hair...

Adriana reached up and again fingered her long locks, grateful to find them intact. All but four of the women she had encountered over the past few days had sported either shaved skulls or closely-cropped hair, and the looks of envy some of them had shot her had made her feel ashamed, even though she didn't quite know what it was she had to be ashamed of, or for. And then there was the matter of her clothes, which were of noticeably better quality. She had no idea where they'd come from, and while they were certainly not new, at least they fit her, which was more than could be said for most of the others she'd seen so far.

She had awakened in a windowless room in the company of four other young women who, like her, had been provided with good clothes and allowed to keep their long hair. But these four others – identical twin sisters Hana and Julianna, as well as Etty and Malva - had but recently arrived and were at a loss to answer her questions. They did, however, mention overhearing their guards mention the need for "one more", which implied that their little group – whatever its purpose – was now complete with her addition.

This was seemingly confirmed when, shortly after Adriana's arrival, they were visited by a sour-faced and horribly thin woman who introduced herself simply as Valy.

Her mission, Valy announced angrily, was to teach them a song.

Bemused, Adriana and the four others looked at one another and immediately burst out in uncontrollable laughter, this certainly being the last thing they had expected to hear. To be ripped from their homes and loved ones, to be transported over hundreds of miles, to endure all this suffering... and then to be expected to learn a silly song? This was more than they could comprehend and all they could do was laugh.

They laughed until tears flooded their cheeks and it took them a moment to take notice of Valy, who was shouting herself hoarse trying to regain control of the situation. The old woman was yelling at them to be quiet, spittle flying for her lips and her face a deep red, and Adriana and her new friends eventually settled down because they suddenly feared she might die on the spot.

"Laugh while you can", the old witch venomously spat at them. "You have no idea where you are. You know *nothing* of this place, with your silly long hair and fancy clothes. You know *nothing* of what happens outside this very door. Enjoy it while it lasts, because I *swear* to you that it won't."

Her chilling words killed the last chortles that still shook their bodies and a seed of fear began to bloom inside the young women.

They were not let out of their room a single time over the following days. Whenever the door opened – usually to admit a guard or Valy – they would have to kneel with their heads pressed against the wall and their hands covering their eyes, to keep them from catching even a glimpse of the outside world. They often heard voices, either angry or pleading, but beyond that, as Valy had said, they really knew nothing of what happened outside their walls.

They soon settled into a mind-numbing routine of sleep and rehearsal. A guard pounded on their door every morning to wake them, shortly before Valy arrived. They paused briefly in mid-morning when a meal was brought, and Valy left for the day when the second meal was delivered in the early evening. The five women slept on thin mattresses of straw and they relieved themselves into a bucket placed in the corner. This brought back unpleasant memories, but at least this bucket had a lid and the guard would take it away whenever they requested.

The relative comfort in which they lived soon became intolerable and the women found themselves teetering on the verge of madness. Their cell grew smaller by the day as the walls seemed to close in on them. The song – repeated a million times a day – turned into a nightmare that haunted their minds. Valy had clearly received extensive musical training and she proved an impossible taskmaster, berating them every time they faltered. Etty, more than the others, bore the brunt of the old woman's anger, since the poor girl was completely tone-deaf and couldn't have carried a tune to save her life – which, in this case, she apparently needed to do.

This, in turn, led to tensions between the women, who began blaming one another for their apparent inability to please Valy and bring this torture to an end. A small fissure formed within their group, with sisters Hana and Julianna in one camp and Adriana, Etty and Malva in the other. Fights and shouting matches broke out daily. The women often ate their last meal of the day in silence, the camaraderie of the first days having given way to an animosity that bordered on hostility.

Then, on what was perhaps the fifth day, everything changed. Valy didn't come in the morning and the guard who brought them their meal ignored their questions. A few hours later, the five women were blindfolded and taken to shower under the watchful eye of several guards. At first they balked at denuding themselves in front of so many men, but it rapidly became very clear that they didn't have a say in the matter. The guards were also quite serious, almost grim, and their whole demeanor indicated that they weren't here for their personal enjoyment; something grave was clearly afoot and the five women sensed they had nothing to fear from them. So they turned their backs to the men and shielded each other's intimacy as best they could while they enjoyed the hot water and fragrant soap and shampoo that were provided.

The guards began shouting "*Raus! Raus!*" after about ten minutes and the women rapidly rinsed off before the water was turned off. Each then donned clean clothes and they were allowed a few minutes to do each other's hair. Again blindfolded, they walked for about fifteen minutes, exiting one building before eventually entering another, and when the blindfolds were removed they found themselves in this room, in what appeared to be a mansion of some sort.

Four guards were in the room with them, one posted in each corner. Adriana looked at each one in turn, but the men ignored her and simply stared vacantly ahead.

"Where do you think we are?" she whispered to Malva, who was sitting next to her. The other woman shrugged. "I don't know, but I'm not liking it at all", she said softly.

The smell of rich, warm food wafted into their room, making their stomachs growl. Adriana fought a new wave of nausea and exhaustion. She buried her face in her hands to steady herself and tried to keep from crying. Images kept flashing through her mind... the Hlinkas bursting into their apartment... the men who tried to rape her... Aaron shot dead on the floor in front of her eyes... her parents missing in the crowd... Sándor Pfircsik, another one killed because of her... the train... all tumbled in her head in a never-ending, nightmarish kaleidoscope.

From somewhere in the distance came the sound of music and people applauding. Adriana looked up just as the door was unlocked and opened.

A young SS officer was standing in the doorway, looking at them. His uniform was crisp and sharp and his jackboots gleamed. He examined each woman in turn, his eyes resting on each for several seconds, and nodded to himself, apparently satisfied. He left without addressing them, but Adriana overheard him tell the guard that he'd be sending for them shortly.

She began to piece things together, and the picture that formed felt like a kick in the stomach. Here they were, five attractive young women, freshly washed and coiffed, dressed nicely, in a manor where a party was clearly being held, if one were to judge by the smell of food and sound of music. An SS had just come to examine them, with the same attention one gives cattle at market, and had pronounced himself satisfied by what he'd seen.

Now, she asked herself, what possible use are five young women at a party of Nazi officials? A single, disgusting possibility instantly flashed through mind and she felt her knees weaken. Then anger flared up at the bottom of her being and she again vowed to fight these monsters with every ounce of strength she possessed. She scanned the room for any potential weapon but it was entirely bare, except for the five chairs in which they sat. The SS officer had, however, clearly indicated that they'd be moved soon, and Adriana resolved to be on the lookout for any opportunity that might present itself.

Let them be stupid enough to lead us through the kitchens or the dining room, she thought. *Even a dull butter knife will do.*

She was about to attempt to share her plan with Malva when the door opened again.

"*Folgen Sie mir*", the Nazi guard ordered roughly while motioning for them to get up. His four colleagues left their posts in each corner of the room and herded the women toward the door.

Adriana found herself at the front of the line, immediately behind the guard. The twins walked behind her, followed by Etty and Malva. She wished Malva had been right behind her, since she knew she could count on her no matter what; Hana and Julianna, on the other hand, could simply be relied on to do whatever most favored them. Of the four men who had guarded them in the room, two now walked on each side of the column while the last two brought up the rear.

They were led down a short corridor and down a flight of stairs. Adriana's heart was beating so fast she feared it might burst. But even through her terror she noticed how luxurious the mansion was, how plush the carpet was, how fine the tapestry was, how high the ceilings were. She had never known anyone who inhabited a residence such as this one.

The noise of a room filled with chattering people grew louder as they neared the bottom of the stairs. The smell of food was also stronger, but she was so nervous that it now made her want to vomit. Her palms were sweaty and she focused on the back of the neck of the guard in front of her. If she got her hands on a blade, where should she strike? Should she go for the jugular, like a rabbi performing *shechita*? After all, the Sicarii rebels entrenched at Masada had dispatched one another in just such a fashion rather than surrender to Roman governor Lucius Flavius Silva and his legion, the famed *X Fretensis*. Should she instead try to plunge it between two vertebrae? Perhaps a strike between the ribs, aimed at the kidneys, would be more effective? Could she even bring herself to kill another human being, if her life or her honor depended on it? Twice already she'd been assaulted and almost killed. And twice already she'd been saved not by her own hand, but by someone else's sacrifice.

Lost in her thoughts she almost bumped into the guard when he stopped abruptly. The guard saluted and only then did Adriana notice the officer who'd visited them a few minutes earlier. The man was standing with his back to a closed door and he looked visibly nervous.

"Heil, herr obersturmführer", the guard said.

"Heil", the officer replied distractedly. "You're dismissed. I'll take it from here."

The five guards all saluted before departing, leaving the five women alone with Otto Mockël. He lined them up one besides the other, facing him, and again examined each one minutely. He stood less than a foot away from Adriana and looked her over completely, from head to toe. He spent an uncomfortable amount of time staring at her breasts, which only confirmed her worst fears. Mockël even leaned in to smell her and his own scent so repulsed her that she thought she might throw up all over his sadistic uniform. She looked down, away from him, and her eyes alighted on the man's sidearm. It was right there, almost touching her, less than six inches from her hand, and she wondered if she might be quick enough to snatch it out of its holster and start shooting. Mockël moved on to the first twin before she'd found the courage to act, leaving her on the verge of tears.

Mockël needed almost ten minutes to complete his examination. By the time he was done, Adriana was shaking like a leaf with fear and anticipation. She could only imagine what fate awaited them on the other side of that door. Regretting her earlier inaction, she cast around for a weapon, any weapon, even a potted plant or a book, but there was nothing she could use. And even if there had been... what use would it have been to kill this one Nazi when there were a thousand others just waiting for her?

"*Sehr gut*", Otto Mockël finally said in a low voice. "*Sehr gut*. You are all very pretty. *Jetzt wirst du singen*."

Adriana could not believe her ears. This was what this was all about? The endless rehearsals with Valy, the humiliating shower, the clean clothes? They had been brought here to sing that silly, silly song for a bunch of Nazi pigs? Of course, now that she put two and two together, it made sense. But she still felt like crying with relief.

Mockël opened the door and strode into a large room filled with eating, smoking and chatting men. The five women instinctively filed in behind him and their appearance quieted the crowd down almost as if by magic. The assembled men stared agape at the five goddesses, two of them absolutely identical and indistinguishable from one another, who had suddenly materialized in their midst, like angels fallen from the heavens straight into Hell. The sudden appearance of Adolf Hitler himself wouldn't have made more of an impact. A silence of almost religious intensity reigned as Mockël proudly led his *piece de resistance* to the front of the room. He paused for a moment to enjoy his triumph and to allow the men a few more seconds to admire the women – *his* women. He caught a man at Höss' table nudging his neighbour suggestively and he didn't need much imagination to guess what some of the guests were thinking.

"Herr obersturmbannführer", he began, addressing Rudolf Höss directly. "We have assembled here today to celebrate your birthday, the birthday of a man who will undoubtedly be remembered as one of the greats of our glorious Reich. And such a man deserves nothing less than the absolute best. So, herr obersturmbannführer, for you..."

Mockël nodded at Adriana, his eyes cold and hard but his meaning absolutely clear. Adriana froze for a moment, petrified by his stare, before looking away. The moment was at hand and there was no avoiding it. So she took a deep breath and asked Aaron to help her get through this.

Heute kann es regnen,
stürmen oder schnei'n,
denn du strahlst ja selber
wie der Sonnenschein.

Adriana had always enjoyed singing, but she had never imagined she would one day be called upon to do so in a setting such as this. She had good voice, strong and clear, and she could hit most high notes without sounding too strained, which probably explained why Valy had chosen her to sing the first verse alone. But tonight, exhausted and terrified as she was, her voice sounded thin and unstable to her ears, and she was relieved when Hana and Julianna's turn to perform came.

Heut ist dein Geburtstag,

darum feiern wir,

alle deine Freunde,

freuen sich mit dir.

Adriana took a few deep breaths to settle her voice. Then, in almost perfect unison, the five women launched into the song's chorus.

Wie schön, dass du geboren bist,
wir hätten dich sonst sehr vermisst.
wie schön, dass wir beisammen sind,
wir gratulieren dir, Geburtstagskind!

Adriana and poor, gentle, harmless but completely tone-deaf Etty had to sing the next verse together, Valy having obviously relied on Adriana's voice to carry them through. She knew Etty had to be even more terrified than she was, so she discreetly reached for her hand. The other woman grabbed it eagerly and squeezed back so hard that Adriana almost winced in pain.

Uns're guten Wünsche
haben ihren Grund:
Bitte bleib noch lange
glücklich und gesund.

Etty stumbled on the last sentence. Her German was less than rudimentary and she was essentially regurgitating sounds she had memorized, rather than words she understood. Adriana felt her stiffen. This was the last thing that needed to happen. If Etty were to make it to the end of the song, she had to stay as relaxed as possible. Adriana gave her hand a squeeze to steady her and they attacked the next verse together.

Dich so froh zu sehen,
ist was uns gefällt,
Tränen gibt es schon
genug auf dieser Welt.

Adriana's eyes filled with tears when they released the last word, so proud was she of Etty. The girl had acquitted herself more than honorably, she had overcome her fears, and since this was the only section of the song that really threatened to expose her limited singing abilities, they were mostly home-free. The five women then sang the chorus one more time, their voices filling the room and mesmerizing the men. Cigarettes smoldered forgotten and glasses remained suspended in mid-air as Malva and the twins launched into the next verse.

Montag, Dienstag, Mittwoch,
das ist ganz egal,
dein Geburtstag kommt im Jahr
doch nur einmal.
Darum lass uns feiern,
dass die Schwarte kracht,
Heute wird getanzt,
gesungen und gelacht.

Adriana had to sing the final verse alone to bring the song full circle, to bring to an end to what she had begun – to kill the infant she had birthed. She stared at the assembled men and for an instant wondered through what perverse logic they could think themselves better than her. They were flesh and blood just like her, they needed food and sleep and love just as much as she did, they voided their bladder and bowels daily, they too experienced pain and joy... and yet here they were, making her perform like a circus animal for their enjoyment, forcing her to entertain them against her will, some of them salivating as they watched, lust etched openly on their features.

She then looked at Rudolf Höss. She really had no idea who he was, but it was obvious that he was a man of some importance, a leader among them. Adriana thought him an ugly, pudgy man who had been cursed with a large nose, meaty lips and oily skin. Him, a member – nay, a leader! - of the so-called "master race"? Please. Höss stared back at her with less interest than a cow gives a passing train as she launched into the final verse of the song. She channeled all her anger through her voice and it came out so powerful and so clear that some of the men visibly recoiled under its assault.

Wieder ein Jahr älter,
nimm es nicht so schwer,
denn am Älterwerden
änderst du nichts mehr.

Now it was Etty's turn to discretely reach for and squeeze Adriana's hand. The girl could feel the intensity of the moment and an electric charge coursed between them. They held on to one another as tightly as they could, reveling in the potency of the spell that Adriana had cast over these monsters who would devour them, enjoying this brief instant of power for they knew, both consciously and unconsciously, that the end of the song would open onto much, much darker times.

Zähle deine Jahre
und denk' stets daran:
Sie sind wie ein Schatz,
den dir keiner nehmen kann.

Adriana held the last note for as long as she could, knowing that the spell would shield them for as long as she kept singing. But in the end, unavoidably, she could sing no longer and she had to let the last word die, hoping that they wouldn't all die along with it. The spell held for a few seconds longer as her voice reverberated across the room – and then it was smashed to pieces as the men began applauding wildly. Adriana wondered if they realized they were ovationing members of a race who they claimed to be inferior to them in all things.

Otto Mockël ran to the front of the room to bathe in the applause as well but hauptsturmführer Robert Mulka beat him to it by half a second. No doubt his superior would have stayed comfortably in his seat if the song hadn't been so triumphantly received. But as it was, Mulka was more than eager to steal his underling's thunder and he proudly and publicly congratulated Mockël for having followed his orders so efficiently. Adriana caught the look of absolute dismay and complete furor that descended on Mockël's face, but the rest was lost to her since the five women, their usefulness spent, were already being hustled out of the room by guards who had appeared out of nowhere.

Adriana glanced behind her one last time before being shoved out the door. She could feel eyes on her, eyes that were tracking her, but there were so many men there that it could have been anyone of them. Then the guards pushed them forward and the door slammed shut behind them.

At the back of the room, transfixed, stood Mattias Traugott.

Night had fallen and the camp was bathed in an unnatural glow by the hundreds of searchlights that swept across it incessantly. They encountered several patrols and many guards were clearly startled by their appearance, but the men who escorted them kept them moving at a brisk pace.

The women were led to a dark building. A guard opened the door and light flooded from inside the building. The five women were shoved inside and the door was closed behind them.

Many, many years later, Adriana would recall this as the exact moment when the ground opened up beneath her feet and she plunged directly into a hell from which she wouldn't emerge for a very long time.

Adriana looked around the room fearfully. She was at first struck by the presence, along the wall to her left, of several chest-high mounds of what appeared to be human hair, roughly sorted by color. There were also piles of clothes, some badly damaged and others not, and shoes; there were three mounds of these, one each for men, women and children.

A dozen guards appeared from an adjoining room, as though they had been waiting for them. These guards appeared bored and jaded, as though what was about to occur was as mind-numbingly routine to them as having a cup of coffee. Several yawned and stretched while they examined the newcomers. And then, just as wolves smell which member of the herd is weakest, they sensed that Etty was the most vulnerable of the five, and they went after her first. The girl screamed in terror when the men grabbed her and pulled her away from the others. She reached back for Adriana and Adriana reached for her and their fingers touched but then Adriana was roughly shoved back by the guards who had taken them here.

Two guards held Etty by the arms as the others expertly and rapidly cut off her clothes. It all took less than five seconds; one moment she was fully clothed, the next she was completely naked. The girl screamed again as the four remaining women huddled together, crying and clinging to each other for safety. Adriana's mind immediately flashed back to the two Hlinka guardsmen who had attempted to rape her, for surely this was the fate that awaited them here. Without thinking she lunged past the guards and almost made it to Etty before the men grabbed her and threw her back.

"Your turn will come", one of them growled sadistically.

"Leave her alone, you pigs," she shouted at the top of her lungs. "Let her go!" She again tried to run to Etty but this time Malva and the twins restrained her, grabbing handful of her clothes and pulling her back.

"Adriana stop!" Malva shouted in her ear. "Stop or they'll kill you!"

"Then let them kill me!" Adriana shouted back defiantly but no matter how hard she struggled, she couldn't break free of them.

The four women watched helplessly as the guards forced Etty to the ground. Two still held her arms and two now grabbed her legs and tried to pull them apart. There was a flash of light on metal and a buzzing like that of an angry swarm of bees as another guard knelt next to Etty's head and began shearing off her hair. Her long, blond locks fell away in clumps and her face was soon covered with hair as she thrashed around, desperately trying to escape.

Another guard was standing next to her feet and Adriana immediately guessed what his purpose was. The two guards holding Etty's ankles were pulling with all their might, but the girl was fighting them with all her strength and they were having no success. She was showing surprising resistance for a girl her size. Tiring of the fight, the guards released her ankles and began mercilessly pummeling her thighs with their fists. Etty howled in pain and she tried kicking her assailants, but there was little she could do.

After a few seconds her kicks grew weaker and the guards knew they had her. They again grabbed her by the ankles and began pulling. Etty was still able to resist, but this time only for a few seconds. The space between her ankles inexorably grew wider. Etty abruptly stopped crying and she raised her head off the floor and clenched her jaws like a woman giving birth, but this was a struggle she could not win. Her bruised muscles betrayed her and her legs finally snapped open. The guard immediately knelt down and carelessly shaved off her thatch of dark hair. Etty whimpered like a wounded animal when he nicked the most sensitive spot of her entire body.

The guards holding her released her and walked away. Another approached with a bottle and doused her from head to toe with a powder that smelled strongly of disinfectant, not caring if she got any in her mouth or eyes. Etty curled up on the floor in the fetal position, crying and muttering words only she could understand. She seemed to be rocking herself, like a baby trying to get to sleep, and there she remained until the guards picked her up by the arms and dragged her away.

Adriana and the three others were petrified with terror, each fearing that she might be next. Malva's nightmare was the next to come true and she cried hysterically when the guards came for her. She clung to Adriana and the twins, and they to her, but the guards were much too strong. The tug-of-war ended when her clothes tore and she was ripped away from her friends. It was as though the sound of her tearing clothes had paralyzed her. She went entirely still, almost catatonic, and stopped fighting back completely. She even spread her legs willingly for the guard to shave her, which elicited more than a few obscene comments from the Nazis.

The guard next grabbed Hana but he froze when he realized that she and Julianna were identical twins, which he had apparently failed to notice until now. He stared at the two of them, then he looked back at his friends over his shoulder, and they all laughed when he grabbed Julianna as well, leaving only Adriana.

The two women were stood next to one another as the men encircled them. The Nazis seemed to find the situation quite amusing, even though the twins were clearly terrified. They were holding hands and clutching one another and crying, but the more fear they showed, the more the men laughed. The guards eventually tired of the sport and Adriana again, uselessly, shouted at them to stop when they attacked the twins as one, tearing their clothes away and leaving them naked in the middle of the room.

There was a brief pause as the men shamelessly examined the twins' bodies, having taking it upon themselves to determine just *how* identical they were. The Nazis were clearly fascinated – in a disgusting, animal way - by the spectacle of two exact copies of the same female. If it's true that most men fantasize about having sex with two women simultaneously, it's even truer that they fantasize about having sex with identical twins. Rude comments were made and ribald jokes flew, and Adriana could sense the situation deteriorating by the second.

A few guards grabbed truncheons with which they began poking Hana and Julianna, making them cry even harder. The women tried to protect themselves and cover their bodies as breasts and buttocks and vaginas were assaulted, but the guards were simply too numerous. The poking grew more intense and more perverse. As Adriana watched, the guards began stroking their truncheons as they would stroke themselves. One leaned in closer and poked Julianna directly in the anus with an upward thrust, making her scream in fear and pain. His friends howled with laughter. The twin spun around, away from him, in the process inadvertently turning her back to another guard who now assaulted her in the same manner. It soon became a sport to see who could strike a direct hit on the women's most private parts, either from the front or from behind, and the men began wagering as to who would actually succeed in *inserting* his truncheon first.

Hana and Julianna were being driven mad by the assault. No matter which way they spun, no matter which baton they swatted away, there was always another man with another truncheon coming at them from somewhere. One man tried to poke Hana in the mouth but instead smashed her nose, flooding the lower half of her face with blood. The sight of blood drove the men to a new frenzy and there was but one thing that could happen. One man unfastened his pants and grabbed Julianna from behind, shoving her to the ground as the other guards cheered. He turned her over so that she lay on her stomach and he positioned himself on top of her from behind, holding her hands behind her back with one hand while with the other he fumbled to extirpate his manhood from his clothes. Hana screamed and tried to shove the man off her sister, but others grabbed her and pulled her away.

The man was still fumbling when he died. He let out a strange, strangled cry - more like a croak, really – and his whole body shuddered before going completely limp. His left foot twitched a few times before it, too, joined the rest of the body in death.

The guards didn't notice anything at first, so excited were they. But after a few seconds, a strange, surreal silence enveloped the room and their cheers died as they finally realized that something was clearly wrong.

One man nudged the would-be rapist gently with the tip of his boot, and then took a quick step back when the guard simply rolled off Julianna's naked body. Julianna quickly scuttled away, crying and whimpering, to join her sister.

The heart attack had been as sudden as it had been unforgiving. The man's vacant eyes stared at the ceiling and his lips had already turned blue. His right hand was still clenched around a quickly deflating dick.

Another man – a low-ranking rottenführer who had been among the ringleaders - knelt next to the man's head and bent down to listen for breath. Finding nothing, he cursed and shook his head in disgust. He then stood up and, with the help of a couple of others, pulled the body away, barking a mixture of profanities and orders all the while.

All the sport now gone out of them, the men made short work of shaving Julianna and Hana before turning their attention to Adriana.

She felt a primal fear wash over her, a fear that urged her desperately to flee, but she refused to yield to it. *Never again*, she vowed. *Never again will I run from them*. She stood her ground and steeled herself for what was to come. When the guard reached for her, she reared back and spit in his face with all the strength she could muster. The man recoiled, took a step back and wiped her saliva from his face with his sleeve before angrily punching her in the stomach as hard as he could. Adriana doubled over, retching, as the man grabbed her by the hair and dragged her to the middle of the room.

Adriana knew what to expect by now, but the guards seemed to her to be angrier than before. These were men who had been fired by lust only to be deprived of their prize at the very last moment, and Adriana now feared that they might relieve their pent-up frustration on her. She tried to free herself from their grasp, she screamed and clawed at the hands holding her, but it was pointless. She was like a dwarf fighting an army of giants.

They began cutting off her clothes, painfully nicking her skin on several occasions, and after a few seconds she, too, found herself lying on her back, naked on the cold concrete floor. She heard the buzz of the approaching razor and a fresh wave of panic washed over her.

Her hair was nothing short of legendary. It was long and dark and thick and curly. His father had often joked that small birds probably hid and nested in her hair, unbeknownst to the rest of the world. Her hair was the envy of all the other women in her neighborhood. It was what had men lined up around the corner at the door of the Zöbel household. Her hair was what most people first mentioned about her. Simply put, it was what defined her. "*Adriana? Adriana who?*" people would ask. "*Adriana Zöbel*", others would reply. "*Adriana with the hair*". "*Aaaah... that Adriana! Now I know who you mean! Adriana with the hair!*" Asking Adriana to part with her hair was like asking her to cut off an arm or a leg.

She twisted her head left and right, hoping for a hand to bite, but the Nazis had done this hundreds of time before and they were staying safely out of reach. When the first clumps fell away, she felt as violated – perhaps even more so – as she had when the Hlinka guardsmen had attempted to rape her several days earlier. By shaving off her hair, the Nazis were ripping away her identity, her uniqueness, they were depriving her of one of the central components of what made her a human being. She was so traumatized by the feeling of the blades scraping against her skull that she barely even noticed when the Nazis shaved her secret garden bald.

And then it was over. They released her, leaving her completely exhausted and utterly dehumanized on the ground. Adriana grabbed a handful of her hair and held it in a closed fist against her mouth and nose, the faint smell of shampoo still perceptible, as she too was doused with disinfectant.

The women were handed thin tunics of striped burlap that scratched their skin and wooden clogs for their feet. No matter what they did, the tunics hung on them like oversized sacks of potatoes and it was simply impossible to be even remotely comfortable in them. The tunics were especially tight under the arms, where they chafed the skin horribly, but at this stage Adriana and the others would have gladly slipped on straight jackets woven of barbed wire, if only to hide their bodies from these monsters.

They were stunned to see that day was dawning when they exited the building. Hadn't it been the middle of the night when they had been taken from Höss' birthday party? Just how long had their ordeal lasted, exactly? The guards led them to a courtyard where they lined up in the cool morning air. They rapidly began shivering in their ridiculous clothes but the guards barked furiously at them when they wrapped their arms around themselves for warmth. They had to stand perfectly straight, with their arms next to their bodies, and not move.

Adriana hated how the cold air felt against her naked scalp. Tears filled her eyes but she fought them back. She glanced at Malva next to her. The girl was staring straight ahead and she had yet to emerge from that trance in which she had plunged earlier, when the guards had seized her. She had the vacant stare of a woman who has gone into hiding deep, deep within herself. Adriana kept staring at her, hoping that Malva would sense her eyes on her and glance her way, but Malva was somewhere else, somewhere far, far away.

Adriana wished she could join her.

10

Mattias Traugott was at war with himself.

He couldn't sleep. He had tried everything, even singing his favorite lullaby to himself in his mind, but always sleep eluded him as he tossed and turned.

All he could think of, all he could see, was that woman. Her face floated behind his closed eyelids, just as it danced in front of him when he stared into nothingness.

Goddamn Jewish bitch, flaunting herself like that in front of a hundred men. Goddamn Jewish whore.

I'll kill you if I ever see you again.

Mattias Traugott sought refuge in the safe haven of his hatred, failing to notice that it didn't burn quite as hot as before.

PART TWO

Six months later, April 1943

1

When they awoke that morning, they found that Etty had died during the night.

Adriana had spent the night with her head resting on her friend's chest and she immediately noticed the silence beneath the ribcage. She opened her eyes slowly and listened more closely, but there was nothing. The lungs didn't breathe and the heart didn't beat. Adriana sighed and closed her eyes again. She had no strength to waste on sorrow or sadness. She needed to sleep, even if only for a few extra minutes.

Etty was the second member of their group to go. Malva had been the first, having lasted not even one day. The Nazis had taken her away on their very first night in the barracks, in camp Fk4. The girl had laid down on the thin mattress of straw that covered their platform and almost immediately begun screaming and flailing at herself as though she'd gone mad.

"Get them off me, get them off me!" she howled, having apparently snapped out of her catatonia.

Adriana grabbed her shoulders to calm her down, but she let go after mere seconds with a scream of her own when she felt the first bites. She looked at her hands and saw dozens of tiny black insects crawling over her skin and invading her body like an army on the march. Repulsed and horrified, she instinctively tried to shake them off, but it was already too late. The lice, starved for warm human blood, weren't going anywhere.

Malva was rolling on the floor, slapping at herself and tearing at her clothes and gibbering like a demented soul. Having laid down first on the mattress, she had instantly been assaulted by millions of lice and this had dealt one ultimate, fatal blow to her sanity. Whatever light burned in her mind winked out, leaving nothing but a dark emptiness.

Alerted by her screams, guards rushed to their section and began pummeling her with their boots. One hard blow landed on her chin, knocking her out, and Malva finally fell silent. Not willing to risk infecting themselves, the guards ordered two other women to drag her away as Adriana,

Etty and the twins watched, stunned and helpless. Had they known they would never see her again, they might have tried to intervene, they might have tried to save her – but truth be told, they had yet, at the time, to take the full measure of this place where they now found themselves. They were still capable, during those first few days, of a naivety and a credulity which they today found laughable, and they believed Malva would be taken to a doctor and then returned to them. Never did they imagine she was being taken directly to the gas chambers.

Adriana grunted as the woman next to her turned over and poked her in the ribs with an elbow, trying to gain an extra inch of space. Adriana had rapidly learned to fight right back and she poked the woman in the stomach. The woman let out a breath of pain and retreated.

They slept eight women to each platform, even though there was only enough space for four. So six of them squeezed in together lengthwise as tightly as they could, while the other two slept crosswise with either their bunkmates' feet or heads on them through the night. This inhumane arrangement, while better than sleeping on the floor, drove people mad after a few days. It turned previously civilized human beings into wild animals ready to scratch and punch and shove and even bite if it gained them just a little bit more space. It wasn't rare for fights to break out in the middle of the night, all over an extra half-an-inch of privacy.

Adriana, Etty and the temporarily-chastened Hana and Julianna rapidly figured out there was strength in numbers. They saw how they could slightly improve their lot if they all slept on the same platform, since between the four of them they controlled half the sleeping spots. That gave them some say over who slept where and they didn't have to worry as much about someone trying to cheat them. Malva's survival would have guaranteed them dominance of their platform, which would have essentially preserved them from ever having to sleep in one of the dreaded crosswise spots.

Etty's death would change everything. There were now only three of them left and the balance of power would shift to their five bunkmates the very next night. Adriana also knew that she could count on the twins to jump ship the first chance they got. Had they remained firm in their alliance, the three of them might have been able to hold their own for a while, but Adriana knew that would never happen. Hana and Julianna would dump her the second it served their purposes to do so, just as they had been playing nice for the past six months solely because it allowed them a small measure of additional comfort.

Adriana sighed again as she realized that she was likely to be relegated to one of the crosswise spots for the foreseeable future.

She didn't even have enough energy left to be angry at Etty for dying. If anything, she was happy that her friend had finally been freed from her torments. Frail and vulnerable Etty should by all rights have been the first to die. That she had survived for this long while others, stronger and fatter and meaner, had succumbed long ago was nothing short of miraculous. But Etty had possessed an inner strength, a burning *fire*, that others had lacked and she had been able to go on day after day. Still, unavoidably, she had fallen sick the week before and stopped eating, instead offering her meager rations to Adriana. Adriana refused at first and tried to force her friend to eat, but she relented when Etty instead gave her food to Hana and Julianna, who devoured it eagerly. Etty then developed a fever and it became obvious she didn't have much longer to live.

Adriana scratched absentmindedly at a louse. She hoped the *kommando* charged with collecting the bodies of the dozens who died each night wouldn't be too busy to take Etty away later. The Nazis' insane bureaucracy demanded that each inmate – living or dead - report for muster every morning. That meant the dead had to be taken along and supported upright by two others while muster was called. If the *kommando* couldn't then take the body away, it had to be returned to its platform and brought back the next morning – a process that, in some instances, was repeated over several days.

Adriana clasped her hands over her distended belly. At some point she had gotten so used to being constantly hungry that she could no longer really recall what *not* being hungry felt like. The watery soup and piece of hard black bread they received daily were just enough to keep them from dying, and not enough to keep them truly alive.

This was the demented world she now inhabited, a world where the dead were considered living until further notice, where hunger was the norm, where people cared only for themselves and not for one another, and where the dead were envied instead of mourned.

Adriana was lost in those thoughts when *reveille* was sounded, marking the dawn of another day of backbreaking and often life-threatening labor. She kept her eyes closed a moment longer and wished Etty well on her journey to whatever world might still exist after this one. She then rolled off the platform and asked Aaron to grant her the strength to fight for her life, one more time.

Mattias Traugott reclined his chair against the wall and crossed his ankles over the edge of the table as he listened to the sweet music of the man's numbers.

"*Zwanzig... dreißig... vierzig... fünfzig*", the man said before pausing. "That makes it five hundred American dollars, herr untersturmführer. One of our better hauls to date."

Traugott pulled deeply on one of the rich, expensive cigars he and his men had appropriated a few days earlier, enjoying the smoothness of the smoke as it filled his lungs. He then released it slowly and smiled as the blue cloud billowed toward the ceiling. Five hundred American dollars in a single week. Not bad indeed. And that was on top of the Hungarian *pengős*, Slovak and Czech *korunas*, Polish *złotys* and currencies from half a dozen other nations that were piled on the table in front of them. A locker at the back of the room – a locker that only Traugott could open – contained the gold, jewelry and other valuables they had found and which would later be liquidated on the black market.

He poured himself another measure of cognac and swirled the amber liquid around in his glass before gulping it down. The men in the room with him were already rich and getting richer by the day, him more than anyone else. He could see greed gleaming in their eyes as they stared at the money and knew that this was a dangerous beast, one he needed to tame lest it ruin everything.

He pulled on his cigar again as he made up his mind, knowing that all eyes rested on him.

"Yes, it's very impressive", he finally said. "But give half of it back to the obersturmbannführer. If we take too much, he'll grow suspicious."

The men gasped and Traugott knew that his authority over them was about to be seriously challenged.

"Half? *Half?*" the man who had counted the bills repeated incredulously, in a tone that Traugott didn't care for. "Half is too much, herr untersturmführer. Let's give back 20 percent. That should be enough."

The other men grunted their assent. Eighty percent of the haul for them and a measly twenty percent for the man who could send them all to jail for fifty years if he so decided struck them as an eminently reasonable proposition. Traugott, on the other hand, knew that it was pure suicide. They had grown greedy as of late, keeping more and more money for themselves as the number of prisoners passing through the camp grew exponentially. Traugott knew Höss was bound to notice, sooner or later, that the loot generated by his *effekten-kommando* wasn't growing at the same rate.

And then questions would be asked. And the last thing Traugott wanted, the last thing he *needed*, was Rudolf Höss asking questions. They were walking a very fine line and one false step could kill the goose that laid the golden eggs.

He removed his feet from the table and began pacing slowly around the room, a cloud of smoke trailing behind him. The men were encouraged that he seemed to be giving their proposal some consideration. Traugott stared at the ground as he walked, his hands linked behind his back, unconsciously mimicking one of Hitler's favorite poses, and he circled the room once before coming to stand directly behind Dieter Lotze, the man who had proposed the 80-20 split.

Lotze was a relative newcomer to their group but Traugott was already beginning to regret recruiting him. The others had recently grown more rebellious under his influence, and for the first time Traugott's decisions were being challenged – sometimes openly, but mostly behind his back. His leadership of the operation was no longer as secure as it had once been and this wasn't something he would tolerate any longer.

"I see", he said slowly. "So you all agree that we should keep more money for ourselves than we send back to Höss."

The men all nodded contentedly, believing he had come around to their way of thinking.

"Herr Lotze", Traugott added with the smoothness of a striking snake. "I'm not sure I quite grasp the wisdom of your proposal. So if you could perhaps enlighten me?"

Lotze smiled self-importantly at the respect and deference Traugott seemed to be showing him. He winked at the others.

"Well, herr untersturmführer, it seems to me that..."

He got no further before Traugott grabbed him by the back of the neck and slammed his head against the table, rendering him half unconscious. Lotze's skull hit the hardwood with a sound like a gunshot. The assembled men gasped and pushed away from the table as the bills scattered like autumn leaves in the wind. The bottle of rare cognac toppled off the table and exploded when it hit the ground.

Dieter Lotze moaned as Traugott pushed down on his neck with all his strength, pressing his bleeding forehead into the table.

"Now why in the name of hell would I care what you think", Traugott growled as he bent closer to the man. "What you think has less value than a pile of rat shit. I made you all richer than you ever thought you would be. I can just as easily send you all back to the shitholes in which your whoring mothers found you."

Traugott put his cigar to his lips and pulled on it until it glowed a bright, incandescent red. He then brought the tip to within an whisker of Lotze's right eye. The man's only visible globe widened and rolled in fear and terror and he tried to wriggle away, but Traugott's hand around his neck was like a vise.

"Take a good look at this money that you like so much, *schwanzlutscher*, because that's the last of it you'll ever see."

Traugott then pressed the burning cigar into the man's eye, bursting it. Lotze howled in pain and his body was wracked by a jolt of agony, but still Traugott wouldn't release him as he pushed the cigar in deeper. A sickening smell of burning flesh filled the room and two of the men turned away to vomit. Lotze finally managed to place both hands against the table and he pushed himself up with every last ounce of strength he possessed, freeing himself from Traugott.

He tottered a few steps back, the cigar still embedded in his eye. He instinctively closed one fist around it and, without thinking, pulled it out. The cigar came out with a sick, sucking sound and a clear liquid ran down the right side of his face. His back now against the wall, Lotze threw the cigar away and scanned the room with his remaining eye - which, incredibly, was filled not with fear or pain, but with hatred. He snarled and, with one hand pressed over his ruined eye, reached for his sidearm when he finally spotted the man who had done this to him.

Traugott didn't wait to be shot dead where he stood. He immediately rushed Lotze, slamming him against the wall and disarming him. He then punched him in the face several times, bloodying his nose and mouth, before kneeing him in the groin. Lotze collapsed to the floor, one hand against his face and the other between his legs.

"Take him to the infirmary", Traugott finally said, breathing hard. "Tell them he had an *accident*. If anyone finds out the truth..."

He let his words hang menacingly, knowing he didn't need to add anything more. His men understood the price they would pay, both individually and collectively, if they talked. Not only would it end this operation once and for all, but they would then spend their days looking over their shoulders, knowing Traugott was coming after them.

Traugott took a look around the room. Chairs had been overturned, bills were scattered all over the place and at least two puddles of vomit were congealing on the floor.

"And clean this mess up", he ordered disgustedly. "It's like a pigsty in here. And do something about that *smell*."

He then calmly walked out without ever looking back.

The women had been walking for two hours and some were on the verge of collapsing with exhaustion.

Adriana looked up at the sky as she walked, turning her face up to the cold April sun. She was sure her feet would have hurt, had they not been frozen solid. The mornings were still brutally cold and the inmates could, at best, hope for a few hours of lukewarm weather around mid-day. At first the wooden clogs had given her terrible blisters, but then thick calluses had formed and provided some relief. Still, these clogs were to shoes what Hitler was to humanitarian aid. They made her legs ache up to the hip if she had to walk in them for any length of time. Some women found them so uncomfortable that they chose to go barefoot, wrapping their feet in rags in winter.

They were following a dirt road that led from the camp to a town called, according to a sign they had seen earlier, Oświęcim. Whether this was their final destination or not, they obviously didn't know, but they seemed to be taking forever getting there - which wasn't really all that surprising, considering how weak with hunger and disease they all were. They didn't walk as much as they crawled.

Adriana had counted about thirty women in their group, but Hana and Julianna had been assigned to a different detail. Adriana didn't know what there was for them to do in Oświęcim, nor did she care, but she was pretty sure the twins had managed to land themselves the best assignment possible. Each barrack had a *kapo*, usually a common criminal recruited by the Nazis to serve as boss and overseer, and theirs was a fat boar of a woman named Hiltrude. The previous kapo, Lyudjilla, had died the month before, her neck snapped by a huge tree log dropped by the inmates who had been loading it onto a truck. The ten women responsible for the so-called accident were immediately sent to the gas chambers, and it was later said they died with a smile on their lips.

Like all bullies, Hiltrude was a creature of great insecurity who needed to make others feel inferior and control everything; the slightest transgression became, in her eyes, a serious challenge to her authority. Hana and Julianna had rapidly understood they could ingratiate themselves with the new boss by snitching on other inmates, and more than one poor woman had felt Hiltrude's baton across her back after being reported by the twins. Adriana now kept her distance from them to keep from being judged guilty by association. She had also moved to another sleeping platform, since it seemed to her more than likely that Hana and Julianna would be murdered in their sleep before too long.

Hiltrude was so obese that she couldn't take more than a few steps before beginning to sweat profusely, even in winter, and having to stop to catch her breath. So her first order of business upon arriving at Auschwitz had been to order the camp's carpenters to build her a two-wheeled chariot in which she sat while four inmates pulled her around like so many horses. The first chariot had collapsed under her immense weight and a second, more robust one had been assembled – but only after she'd beaten the head carpenter to within an inch of his life. The beating had almost killed her as well – she was taken to the infirmary complaining of chest pains from which, unfortunately, she recovered.

It was in this chariot that Hiltrude now rode at the head of their pitiful column, like a general leading his army through the streets of a conquered city, comfortably wrapped in a warm blanket against the cold while her four slaves strained to drag her over the uneven road. Hiltrude was jostled roughly when the chariot ran over a pothole and she berated the four women pulling her. Adriana wondered what might happen if the chariot were - accidentally, of course – to tumble into the ditch, taking Hiltrude with it. Might she, too, die of a broken neck?

She put the thought away, knowing it was pointless to entertain such fantasies. If such a thing were to happen, here and now, the six guards escorting them would certainly execute them all on the spot and dump their bodies in the ditch alongside Hiltrude's. And while some would have undoubtedly welcomed the sweet release of death, Adriana wasn't one of them. Not yet, anyway.

The sound of an engine came from behind and the guards ordered them off the road. The inmates obeyed so slowly that the convoy was on top of them by the time the last woman finally got out of the way; if she hadn't, Adriana doubted very much the trucks would have slowed down to keep from running her over. A human life, and specially a *Jew's* life, wasn't worth a whole lot at

Auschwitz.

Six Wehrmacht trucks roared past them, showering them with dust. Adriana raised an arm and closed her eyes to keep from being blinded, but she still managed to catch a glimpse of the soldiers who sat in the last truck. Two of them were staring open-mouthed at the spectacle before their eyes, wondering where this battalion of living-dead that stood by the side of the road might have come from. One of the two, a young man who couldn't have been more than 20, looked directly at Adriana and there was such a look of confusion in his eyes that she couldn't help, despite everything, but feel a tinge of pity for him. This young man had probably been told that he was fighting for Germany's right to exist, not for Germany's right to starve harmless women to death. He, like her, was but a cog in an infernal machine much larger than himself – a machine that would spit him out the second his usefulness was spent.

The moment lasted for a mere instant, and then the young man was swallowed by the hurricane of dust that trailed behind the convoy and he was lost from view.

The inmates' march ended at a long brick wall next to which a truck had been parked. The wall was about twelve feet long and almost eight feet high, but what purpose it served was a complete mystery. It stood by itself, apart from the four or five other buildings in that area. It looked as though it had been erected there before being promptly forgotten. Adriana surmised that it was probably all that remained of a huge building that had once stood in this spot.

Hiltrude climbed off her chariot and conferred briefly with the two guards who had driven the truck here. One of them then lowered the rear gate of the truck and began taking out metal rods that each measured about four feet in length.

"Listen to me, you lazy bitches", Hiltrude said before pausing, winded by the few steps she had taken. "You're going to take this wall apart brick by brick. So grab a bar and get to work."

That was it. The inmates knew better than to expect any type of explanation. They were expected to obey, no questions asked, and that's exactly what they did. Hiltrude returned to her chariot and had the four women pull her to a spot in the sun while the workers picked up the rods. These might have constituted dangerous weapons had the women not been so weak, but the guards knew they had nothing to fear from inmates who had been beaten and starved to death for months. And even if the women attacked the guards and somehow managed to disable them... what purpose would that serve, other than perhaps hastening their own deaths, in a country positively crawling with German soldiers? They wouldn't have lasted an hour on the lam.

So the women grabbed the rods and got to work. Not that any of them had any idea how they were supposed to safely demolish a brick wall this size. The first thing they figured out was that they had to protect their hands from the the rods, otherwise blisters formed almost instantly where the metal rubbed the skin. So they tore strips from their clothes and bandaged each other's hands.

"What's your name?" the woman Adriana was helping whispered almost inaudibly.

Adriana glanced nervously in Hiltrude's direction, but the fat woman's head had fallen against her chest and she seemed to be sleeping. The guards were standing several yards away, chatting among themselves and looking completely bored.

Judging it safe to reply, Adriana answered. "Adriana Zöbel", she said. The woman nodded, as though the name meant something to her. "Simeon and Raanah's daughter, from Rimavská Sobota. *Adriana with the hair*. Yes, I thought it was you."

Adriana froze and stared at the other woman suspiciously, trying to recognize her. "I don't know you. Who are you?" she whispered.

The other woman shrugged as she wrapped Adriana's hands. "It was a long time ago. I'm Magrita, Magrita Adamčiaková. We were in school together when we were little. But then we moved away and..." She shrugged again.

Adriana stared at her again and mouthed her name silently, but she still couldn't place her. "I'm sorry, but...", she began before Magrita interrupted her. "Do not worry yourself about it. Like I said, it was a long time ago. But I remember your hair, though today you seem to have misplaced it."

Adriana touched her bald head and smiled despite herself. Magrita smiled as well. "It's good to have friends in a place like this. Let's get to work before she wakes up", Magrita said, nodding in Hiltrude's direction.

They quickly realized it was pointless to try to dislodge the bricks by hammering directly at them.

So, holding the rods horizontally with both hands, they pounded at the mortar with the tips until they pierced an opening into which they could insert the bar, which then allowed them – if they had sufficient purchase and leverage - to pry the bricks loose. It was still very dangerous work. At all times the women risked being struck by a dislodged chunk of mortar or by a wayward rod, and after an hour most sported shallow cuts to their faces or hands.

It was also very slow work. The rods only weighed a couple of pounds each, but the women lacked the strength to wield them for more than a few minutes before needing to rest. Of the thirty of them, no more than a dozen were actually working at any given time while the others caught their breaths and rested burning arms. And to add to their misery, the wall was about two feet taller than the tallest one among them, which meant that no one could reach the top portion safely. They had to work above their heads, holding the rods with extended arms, until their shoulders were on fire.

A woman then came up with an idea that struck them as being quite sensible: instead of demolishing the wall from top to bottom, as they'd been doing, they'd dismantle it from left to right. They'd select a section that measured, say, two feet in width and remove the mortar linking it to the rest of the wall. Once the section had been separated, they would just topple it to the ground, where it would be much easier – and less tiring - to take it apart. With any luck, the impact would also smash the section into smaller pieces, speeding up their work even further. Encouraged by this brilliant strategy, the women got to work with renewed energy, and with teams attacking the wall from both sides, they had first section on the ground in less than twenty minutes.

It then took them another fifteen minutes to separate the individual bricks and load them into the truck. The women were quite pleased with this new method, having found it much less tiring. Once the section had been toppled, they no longer had to fight gravity to hold their rods horizontally to work; now that they worked vertically, gravity even became their ally as they raised and lowered the bars to smash the mortar.

The women worked tirelessly through the day, managing to dismantle one section every hour or so, but about six feet of wall – representing about three more hours of work - still stood when

Hiltrude finally woke up from her nap.

"Lazy whores!" she thundered as she climbed down from her throne. The women froze as they watched her waddling in their direction, and a few gasped when Hiltrude pulled from her pocket the rubber baton that she carried with her at all times. "Work faster before I lose my temper!" she roared, emphasizing her threat by slapping her open palm with the baton several times.

Fearing the worst, a few of the women panicked and tried to topple the section on which they were working, even though it hadn't yet been fully detached from the rest of the wall. Sufficient mortar remained to hold it in place and the women, seeing Hiltrude coming ever closer, pushed even harder.

There was a loud sound, like the crack of a whip, and the whole wall shuddered.

Adriana's newfound friend, Magrita, had been standing a bit apart while she re-bandaged her hands. She looked up at the sound and immediately saw that a crack had formed, snaking its way through the mortar and around the bricks from one end of the wall to the other, approximately one foot off the ground.

Then, as she watched, time seemed to stand still, and what remained of the wall began to topple over.

"Adriana! Look out!" she shouted, but she was too late.

The entire remaining six-foot section of wall - thousands of bricks weighting tens of thousands of pounds - thundered to the ground, crushing the half-dozen unsuspecting women standing next to it. The earth shook and a cloud of dust filled the air.

"Adriana! Adriana!" Magrita screamed.

But there was no reply.

4

Berlin

The Mercedes 260D pulled up alongside the curb and stopped smoothly. Two men emerged from the back of the powerful car that had fetched them at the train station. One was dressed in the impeccable uniform of an SS officer while the other, a bit more disheveled, wore a black patch over his right eye.

"Just remember to keep your mouth shut until I give you leave to speak", the officer growled at his companion. The other man nodded meekly and kept his gaze lowered, as though he feared looking the SS in the eye.

Otto Mockël stretched to relieve the tension in his back. The train ride from Auschwitz to Berlin had taken almost a full day, twice as long as he'd expected; passenger trains had very low priority and were constantly being sidetracked by those rushing either goods or troops to the front, which made it impossible to predict how long it would take to reach one's destination. To make matters even worse, his travel companion had proved to be a completely uneducated oaf whose sole topic of interest had been the women on the train with them, and more specifically the size and shape of their breasts.

Exasperated, Mockël had finally ordered the man to remain silent or he'd have him court-martialled for gross insubordination.

Mockël looked to his left and right, up and down Prinz-Albrecht-Strasse, and he felt a small thrill at finding himself at the very heart of the glorious Third Reich he served so proudly. Soon, this would be the center of the civilized world, a megalopolis whose power and splendor would surpass even that of ancient Rome. A beautiful blond woman taking her dog for a stroll on a warm spring day smiled boldly at him, visibly seduced by his resplendent SS uniform. Mockël smiled back and bowed slightly, hoping to strike up a conversation and perhaps make the most of his few hours in town, but then the woman noticed that other man ogling her chest and she quickened her pace. Mockël watched her walk away wistfully and, neither for the first nor the last time, wished it weren't against the law for officers to kill their subordinates.

He looked up at the massive building they were about to enter and the sight sobered him up instantly. Some men who had entered it had never been seen again, and he had no intention of joining their ranks. He had come to Berlin on a very special mission, to meet some extremely important and powerful men, with whom he proposed to share some potentially explosive information – the type of information that could make or break a career with equal indifference.

"Right", he said as he reflexively straightened a uniform that couldn't have been any straighter. "Let's go in. And don't you dare say a single word or I'll cut out your tongue and feed it to my dog."

Möckel had acquired a wolfhound the month before and he hardly ever left the gigantic beast – it stood taller than him when it reared up on its hind legs - out of his sight, since he was in the process of training it as an attack dog. He'd left it behind at Auschwitz and he couldn't wait to be reunited with it. He'd thought about naming it *Adolf*, but fearing that the name might be perceived as an insult by some, he'd instead settled on *Achtzehn*, which meant "eighteen". To those who asked he explained that the dog was the eighteenth son of a world champion, hence its name; in truth, the number 1 stood for the letter "A" and the number 8 for the letter "H" - Adolf Hitler's initials.

Möckel saluted the two guards posted at the entrance and, mustering all the confidence he could, walked into the building.

"*Guten Tag*", the young woman sitting at a massive desk greeted them. "How may I help you?"

Möckel bowed politely. "*Guten Tag, fräulein*", he said. "I am obersturmführer Otto Möckel. I have an appointment with gruppenführer Heinrich Müller."

If Möckel had hoped to impress her by mentioning the Gestapo chief, he failed. She'd heard it all before. The young woman didn't bat an eyelash as she opened a ledger on her desk, found today's date and ran her finger down a long column of names. She then emitted a small sound that Möckel found quite worrisome.

"I'm very sorry, herr obersturmführer", she began, "but I don't see your name anywhere and... Ah yes, here it is!"

She had moved her finger to the previous page to scan the names written on that side of the ledger. "It seems that your appointment was yesterday, not today."

Mockël felt himself redden slightly. "Yes, *mein fräulein*, but as you know travel by rail is quite unreliable and we arrived just a few minutes ago. We have come straight from the train station. I'm sure the gruppenführer won't hold that against us."

The receptionist looked down at her ledger again, visibly troubled and pensive. She hated finding herself stuck in the middle of such situations.

"I must apologize again, herr obersturmführer", she explained, looking up meekly at the SS officer who stood before her, "but gruppenführer Müller left very early this morning and he won't return until next week. I don't see what..."

Mockël emitted an involuntary growl that silenced her instantly. "My dear *fräulein*, we have traveled all the way from Poland on a mission for Maximilian Grabner, the Gestapo chief at Auschwitz", he said, probably revealing more information than was necessary. "We are here for the sole purpose of meeting with gruppenführer Müller, to whom we are to present some very sensitive information. It would *not* be wise for you to simply turn us away."

The young woman was on the verge of tears. Her job was to receive the mail, answer the phone, greet visitors and perhaps offer them coffee while they waited. Her job was *not* to handle the outsized egos of men such as this one. What did she know of secret missions and sensitive information? How could it be her fault that this man was showing up for his appointment with the gruppenführer late by a full day? How could she be expected to fix such a thing?

But then she thought of a way out of her predicament and her tears receded.

"*Bitte*, herr obersturmführer", she said, "if you and your companion would just take a seat over there, I'll see what I can do. I'll just be moment."

Mockël hesitated but then he bowed and reluctantly went to sit in one the leather chairs that lined the wall.

The receptionist lifted a massive black telephone off its cradle. She spun the dial a few times and waited expectantly for a reply.

"Albert Duchstein", a man answered.

The young woman breathed an internal sigh of relief at finding Albert at his desk. She was suddenly very glad that she had finally agreed to go for coffee with him the week before, after holding him at bay for so long. "Albert, this is Emma", she said in a very, very low voice, all the while covering her mouth with her hand. "I have a problem."

A few minutes later she rose from her desk and went to Mockël. "The gruppenführer's adjutant will see you, herr obersturmführer."

"His adjutant?" Mockël asked skeptically.

"Yes, herr obersturmführer", Emma said with a touch of impatience. "Untersturmführer Albert Duchstein will grant you a few minutes of his time, even though your appointment was yesterday."

Mockël was boiling inside. Not only was this impertinent tart again reminding him of his tardiness, but now he would have to deal with *another untersturmführer*, just like Traugott. He had come here expecting to meet a gruppenführer, but now he was instead being graciously "granted" an audience by a man he outranked.

Ever conscious of his appearance, Mockël stood up and ran his hands over his uniform to smooth out any wrinkles. When his companion failed to rise, Mockël looked at him and was mortified to see that the man seemed to have fallen asleep. A rivulet of thick drool ran from the corner of his mouth and had stained his uniform. And to think that he had almost met the highest-ranking man in the Gestapo in the company of such a buffoon! The man awoke with a grunt when Mockël kicked him none-so-gently.

Emma smiled discretely. "Gustav will take you to untersturmführer Duchstein's office", she said, pointing at a man who stood slightly behind her.

"Right this way, herr obersturmführer", Gustav, who was 143 if he was a day and wore the dress of a civilian, said immediately.

Mockël stared at the man but the man stared right back at him, not the least bit intimidated. There was something hard and merciless in his eyes. Mockël guessed him to be a veteran of the First World War who was now too old to serve at the front but who still managed to do his part this time around. He thanked Emma with a barely perceptible nod of the head and followed Gustav as the man led them through a maze of stairways and corridors. Their escort finally stopped in front of a wooden door and knocked sharply.

"Enter", came a voice from the other side.

Gustav opened the door and stepped aside to let Mockël and his companion through. He then closed it, leaving the two men alone with untersturmführer Duchstein.

Duchstein had risen to greet a superior officer and was standing at attention behind his desk. Mindful that he outranked the man, Mockël took longer than was proper before addressing him. He looked around the office, trying to appear disdainful and jaded, but he was still impressed by the quality of the furniture. The room was small, no bigger than a regular bedroom, but it had a window that let in plenty of sunlight.

He sighed loudly to show his irritation and finally saluted, sloppily, untersturmführer Duchstein.

"At ease, untersturmführer", he said. "At ease".

Duchstein relaxed. "Please have a seat, obersturmführer", he said, but Mockël was already in the process of appropriating the only chair available. The man with him, it seemed, was meant to remain standing. Duchstein looked at him briefly and wondered in which battle he had suffered such a hideous, disfiguring wound. "How may I be of assistance?" he asked, turning his attention back to Mockël, though Emma had briefed him as to what this was about.

"Oh I'm sure that little *flittchen* down there has already told you why I'm here", Mockël said aggressively, purposefully insulting the woman to see how Duchstein would react. Anger flashed ever-so-briefly in the man's eyes and Mockël smiled at having scored the first point so easily. "So let's not play games, untersturmführer. Maximilian Grabner has sent me here to deliver very sensitive information to gruppenführer Müller. I need to see him immediately."

Duchstein noted that Mockël kept referring to himself, and solely to himself, as though the man with him was of no importance. "You could have seen him yesterday", he replied very slowly, "Had you not been... *delayed*, shall we say?"

"You will do well to keep your impertinence in check, untersturmführer Duchstein", he snapped back at the man. "If we were *delayed*, it was only by trains carrying our valiant *streitkräfte* to the front. Not all of us are afforded the luxury of fighting the war sitting behind a desk."

Duchstein smiled at the weak jab, guessing correctly that Mockël had seen as little combat as he had since the outbreak of the war. "Be that as it may, herr obersturmführer", he said, "gruppenführer Müller is simply not here. As you were told, he left early this morning and is not expected back until next week at the earliest. There is nothing either one of us can do about that."

Mockël exhaled sharply through his nose. "Yes, I realize that", he replied. "But surely, there must be someone else who can see me."

Duchstein almost asked whether, by "someone else", Mockël meant someone other than gruppenführer Müller or someone other than himself, but he knew the answer to that question. In any case, he had been expecting just such a condescending comment and his riposte was ready. "Well yes, now that you mention it, as a matter of fact there is someone else here who might be willing to see you", he said. He watched in amused anticipation as Mockël puffed himself up self-importantly, as though he had just scored a major victory. "Obergruppenführer Ernst Kaltenbrunner happens to be in the building for some meetings. I'm sure he might be able to give you a few minutes of his time."

Mockël felt as though he'd been punched in the stomach and he swallowed hard. Kaltenbrunner was the head of the RHSA, the Reich Main Security Office, the agency that oversaw the Gestapo. That made Kaltenbrunner Heinrich Müller's superior, but that was a bit like calling the Pope a simple priest. The reality was much, *much* scarier. In an instant, Mockël had to judge whether the information he was carrying was worthy of troubling such a powerful and influential man.

He was about to accept Duchstein's offer when he remembered the man behind him. Dare he appear before obergruppenführer Kaltenbrunner with such a man, such a *lümmel,* as his sole proof and witness? Did he really have that much faith in the man? The answer was an obvious no. That was part of the reason why Mockël hadn't wanted to take him along on this mission, to distance himself from him, but Max Grabner had been of a different mind and had overruled him.

Mockël capitulated. He pulled an envelope from his breast pocket and let it drop on Duchstein's desk. "This is the letter of introduction herr Grabner gave me", he said as Duchstein pulled it from the envelope and began reading it. "It contains most of what this man claims to have witnessed at

Auschwitz."

The men sat in silence as Duchstein read the document, which ran for almost five pages. "I see", he said once he was done. "These are most serious accusations. And obersturmbannführer Höss knows nothing of this?"

"I have told him nothing."

"May I ask why?"

Mockël barely hesitated. "Because he may be complicit in the whole thing."

"I see", Duchstein repeated. "Allow me to be quite frank, herr obersturmführer."

"By all means", Mockël said icily.

"Gruppenführer Müller is, more than anything else, a policeman, perhaps the best I have ever encountered", he explained. "And as such, he will want proof... real, concrete proof... of these alleged events before acting on this information."

"But I *have* proof", Mockël protested. "I have the testimony of a man who was there, who saw everything."

"What you have, herr Mockël", Duchstein countered, dropping the man's rank on purpose, "is the testimony of a common thief who should be taken outside and shot before he disgraces his uniform any further."

The two men stared at one another for a moment. "This letter makes amply clear that your sole witness has a score to settle, and that makes him less than trustworthy", Duchstein resumed when Mockël remained silent. "He will swear to anything to get his revenge, but also to save his own skin. Put yourself in my shoes for an instant! Unless further proof is found, it would be this man's word against another's, and that's simply not good enough."

"But he was *there*, he saw *everything*", Mockël repeated indignantly.

"Yes, yes, so you say and so he says", Duchstein replied, now dropping all pretense of deference and waving the comment aside as though it were a troublesome insect buzzing around his head. "Now, don't get me wrong. I'm not saying an investigation isn't warranted. But before I take this to gruppenführer Müller, you'll have to give me something more."

"There is nothing more", Mockël growled. "That's all I have."

Duchstein smiled. "That's quite unfortunate. But... perhaps if I were to hear your man's testimony for myself? Maybe I would then be better able to judge for myself?"

Mockël's heart sank. Allowing that man to speak was the last thing in the world he wanted. If the idiot wavered in the least from his earlier testimony, if holes or contradictions appeared in his tale, then he'd lose all credibility and this whole thing would collapse like a house of cards. But at the same time, Mockël couldn't deny Duchstein's request. If he did, he'd look as though he didn't have faith in his star witness and the end result would be the same.

He had no other choice but to let the man speak and hope for the best.

"If you think it wise", he finally conceded.

"I do", Duchstein said with a smile that infuriated Mockël. He then turned to the man who had been standing at the back of the room this whole time, listening as the two men discussed him as though he weren't present.

"Step forward, don't be afraid", Duchstein said as he motioned for the man to come closer.

The man took a few hesitant steps and coughed to clear his throat. "Yes, herr untersturmführer... I mean, thank you herr untersturmführer", he finally managed to say. Mockël could have wept with despair.

"Please begin by confirming your identity", Duchstein ordered.

"Yes, herr untersturmführer", he said tentatively. "My name is Lotze. Dieter Lotze."

Magrita blew on her frozen fingers, but her breath felt as cold as the howling wind. She flexed and shook the icy digits, trying to get warm blood flowing, but they might as well have been dried twigs.

She knelt down and clawed at the still frozen ground, looking for blackened potatoes left over from last year's harvest. When she found one, she dug it up with her bare hands, broke the icy soil into chunks to get at the tuber - tearing off her fingernails in the process – and dumped it into a bag slung around her shoulders. Like most other tasks they were assigned, this one appeared entirely futile and pointless, but she suspected the inedible vegetables would find their way into tomorrow's soup.

Magrita wondered whether she'd ever see Adriana again. Her friend had been knocked unconscious by the falling wall and she'd sustained a nasty cut to the back of the head. Hiltrude had immediately proclaimed that all those who couldn't walk back to Auschwitz would be shot and left to rot in the ditch. That fate had befallen five injured women, but Magrita and another woman had pulled Adriana from the rubble and promised to drag her back to camp. Hiltrude had shrugged and walked away, but only after swearing to kill all three of them on the spot if they lagged behind.

Adriana began coming to after a few minutes, but there was no way she could have walked back to camp on her own. Her legs were wobbly and she stumbled more than she walked as Magrita and the other inmate carried her. The two women had gone less than a mile when it became crystal-clear to them that - despite their best intentions – returning Adriana to Auschwitz was quite simply beyond their exhausted strength. They were already panting and Hiltrude – whom the women now nicknamed *Hell*trude behind her back – was watching them relentlessly, hoping for the slightest sign of weakness.

"Adriana, either you help us or you'll die here", Magrita whispered into her ear, glancing at the fat woman over her shoulder. "Don't give her the pleasure. *Please*."

From that moment on it seemed to Magrita that Adriana supported more of her own weight until, at long last and just as the sun was setting, the camp came into view. Magrita had never imagined she'd ever be happy to see the place, but on this night she was.

But they weren't out of the woods yet. Not by a long shot. Auschwitz was a merciless place. With trains delivering thousands of new inmates every week, workers who fell sick or were injured became instantly expendable and were routinely sent to the gas chambers, no questions asked. This was the fate that certainly awaited Adriana. If she couldn't answer roll-call the next morning, Hiltrude wouldn't think twice about shipping her off to the gas chambers.

The women had almost returned to their barracks and Magrita was at a loss as to what she should do now. Her only goal for the past few hours had been bringing Adriana back to camp alive. She hadn't planned beyond that. But now that they were here, she had to figure out how to keep her friend alive until morning and beyond. Simply returning Adriana to her platform and praying that she felt better the next morning didn't seem quite sufficient.

The answer came in the form of a short, stocky woman she spotted, her head bent and lost in her thoughts, about fifty yards away. Magrita made up her mind in an instant.

"Follow me", she ordered the other woman in a very low voice, not giving her any choice in the matter.

At the last moment she veered to the left, away from the rest of the group. Such a transgression was punishable by summary execution and the other woman hesitated but Magrita kept walking, giving her unwilling accomplice a choice between following her and dropping Adriana. The woman was clearly scared and her instinct was to follow the rules, but in the end she kept hold of Adriana and went along with Magrita.

They had taken less than five steps when Hiltrude noticed the straying trio.

"You three, fall back in line immediately!" the fat *kapo* roared.

"Ignore her, I have a plan", Magrita ordered.

She began walking faster, adrenaline now coursing through her veins. Magrita felt as though she could have carried Adriana alone – which is exactly what she ended up having to do less than ten seconds later.

"I said, fall back in line immediately *or I'll have you shot!*" Hiltrude bawled again.

This proved too much for the other woman. Seized by a mortal fear, she panicked and bolted back to the rest of the work party without any warning. Magrita almost dropped Adriana when her partner suddenly let go, but she wrapped an arm around her friend's waist at the last second and kept walking. She could feel half a dozen rifles trained on the two of them and knew that the fatal bullet might be fired at any moment.

She locked her eyes on the woman she had spotted, forcing herself to think of nothing else and knowing that each step improved her chances of pulling this off. She was now less than thirty yards away.

"Doctor Ada! Doctor Ada!" she yelled as loudly as she could.

The woman's head snapped up and she looked in Magrita's general direction. But the hundreds of inmates who milled about in the courtyard made it hard for her to determine which one of them was calling her name.

"This is your last warning!" Magrita heard Hiltrude howl hysterically behind her.

"Doctor Ada, over here! Doctor Ada!" Magrita shouted again, this time waving her free hand above her head. She was on the verge of tears.

"Guards, shoot them!" Hiltrude ordered. Magrita ducked and cringed, waiting for the impact of lead against flesh that would end their lives.

"Hold your fire! Hold your fire!" Doctor Ada hollered, having finally spotted the two women stumbling in her direction. It was far from certain that she had the necessary authority to countermand a *kapo*'s orders, but in the confusion no shots were fired and the two women finally collapsed at her feet, exhausted beyond belief.

"What's going on here, exactly?" she asked, but Magrita was too winded to answer.

"Mind your own business, *doctor*", Hiltrude said rudely. "These inmates are mine. I'll deal with them."

The fat woman was panting and sweating, and her face had gone the color of overcooked beets. Two armed guards accompanied her and seemed unsure what was expected of them.

Hadassah (Ada) Bimko Rosensaft was a Pole who had studied medicine in France. She had been brought to Auschwitz along with her husband and 5 1/2-year-old son, Benjamin, and while her loved ones had rapidly been killed, she had been spared because of her medical training and put in charge of what passed for the Jewish infirmary. Her job wasn't so much to treat the inmates as to determine who could still work and who had reached the end of the line.

Having said that, the imagination and resourcefulness she displayed when time came to demonstrate who was still strong enough to work, and who should thus be spared the gas chambers, had rapidly become legendary among the inmates. She had been on her way back to the infirmary when Magrita had spotted her.

And after what she'd been through over the previous months, Doctor Ada wasn't about to be browbeaten by an uneducated bully.

"Well, hello Hiltrude", she said pleasantly, but sounding as though she was addressing a retarded child. "How are you this evening."

The kapo stared at her with daggers in her eyes. "I said mind your own business, *doctor*", she repeated, showing none of the deference Germans usually grant physicians – even Jewish physicians. "These inmates disobeyed the rules and now they'll be punished."

Ada Rosensaft smiled at her the way she might have had Hiltrude complimented her on her new hair color. "But I *am* minding my own business, my dear Hiltrude", she replied patiently. "These inmates are clearly in need of medical attention. I'll just be a minute, then you can have them back."

She then turned her attention to Adriana and Magrita, kneeling down next to them and effectively dismissing Hiltrude. The kapo was outraged and seemed about to explode. "I don't know who the hell you think you are, but I can...", the fat woman began.

Doctor Ada immediately stood back up and moved closer to the massive *kapo*, who towered over her by at least six inches. "I was wondering, Hiltrude", she said, but this time with a voice harder than Damascus steel. "How is that rash of yours? Did the ointment I give you relieve the chafing between your buttocks?"

There was something in Ada's tone and words that hinted at more hidden secrets, at more embarrassing details that would be revealed if the *kapo* didn't back down and shut the hell up.

Hiltrude caught the hint and her eyes bulged out of her head. She opened and closed her mouth several times, gasping like a fish out of water. Ada didn't give her a chance to recover. "Give me a minute with these inmates and then *maybe* you can have them back", she repeated, the added word like a slap in the face.

"You'll pay for this, I swear you will", Hiltrude spat at her, jabbing in her direction with a finger that looked like an overstuffed sausage link. She then spun around and waddled back to the work party.

"I think you've just made an enemy on our account", Magrita said feebly.

Doctor Ada exhaled slowly through her nose as she knelt down again. "Don't worry about me", she said. "I still have more friends than I have enemies. Tell me what's wrong."

Magrita summed up the events of the previous hours. Ada nodded as she listened pensively.

"Your friend has a concussion", she said as she examined Adriana, who was moaning softly. "It doesn't look as though she has any broken bones, which is a very good thing. I can keep her in the infirmary until the morning, and then we'll see. But you..."

Magrita was puzzled. "What about me?"

Doctor Ada shook her head. "There's nothing I can do for you. I have to send you back to your barracks to face Hiltrude. And I don't think I'm the only one who's made an enemy tonight."

Magrita smiled. "Just take care of Adriana. I, too, still have more friends than I have enemies."

Doctor Ada then picked up Adriana as though she weighed no more than a newborn child and walked away with her, heading for the infirmary.

That had been two days ago. Magrita had feared Hiltrude's retribution, but the fat kapo had been nowhere in sight upon her return. The rumor of her medical condition, on the other hand, had already spread like wildfire through the barrack, which perhaps explained her disappearance. But the next morning, Magrita found herself assigned to this kommando, tasked with pulling rotten vegetables out of the frozen ground, which clearly demonstrated that her defiance had gone neither unnoticed nor unpunished.

A guard's whistle sounded, marking the end of the workday. Magrita dropped one last potato into her sack and the long walk back to Auschwitz began.

6

The young soldier Otto Mockël had entrusted with the care of his wolfhound in his absence was becoming more afraid of the beast by the day.

Achtzehn spent its days curled up in a corner of his room, awaiting the return of its master. But it never seemed to sleep. Whenever the soldier looked at him, the dog was watching him, tracking him like prey. It growled whenever he came near. The dog had almost ripped off his arm the first time he'd approached it with a bowl of food. The soldier had thus learned to prepare the monster's evening meal in a separate room, keeping the door closed as the dog growled and barked and paced on the other side. The soldier had also learned that it was wise to flatten himself against the wall *before* opening the door, lest he get knocked down by the charging dog one more time.

The only time Achtzehn displayed anything resembling happiness was when the soldier took its leash off a hook on the wall, indicating that it was time for one of the three daily walks Mockël had mandated.

Anyone observing them this evening would have been left with absolutely no doubt as to who was in charge, as to *who* was taking *who* for a walk. Achtzehn was such a powerful animal that the young soldier had to hang on to the leash with both hands. No matter how deep the steel choker bit into its neck, no matter how hard this silly human pulled, Achtzehn could pull twice as hard and the young man usually ended up jogging most of the way. The only respite he got came when the animal stopped to relieve himself or to bark at an inmate. Combined with the fits of rage that seized Achtzehn whenever they encountered another one of the numerous dogs that also inhabited Auschwitz, the young soldier usually returned from these walks exhausted, his uniform soaked with sweat and the muscles in his arms throbbing.

The young man doubled over and rested his hands on his knees to catch his breath when Achtzehn froze suddenly, intrigued by a scent on the ground. Maybe someone had bled to death here the day before or the week before or even the month before. It didn't really matter to the young soldier, just as long as they stopped for a few seconds. He looked up when he heard Achtzehn begin to growl and his heart skipped a beat.

"That's Mockël's mutt, isn't it?" Mattias Traugott asked without any preamble.

The soldier was paralyzed by indecision. On the one hand, if he failed to salute a superior officer, he could be punished. On the other, if he took one hand off the leash and Achtzehn chose that moment to take off, he'd never catch it. And to top it all off, Achtzehn was growling and baring its teeth at an untersturmführer who was said to be among obersturmbannführer Höss' favorites.

"I asked you a question... Is that Mockël's mutt or not?" Traugott repeated, saving the young man from his dilemma.

"Yes, herr untersturmführer", he finally managed to say, all the while wondering how there could be any doubt as to whose beast this was. "I'm sorry it's growling at you like this."

He tugged at the leash as hard as he could several times, hoping to distract the dog, but the leash might as well have been tethered to the Rock of Gibraltar.

"Its master trained it well", Traugott snickered. "It probably knows how I feel about it."

"Yes, herr untersturmführer", the man said, for lack of anything else to respond.

Traugott was staring at the dog, as if daring it to lunge at him – which is exactly what Achtzehn, sensing the challenge, did. The animal tried to leap at Traugott's throat, certainly meaning to rip it out with a single bite, but the young soldier had sensed its mood and was ready for it. Praying it didn't snap, he yanked on the leash with every ounce of strength he possessed just as Achtzehn leaped. The dog was brought up sharp, which only increased its fury. The soldier felt as though his arms were being pulled out of their sockets as he fought to control the rearing monster.

Traugott didn't even flinch. Two soldiers who happened to witness the scene immediately aimed their rifles at the dog, thinking to save an officer from a horrible death, but Traugott waved them away without even glancing in their direction. The two soldiers walked away reluctantly.

The young soldier was silently hoping that Traugott would go with them before he lost control of Achtzehn. But the untersturmführer just stood there, cold as ice, and in the end something unbelievable happened. Achtzehn's fury evaporated as quickly as it had materialized and, in a flash, the beast seemed to lose all interest in Traugott. It stopped straining at its leash and simply sat there panting, calmer than the young man had ever seen it.

Traugott smiled as the soldier stared at him, flabbergasted.

"The beast is like its master", he explained without being asked. "It feeds on fear. Deprive him of that fear and it loses all power over you."

The young man wondered how one could refrain from displaying fear when faced with such a monster, but he remained silent. He had no interest in engaging in a discussion on dog training with an officer.

"But why isn't Mockël walking his mutt himself?" Traugott then asked with a smirk. "Has the dog already grown too big for him to handle?"

""No, herr untersturmführer", the soldier replied. "Obersturmführer Mockël has gone to Berlin for a few days and he ordered me to look after Achtzehn in his absence. He left a few days ago."

Traugott was immediately intrigued. "Berlin? Why?" he asked. A work kommando walked slowly by them, eliciting a disinterested growl from Achtzehn.

"I don't know, herr untersturmführer", the young soldier said truthfully. "All I know is that he and another man left by train a few days ago."

Traugott was even more intrigued. "Who was the other man?" he asked.

The young soldier shrugged. "I don't know, herr untersturmführer. I am new here. I don't really know anybody."

But Traugott's senses were now on full alert and he wouldn't be denied. He took a step closer to the young soldier, coming within easy reach of Achtzehn's powerful jaws. The dog paid him no attention.

"Describe that other man", he ordered. "Tell me what he looked like."

The young man stared at Achtzehn, silently praying for the dog to chase something, anything, and drag him away from this officer's questions. But instead, Achtzehn laid down and began noisily licking its paws.

The soldier closed his eyes and tried to think. "I'm sorry, herr untersturmführer, but I didn't get a good look at him. I wasn't really paying attention."

Traugott took another step closer. "Think harder", he said.

Then an image flashed through the young man's mind, saving him. "The man... herr untersturmführer, I remember his face was wounded on the right side. He had a black eye patch on that side of his face."

Traugott felt a chill seize his heart. "An eye patch. On the right side. You're sure", he demanded slowly.

The soldier wondered what he had got himself into. "Yes, herr untersturmführer, I'm certain. It looked like..."

But Traugott was already walking away. Achtzehn watched him go for a moment before returning its attention to its paws.

Doctor Ada held her patient's wrist for a full minute, checking the pulse, before setting it down gently. She pursed her lips. This one had reached the end of her life and would be dead before morning. The heart beat irregularly - sometimes five times in quick succession, sometimes not at all for several long seconds – but always it fluttered weakly, like a bird that beats its wings helplessly against the bars of its cage.

It was just a matter of time before it fell silent forever. There was nothing Doctor Ada could do for that poor woman, who had been brought to her earlier that day after being beaten bloody by the officer who ran Kanada. In another time and place, yes, perhaps she might have been able to save her, but here? It was all so futile. She tried as hard as she could, *desperately* hard, to keep her patients alive for as long as possible, always hoping that tomorrow might be better than today, always believing, but sometimes it was better to just let them go.

And God knew how easy Auschwitz made it to give up. Sometimes Ada Rosensaft asked herself why she fought so hard against Death in a place such as this, since in the end Death always triumphed. Death was the inevitable outcome for all those who passed underneath the *Arbeit Macht Frei* sign. The only unknown was the manner in which Death would claim them; even those who managed to avoid the *kapos*' blows and the guards' bullets, even those who withstood disease and starvation for longer than should be possible – all, ultimately, would be claimed by the gas chambers, no matter what she did.

In a way, it would be more sensible to help as many people die as rapidly and as painlessly as possible. Better a quick injection or a pill slipped under the tongue than weeks and months of hopeless suffering. There was no point in living for as long as possible if the only issue was an agonizing, suffocating death in the gas chambers.

But perhaps fighting for Life wasn't the same as fighting against Death. In her previous existence, Doctor Ada had fought for Life – for the lives of patients who wanted to live, for the lives of their loved ones, for the lives of all those who still dared hope for a brighter tomorrow. But here, at Auschwitz, she spent every single waking moment fighting against Death, and she had learned to cherish even the tiniest of victories in the face of so many massive defeats.

She went to check on her newest patient, the one called Adriana. The woman had been sleeping for several hours and it was time to wake her up; she had sustained a severe blow to the head and with such injuries, it was better to avoid prolonged sleep lest it turn into a coma from which the patient might never awaken.

"Wake up, dear one, wake up", Doctor Ada said quietly. "Wake up, Adriana. We need to have a chat."

She shook the young woman gently, trying to rouse her as softly as she could. The last thing she wanted was for her to come to with a shock. After a few minutes of stubborn efforts, Adriana's eyelids finally began to flutter as she returned from whatever dream world she had been visiting.

"Where... who... where am I?" she asked in a weak voice as she tried to push herself up on an elbow.

Doctor Ada pushed her back down, gently but firmly. "Don't try to rise just yet, please. My name is Ada. You're safe here."

Adriana looked at her. "Yes, of course, I know you. You're Doctor Ada. Everybody knows you." The two women shared a smile.

"What am I doing here?" Adriana asked.

"Your friend Magrita brought you back. How much do you remember?"

"Magrita... ooowww, my head", Adriana moaned as she placed a hand against her forehead.

Doctor Ada took Adriana's hand in hers and checked her pulse. She was relieved to find it regular and strong. But in so doing she also got a look at Adriana's tattoo and was stunned by what she saw. Doctor Ada herself bore number 52406, but Adriana's was only 1971.

This one had been here a long time. Much too long.

"I'm afraid you'll have quite a headache for a few days", she said.

Adriana was breathing deeply and after a moment the pain seemed to abate somewhat. "I remember we were working on a wall, then there was a loud cracking noise and..."

She also had vague memories of *someone* asking her to walk, of *someone* begging her not to give *her* the pleasure, but these were mere flashes, disjointed images taken out of their context, and she was unsure what they meant. Doctor Ada nodded pensively.

"Don't worry", she said. "This is all quite normal. For now you need to rest. I'll have to wake you regularly, but for now try to sleep."

"How long will I stay here?" Adriana asked groggily.

Doctor Ada thought for a moment before replying. "For as long as I can keep you", she said, knowing that this meant mere hours.

This patient, more than anything, needed rest. The next time they sent her out to carry sacks of crushed stone or to push a wheelbarrow all day, she'd certainly die. And thence lay Doctor Ada's impossible dilemma – if Adriana worked, she'd die; if she didn't work, she'd also die. Adriana wasn't strong enough to engage in any of the exerting work that would certainly be demanded of her. But if Adriana wasn't strong enough to report for roll-call the next morning, she'd be taken directly to the gas chambers.

Doctor Ada looked at her other patient, the one whose death was imminent. A plan began to form in her mind and she smiled.

She'd fight Death one more time.

Traugott wanted to run but he couldn't, since doing so would have betrayed the worry gnawing at him. So he walked as rapidly as he dared, all the while fearing that he'd be too late.

And he was.

He shoved open the door and rushed through *Kanada*'s work area, which was deserted at this time of night. He headed straight for his office and his worst fears were realized when he saw a guard posted in front of his door. He immediately retreated out of sight and took a moment to compose himself.

He'd only have one chance to get this right.

He took a long, slow walk around the work area to clear his mind, kicking discarded items as he went, and finally headed back to his office. He walked calmly and confidently, as if he didn't have a care in the world, and the soldier snapped to attention when he came into view.

Traugott feigned surprise at seeing the man. "What's the meaning of this? What are you doing here?" he asked, managing to sound indignant.

The soldier was visibly quite uncomfortable. He hadn't expected to be confronted by an angry officer in the middle of the night – and certainly not by *this* angry officer. He stood to attention even straighter and looked directly ahead. "Begging the untersturmführer's pardon, but I'm just following orders", he said rapidly.

Traugott sighed impatiently at such an obtuse explanation. "And what orders are those? To keep an eye on an empty warehouse to make sure it doesn't fly away?" Traugott was trying to sound jovial and carefree, but he was desperately worried by what might await him on the other side of the door. To find out, he'd first have to get past this man.

"Again begging the untersturmführer's pardon, but I'm to make sure that no one enters this office until morning", the man said.

Traugott sighed again, as if this was the most ridiculous thing he'd ever heard. "This if my office. I need papers inside. By standing in my way, you are interfering with the Reich's business".

His attempt to intimidate the man failed. "That's not my purpose, herr untersturmführer, but I must follow orders", the man repeated stubbornly, still looking straight ahead and never directly at Traugott.

Traugott decided to fish for information. "Whose orders? Obersturmbannführer Höss'?" he asked, hoping that the camp commander hadn't suddenly decided to turn on him.

The question clearly made the man uneasy. "*Nein*, herr untersturmführer. I was ordered here by untersturmführer Maximilian Grabner, who is acting on behalf of sturmbannführer Konrad Morgen."

A wave of dizziness washed over Traugott. *Well, it could have been worse*, he thought to himself. *He could have told me that Himmler himself was investigating me.*

Georg Konrad Morgen was the most feared SS judge in the whole of the Third Reich. His intolerance for corruption was legendary and he'd stop at nothing to catch and punish those responsible, hence his nickname - "The Bloodhound Judge". The fact that he and Grabner – who would himself find himself in Morgen's crosshairs less than a year later – had locked him out of his office proved beyond any possible doubt that Mockël and Lotze had leaked word of his lucrative little scheme to Berlin

Traugott also knew that the Gestapo's involvement meant that Höss wouldn't lift the smallest finger to help him. He was on his own, and he *had* to gain access to his office.

"I find your sense of duty quite commendable", he told the guard more amiably. "I don't know what's going on here, but I'm sure it's just a misunderstanding. In any case, I simply need a file on my desk, that's all."

"I'm sorry, herr untersturmführer, but my orders are clear and I can't allow anyone to enter this office. Not even you", the man replied.

"Then, by all means, follow your orders to the letter and don't let me in. Open the door, get the file for me and I'll be on my way. I'll stay out here the whole time", Traugott suggested. He even took a few steps back and spread his hands as proof of his good faith.

The man thought about it for an instant before taking the bait. "Very well, herr untersturmführer", he said. "This sounds acceptable."

Traugott waited until the man had opened the door and entered his office before rushing him from behind. He wrapped his left arm around the man's throat and pulled on his wrist with his other hand, compressing the guard's airways with his forearm. The man let out a strangled cry and tried to pry Traugott's arm away from his throat, but his fingers only slipped against Traugott's muscles. The man then began spinning around in circles, trying to slam Traugott against the walls, but he only managed to shut the door, which muffled the sounds of their struggle.

The men fought for several long seconds, thoroughly trashing Traugott's office, before the guard began to falter and weaken. Or at least that's what Traugott thought. The instant he loosened his hold on the guard's throat, the man came alive and pulled out his knife. Traugott grabbed his hand just as the guard was stabbing backward, but the tip of the blade still pierced Traugott's uniform and nicked the top of his right thigh. Warm blood began flowing down his leg.

Traugott fought to turn the knife away from his body and toward his adversary, but neither man had a clear advantage over the other. Now that Traugott no longer had his arm wrapped around the guard's throat, the man was once again breathing freely and he was quickly regaining his strength. He was also fighting with the fierce desperation of a man who knows he's about to die.

Traugott grabbed the guard's forehead with his only free hand and began pulling the head backward. He had no illusion that he might break the man's neck, but he wanted to divert his attention away from the struggle for control of the knife. When that didn't work, Traugott let his hand slip down the man's face until he found the eyes and that did the trick. The second Traugott's fingers began pressing down on his eyeballs, the man's attention wandered and he was doomed. Traugott twisted the knife inwards and slammed the man into the wall, pushing the blade deep into his lower back.

The man's whole body stiffened and he let out a gargled cry. Traugott pulled him away from the wall and slammed him into it again. The man's blood spurted all over his hand and Traugott knew he had severed a major blood vessel. This time, the man's body went completely limp and he slipped lifelessly to the floor when Traugott released him.

Breathing hard, Traugott took a few steps back and wiped his bloody, shaking hands on his uniform. He looked around his destroyed office and immediately saw how he would explain what had happened. He then placed a boot on the man's chest, wanting to see if it still rose and fell, but there was no movement. Satisfied that he had taken care of that problem, he turned his attention to the next one.

The locker at the back of the room in which he kept the gold, jewelry and other valuables destined for the black market had been sealed with a new padlock. His own lock looked intact, but someone – he guessed Grabner on Morgen's orders - had installed a second lock, which prevented him from opening the locker and removing the contents.

This was quite clever. Had the investigators smashed his lock and opened the locker, Traugott could have credibly pretended that whatever incriminating material was found had, in fact, been planted. This way, the locker would only be opened once all those concerned were present, and Traugott would be hard-pressed to deny knowing anything about its contents.

He shook the new lock hard, hoping against hope that it might pop open, and he hit the locker with his fist in frustration when it obviously didn't. He then examined the hinges on both doors, but quickly came to the conclusion that he couldn't remove them without risking damage that might be noticed later on. He considered procuring a crowbar or an ax with which to smash the locker open, and then claiming to have been robbed, but Konrad Morgen hadn't acquired his fearsome reputation by being an imbecile. The main suspect in an investigation for theft and corruption being the victim of such a convenient burglary would simply further arouse The Bloodhound Judge's suspicions.

Traugott needed to come up with something that would get both Morgen and Grabner off his back for good. Either that, or he had better start fleeing right now because the instant they saw what was in that locker, he was a dead man.

He began running his hands along the edges, looking for any way in, and he was just about to give up when his fingers encountered, behind the locker, something that finally gave him hope. Almost trembling with excitement, he pulled the heavy unit away from the wall and examined the back side. It was nothing more than a thin sheet of wood that had been screwed in place. Traugott's fingers had miraculously run over one of these screws, which was beginning to come loose and was slightly raised.

Using the tip of his knife as a screwdriver, it took him about twenty minutes to remove all the screws. He was careful to drop them all into his pocket, since a single missing one – should it be noticed – might be enough to arouse someone's doubts later on. He then removed the sheet of wood, exposing the inside of the locker. Traugott smiled.

He grabbed two tote bags into which he quickly dropped all of the incriminating valuables. He kept a gold watch and a diamond ring, which he placed in the dead guard's pockets, while in a third bag he put a wad of bills worth several hundred dollars and two bottles of expensive liquor. There was a small fortune here, enough to allow someone to live comfortably for a few years, and he was briefly tempted to disappear into the night with his loot. But since life as a fugitive from the Gestapo probably wasn't all that pleasant, he put the locker back together as carefully as he could and pushed it back against the wall.

He then stepped back and examined his handiwork. The locker appeared absolutely the same as it had before. Traugott nodded contentedly and checked to make sure that the guard was indeed dead before exiting his office and slipping away silently.

He still had two things to take care of, then he'd go wake up Rudolf Höss to report a murder.

"Why are you doing this for me?" Adriana asked.

The question made Doctor Ada smile. "I don't think I could explain it to you", she said. "That poor woman is already with God and you're not. If we don't do this, you too will die."

She then shrugged, indicating this was the only explanation she could provide, and the two women fell silent as Doctor Ada helped Adriana slip into the deceased woman's clothes.

"Hurry", she whispered, "we only have a few minutes before roll-call".

The other woman had been much smaller than Adriana, and even in her famished state, the clothes were a very tight fit for her. The shoes, however, were simply too small and Adriana would have to make do with her wooden clogs. Doctor Ada then dressed the dead body in Adriana's clothes and they were done. They were under no illusion that their subterfuge would go unnoticed for very long, but who knew what difference a few hours could make?

Roll-call was sounded outside and it was time for Adriana to go.

"Thank you, Doctor Ada", she said, hugging the small woman. "I'll never forget you."

"Oh, please see that you do", Ada Rosensaft immediately replied. "Live a long, long life and forget all about me and this place. Be happier than you've ever been. Now go before they come looking for you."

No sooner had she uttered those words that two SS guards barged into her tiny infirmary. Doctor Ada stared at them with a mixture of contempt and pity, as though she was torn between hating them for being such monsters and pitying them for being such idiots.

"That one died", she said, nodding at the dead woman. "This one is going back to work."

The rest was lost to Adriana as she emerged from the building. Her head was pounding, her legs were wobbly, but at least she was alive.

She took a moment to get her bearings, while all around her inmates quickly lined up outside their barracks. She would only return to her own barrack later that evening, assuming she was still alive by then, and she looked forward to being reunited with Magrita and thanking her friend for saving her life. Unsure of where she was supposed to go, but knowing that she couldn't just stand there forever, Adriana began walking about randomly until she finally spotted two women dressed as she was. She hurried after them.

Adriana knew she was risking her life, but she felt strangely calm. She had stared Death in the face on several occasions over the past few months and she was still here, defiantly staring back. While it terrifies most people, the prospect of dying now left her almost completely indifferent. She felt as though she had very little to lose, like a gambler who hits Monte Carlo his pockets filled with someone else's money. Who cared if she won or lost? Who cared if she lived or died? With the sole exception of Magrita and Doctor Ada, whom she had only met over the last few hours, no one cared about her here, just as she herself didn't care about anyone else.

Adriana had long ago come to terms with how little value was placed on her existence at Auschwitz. Her life could end at any moment, for any reason. It was simply the way things were here. At Auschwitz, you risked your life simply by awakening in the morning. There were no right choices here, no wrong choices. There were simply the choices that you made, for better and for worse, and those that you didn't, also for better or for worse. There was absolutely nothing that would, or could, guarantee your survival until the next day. So, sometimes, since one had absolutely nothing to lose, it made complete sense for one to take apparently foolish risks, risks one would never contemplate outside Auschwitz's walls of barbed wire, all for the chance of a small reward.

And today, Adriana had decided to go along with Doctor Ada's plan. Whether this was the right choice or not was impossible to ascertain. It also didn't matter in the least. The kind Pole had been adamant: this was her only chance, and Adriana agreed. As weak as she felt, she didn't need a medical degree to know that the least exertion might prove fatal.

There were more women dressed like her ahead. They all wore a white handkerchief, pirate-style, over their heads. This marked them as members of the *weißköpfchen*, one of the most desirable kommandos in all of Auschwitz. As she drew closer, Adriana immediately noticed that these women appeared better fed and more rested than the other inmates. She even spotted the odd tuft of hair sprouting from underneath their handkerchiefs, a rare sight in a place where any body hair was immediately colonized by lice.

Adriana caught up to the two women she had been following and lined up next to them. She stared directly ahead and tried to empty her mind. She focused on a point far in the distance and willed herself to become invisible to the eyes of all those who might notice that she didn't belong here. More women were arriving and lining up, until there were about one hundred of them. Adriana tried to lose herself in this small crowd, to become one with these women. She had no right to be here but she had to convince herself otherwise, she had to project an image of confidence and self-confidence to the outside world; if she didn't, her doubts would be like blood to these sharks, and she would be found out and devoured alive.

A *kapo* Adriana had never seen before arrived along with the last few women. Where Hiltrude exuded the arrogance and violence of a true psychopath, this *kapo* more closely resembled someone's dear old grandmother. The woman walked slowly and deliberately, her back slightly stooped, and her hair, though very short, was entirely white. Adriana was immediately struck by her caring eyes and she wondered how such a woman had ended up in a place such as this.

The kapo took a moment to count them, mouthing the numbers silently, and seemed satisfied that all were accounted for. Adriana was relieved not to have been noticed.

"Very well *damen*", the woman began in a voice that, while velvety soft, carried a hundred times more authority than Hiltrude's bellows. "You know how it's done. In a single file, one behind the other, and let's be on our way."

The women filed out docilely. Adriana kept her head down and matched the pace of the woman in front of her. She felt terribly exposed, now that she no longer was one among a hundred. She knew she might be noticed at any moment. And she was.

"What's your name?" someone walking next to her suddenly asked. Adriana jumped and looked to her right. The old kapo had sidled up silently next to her and was watching her with inquisitive eyes. Adriana didn't reply.

"My name is Rita and I'm in charge of this kommando", the old woman said.

Still, Adriana remained silent. Rita walked with her for a moment. She seemed to be in no hurry.

"You're not supposed to be here", she finally said, stating the obvious. When Adriana still didn't say anything, she added: "It's the shoes, child. You don't have any shoes."

Adriana bit her lower lip and kept her head down. Rita was right, of course. All the other women who were part of this kommando had on regular shoes, while she still wore her wooden clogs. The dead woman's shoes had been too small for her and she'd left them behind. And now this tiny detail would probably cost her her life.

Rita remained pensive for a moment. "I don't know how you got here but I have no choice but to report you", she said. "And then they'll assign you to the S.K. and you'll die."

Adriana bit down on her lip harder until she tasted blood. Tears welled in her eyes and she fought to hold them back. The S.K. was the strafekommando, one of the worst work details imaginable at Auschwitz, right alongside the sonderkommando who burned the bodies in the crematoria. Those assigned to the S.K. worked in the swamps, in the cold and damp, immersed up to their hips in freezing water for hours. It was a penal kommando, one reserved for those inmates who had broken the rules but who could still work. It was also a guaranteed death sentence.

Rita let the weight of what she'd just said sink in before she went on. "So here's what we'll do", she said, never raising her voice. "I'll count ten steps. If you're still here, I'll report you to the untersturmführer and we both know what will happen then. But during those ten steps, maybe you'll decide to walk away and take your chances somewhere else. If you do, I won't say anything."

Rita wasn't truly being magnanimous and generous. Returning to Hiltrude and throwing herself at the fat kapo's mercy simply wasn't an option for Adriana. The beating she'd receive if she did would kill her. She'd rather take her chances in the swamps. So she counted ten steps, and then eleven, and then twelve, and then...

Rita sighed. "Very well", she finally said. "I wish you well, child."

The old woman walked away, leaving Adriana alone with her somber thoughts.

10

Konrad Morgen arrived at Auschwitz just after dawn. He was immediately impressed by the size of the camp and by how it fairly buzzed with activity, but that wasn't why he was here.

If what Mockël and Lotze had reported were true, Auschwitz had sprouted a pustule of corruption that needed to be lanced immediately before the infection got out of hand. Assuming, of course, that it wasn't already too late.

Otto Mockël had traveled with him and the young officer, despite the early hour, eagerly led them directly to Rudolf Höss' office. But the obersturmbannführer wasn't present and the two men then went in search of Maximilian Grabner. The Gestapo chief was also absent but one of his aides, upon Konrad Morgen introducing himself, told them where to find him.

Mockël felt the first few arrows of worry strike his soul.

The two men crossed the camp rapidly and Mockël was careful to hide his smile when Morgen covered his mouth and nose with a gloved hand. The smell of the crematoria was particularly strong and made for a perfect backdrop to the day's business. There definitely was a stench that permeated Auschwitz, and as far as Mockël was concerned, it didn't only come from the burning of filthy corpses.

A guard posted at the door of the building blocked their path, explaining that an investigation was ongoing and that he was under strict orders from Rudolf Höss not to allow anyone inside. He only relented when, again, Konrad Morgen introduced himself. The Bloodhound Judge's reputation preceded him throughout the Reich and rare were those foolhardy enough to interfere with his business.

They found Höss, Grabner and Traugott in deep discussion in the middle of Kanada's work area. The three men spun around when the door opened and Mockël was pleased by the look of fury that descended upon Traugott's face when their eyes met. Höss, for his part, was a bit stunned by Konrad Morgen's appearance at Auschwitz without his having been forewarned of the judge's visit. He rapidly overcame his shock, reassured by the fact that he remained the highest-ranking man in the room, and the men hid behind a facade of salutes and handshakes while they took each other's measure.

"Welcome to Auschwitz, sturmbannführer Morgen", Höss began. "I wish I had been told of your visit. I would have greeted you properly."

Höss glanced at Grabner and immediately noticed that the Gestapo chief, on the other hand, didn't seem all that surprised by Morgen's arrival. He narrowed his eyes at him suspiciously.

"The guard outside told us of an investigation", Morgen replied, cutting straight to the chase. "Perhaps I can be of assistance."

Höss nodded. "Of course", he said. "This man here, untersturmführer Mattias Traugott, came to me early this morning with a very peculiar story and we're trying to sort out what, exactly, transpired here. He was just about to retell it for untersturmführer Grabner's benefit. I would certainly value your input in the matter."

Höss then nodded at Traugott, who coughed discretely into his fist.

"As I told the obersturmbannführer earlier", he began, adopting a tone that was suitably meek, "I had left a file in my office last night. When I came by to retrieve it a few hours later, I caught an intruder rifling through my desk."

Morgen immediately raised a hand to silence him.

This man, this Traugott, was the one he'd come here to investigate, and less than five minutes after meeting him for the first time he was already spouting a tale that seemed destined to exonerate from whatever had happened.

This one was a slick one, and Morgen's senses were on full alert.

"You returned in the middle of the night to fetch a file?" he asked. "Could it not have waited until morning?"

Traugott shrugged nonchalantly. The soldier he'd killed had told him that Grabner had ordered his office guarded, on Morgen's orders, so he, too, knew who he was dealing with. He also knew he had to thread very carefully. "I suppose it could have, herr sturmbannführer", he said innocently. "But I was awake so I decided to take care of it right away."

"And who was the intruder? An inmate, of course?" Morgen went on suspiciously.

"*Nein*, herr sturmbannführer", Traugott explained. "This is what's most puzzling. The intruder was a guard."

Morgen raised his eyebrows and Grabner looked uncomfortable.

"Quite puzzling indeed", the judge conceded cynically. "Go on."

Traugott nodded. "This intruder attacked me before I could say a word. He stabbed me, but I fought back and eventually killed him." Traugott hadn't changed out of his bloody uniform, which added a layer of credibility to his tale.

"You killed one of our brethren? This is quite a serious matter", Grabner intervened.

"I was acting in self-defense", Traugott immediately replied. The two men were of equal rank, so no deference was required.

"Yes, we'll see", Grabner said. "What else?"

Traugott shrugged again. "Someone has locked me out of my locker, to keep me from accessing its contents. I have no idea what..."

Konrad Morgen again raised a hand and Traugott fell silent. "You two are dismissed for the moment", he said abruptly, addressing the two junior officers. "I need to confer with obersturmbannführer Höss and with herr Grabner. Leave us."

Having no say in the matter, Traugott and Mockël clicked their heels together obediently and retreated to the far corner of the warehouse while the three other men bent their heads together.

"How is my good friend Lotze doing?" Traugott asked sarcastically in a very low voice.

"I found him to be a fascinating man", Mockël said, not even bothering to deny knowing Dieter Lotze. "He told the most *verwunderlich* stories. At first I found it quite hard to believe that an SS officer could be so dishonest. But then he told me who the officer was, and then obviously it all made sense."

Traugott ignored the barb and said: "Personally, Lotze reminded me of your mutt. All bark and no bite. Lotze probably licks his own balls, too."

Color rose to Mockël's face and he was about to respond when he was interrupted by an outburst from the camp commander.

"Why wasn't I informed of this! This is entirely unacceptable!" Höss shouted before lowering his voice again. A moment later he raised it again, enough for Traugott to catch "...report to the Reichsführer myself...", but then he regained control of his emotions and the rest of what he said was unintelligible.

Höss then summoned Traugott and Mockël. The obersturmbannführer was both flabbergasted by what he'd just heard and furious at all that had been happening right under his nose. He shot a glance at Traugott that Mattias didn't really care for.

"The body is still in your office?" Morgen asked.

Traugott nodded. "Yes, herr sturmbannführer. I didn't touch it."

"Let's have a look", the judge ordered.

The five men made their way to Traugott's office, where they found the dead guard still sprawled face down, his head against the wall, just as Traugott had left him a few hours earlier. Morgen surveyed the entire room, noticing that it had been thoroughly trashed, and sighed.

"Well, there definitely was a fight here, that much seems obvious", he stated. "But the coincidence of it all strikes me as being quite fantastic."

"Coincidence, herr sturmbannführer?" Traugott asked innocently, playing his cards as artfully as he could. He was also very glad not to have underestimated Morgen's intelligence. "I'm afraid I don't quite understand."

Morgen turned to face him and grew even more serious, if such a thing was possible. "Untersturmführer Mattias Traugott, allegations of theft and corruption have been leveled against you. I have come here to investigate these serious charges. Access to your locker was restricted on my orders, to prevent the disappearance of any potential evidence prior to my arrival. And now I find you also involved in a murder, and your office completely ransacked. *That* coincidence, untersturmführer."

Traugott managed to appear both outraged and shocked. He stared at Rudolf Höss, who simply stared back, and then put on a show of searching for a suitable response. "And may I ask who leveled these allegations, herr sturmbannführer?" he finally asked.

"Their names shall remain confidential for the moment", Morgen said, unwittingly confirming that there had been more than one accuser. "Suffice it to say that a witness came forward, and his testimony was judged credible enough to warrant an investigation."

"It's very difficult for me to defend myself against such vague accusations, herr sturmbannführer. What am I accused of stealing? And how am I corrupt?" Traugott protested feebly. "But I have nothing to hide and I'm sure this is nothing more than a misunderstanding. Here's the key to my locker. Please search it at your convenience."

He handed a small silver key to Morgen, who pinched it between two fingers as though he was afraid it might burn his skin. The Bloodhound Judge then looked expectantly at Grabner, who finally fished another key out of his pocket and gave it to him. Armed with the two keys, the SS judge walked to Traugott's locker, threading his way carefully through the debris that littered the floor, and opened it.

He stared, dumbfounded and angry, at the half-empty locker. Where his sources had sworn he'd find a fortune in stolen goods, he saw only shelves that held nothing more than a couple of clean uniforms, a few towels and several personal items of absolutely no value. He grabbed a shaving kit from the top shelf and took much longer than was necessary to look through it. He then took several deep breaths before turning around.

"Someone tell me why I have traveled all the way from Berlin to investigate a shaving kit?" he thundered, addressing all four men but staring directly at a stupefied Otto Mockël.

When no one could provide an answer to the judge's question, Traugott knew time had come to drop the ace hidden up his sleeve. "If I may, herr sturmbannführer, I believe I may have an explanation", he said. "Or at least a hypothesis."

"By all means, untersturmführer Traugott, enlighten us", Konrad Morgen growled impatiently.

Traugott pretended to be weighing what to say, while in fact he had rehearsed this part endlessly in his own mind. "As I'm sure obersturmbannführer Höss will attest, my presence here has earned me several enemies", he began. He was relieved to see Höss nodding in agreement. "There were those who, before my arrival, would enrich themselves at the Reich's expense. This has stopped and the yield generated by this operation has increased by a factor of at least five over the past several months".

Höss nodded again. "What he says is true", the camp commander confirmed. "His performance has been stellar."

Traugott bowed in silent thanks. "Could it then be, herr sturmbannführer, that I am the victim of a plot orchestrated by those whom my arrival has displeased?"

Morgen narrowed his eyes at him. "You claim to have been set up? By whom?"

"I'll get to that in a moment, herr sturmbannführer", Traugott said. "But like you, I am struck by such a fantastic coincidence. Hours before your arrival, an intruder breaks into my office... Could he have been on a mission to plant evidence to incriminate me?"

Morgen pursed his lips. "That's easy enough to verify", he said. "Mockël, search the body."

Mockël's jaw dropped open and he was about to ask why he should, when he remembered that it was essentially on his account that Konrad Morgen was here. Thinking it wiser not to antagonize the judge further, he knelt, fuming, next to the dead man and began rifling through his pockets. He rapidly found the gold watch and diamond ring Traugott had concealed there earlier.

Traugott smiled, but he managed to appear sorry rather than triumphant. "It seems that my enemies will stop at nothing, herr sturmbannführer", he deplored. "Including wasting the time of a man such as yourself."

Morgen seemed on the verge of exploding. "I demand to know who is behind this!" he roared. "Grabner! You sent this guard here! You picked him! Are you responsible for this nonsense?"

Maximilian Grabner shook his head. "No, of course not, herr sturmbannführer", the Gestapo chief replied quickly, desperate to extricate himself from this mess as rapidly and cleanly as possible. "I simply followed your orders to the best of my abilities."

"Don't blame this on me!" Morgen thundered, even though Grabner was doing no such thing. "You're the one who..."

As much as he relished watching his enemies tear each other apart, Traugott knew that he couldn't allow his carefully orchestrated plan to morph into a personal quarrel between the two men. He still had one more card to play. So he went to Rudolf Höss and whispered something in his ear while Grabner – who, as a member of the Gestapo, was accountable to the SS – and Morgen kept screaming at each other. The obersturmbannführer nodded and interrupted the shouting match by stepping between the two men.

"This will get us nowhere", he said. "The first person we need to interrogate is the one who leveled these charges against Traugott. That person is clearly the one who had the most to gain from these malicious allegations."

Traugott lowered his head to hide a smile. Höss had apparently already forgotten the doubts he'd briefly entertained about him and was again following his advice blindly. Instead of destroying him, Mockël's plot had only reinforced Traugott' standing in Höss' eyes. Unbelievable.

Konrad Morgen stared at Höss for a moment before turning his gaze to Otto Mockël. He then looked back at Höss. "You're right, of course", he finally said, nodding. "I apologize for losing my temper, herr obersturmbannführer". He then looked at Traugott. "It seems you were unjustly accused, herr Traugott. Please accept my apologies. But also please remain at my disposal until my departure. I may yet send for you."

Traugott bowed obediently as the four men filed out of his office. He taunted Mockël with his eyes when the other man walked by him, and Mockël replied with a murderous stare, but Traugott knew he'd have the last laugh today. He'd gladly have paid a small fortune to be present when they found the money and liquor he'd hidden in Mockël's locker, again by removing the back panel.

He exited his office after them and was about to send for two guards to come remove the body when the soldier he had posted at the door of the warehouse appeared before him.

"What the hell are you doing here?" Traugott asked angrily. "Why have you left your post?"

The man was almost trembling with fear. "My apologies, herr untersturmführer, but the workers have arrived and I was unsure whether I should let them in or not. I left them waiting outside."

Traugott closed his eyes and pinched the bridge of his nose. The workers. Of course. Through all this madness, he still had an operation to run.

"Let them in but keep them confined to the work area", he ordered. The guard nodded in acknowledgment but remained where he was. "Was there something else?" Traugott asked impatiently.

The guard swallowed hard. "Begging the untersturmführer's indulgence in advance, but *kapo* Rita is asking to speak with you urgently", the man said.

A kapo demanding to speak with an SS officer was an insolence of almost unimaginable proportions, but Traugott's anger was all spent. He sighed wearily and shook his head in disbelief, wondering what else this day had in store for him.

"Very well", he finally said. "Send her to me."

11

Trying to make herself as small as possible, Adriana stood, bewildered and trembling, in a corner of the room as the other women got to work.

She watched in amazement as they began sorting through piles of clothes, examining each garment minutely before disposing of it. Sometimes they found objects that they dropped into locked boxes in the middle of the room. If she craned her neck, she could see other women doing the same thing with piles of shoes in the next room. There were also rooms beyond that one, and while she couldn't see what went on in those, in all logic it had to be something similar.

The women worked rapidly and efficiently. The clothes had already been sorted into giant mounds of dresses and shirts and pants and so on. Once a worker had examined ten dresses, for example, she'd bring them to another woman standing next to a very long table. This woman would fold the dresses cleanly and bundle them up with a length of string. The bale was then set aside, by which time the first woman was just about ready to return with ten new dresses. But what struck Adriana the most was that nobody got yelled at, nobody was threatened, nobody was harassed or hurried or even beaten. Assuming that you provided an honest effort, you were left alone.

Hiltrude would have been completely lost here.

Adriana was stunned. It was a poorly kept secret that these mysterious women with the white scarves had been assigned to the most desirable *kommando* around, but now she knew what it was, exactly, that made it so desirable – and this, in turn, had to be one of the best kept secrets at Auschwitz, and for good reason. The *weißköpfchen* themselves, as they were known, meaning the ones with the white heads, were notoriously tight-lipped about what they did. This Adriana now also understood better. A job like this could get you killed in your sleep by someone looking to steal it away from you. Better not to brag about it too much.

Adriana herself owed her presence here, however short-lived it might eventually prove to be, solely to someone else's death.

The *weißköpfchen* got to escape Auschwitz daily to rejoin the outside world. Even though they never went past the camp gates, these women might as well have gone to work in a regular factory a thousand miles away from here. They were treated like human beings. They worked in a safe environment, sheltered from the heat in summer and the cold in winter. They knew nothing of collapsing brick walls or freezing swamps. They knew nothing of starvation and disease and arbitrary beatings.

This couldn't be real. This had to be a dream, an illusion. And soon she'd wake up.

The kind old kapo, Rita, had told Adriana to wait quietly while she went to fetch the SS officer in charge of the warehouse, all the while looking like she was fetching the Devil himself. And now Rita was returning, accompanied by a disheveled officer dressed in a bloody uniform. The old woman shook her head when she saw that Adriana was still obediently standing there, as though she'd expected her to have fled – or perhaps hoped that she would have.

Rita stepped aside and the SS officer walked right up to Adriana. He had the coldest, meanest, most vicious eyes Adriana had ever seen in her entire life. The man's whole body radiated evil and Adriana shivered. She knew she could expect no mercy from such a monster.

Traugott looked Adriana up and down, taking a moment to note the clogs she still wore, and he sighed in exasperation.

"What are you doing here? Where did you steal these clothes?" he asked.

Adriana simply dropped her eyes and remained silent. She wasn't about to betray Doctor Ada by revealing how she'd come to be here. Nothing she said would make any difference anyway.

She could feel the weight of the man's stare on her, pressuring her to respond, but still she kept silent.

Under normal circumstances, Traugott would probably have slapped the truth out of her. But on that morning, after all he'd been through over the previous hours, he was simply too exhausted to get worked up over an insolent Jewess. So he shrugged and turned to Rita.

"She can stay here for today", he told the *kapo*. "Find her something to do. But tomorrow I'm assigning her to the strafekommando. I don't have time for this."

He then walked away from the two women, his mind already concentrating on the task of removing the dead body that still lay in his office. He had almost exited the work area when a single sob escaped from the woman he'd just condemned to the strafekommando – a woman who, until that moment, had remained entirely silent and whose voice he hadn't heard.

Traugott froze in his tracks and he felt his entire mind go numb. Then, against his better judgment, he spun around slowly and looked at the woman more closely. The numbness spread from his mind to the rest of his body and for a moment he felt as though he'd been encased in ice. He couldn't have moved an inch to save his skin had an entire battalion of Russian T-34 tanks been barreling down on him.

He took one step, then another, and another, and then he was standing behind Rita who had his back turned to him and seemed to be comforting the inmate. The *kapo* quickly jumped out of the way when she sensed his presence behind her but she was invisible to Traugott. His entire attention was focused on the other woman.

Adriana again looked into his eyes and she was astonished by what she saw there. Gone were the hatred and violence, replaced by a mixture of stupefaction and uneasiness and benign curiosity – and even fear.

"Sing for me", Traugott demanded softly.

Adriana was taken completely aback by his request. That was the last thing she'd expected. Was this a sick joke? This man wanted her to sing for him? Here and now? After he'd just sentenced her to death? Like hell she would.

"No", was her sole reply, and she managed to make the word sound as though it contained more than one syllable. Rita gasped audibly.

The SS officer raised his chin a bit and joined his hands together behind his back, but his eyes never left hers. Adriana held his stare while Rita observed the scene, completely flabbergasted by what she was witnessing. Traugott seemed about to say something else, but instead he swallowed hard and took a few deep breaths.

"Sing... *Bitte, sing für mich*", he finally said.

Adriana couldn't believe her ears. This SS officer was not ordering her to sing for him. He was *asking* her to sing for him. And not only was he asking her to sing for him, but he was asking her to *please* sing for him? For a Nazi to ask a Jew to *please* do something defied all the laws that now governed her world. It was simply inconceivable.

She stared deeper into the man's eyes and what she saw there troubled her. She would have been hard-pressed to explain what it was, exactly, that she read there, but she felt like she'd finally spotted a flickering light through the trees after wandering aimlessly through the dark woods for days. Is this light a lamp hung outside a cottage where she'll find safety, or are they the glowing eyes of a wolf tracking her?

Adriana bet on the cottage.

"What... what should I sing, herr offizier?" she asked respectfully, unaware that all worked had stopped around them and that all were watching the unfolding scene. The SS shivered visibly when she spoke and his whole body seemed to resonate.

Traugott didn't have to search long for an answer. "*Bitte*... Sing like you did at the birthday party."

Again that word. *Bitte*. Please.

Adriana had to think for a moment before understanding what he meant. Of course, it had to be Rudolf Höss' birthday party, a few days after she'd arrived at Auschwitz but at the same time, a lifetime ago. That was the only occasion he'd have had to hear her. She lowered her eyes and concentrated, trying to remember the words, and cleared her throat discretely.

This was hard. Inside she was shaking like a leaf and she was finding it impossible to concentrate. She knew the lyrics were hidden in her mind somewhere, but they remained elusively out of her grasp. The more she reached for them, the more they seemed to slither away. She was scared, she was exhausted, she'd been concussed and beaten and starved, and her memory was failing her. In the end she could only remember the last verse, recalling the spell it had cast over the guests at the party, so she sang it, hoping that its magic would operate once more.

Zähle deine Jahre
und denk' stets daran:
Sie sind wie ein Schatz,
den dir keiner nehmen kann.

But on this day, there would be no spell. Adriana's powers of enchantment had vanished. The outrage that had previously powered her voice had been replaced by despair, anger had yielded to loss and hope had been slain by sorrow. Even though she sang for less than ten seconds, by the time she was done tears were streaming down her face. All she could see was poor little Aaron lying dead on the floor in front of her, his soul escaping the tiny body. Then she thought of her parents, who were certainly dead by now, and she thought of kind old Sándor Pfircsik who had sacrificed his life so that she could live, and she thought of Etty and Malva, destroyed by the evil who was overlord of Auschwitz, and she cried uncontrollably. To be here today, singing for a man dressed in that monstrous uniform after all that had happened to her, was more than she could bear.

Traugott took a step back when the song ended. A silence deeper than that of the catacombs reigned inside the warehouse. Those who had witnessed the scene would never forget it. Rita had clasped her hands to her bosom and seemed to be praying. The inmates had stopped working and the guards whose job it was to keep them productive were paralyzed by indecision, fearing that any intervention might incur them the wrath of their untersturmführer.

Adriana kept her head down as she collected herself. When she finally looked up and into the SS' eyes, the fear she read there almost made her feel sorry for him. How could she possibly have frightened him so with a simple song? What the hell was going on here, exactly?

Traugott stared at her for a moment longer before turning to Rita.

"I'm assigning her to this kommando from this moment", he said in a voice that reverberated from a thousand miles away. "Take her to have a shower, and then give her some better clothes."

Then, almost as an afterthought, he added: "And find her some proper shoes".

One month later, 24 May 1943

The SS-Hauptsturmführer stepped out of the car, set down his leather suitcase, brushed the dust from his clothes and grinned.

He liked the place already and his eyes sparkled in eager anticipation. Great things would be accomplished here, he thought, all in the service of the Fatherland.

He was already a war hero. He had been awarded the *Eisernes Kreuz 2. Klasse*, and then the much more prestigious *Eisernes Kreuz 1. Klasse*, for various acts of bravery while battling the Russians. He had been a bit despondent at being declared unfit for duty after being wounded, but that turned out to be a blessing in disguise.

After his recovery, he visited the *Kaiser-Wilhelm-Institut für Anthropologie, menschliche Erblehre, und Eugenik* in Berlin, where he happened to bump into a man who had been his mentor several years earlier, Otmar Freiherr von Verschuer. The two men renewed their association and von Verschuer, recognizing a kindred spirit when he encountered one, pulled a few strings to get him this assignment.

The hauptsturmführer picked up his suitcase. He then fished out of his pocket a scrap of paper on which he had scribbled the name of the man who would be his superior and who he needed to report to: standortarzt Eduard Wirths, chief SS doctor of the Auschwitz concentration camp.

He took another look around and smiled contentedly. Yes, here he would go on serving the Fatherland, but in a completely different manner.

He set off in search of Wirths.

"Here comes your boyfriend", Magrita whispered mischievously.

Adriana looked to her right and saw Traugott approaching. He was progressing slowly, putting each foot down deliberately, his heels clicking against the ground. He looked like a man walking a tightrope – or, perhaps more accurately, like a prisoner sent on ahead of soldiers advancing through a minefield. Hands linked behind his back, he'd stop next to each worker and make great show of examining her work. Every once in a while he'd pick up a garment and give it a once-over to make sure nothing had been missed. He'd then nod approvingly before dropping it and resuming his rounds.

Adriana groaned.

"He's not my boyfriend", she whispered back with a touch of anger. "I hate him. He's a *Nazi*."

"I don't think he knows that", Magrita shot right back, but just as lightly as before. "That he's not your boyfriend and that you hate him, I mean. I'm pretty sure he knows he's a Nazi."

Someone tutted behind them. Adriana looked over her shoulder. Kapo Rita was staring at them sternly, like a teacher who's caught two of her pupils cheating during an exam.

"Work in silence", she chastised them. "The rules apply to *all* of you."

Adriana and Magrita dropped their eyes apologetically. Adriana wondered if the emphasis Rita had put on the word "all" had been directed at her. She finished folding yet another shirt and added it to the pile on the table in front of her.

Word of how she'd found herself assigned to the *weißköpfchen* had spread through the camp like the plague. Traugott hadn't said a single word to her since that day, a month ago, when she'd sung for him, but that hadn't stopped tongues from wagging. Especially considering the fact that, less than a week later, Magrita had also found herself one of the *weißköpfchen*. It was widely assumed that Adriana had intervened on her friend's behalf, while in truth she'd had nothing to do with it. It had all been Traugott's doing. He somehow figured out who Adriana's best friend here was and had her transferred to his kommando.

But the truth didn't matter much. Some spiteful inmates had now taken to calling Adriana

"Queen Esther", both behind her back and to her face – a none-too-subtle evocation of the Jewish orphan who eventually became the wife of King Ahasuerus of Persia.

Auschwitz wasn't a place where one liked to stand out and now Adriana's name was on a thousand lips, through no fault of her own. She tried to concentrate on her work and repeated to herself, for the thousandth time, that she'd done nothing wrong. If it was painfully obvious that Traugott had taken a special liking to her, it should also have been obvious that she'd done nothing to attract his attention, let alone seduce him. She'd also done nothing to take advantage of this special position that she now found herself in.

Or had she?

She owed her being here to some other unfortunate soul's death and to Doctor Ada's ingenuity. She was essentially here fraudulently. If she hadn't gone along with Doctor Ada's subterfuge, someone else would have been assigned to the *weißköpfchen*, not her. Someone else would have lived while she, in all likelihood, would have died. Her survival was directly responsible for someone else's demise.

And when she'd been found out, when her fraud had been exposed, she'd only been saved by this crazy SS' fascination with her. If not for his intercession, she'd have frozen to death in the swamps by now. The thought of renouncing her position, of admitting that it wasn't rightfully hers and that it should be given to someone else, had obviously never entered her mind. So now here she was, assigned to an indoor job that would never be described as strenuous, showering every few days, with an inch of hair on her head, growing stronger on whatever food the previous owners of these clothes had stuffed in their pockets, living, surviving, thriving even.

Her swollen belly had returned to its normal size now that she was no longer systematically famished. Her waxy, translucent skin had regained its elasticity and her gums no longer bled. Sores had healed and the bone-deep exhaustion that she'd never fully grown accustomed to had somewhat receded. She was essentially lice-free. And the lancing pain that she felt in her lower abdomen warned her of the impending return of an old enemy whom she hadn't really missed these past few months.

Had she not been at Auschwitz, Adriana would have considered her situation to be almost tolerable.

Traugott was now standing directly behind her. Adriana knew he was staring at her but she refused to turn around and acknowledge him. She concentrated on the shirt she was folding, trying to block his presence out of her mind. Others had warned her of the type of man he was and she was determined to stay as far away from him as she could. She'd been told of the violence that simmered just beneath the skin, threatening to erupt at any moment, of the cruelty and ruthlessness of which he was capable, and while she'd yet to witness it herself, she was afraid.

Adriana was also troubled. On the few occasions that their eyes had met, she'd seen nothing of the savage monster she'd been told to fear. Rather, she'd found herself gazing into the eyes of an orphan, lost and alone in the world, desperate for some love and attention. His eyes would lit up with a mixture of hope and trepidation, as though her looking at him filled him with indescribable pleasure, as though this brief exchange might give birth to something else, as though he hoped that it might ignite in her the fire that already consumed his soul. But all Adriana felt for him was a cold hatred and she knew that he sensed it. The hurt she read in his eyes when he saw that her own eyes reflected none of what he felt spoke volumes.

She could have faked it, had she wanted to. She'd had enough suitors to know how. A naughty wink here and a conspiratorial smile there would have done it. Of course, such acts might have encouraged him to ask for more, but she didn't feel that she had much to fear on that front; she knew how absolutely *verboten* physical relations between Nazis and Jews were. Would he still have risked it? Perhaps. But he'd never get the chance because there would be no wink and there would be no smile. She found the thought of dishonoring both herself and the memories of all those she'd lost so far by prostituting herself to him so repugnant that she remained cold and distant – all the while being perfectly aware that such an attitude might cut her time here very short.

Traugott walked on. Adriana breathed a silent sigh of relief and grabbed another shirt to fold. She spread out the garment on the table in front of her. She smoothed out the wrinkles and was struck by how small it was, as though it had belonged to a child. She was about to fold it into a rough square when the faintest scent rose to her nostrils. Her mind immediately went blank. She looked at the shirt again, perhaps truly seeing it for the first time, and then she grabbed it with both hands and brought it to her face, inhaling the odor that it still held.

It was barely there, but it was enough. *Pine needles.*

No. It couldn't be. Not even God could be that cruel. She frantically turned the shirt over in her hands, looking for the small tear in the back, the small tear that a skilled seamstress had almost made vanish, the small tear that wouldn't be there because this wasn't *his* shirt, this was just *a* shirt that happened to smell like *him*.

Adriana's fingers found the small tear. She let out a sharp cry and shoved away from the table, letting the shirt drop to the floor. She cried out again.

"Adriana, what's wrong?" Magrita asked.

"What's going on? Why are you screaming?" Rita demanded almost at the same time.

Both women were staring at her but all Adriana could see was the crumpled shirt on the ground.

A shirt that smelled of pine needles.

A shirt that smelled of her father.

Adriana's entire body was shaking. She was shrieking hysterically. Rita was standing directly in front or her, holding her by the wrists and trying to get through to her. "Adriana?" the old woman was shouting. "What's wrong, child? For the love of God tell me what's wrong!"

But Adriana was gone. That shirt could mean only one thing: her father - and in all likelihood, her mother along with him - had been brought to Auschwitz and gassed. They were both dead. She had long supposed them to have been, but to actually have proof of their deaths annihilated any possibility she may have been wrong. In her mind suddenly formed an image of them clinging to each other as the yellow gas filled their lungs, Simeon Zöbel finding enough breath to tell Raanah that he loved her one last time before they began vomiting over one another, condemned to a suffocating, agonizing death by animals who had decided that they, who had always strove to lead the most harmless lives possible, were to blame for all that was wrong with the world.

Adriana felt a sting on her cheek and she finally managed to tear her eyes away from the shirt.

When she looked at Rita, the woman's hand was raised, ready to strike again. Rita dropped her hand and Adriana began to cry uncontrollably

"That shirt... it was my father's", she finally said. "He's... he's dead. And my..."

She passed out before finishing her sentence.

"What's going on here?" Traugott thundered. "Why aren't you working? Why..."

He stopped short when he saw Adriana lying unconscious on the ground. He looked at Rita, then back at the inert body.

"What happened?" he demanded in a slightly mollified tone. Rita explained that Adriana had fainted after finding her father's shirt. Traugott nodded and seemed to make up his mind very quickly.

"You two", he ordered Rita and Margita. "Grab her by the wrists and follow me."

The two women obeyed immediately and followed him as he led them behind some shelves on which were stacked the clothes ready to be shipped out.

"Rita, you stay with her and get her back to work as rapidly as you can", he said. "You, back to work now."

Magrita vanished without a word.

"Make it quick", he told Rita again. "Or there might be more trouble than you know."

Traugott normally ruled as complete Lord and Master over all that happened inside the *Aufräumungskommando* and on any other day such an event wouldn't have caused him any worries. But after the occurrences of the previous month, Rudolf Höss had grown more careful and suspicious. He'd formed a *qualitätskontrollgruppe* that he'd entrusted to his faithful adjutant, the sour-faced hauptsturmführer Robert Mulka. This new group conducted surprise inspections of the various kommandos, hoping to keep them honest and efficient with the constant threat of an unannounced visit.

Traugott had yet to be inspected, but he knew that today was his day. Someone who worked under Mulka had agreed, in exchange for a bottle of scotch, to warn him in advance of any spot inspection coming his way. Adriana's little fainting spell couldn't have come at a worst time. He knew that Mulka and his men would take a census of all the workers who were supposed to be here, and if a single one was found to be missing, there'd be hell to pay.

Traugott had barely returned to the work area when the door slammed open and Mulka strode in, right on cue and looking even less cheerful than usual. He was followed by a coterie of half a dozen men, among whom Traugott was stunned to recognize Otto Möckel. He hadn't seen his old enemy since the day he'd planted stolen goods in his locker, a month ago, and he'd essentially assumed him to have been thrown down the Reich's deepest and darkest dungeon by Konrad Morgen. The fact that he was here demonstrated either that the Bloodhound Judge's reputation was overblown, or that Möckel could count on the backing of some powerful people. In either case, he was back and Traugott knew that only death would now settle things between them.

Traugott and the other SS saluted sharply while the prisoners just stood there, frozen with fear. Mulka returned the salute and took a moment to remove the leather gloves he always wore, peeling them off one finger at a time and clearly relishing the respect in which he now basked.

"At ease", he finally said. Then, addressing the inmates, he snarled: "Get back to work before I have you all crucified like your God. This is Reich's business."

He then shot Traugott a look that made Mattias wonder what he knew of the events that had transpired here a month ago. While Höss might have kept Konrad Morgen's visit secret from his adjutant to protect his own image, Traugott didn't doubt that Möckel would have informed his boss of the aborted investigation – especially now that he was himself part of a squad tasked with rooting out corruption and inefficiencies. If ever proof was needed, he need simply look at the uncanny coincidence of Möckel's return and this first inspection.

"Heil Hitler", Mulka said.

"Heil Hitler", Traugott replied. "Welcome to the Aufräumungskommando, herr hauptsturmführer. How may I be of assistance?"

"Oh, I think you know why we're here", Mulka said with a thin, knowing smile that made Traugott shiver. "Lead me to your office while my men attend to their business."

The last thing Traugott wanted was to let Mulka's minions go over his operation with a fine-toothed comb, but he really didn't have much choice in the matter. He also had a good idea why Mulka wanted to see his office, but the man had to be a complete idiot if he thought that Traugott would still be keeping his loot in his locker.

He bowed subserviently. "Of course, herr hauptsturmführer. Right this way."

As they left the work area together, Traugott caught a murderous glance from Mockël. He also noticed with some worry that Rita and Adriana hadn't yet returned.

Adriana was vaguely aware of the smell of pine needles.

At first the scent came to her from very far away, as though it had been carried by the breeze over a great distance. Then, the closer she came to regaining consciousness, the more powerful it grew. So that when she awoke, she was 10 years old, she had just taken a bath, her father had just showered, and he was reading her her favorite bedtime story. She was sitting in his lap with her head resting against his shoulder, breathing in the familiar smell of that unique cologne.

But then she opened her eyes and the scent vanished, like a candle snuffed out by the wind. Rita was kneeling next to her, holding her hand. She could hear voices in the distance, some that sounded quite angry, but for now she felt safe.

"Welcome back", Rita said gently.

Adriana looked at her for a moment, trying to reconnect with reality. When she finally did, she found herself instantly besieged by images and memories and sensations that threatened to submerge her all over again. She closed her eyes to fight them off, gripping Rita's hand harder, and she shivered one last time. She re-opened her eyes.

"Better now?" Rita asked with a smile.

Adriana nodded, not yet trusting herself to speak. She swallowed hard.

"That was... that was his shirt, Rita", she finally whispered. "My father's shirt. That was just too much."

Rita nodded. "Yes, I know", the old woman said. "No matter how strong you are, you'll never be strong enough to defeat Auschwitz. Some days you'll win, but in the end..."

She let the rest of her sentence hang. More angry voices echoed in the warehouse. The two women fell silent and Adriana sat up, a bit alarmed. Her head spun and she placed a hand against her forehead. The voices died down.

Adriana was still holding Rita's hand and she didn't want to let go. The old *kapo* radiated an inner strength, a powerful calm that Adriana found very comforting. Nothing ever seemed to phase her. Adriana had observed her praying on numerous occasions and it was clear that her spirituality had yet to fall victim to the horror that was now their daily existence.

Adriana once again wondered how Rita had ended up here, what crime she could possibly have committed, but she felt that such a question should probably remain unspoken.

"Tell me why this is happening to us", Adriana asked on the spur of the moment. "What did we do to deserve this? Why is God allowing this to happen?"

It was Rita's turn to sigh and she looked at Adriana for a long time before answering. "I don't know, child", she said. "I truly wish that I did, but I don't. I pray every day, sometimes more than once a day, and I still don't know. Sometimes I think that there is no God here. I think God saw what was happening and He decided not to come here. Even He can't bear to see what His children are doing."

This was the most sensible thing Adriana had heard in a long time, but she wasn't given much time to reflect upon it. Men were arguing nearby, their voices loud enough to be heard, something about an incomplete head count and missing workers.

The two women jumped to their feet, Adriana hanging on to Rita for balance.

"What do we do?" she asked.

"I don't know", Rita admitted, remembering Traugott's warning about there being more trouble than she knew if they were found to be missing. "But we can't stay here. If they find us, we're dead."

Adriana looked around her. They were in a small room whose only exit led to the work area. Shelves reached to the ceiling, piled high with bundles of clothes ready to be shipped back to Germany. Inspiration struck. Adriana quickly grabbed two bundles and gave them to Rita. She then gave her two more, before grabbing four for herself.

"What are you doing?" Rita asked.

"No time to explain", Adriana said. "Just follow me and do what I do."

Adriana led the way as they exited the storage room. As soon as they rounded a bend in the hallway, they were spotted by a trio of men standing outside Traugott's office.

"You there, halt!" one of the men immediately barked. Adriana and Rita froze in place as Mulka, Traugott and Mockël walked rapidly in their direction.

"What's going on here?" Mulka demanded. "Where have you been hiding?"

Adriana kept her eyes lowered as she replied. "Begging your pardon, herr hauptsturmführer, but we're not hiding. We're following the untersturmführer's orders and working."

Mulka looked back at Traugott over his shoulder and exhaled impatiently through his nose. He had been thrilled when Mockël had reported two missing workers a few minutes ago, one kapo and one inmate, but not as thrilled as Mockël had been when Traugott had proved unable to explain their whereabouts.

"And what orders are those?" Mulka asked sharply.

Adriana risked looking at Traugott, hoping he might be able to help them. But all she saw in his face was a mixture of incomprehension and despair, with a dose of panic thrown in for good measure. She was on her own.

"Herr hauptsturmführer, we're to select bundles of clothes at random for re-inspection", she explained.

Mulka seemed perplexed while Mockël was clearly fuming. Traugott, on the other hand, suddenly appeared relieved.

"To what end?" Mulka demanded.

Adriana was about to reply but Traugott cut her off, having finally caught on to her plan. "To make sure the work was done correctly the first time, of course", he said. "These clothes have already been inspected and sorted. But if we find that they still contain valuables, we'll know that the work isn't being done properly and we can correct the situation. These two women must each inspect fifty bundles every day. It's a small fraction of the total, but it's enough."

Mulka looked dubious. "Why didn't you mention it earlier?"

Traugott shrugged. "It simply slipped my mind, herr hauptsturmführer. I'm sorry, but with over 600 workers to supervise, I can't be expected to know where each one is at any given moment."

Mulka rounded on him. "Oh yes, you most certainly can, and see that you do from now on", he growled. He then looked at Otto Mockël. "We're done here. Let's go."

The two men walked away, leaving Traugott alone with the two women. He looked at Adriana and the gratitude that she read in his eyes horrified her. She could tell he was about to thank her for her quick thinking, so she cut him off.

"I was saving myself and Rita, not you", she snapped. "Go to h..."

His reaction was immediate. He had guessed what she was about to say, and this he wouldn't tolerate. Not from her, not from anyone. He grasped her by the arm and pulled her to him, bringing his face to within an inch of hers.

"Don't forget yourself, *neunzehnhunderteinundsiebzig*", he said, his eyes blazing and his fingers digging painfully into her muscle. "Don't you ever forget who's in charge around here."

He then released her arm. "Now get back to work. The two of you."

Hiltrude feared neither man nor beast, neither god nor demon.

Thirteen years ago she had been sentenced to life in prison for the kidnap, rape and murder of a neighbor who had spurned her amorous overtures.

The man had been foolish enough to snicker when she suggested they go for a stroll in the forest together – more specifically, a section of the forest couples looking for a bit of intimacy were known to frequent.

For that offense, she snatched him from his home and dragged him to her barn, where she proceeded to force herself on him. When the terrified, disgusted man failed to rise to the occasion, she sodomized him with a loaded shotgun before throwing him – bound and gagged and bleeding profusely from the internal injuries he had sustained – to her hogs. She then pleasured herself as she watched the beasts tear him apart, his moans of terror and pain mixing with her own moans of pleasure and delight.

She would have gotten away with the crime had a policeman not discovered an unconsumed phalanx in the hogs' pen.

But the hauptsturmführer who had summoned her was neither man nor beast, neither god nor demon, and Hiltrude was quaking in her own skin.

"I trust I have made myself clear?" the officer asked again.

Hiltrude was sweating profusely. "Perfectly clear, herr hauptsturmführer", she said, wringing her hands anxiously. "I think I have just what you need. I'll send them to you this evening."

As repulsed as he was by the obese creature in his presence, the hauptsturmführer's professional curiosity was still aroused. He was trying to determine whether anything useful might be learned from the dissection of such a specimen. He might have liked, for example, to ascertain whether certain organs retain more fat than others. Or might he discover a malfunctioning organ that could account for her condition? If he sliced her open, would he be able to determine whether a diseased organ was, in fact, a cause or a consequence of her obesity?

The lines of investigation seemed endless but he shook them off. He had not come here to study walking barrels of lard. His other work was much, much more interesting, and potentially much, much more vital to the Reich's survival.

"Is there anything else, herr doktor?" Hiltrude risked asking timidly.

She had never encountered anyone like him and she wanted to leave as soon as possible. In a place where evil was the norm, this SS stood head and shoulders above all the others. The man *smelled* of evil, and she was absolutely terrified of him.

The hauptsturmführer seemed to have forgotten her presence.

"No, that will be all", he finally said in a voice tinted with lassitude. "Send me the two specimens tonight. And see that they are satisfactory. Otherwise, I will be most... displeased."

The implicit threat wasn't lost on Hiltrude. The fat kapo bowed obediently and scurried away, cursing for one of the few times in her life a massive weight that kept her from fleeing faster.

Mulka and Möckel exchanged incredulous glances. The obersturmbannführer couldn't possibly be serious.

And yet he was.

"I received the orders directly from obergruppeführer Pohl", Höss said, referring to Oswald Pohl, the head of the SS-WHVA. "The decision was made by the Reichsführer himself and we're to implement it immediately."

Mulka couldn't believe his ears.

"And where...", he began, before stopping to clear his throat. "And where are we supposed to locate this new facility, herr obersturmbannführer?"

Höss shrugged. "Block 24 will do nicely", he said. "It's close to the main gate and a bit out of the way."

"And what of the prisoners who are currently in Block 24?" Möckel inquired.

Höss stared at him as if he'd just asked the stupidest question ever heard and Möckel dropped his eyes apologetically. He knew he only owed his continued presence here to Mulka's protection and that he wasn't yet entirely off Höss' black list. He'd escaped Konrad Morgen' investigation with a slap on the wrist, but others hadn't been so fortunate. Morgen had searched dozens of lockers and rumor had it he'd found a fortune in gold, jewelry and other valuables. Some guards had vanished overnight, their fate unknown.

Höss got up and began pacing, hands behind his back.

"Listen", he said. "I agree with you that these orders are most... unusual, shall we say? But when I raised a few objections with obergruppeführer Pohl, he was adamant: this is what the Reichsführer wants, and what the Reichsführer wants, the Reichsführer gets. He believes it will give inmates an incentive to work harder. Such a facility has existed at Mathausen since 1942 and they're reporting some success. One is also set to open at Buchenwald in a few weeks. So we're not alone in this."

Mulka tried to conceal his impatience and contempt. To him, this smelled of a brilliant initiative dreamed up by pencil-pushers in Berlin, bureaucrats with absolutely no understanding of life in the field. They came up with these cockamamie ideas, and then it fell to men such as himself to clean up the mess.

But since the idea had the backing of Heinrich Himmler himself, Mulka knew that opposing it would be futile: what he thought mattered not, and Auschwitz would soon have its very own brothel. So he decided to gather as much information as he could.

"Did obergruppeführer Pohl provide any further details?" he asked. "Is this *lagerbordell* to be accessible to all prisoners? Where are we to find the women needed?"

Höss pursed his lips. "Vouchers will be issued to our most valuable prisoners, such as members of the fire brigade", he explained. "Under no circumstances are they to be handed to Jewish prisoners. As for the women..." He stopped and shrugged as if it were of little importance. "Get them where you may. I don't expect the patrons will be too picky."

In this he was probably right, but at the same time Mulka and Mockël couldn't help but wonder whether Rudolf Höss had taken a good look, lately, at the women of Auschwitz. Could an inmate be so desperate for physical relations as to copulate with a bloated, sore-covered, lice-infested woman? Time would tell, they guessed.

"Now get to work", Höss ordered. "I want the brothel operational within a month."

Mulka and Mockël got up and saluted before exiting the room, wondering what the hell they had just gotten themselves into.

Adriana, Magrita and the other *weißköpfchen* had been standing in the pouring rain for over six hours and several of them had already collapsed. They lay where they had fallen, slowly freezing to death under the indifferent gaze of a few guards.

Adriana knew the same scene was being replayed across Auschwitz.

It had been raining almost without interruption for three days. The previous evening, two inmates had taken advantage of one of the most violent storms in recent memory to hide under a pile of construction materials instead of returning to their barracks. They remained concealed until night fell, intending to escape under the storm's cover. And they might have succeeded, had it not been for an ill-timed flash of lightning that lit up the darkness just as they were making a run for it. Both men were immediately shot dead and now, as was the usual practice at Auschwitz, the entire camp was being made to pay for their sins.

The prisoners had been ordered out of their barracks just before midnight and made to stand in the rain while, officially, the guards checked to make sure that no one else was missing. But the prisoners knew they were being both punished for the aborted escape and warned against themselves attempting to flee. Adriana counted herself lucky that, at least, they were allowed to stand; guards had been known to make inmates kneel or crouch or even stand on their heads for hours on end.

She also counted herself lucky that this was happening today instead of a few weeks ago, before she joined the *weißköpfchen*. She had been so weak at the time that a night spent in the cold rain would probably have killed her. A dozen women had already collapsed around her and she hated to think what was happening elsewhere. If the women of the *weißköpfchen*, who were among the healthiest and strongest and best-fed inmates at Auschwitz, were falling and dying, what chance did the others stand?

Adriana was soaked to the bone and she was shuddering uncontrollably. Her teeth chattered so hard she feared they might shatter. Her entire body ached, her muscles tortured by wave after relentless wave of shivers. Water had seeped into every nook and cranny of her body. She was also desperately worried about her friend Magrita. The young woman had awakened with a fever a few days ago and had grown weaker ever since. Adriana didn't know whether she counted among those who had collapsed, but if she did, she was as good as dead.

Adriana blinked the water out of her eyes and spotted Rita standing both a few meters from her *weißköpfchen* and purposely away from the guards, as though she wished she could have lined up with the former and wanted nothing to do with the latter. The old woman had on a worn out raincoat that likely did little to keep her dry. Adriana guessed that as a kapo, Rita could probably have sought refuge somewhere, but she was still there, sharing the fate of her wards. Their eyes met and no words were necessary to express what passed between them.

An SS officer dressed in a long, oily trench coat, a cap with the habitual skull and bones and knee-high jackboots appeared out of the rain and came to stand next to Rita. A new wave of cold washed over Adriana when she recognized Mattias Traugott. The man had kept his distance since their little altercation of the previous week, and she guessed he had come to inquire as to his workers' whereabouts. The *weißköpfchen* should have reported for duty by now and without them, no work was getting done.

Or maybe he'd come looking for her.

Traugott raised a hand to shield his eyes from the rain. He seemed to be scanning the assembled women as he exchanged a few words with Rita. Adriana lowered her head and dropped her eyes as much as she dared, fearing he might be searching for her. If he saw her, she thought he might be tempted to do her a favor - in his perverted mind, at least - by pulling her out of the rain. The last thing Adriana wanted was to be singled out in front of all the other women. She had enough rumors and hurtful innuendos to contend with as it were. But either Traugott didn't see her, or he did and chose not to act, because he then went to speak with one of the guards. The man saluted and Traugott seemed to ask him a few questions. Their conversation grew animated and Traugott kept pointing at the workers and then back in the general direction of his warehouses, his meaning amply clear.

In the end, defeated, he simply stomped away angrily.

Adriana's eyes snapped open when she heard Rita's voice. She had dozed off on her feet. The rain had lessened and the sun appeared as a pale disk of weak light behind thinning clouds. She had no idea what time it was. Adriana shook her head to clear her mind and thousands of droplets of water showered from her short hair.

Rita was speaking again. *You know how it's done. In a single file, one behind the other, and let's be on our way*, which was what she always said when time came for the *weißköpfchen* to go somewhere.

The women reacted instinctively to her command and lined up like well-trained kindergartners on their way to the playground. Some tried to help their fallen comrades, some of whom managed to make it back to their feet, but many had to be left where they had fallen and would never be seen again. Adriana looked for Magrita, but she couldn't find her anywhere. Fear gnawed at her that the friend who had saved her life might be one of those piles of sodden clothes they were now leaving behind.

Magrita might have died, cold and alone and abandoned, during the night, and Adriana begged Aaron to welcome her and take care of her if she had.

Adriana was surprised to see that Rita was marching them to the warehouses. She had expected them to return to the barracks, if only to change into some dry clothes, but this was Auschwitz and Auschwitz was unlike any other place on Earth - a place where hypothermic workers who had spent the night standing in the freezing rain would be expected to perform as if they'd just returned from a beach vacation.

The sun finally pierced through the clouds and steam soon began to rise from the rooftops. The giant fans that fed the flames of the crematoria were suddenly switched on, filling the air with a sinister roar like that of an angry dragon furiously demanding its daily ration of human flesh. The sound made the women walk a little faster, until they essentially stumbled into the warehouses.

Traugott was there, impatiently waiting for them.

"To work, all of you", he barked as soon as they entered. "We've lost half a day already. You'll have to make up for it."

Then he added: "*Neunzehnhunderteinundsiebzig,* come with me".

Adriana felt as if she'd been slapped. All the other women stopped wringing the water out of their clothes and stared at her. Adriana was frozen in place and she could feel herself turning red. This was her worst nightmare: that idiot had finally and openly singled her out in front of all the others. She wanted to scream at him, to tell him to go to hell, that she'd never go anywhere with a Nazi pig, but what choice did she have, really?

Adriana looked at Rita. The old woman pinched her lips, understanding the impossible dilemma Adriana now found herself in, before discretely nodding at her to go with Traugott. But still Adriana didn't move. Then someone came up behind her and placed a gentle hand on her shoulder.

Adriana turned around. Magrita was standing there, half-dead. She was visibly shaking and there were unnaturally dark circles under her sunken eyes, but she was alive. Adriana hugged her with relief.

"Do as he asks", Magrita whispered in her ear. "We need him. *We* need *you*. So go."

Adriana held on for a moment longer, feeling the feverish heat that came off her friend, before finally letting go. She dropped her head, not daring to look anyone else in the eyes, and made her way to Traugott's office while the other women watched her go.

She felt like a condemned man walking to the gallows and she feared imagining what he could possibly want with her. Certain guards were known to prey mercilessly on the inmates, both male and female, to satisfy their basest instincts. The rules against such behavior were impossibly strict, but rumor had it that Rudolf Höss himself had taken a mistress from among the inmates, although a non-Jewish one. The commander of another camp called Buchenwald had also supposedly been executed on similar charges. Given such examples, most guards now assumed they could do as they pleased, though discretely.

But Adriana had worked at Kanada for well over a month now and if Traugott meant to rape her, he would certainly have done so by now. Why would he have waited all this time? Still, she found herself wondering how she would react if he demanded sex from her. Could she bring herself to do it? Probably not.

Traugott was waiting for her outside his office. He motioned for her to come closer, but Adriana stopped about three feet away from him. She would come no nearer.

"How are you feeling?" he asked nervously.

She couldn't believe he'd just asked her that. "Fine, herr untersturmführer", she said dully. She kept her head down and her eyes fixated on the puddle of water that was now spreading around her feet. Water also flowed from her hair and into her face, dripping off the tip of her nose.

"I tried to get you out of there, *all* of you I mean, but there was nothing I could do", he explained, and Adriana wondered why he thought she might care. She remained silent.

There was a long silence and Traugott seemed at a loss as to what to say next. "I... I got this for you", he finally said. He tried to hand her something he'd kept hidden behind his back.

Adriana instinctively looked up and saw he was holding a towel and a change of clothes. She wouldn't have been more horrified had he been holding a venomous snake. She almost took a step back but caught herself. She then dropped her head again and crossed her arms in front of her.

"I thank the untersturmführer for his consideration, but I'm fine as I am", she said as coldly and as formally as she could manage.

What a complete imbecile. Did he have any idea how she'd been treated if she returned to the work area dressed in warm, dry clothes? As if her life weren't sufficiently hellish as it were.

Traugott's hand dropped away after a moment and he exhaled impatiently through his nostrils, a sure sign he was getting angry.

"I've been nothing but kind to you, I've already saved your life twice, and yet you can't even look me in the eyes", he stated impatiently. "What have I done to you that you so despise me?"

Adriana closed her eyes and bit her lip to keep from shouting at him. She dug her fingers into her own flesh, trying to concentrate on the pain, but to no avail. This was too much. She couldn't believe Traugott expected gratefulness and warmth and friendship – and perhaps more – from her. What world did he live in?

She looked up at him and the change that came over his face told her that much of the anger she felt was reflected in her eyes.

"My father was a good, honest, decent, hard-working man, and my mother was the kindest person you'd ever meet should you live to be one thousand years old. Then, one night, men came to our home", she began slowly, hammering each word.

She stopped and stared at him. "Men. Like. You", she whispered. Understanding suddenly dawned in his eyes and he looked away. Adriana could have stopped there, but she didn't.

"These men grabbed my father by his beard and they made him beg for his life", she said, tears welling in her eyes. "Then they took him and my mother away to die like animals. And then they tried to rape me. They might have succeeded too, had my little brother, his name was Aaron, not saved me. What happened to Aaron, you ask? How kind of the untersturmführer to care." Her sarcasm was like whip across his back. "Aaron is dead now. They shot him like a dog. He was 11 years old."

She stopped again, giving her words time to sink in. She could tell he was troubled, but she could hardly have cared less.

"You think I *despise* you, Nazi?" she snarled. "You're not even close. I *hate* you with every cell in my body. And you have the nerve to ask me why? Are you that blind and stupid? Look around yourself and see what *men... like... you...* are doing to people like me. Why would I *not* hate you? And you think to make everything alright *with a dry towel*?"

She stopped to laugh coldly. "And what happens after that? We become buddies and every now and then you call me to your office so I can suck your Nazi dick?"

Traugott still could not look at her. He was fidgeting with the clothes he had prepared for her, trying to regain some of his composure but failing badly. Her words had plunged into him like so many daggers and he had felt something snap inside him.

When he finally looked at Adriana, she too noticed a new light in his eyes, though she was unsure of its meaning.

"Is that all you see when you look at me?" he asked. "An SS uniform? Not a man?"

She shook her head. "There is no man. Just a Nazi."

Traugott dropped his head again, apparently hurt. Then, for some reason, Adriana remembered

Magrita's words from a moment ago. *We need him. We need you.* Maybe this is what she'd meant. Maybe some good could come from this. Maybe this power she had over him, whatever its nature, could be put to good use.

"My friend Magrita is very ill", she said after a moment. "She needs to see Doctor Ada. And not just for a few hours; for as long as it takes for her to heal. Doctor Ada will need medicines to help her. And Magrita needs to return here when she's better."

Traugott nodded almost immediately. "Yes, of course", he said.

"I'll accept the untersturmführer's offer", Adriana then said. "But not just for myself. I'll accept it for all of us. Everyone gets a towel and everyone gets dry clothes, not just me."

"For you I'd do anything", he said.

Adriana was speechless. Had he really just said such a thing? She turned around to walk away, but then she thought of something else.

"And the untersturmführer would be most kind to order his men to have the decency to turn their backs while we change our clothes", she said meekly, as though she were merely making a suggestion.

She left without awaiting his reply. There was no need.

17

That day's events inevitably gave birth to two rumors that circled back directly to Adriana.

The first was that several of the *weißköpfchen* had died in the storm and that there were, therefore, many openings within the ranks of that mysterious, but so desirable, kommando.

The second was that you needed to speak to Adriana about it. A word from her, it was now said, could get you just about anything you wanted, short of your freedom.

Hana and Julianna - the vampiristic twin sisters who had sung with Adriana, Etty and Malva at Rudolf Höss' birthday party – were all smiles when Adriana returned to the barracks later that evening. They asked a few perfunctory questions about her health and well-being, they who had not addressed her in months, before smoothly requesting to join the *weißköpfchen*.

Adriana was both floored and angered by their nerve.

"Maybe you should ask Hiltrude to help you", she replied coldly.

The sisters exchanged a worried glance. Their survival depended on the help and favor of those more powerful than themselves, hence their closeness to Hiltrude. But in Adriana, they had found someone even more influent than a mere kapo, someone who reportedly pulled the strings of an SS-Untersturmführer. Short of having direct access to Rudolf Höss, this was probably the best they could ever hope for.

They were momentarily destabilized by Adriana's hostility, but they recovered rapidly. Julianna bent closer to Adriana.

"Truth is, we don't much like her", she whispered conspiratorially.

Adriana feigned surprise. "You don't say. You could have fooled me."

"We're just using her", Hana added most unhelpfully. Her sister elbowed her in the ribs to shut her up, but she was a fraction of a second too late; the damage was done.

"Just like you mean to use me now", Adriana shot right back, scoring a critical hit. The sisters fell silent for a moment. This was going badly and they needed a new tactic.

"Very well", Hana backpedaled contritely. "I believe we owe you an apology. We haven't been the best of friends to you recently. But we're more than ready to make amends, if you'll just give us a chance."

Julianna was nodding emphatically, but Adriana wasn't really listening to them. The repercussions of her earlier intercession on behalf of Magrita and the other *weißköpfchen* were just beginning to dawn on her. These two would be but the first to come to her with their requests. Every inmate she met from now on would demand this or that, expecting her to simply snap her fingers and make it happen. Already, a half-dozen women were hovering innocently behind Hana and Julianna, like customers waiting on a busy clerk, just hoping for a word with her.

But there was simply no way she could help them all. Truth was, she didn't even know if she could help a single one of them. Yes, Traugott had immediately sent Magrita to Doctor Ada, and yes he'd kept his word and allowed the *weißköpfchen* to change into some dry clothes, but what of it? What might he ask of her in return the next day? How much power did she really wield over this SS?

She truly wished she could help as many people as possible. She truly wished she could give them some hope. But in truth, she didn't know that she could – so she felt it was safer to nip this whole thing in the bud. Every single person she helped would generate how many new requests? Ten, twenty, fifty? What might happen to those for whom she could do nothing? What might happen to *her* if she began turning people down? She needed to keep this from getting out of control, both to protect herself and to protect those who sought to rely on her.

The more help she gave, she feared, the more help would be asked of her – help she might then not be able to provide.

"...Berlin?" Hana was saying.

Adriana looked at her. "What did you say? I wasn't listening."

Hana smiled at her with exaggerated indulgence. "I said, such a simple request is certainly within the power of someone who got a friend transferred to a hospital in Berlin?"

Adriana was flabbergasted. "What are you talking about?"

Hana smiled again, barely concealing her impatience. "Your friend Margarita..."

"Magrita", Adriana immediately corrected her.

"Yes, Magrita", Hana said a bit rudely, as if it were of little importance. "She was quite sick. Didn't your *friend* send her for treatment to a hospital in Berlin at your request?"

And there it was, illustrated in all its absurd glory, the danger in which she now found herself. After mere hours, word of mouth had already conferred upon Adriana the power to have a feverish prisoner shipped to Berlin. Soon, people would believe her capable of ordering the guards to simply shut off the ovens, throw the gates open and send everyone home with an apology and a slap on the back.

Adriana almost laughed out loud at such a ridiculous question. "Magrita is with Doctor Ada", she simply said, taking care to neither confirm nor deny her role in the matter. "Where did you hear she'd been sent to Berlin?"

The twins looked at one another. "Someone told us..."

"What the hell is going on here?" someone roared next to them.

The three women jumped when they saw Hiltrude glaring at them. Hana and Julianna looked ashamed, like schoolchildren who've been caught with a dirty caricature of the school principal. They clearly feared the reaction of their protector and benefactor. Adriana, on the other hand, now believed she didn't quite have as much to fear from the fat kapo.

"They were just inquiring about Magrita", Adriana explained.

Hiltrude looked around her. "And where is the lazy little bitch?" she asked angrily.

Adriana took a moment before responding, anticipating with relish Hiltrude's reaction. "She's been sent to Doctor Ada. She'll be there for a few days."

Hiltrude's eyes bulged out of her head and she turned red with outrage. "What? I'm the only one who can authorize that!"

Adriana smiled at her condescendingly. "That's not quite true, since the decision was taken by someone who didn't see fit to consult you", she said slowly.

Hiltrude sputtered and seemed about to explode. "Who?" she finally demanded angrily.

"SS-Untersturmführer Mattias Traugott", Adriana said. She felt a tinge of shame at the pleasure the use of his name, and inferred power, provided her. There was a real danger she might get addicted to this, she realized.

Hiltrude had very little sense in her brain, but she knew a losing battle when she saw one. If there was nothing she could do about an SS officer meddling in what she considered to be *her* business, there was definitely something she could do about an insolent and insubordinate inmate. She was about to order Adriana to go clean the latrines, just because she could, when she saw Hana and Julianna, who were trying to make themselves invisible, and she remembered why she'd come here in the first place.

"You two", she said loudly, pointing a finger at them. The twins took a step back. "Someone wants to see you."

The sisters sensed that nothing good could come of this and they clung reflexively to one another. "Who?" Julianna demanded with a shaky voice.

"A new hauptsturmführer who arrived just a few days ago", Hiltrude said. "You're to report to him immediately."

The twins looked at one another. "There are probably a hundred hauptsturmführers at Auschwitz", Hana said with uncharacteristic boldness. "Do you know his name?"

Hiltrude shivered as she recalled her brief encounter with the man. "Yes", she finally said. "He's a doctor. His name is Mengele."

19

The day was stifling hot and there was not a whiff of breeze to relieve the heat.

Traugott could feel sweat running down his back, soaking into his uniform. He half-closed his eyes to protect them from the glaring sun and blindingly blue sky. He wiped his sweaty palms discretely against his pants, but that did little to alleviate his discomfort. He knew a dozen others were suffering as he was on each side of him, but that brought him no solace.

If only the bloody train would come already.

Traugott glanced to his right. Rudolf Höss was still deep in conversation with an officer he didn't know but whom he'd seen around over the past few days. The man was out of uniform and dressed only in a white lab coat, and as Traugott watched, Höss nodded pensively, apparently agreeing with a suggestion the man was making.

Otto Mockël was standing slightly behind them and to Traugott it looked as though he might be eavesdropping on their conversation. Observing his enemy, Traugott again wondered how the man had escaped so easily from the claws of the Bloodhound Judge. It then dawned on him that Mockël had possibly struck a deal with Konrad Morgen, perhaps agreeing to become his eyes and ears inside Auschwitz. That would explain his incredibly lenient punishment. It would also be completely in keeping with Mockël's character.

Little did Traugott know that Robert Mulka had, in fact, tasked Mockël with staffing Höss' new brothel with a sufficient number of what the adjutant had called "suitable workers". Since this excluded just about every woman at Auschwitz, with a few exceptions he'd already identified, Mockël was essentially here to appropriate any newcomer who might suit their needs.

He had vowed to be extremely thorough in his selection, and he had a long night ahead of him.

The familiar rumble came as the train finally appeared in the distance. It seemed to be moving incredibly slowly in the heat and tension increased by a notch. Traugott blinked the sweat out of his eyes, but still the train appeared to be surrounded by a shimmering haze as it drew progressively closer to the ramp where hundreds of new inmates would shortly disembark.

The train stopped with hissing and screeching brakes, as it had countless times before, and there followed a surreal moment of calm and silence during which the whole world seemed to be holding its breath.

Traugott had been through this a million times already, but today the oppressive heat was making him edgy and restless. His heart was beating much too rapidly and he was feeling a bit nauseous. He kept opening and closing his fists reflexively, wanting for this to be over as soon as possible so he could return to the comparative cool and comfort of his warehouses. His mouth was dry and he was having difficulty swallowing.

Now that the train had stopped, the cogs of a well-oiled machine would begin turning: the guards would unlock and open the sliding doors, some prisoners would stumble out, others would emerge tentatively, orders would be barked, shots might be fired, whips would crack, blows would be dispensed and mayhem would ensue for about twenty minutes.

Then, mercifully, it would be over.

But before any of this could happen, Höss and the officer in the white lab coat moved to the center of the ramp. The camp commander raised his hands, like a speaker motioning for his audience to settle down. He then called one of the guards to him and whispered his instructions into the man's ear. The guard appeared surprised, but he saluted and ran back to his comrades. A minute later, the men did unlock and open the sliding doors, but then they stepped back silently.

Traugott was stunned. What the hell was going on? Why weren't the newcomers being cowed into submission by the usual explosion of violence? Why weren't they being threatened and beaten? What had got into Höss? Didn't he realize that the inmates might seize this opportunity to rush out of the boxcars and attack them?

As these thoughts were going through his mind, the camp commander also stepped aside, leaving the white-coated officer apparently in charge of the operation for now. The man turned his back on the assembled SS and faced the train.

"Welcome to Auschwitz", he called in a loud, but calm and reassuring, voice. "Please don't be afraid and show yourselves. You'll be well taken care of here."

He then fell silent and waited patiently. An eye-watering, throat-constricting stench emanated from inside the wagons. That was nothing new and Traugott liked to think that he'd got used to it, but today the smell of putrefying bodies mixed with that of feces and hundreds of unwashed bodies made him want to vomit.

A full minute elapsed before the first dirty, sweaty and emaciated faces appeared tentatively in the open doors. The officer smiled benevolently and motioned for them to disembark.

"Welcome, welcome", he repeated. "My name is doctor Josef Mengele. I am a physician. Anyone needing medical attention will be seen to. Please get off the train. We have food and water."

Still no one moved and Traugott wondered how many of the inmates had survived the journey. It wasn't unusual for dozens of bodies to be pulled from the trains and taken directly to the crematoria. He also knew that Mengele was lying: the only medical help they could expect was a trip to the gas chambers and the only food they were likely to be offered was a watery soup of rotten vegetables.

At long last a single man dressed in a torn black cassock appeared in the door. He pushed his round glasses up his nose and surveyed the scene before him for a moment before lightly jumping off the train and onto the ramp. He then walked confidently toward Mengele.

"I am father Maximilian Kolbe", he introduced himself. "I am the founder of the Franciscan friary of Niepokalanów, in Poland. Where are we and why have you brought us here?"

The man had the ascetic face of a religious fanatic. His salt and pepper hair was cropped very short and he radiated a self-confidence Traugott found a bit disconcerting. It was as though deep in his soul burned the unshakable conviction that nothing in this world could ever harm him.

Kolbe came to stand very close to Mengele, forcing the doctor to take a step back. Traugott was left with the impression that two powerful but opposing forces – love and hate, light and darkness, good and evil - had just briefly engaged in battle and that one had temporarily forced the other to yield.

Mengele smiled. "Welcome, father Kolbe", he said with an friendliness Traugott almost found believable. "You have arrived at Auschwitz. This is a work *katzet* where..."

"This is a place of death", Kolbe interrupted him sharply. "It smells of nothing but death."

Mengele's smile froze on his face and he chose not to debate the point. "Father Kolbe", he said with a slight grimace, as though the words tasted bitter on his tongue, "Please, let's not argue. If you'll just ask your... *companions?*... to get off the train, I can assure you that you'll not be mistreated. You can see for yourself that..."

The friar raised his right hand and slowly drew the sign of the Cross in mid-air, as though he were erecting an invisible barrier between the two of them. "*Thy tongue deviseth mischiefs; like a sharp razor, working deceitfully. Thou lovest evil more than good; and lying rather than to speak righteousness*", Kolbe recited with closed eyes. "Keep your assurances to yourself. I don't believe any of your lies."

Mengele stared at him and his whole demeanor changed. Like a moulting snake, the scales of his friendliness fell away to reveal a malevolent iciness that made Traugott flinch. In a very low voice that was still loud enough for Traugott to hear, he said: "You wish to quote Scripture, *pater*? Then let's: *And the God who answers by fire, he is God.* So hear me well: I am God here. Either you get them off the train or I'll have my men lock the doors and set the cars on fire. Then you and I can just stand here and watch them burn. It should improve the smell."

Kolbe staggered back as though he'd been struck and a few gasps came from inside the wagons when he fell to his knees and signed himself. He then crossed his arms over his heart and began praying, his mouth mumbling words that remained between him and his God. To anyone arriving upon the scene at that very moment, it might have looked as though Kolbe was praying to the almighty Mengele, while in fact he was seeking guidance as to how best stand up to this demon he had encountered.

The two men remained as they were, sweating in the heat. Finally, after several long minutes, Kolbe swallowed hard a few times and opened his eyes.

"Come out", he called out, completely ignoring Mengele. "If we do as they say, we'll not be harmed."

Traugott saw that Kolbe had managed to keep part of the truth concealed without actually lying. What he had said was true: as long as the inmates complied with the guards' demands, no harm would come to them – in the extremely short term, at least. Only their disobedience would put their safety at risk.

Maximilian Kolbe got back to his feet and went to help an old man off the train. As he led him by the arm to take his place on the ramp, he stopped in front of Mengele and said softly: "Next time you and I meet, officer, I expect to be looking *down* on you."

It took less than ten minutes to empty the wagons and for all the newcomers to be neatly lined up on the ramp – men on one side, women and children on the other. It was always thus: like sheep jumping off a cliff, once a few of them had risked it, the others just followed blindly without thinking.

Rudolf Höss was still stunned by what Mengele had accomplished. Hundreds of Jewish prisoners had been talked off the train and organized, all without having to resort to violence – if the threat to burn them alive was set aside for a moment. There had been no fights, no blood, no cries, none of the usual mayhem. Even more impressive, the desired result had been attained in about half the usual time. It seemed that the doctor had been right all along: the prisoners were so scared that they would essentially believe anything you told them, a fact the Nazis could use to their advantage. The newcomers so desperately wanted to believe no harm would come to them that they would deny their own senses and blindly put their trust into any falsehood they were fed.

This, a death camp? No, of course not, that's completely ridiculous. This is just a work camp. That smokestack over there? Just a plain incinerator to dispose of our trash. And yes, we're taking you to the showers; not all are as clean as you are, you understand. No, don't worry about your bags, they'll be returned to you in no time at all. Right this way, my friend, right this way. You have nothing to worry about. We'll turn on the water in just a minute.

From now on, instead of being threatened and beaten, arriving inmates would be promised a warm shower and a soft bed. It seemed that such promises would keep them docile and compliant for as long as was needed - until it was too late.

Traugott would have been impressed as well, had he not been busy fighting off a wave of vertigo that made his head swim and his knees weak.

In the crowd he had spotted a Jew who had two children by the hand. The man had a long flowing beard and his children, a boy and a girl, appeared to be twins of perhaps ten or twelve. The girl had long, luxurious black hair while her brother had an confident, defiant air about him. The look he shot Traugott showed he understood better than the adults around him what was happening here. He wasn't fooled for a second, and yet he showed no fear.

Traugott's sight narrowed to a single point and he felt as though he might faint.

These men – men like you! - grabbed my father by his beard and they made him beg for his life, she had said. *My brother saved me, but Aaron is dead now. They shot him like a dog. He was 11 years old.*

Men like you!

Männer wie mich.

Traugott was reeling. His mind took him back several months, to one of the first transports he'd witnessed. A woman had been left behind in one of the wagons and he'd almost put a bullet in her brain. He'd dragged her out into the daylight and Mockël had taken her from him, claiming to have a *use* for her. Then Mockël had produced five stunningly beautiful women to sing at Höss' birthday party.

It had been her. *Neunzehnhunderteinundsiebzig.* She'd been here and he'd almost killed her. She'd asked for her brother, Aaron. She'd been one of them, and he'd been a man like them. And their encounter had almost ended as encounters between people like her and men like him always did.

The more the jigsaw pieces clicked together in Traugott's mind, the sicker he felt.

As Traugott watched, Mengele walked to the man and his twins. He knelt down and handed them a few sweets that he fished out of his pocket. He seemed fascinated by the children. The girl accepted the treat eagerly and immediately stuffed it in her mouth; her brother stubbornly refused to touch it, despite the fact that – like her – he had probably not eaten in days. His father gently urged him to take it, probably telling him not to be rude, but the boy kept his hands behind his back and seemed to be challenging Mengele to make him change his mind.

Mengele finally burst out laughing and gave the second treat to the girl, who devoured it in less than two seconds. He then tousled the boy's hair, like some benevolent uncle, but the child flinched when the doctor touched him.

Mengele's face, when he hurried by Traugott, was that of a madman.

"Untersturmführer, are you alright?"

The ramp was empty. All the inmates had been led away. A guard was staring quizzically at Traugott, who suddenly realized that he had no recollection of the last few minutes. He stared back silently at the guard.

"Apologies, untersturmführer, but maybe you should see a doctor", the man said tentatively.

"I'm fine, leave me", Traugott snapped with all the authority he could muster.

The man saluted sharply and left. As soon as he was gone, Traugott rushed out of sight and vomited in the tall grass. He stayed there, bent over and retching, for several minutes.

Verdammte Hitze. Damn heat.

20

Achtzehn whined plaintively as it stared at the seven women cowering in the far corner of the room. Every once in a while it lunged at them, only to be stopped short by a rope tied to its collar and fastened to the wall. Then it crouched down again, growling and staring.

Otto Mockël knelt next to the beast and patted its head.

"Be patient my boy, you'll have what you want shortly", he said reassuringly. The dog ignored him completely, fascinated that it was by the women.

Mockël brought them here straight off the train. He lined them up outside and ordered them to strip. When they refused and began crying, he picked one at random and threw her to the ground. Three guards then ripped off the woman's clothes, after which Mockël again ordered them to strip. This time, they all complied reluctantly – all but one, who was dispatched to the gas chambers. Stubbornness and defiance weren't qualities he sought in his whores.

The women kept covering their bodies with their hands, so Mockël had their wrists bound behind their backs so he could examine them freely. The youngest one appeared to be no more than fourteen and barely had hair between her legs; the eldest was in her mid-thirties and her sagging tits and wide hips showed that she had already borne at least one infant.

Not that their current appearance mattered much. In a few weeks, they'd all look 100 years old.

It took Mockël a few minutes to realize the horrible smell that had been bothering him in fact radiated from them. After days on board a stifling train, deprived of all hygiene, these women *stank*. The smell was so bad he could detect it even over the stench of incinerated human flesh given off by the crematoria. Their skin was gray with filth, their hair was a matted mess and bodily fluids of various colors had run down their thighs, staining them a dark, reddish brown. They were utterly repulsive.

Mockël ordered one of the guards to turn a fire hose on them. At first the women howled and turned their backs to the stinging spray, but after a moment they began exposing certain parts of their bodies to the water, incapable of passing up this opportunity to clean themselves. The guard cackled as the women spread their legs and allowed him to shoot the powerful stream directly at their private parts, if only for a couple of seconds.

The women's hands were untied so they could wring the water out of their hair. Those whose hair was long enough wrung as much water as they could directly into their mouths. Those whose hair wasn't looked on with envy and had to be content with licking their palms.

The sun was beginning to set but the heat was still oppressive. It was even worse inside the small room Mockël had commandeered for his experiment. It lacked any windows through which a merciful breeze might have blown, Mockël had closed the door and the only light came from a single bulb that swung from the ceiling. The room felt like a sauna and Achtzehn was panting heavily.

This didn't keep the naked women from shivering as they huddled together. An hour ago, they had been complete strangers. Now, their nude bodies were pressed against one another, as intimate as lovers.

"You", Mockël said, pointing a finger at the teenage girl. "Come here." He then pointed at the middle of the room.

He didn't know whether she had any German, but it didn't matter. His order would have been understood anywhere on the surface of the planet.

The girl shrieked and tried to hide behind the woman next to her. The woman wrapped her arms around her and pressed the girl's face into her shoulder, trying to comfort her.

"I said here, now!" Mockël barked again. Achtzehn growled behind him.

The girl shrieked again and Mockël felt anger rise inside him. He went to grab the girl but the woman who had already borne a child came to stand before him.

"*Nein*", she said, making a slashing gesture with both hands. "*Nein*", she repeated, which seemed to be the only German she knew.

She pointed at Mockël and then at herself. When Mockël failed to react, she pointed at him again, and then at herself again, and then she lifted both of her breasts in her hands.

Mockël smiled. The woman was offering herself to him to save the child from being raped. Mistaking his smile for an invitation, she reached out with her left hand to touch him between the legs, but he batted her hand away with a mixture of disgust and impatience.

"Don't you ever touch me", he snarled.

He grabbed her by the hair and pulled her to the middle of the room. His fist still wrapped in her hair, he forced her down on all fours.

He then went to fetch Achtzehn, who began barking excitedly.

The woman let out an inhuman cry and tried to get back up when she suddenly understood what the SS had in mind, but Mockël was quicker. He whipped out his gun and pressed the barrel into the back of her neck, forcing her to stay where she was.

He still had Achtzehn's leash in his other hand. He led the beast behind the woman and it immediately buried its muzzle in her buttocks. She cried out – *nein, nein, nein!* - when its wet nose touched her intimate flesh. The dog sniffed her for several seconds before letting out a lusty howl and attempting to mount her. The woman instinctively crawled forward, trying to get away from the beast. She froze when Mockël cocked his gun next to her ear. She was crying and shaking so hard that her whole body was trembling.

Achtzehn sniffed her again.

The woman vomited and began babbling incoherently when the dog mounted her, its front claws drawing lines of blood into the skin of her back as it thrust in and out of her. After a few seconds, Achtzehn sat back and contentedly began licking its bright red penis.

Mockël holstered his weapon. He shoved the woman with his boot and she simply toppled over without a sound. She then curled into a ball and began rocking herself.

The other women, transfixed with horror, had fallen silent. Mockël turned to look at them.

"Very well", he said. "Who's next?"

21

Josef Mengele removed his white lab coat and threw it over the back of a chair.

He immediately began making notes about the twins he'd found on the ramp, the boy and the girl. Too bad they were dizygotic twins, which in his mind made them less interesting than monozygotic twins, but they still displayed other characteristics that intrigued him.

How similar they were, and yet how so different.

There were a few physical differences between them; the boy was slightly taller and the eye color wasn't exactly the same. But he had been mostly struck by their psychological uniqueness. The girl had been shy and compliant and docile where her brother had been self-confident and defiant and headstrong.

Mengele wondered how much of this uniqueness was innate and how much was an acquired behavior. It was an interesting question, since it could be assumed the twins had been raised in the same household by the same parents, that they'd both attended the same school, that they'd essentially led the same lives since the day of their birth.

What, then, accounted for their radically different personalities? Perhaps a study of their brains would bring him closer to an answer.

Someone knocked discretely on the door to his office.

"Forgive me, herr doktor, but the subjects you requested are here".

Mengele looked up from his notes. Miklos Nyiszly was a seasoned Jewish pathologist Mengele had recruited straight off the train. Standing on the ramp amid the terrified prisoners, Mengele had asked for anyone with medical expertise and Nyiszly had stepped forward. Mengele had questioned him about his qualifications and made him a member of his staff, but only after warning him that any deception would be severely punished.

The man was in his early forties and he vainly tried to conceal his baldness with a long lock of hair combed over his gleaming skull. He was in all respects an insanely boring individual, but he was also quite competent and that was all that really mattered to Mengele.

Mengele had almost forgotten about the twins that fat kapo had promised him. This had to be who Nyiszly meant. They held much less interest for him since his encounter with the children, but since they were here, he might as well see if he had any use for them.

"Let me see them", he said, slowly getting up from behind his desk.

He followed Nyiszly into the next room. Hana and Juliana were sitting on a bench, holding hands and looking scared out of their minds. Nyiszly had already changed them out of their thin tunics of striped burlap and into medical gowns.

Mengele analyzed them silently for several minutes. He motioned for them to stand up and then had them turn around, slowly, so he could examine them from various angles. The only good thing was that they were identical. There were other issues that irritated him. For starters, they were much older than the kapo had indicated. He had understood them to be in their late teens, but they were clearly in their mid-twenties. These two had also visibly been at Auschwitz for some time, and their severely damaged bodies limited their usefulness.

Overall, Mengele was disappointed, and that deceitful kapo would soon become acutely aware of it.

Hana and Juliana sat back down on the bench, still holding hands. Watching them, Mengele thought of something. He left the room without having said a single word, Nyiszly right on his heels.

"Here's what we'll do with them", he said, before explaining in detail the procedure he wished to perform.

A heavy ball of lead began forming in the pit of Nyiszly's stomach as Mengele handed him his instructions and he hoped he wasn't sweating too visibly.

He knew he had to be careful not to let any of his discomfort show. For if he did, Mengele would simply replace him with someone else.

Ich liebe dich.

I love you.

Adriana didn't want to touch the scrap of paper Traugott had placed in front of her, but neither could she leave it there, in plain sight for all to see. So she scooped it up rapidly and crumpled it into a pellet that she popped into her mouth. She chewed it a few times and almost choked when she tried swallowing.

Magrita patted her on the back.

"Are you alright?" she asked. Adriana nodded and gave her friend a grateful smile. Traugott had kept his word and Magrita had returned from Doctor Ada's weeks ago. Her health was still fragile, but she was no longer on death's doorstep and Adriana was glad to have her back.

She finally managed to swallow the ball of paper.

This wasn't the first time Traugott had done something of the kind. He'd sneak up behind her and drop his message on the shirt she was folding. *I'm glad you're here. I'm thinking about you. Please be careful. Do you need anything? You're beautiful.*

This was the first *I love you*. Now that the line had been crossed, it probably wouldn't be the last.

He had also come up with a nickname for her: he called her *meiner Auschwitz rose*, my Auschwitz rose, explaining that roses sometimes sprout on top of dunghills. He obviously meant for the nickname to be flattering, but she wasn't sure how she felt about it, let alone about the man who had invented it.

Love was elusive enough under the best of circumstances. Adriana could count on the fingers of a single hand the people who had loved her – truly and sincerely loved her - since the day of her birth. But here, at Auschwitz? People didn't love one another. They had no other choice but to tolerate each other, and after a while they might even come to like one another, but love? Please. Whoever you loved would probably be dead the next morning, so why bother? Life here was hard enough without adding love to the mix. Love belonged at Auschwitz as much as the Pope belonged on board a tank.

And yet... there It was. She had apparently found It, or rather *It* had found *her*, here, in the depths of this seventh circle of Hell. And if she were honest about it, if she didn't try to fool herself, she had to admit that the horror and disgust this monster's love had originally sowed deep inside her were slowing giving way to a kind of warm glow that made her life a tiny bit less unbearable. Adriana had found something she could cherish, something that was hers and hers alone, something she didn't have to share with anyone else, something she *couldn't* share with anyone else, but also something very fragile and potentially quite dangerous she needed to protect.

Traugott's feelings for her could no longer be ignored. An infatuation would long ago have been slain by her indifference and hostility, while a vulgar carnal desire would by now have been quenched — by will or by force. No. What Traugott felt for her, as scary as she may find it, was undeniably love. Now, the only unanswered question that remained was, what was she going to do about it?

Adriana could sense a difference in Traugott, they *all* could, but she remained wary. What could possibly have happened to change him so? It had been days since he'd yelled at anyone and even longer since he'd struck an inmate. He had, on the other hand, threatened to court-martial a guard who'd slapped — needlessly, it appeared — a prisoner. To everyone's stupefaction, Traugott had suddenly decided to take to heart Himmler's orders regarding the mistreatment of valuable workers.

The man remained hard and demanding and it certainly would have been far-fetched to have called him "friendly". One also got the feeling the violence he'd exhibited time and again hadn't been completely eradicated, that some fragments of it still remained, like mines forgotten in a field that threaten to detonate at the slightest misstep. All they knew was that the mad dog of the past hadn't been seen in days.

Adriana could feel his eyes on her. She usually ignored him until he stopped, but this time she looked up. He was standing across the room from her, staring. When he saw her looking at him, he inclined his head to the right and headed for his office. His meaning was clear.

Adriana sighed. She didn't want to go, she *never* wanted to go, but as always, she didn't have much of a say in the matter. At least this time he hadn't called her name, her *number*, out loud. Not that it much mattered anymore. The other women had almost gotten used to her being called away, and while she could easily guess what they imagined went on between the two of them, at least all work no longer stopped when she went.

Adriana slowly finished folding the shirt in her hands and placed it on top of her pile. She then glanced at Magrita, who shrugged helplessly. *What can you do?*, her friend seemed to be saying.

What can I do indeed.

Traugott was sitting behind his desk. He waved for her to come in and close the door behind her. They'd done this many times and she knew how things would go. Since she had vowed never to give him the satisfaction of speaking first, and since he often seemed at a loss for words in her presence, sometimes the silence would stretch on for several long seconds, perhaps for a few minutes. She'd just stand there, immobile and silent, staring at the ground while he stared at her, sweeping her body from head to toe with his eyes until he found something to say.

Topics of conversation were rare and few in between between an SS officer and a Jewish inmate, and once, frustrated, he had sent her away after almost five full minutes of uncomfortable silence.

"Your friend Magrita is doing better", he finally said.

She nodded without looking up. "She is", she replied. Then, almost against her will, she added: "Thank... thank you for your help."

Had Adriana looked at Traugott at that very moment, she would have seen him smile for the first time. "For you I'd do anything", he said. She recognized the words from a few weeks earlier. She nodded again and silence returned.

"And... and how is life in the barracks?" he asked, clearly for lack of anything better to say. The question was so absurd it almost made her laugh. How did he think life was in the barracks?

She looked at him. "Something happened the other day. Maybe you heard about it."

He seemed puzzled and frowned. "Two men died", she explained very calmly. "A man and his son. They threw themselves against the electric fence rather than go on living here. I was there and I saw them. Their hands and their feet were completely burnt off and their eyeballs exploded and their hair caught on fire. They died a very horrible death, but they still found it preferable to life here. Why would someone do that, do you think?"

He sighed and looked away uneasily. Her point was clear and he wanted to change the subject, but she wasn't done. "And then the guards picked twenty inmates at random, ten for each man that died, and they beat them with iron bars because they didn't keep the men from killing themselves. One threw himself to the ground and wrapped his arms around his head and begged for them to stop, but they kept hitting him until he fell silent. They killed him. There was brains oozing out of his ears. I saw that, too."

Traugott remained silent. What was he supposed to say or do? Did she expect him to apologize or blandly tell her that "these things happen"? This wasn't a summer camp and he knew that better than most. He was also beginning to fear they might all be held to account one day. Over the past few weeks, the Allies had mercilessly bombed Hamburg and the *Kriegsmarine* had begun withdrawing its U-boats from the North Atlantic in anticipation of the Allied invasion of Europe.

Traugott had always been a survivalist, and he could sense the tide of the war turning against the Reich. Maybe it was time to begin hedging his bets.

"I meant, how is life in *your* barracks", he asked.

Adriana smiled inwardly when she saw how uncomfortable she had made him. "It's fine", she said noncommittally, dropping her eyes again. "We're getting a new kapo. Our old one, Hiltrude, is gone."

"What happened to her?" he asked immediately, happy to have engaged her in a semblance of conversation.

Adriana shrugged. "Obviously, nobody told us", she said.

"Would you like me to look into it?" he demanded.

Adriana shrugged again. "She won't be missed. She wasn't very nice."

There was a slight hissing sound when he pulled a drawer open. Her curiosity got the better of her and she saw him place a small wooden box on the desk in front of him. He opened it but she looked down before seeing what it contained – and before he noticed her interest.

"Someone gave me this a few days ago", he explained. That was a lie and they both knew it. Like just about anything else of value he owned, the box had been stolen from the luggage of a Jewish inmate. "It's a manicure kit. Some of the instruments are plated with gold. It's very nice."

Adriana kept her head down. She knew what was coming next, so she readied herself. "But I'm not sure how to use it", he went on. "Come show me."

His words made her flesh crawl. There was no way she would ever touch him. She raised her head and stared at him again. A strange calm had enveloped her. "Have you ever killed someone?" she asked.

He seemed surprised. "By someone, you mean...?" he said. Apparently, in his mind, killing a Jew wasn't the same as killing another human being, and he needed her to clarify which of the two she meant.

She kept staring at him. "Have you ever killed someone?" she repeated.

His gaze hardened as he stared back. "No", he said flatly. Another lie. What he meant was that he had yet to kill anyone here, at Auschwitz. His previous life was another story. There was also the matter of that inmate he had beaten to death for stealing a mouthful of bread. And the matter of Dieter Lotze, whom he had wanted to kill but whom he had instead maimed and disfigured.

And the matter, of course, of that Jewish inmate he had found unconscious on board a train and whom he had come within an inch of shooting in the head.

"No", he repeated. He could tell that she didn't believe him. For some reason that troubled him deeply, he *needed* her to believe him. "Now come give me a manicure. I want to look at you for a minute."

They both understood that much more than a manicure was at stake here. The manicure was but the field on which they were jousting, like medieval knights trying to ascertain their supremacy over one another. Traugott wanted to see how much progress he had made, whether he had tamed her enough to bend her to his will. But for Adriana, acceding to his demand would have been tantamount to acknowledging the existence of a certain intimacy between them, something that would never happen.

"I'm not giving you a manicure", she said calmly. "And stop calling me into your office. You're making me look like a whore. Now I'm leaving."

Adriana spun around and grabbed the doorknob. The sound of the chair legs scraping angrily against the concrete behind her warned her she had just stepped on one of those forgotten mines.

"Stay where you are, *neunzehnhunderteinundsiebzig*", he growled. She winced. How she hated to be called that. She knew that he knew her real name, and yet he chose to address her by her number. How demeaning she found it, how humiliating. But then again, that was the whole point, wasn't it? It was his way of reminding her who was in charge here, as if there was the slightest chance she would ever forget.

She turned around to look at him. Strangely, she felt no fear. "This is all a game to you, isn't it?" she asked with a humorless smirk. "Just a silly game. You want me to like you, and yet you treat me like your slave. Is that why the untersturmführer is so nice to me?" She couldn't return the favor by using his number, but she could hurl his rank at him like an insult. "Because he expects me to come into his office to do *things* for him in return? You're nice to me so I'll be nice to you, is that it? You want me to like you, and yet you can't help but behave like a Nazi who sees me as a plaything. But I probably shouldn't be surprised. It seems to me you were a Nazi long before you put on that uniform."

She could tell he was struggling to contain his emotions. His upper lip was trembling and he seemed about to explode. Adriana decided to quit while she was ahead. "Now I'm leaving", she announced. "I can't stand to look at you any longer."

She found herself staring down the barrel of his pistol before she had taken a single step. "Who the hell do you think you are", he snarled. "You'll leave when I tell you to leave."

Looking at him, Adriana saw that his pride and honor had been wounded, something that even his love for her couldn't overcome. "If you truly saw me as a human being, you wouldn't be pointing that thing at me", she said slowly. "If you truly saw me as an equal, you'd respect my right to decide for myself, to make choices with which you might disagree. You want to *make me* give you a manicure just like you want to *make me* love you. You think it's for you to dictate my actions and even my feelings. I'm nothing but a toy to you. Well, untersturmführer, I'm no one's toy, and certainly not yours. And now I'm leaving."

He cocked the gun as she touched the doorknob.

"I'll shoot you dead if you walk out that door", he threatened behind her.

Adriana barely paused. "Then shoot me. Kill me, here and now. I'd rather die than keep playing this game with you."

She waited for a second, and then she opened the door and left.

"Can you see anything?" a woman whispered urgently.

Her voice was like a clap of thunder in the silence. A dozen women were huddled around Magrita, whom they had propped up so she could look out a tiny, dirty window at the top of the wall.

"Shhh", Magrita replied impatiently. "I'm trying to see if I... Wait, here they come."

A million volts ran through the women, who all began talking over one another. They always wanted to know the same things. *Where do they look like they're from? How many of them are there?* Then the questions turned more personal. *My husband, he walks with a limp, can.... A woman with five children, maybe it's my sister... Look for my brother. He's very tall and... My uncle, my aunt, my cousin...* In her eagerness, one woman forgot herself and asked after her baker, which earned her quizzical looks from the other inmates. The woman had the grace to turn red before falling silent.

The SS had begun locking down the camp every time a new transport arrived. This was part of their new strategy to maintain order at all times. There had been too many incidents of inmates needing to be subdued after recognizing a loved one – or even just someone they had met once twenty years ago - among the newcomers being led to the gas chambers. Such encounters also created problems for those who had just arrived and who the SS wanted to maintain in complete ignorance until the very last moment. Meeting someone they knew but who appeared half-dead had the unfortunate effect of dispelling the myth that they had nothing to fear.

Magrita counted about four hundred people marching through the courtyard outside their barrack. Mostly women and children, as usual, but also a good number of men, both young and old, both seemingly fit or clearly infirm, who for some reason had been judged to be of no use to the Reich. She knew what was coming. Once they they got to a certain spot in the courtyard, one of the newcomers would look to his right and... There, it had just happened again. Someone had spotted the two faucets that sprouted from the building across the courtyard. She had witnessed the scene several times, and it almost always played out the same way: the second someone noticed those faucets, people that otherwise appeared listless and defeated became raving lunatics ready to kill for a single mouthful of tepid water.

Like a school of fish that move as one to escape a shark, the newcomers rushed the faucets.

A few years ago Magrita had struck up an unlikely friendship with an Irish priest, Father O'Donnell, who'd been endowed with the most mystical green eyes she'd ever seen in her life. She'd been more than a little infatuated with him but the man had been strong in his vows of celibacy. Still, sensing a potential convert, he'd given her a Bible she'd read in the utmost secrecy. Watching the deportees run for the faucets, she was reminded of a story from the Gospel of Mark:

And immediately Jesus gave them leave. And the unclean spirits went out, and entered into the swine: and the herd ran violently down a steep place into the sea, (they were about two thousand;) and were choked in the sea.

As she watched the newcomers punch and kick and shove and trip one another to reach the water first, Magrita had to fight the urge to find them contemptible, to sneer at them for debasing themselves in such a manner. She knew she wasn't witnessing their true nature. These were desperate people desperate to live. Just like the swine in Mark's story, without even being aware of it, they had fallen prey to a power – the desire to survive - over which they had no control, and they were being compelled into acts that went completely against their nature.

And acts that, she was sure, would have given them great shame later on, had they not been destined to die in the next fifteen minutes.

The SS had finally learned it was futile to seek to deny a drink of water to those who had gone without for days. The stampede was inevitable; it couldn't be prevented, only contained. So they were content to just stand by and watch as the soon-to-be-gassed filled whatever containers hadn't been left on the ramp – pots and pans but also shoes and hats and even chamber pots – and drank greedily. Those who hogged the faucet for more than a few seconds were mercilessly shoved aside by those waiting their turn, and the guards intervened on a few occasions – though their efforts were clearly half-hearted – to break up sad fistfights between parents desperate to provide for their children.

Magrita observed the deportees, trying to determine where they might be from. Sometimes their clothes hinted at their country of origin. Sometimes she'd catch a word here and there and recognize the language. When nothing else worked, she judged by their overall filthiness how long they'd spent on board the train; those most filthy, she assumed, had come from farther away, though she knew that measure to be quite imprecise. But today she wasn't having much luck. The newcomers looked as though they might be from northern Europe, perhaps Belgium or the Netherlands, but she couldn't be sure.

This was both good and bad news. Good, since it meant these people weren't *their* people, so they weren't likely to know those who would die today. Bad, since among the new workers they would meet tomorrow there wouldn't be anyone with news from home.

"Let me down", she finally said. "I can't see anything."

The women immediately lowered her and another – one of the *weißköpfchen*, as it happened – took her place. Each was desperate for a glimpse of a familiar face, but Magrita had had enough. She went in search of Adriana.

She found her friend huddled on the sleeping platform they shared with six other women. Adriana always retreated from the group whenever the camp was locked down. *I've already lost my mother and father to this place. What good does it do me to know that my cousin or my nephew is also here?*, she'd once explained. *There's nothing I can do to save them. I'll learn of their deaths soon enough. So please don't tell me if you see someone I might know.*

Still, there was a silent question in her eyes when she looked at Magrita, who simply gave a tiny shake of the head. Adriana sighed, relieved, and Magrita sat next to her.

The atmosphere in the barrack had changed dramatically with Hiltrude's mysterious disappearance. The fat kapo had yet to be replaced and, for the time being, the inmates were more or less left to themselves. Guards had been posted outside to maintain order, but that was the extent of it. They wanted nothing to do with being posted *inside* such a dirty, smelly, lice-infested place.

With Hiltrude gone, and with nature abhorring a vacuum, Adriana had been elevated to a position of some authority due to her seniority. She could hardly believe she had been at Auschwitz longer than most. Here she was, not yet 25 years on this Earth, being asked what to do and where to go and who to talk to by women twice her age. Some of these women sought her out because, in their eyes, she seemed to have figured out how to remain alive here. If there is a secret to surviving Auschwitz, they thought, then certainly this young one has it and maybe she'll share it with us.

If they only knew how helpless and terrified she felt most of the time. Didn't they know she owed her life not to her cunning or her street-smarts, but to some crazy SS officer who probably envisioned the two of them living together happily ever after the war? Didn't they know that without Traugott, she'd have been as dead as the rest of them a long time ago?

But of course they knew, and what a double-edged sword that relationship was proving to be. Yes, it had saved her life, but it had also made it immensely difficult. Adriana now found herself constantly on her guard, constantly wary, constantly questioning why this woman was suddenly wishing her "a good day" or why that one was holding the door open for her. Did they have any ulterior motives? Maybe they didn't, but then again maybe they did. How could she tell who really liked her and who was just angling to use her? She often got her answer when she explained that despite what they might have heard, there really was little she could do to help them. Some women broke down in tears, some turned their backs and never spoke to her again, but on a few occasions Adriana had also been slapped and spat on and called a whore.

"If he'd seen me first, I'm the one he'd be in love with", one woman screamed at her before attempting to claw off her face.

She tried to help as many of them as possible, but she only agreed to pass on to Traugott the most innocuous demands – *Could I take a shower? My stomach hurts, could I go to Doctor Ada's for a few hours? Could I get a note to my brother in another part of the camp?* Those women who came to her with insane requests – *Can you* (by which they really meant Traugott) *get me out of here? Could I not go to work anymore?* and, in one I-must-have-misheard-you instance, *Could I get a night alone with my husband?* - were the ones who went away most disappointed or most angry.

Adriana knew there was no point in asking him these things, his vow to do anything for her notwithstanding.

She was walking a very, very fine line with him: she had to be cold enough to keep him at bay, but no so hostile that it cost her this unique opportunity to help her fellow inmates if he gave up on her. Straying too far to one side of the line or the other might ruin everything.

She also wanted to limit how indebted she felt to him – or more to the point, how indebted he might come to feel she should be to him. Small requests, she hoped, would only generate small expectations on his part. Major favors, on the other hand, she felt were best avoided, lest they give birth to an even bigger problem.

She turned her attention back to Magrita. "What do you think happened to her?" Adriana asked, without needing to specify to whom she was referring.

Magrita shrugged. "Maybe they rendered her into cooking oil", she replied.

The two women began giggling uncontrollably until tears of laughter ran down their cheeks. "That's kind of gross, actually", Adriana said after a moment, wiping her eyes with both palms.

Magrita nodded. "You're right. Anyway, I think it's more likely they sent her to the Eastern Front to keep their tanks lubed up."

More helpless laughter ensued, after which Magrita said: "But you know, I'm more worried about your friends, Hana and Juliana."

That sobered them up instantly. Just like Hiltrude, the twins had vanished mysteriously. Adriana had a feeling these disappearances were all linked, though she couldn't figure out how, exactly.

A heart-rending shriek tore through the barrack and the two friends jumped to their feet. There were screams and shouts and the *weißköpfchen* who had climbed up to look out the window a few minutes ago came running around the corner, a look of pure terror and madness on her face. The woman saved her life by stopping just in time to avoid colliding with the guards who had burst through the door with guns drawn.

But she only stopped for a moment. After an instant, to Adriana's and Magrita's complete dismay, the woman tried to push past the guards. Taken by surprise, the the two men didn't fire but instead just shoved her back, right into the arms of the women who by now had been attracted by the commotion. The *weißköpfchen* tried to rush forward again, but with a dozen hands holding her firmly, all she could do was flail like a fish caught in a net.

"Let me go, let me go", she screamed hysterically. "I must save them, let me go, for the love of God!"

The guards now had their weapons trained on her. The camp was still locked down and any inmate seen outside the barracks would simply be shot on sight. The guards appeared ready to pull the trigger at any moment.

"Who, who did you see?" Adriana asked loudly. She positioned herself directly in front of the woman, with her back turned to the guards to block their view of the distressed prisoner. She was desperately trying to recall the woman's name, and it finally came to her. "Bea, tell me who you saw?" she repeated when the woman failed to respond.

Beatrijs Spaans – nicknamed Bea - hailed from a small Dutch village near the border with Belgium. Her story was that of countless others: she'd been traveling to a neighboring village to visit her future husband and her papers had been in perfect order, until a patrol decided they weren't and she'd been shipped here. She'd been completely cut off from the rest of her family and she had no idea what had become of them, just like they had no idea what had become of her.

Bea finally focused on Adriana at the sound of her first name and her eyes filled with tears.

"*Mijn opa en mijn oma*, I just saw them, they're outside, I have to... I have to...", she said. Then she stopped and began struggling with renewed despair, trying to break free.

Seized by an impulse that she couldn't have explained, Adriana turned to the guards. "Go back outside", she said firmly. "I've got this under control, I'll handle it."

The two men appeared stunned at being ordered around by an inmate. They remained where they were, but Adriana caught one glancing at the other out of the corner of his eye, as though seeking guidance. This was clearly virgin territory for them and they didn't know how to handle the situation. She took advantage of their indecision. "This doesn't concern you", she added in the tone of a mother rebuking an impertinent child. "There's nothing for you to do here. Leave us."

There was another moment of hesitation, after which they finally holstered their weapons. One of them pointed a finger at Adriana. "Is she comes out that door, she dies", he warned needlessly, firing a parting shot to save face. The two men then left.

A few women breathed an audible sigh of relief and the tension decreased by a notch when the guards closed the door behind them. Only later did Adriana wonder whether they had been so docile because they, too, knew who her *friend* was. And only later would she come to regret their obedience, which gave about fifty women the impression she had the power to order SS guards around.

Bea was sobbing. She appeared completely exhausted and Adriana began stroking her short hair. "There's nothing you can do to save them", she said gently. "You know that."

Bea dropped her head and nodded as tears rolled down her cheeks. "If you go out there, you'll just get shot in front of their eyes", Adriana added. "They'll see you die and that'll be the last thing they see. That's not what you want, is it?"

Bea shook her head and remained silent. "We've all lost people we love", Adriana went on. She then motioned for the women who were still holding Bea to release her. "You know I lost my father and my mother to this place. But we have to live, to make sure that those who did this are held accountable one day."

Bea nodded in resignation, but then a new energy flowed through her and she lifted her head and the glimmer of hope in her eyes made Adriana's stomach sink. "*You* go out there and get them", the woman suggested, eagerly grabbing Adriana's hands. "They won't shoot *you*. Or ask *Krumme* to save them. That's easy enough", she said, using the nickname some inmates had taken to calling Traugott behind his back. It simply meant "crooked".

Oh yes, how so easy it all was, wasn't it? How very simple. If the mighty Queen Esther would simply snap her royal fingers, she'd spare the lives of two of her beloved subjects. How very convenient to be so powerful that all would unquestioningly do her bidding.

Adriana wanted to cry. What did Bea expect from her, exactly? What did they *all* expect her to do? To descend from the heavens into the courtyard like some Messiah and miraculously pluck two people to safety? Or perhaps she should simply order the guards to summon untersturmführer

Mattias Traugott – yes, right away, snap to it! - and then request his merciful intercession?

There was no doubt in her mind she'd be the one getting a bullet in the head if she walked out that door. Nothing and no one could change that. But there was simply no way she'd ever get Bea to accept that answer. There was no point even arguing about it.

"I'm sorry, Bea", Adriana said as calmly as she could. "There's nothing I can do."

Bea stared at Adriana incredulously for a moment, and then she pulled her hands away as if she'd been bit. "You selfish bitch", she said. "You're just going to let them *die*?"

"I'm so sorry, Bea", Adriana said. "I really wish I could save them but... I simply can't."

"You can't or you won't?" another woman asked, inevitably voicing out loud what they'd probably all been thinking.

Adriana searched the crowd to see who had spoken, but all she saw was a sea of a hundred hateful eyes staring at her. *If I could save them, why wouldn't I?*, she almost shot back, but in her heart she knew it didn't matter. There was nothing she could say that would make any difference. Not now, not ever.

"I'm sorry", Adriana repeated before turning away to return to her sleeping platform.

There was a ghoulish shriek behind her and Magrita shoved her with surprising strength. Adriana tripped and fell and Bea's claws encountered empty air where Adriana's head had been less than a second before. Adriana looked over her shoulder and cringed when she saw Bea still coming after her, but now Magrita was also standing protectively over her. There was a smacking sound and then Bea was sitting on the floor with a hand over her bloody mouth.

Adriana scrambled to her feet. "I didn't know you could hit like that", she told Magrita.

"I didn't know I could", her friend replied, massaging her sore right hand.

Bea was still on the floor, staring up angrily at them and preparing to attack again, when the door opened suddenly. The women all jumped, expecting the guards to barge in and start shooting.

"Well, this is quite the welcome", Rita said as calmly as ever as she took in the scene before her eyes. "I can see why you ladies can't be left without adult supervision for very long."

The few *weißköpfchen* in the room stared, dumbfounded, at their kapo, while the others

186

wondered who this old woman was.

"Rita... what are you doing here? The lockdown...?" Adriana demanded.

"The lockdown was lifted ten minutes ago", Rita replied. "I think you were too busy to notice."

Bea got to her feet, all the anger suddenly drained out of her. If the lockdown had been lifted, it meant the courtyard was empty. And if the courtyard was empty... She buried her face in her hands and allowed herself to be led away by a few women.

"As for what I'm doing here, maybe you can tell me", Rita went on. "It seems your old kapo has gone missing, so I'm to be in charge around here from now on."

Adriana just stared at her, as she remembered telling Traugott that Hiltrude had vanished and wouldn't be missed.

"I think I may have you to thank for this new choice assignment?" the old woman asked Adriana with more than a hint of sarcasm.

24

Pain.

Pain that ebbed and flowed like the tide. Searing pain, freezing pain. Pain as bright as the sun and as dark as a moonless night. The kiss of a lover and the sting of a whip. Pain that pushed you to the edge of madness, pain that kept you chained to the realm of the sane. Pain that promised eternal salvation and pain that threatened eternal damnation.

They had no more thoughts, no more consciousness, no more feelings, no more awareness. Pain had claimed their souls as its exclusive playground and it brooked no rivalry. Pain had become the alpha and the omega of their lives. Pain greeted them in the morning and haunted their nights, keeping from them the sleep that might have offered ephemeral relief.

Miklos Nyiszly tied the surgical mask behind his neck before entering the room. The stench of putrefying flesh had become quite strong, so he had daubed some oil of lilac onto the mask to fight the smell. He hoped Mengele wouldn't notice this sign of weakness.

They found Hana and Juliana as they had left them the night before. The twins were lying on adjacent beds, with Hana's right hand and Juliana's left bandaged together. Their other limbs had been secured with restraints to keep the two women from thrashing around. More blood had seeped into the bandage, staining it a reddish, dark brown.

"Remove the bandage", Mengele ordered indifferently.

Miklos Nyiszly steeled himself for what was about to come. In his mind, he flipped the switch that allowed him to do such things, the switch that transformed him from a loving husband and doting father into a cold clinician fueled by medical curiosity. If he was to do what was expected of him, he had to transport himself to a world in which he was engaged in nothing more than a quest for scientific knowledge. If he did not, he would be repelled by the task set to him, and he would die.

He glanced at Mengele. The doctor had retreated behind his usual glacial demeanor. He was busy examining the fingernails of his right hand and might as well have been waiting for the bus on a street corner for all the concern he displayed.

Nyiszly slowly began unwrapping the gauze and the stench immediately increased by a factor of a million, completely overpowering his meager defenses. The layers had stuck together and he pulled them apart as gently as he could, but the twins' moans told him he wasn't being gentle enough. And as if the smell didn't suffice, he could feel their burning skin even through his rubber gloves, a sure sign infection had set in.

He took a breath and uncoiled the last length of bandage. He needed no more than a cursory examination to determine that their experiment – *Mengele's experiment*, he chided himself - had been a complete failure. Not only was the skin hot, but it was also red and swollen and inflamed, and a greenish liquid oozed from between the sutures. The fingertips had taken on a blackish hue from the lack of oxygen and, as he watched, the twins tried to pull their hands apart. A few of the sutures popped from the rotting flesh with a stomach-wrenching sound, but the others held.

Nyiszly took a quick step back.

"Well?" Mengele asked nonchalantly.

"See... See for yourself, herr doktor", Nyiszly replied haltingly through his mask. "There seems to have been a problem."

Mengele came closer and bent over the suppurating wound, apparently completely unbothered by the stench, and adjusted his glasses on the tip of his nose as he examined it.

"Quite", he said after a moment. "It seems our experiment has failed. We will try again later, but we must first come up with a different procedure."

Nyiszly wondered who Mengele's "we" referred to. It had certainly not been his – Nyiszly's - idea to attempt to create conjoined twins by stitching these two identical women together. But Nyiszly also wondered whether he would have been so quick to distance himself from this monstrous experiment if it had succeeded. Wouldn't his professional ego have then demanded some credit?

"Make a final note of their vital signs", Mengele ordered. "And then prepare for the experiment to be terminated."

Nyiszly jotted down the twins' heart rate, blood pressure and temperature while Mengele filled two syringes from a bottle of clear liquid. Nyiszly couldn't read the label from where he stood, but the smell told him that the bottle contained chloroform.

He was measuring Hana's dilated pupils when the dying woman breathed a few words. Nyiszly was so surprised he released her eyelids with a start and dropped his pupillometer, thinking he must be imagining things. But her lips were definitely moving and, somehow, Mengele heard her as well.

"What is she saying?" the doctor asked.

"I... I don't know", Nyiszly confessed, knowing there was only one way of finding out.

He bent closer to Hana, placing his ear against her lips. Her breath was impossibly hot and smelled of a dead animal that has been rotting in the summer sun. It took almost a full minute before the words came again.

"*Heut ist dein Geburtstag... Darum feiern wir... Alle deine Freunde... Freuen sich mit dir*", Hana whispered.

Nyiszly was stunned.

"What did she say?" Mengele asked again, this time with a note of impatience.

Nyiszly hesitated. "She's delirious, herr doktor", he said. "She has a temperature of almost 105 Farenheit. Her mind is gone."

"That's not what I asked", Mengele replied tersely. "I asked you what she said."

Nyiszly sighed. "She's singing, herr doktor", he finally said.

"Singing?" Mengele asked.

"Yes, herr doktor", he confirmed. "Singing. A birthday song."

It was Mengele's turn to sigh. He finished filling his syringe and came to stand next to Hana. He sought a precise spot between her ribs, on the left side of her body, with the tips of his fingers. He then inserted the long needle into her heart and injected the chloroform directly into her left ventricle.

Nyiszly watched, mesmerized. Though Auschwitz was a place of death, he had never before seen Mengele kill anyone. He was frozen in place, his limbs paralyzed by the murder – what else could one possibly call it? - he had just witnessed. Mengele's movements had been precise and professional and confident, and his hands hadn't trembled in the least when he'd injected the chloroform. There had been no hesitation, no second thoughts, no remorse, no burdensome conscience... Just the deliberate act of a man for whom human life has lost all value.

Mengele had killed the woman with the cold detachment of a pure sociopath. Nyiszly had seen doctors inoculating a crying infant display more emotion.

Hana shuddered one last time when the blood in her ventricle congealed, causing instant death. Mengele withdrew the needle and a tiny bead of bright red blood formed above the skin.

"Make a note of the time of death", Mengele ordered.

Juliana died in the same manner less than a minute later.

Rudolf Höss tossed the report dismissively aside and cursed under his breath. Stupid fool. Stupid, stupid fool.

"What do you think?" Maximilian Grabner asked.

"I don't believe it", Höss said after a moment. "Not a word of it. No one can be that idiotic."

The Auschwitz Gestapo chief stared at the camp commander through slitted eyelids. This wasn't quite the reaction he had expected, though he now wondered what else, exactly, he should have expected.

Höss deluded himself if he thought his relationship with Eleanor Hodys, the young Austrian political prisoner he had taken as his reluctant mistress the year before, had gone unnoticed. In truth, Grabner was well aware of it and Berlin had also been making inquiries. So far Grabner had only confirmed that Höss had ordered Hodys transferred to the special prison underneath the main administrative building. He hadn't yet said anything about Höss visiting her almost nightly by sneaking through an air raid shelter, in an attempt to escape the guards' notice.

Grabner also knew others, including Höss' adjutant Robert Mulka, had taken notice of the commander' nightly escapades. Just because he had decided to keep some information to himself for later use didn't mean all had made the same choice.

And now Höss was being made to discipline not only an officer, but one of *his* officers over an infraction of which he was himself essentially guilty. Perhaps this explained his reaction, Grabner thought. Höss still believed that no one knew about Hodys, and he wanted to keep it that way. If he were to sanction one of his officers over an illicit relationship with an inmate, who knew what events this might set into motion? Might it not then become impossible for him to pursue his affair?

Höss certainly feared some unforeseen repercussions for him, so his first instinct was to deny everything.

"I just don't believe it", the obersturmbannführer repeated stubbornly.

"This came directly from the Hauptamt SS-Gericht", Grabner said. "Someone apparently talked to Konrad Morgen during his visit and he's been investigating ever since."

Grabner thought he knew who Morgen's source was, and if he was right, he would have bet the farm the SS Court Head Office was holding a lot more information than it was letting on. "We should count ourselves lucky he's trusting us to handle this ourselves", he added.

Höss had to concede Grabner's point. The last thing they all needed was another impromptu visit by the Bloodhound Judge. But he wasn't sure they should rely too much on Morgen's alleged "trust" in them. Now that the judge had gotten wind of this matter, he'd be watching very closely from afar: if they failed to act decisively, he'd pounce on the occasion to come down hard on all of them instead of on a single culprit.

"This is the second time Morgen has come sniffing around my business", Höss said angrily. "Maybe he's forgotten I was named by the Reichsführer himself and that I'm under his protection."

And when you were a kid, you probably had your older brother beat up that bully who stole your shoes, you miserable little feigling, Grabner thought contemptuously.

He was tempted to reply that Morgen wouldn't be sniffing around Höss' business if it didn't stink like carrion, but he didn't think his comment would be well received.

"Morgen doesn't really answer to anyone", Grabner reminded the camp commander. "He makes his own rules and he's as tough and as straight as they come. If you go up against him, you'll lose."

"Perhaps, but I'll also make sure not to go down alone", Höss replied aggressively and Grabner worried what, exactly, he meant by that.

Grabner pulled a handkerchief from his pocket and wiped the sweat from his ample forehead. The camp commander was in a fighting mood and his belligerence was making Grabner nervous, since he had his own reasons for wanting Morgen to turn his attention away from Auschwitz. The Bloodhound Judge had apparently recently expressed an interest in certain things that... well, suffice it to say that the sooner something other than Auschwitz caught Morgen's fancy, the better for all concerned. On the other hand, if Höss decided to phone Himmler and pick a fight with Morgen, the war that would ensue would be epic and the collateral victims numerous.

Grabner doubted Höss was endowed with sufficient intelligence to perceive the potential repercussions of going up against Konrad Morgen, even with Heinrich Himmler potentially in his corner. He only knew one thing for sure: he had no intention of finding himself caught in the crossfire, and that meant getting Höss to see the light and listen to reason.

"The Gestapo has files on tens of thousands of people", Grabner said. "Morgen has files *on* the Gestapo. He knows things about us we probably don't even know about ourselves. Or that we think no one knows about ourselves."

The threat struck home. Höss dropped his head and looked to the side, avoiding Grabner's eyes. He began gnawing on the nail of his right thumb.

"I need to get him off my back", Höss finally said.

Grabner breathed a silent sigh of relief. This was the opening he'd been waiting for. "If you don't want Morgen snooping around here, don't give him any excuse to be snooping around here", he said. "Do your job, do what you have to do, and he'll go away."

Höss grabbed the file from the table in front of him and began leafing through it, even though he'd already read it from cover to cover twice. He then picked up his phone and summoned Robert Mulka, who arrived less than a minute later.

The adjutant saluted and stood to attention, awaiting his instructions. Höss seemed to hesitate and Grabner could almost hear him second-guessing himself. He feared Höss was about to choke and in the end, he almost did.

For his orders weren't exactly the ones that Grabner had expected – or hoped for.

"Hauptsturmführer", he said. "Find inmate *neunzehnhunderteinundsiebzig* and bring her to me. Now."

26

At that moment, inmate *neunzehnhunderteinundsiebzig* was slowly suffocating, as though she had been buried alive.

Adriana was kneeling on the ground, grimacing and trying not to panic as she tried to catch her breath after getting the wind knocked out of her. She wrapped both arms around her midsection and took a wheezing, painful breath. She felt as though she were breathing through a tiny straw.

No matter how hard she inhaled, no air would flow into her screaming lungs. She couldn't open her eyes and her mind was filled with exploding stars. She removed one hand from her stomach and placed it against the ground to keep from toppling over. She heaved with all her strength, desperately trying to pull air into her body.

Finally, just as she was about to pass out, a trickle of oxygen found its way into her system, feeding her starving cells and somewhat alleviating her distress.

"What happened? What's wrong?" she heard someone, probably Magrita, ask.

Adriana raised a finger in the universal gesture and took another, deeper breath. Her lungs burned but at least she was breathing again. She placed both hands against her thighs and wiped the tears from her eyes with her palms. She took several more gulps of air, pulling it as deeply into her lungs as she could, and her mind began to clear.

"It was... it was an accident", Adriana whispered with a croaking voice. "It was my fault. I wasn't paying attention."

Her breathing had almost returned to normal, though it remained a bit labored.

"What happened?" Magrita repeated.

"Are you deaf or stupid? She just told you. An ac... ci... dent", someone else replied angrily. Magrita looked to see who had spoken and saw that it was Beatrijs, the woman whose grandparents had been gassed a few days earlier. "I threw the bale at her, she wasn't looking and it struck her in the stomach." There indeed was a bale of clothes lying next to Adriana.

At the end of the week, the women would load the clothes they had sorted and bundled over the previous days onto trucks headed back to Germany. But rather than each woman carrying a bale to the truck and returning to fetch another, the inmates had discovered it was much more efficient to throw the bundles from person to person along a sort of human conveyor belt. That way of doing things was quicker, but it was also somewhat more dangerous: the bundles weighed 15 or 20 pounds each, and as worked progressed and the women fell into a rhythm, the task seem to take on a life of its own and coordination became absolutely essential. If you threw the bale before the next woman was ready to catch it, at best you might have to refold and rebundle the clothes; at worst, injuries had been known to occur, from broken fingers to outright concussions.

Shouts echoed in the warehouse as other women demanded to know why work had stopped. As well as being hazardous, the task was tiresome and they all wanted to be done as quickly as possible. Dropping too many bundles, and thus paralyzing the whole operation too often, was cause for expulsion from the *weißköpfchen*.

Magrita grabbed Adriana's hand and helped her to her feet.

"Can you go on?" she asked.

Adriana simply nodded. Magrita looked at Beatrijs, who stared back at her defiantly with arms crossed over her chest, as though challenging her to dispute it hadn't been a silly accident.

A minute later bundles were again flying down the line in a carefully choreographed, graceful ballet, but Magrita could tell that something was wrong. She and Adriana always performed this task next to one another, knowing they could rely on each other, and Adriana's throws were usually precise and perfectly timed. But now, Adriana seemed to be throwing off-balance, which meant she was also catching Beatrijs' bundles off-balance. Her throws had a rushed, careless feel that was completely uncharacteristic of her.

Magrita threw the bale she had just received from Adriana to the next woman before quickly spinning to her right to catch Adriana's next throw – but that throw never came.

Possibly because she had injured her ribs in the "accident" a moment ago, Adriana was a bit slow spinning to her own right to catch Beatrij's next bale. No matter; Beatrijs should have noticed Adriana wasn't ready and withheld her throw for a fraction of a second. Instead, as Magrita watched, Bea hurriedly threw the bale she was holding. The woman had clearly precipitated her throw, giving Adriana no chance.

The heavy bale struck Adriana squarely in the face and she collapsed like a puppet whose strings have been cut.

"Adriana!" Magrita screamed.

She again rushed to her friend's side, kneeling down next to her. Adriana had been knocked unconscious. Her nose was broken and bright red blood flowed from her nostrils. Magrita rapidly lifted her head off the ground to keep her from choking.

"Adriana! Wake up!" she screamed again.

Adriana coughed. She was already coming around. She shook her head and winced in pain. Before Magrita could stop her, she touched her nose with the tip of her fingers and let out a shout of pain.

"Don't move, we'll get Doctor Ada", Magrita said, but Adriana waved her away.

"No, I'm fine", she said. "I just didn't see it coming."

"Of course you didn't", Magrita said. She looked at Beatrijs, who was observing them with a self-satisfied smirk. She then read the woman's lips as Bea mouthed: *The mighty Queen Esther, finally knocked back down to Earth.*

Magrita was stunned. "You did this on purpose", she accused Beatrijs. "I saw you do it."

"Magrita, please don't", Adriana said feebly. "Leave it be. Just help me get up. I'm fine."

Adriana was struggling to get back on her feet and Magrita had to support her to keep her from collapsing again. The blood that still flowed from her broken nose had stained her clothes.

"I saw her do it, Adriana", Magrita protested. "She *wanted* to hit you. She..."

Adriana quickly wrapped both arms around Magrita's neck in an awkward hug, as though hanging on to her to keep her knees from buckling. She whispered into her friend's ear: "I know all that. But I'm begging you, be quiet. Don't make a scene. *Please Magrita. Pleeeease.*"

Magrita recoiled. "But why? Why are you protecting her? She's just..."

"What the hell is going on here? Why aren't you women working?" someone barked from across the room. Magrita heard Adriana groan.

"Someone answer me!" Mattias Traugott roared. "Why has all work stopped?"

Most women simply stared at the ground as the dreaded untersturmführer strode through the silent warehouse, his heels clicking sinisterly against the concrete. Traugott was again about to demand an explanation when he spotted Adriana's bloodied face and clothes. His entire demeanor changed instantly and he walked rapidly over to her.

"What's happened here?" he asked with unmistakable worry.

"A simple accident, herr untersturmführer", Adriana answered uneasily, before Magrita had a chance to say anything else. Her nose was clogged with blood and she sounded as though she had a massive cold. "The bale flew through my hands and struck me in the face."

Traugott narrowed his eyes at her. He was clearly skeptical. "Is this true? An accident?" he asked, turning to Magrita.

Magrita froze. She had never dealt with Traugott personally and she didn't know how to handle the situation. Tell the truth and betray her best friend, or lie to a man who could order her death with a simple nod? She looked at Adriana, and all of a sudden everything became clear. She understood why Adriana was lying: if Traugott found out Beatrijs had intentionally injured her, he'd send her directly to the gas chambers.

And no matter what Beatrijs might have done, no matter what she might be, she didn't deserve such a fate. Nobody did.

"Yes, herr untersturmführer", Magrita finally breathed. "It was simply an accident."

Adriana placed a grateful hand on Magrita' shoulder and wiped the drying blood from her face with the back of her sleeve. Traugott stared at them. He knew they were lying, but there was nothing he could do about it. He was about to say something else when another voice reverberated throughout the warehouse.

"Untersturmführer Traugott, why has all activity here stopped?".

Traugott spun around and his stomach dropped to the floor when he spotted Robert Mulka striding rapidly in his direction, with Otto Möckel and that gigantic Irish wolfhound of his, Achtzehn, right on his heels. The powerful dog was straining madly at his leash and giving Möckel all that he could handle.

Traugott clicked his heels together and saluted Höss' adjutant. He tried to ignore Möckel, who was staring at him smugly.

"A simple accident, herr hauptsturmführer", he explained. "A worker has been injured but it's nothing to be concerned about. I was getting them back to work as you arrived."

Mulka returned the salute and Traugott relaxed a little bit. "It isn't the first time I've found your inmates twiddling their thumbs in your presence", the adjutant reprimanded him maliciously. "This situation seems to keep repeating itself. Maybe I need to keep a closer eye on your operation."

Traugott clenched his gloved fists behind his back. He knew better than to try and win an argument with Mulka. If the adjutant was determined to find fault with him tonight, which he seemed to be, fault he would find and there was nothing Traugott could say or do that would stop him. But his anger had still been roused by Mulka's blatantly unjust assessment of his performance and he couldn't remain silent. He was about to protest when Mulka silenced him with a raised hand.

"Be quiet, that's not why I'm here", he said tiredly, as if he couldn't believe Traugott would even try to defend himself in the face of such irrefutable evidence. "I'm looking for inmate *neunzehnhunderteinundsiebzig*. Where is she?"

Several inmates gasped and Adriana bit her lower lip to keep from doing the same. Traugott was left momentarily speechless. That was perhaps the last thing he'd expected. Why the hell would Mulka be looking for that specific prisoner, out of the thousands now at Auschwitz? What did he want with her? There was only one reason he could think of, and he didn't like the potential ramifications.

"*Neunzehnhunderteinundsiebzig,* untersturmführer", Mulka insisted impatiently. "She's one of yours, isn't she? Where is she? Do you even know?"

Traugott again bristled at this new insinuation of his incompetence. Mulka really seemed to have it in for him tonight. He tried to think of a way to stall the adjutant, to gain a few precious moments, but in truth, he was stuck. Adriana was standing right next to him and he couldn't risk lying. He had no other choice but to tell the truth.

But in the end, Mulka sighed exasperatedly before he could speak. "Never mind, I'll find her myself. You", he said, singling out a woman who had joined the *weißköpfchen* less than two weeks earlier, "go stand over there."

The terrified woman hesitated for just a moment before complying. She was shaking like a leaf. "Which one is *neunzehnhunderteinundsiebzig*?" he asked.

"I... I don't know, herr hauptsturmführer", the woman replied truthfully, with a tremulous voice that betrayed her fear. "I'm sorry, but I don't know."

"No, of course you don't", Mulka said, as if wondering why he'd even asked. "Mockël, I think your hound could use some exercise, could it not?"

"Indeed it could, herr hauptsturmführer", Mockël replied immediately with an eagerness he didn't even try to conceal. As excited as a kid on Christmas morning, he bent down and whispered something into Achtzehn's ear. The beast's entire demeanor changed instantly: its muscles tensed, the hair on its back bristled, it lowered itself on its haunches, a low growl arose from its entire body and its upper lip raised into a vicious snarl that exposed almost two inches of fangs.

Whatever command Mockël had given it, Achtzehn was now ready not only to attack, but also to kill.

The poor woman cried in fear and took a step back, but there was really nowhere for her to go.

Traugott couldn't believe what was happening. What the hell was Mulka doing? He could simply have ordered the inmates to roll up their sleeves to check their numbers. Yes, that would have taken a bit longer, but... this? What purpose did this sick game serve?

And then he got it: Mulka was testing him. The adjutant had ordered him to identify Adriana, but he'd never really given him a chance to obey. He'd never intended to play fair. This was a trap and the game was rigged against him. Mulka wanted to see how far he was ready to go to protect this mysterious *neunzehnhunderteinundsiebzig*. Would he allow an innocent woman to be mauled to death to keep her identity hidden just a few minutes longer? If he did, wouldn't that say all there was to be said about the matter? Why would an SS officer go to such lengths to protect a Jewish inmate, if he had nothing to hide? Remaining silent would have been tantamount to proclaiming himself guilty of whatever he was charged with.

He had no other choice but to give up Adriana. If he didn't, another inmate might speak up to prevent the impending massacre. His silence certainly didn't guarantee Adriana's safety. He had to do it now. Traugott wanted to speak, he was *positive* he wanted to speak, but his mouth remained stubbornly shut. He couldn't have pried his jaws apart with a crowbar if he'd tried.

Mockël reached down to release Achtzehn.

The monster growled and got ready to tear out the woman's throat.

Traugott began to sweat and tremble.

Adriana took a step forward.

"I'm the one you're looking for, herr hauptsturmführer", she said calmly. "My name is Adriana Zöbel. My parents, Simeon and Raanah Zöbel from Rimavská Sobota, Czechoslovakia, were murdered in this place. But I still live."

She stared straight ahead, hands linked behind her back, and waited. She appeared as impassive as a statue. Traugott immediately noticed she hadn't mentioned her number. She'd stated her name loud and clear, and she'd proclaimed herself unbowed and unbroken by accusing them all of her parents' murders, and never would she refer to herself as a number.

Mulka stared at her suspiciously. He took a couple of steps, roughly grabbed her arm and checked her number to confirm her identity. He sighed. "Stand down, Mockël", he said. "We've found her."

Mockël appeared positively dejected. He whispered another command and Achtzehn instantly reverted to its normal, out-of-control self, as though Mockël had flipped a switch.

"I was just inquiring as to her injuries", Traugott finally managed to say.

The remark elicited a rare smile from Robert Mulka and Traugott saw he'd made a mistake. "Really? What a strange coincidence", the adjutant said. Behind him, Mockël was also smiling broadly, as if he couldn't believe such stupidity, and Traugott wanted to kill him and his dog on the spot. "And why would you be so concerned about this specific inmate's well-being over that of all the others?"

The comment was again unjust and unfounded, but Traugott managed to keep his anger in check. He knew any protest he offered would simply make him look even more guilty. "She's one of my best workers", he simply said.

"I'm sure she is", Mulka immediately replied, with a massive dose of sarcasm. "But for now, you'll have to do without her. She's coming with me."

This time Adriana couldn't keep her gasp silent and Magrita grabbed her hand from behind her.

No good could possibly come of this.

"May I ask why?" Traugott demanded nervously, all the while knowing it would have been much preferable for him to appear not to care in the least what happened to this woman.

"You may not", Mulka said. He then turned his attention to Adriana, dismissing Traugott completely. "Clean yourself up", he ordered her, his voice dripping with disgust and disdain. Then, after Adriana had wiped most of the blood from her face, he said: "Follow us and keep silent".

Magrita was still holding Adriana's hand and she gave her a squeeze before finally letting go. Adriana did her best to ignore Traugott, who was staring at her hard. The last thing she needed was to be caught exchanging glances and silent messages with this officer. Achtzehn began barking wildly and its glistening red penis emerged when she approached. Mockël silenced the dog with a slap, but Adriana remained well out of reach of the beast as the two men led her away.

Traugott watched them go helplessly. At the last moment, Mockël turned around and the evil smile he gave him told him that worse, much worse was yet to come.

27

Five days later.
Block 11. The "Death Block".
August 1943

A prisoner was being flogged outside.

The sound of leather tearing flesh reached Adriana through the tiny window. The inmate had stopped crying a while ago, but still they kept whipping him. Perhaps the man had passed out. Or perhaps he had mercifully passed away. In either case, at least he no longer felt any pain.

Adriana feared she, too, might get flogged before too long. She shuddered at the thought. It was said a Nazi by the name of Eichmann had invented a whip lined with barbed fishhooks all along the thong. It allegedly ripped out fist-sized chunks of flesh, until the victim died of massive blood loss. At least that's what the stories said. Just a few years ago, Adriana would never have believed the human mind capable of dreaming up such a nightmarish device. But now, after all she'd seen and experienced... she wasn't so sure what to believe anymore.

Another cry arose from deep within the bowels of the building. Adriana tried to block it out of her mind. Such demented cries were heard at all times, haunting her days and nights, and to her they sounded like damned souls burning in hell – which, in a sense, they were. For the prisoners whose fingernails were being ripped out or who had been hung from the ceiling by their wrists with their arms twisted behind their backs or locked for days in cages too small to either stand or sit or lie down probably thought they had died and gone straight to hell.

Adriana looked up at her own shackled wrists. The guards had thrown the chain over a hook screwed into the ceiling, forcing her to keep her arms raised above her head. Or so they thought. Adriana had yanked down on the hook as soon as she'd been left alone and to her immense surprise, it had dropped by a few inches in a shower of dust. Now, if she raised herself up on tiptoes, she could just manage to slip the chain off the hook and free herself. She simply had to be careful to return to her original position and fake extreme discomfort whenever she heard the guards coming.

She almost got caught the day before yesterday, when she was distracted by the sound of dozens of footsteps in the narrow alleyway between Blocks 10 and 11. Adriana went to the window and saw a dozen blindfolded inmates being escorted by a handful of laughing guards. The guards lined up the inmates against the wall, and she immediately guessed what was about to happen. She still gasped and recoiled in horror when the guards opened fire, machine-gunning the prisoners where they stood. Adriana had to duck out of the way when bullets and chunks of mortar and brick began ricocheting up the wall.

Then the guards, still laughing and joking and probably completely drunk, began making fun of those inmates who'd soiled themselves in the last seconds of their lives. They were particularly amused by a young man whose stiff penis still protruded from his pants and who had ejaculated a fraction of a second before dying. Adriana watched as a guard grabbed the penis with his fingertips and sliced it off with a swift gesture, before holding the dripping member up for his friends' amusement.

Adriana was so engrossed by the macabre spectacle unfolding twenty feet below that she never heard the guards' footsteps that always forewarned her of their arrival. All she heard was the soul-chilling sound of the key sliding into the lock and she threw the chain of her shackles over the hook just as the door swung open. The guards found her as they always did, hanging limply from the hook with her feet barely supporting her. If they noticed that she seemed to be breathing a bit harder than usual, they made no mention of it.

Her mind returned to the inmate who had just been flogged to death right outside her window.

Adriana resolved to tell the SS whatever they wanted to hear if she should ever find herself threatened with the same fate. Why should she insist on telling the truth when they obviously cared nothing for it? For five days they'd stubbornly asked her the same questions, and for five days she'd stubbornly provided them with the same answers. But again and again they asked, unconvinced and unsatisfied, and again and again she answered until she felt she might go mad from the endless repetition. She'd been slapped a few times, and one of them had once grabbed her short hair, but that was only to be expected. She knew these monsters to be capable of much worse. For one, the man with the huge dog, the same one who'd forced her to sing at Höss' birthday party a lifetime ago, clearly wanted nothing more than to beat what they believed to be the truth out of her. She wondered that he hadn't yet recognized her. Still, to Adriana, it felt as if they were almost holding back for some reason. She got the feeling someone or something was keeping them from doing all they really wanted.

She heard the sound of footsteps echoing in the hallway. Here they came again. Knowing she had ample time, she looped the chain over the hook and feigned sleep. The rusty hinges creaked when the door was pushed open.

Someone entered the room. A single man, alone, judging by the sound of his heels against the concrete floor. That damn sound would haunt her sleep for decades to come. Click. Clack. Click. Clack. Like some doomsday clock counting down the last seconds of her life. Even once safely away, thousands of miles away from here, she'd still jolt awake in the dead of night, in a cold sweat, certain she'd heard heels clicking against the floor just outside her door.

So a single man, alone. That was unusual. They always interrogated her three or four at a time. The man with the dog was always there, and so was the one who never smiled and who seemed to be his boss. Once the camp commander himself also came, but he appeared very ill at ease. He left after just a few minutes without having said a single word.

The hook had been positioned so she'd have her back to the door at all times, so she had no idea which one of them it was.

The hinges creaked again when her visitor shut the door. Then there was a click as he locked it, and Adriana felt the first tentacles of fear snake around her heart. This was also unusual. They always, always left the door unlocked, in case they suddenly had to leave the room for whatever reason.

The man took a couple of steps... *click, clack, click, clack*... and came to stand directly behind her. She could hear his breathing and smell his sweat. He was standing so close she could feel his body heat against her skin. She kept her eyes shut and her head down, pretending to have passed out and hoping the man would simply leave and return at another moment.

She really should have known better.

"Wake up", the man said in a soft voice, almost as though he feared being heard from the outside.

Adriana ignored him. She concentrated on keeping all her muscles relaxed to preserve the illusion she had truly passed out. The slightest twitch could betray her.

She tried to block out the burning pain that was blooming in her shoulders. Hanging like this, with her legs nothing but dead weight under her, she got an inkling of the unbearable torture this was meant to be. All her weight was pulling down on her arms and already her hands had gone numb from the lack of blood, while the joints in her shoulders were being stretched beyond their breaking point.

She wouldn't be able to remain like this for very long before giving herself away.

"Wake up", the man repeated more forcefully. He bent down to speak directly into her ear and she shivered with fear when she recognized his voice: the man with the huge dog.

Adriana moaned. She shifted her weight to try and relieve the pain, but it only seemed to make it worse. She moaned again. She was suddenly dead certain that unless she found a way to make him leave, something very bad would happen to her.

Otto Mockël was still standing directly behind her. Thinking she was finally coming to, he reached around and placed a gloved hand under her jaw and tried to pull her up onto her feet. Adriana wished herself to be as heavy and as limp as she could, but as soon as Mockël lifted her up, blood flowed back into her hands and her shoulders screamed their gratitude.

The relief she felt was unspeakable and it was almost against her will that she placed her feet beneath her.

Satisfied, Mockël came to stand in front of her. Adriana kept her eyes closed, refusing to look at him, but then Mockël violently grabbed her jaw in a vise, digging his fingers into her cheeks.

The shock made Adriana open her eyes. Mockël's face was less than two inches from hers and he was staring at her hard. She stared back, unsure of what he wanted, and saw his expression change completely.

He seemed stupefied.

"You", he whispered. "I know who you are. I should have let you die on board that train."

Their paths had crossed a few times since Höss' birthday party, most notably when Mulka had come looking for her a few days ago, but this was the first time in a year they'd actually come face to face. Even over the course of the previous interrogations, Mockël had remained threateningly in the background with his dog while others asked the questions. It seemed he hadn't taken a good look at her before today.

Adriana's appearance had radically altered over the past year. She'd been pushed to the brink of death and dragged back, some of her subsisting teenage softness – both mental and physical - had been replaced by a new toughness she didn't find unappealing, her hair was obviously mostly gone, and although she'd regained some of her health since joining Traugott's *weißköpfchen*, she doubted someone other than her immediate family would have known her at first glance.

This was the first time Mockël had really seen her since Höss' birthday party, for which she'd been made to look absolutely radiant, so perhaps it wasn't all that surprising he hadn't recognized her until today.

"You should be dead by now", Mockël said. "No one survives Auschwitz for this long."

"And yet I still live", she spontaneously spat back, before pondering the wisdom of engaging him in such a fashion.

"Yes, you still live... for now", he inevitably replied with a smirk. "But that you do only proves what we've been suspecting. Traugott made you his whore. That's why you still live, isn't it? You're Traugott's whore."

"I'm no one's whore", Adriana said angrily. "Not his, not yours, not anybody's. I'm still alive because I won't let animals like you kill me."

Mockël smiled, as though her anger and her insults amused him. He walked slowly around her and again came to stand behind her, so she couldn't look at him. He placed his mouth directly next to her ear.

"Tell me the truth and you'll live even longer", he said in a tone another man might have used to profess his undying love to his soul mate. "Tell me what he likes. Do you let him fuck you in your other hole?"

He rubbed his hand suggestively between her buttocks. Adriana tried to twist away and she bit her lower lip to keep from yelping in pain when he pressed his fingers, hard, against her anus.

"Do you take him in your mouth until he comes?"

Adriana was a virgin. Once, and only for a couple of seconds, she'd let the handsome Julius Gaàl slip his tongue inside her mouth, and even that had made her feel ashamed. But now, those things Mockël was mentioning... well, she'd *heard* about them, but did really people engage in such depraved acts?

The feeling something extremely bad was about to happen to her grew even more intense.

"Does he bend you over his desk or do you do it on the floor? We know what's really going on. Just tell me and I'll let you go."

His breath smelled of beer and onions, and it made Adriana want to gag.

"I've got nothing to tell you, you pig", she said. "There's nothing going on. Go to hell."

Mockël snickered. He placed his hands on her hips and pulled her to him. She felt his stiff member between her buttocks and he began grinding his hips against her. Adriana gasped and tried to pull away, but there was nowhere for her to go. Mockël snickered again.

"We all know you're a whore", he said lustily. "But if you're not Traugott's, then you'll be mine."

His hands slid up from her hips onto her ribcage and then onto her breasts. He grabbed them hard and began licking her neck. Adriana screamed, but she knew that in a place where pain and despair ruled like tyrants, screams held no power.

Mockël removed a hand from her breasts and unbuttoned his trousers. He then began lifting up her uniform, and Adriana felt the cold air against the skin of her bare legs.

Something snaps in her mind. This is not happening to her, not again. She loses contact with reality for a few seconds. One moment she's standing there helplessly as Mockël is viciously pawing at her underpants, the next she's slipped her shackles off the hook and she's sitting astride his back with the chain around his neck, riding him like a wild bronco, choking him.

How this happened, she never knew.

Adriana pulled on the chain with all the strength she could muster. Mockël made a strangled noise as the steel links dug into his neck.

"Let me go", he croaked.

Adriana placed one knee against Mockël's back to give herself additional leverage. She gritted her teeth and pulled even harder. Beads of sweat began to roll down her face, mixing with tears of rage.

Mockël began to panic.

He raised himself onto his knees, sliding Adriana off his back, and clawed at the chain with both hands. Unable to find any purchase, he reached over his head and behind him, looking for her face or her head, but she managed to remain safely out of reach.

Then, almost by accident, as though God had decided to help him instead of her, his hands found her wrists. He pulled her forward as hard as he could, and the chain slackened just enough for him to slip his fingers between the steel links and his flesh.

Adriana knew she was in trouble. She tried pulling harder on the chain, but her muscles were already tiring and Mockël was fighting to save his life.

The SS then yanked the chain forward with both hands at the same time he threw his head back. Caught by surprise, Adriana lost her balance and toppled forward, and her injured nose connected with the back of Mockël's skull. A lightning storm of blinding pain exploded behind her eyes and she collapsed to the ground.

Mockël freed himself and came to stand well away from her, choking and coughing and retching. His penis was still hanging limply out of his trousers, but he didn't seem to notice.

"You're dead, I'll kill you", he finally managed to say.

Adriana laughed through her pain. "No you won't", she said feebly as she pressed her back against the wall. "They won't let you."

It was Mockël's turn to laugh, but his laughter turned into a coughing fit. "Who won't let me, Traugott?" he asked after it had finally subsided. "You Jews really are as stupid as they say. He's gone. And besides, I *outrank* fucking Mattias Traugott. You're dead, bitch. This is your last day."

Adriana shook her head. "No, not Traugott. He's nothing. You can't touch me and you know it. Otherwise I'd *already* be dead."

Mockël was stunned.

Konrad Morgen was still looking to clean up Auschwitz of its rampant corruption, and he seemed to believe he'd be able to do so one individual at a time, jumping from one to the next, demanding of each new suspect the names of others he could take down. He probably cared little if those fingered by their colleagues were actually guilty of anything, as long as all were eventually scared straight.

And the first name on his list, despite his earlier failure and borderline humiliation, was still that of Mattias Traugott. So when he heard of an inmate who'd developed a special relationship with his main suspect, he immediately ordered she be interrogated. But he also ordered she be kept alive until she'd given them Traugott, arguing that Traugott would then become but the first in a long line of falling dominoes.

And since she hadn't yet talked, Adriana was right: there was absolutely nothing he could do to her without risking the wrath of both Robert Mulka and the Bloodhound Judge.

Adriana, obviously, knew absolutely nothing of Morgen's scheme. She was bluffing to save her life. All she knew was they'd treated her with kids' glove over the past five days. She knew what an Auschwitz interrogation could be like, and this most definitely wasn't it. So clearly someone, somewhere, was protecting her. And if not Traugott, then someone much more powerful than him. That's what she was betting on, and she seemed to be winning.

Mockël was staring at her. He licked his lips and, to her horror, she saw his penis begin to stiffen again.

"I may not be allowed to kill you, but you'll soon wish you were dead", he said as he took a step in her direction.

Adriana pressed her back against the wall even harder, instinctively trying to scuttle away, but she was trapped. She knew she wouldn't be able to fight him off again. She wondered if it might not be better for her to simply lie on her back and open her thighs to him. That way, perhaps he wouldn't beat her too badly. It was sometimes wiser to surrender and live to fight another day than to engage the enemy in a hopeless battle.

Mockël was standing right in front of her, and she was hypnotized by the quivering penis rising out of his trousers. She wanted to look away, she knew she *had* to look away, but she couldn't. She was the rodent and he the king cobra.

She raised her shackled hands in self-defense when he bent down to grab her, and she knew it was all over when she felt his fists close around her wrists.

She opened her mouth to scream, but no sound came.

She tried kicking him when he lifted her off the floor, but he deftly evaded her blows.

She winced when he reared back and cringed in anticipation of a blow that never came.

Someone slid a key into the lock.

They both froze for a second, Mockël in stupefaction and Adriana in relief. He immediately released her and Adriana collapsed, sobbing and hurting, against the wall. Had she looked up at that very moment, she would have seen Mockël hurriedly trying – and failing - to stuff his swollen member back into his pants, like a teenager caught *in flagrante delicto* by his puritan mother.

Mockël turned his back to the door when it creaked open. He was still fumbling with his clothes when Robert Mulka walked in.

Behind him, Adriana saw in disbelief, came Rita, the old kapo, and Doctor Ada.

Höss' adjutant stopped short. He clearly hadn't expected to find anyone in the cell with the prisoner, and he was trying to make sense of the scene before his eyes.

Mockël spun around and turned a deep red when he found himself face to face with his immediate superior. He saluted hurriedly, all the while hoping he'd buttoned his trousers correctly.

"Heil... Heil Hitler!" he said, trying to regain his composure.

Mulka scowled at him and didn't return the salute. "What are you doing here, Mockël? It's absolutely irregular for you to be alone with this prisoner."

Adriana immediately noticed he'd said *this* prisoner and not *a* prisoner, which confirmed that she enjoyed a special status of some sort. She then looked at the two women with Mulka, and the sympathy she read in their eyes made her want to weep.

"Yes, herr hauptsturmführer, I am well aware of the rules", Mockël stammered. "I simply thought that perhaps, alone with the prisoner, I might be able to..."

"I don't really care what you thought", Mulka interrupted him. "You disobeyed a direct order and you'll have to answer for that decision."

"Yes, herr hauptsturmführer", Mockël simply said, standing as rigidly to attention as he could.

Mulka narrowed his eyes at him.

"And what the hell happened to your neck, Mockël?" he asked suspiciously.

Mockël flushed again. "It's nothing, herr hauptsturmführer", he said. "Razor burn, nothing more."

Mulka narrowed his eyes at him even more. "You're in enough trouble as it is, Mockël", he said angrily. "Don't lie to me. That's not razor burn. It looks as though..."

He stopped and a look of absolute stupor descended over his face. "Did the prisoner attack you, Mockël? I can see the chain imprinted into your flesh!"

Mockël had no choice but to keep lying. He couldn't admit that he'd tried to rape Adriana, nor that she'd come within an inch of killing him. The first confession could end his life, and the second his career. Any other prisoner he could have and would have sent to the gas chambers, but not this one. This one's death would raise too many questions he didn't care to answer.

This one was untouchable. For now, anyway.

"Herr hauptsturmführer, if the prisoner had attacked me, she'd be dead by now", Mockël said. "I'd have killed her."

"In that case, if I were you, I'd be extremely grateful that no such thing happened", Mulka said in a tone ladened with unspoken consequences. He then turned his attention to Hadassah Bimko Rosensaft.

"You", he barked. "You'll examine the prisoner and confirm she hasn't been harmed and she's fit to return to work."

The way he said it made it amply clear that Doctor Ada had no choice in the matter. She was to declare Adriana safe and sound, even if she found her to have suffered two broken arms, two broken legs, a concussion, a collapsed lung and a lacerated liver.

Mulka motioned for Mockël to follow him and the two men exited the cell. A lively one-sided discussion, with Mulka screaming at Mockël to shut up every time the man uttered more than three consecutive words in his own defense, erupted in the hallway, but the three women paid it no attention.

Ada knelt in front of Adriana.

"Has he harmed you?" she whispered in her ear as she made great show of examining the back of her neck.

"I'm fine, Ada", Adriana replied.

"That's not what I asked you."

"Don't get involved in this, Ada. There's no need. I'm fine."

"I'm already involved", the doctor said. "They're making me sign a document confirming you are as healthy and unblemished as the Virgin Mary Herself. I just want to know how big a lie I'm telling."

"I'm fine", Adriana repeated stubbornly, and Ada sighed just as Mulka and Mockël returned.

"Well?" Mulka asked rudely.

Ada stared at Adriana for one more moment. "Not even a broken fingernail, herr hauptsturmführer", she lied. "She's perfectly... fine."

Mulka nodded contentedly, as if the issue had ever been in any doubt. "Very well. You", he said, now addressing Rita. "I'm returning this prisoner to your custody. Take her away."

Rita seemed to hesitate for an instant.

"I'm sure the hauptsturmführer would agree this prisoner will be much more efficient in the Reich's service if her hands are unshackled?" she stated, managing to hide her contempt beneath a layer of fake subservience.

Mulka sighed impatiently and fished a tiny key out of his pocket. Adriana got back onto her feet with Ada's help and held up her wrists without meeting Mulka's eyes. Her shackles clattered to the floor a second later.

Rita then grabbed her by the shoulder and hurried her out of the cell. The two women walked rapidly and Rita remained silent until they were safely out of earshot.

"Now tell me what really happened in there and what they want with you", she then said softly. "Then I'll tell you a story."

28

One week later
Somewhere between Auschwitz and Vienna
August 1943

Mattias Traugott was so groggy he could barely keep his eyes open.

The heat inside the car was stifling. He'd been on the train for almost thirty hours and it was beginning to feel as though this hellish trip might never end. The meager provisions he'd taken along had long ago been exhausted and he hadn't had anything to drink since he could remember. His mouth was parched and the muscles in his thighs had begun to cramp, both from dehydration and from the prolonged immobility.

He also smelled horrifyingly bad and his uniform, soaked with sweat and covered in grime, was a disgrace. Such an appearance would have earned him a severe reprimand back at Auschwitz but here, nobody seemed to be paying him any attention. All the other passengers were mired in their own misery and discomfort, and they had absolutely no interest in him.

The few who had looked at him when he'd come on board had quickly looked away. Where Traugott had expected admiration, he'd encountered a dislike so intense it bordered on hatred. He found the whole thing a bit unsettling. He was used to his uniform inspiring respect and fear, not contempt and resentment. He almost felt a pariah wearing it, and it was clear he could expect no favors from the other passengers during his journey.

It was true the war was going badly for the Axis. Vienna, where most of these people were probably headed, had been bombed the previous September, and less than a year from now the city would be pounded by Allied bombers. And over the past few weeks, the Allies had pummeled Sicily and the Italian mainland, including Rome for the first time, while continuing attacks against the Ruhr industrial valley had forced the Reich to evacuate thousands of German civilians from the area. The Nazi forces had also been routed by the Red Army near Kursk, forcing Hitler to call off Operation Citadel.

Perhaps this explained why the other passengers seemed to be ignoring him. Perhaps it had nothing to do with his disheveled and unkempt allure. Maybe he simply made an easy and convenient scapegoat for all that was wrong with their lives.

Traugott's nerves were frayed and he wondered how long he'd be able to keep his temper in check. He'd boarded the train too late to sit by the window, where he might at least have got some air, but he now saw it made little difference. The train was usually stopped for one reason or another, and then it turned into an oven and the heat became inhuman. Even the previous night had brought limited relief. And even when the train finally rolled, it moved so slowly that little air came in through the narrow windows.

Sitting by the window would have done nothing to make this more bearable.

Traugott ended up sitting next to an overweight man who occupied much more than the half of the seat to which his ticket logically entitled him. The man's massive right thigh inconsiderately spilled over the imaginary border between them, forcing Traugott to sit slightly sideways and making him want to smash the fat man's face into a bloody pulp.

To make matters even worse, if such a thing was possible, the man had procured several links of the stinkiest, smelliest sausage Traugott had ever come across and he'd been munching on it almost without interruption since the start of the trip. Not only did he sound like a ruminating cow but now, after almost two days spent traversing the man's digestive system, the spicy meat had reached the end of its journey, resulting in a seemingly endless cannonade of thunderous and odoriferous flatulence.

It was probably a good thing Höss had forced him to surrender his sidearm when he'd suspended him for a week. Otherwise, the next time the man made to lift his right buttock to relieve the pressure building up in his intestines, Traugott might have saved him the trouble and bore him another hole through which to vent his gases.

The train eventually pulled into the *Wien Westbahnhof* station, on Vienna's west side, after what felt like an eternity. Some passengers clapped and cheered sarcastically, but Traugott hurried off and hailed a cab. His mother's house was only fifteen minutes away and he normally would have strolled there, but after the interminable ordeal he'd just endured, he was eager to arrive as rapidly as possible.

The cab driver nervously eyed the uniformed man in his rear-view mirror and tried to engage him in a conversation about how the war was going, but Traugott couldn't have been less interested. His only replies were distracted *das* and *neins* and *vielleichts*. The driver then assured him he was a loyal citizen of the Reich, who was doing his part to help win the war.

That shook Traugott out of his moroseness. He snorted impatiently and stared at the man directly for the first time. He asked him why, exactly, he wasn't at the front fighting the Russians or helping prepare to repulse the Allied invasion that was certainly coming. The driver turned red as a beet and muttered something about an old back injury. He then thought it wiser to drive the rest of the way in silence, leaving Traugott to his somber thoughts.

He wondered how his mother would receive him. There had been no time to write or call and she had no idea he was coming. Not that it mattered, since he really had nowhere else to go. Going to his father in Germany had certainly not been an option, even though he'd lived with him for a while after his parents' divorce. That ended on the day Leonhard Traugott discovered his teenage son parading in front of the mirror in his brand new *Hitlerjugend* uniform. Claiming Hitler was a madman who would lead Germany to its destruction, he flew into a rage and presented Mattias with an ultimatum: quit that band of thugs, as he'd called them, or leave my house.

Stung by his father's cowardice and lack of patriotism, Traugott went to find his mother Teresia, who had moved back to Vienna after the divorce. She hadn't been overjoyed by his decision to join the Hitler Youth but at least she'd been willing to tolerate it, seeing it as no more than an adolescent fad that would rapidly fade away. She might have reacted differently, had she known it would lead to a career in the SS.

The two of them learned to get along by avoiding certain issues on which their views differed radically. Their relationship would never be described as warm and loving, but at least they still talked every once in a while. The fact that they never discussed anything of substance anymore – *How's the weather where you are? Here it's been raining for days. Did I tell you old Mrs Wimmer died? Yes, she'd been quite sick* - was best left unmentioned.

Traugott smiled thinly when the cab drove past the *biergarten* where he and other members of his HJ unit had gotten completely drunk one memorable night after he'd been bestowed with the single *sig* rune, the victory symbol, by the SS. That honor had practically guaranteed his admittance to the *Schutzstaffel* less than a year later. It still counted as one of the proudest days of his life. How old had he been at the time? Eighteen? Nineteen, maybe? He mostly remembered feeling completely invulnerable and indestructible. It was Germany's destiny to rule the world, and he'd been chosen to help her do it.

If he'd only known.

The cab pulled up slowly alongside the curb, startling Traugott out of his reverie. They'd arrived. He exited the car after distractedly handing the driver a few Reichsmarks and grabbing his bag on the seat next to him. He closed the car door discretely, not wishing to alert the house to his arrival. He needed a moment to collect his thoughts before making himself known.

He stared at the small wooden door in front of him, again wondering how he'd be welcomed. The name *T. Schlamelcher* – his mother had reverted to her maiden name after the divorce – was painted in small white letters across the middle. The yellow flower boxes were still there. Traugott then looked down at his filthy uniform and scuffed jackboots, and wished he cut a better, more impressive figure. It wouldn't make one iota of difference to his mother, but at least he would have felt better about himself, more confident.

He let out a wary sigh and rang the doorbell. The familiar chime echoed in the vast residence, but nothing happened. Perhaps she wasn't home? He rang again, and this time he was rewarded by the sound of cautious footsteps on the other side of the door.

"*Wer ist da?*" a voice he instantly recognized asked.

He smiled in spite of himself. His mother had always been very prudent, though her caution perhaps made more sense in this day and age. "*Es ist mir, Mutti*", he said. "Mattias."

He could have sworn he heard her gasp, and in his mind he imagined her stepping away from the door and raising a hand to her mouth to cover her shock. He waited for the door to open, but it remained firmly closed and locked. Maybe she hadn't heard him clearly.

He stepped closer to the door and knocked gently.

"Are you there, Mutti?" he said a bit louder. "It's me. Ty. Please open the door."

If she hadn't recognized his voice, she would certainly recognize his nickname since childhood.

An old man shuffled by on the the sidewalk behind him. Alerted by the sound of slippers scraping against the cement, Traugott turned and saluted politely, but the old man just glanced at his dirty uniform and muttered under his breath something that sounded suspiciously like "*no wonder we're losing the war*" before noisily gliding away.

Traugott was growing somewhat worried, and more than a bit annoyed, at being kept waiting for so long. Why wasn't she opening the door? Had she suddenly lost her mind, to the point that she no longer knew him?

"Mutti, it's me, Mattias. *Your son*", he said forcefully. "Open the door. There's nothing to worry about. Please let me in."

A few more seconds elapsed before bolts were finally pulled and locks snapped. The door slowly yawned open, but only by a couple of inches. Traugott saw that one final security chain hadn't been unfastened. An old woman, her snowy white hair pulled back in a tight bun, peered through the opening. She raised a hand to her mouth and her eyes grew wide, just as Traugott had imagined a few seconds ago. He smiled at her.

"Hello Mutti", he said gently.

"*Ach du lieber*", Teresia Schlamelcher breathed in a barely audible voice. "Ty. You're alive. You're back."

They stared at each other for a moment, speechless. "Mutti... the chain?" Traugott finally said. His mother looked at the security device and seemed startled, as though she hadn't noticed it before. She closed the door, unfastened the chain, and opened the door again, this time completely.

She took a step back, which Traugott interpreted as permission to come in. He stepped inside and slowly closed the door behind him. He put his bag down and smiled at finding himself here, now, again, after all that had happened.

The house was as he remembered it, as if it had been frozen in time when he left. Even the ugly wallpaper was the same. On his right, a staircase climbed along the wall to the second floor, where all the bedrooms were. Directly in front of him, behind his mother and splitting the house in two, ran a corridor that led to the kitchen – his favorite room, since it was always bathed by the morning sun. And on his left a double door, currently closed, gave access to a large room that served both as living room and dining room.

He returned his gaze to his mother and smiled again. She, too, was as he remembered her, even though he'd only seen her once or twice since the start of the war. Her hair was whiter than he recalled and her wrinkles were perhaps a bit deeper, but her sea-blue eyes were as alive and as piercing as ever.

He was, on the other hand, a bit unsettled by her reaction to his sudden arrival. She seemed completely stunned, and while he hadn't expected to be showered with hugs and kisses, neither had he expected her to stare at him silently as she was now, as though she didn't quite know what to make of this filthy stranger who'd been dropped on her doorstep.

She looked him up and down, and he felt compelled to apologize for his appearance. "I've been traveling for almost two days", he explained. "The conditions on board the train were... well, the war is hard on us all."

Still, Teresia remained silent. "I'd offer you a hug, but I'm afraid you'd stink for a week", he joked, hoping to alleviate the uneasiness between them.

That seemed to break her paralysis. She came to him rapidly and wrapped her arms around his neck, pulling him to her. He hugged her back gratefully.

"Forgive me, Ty", she said softly. "It's just that..." She stopped in mid-sentence, as though she'd caught herself just in time. "You're my son and I love you. No matter how bad you look. Or how horrible you smell."

They both laughed as they broke the embrace.

"But what are you doing here?" she asked.

"My... my commanding officer gave me some time off", he half-lied. "It all happened very rapidly and there was no time to write or call to warn you. I'll tell you more about it later."

She nodded a bit too quickly and Traugott narrowed his eyes at her. Was she even listening to him? He again got the feeling his impromptu arrival had deeply unsettled her. A small alarm bell went off at the back of his skull.

"I just finished baking some chocolate *lebkuchen*", she said. His stomach grumbled at the mouth-watering smell; his brain worried how she'd been able to procure chocolate. "I'll put some tea on the stove. But first..."

He took the hint. "I'll go take a shower", he said with a smile.

She nodded again. "I've still got some of your old clothes upstairs", she said. "I'll bring them down so you can change out of whatever that *thing* is you're wearing."

Was she referring to his filthy clothes or to a uniform for which he knew she held no love? He decided to let it pass. He gave her a peck on the cheek and made a beeline for the bathroom.

As soon as she heard him close the door, Teresia buried her face in her hands and fought the panic that threatened to submerge her.

What was she going to do now?

29

Block 24
Auschwitz brothel
August 1943

The inmate fingered his voucher nervously and tried to summon the courage to speak.

"But, herr obersturmführer...", he began timidly. "She is but a child... and her mind seems to be gone."

Mockël sneered at the emaciated man before him.

"What do you care?" he growled. "You haven't been with a woman in years!"

The inmate glanced at the girl lying in the small room. The 14-year-old Mockël had conscripted earlier had never recovered from being raped – or, as Mockël liked to think of it, *broken* - by

Achtzehn. She had to be hand-fed three times a day and she'd been known to soil herself at the most inopportune moments. She was also prone to sudden fits of mad shrieking.

Otherwise, she spent her days staring at the ceiling, unblinking.

"Get to it!" Mockël roared, shoving the man into the room. "You've only got 13 minutes left."

He shut the door and looked at his watch. He noted the time to make sure the inmate didn't stay in there one second longer than the 15 minutes he was allowed. If he wasn't done by then, well, better luck next time.

This was still getting to be a problem. This inmate wasn't the first to complain about the girl. Most of those who'd been assigned to her had been too needy to make trouble. Mockël doubted they'd even noticed who they were rutting with. Most had simply jumped on top of the girl, lifted her thin gown above her hips and been done before Mockël had smoked a cigarette.

Animals.

But there had also been a few puritan prudes who'd balked at being presented with such a "reward" for their good behavior and hard work. Some had even handed Mockël their voucher and walked away, shaking their heads in disbelief. Others had grumbled about the girl's lack of vivacity.

Mockël found their complaints infuriating. What had the ungrateful bastards expected, exactly? A night with Hedy Lamarr? If they wished to pass up a few minutes of carnal pleasure with a woman after going without for months and years, let them. The girl was the perfect whore, as far as Mockël was concerned, since the men could do whatever they wanted to her. Nothing, no matter how perverse, was off-limits.

Mockël didn't care the first thing about the inmates' dissatisfaction. What he did care about, on the other hand, was word of the situation eventually reaching Robert Mulka or, even worse, Rudolf Höss.

The brothel was the camp commander's pet project of the moment. Höss truly believed inmates promised unrestrained access to a female body would work harder and be better behaved. But a rumor – even a greatly exaggerated one - that the waiting women were nothing more than catatonic children could undermine the whole thing. Mockël knew he had to get a grip on the situation before it got out of hand.

The door opened behind him and the inmate exited sheepishly, his shoulders stooped in shame.

Mockël smiled sadistically as he watched him go. So the man had overcome his scruples after all.

On the other side of the door, the girl began to howl.

Traugott tore in half one of the barley rolls his mother had reheated in the oven and wiped the last of his oatmeal off the bottom of his bowl. After years of war and deprivation, this simple meal tasted heavenly.

All that was missing was a cup of real coffee, but the stuff was simply no longer obtainable. Instead, they had to make do with what passed for coffee in wartime - acorns, chicory or grain that had been roasted and ground up, depending on what was at hand. The end product usually smelled horrible and tasted even worse, but at least it was hot.

He raised a fist to his mouth and burped as softly and discretely as he could. His mother still noticed and smiled benevolently at him.

"Sorry about my military manners", he apologized.

She smiled again. "It's good to have you home, Ty", she said.

He couldn't help but wonder whether she truly meant it, after the strange welcome he'd received the day before. Even this morning she still felt distant and wary, as though there had appeared between them a small chasm he was unable to bridge.

Teresia took a sip of her own *ersatz* coffee and grimaced. "Worst ever", she pronounced it. "The last letter I received from you mentioned you were being transferred to a camp in Poland", she went on, changing the subject.

Traugott's eyebrows shot up. "Really? That's the last one you got? I've written at least twice since then, as best as I can remember." He shrugged and smirked. "I think the *Reichspost* is struggling to keep up with the Wehrmacht."

She offered him a smile devoid of all warmth, as though she were merely being polite. "I'm sure the Reich's leaders have more urgent matters to attend to than delivering our mail on time", she said, again prompting him to wonder what, exactly, she meant.

"Tell me about this camp of yours", Teresia went on, once again changing the subject.

Traugott cleared his dishes and went to dump them in the sink before answering. He needed a few seconds to think of an appropriate reply, since he knew he couldn't tell her the truth. As he gathered his thoughts, he noticed the cupboard above the sink hadn't been shut all the way, and inside he glanced half a dozen *Deutsches Rotes Kreuz* Chocolate Tins.

Slowly, he pushed the door closed. That explained the *lebkuchen* his mother had baked the previous evening. It did not, on the other hand, explain how she had procured emergency foodstuffs those the Red Cross didn't deem needy could only obtain on the black market – and even then solely at an absurd price.

He let the matter go for the moment. Teresia was still waiting for his answer and in the end, he opted for a simple lie that wasn't too far removed from the truth.

He returned to the table and downed the last of his coffee. "It's just a prisoner of war camp", he said. "Nothing special."

"You mean... like Russian soldiers?" she asked, trying to sound indifferent.

He felt as though they were sparring, each probing the other's defenses, looking for a weakness, a vulnerability.

"Yes, something of the kind", Traugott said. Then, almost without thinking, he added: "We also get criminals that pose a threat to the Reich."

That intrigued her. "Criminals? What do you mean?"

Traugott immediately wished he could take back the last ten seconds. How could he explain the criminals he meant were Jews and gypsies and homosexuals and crippled and other so-called *deviants*? He firmly believed these people needed to be kept under control, that their elimination was an absolute necessity, but he also knew enough about his mother's views to understand this wasn't a conversation he could have with her.

So the sparring continued.

"Criminals, Mutti", he said after a moment. "Murderers and rapists and such. We make sure they can't harm anyone anymore."

This last sentence was true, at least. Anyone sent to Auschwitz rapidly became incapable of committing any further harm.

His mother was staring at him in a manner that made him uncomfortable. "There are stories,

Ty", she finally said slowly, as though each word weighed a ton. "Stories of camps were people are being sent to die. Not prisons, not camps for prisoners of war, but... *death camps*, some are calling them."

He knew she was watching his reaction closely and he tried to remain as impassive as possible.

Reich Minister of Propaganda Joseph Goebbels had done a masterful job mobilizing the population in favor of the war effort. The movies his ministry had produced, and which invariably presented the German soldier as civilization's last rampart against hordes of demented and bloodthirsty barbarians, were truly rousing. Those movies exposing the Jews' dishonesty and avarice had also opened many eyes.

But pockets of skepticism still remained. There were still those who failed to see the danger at hand, those who didn't have the stomach to do what needed to be done, those who simply... didn't... understand. Those were the ones that couldn't be told the truth, lest they then contaminate the others with their plague of doubt and dissent.

The truth needed to be hidden from people like Teresia Schlamelcher.

Still, Traugott knew that any attempt to talk his way around his mother's question would simply make him look guilty. He had to meet it head on. So in his mind he flipped the switch from *loving son* to *SS soldier* and he tried to view her not as his mother, but as an enemy of the Reich. He didn't succeed entirely, but enough to keep from betraying anything.

"Stories, Mutti, nothing more", he replied coldly. "Stories told by people trying to undermine what we're building. Stories told by traitors to our cause. You should take care who you repeat these stories to. They could cause you much trouble if they fell upon the wrong ears."

Is he threatening me?, Teresia Schlamelcher wondered. *Is my own son threatening me in my own home? Has it come to this?*

Traugott sensed her uneasiness and smiled. "But you obviously have nothing to fear from me", he tried to reassure her. "I'm just asking you to be careful, that's all."

A noise came from upstairs before she could reply, startling him.

"What was that?" he asked.

His mother looked flustered. "I think there's a rat", she said rapidly.

"A rat? I'll take care of it. Just give me a broom", he immediately offered.

"No, no, no, there's no need", she protested. "I'll just borrow Mr Schmidt's cat. He'll take care of it."

"Mutti, you're allergic to cats", he reminded her. His pulse began to race. "What's going on here?"

His mother remained silent and looked down. Traugott pushed his chair away from the table and got up.

"Where are you going?" Teresia asked, clearly worried.

"Upstairs, to find your *rat*", he said angrily as he headed for the staircase that led to the second floor.

"Ty, don't!" she almost screamed as she sprang up to come after him. He ignored her as he bounded up the stairs, two at a time.

He went first to the room where he'd slept the previous night, though he knew he'd find nothing there. If there had been a rat, he'd have heard it. He still checked under the bed and behind the curtains and in the closet, but came up empty-handed.

There were two other bedrooms, including his mother's, and a bathroom on that floor. He checked the second guest bedroom, but it only held a single bed and a small three-drawer dresser. There was nowhere for anything to hide. He still checked under the bed and in each drawer just in case.

He didn't find as much as a dried-up pellet of rat droppings.

"Ty, please, there's really no need to trouble yourself", his mother pleaded as he headed for her own bedroom. "Please, let's go back downstairs and finish our coffee."

He barely heard her

He paused before entering the room. As a child, before his parents' divorce, their bedroom had been his favorite room in the whole house. He'd crawl into bed between the two of them almost every morning and his mother, only half-awake, would cradle him in her arms while his father snored softly next to them. Never in his life had he felt safer than on those mornings, cocooned under the thick covers as his mother stroked his hair.

Then one morning he found Teresia alone in the wide bed, her pillow still wet from the tears she'd shed during the night. She'd explained things he'd been too young to understand, about love coming in different shapes and colors, about love being a living thing that's constantly changing and evolving, about how those changes are sometimes for the best and sometimes not, about his father and her still loving one another but no longer being *in* love... He tuned her out when he finally understood the three of them would never again cuddle in the same bed, his feeling of safety gone and never to return.

He shook his head to clear the memories and entered the bedroom.

His mother had always been tidy to the point of obsession, and she still was today. Her bed looked as though she'd gone over the edges with a straight razor. Her shoes were neatly lined up along the far wall. Iif he opened the closet, he'd find her blouses sorted by size and color and each skirt hung on a separate hanger. Her bathrobe would be on a hook behind the door and each hat stored in its own box on the shelf. The surface of her dresser was entirely bare and looked clean enough to perform surgery.

His father had sometimes joked Teresia could dress in complete darkness and still manage to look sharp, since she knew with unerring precision where each article of clothing she owned could be found.

Traugott gazed around the room, looking for any sign of a furry, four-footed and long-tailed intruder. He was loathe to invade his mother's privacy by going through her things. If he did, she'd later spend countless hours returning everything to its proper place – including those items he hadn't disturbed.

He sighed.

"I'll check the bathroom first", he said to no one in particular. His mother simply stood with her back against the wall, wringing her hands and looking distraught.

The bathroom was at the other end of the hallway, but he was stopped short by a strange smell.

This was a smell he knew from somewhere, though definitely not one he associated with his childhood or his mother. He needed a couple of seconds to remember where he'd encountered it before and when the memory finally came to him, it turned his insides to water.

Traugott lived in a world where everything was possible, where everything could happen. Wasn't he himself proof that this was the truth of it? Who could have imagined an SS guard – dare he admit it to himself? - falling in love with a Jewish inmate? If this didn't prove anything could, and usually did, happen, he didn't know what did.

But this? No, *this* couldn't be.

His first thought, his first hope, was that the smell emanated from the bathroom, but *that* also couldn't be. His mother's fastidiousness would never, ever tolerate such a thing. So the smell had to come from somewhere else, and he'd already checked every other room on this floor. The smell was also not noticeable on the first floor.

That left only one possibility.

He looked up and pulled on the rope that slowly lowered the narrow staircase that climbed into the attic. The abominable stench that immediately cascaded down through the opening confirmed his worst fears. He took a step back and placed a hand against his mouth to keep from gagging.

He looked at his mother with eyes of fury.

"Oh you silly woman", he said angrily. "How can you have been so stupid."

Teresia Schlamelcher buried her face in her hands and burst out in tears.

31

"You understand they're using you, don't you?" Rita said softly. "*All* of them."

The two women were making their way back to their barracks, but their progress was slowed by columns of shuffling prisoners or by guards demanding to know where they were going. Two inmates walking about by themselves could only arouse suspicions, but Robert Mulka had given Rita the necessary passes and they were allowed to be on their way.

Most of the guards also knew Rita by sight, if not by name, and they implicitly trusted the old woman. Still, Auschwitz's inner courtyard was a maze of dozens of sectors divided by miles and miles of fences, and they'd have to go through at least ten gates before reaching their destination.

Adriana nodded. She had just finished telling the kapo about her ordeal of the previous five days, about the questions she'd been asked concerning her relationship with Traugott and about her feeling that someone very powerful was protecting her.

She had, however, stopped short of telling her about Mockël's attempted rape, though she was sure Rita had guessed what had happened.

"Whatever you're involved in is very, very dangerous", Rita continued. Adriana opened her mouth to protest she wasn't involved in *anything*, but Rita silenced her with a gentle wave of the hand, as though it didn't matter. "These men have no honor and they can't be trusted. Whatever you've been told is a lie. Whatever promises you were made won't be kept. Whatever you think you know is certainly wrong. All you are to them is a club with which to bash their enemies."

"But I didn't tell them anything, because there was nothing to tell", Adriana replied.

Rita's smile told Adriana she wasn't fooling the old woman. "You don't need me to tell you the truth is of no relevance", she said, echoing Adriana's earlier thoughts. "All that matters is what they believe to be the truth. And right now, someone, somewhere believes you've still got information they need. Otherwise, you'd be dead."

Adriana had figured out as much by herself, but hearing someone else say it made her shiver. "So...", she began.

They were stopped at yet another checkpoint and showed the guard their papers. He looked them over briefly before allowing them through the gate and into the next sector.

"So", Rita repeated once they were through, "this isn't even close to being over. They'll come for you again and again and again, until you either tell them what they want to hear, or they decide you aren't of any use to them any longer. And when that happens..."

"When that happens", Adriana completed. "I'm dead, since the truth doesn't matter."

"The truth doesn't matter", Rita echoed. "But that's pretty much the way of the world, believe me."

Adriana remained silent, sensing more was coming. Rita seemed to be in a very pensive and reflexive mood, even by her own standards.

"There was a man in the village where I lived", the old kapo began. "A strange man, who lived alone and never bathed. The kind of man some people threaten their children with if they won't go to sleep quietly. *If you're not asleep in two minutes, the bad man will come and take you away!* How stupid I was."

"Stupid?" Adriana asked.

"Stupid to have taken him so lightly, to have thought him a harmless fool who had perhaps been touched by a spirit", Rita explained after a moment. There was a rare note of impatience in her voice, as though these events still troubled her greatly. "He'd been touched alright, but not by a spirit. He'd been touched by a demon."

Rita signed herself and seemed to mutter a quick prayer. The guard checking their passes at that moment gave her a strange look before allowing them through.

"I choose to believe people are good until they give me cause to think otherwise. Why should I fear him simply because of the way he lives his life? Maybe some great misfortune had befallen him and explained his behavior. Who was I to judge this man? *He that is without sin among you, let him first cast a stone.* So I used to visit him to bring him a bit of food", Rita said. "I'd go whenever I could, whenever I'd baked an extra loaf of bread or in the fall to share my preserves. I don't think we ever exchanged more than ten words. Most of the time he simply ignored me. I don't think he even knew I was there."

"Why did you take care of him like this?" Adriana asked.

Rita smiled again. "Always that question... Why, why, why?" the old kapo said. "All the time the other villagers asked me... *Rita, why do you go over there? You shouldn't mind him, he's dangerous! If you keep feeding him he'll never go away!* So I'll tell you what I used to tell them: I did it simply because it was the right thing to do. Because if you do right by people, then people will do right by you. Nothing more, nothing less."

Adriana waited for the rest of the tale. Rita stopped walking and stared at the ground, as though her mind was a million miles away.

"Then one day seven children disappeared", she breathed. "Seven boys and girls, all gone at once. Seven little angels, Adriana. *Seven.*"

Rita then fell silent for a long time and Adriana thought perhaps she didn't have the strength to go on. She placed a hand on her friend's shoulder.

"Rita, please... You don't have to...", she began.

The kapo grabbed Adriana's hand and squeezed it hard. "It's alright", she said. "I'm almost done."

"The children were found in the woods behind this man's cabin", Rita went on. "Hung by their feet from the trees and their throats slit, like hogs. The man was collecting their blood in large bowls. He was drenched in it from head to toe when the villagers arrived."

"And they killed him", Adriana guessed.

Rita laughed again, but her laughter was one of derision. "Oh Lord no", she said. "They did much worse than that. They tied him to a tree and each parent took turns slashing him and burning him. They gouged out his eyes and they cut off his genitals and they did all sorts of unspeakable things to him. But they also made sure to keep him alive. Then they set him afire and sent him back to the hell from whence he'd come."

"The police didn't stop them?"

"The police weren't there. Obviously no one called them."

"But the children... Why seven?" Adriana asked.

Rita shrugged. "Who knows?" she said. "There were dozens of Bibles in his cabin. Stacks upon stacks and rows upon rows of Bibles. And in the Bible are mentioned the seven days of Genesis, the seven seals of Revelation, the seven devils cast out of Mary Magdalene, the seven spirits of God, the seven last plagues, the voice of the seventh angel, and of course the seven deadly sins.. Or maybe he just took seven because that's how many he found. We'll never know."

"Were you one of those villagers?" Adriana asked. "Is that why you're here? Because you took part in..."

"No, that's not why I'm here", Rita interrupted her, finally looking up. Adriana saw tears in her eyes. "The villagers weren't satisfied with his death. Their rage and their grief demanded more blood. Then one of them remembered I'd fed him. And another noticed my own daughter hadn't been taken."

"Oh no...", Adriana whispered, but Rita didn't hear her.

"I can still see the mob outside my house", the old woman said. "They had pitchforks and axes and hammers and torches and..." She closed her eyes and shook her head, as though to dispel the memory. "But luckily I heard them coming and I was able to grab a gun my husband had left me. That allowed me to hold them off just long enough for the police to arrive and save us, my daughter and me. They took us away and I thought we were safe."

"But you weren't", Adriana said.

"Far from it", Rita confirmed. "The police chief was the godfather of one of the dead children. The villagers began telling him how I'd been friends with this man, how I'd encouraged him to remain in the village... It was completely ludicrous. In the end, I think they had me celebrating dark masses with him by the full Moon."

"And he believed them?" Adriana asked.

Rita smiled at her mischievously. "If you think that's of any relevance, then you haven't been paying attention", she said. "The police chief had lost his goddaughter. His own family was demanding... *demanding!*... some retribution, some sort of justice. And these were people he'd have to live with the next day, and the week after that, and the month after that... And there I was, sitting in a cell, and he had dozens of so-called witnesses all ready to swear upon their souls that I'd committed some of the worst crimes you can imagine."

"The truth didn't matter", Adriana whispered.

"No, Adriana", Rita said. "The truth. Most certainly. Did not matter."

32

Traugott couldn't bring himself to climb up into the attic.

For if he did, he would see. And if he saw, he would know for sure. And once he knew for sure, he could never revert to not knowing. And once his claim to plausible deniability slain... well, what then?

Perhaps thinking the same thoughts, Teresia Schlamelcher tried one last time to dissuade him. "You don't have to go up there, Mattias", she said in a strangled voice. He noticed she hadn't called him by his nickname. "Just turn around and go back downstairs. Your coffee is getting cold."

She was right. He was under no obligation to do anything. He wasn't on duty, she was his mother, and he could simply pretend not to have noticed anything. No one would ever know, but for the two of them.

Except he couldn't simply shrug and walk away. The Reich, his Führer, the SS... all had taken him in and given him a sense of purpose at a time when he'd been dangerously adrift. They'd offered him a family at a time when he'd had none. If not for them, he might have ended up in prison or dead in the gutter. They had molded him into the man he was today and he could never live with himself if he were to repay their trust with such an act of cowardice and treason.

So instead of taking a step back, he took a step forward and placed a foot on the first step. The staircase groaned under his weight. It groaned again, as if to warn him against his decision, when, slowly and deliberately, his foot came to rest on the second step.

"Ty, don't", his mother said. "There's no need."

She was standing at the foot of the staircase. He hadn't noticed her coming up silently behind him. When he looked at her over his shoulder, the eyes he encountered had lost all fear and sadness. Her gaze was steady and her features had hardened into a mask of resignation and determination. It made him pause.

"I don't have a choice Mutti", he said. "Don't try to stop me."

"There's always a choice", she replied immediately, "but that's not what I meant."

She stared at him a moment longer, hoping against hope he might change his mind at the last second. When he didn't move, she called out in a louder voice: "Please come down, Mrs Pflaumlocher. He knows you're up there. There's nothing more we can do."

Traugott wasn't really surprised. He had already guessed his mother, for reasons he couldn't begin to fathom, was harboring Jews in her attic. Though he'd occasionally heard of such things happening across the Reich, it still shocked him that some would be willing to take such a risk; those caught in the act were shipped off to concentration camps, when they were not simply sentenced to die.

He climbed back down slowly, all the while keeping his eyes locked on the dark opening in the ceiling, but nothing happened.

"Mrs Pflaumlocher, please...", Teresia called out again. "I know you're scared, but please come down. If you don't, he'll come up and find you. And we don't want that, I assure you."

Traugott's head snapped around and he stared at his mother with both surprise and dismay. What had she meant by that last comment? What kind of monster did she believe him to be? What did she fear he might do? Rush up into the attic and smash everything and hurt – nay, slaughter! - whoever was hiding up there? How could she know him so badly? How could she possibly think such a thing?

Or maybe she knows you better than you think, a little voice whispered from the dark recesses of his mind.

And that name, Pflaumlocher... It hadn't struck him at first but now, hearing it a second time, a memory arose from his past to take a swipe at him, for the moment as blurred and hazy and terrifying as a medieval knight charging through thick fog.

A noise came from the attic, distracting him. He immediately looked up.

A pair of dirty slippers had appeared in the opening. He could see feet socked in gray in the slippers and the hem of a gown, but nothing more. The feet remained motionless for several seconds before finally beginning their slow descent. And the further down they came, the more they revealed of Teresia Schlamelcher's alleged rat.

The woman looked to be at least 100 years old. Her grimy face was heavily wrinkled and her dirty white hair had been tied in a loose ponytail. She was wearing a threadbare gown Traugott recognized as having once belonged to his mother. She kept her hands clasped in front of her, revealing a network a dark blue veins under the parchment-like skin.

She also smelled horribly bad, showing that she hadn't bathed in weeks. And that was the smell that had given her away, the smell that he'd noticed – the stench of a train delivering Jews at Auschwitz.

He took a step back when she reached the bottom of the staircase. The woman appeared vaguely familiar when she came to stand directly in front of him.

She stared at him with eyes that were remarkably calm and serene.

"Hello, Ty", she said. "Forgive my appearance, but I don't get out much these days. How have you been?"

Washington D.C.

The small man sat on the edge of his chair with his hands clasped between his knees.

So much depended on his mission, it was hard to believe. The next few minutes, and the men on the other side of that door, would determine the fate of hundreds of thousands, of millions, of human beings.

And yet such was his faith in his cause that he hardly felt nervous at all. If anything, he felt a bit too confident and he knew he'd have to be careful, lest he come across as arrogant and hinder his chances. He'd already had half a dozen such meetings all over Europe with representatives from at least four governments. He was becoming an old hand at this. He already knew what he'd say, the questions they'd ask, the answers he'd provide, the objections they'd raise and the arguments with which he'd counterattack. He was ready.

But his confidence mostly came from his unshakable belief in the righteousness of his cause. When he told them what he knew, when he shared with them what he'd seen and heard and done, what choice would they have but to grant him the assistance he sought? Who could possibly remain impassive and indifferent in the face of such evil?

And if these men wouldn't listen, if they wouldn't believe and if they wouldn't help, he'd find others who would. No later than this evening he was scheduled to have dinner with Cardinal Samuel Stritch, the powerful and influential Archbishop of Chicago, who happened to be in town for a conference. It was his hope the cardinal would then inform pope Pius XII. And tomorrow he'd board a train for Los Angeles where a friend had promised to introduce him to some of Hollywood's biggest stars.

Someone, somewhere, would listen and believe. He wouldn't stop until they did.

The door opened silently and a woman emerged. "The President will see you now, Mr Kozielewski", she said.

He immediately got up and bowed politely. "Thank you, Mrs Tully".

Despite the confidence that fueled his demeanor, Jan Romuald Kozielewski still felt a tinge of trepidation when he crossed the threshold of the Oval Office and entered the inner sanctum of the most powerful nation on Earth. No matter what he told himself, this meeting wouldn't be like the previous ones.

The President's personal secretary, Grace Tully, shut the door behind him but he hardly noticed.

Three men were standing around Franklin Delano Roosevelt's desk at the far end of the room, conferring busily with the President. The three huge windows behind the presidential desk let in a flood of sunlight that outlined the men in shadows, but Kozielewski had done his homework and knew who they were: Secretary of State Cordell Hull; admiral William D. Leahy, the chairman of the Joint Chiefs of Staff; and Harry Hopkins, one of the President's top aides.

The men were so absorbed by their discussion that they didn't notice him at first, which gave Kozielewski time to look around. He was immediately struck by how sparsely furnished the room was: several chairs were arranged around the desk, a few others lined the walls, as did a dark-colored couch, and a model of a three-masted schooner sailed on a small wooden table on his right, but that was pretty much it. The walls were also essentially bare, and the room had a strangely austere and spartan, almost monastic, air. It seemed to have been furnished in haste with whatever furniture was available.

Kozielewski felt slightly disappointed. The office of the President of the United States looked like that of a second-rate accountant. He sighed.

Hopkins finally noticed him. He broke away from the group and came toward him with an outstretched hand.

"Mr Kozielewski, welcome", he said warmly, shaking his guest's hand. "I'm sorry to have kept you waiting."

"Not at all, Mr Hopkins", Kozielewski immediately replied. "I appreciate the President granting me a few minutes of his time. I'll make it worth his while, I assure you."

"I'm sure you will", Hopkins said. "Please come this way."

Kozielewski allowed Hopkins to introduce him to the assembled men, even though he already knew who they were. Handshakes were exchanged, but Roosevelt remained seated. He neither apologized nor explained, nor did he need to. The President had been paralyzed from the waist down by polio over 20 years earlier, and the strain of leading the country in this time of war was said to be taking its toll on his already fragile health.

The fact that he only moved around in a wheelchair also probably explained the scarcity of furniture in the Oval Office.

"Please be seated", Roosevelt said sternly. The men arrayed the chairs in a rough semi-circle in front of his desk and Kozielewski found himself sitting directly across from the President, with Hopkins on his left and Hull on his right. Admiral Leahy remained standing and kept pacing in a tight circle, his chin resting in the palm of his hand.

A moment of uneasy silence followed, until Kozielewski realized the men were waiting for him to say something. He found himself staring directly into the grayish eyes of the President of the United States, and for a very brief instant his confidence faltered.

But only for a very, very brief instant.

"One year ago members of the Jewish resistance in Europe smuggled me into the Warsaw Ghetto", he began in a tone that immediately told them they needed to pay close attention to what he had to say. "I only wish I possessed the eloquence required to convey to you what I witnessed there, but I unfortunately do not. All I can do, Mr President, gentlemen, is share with you what I saw."

He paused and closed his eyes, reliving the scene in his mind.

"A young Jewish woman was walking down the street", Kozielewski said slowly. "She had a child of no more than one in her arms. As I watched, four German soldiers surrounded her and one of them snatched the child from her arms while the three others restrained her. The woman began screaming, but they just laughed. Then the soldier grabbed the child by the ankles, swung him around his head a few times and slammed his head against the edge of a brick wall. The impact almost ripped the child's head from his body."

He paused again to allow the image to be seared into their minds.

"I have never, never heard anyone scream like that poor woman did when they killed her child, and I hope I never do again", Kozielewski went on. "The soldier just dropped the body of the child and walked away. I heard him curse because some blood had splattered his uniform. He sounded quite upset."

"What happened to the woman?" Cordell Hull asked somberly.

Kozielewski looked at the Secretary of State. "When they released her, she simply collapsed", he said. "Then she began crawling toward the body of her child, but she didn't make it. After a few seconds her eyes rolled up into her head and she began foaming at the mouth. Her body shook uncontrollably for what seemed like a long, long time, quivering in the dirt, and then she just... died."

Another silence followed. But this time, it was the silence of men unable to think of anything to say. Hopkins wanted to ask why no one had intervened, why no one had helped the woman, but he didn't. The answer was too obvious.

"War is a nasty, horrible business", Franklin Roosevelt finally stated. "I can assure you our American boys fighting in the Pacific aren't spending their days lounging on a beach."

Kozielewski had expected a reply of the sort, and he was ready. "I would respectfully point out, Mr President, that at least your soldiers have a chance to fight back and defend themselves", he said. "This poor woman did not. All she could do was watch as the Germans murdered her baby in front of her eyes."

"Atrocities are an unfortunate part of war", admiral Leahy contributed from behind them.

"*Unfortunate* is hardly the word I would choose, admiral", Kozielewski replied icily.

The chairman of the Joint Chiefs of Staff waved the remark aside. "My point is this", he said. "In all armies since the beginning of mankind, going as far back as Genghis Khan and Alexander the Great and even the mighty Roman legions, there have been individuals who become so corrupted by war they commit acts of which they'd be incapable in peacetime. History books are filled to the brim with officers trying to keep their men from burning and looting and raping. Sometimes they succeed, but often they do not."

Admiral Leahy was apparently trying to minimize the relevance of Kozielewski's tale by arguing, in essence, that the four German soldiers he'd encountered had been nothing more than the proverbial bad apples. Surely, he was saying, the entire German army isn't composed of such monsters?

Jan Kozielewski wasn't really surprised. He'd encountered such skepticism before. It was only to be expected from those who hadn't been there, who hadn't seen and heard as he had. Despite all its failings, the human soul always clings to the last possible shreds of decency. It refuses to believe another human being capable of such things, until such time as it is presented with irrefutable proof.

Still, Kozielewski chose not to debate the point with the admiral. He didn't need to. He turned his attention back to Roosevelt.

"A few weeks later I found myself in the town of Izbica Lubelska, in eastern Poland", he continued. "There, disguised as an Ukrainian camp guard, I tried to infiltrate the Bełżec death camp."

Roosevelt interrupted him with a raised hand. "A death camp, you say? I've never heard of such a thing. Has anyone?"

Roosevelt was lying. He had, in fact, been informed of the existence of such camps back in 1942, during a very private meeting with Jewish leaders, but it would be almost 60 years before the world found out, completely by accident, that the atrocities happening in Europe had been known to him almost since the start. So for now, the American president chose the only option available to him: he feigned ignorance and outrage.

Cordell and Leahy shook their heads. Hopkins was the only one to speak up. "I've heard rumors, Mr President", he confessed. "But nothing more. I certainly didn't have sufficient proof to even contemplate bringing it to your attention. This is the first first-hand account I've ever come across. In all honesty, before today, it sounded like propaganda to me."

Roosevelt stared at Kozielewski. "Please continue", he demanded.

"We are aware of six such camps", Kozielewski said. "In addition to Bełżec, there are Sobibor,

Treblinka, Chelmno and Majdanek. The sixth one is said to be the worst of all, and it is also the most feared."

"It's called Auschwitz."

Traugott was stunned. He wanted to ask the old woman how she knew him, but his mother spoke first.

"You too, children", she called out, looking defiantly at her son. "Benny, Renata... Come down and join us. You have nothing to fear."

Traugott's head snapped around again. Children? *Children?*

More feet, these ones much smaller, appeared at the top of the staircase and began the slow descent. The children, one boy and one girl, were as smelly and as dirty as the old woman. They came to stand on each side of her, each grabbing a hand for safety and reassurance. They kept their eyes down and refused to look at him, as though they feared him terribly.

For a brief instant, Traugott was reminded of the brother and sister he'd seen on the ramp at Auschwitz, those Mengele had seemed to find so fascinating. He wondered what had become of them.

"Mattias", his mother began assuredly, "I'm sure you remember Mrs Pflaumlocher. And these are her grandchildren, Renata and Benjamin. But we call him Benny. And before you ask, no, they're not twins. Benjamin is actually two years older, but Renata is very big for her age."

The look of utter stupefaction on his face told her that no, he did not remember a Mrs Pflaumlocher. It also told her he didn't care the first thing about these children's age, about them being or not being twins.

His mother smiled slightly, apparently already enjoying the shock she was about to inflict upon him.

"Son, Mrs Pflaumlocher is your old babysitter", she announced slowly. "This is the woman you used to call Mrs P."

And with that, the medieval knight emerged from the fog with visor lowered and lance leveled at the center of his chest, his mighty warhorse churning up the earth with iron-shod hooves. Traugott was too slow reacting and couldn't duck out of the way in time to avoid the crushing blow.

Rosche Pflaumlocher and her husband had lived next door to them in Germany, before his parents' divorce. She had indeed babysat him many times, and to this day he retained fond memories of the warm bread she'd bake for him and her own kids whenever he went over.

But since her last name had been impossible to pronounce for a five-year-old, he'd always called her Mrs P – which he'd found irresistibly funny at first since *p* was also the first letter of *pinkeln*, the German word for pee.

Nothing funnier than pee when you're five.

But surely this couldn't be the same woman? He remembered Mrs P as a jowly, big-boned, slightly heavyset *fräulein* who could have squashed between her thumb and forefinger this frail, birdlike creature who now claimed to be her. Or maybe she had never really been that big but had only appeared so to a child's eyes? He had also not seen her in over fifteen years; Mrs P had moved away shortly after his parents' divorce, after her husband's sudden passing.

"How... what...", Traugott stammered before pausing to collect his thoughts. "Why is she here?"

The Pflaumlochers were Jews so the answer to that question was clear as day, but he still needed to ask it.

Rosche Pflaumlocher answered before Teresia could.

"I'm here because I had nowhere else to go", she explained gently. "These are my son's children. My son and his wife were taken almost two years ago."

She stopped. She didn't need to explain what she meant by "taken". Traugott looked aside, surprised by the tinge of guilt he felt.

"Luckily the children were staying with me at that moment", she went on. "When I heard what had happened, I knew they'd be coming for me as well, so I fled with the children and only the clothes on our backs."

She stopped again. Again, she didn't need to explain who "they" were.

"I had no family left and I knew I couldn't stay in Germany", Mrs P said. "And then I remembered your mother had moved to Austria, which wasn't much better but at least no one would know me here. A few kind and decent people I met along the way helped us, and with a lot of good fortune, I was able to find her."

"I didn't know her when she showed up on my doorstep", Teresia admitted. "But when I recognized her and she told me what had happened, there was no question in my mind what I needed to do."

"You mean you've been hiding them here for almost two years?" Traugott asked incredulously.

His mother raised her chin and stared at him angrily. "And what would you have me do? Turn her in so she could be sent to one of your *camps*? Look at them. An old woman and two children. What threat are they to your precious Reich? Answer me that!"

So that was the way of it, then. As far as she was concerned, it was *his* Reich, not *her* Reich and certainly not *their* Reich.

Here, in this house, he stood alone.

At least Mrs P's presence explained the chocolate he'd found downstairs. He remembered the Pflaumlochers as being somewhat wealthy, and Rosche was probably not being entirely truthful when she claimed to have fled with the children and nothing but the clothes on their backs. It was more likely she'd shown up with some money stashed away somewhere.

He looked at his mother. "How could you take such a risk, Mutti? Do you know what'll happen to you if these people are found here?"

Teresia narrowed her eyes at him. "You'll show some respect while under my roof, son", she chastised him. "*These people*, as you call them, have been my friends longer than you've been alive, and you'll not treat them like cattle. Rosche's husband worked to provide for his family until his heart gave out. You'll not meet a more hardworking man in your entire life."

She paused and smirked. "And besides... is it me you're worried about, or yourself?"

Her question left him speechless. Those who sheltered Jews put not only themselves at risk, but their entire families. If caught, all were shot or sent to die in the camps. Might the same thing happen to him? It might – unless he did the only sane thing and denounced the whole situation to the authorities immediately. Only then would he be safe from any repercussions.

But... saving himself by condemning his mother? Could he really bring himself to do such a thing?

There was only one thing he could do.

"You have nothing to fear from me, Mutti, none of you do", he began. "But don't expect to hear from me again until the war is over. Now I have to leave. I can't stay here one moment longer."

He'd only been here a few hours, so he could still plausibly claim not to have seen or heard anything. But the longer he stayed, the less believable his story became. Each minute he spent in this house increased the danger he faced.

He spun around and went to collect his things without another word. He'd go back to Auschwitz and serve out the rest of his suspension there. Or perhaps he'd throw himself at Höss' mercy and hope for a bit of leniency.

He only knew he could stay here no more.

Roosevelt mouthed the unfamiliar name silently.

Auschwitz.

"What is the purpose of these death camps?" Cordell Hull asked.

"To kill as many people as possible in the shortest possible amount of time, Mr Secretary", Kozielewski stated coldly, as if the name weren't sufficiently self-explanatory. "In America you have mighty factories that produce hundreds of tanks a day. Imagine applying the same efficiency, the same determination and the same organization to the systematic extermination of those you judge to be your enemies. Or simply your inferiors. This is what the Nazis are doing in Europe."

"Impossible!" Roosevelt and admiral Leahy thundered at the same time.

"Have you got any proof of these outrageous claims?" Cordell Hull asked. "You say you infiltrated this camp? What did you call it?"

"Bełżec, Mr Secretary", Kozielewski answered patiently. "And no, I could not infiltrate the camp. But I did get close enough to witness what the Germans call a *durchgangslader*, which appeared to be a sort of transit station where prisoners were herded before being shipped off to various camps. I saw hundreds and hundreds of people, men and women and children, young and old, sick and healthy, crowded together in the filthiest conditions you can imagine, hungry and thirsty and cold and desperate, just... waiting."

"Waiting... for what?" Hopkins asked.

"For the train, Mr Hopkins", Kozielewski said.

"The train? What train?" Roosevelt demanded.

Harry Hopkins shook out a cigarette and lit it, inspiring Cordell Hull to do the same. Soon, Jan Kozielewski was enveloped by a cloud of blue smoke.

"Every three hours, like clockwork, a train comes", he explained. "Maybe fifteen or twenty cars normally used to transport cattle or freight, but certainly not human beings. Hundreds of people are then made to board these trains, never to be seen again. Sometimes families stay together, but most often they do not. Imagine a mother and father made to leave their 5-year-old daughter behind, to be cared for by complete strangers. Imagine their panic and distress. Imagine *the child's* panic and distress. I witnessed such a scene, and many others far worse, on several occasions."

"That's absurd", admiral Leahy growled from behind him. "If such a thing were happening, surely we'd know about it."

Kozielewski twisted around in his chair to look at him. "Would you, admiral?" he asked with just a touch of sarcasm. "You don't have a single soldier on the ground anywhere in Europe today. You're no closer than London, and that's almost 1000 miles away. And while I'm sure you've managed to set up an impressive network of spies and informers, I'm also certain these spies are far too busy keeping an eye on Hitler and Himmler and Goering to be bothered with the fate of a few silly Jews."

Cordell Hull almost jumped out of his chair. "That is totally unfair, Mr Kozliweski", the Secretary of State thundered, mercilessly mangling his last name. "If we didn't care about the fate of a few silly Jews, as you put it, you wouldn't be here today."

Kozielewski almost laughed out loud. *What a dirty business politics is,* he thought. Unlike the Roosevelt administration, the Jewish community in America was increasingly aware of the atrocities sweeping Europe, having heard from relatives across the Atlantic. And some members of this community also happened to be wealthy and influential individuals who contributed heavily to the Democratic Party. It was only thanks to their persistent intercession that Kozielewski had finally been granted a meeting with the President.

He was tempted to ask Hull whether their newfound concern for these silly Jews might have something to do with upcoming elections, but he thought better of it.

"So we're not talking about a few hundred people, are we?" the President demanded calmly, in an attempt to keep the meeting from derailing.

"No sir", Kozielewski said after Hull had sat back down. "We estimate that tens of thousands of people are being sent to their deaths every single day."

"But again, you have no proof", admiral Leahy once more protested. "Just hearsay and, with all due respect, what you claim to have personally witnessed."

"You think me a liar?" Kozielewski asked without bothering to look at the chairman.

"Not at all", the admiral backtracked. "I'm sure these events you just described actually happened. But you are one man who witnessed a couple of events on a couple of occasions. It's one thing to ask us to believe this. It's quite another to ask us to believe that such atrocities are happening across Europe, in a systematic and organized fashion. What you are describing is just... unthinkable. And as you yourself just admitted, you've never even seen one of these camps."

Kozielewski sighed and tried to keep from smiling. He had been waiting for just such an opening. Now was the time to play his trump card.

He slipped a hand inside his jacket and pulled out a sheaf of papers bound together. He placed the packet on the President's desk.

"Just before traveling to Washington, I met with Captain Witold Pilecki, of the Polish Army", he explained. "At no little risk to himself, Captain Pilecki managed to be imprisoned at Auschwitz in October of 1940. He spent almost 1000 days there before finally escaping last April. This is his final report. I strongly suggest you avoid reading it just before bedtime."

Harry Hopkins appeared thunderstruck. "Mr President", he began. "I've heard that name before. Pilecki. Wild Bill mentioned him to me a couple of months ago. The Brits have been receiving reports from a man of the same name at least since 1941. But..."

Kozielewski grinned inwardly. Wild Bill had to be William Joseph "Wild Bill" Donovan, the head of the Office of Strategic Services, the OSS. The fact that he'd also heard of Captain Pilecki would add a veneer of credibility to his story.

"But what, Mr Hopkins?" Roosevelt demanded impatiently.

"The reports were passed on to them by the Polish Home Army, the *Armia Krajowa*, essentially the Polish Resistance", Hopkins explained. "But the claims in these reports were so outrageous and so exaggerated they were judged to be of little credibility. We weren't even sure Pilecki was real. No one paid them much attention."

Roosevelt was leafing through the document as Hopkins spoke. His eyebrows shut up in surprise. "I can see why, Mr Hopkins", the President said. "This passage right here tells of gas chambers camouflaged as showers and of corpses being incinerated in ovens... But why is there no mention of the condition of horses in occupied Poland?"

At first Kozielewski thought he'd misheard, then he wondered whether the President might be joking to relieve a bit of the tension. But when Hopkins discretely kicked his ankle, and when he noticed Hull staring embarrassedly at the tip of his shoes, he knew he hadn't misheard and the President hadn't been joking. Apparently, Roosevelt's health wasn't failing solely on the physical plane.

Kozielewski coughed in his fist to disguise his discomfort. "I can assure you that every word in there is true, Mr President", he said. "I spent several days with Captain Pilecki. I only wish he could have traveled here with me. One look into his eyes would have utterly convinced you. There is a... sadness, I guess I'd call it... that now resides in his soul, like he emerged from Auschwitz damaged and broken. What he went through is simply indescribable."

"Either that or it's one gigantic hoax", admiral Leahy muttered. No one paid him any attention.

"What do you want from us, Mr Kozielewski?" Roosevelt demanded.

Kozielewski could hardly believe his ears. He'd just told them tens of thousands of people were being massacred every day, and they were asking him what they were supposed to do about it?

I want you to dispatch hundreds of bombers to obliterate these camps, he wanted to scream. *I want you to save these people from a death so horrible you wouldn't wish it on your worst enemy. I want you to stop this madness that's descended upon the world.*

"You must understand our resources are already stretched very thin", the President was saying. "I'm not sure what we could..."

"Sir, with all due respect", Kozielewski interrupted him. "You've got at your fingertips the most powerful army in the world today, perhaps the most powerful that's ever been assembled."

"The Russians might not agree with that statement", admiral Leahy said.

"Be that as it may", Kozielewski continued. "We're talking about tens of thousands of lives at stake, perhaps even millions of lives. I'm sure you'll agree that..."

"Millions of lives are also at stake in the Pacific", Roosevelt reminded him. "Last year, in Hong

Kong, Japanese soldiers bayoneted to death a hundred injured soldiers hiding in St. Stephen's College. Some were tortured first and women were gang-raped. By the time it's all said and done, they'll have killed millions in China and the Philippines and Malaysia and wherever else!"

"But..."

"It's the same everywhere", Roosevelt went on vehemently, ignoring him. "The RAF managed to give the Nazis a bloody nose and sent them running back across the English Channel with their tails tucked between their legs, but in the space of just eight months, forty thousand people were killed in the UK and a million houses were destroyed or damaged in London alone. And that's the price of *victory*, Mr Kozielewski. Winston and his boys actually *won* that battle. Imagine the toll of defeat."

"The point the President is making is this", Cordell Hull explained with little patience. "The world is at war, Mr Kozielewski. People are being killed and massacred from one end of the globe to the other. America can't reasonably be expected to protect and save them all. We've got our own battles to fight. That may sound harsh to you, but that's just the way it is."

"It seems to me, Mr Secretary, all that's missing is a bowl of water in which to wash your hands", Kozielewski snapped.

Hopkins and Hull both stood up, indicating the meeting had come to an end. Kozielewski sighed and also stood up. The men exchanged rapid handshakes.

"Thank you for bringing the situation to our attention", Roosevelt said, before picking up his phone. "Mrs Tully, our guest will be leaving".

The door opened almost immediately. "Right this way, Mr Kozielewski", the President's secretary called to him. Kozielewski left the Oval Office without another word.

"Well, that was something", Hopkins said after he'd gone.

"I still have a hard time believing it's all true", admiral Leahy repeated. "Tens of thousands of people killed every single day? Entire camps built for the sole purpose of extermination? I mean..."

"Well I, for one, believe him", Hopkins said. "I don't think he was lying. It's just too fantastic to be false. I just wish..."

"Mr President", Cordell Hull interrupted. "We shouldn't dismiss the possibility that the Russians are behind this. They're desperate for us to open a second front in Europe. They may have invented everything to lure us into invading before we're ready."

"You think Kozielewski is a Russian agent?" Hopkins asked.

"He may not even know it himself. Maybe the Russians just fed him what he wanted to hear. Maybe this Pilecki is the actual Russian agent", Hull hypothesized. "But I don't know what I think anymore. I'm just trying to be cover all the bases."

"I agree we shouldn't rush into anything", Roosevelt said. "But I'm also not ready to simply forget all we've heard today. If this should be true and if we should be found to have known and done nothing... God above, how would History judge us?"

Recalling his experience on board the train the day before, Traugott chose not to wear his uniform for the return trip to Auschwitz. He folded it neatly and placed it at the bottom of his bag, dressing instead in some of the clothes his mother had found for him.

He left without saying goodbye, a few hours after discovering Mrs P and her grandchildren hiding in the attic. He could have gone sooner but instead he lingered in his room, hoping in vain his mother might come sort things out with him. And since he was too proud and too righteous to go to her, the ice remained unbroken and his volcanic anger began building inside him, burning hotter and hotter with each passing minute.

He chose to go before it erupted.

He closed the front door gently and headed for the train station. This time he'd walk. He thought he spied a dark shape behind the curtains of the living room, but he stared stubbornly ahead and refused to look in that direction. If Teresia were indeed watching him go, then let her; he wouldn't give her the satisfaction of acknowledging her presence. She had chosen her path, he had chosen his, and at least for now, those paths traveled in diametrically opposite directions. He knew what he had to do, even if she didn't.

A train was scheduled to travel to Krakow, which was only 40 miles from Katowice, the town closest to Auschwitz, every day at 4pm, over an hour from now. But when he asked for a ticket, the attendant informed him the train had left an hour ago. Fuming, Traugott demanded an explanation, but the attendant could only shrug and suggest he catch the train going – hopefully - to Warsaw at 6:15.

Traugott declined angrily. Warsaw was over 160 miles from Katowice, and then he'd have to find either a bus or a regional train to travel the rest of the way. Furious with himself, he instead purchased a ticket for tomorrow's train to Katowice, and the attendant politely suggested he be at the station no later than noon, you know, just in case... Traugott thanked him curtly and left, wondering where he was supposed to go now.

He briefly considered spending the night inside the vast station – at least he wouldn't miss his train again if he did - but the thought of trying to sleep on a bench surrounded by drunks and crippled was more than he could contemplate. So he began walking aimlessly, until he realized he was unconsciously making his way back to his mother's house.

Hi Mutti, I know we just had a huge fight, but I missed my train and could you take me in for just one more night? Right. Splendid idea.

Traugott shook himself out of his reverie and was surprised to find himself standing in front of the *biergarten* where he had celebrated his single *sig* rune a few years ago. He hesitated only briefly before walking in.

He smiled nostalgically when he found the place as rowdy and noisy and smoky as he remembered it. He spotted a vacant table to his right, one where he could sit with his back against the wall and an eye on the door, and made a beeline for it. He placed his bag carefully under his chair and allowed himself to enjoy the moment.

It was hard to believe he was back here after all those years. Directly across the room from him was the table where he and his friends had drunk themselves into a stupor in honor of his good fortune. He could still remember the blinding headache that had awakened him the next morning, but also the intoxicating sense of pride and purpose he'd felt at the time. The table was currently occupied by three unkempt, middle-aged men who looked as though they'd been anchored there for a few days. One of them glanced at him over his shoulder for a moment. When he turned back around, the man said something that made his two friends laugh. Traugott ignored them.

The *biergarten* was doing good business tonight. There was hardly an empty chair to be found as people ate and drank and smoked and laughed, apparently unconcerned by the war raging outside. Or perhaps it was the other way around. Perhaps they chose to eat and drink and smoke and laugh tonight because they knew a bomb might blow their heads off tomorrow.

There were also a few uniformed men in the room, but they all appeared to be either Wehrmacht or Luftwaffe. Traugott didn't spot a single SS uniform, and he was suddenly glad his own uniform was safely hidden out of sight at the bottom of his bag. This was one night where he didn't feel like standing out.

He was startled when someone placed a large glass of foaming beer on the table in front of him. He found himself looking up at a pretty young waitress with short blond hair and large breasts.

"I didn't order this", he protested.

She smiled at him. "No, but you would have sooner or later. I just saved you some time. Haven't seen you in here before. What's your name?"

Traugott was caught a bit short by her forthrightness. Must be the war again. No time lost, no opportunity wasted, for tomorrow we may all be dead. "Mattias", he replied. "You?"

"I'm Gundula. I know. It's ironic isn't it?"

Traugott smiled. *Gund* was the German word for *war*.

"So tell me, Mattias... What would you like tonight?" she asked. Something in Gundula's eyes and voice told him she wasn't necessarily referring to food and drink. He felt the first stirrings of a physical reaction, but for now he chose to play it safe. If there was more to be had from her, he'd find out in due time.

"I'm sure you can come up with something I'd like", he said, following her lead. Gundula winked at him and walked away with an exaggerated sway of the hips he hoped was meant to seal the deal.

He watched her go until she was swallowed by the crowd. He took a first sip of his cold beer and noticed the same man as before staring at him again, but this time with a decidedly much less friendly air. Intrigued and annoyed, he returned the man's stare for a few seconds before raising his glass in a silent toast. The man glowered at him a moment longer before turning back to his friends.

What the hell was that about?

Traugott put him out of his mind and tried to relax. As long as he were here, he might as well enjoy himself. He couldn't remember the last time he'd had an entire evening to himself, free of all responsibilities. Even at Auschwitz, the nights spent drinking the liquor and counting the money stolen from the Jews with a few other SS were little more than oases - temporary escapes from the inhuman reality around them. Those evenings always had a guarded feeling about them, they felt both artificial and superficial, and he never allowed himself to be completely at ease. He always kept a few barriers up, wary and suspicious of those who pretended to be his friends – but who, in fact, were certainly using him just as much as he was using them.

His thoughts then turned to prisoner *neunzehnhunderteinundsiebzig.* He glanced at his watch and tried to imagine what Adriana might be doing right now. Probably returning to her barracks, having survived yet another day. He was more worried than he cared to admit. He'd heard nothing since Mulka and Mockël had taken her away, almost ten days ago. He hadn't dared ask too many questions, but those questions he'd asked had yielded nothing. Nobody seemed to know what had become of her. He doubted they'd killed her, but at Auschwitz there were fates worse than death.

And then Höss had suspended him and he'd been forced to leave Auschwitz for a while, and here he was. Thinking about Adriana deeply troubled and unsettled him. He shifted uneasily in his chair and gulped down some more beer.

What, exactly, were his feelings for her? The physical attraction, at least on his part, was undeniably powerful. She was by far the most beautiful woman he'd ever seen, despite also being a Jewess. But beyond that? If all he desired was her body, he could take it – by force, if need be - anytime he wanted. No one would even think of trying to stop him. The fact he hadn't yet told him there was something deeper hidden there, something he'd have to face one day.

So it clearly wasn't solely physical. There was a fierceness about her, a steely inner strength, a wildness one might call it, he also found quite alluring. Auschwitz was filled with women who, under similar circumstances, would have jumped into his bed to save their lives. But not Adriana. She'd told him to go to hell. She'd made it amply clear he could keep his affections and his favors, and that he could expect absolutely nothing from her in return.

She had refused, and still she refused, to compromise her principles, to deny her true identity, no matter the price she paid at the end.

Yes, he'd told her he loved her, but did he really mean it? Were those his true feelings or was he just trying to lure her into giving herself willingly to him? Could he truly be in love with her and put on that uniform, defending all it stood for, every morning?

And what if he were in love with her? Nothing would ever come of it. She had made her feelings for him amply clear on more than one occasion. He had no cause to think they'd ever change. His sole consolation, as thin and fragile as it might be, was that it was not him personally she hated, but all Nazis. No matter the man underneath, all she saw was that uniform. She'd told him as much: *There is no man. Just a Nazi. Men like you.* In her eyes, they were all the same, the interchangeable cogs of an infernal machine whose sole purpose it was to destroy her and her kind.

A plate covered with sauerkraut and steaming sausages materialized on the table in front of him, startling him again.

"Thank you", he said, gazing up at a smiling Gundula. "Care to sit down for a few minutes?" He half stood up when she grabbed the chair across from him.

"The manager doesn't really like it when I'm not on my feet working", she said. "But he won't sack me. I know where and how he gets all this food while everybody else is starving, so I'm good."

"That, and the fact half the men only come here to peek inside my shirt every chance they get, and he knows it."

Traugott needed all his willpower to keep his gaze from dropping down to her chest when she said that. He kept his eyes locked on hers, and prayed he wasn't blushing like an idiot.

"You're quite... unusual", was all he could think of saying before attacking his sauerkraut.

"These are unusual times", she understated, essentially echoing what he'd surmised earlier. "What brings you to Vienna?"

She was really asking why he wasn't at the front, fighting. He shrugged. "I'm just passing through", he said without answering her question.

He knew she'd notice his evasiveness and was relieved when she chose not to pry. "I've only been in town for a month myself", she explained. "I couldn't stay where I was before any longer."

Gundula didn't say anything more, choosing to keep her own secrets and daring him to pry into her life as she hadn't in his. Traugott smelled the trap and walked around it. "You look like you landed on your feet".

"I got lucky", she said. "The owner was outside having a smoke when I walked by. He took one look at me and asked if I wanted a job."

"It's always better to be lucky than good", Traugott said.

Gundula was about to reply when a waitress passing behind her intentionally bumped her chair, hard. The other woman didn't look back or stop to apologize.

Gundula smiled. "That's her very subtle way of telling me to get back to work", she explained. "The other girls don't like me much. Something about their tips being half of what they were before I started working here." She winked at Traugott. "How long will you be passing through town?"

"I missed my train so I have to wait until tomorrow for the next one", he said.

"That must mean you have nowhere to sleep tonight". As she stood up to go, she bent forward to offer him a glimpse of her ample cleavage. Traugott almost dropped his fork.

"You could say that", he conceded. She discretely slipped a small square of paper underneath his plate.

"Well now you do, if you want", she said. "I have to get back to work. Maybe I'll see you later?"

"I'm certain you will", he promised.

He watched her walk away, again, before unfolding the square. It contained an address, presumably hers, in black ink. It was less than three blocks away and he'd have no trouble finding it. He slipped it into his pocket, smiling.

He'd almost finished his meal when a strange rhythmic, knocking sound rose above the ambient noise. Looking up, he saw coming in his direction the man who'd been giving him the evil eye since the beginning of the evening. The man's left leg was gone below the knee and he ambled along awkwardly on a crooked crutch carved out of a stout tree limb.

An unhealthy fire burned in the man's eyes. Uninvited, he collapsed into the chair Gundula had vacated a few seconds earlier.

"You've got the look of an officer about you", the man growled.

Traugott didn't reply. Instead, his eyes never leaving the man, he discretely grabbed the knife with which he'd sliced his sausage, hiding the blade in his hand and along the inside of his forearm.

If the man noticed his move, he gave no sign of it.

"I'll finish my meal and then I'll go", Traugott said slowly. "I suggest you do the same."

The man sneered at him. "You're an officer alright", he said. "First sign of trouble you take off like jackrabbits. That's how come I lost my leg at Stalingrad. Our brave *obergefreiter* fled the second the Reds started shooting back. He left us behind, I stepped on a landmine and..." He angrily slammed the tip of his crutch against the floor to emphasize his point. "All officers are cowards. That's why you're here, having a beer, and not at the front."

The man spit on the ground to illustrate his disgust. Traugott tightened his grip on the knife's handle. If the man made a sudden move, he'd stick the blade in his throat.

Traugott had earlier been glad he hadn't worn his SS uniform; now he almost wished he had. That uniform could still inspire a good dose of fear, even if it no longer commanded the respect it once did. The twin thunderbolts on his collar might have given this bitter drunk cause to think twice about picking a fight with him.

"Go back to your friends", Traugott said with all the calm he could muster. "I don't want any trouble and neither do you."

That remark seemed to inflame the man even further. "You should have thought about that before hitting on *my* Gundula", he said, his eyes now big as saucers.

Traugott was momentarily thrown. In a flash, the man had gone from angry veteran to jealous lover. If further proof had been needed of his mental unstability, it had just been proffered.

"I don't have to explain myself to you", he said. "You're drunk. You need to walk away while you still have one leg to do it on."

There would be no reasoning his way out of this situation, Traugott knew. The man was crazy. Either he got him to back down verbally, or he'd have to do it physically. Both were absolutely fine with him.

"Why you little...", the man screamed. He tried to place his crutch under his arm to stand up, but his advanced state of drunkenness was playing havoc with his equilibrium. Still, Traugott flipped the knife around in his hand and reared his elbow back, preparing to strike upward. The second the drunk reached for him, he'd shove the blade under his chin, through his tongue and into his palate. The strike wouldn't be enough to kill the man, but it'd certainly incapacitate him.

The man finally managed to get his crutch in place. As he pushed against it to stand up, a pair of feminine hands landed on his shoulders and shoved him back into his chair.

"I'll have none of this here, gentlemen", Gundula said. She was staring directly at Traugott, who made the knife disappear. "There's already more than enough fighting in the world as it is, wouldn't you say?"

"But Gundula...", the man began.

"*Die Klappe halten, Hermann*", she snapped in a tone that brooked no reply. "Go back to your table before I have you kicked out. For good, this time. Now."

Hermann seemed about to argue with her, but then thought better of it and got up. "I still say you're a coward officer", he spat at Traugott before turning his back and returning to his friends, who welcomed him like the war hero he'd never be.

Gundula was still standing there, staring at him. "I saw the knife", she said. "You would have killed him, wouldn't you?"

Traugott stared back. There was no point trying to deny it. "If need be, yes", he admitted.

"You've killed before." It was a statement, not a question. Traugott didn't reply. He didn't need to.

"I should have guessed you were a soldier. Those plans you had for later tonight?" Gundula said after a moment, her earlier enthusiasm and cheerfulness now completely gone. "Either you leave the war at the door, or don't bother showing up."

Her words stung.

"Don't you dare judge me", he snarled. "I'm all that's standing between you and a battalion of Russians who haven't seen a woman in months."

"Seems to me the Russians wouldn't be coming for me if you'd left them alone", she fired back. "Or us, for that matter." Traugott could feel his temper rising.

"The Bolcheviks were about to sweep over Europe like a tidal wave", he retorted. "Only the

Fuhrer had the foresight to strike them first. If not for him, you and me and millions of others, we'd be bowing to our Red masters today."

Gundula refused to back down. "Spare me the lecture", she said. "I have to get back to work. Just remember what I said about later. The man can come. The soldier can just go to hell."

Traugott exited the *biergarten* a few minutes later. Night had fallen and the streets were dark. He felt strangely numb. Disappointed? Yes, of course. But hurt? Absolutely not. Women rejecting him for who he was – or, to be truly honest about it, *what* he was - seemed to be a recurring theme in his life as of late: Adriana, then his mother, now her... Gundula was a splendid specimen of Aryan womanhood, worthy of the *lebensborn* centers, but nothing more. A few hours with her would have been pleasurable, but also devoid of all meaning.

Adriana's hatred and anger were much more difficult to bear.

Traugott fished the square of paper out of his pocket and tore it up. He let the scraps fall to the ground.

"You really shouldn't litter, *officer*", someone said behind him.

He turned around just in time to see Hermann the One-Legged Drunk and his two friends emerging from an alley he had just passed. One of the men was holding the neck of a broken bottle and the other a small pocketknife with a ridiculously short blade. They had obviously been waiting for him after sneaking out of the *biergarten* first. Traugott placed his bag on the ground and cracked his knuckles menacingly.

"I got nothing to say to you", he announced.

Hermann smiled as his two friends moved to flank Traugott on each side. "That's good, because we're not here to t..."

Traugott rushed him, taking the trio by surprise. He hit Hermann in the sternum with his open palm and grabbed the crutch with the other hand. The man immediately toppled backward, but Traugott had already forgotten about him. He spun around as rapidly as he could, swinging the crutch at head-level. The wood exploded against the skull of the man who had been about to skewer him from behind with the broken bottle, knocking him out cold. Seeing the odds thus reduced dramatically against him, the remaining man dropped his knife, turned tail and ran. Traugott didn't pursue him.

He instead walked back toward Hermann, who was trying to drag himself away on his belly. Traugott tapped him on the buttocks with the three-foot length of crutch he was still holding. Hermann began whimpering and tried to crawl away faster. Traugott tapped him again. Hermann seemed to be on the verge of tears.

"Where are you going, Hermann?" Traugott taunted him. "I thought you wanted to talk?"

He tapped him a third time.

"So you were at Stalingrad, uh? I don't think so," Traugott taunted him.

"I was!" Hermann whimpered.

"What unit? Under which general? Rommel or von Rundstedt?" Traugott pressed him, naming two of the most famous generals of the time.

"Rommel! I was with Rommel!" Hermann replied hurriedly.

Traugott's laughter slashed the darkness. "Rommel was never at Stalingrad, you dumbass", he sneered. "Might have turned out differently for us if he had, but in January he was in Tripoli running from Montgomery. And you're way too old to have been at Stalingrad. What are you? Forty? Fifty? No, I think you lost your leg when you shoved your foot up some whore's ass and she gave you syphilis. *That's* what happened to your leg."

Hermann knew he'd never get away, so he flopped onto his back to face his would-be victim.

"Leave me alone, please", he begged, all defiance and arrogance now gone.

Traugott placed the jagged end of the crutch against his throat, freezing him. "Why should I?" he growled, slightly increasing the pressure. Hermann tried to swat the crutch away, but he lacked the strength. A trickle of blood ran down the side of his throat. "I should just pin you to the ground like the insect that you are."

And he might have done it, too, had someone not grabbed the crutch at that moment.

"Leave him alone", a voice said. "He's just a stupid drunk."

Traugott looked up. Gundula was staring at him. She was holding the broken crutch with one hand and, after a moment, he allowed her to yank it away. Only then did he notice the fight had inadvertently brought them back to the *biergarten*.

"I saw them leave two minutes before you did", she explained before throwing the crutch away. It clattered on the sidewalk and rolled into the street. "I guessed they'd be up to no good."

He opened his mouth to say something but she spoke first.

"Just leave before someone calls the police", she said. "You've already attracted too much attention."

A dozen people had stopped to watch, but a few were already leaving now that the fight was over. A middle-aged woman fearfully buried her face in her husband's shoulder and pulled him away when Traugott looked in their direction. The others began dispersing as well, but Gundula was right: he had to disappear before the police showed up.

Traugott took one last look at Hermann before retrieving his bag and heading for the train station. He stopped after a few steps and turned back to look at her.

"Maybe after the war?" he called out loudly.

"Maybe", she replied.

He nodded and left. He wouldn't miss his train a second time.

Otto Mockël crouched to rub Achtzehn's ears. The gigantic wolfhound blissfully closed its eyes before licking its master's face.

The three men accompanying Mockël exchanged glances that conveyed a single thought: never, *ever*, would they dare bring their own throats so close to that monster's jaws.

"Watch the old hag", he warned them. "She's a tough old bitch."

Mockël stood up and stretched lazily. Achtzehn looked up at him, expectantly licking its chops.

"Let's go", Mockël ordered.

He pushed the door and they entered the barracks.

Traugott got off the train at Katowice and walked rapidly to the bus station. A yellowed, barely legible schedule glued to the wall informed him the next bus for Oświęcim left less than an hour from now.

He purchased a ticket before locating a public restroom, where he washed up and changed into his SS uniform. Feeling refreshed and bit more like himself again, he got a sandwich from a small shop. The young girl manning the counter kept her eyes down and trembled visibly when she handed him his change.

A dozen other passengers were already waiting to board the bus. The driver opened the doors to let them on just as Traugott stepped onto the platform. Never slowing his pace, he cut in front of the line and climbed aboard with a smirk, completely oblivious to the angry stares his rudeness generated.

He didn't care. He was feeling strangely elated. He was going home.

Home. The word surprised him, but that's how he felt. As strange as that may be, to him Auschwitz, a place of death and despair, was now home.

He took the first seat at the front of the bus, slightly behind and to the driver's right, so as to have an unobstructed view of the road ahead. He finished his sandwich nonchalantly while the other passengers boarded, safe in the knowledge that his uniform protected him from any recriminations. No one would dare say a word.

"Let's go", he ordered as soon as the last passenger was on board.

The driver almost jumped out of his seat and looked nervously at his watch. "But, herr untersturmführer, departure time is only 12 minutes from now", the man protested feebly. "Others might arrive."

Traugott looked at his own watch and smiled. "My watch says it's time", he said coldly. "Shut the doors and go."

The man looked back at his watch and began sweating, even though the evening was a bit chilly. He knew he *might* get in serious trouble if he departed early. On the other hand, it was quite obvious he *would* get in serious trouble if he didn't depart early. The decision was easy to make. "You're right, of course, herr untersturmführer", he finally yielded. "My watch must be slow."

The driver shut the door and turned the key in the ignition. Nothing happened. He turned it to the left again, made sure the clutch was fully depressed, and almost had a heart attack when he turned it back to the right and still nothing happened.

"What the hell's going on?" Traugott growled.

The man licked his lips as he fidgeted with the controls, trying desperately to get the engine started. "It must be the battery, herr untersturmführer", he explained. "It's very, very old. Sometimes it just... dies."

The driver immediately wished he had picked another word to describe the battery's current state. "Well, go find another one and fix this!" Traugott barked.

The man looked at him as though he'd just dropped from the heavens. "Begging the untersturmführer's pardon, but if the *Armia Krajowa* hadn't stolen my good battery last week, there wouldn't be a problem", he said in a tone that he hoped didn't betray his impatience with this obnoxious officer. He was also lying: his battery hadn't been taken by the Polish Resistance, but by a couple of drunken Wehrmacht soldiers who hadn't even needed it. This was obviously not a detail he felt comfortable sharing with a member of the SS. "Now we'll just have to wait for another bus to recharge our battery and get going."

Traugott sighed and looked out his window. They were the only ones here. "And when's the next bus due?" he asked.

The man consulted his watch for an inordinately long time before answering. "The next bus goes to Częstochowa", he began. "Unless my watch is running slow again, it leaves in seven hours."

Rita looked up at the SS officer.

"She's under my responsibility", she said calmly. "I need to know where you're taking her and on whose orders you're acting."

Mockël clenched his jaws and Achtzehn, sensing its master's anger, growled. "You impertinent bitch", he said. "I don't answer to you. Fetch me *neunzehnhunderteinundsiebzig* or you won't live to see the next sunrise."

Rita managed to remain outwardly impassive, even though her entire being was vibrating with a terror borne of helplessness. There was nothing she could do to keep him from taking Adriana. All she could do was stall him for as long as possible, and perhaps hope to bluff her way out. "No, of course you don't answer to me", she said. "But I've been ordered to make sure no harm comes to her. Someone very powerful has entrusted me personally with her safety."

Mockël inhaled sharply. Could this be true? Had Konrad Morgen truly asked this lowly kapo to protect the prisoner? He doubted it very much and decided to follow his instinct.

He grabbed Rita by the back of the hair and pulled her backward, almost bending her in half. "You think to intimidate me, you witch?" he snarled, his face less than an inch from hers. "You *know* nothing and you *are* nothing. You've got five seconds to comply before I sic my dog on you."

Achtzehn began barking furiously and Mockël was glad to finally see a lightning bolt of fear streak across Rita's eyes.

"She's... she's not here", she tried to lie, but her voice had lost all conviction. This man simply terrified her. "She was sick and I sent her to the infirmary."

Mockël smiled. "You lie", he simply said.

He shoved the old woman to the ground and Achtzehn went into a frenzy. A few of the women who had gathered to witness the scene screamed in fear when Mockël bent down to unfasten the leash from the beast's collar. Achtzehn reared up on its hind legs and began slobbering heavily.

Magrita was standing at the back of the crowd. Seeing Rita about to be dismembered, she tried to push her way through the assembled women but Beatrijs, the woman who'd asked Adriana to save her grandparents, was blocking her way.

"Move Bea!" Magrita said. "She needs help!"

But Beatrijs refused to budge. Instead, she innocently but sharply threw her elbow back, catching Magrita in the solar plexus. Magrita doubled over, unable to breathe or move and unnoticed in the commotion of the moment.

Achtzehn was pulling on its leash so strongly Mockël was having a hard time unfastening it. That extra second saved Rita's life.

"I'm here", Adriana said as she stepped between the old woman and the hound. "I'll go with you. There's no need for this."

She had been watching from the sides, partly hidden in the shadows. She knew what was coming. She knew Mockël wanted nothing better than to let his dog tear Rita apart. He wouldn't hesitate for a single second. She'd seen it all before, two weeks earlier when Mockël and Mulka had come to find her in the warehouse and Traugott hadn't wanted to give her up. Mockël had used the same tactic then, forcing her to step forward to keep another from being mauled to death.

One day, she told herself, *they'll be stripped of their uniforms and their dogs and their guns, and then we'll see who cowers on the floor in fear.*

"You don't have to go with him", Rita said as she picked herself up and brushed the dirt from her clothes.

"Shut up, you old hag", Mockël snapped at the old kapo. He grabbed Adriana by the arm and pulled her to him. The three guards then led her away, all the while making sure to keep out of Achtzehn's reach.

"Where are you taking her?" Rita demanded one last time.

Mockël just stared at her and smiled. He pointed his thumb and forefinger at her, dropped the thumb and left without another word.

Traugott stormed off the bus, traversed the deserted station rapidly and exited onto the dark and empty streets.

No way in hell was he going to spend *seven hours* here, just waiting for some stupid bus to show up. There had to be some other way for him to get to Auschwitz.

He looked around, hoping against hope he might find a cab for hire. A single car was parked next to the curb about 100 feet away, but the elderly woman behind the wheel looked like a cab driver about as much as he looked like Josef Stalin. Probably some wife waiting for her husband. He briefly considered commandeering her vehicle – it would have been *soooo* easy to rip open the door and dump her out - but there were things even *he* wouldn't do. Stealing some grandmother's car was one of those things.

He had to get out of here.

His impatience growing, he began walking randomly through the streets, hoping for some miracle but never straying too far from the station. Poland was crawling with resistance fighters emboldened by the Nazis' latest setbacks and the last thing he needed was to get lost in an unfamiliar city. A new group backed by the Soviet Union, the *Armia Ludowa*, had recently been making a name for itself and was increasingly competing with the much larger *Armia Krajowa* – who, in just a few years, would see its lightly-armed forces obliterated by German tanks in the streets of Warsaw after being lured by Moscow into a suicidal assault against the Nazis, an operation that cost hundreds of thousands of lives and essentially eliminated all Western sympathizers from the Polish resistance.

But for now, lynching an SS officer from the nearest lamppost would be a great coup for either group.

One turn down the wrong street and Traugott's uniform could land him in a world of trouble from which he might not emerge alive.

After about ten minutes of pointless meanderings he was ready to give up and turn back, but at that moment a man materialized out of the night and began following him. Traugott first heard footsteps echoing in the empty streets, and he became slightly worried when it seemed the stranger might be tailing him. He looked discretely over his shoulder. The man was about one hundred and fifty feet behind him, and he appeared young and fit.

The old woman at the station. She had looked inoffensive enough, but she had probably been on the lookout for German officers. She had to be the one who'd tipped off the man. *Damn her dry cunt.*

There was one sure way for him to check whether he was truly being followed: he suddenly quickened his pace and listened for the man's reaction. All doubts would be dispelled if he, too, began walking more rapidly. On the other hand, if he stayed where he was, Traugott could forget about him.

The man's footsteps began echoing more rapidly and Traugott snarled.

Oh yeah? I'll show you how this game is played.

He slowed down imperceptibly, allowing the man to come just that much closer, and counted down from five... four... three... two... one... He was about to spin around and charge – the last thing the man would expect - when the stranger began retching horribly.

Traugott stopped. The man had his head down and both hands against the wall, and he seemed about to throw up. He dry-heaved a few times and a thin rivulet of sticky saliva stretched from his mouth and almost to the ground. As Traugott watched, the man tottered and collapsed with his back against a wall. He broke out into a vulgar drunken song and then began crying.

Traugott began to breathe a bit easier. Seemed he had been wrong about the whole thing.

He looked around for any mode of transportation, even a child's rusty old bike would do, but there was nothing. Most cars had vanished from the streets, owing to petrol being so rare, and those who owned bicycles guarded them jealously.

Traugott turned the corner and was stopped dead in his tracks by three other men arriving from the opposite direction. The men didn't even try to conceal they were coming for him. They looked straight at him, took their hands out of their pockets and began to hurry.

Traugott wondered how he'd gotten himself in this mess, but wasted no time thinking about it; he knew he had just a few seconds to extirpate himself from this situation. There were at least four of them – the drunken song had clearly signaled the others he was coming – and this time he wasn't dealing with an old *Säufer* like one-legged Hermann. The first man had expertly fooled him and now he was almost trapped.

Cursing the fact that he was unarmed, his first instinct was to return to the relative safety of the bus station. Why he'd be safer there than here, he couldn't have said, but he could think of no other plan.

Now if he could only remember which way to go.

The newcomers were still about fifty feet away, but they were closing in on him fast. He then heard running footsteps coming from behind him and his mind protested that a single man, not several, ought to be arriving from that direction. He looked back at the three men and one smiled viciously, his eyes gleaming in the darkness. The game was up. They all knew what was happening here, and they all understood there was but one possible outcome: either he got away, or they'd kill him.

Traugott spun around and began running. He reached the intersection at the same time as three partisans – one of them the fake drunk who'd followed him, and where in the hell had the other two come from? - and almost ran into them. They tried to grab him but he threw his bag at them as hard as he could. Reacting instinctively, the men caught it and that gave Traugott the half-second he needed to escape.

One of the men let out a loud curse and they set off after him.

He thought the bus station was somewhere to his left, but that was also the one direction in which he now couldn't go. So he cut sharply to his right, away from his six pursuers, and took off through the unfamiliar streets with all the speed he could muster.

The men were right behind him. They were so close he could hear them breathing hard as they ran. One of them was also screaming at him, and even though Traugott didn't speak a single word of Polish, he doubted very much the man was inviting him to have a glass of vodka with them.

He, the predator, had become prey, and he hated it.

He couldn't let them catch him. Yes, they'd eventually string him upside down for all to see and jeer and spit on, but there would be nothing swift or clean about the manner in which they killed him. His death, when it finally came, would only release him from a fate he dared not even contemplate. An SS officer would be a prized catch, a treasure trove of information, but when he proved unable to tell them what they wanted to know, they'd take out his eyes and rip out his fingernails and slice off his dick.

He was out of breath and a painful stitch burned in his side. Traugott knew he had to keep looking ahead. But when he felt the brush of fingertips against the back of his clothes, he found himself looking back over his shoulder at the partisans.

They were... right... there, so close he could count the beads of sweat on their faces and read the hatred in their eyes and smell their rotten breath and know the despair of the fox about to be ripped apart by a pack of hounds.

That despair sent a jolt of adrenaline coursing through his system and gave him a sudden burst of speed. The distance between him and his pursuers increased slightly, but there was only so much he could do. If only he could have kicked off his shiny leather boots! They were great for parading around and looking like a crazed killer, but when one had to run for one's life, they left much to be desired.

His head hadn't finished swiveling back to the front when he fell. Whether one of the men tripped him or whether he got tangled up in his own feet or whether he stepped on something, he never knew, but the end result was the same. He pitched forward uncontrollably and tumbled against the pavement. The men yelped in victory and then a dozen hands pulled him to his feet.

One man punched him in the stomach, twice, before grabbing him by the hair and tilting his head back while the others held him. The man spat in his face and hit him again in the ribs. Traugott both heard and felt a bone snap like a dry twig.

Traugott tried to free himself, but the hands holding him were too numerous and too powerful.

His broken rib felt like a white-hot blade stuck in his gut and he could barely breathe. He still tried to fight back, but the only damage he managed to inflict were some toes crushed under the heel of his boot.

The man was about to hit him again when a divine white light suddenly tore through the darkness, bathing them in its holiness.

The partisans froze. The man kneed him in the balls after a moment and then they let him go. He collapsed to his knees as they disappeared, running, into the night.

The divine light came closer and closer, glowing brighter and brighter, sounding louder and louder, until it finally stopped directly in front of him.

"Need a ride, *officer*?" a man asked with unconcealed glee.

Traugott looked up and, through eyes swimming in tears of pain, found himself staring at the smug smile of a Wehrmacht soldier at the wheel of a transport truck.

Mockël massaged his still-sore throat with his free hand as he followed Adriana and the soldiers into the night.

You wanted to kill me, bitch?, he thought. *You'll die a thousand deaths before I'm through with you.*

It was a brazen gamble to once again be going after a woman who, despite being a filthy Jewess, was officially under Konrad Morgen's protection. But Robert Mulka, at first reluctant and cautious, had finally agreed that the risk was worth it: if they could break her and hand Morgen Traugott's head on a silver platter, why would the Bloodhound Judge complain? Only the results mattered.

Not to mention the fact that Morgen was increasingly rumored to be taking a close look at Rudolf Höss. If the axe ever came down on the obersturmbannführer's fat neck, it sure as hell wouldn't hurt to be in the judge's good graces.

The tricky part would be keeping Adriana both alive and relatively sane. If she died without having spoken, Mulka and Mockël knew there would be no stone in the Reich big enough for them to hide under.

Mockël had finally convinced Mulka by suggesting they conscript *neunzehnhunderteinundsiebzig* to replace the mad teenager, who had been sent to the gas chambers after trying to bite off a visitor's *Schwanz*. She'd become too big of a liability and been eliminated before she caused an even bigger problem.

Her execution meant there was now an empty room, and an empty bed, in Block 24.

It seemed like the perfect opportunity. Since they couldn't beat and torture Adriana into talking, like they would have any other prisoner, they'd cast her down into hell for a few days and soften her up a bit.

Risk to her body was minimal. The whores were valuable and the prisoners had been warned not to mistreat them – not too much, anyway. Risk to her mind, on the other hand, was considerably greater, but Mockël wasn't overly concerned; women got raped every day and they didn't all go crazy. Besides, he was convinced *neunzehnhunderteinundsiebzig* wouldn't last more than a couple of days. She'd grasp quickly enough that she only had to tell them what she knew in order to be sent back to her beloved Kanada, and then she'd talk. He figured she'd break after her fifth "client", or perhaps she'd last long enough to service her tenth or her twelfth, but certainly no longer than that.

He'd seen her face when he'd come at her a couple of weeks earlier. She was clearly inexperienced sexually, and the trauma she was about to endure would completely annihilate her spirit. Getting her to talk after that would be child's play. She'd tell them everything they wanted to know, and then some.

They had reached the brothel and the soldiers, who weren't allowed inside, stopped at the door.

"I'll take it from here", Mockël said. "Hold my dog."

He thrust the leash into the nearest soldier's hands, who recoiled as though he'd been handed a live snake. Achtzehn immediately began to growl and the guard almost wet himself.

Mockël grabbed Adriana's arm, pushed open the door and pulled her inside. She tried to resist, but he dug his fingers into her flesh hard enough to make her wince.

"What is this place?" she asked as he dragged her along. "Where have you brought me?"

"Shut your mouth", he snapped at her. Then, snickering, he added: "You'll get plenty of occasions to open it later."

There were five doors on each side of the corridor. Adriana heard muffled screams and moans and even a few laughs, but still she couldn't make sense of this place.

Mockël led her to the last door on the left, unlocked it and shoved her inside.

"Get some rest", he said with a sarcastic smile. "Your first one will be here at 5 in the morning."

"My first one? What are you talking about? You can't...", Adriana began.

Then she took her first good look at the tiny room, saw the small bed, and it all came together in her mind. There had been rumors, but... She blanched, still fighting against the reality imposing itself upon her. And then the door directly across from her room opened to let a man out. Before it shut again, she glimpsed a heavyset woman shoving humongous breasts back inside her smock.

Mockël glanced over his shoulder, saw what she'd seen, and smiled again.

"You wanted to be Traugott's whore, now you'll be the whole camp's", he said. "Sweet dreams".

Adriana screamed when he closed the door and locked it, abandoning her to her terror.

There was no love lost between the SS and the Wehrmacht, and Traugott was almost surprised to have been rescued. It would not have been unheard of for the soldiers to simple drive by and wave merrily as the partisans beat him to a bloody pulp - far from it.

Claiming there was no room in the cab, the driver sent him to sit in the back, with the grunts.

And now Traugott knew why they'd stopped. They weren't about to pass up a chance to knock an arrogant SS son of a bitch down a few notches.

No one offered him a hand to climb aboard, a simple task rendered almost impossible by his broken rib. Instead, they watched with an unconcealed glint of amusement as he twisted this way and that, like a stranded fish, until he finally managed to hoist himself up. He had no sooner regained his feet that the driver accelerated away, almost toppling him off the truck and into the street again.

Traugott thought the man had perhaps tried to do just that.

But instead of tumbling out, he managed to spin to his left and collapsed onto one of the two wooden benches, forcing himself in between two men who grunted in displeasure. The impact jarred his whole battered body and he almost cried out in pain. He clenched his teeth and closed his eyes, fighting off tears of agony, and after a moment the pain began to subside somewhat.

The 20-odd men in the back were not exactly what one would have considered crack, elite troops. In the darkness Traugott caught flashes of gray and silver in their beards and hair, and their unkempt appearance, the manner in which they carried themselves, told him they'd already lost whatever battle they'd be asked to fight.

With men like these to defend it, the Reich was doomed.

He thought briefly of Hermann, the drunk he'd beaten up outside the *biergarten*. Perhaps the man had been at Stalingrad after all, despite his ridiculous claim to have fought under Rommel.

They rode in silence for a few minutes, until Traugott noticed the men were all staring at him with obvious amusement. Barely audible whispers and mocking snickers also assaulted him in the darkness, and while he knew it'd be wiser to just ignore them, he was in no mood to be made fun of by the Wehrmacht's Old Farts' Association.

"You see something you find amusing, soldier?" he asked the man sitting directly across from him.

The man almost seemed offended to be singled out. "Who, me? No", he replied slowly. He spoke with an accent Traugott couldn't quite place.

"No, *sir*", Traugott corrected him harshly, though technically a Wehrmacht soldier didn't owe an SS officer any deference.

The man hesitated for much too long before complying. "No, *sir*", he said. Then, his voice carrying a heavy load of sarcasm, he added: "Enjoying the nightlife, *sir*?"

Safely concealed by the darkness, several of his comrades giggled. Traugott ignored them. "A sense of humor, I like that", he said coldly. "You'll be needing it soon."

The man's smile winked out like a candle, extinguishing his arrogance as well, and suddenly he didn't seem quite so sure of himself. "What do you mean?" he asked. He once again dropped the *sir*, but this time Traugott let it go.

"It seems to me a man like you, a man of your immense talents, would be much more useful to the Reich in another capacity", he said. The truck hit a pothole as it rounded a corner, sending fresh waves of pain to wash over his body.

When Traugott could once again open his eyes, he saw the man was staring at him expectantly. He shot him a smile devoid of all humor.

"I see a promotion and perhaps even your own command in a near future", Traugott said.

The man was momentarily speechless.

"The *Volkssturm* is always in need of qualified officers", Traugott said.

The man's eyes grew wide in the darkness. The *Volkssturm* was a national militia composed of boys and old men who, officially, were not supposed to be younger than 16 or older than 60, but who were in fact quite often as young as 13 or 14 and as old as 70. That militia was as ill-equipped as it was ill-trained, and its casualty rate was among the highest of all German forces, since it was usually sent on missions too hopeless to justify the sacrifice of regular troops. And yet stories of the *Volkssturm*'s almost suicidal bravery abounded – the young being too young to fear death and the old apparently seeking a valorous end to lives often spent in complete anonymity.

Still, being assigned to the *Volkssturm* seriously shortened one's life expectancy, and the man knew it. A mask of anger descended on his face and he made to get up.

"Sit down", Traugott barked immediately. "One more move, one more insolent word out of you, and the *Volkssturm* will be the least of your problems. That goes for all of you."

There were twenty of them and only one of him, and he was injured. If they so chose, they could strangle him and dump him off the truck and that'd be the end of him. Or they could just throw him out and let the partisans finish him off. No one would say a word, no one would care.

Traugott had just a few seconds to make them sufficiently afraid to save his life. "Now, unless you want to be sent to the Eastern Front with some zit-faced teenagers and incontinent *Greis*, tell me where this truck is going."

Traugott grinned when the man told him. It seemed that Lady Fortune had finally decided to smile upon him once again.

Adriana was completely cut off from the world.

She wondered what time it was, how long she'd been here and how long she'd *be* here, whether the other inmates had begun their day of backbreaking work, whether Rita and Magrita were looking for her and whether *anyone* would ever look for her ever again...

There were no windows in her room. The only light came from a single bulb dangling from the ceiling that remained lit at all times. She tried standing on the bed to grab and unscrew it, but it was just out of reach – probably purposely so. She gave up after twenty minutes wasted swinging and flailing at it.

The light made it impossible for her to sleep. Besides, the thin sheets were covered with yellowish, disgusting stains. She almost threw up when she accidentally touched one that was still slightly wet and sticky.

If the walls to her cell – as she now thought of this room – quite efficiently blocked out any light, they failed to do the same for noise. All night she heard people coming and going, doors creaking open and slamming shut, laughs and screams and shouts, once what sounded like a woman crying, then two people arguing loudly, though she couldn't quite make out their words... It all melded into a maddening cacophony like that of an insane asylum until, suddenly, it all stopped. There was silence. Total and utter silence. Like someone had flipped a switch. It was almost quiet enough for her to hear her own heartbeat.

There was also darkness. The light was snuffed out like a candle, plunging the room into a darkness that wouldn't have been any deeper and more complete had she suddenly gone blind. At first she was afraid, but then her fear yielded to a strange sensation of relief and safety. Tension drained out of her and she felt incredibly tired.

Adriana thought of the bed, wondering if she could bring herself to lie in it, but instead she curled up on the floor and began to cry softly. She closed her eyes and, for the first time in a long while, she thought of her dead brother, Aaron, and she begged him to come get her.

She wanted to die, but instead she slept.

She awoke with a start. There was someone outside her door. She could hear breathing and panting.

The bulb flickered alive. A key turned in the lock. Then the door slowly swung open on creaky hinges.

She jumped in fear and instinctively ran to the back of the room, pressing herself against the wall as though she might melt through the brick.

Otto Mockël was standing in the doorway. He had his huge dog with him.

"It's five o'clock", he announced coldly. "Your first client is here."

Then he grabbed Achtzenh's collar and began unfastening the leash.

It was still dark when the soldiers dropped Traugott off about two miles from Auschwitz, but the sky was beginning to lighten in the east and day would break in less than an hour.

He heard laughter and what sounded like an obscene remark concerning his manhood as the truck drove away, but he was beyond caring. Those men would be dead before the month was out.

His broken rib made it hard for him to walk, so he ambled slowly along the side of the road. He threaded carefully, afraid he might trip and fall and not be able to pick himself up. With any luck a vehicle would come along and take him the rest of the way, but this early in the day, he had the road to himself. All he heard were chirping crickets and birds merrily greeting the dawning day.

Then the wind shifted and brought him the familiar odor of the camp's ovens. Traugott had heard some inmates say that it smelled like roasted chicken or perhaps roasted pork. Some had even wondered, upon first arriving, whether it might be the smell of a meal being prepared for them.

Others who'd had the additional misfortune of arriving during the night had sometimes exchanged worried glances after spotting the infernal, reddish glow of the furnaces against the night sky.

He smiled. To him, it simply smelled and looked like victory.

He painfully crested a low hill and, in the distance, finally spotted the huge expanse of the camp. It was so brightly lit that it repelled the night by several hundred feet and banished the stars from the sky. It looked like a small city, or perhaps like an oasis of light in a desert of darkness.

Even at this distance he could hear barking dogs and shouting guards. The noise never stopped, the camp never slept, and he loved it for it.

Stopping to catch his breath, Traugott admired Auschwitz for a moment. He felt an odd sense of pride looking at it, as though it somehow belonged to him, as though it was somehow a creation of his doing. It radiated a power he found incredibly intoxicating. Out here, he was just a simple man that any half-dozen unwashed, uncivilized barbarians could manhandle in all impunity. In there, he was a semi-god with a power of life and death over thousands of lesser beings.

Traugott grinned. Auschwitz was calling him. He pressed a hand against his broken rib and quickened his pace. He was almost there.

The big dog bounded and Adriana screamed.

It moved deceptively rapidly for a beast its size. It was on her in less than a second and it placed its front paws on her shoulders. She tried pushing it down, all the while desperately twisting her head to the side as far as it would go, away from its massive jaws, to keep the hound from ripping out her throat.

Achtzehn was incredibly powerful and she couldn't get it off her.

She won a brief victory when she grabbed a front paw in each hand, lifted them off her shoulders and threw the beast to the side. The dog landed awkwardly, rolled onto its back with a surprised yelp, but immediately got back up and came at her again.

"Make it stop! Make it stop!" she pleaded, by Mockël just kept watching in amusement.

Adriana tried to kick it in the snout, but her blow missed and she lost her balance when her other foot slipped. Suddenly finding herself at the dog's complete mercy, she hurriedly curled into a ball.

She drew her knees up underneath her stomach, ducked her head between her shoulders and placed her hands behind her neck. There was nothing else she could do.

The wolfhound began sniffing her crazily. It ran its wet muzzle all over her body, as though it were looking for something, and Adriana whimpered in fear. She tried to make herself even smaller, to make the ball even tighter, so sure was she that the dog would kill her the second it found her throat.

Achtzehn made a strange sound and stopped. It took Adriana a second to realize the hound had now positioned itself behind her. It was clumsily attempting to mount her, but its paws kept slipping against her thin dress.

She shrieked and tried to scramble away, but the dog's weight pinned her in place. She reached behind her and tried to bat it away with a hand, her fingertips brushed against the rough fur, but she could barely reach it. She was a fly trying to move a brick wall.

Achtzehn began thrusting blindly.

Adriana screamed.

Mockël threw back his head and laughed.

"Achtzehn... *Platz! Fuß!*" he called loudly. The dog immediately got off Adriana and obediently came to sit by his left boot.

Adriana began sobbing, her face hidden in the crook of her arm. Mockël was crying too, but his were tears of laughter.

"Next time you'll be naked and I won't call it off", he warned after a moment. "You got two hours to give us Traugott. If you don't, I won't ask again for another five days. Think about that, bitch. Five long days. And Achtzehn will be your first client, every single morning. But only the first."

Mockël didn't even bother closing the door when he left. Where the hell could she go?

There was a checkpoint about a mile from Auschwitz's main gate, but the guard manning it was asleep when Traugott arrived.

The soldier had probably counted on being awakened by the sound of an approaching car or truck. His plan had been defeated by the stealthy arrival of a visitor on foot.

And also, more than likely, by the empty bottle of alcohol under his chair.

Traugott observed the man for a few seconds and briefly considered grabbing him by the throat to teach him a lesson. Instead, he quietly picked up the rifle – an old Karabiner 98 Kurz bolt-action rifle that had seen better days – the guard had leaned against the wall next to him and resumed his walk.

Good luck explaining to your commanding officer where your rifle went, Traugott thought with a smirk.

He was soaked with sweat, panting heavily and in serious pain by the time he arrived at the camp's main gate. Unlike his colleague, the sentinel posted there was wide awake and more than a little startled by this dirty and disheveled officer arriving with the dawn.

There was a moment of uneasy silence as the two men stared at one another, Traugott clearly expecting to be let in instantly and the guard unsure what was expected of him. Luckily, the man recognized Traugott just in time to salute hastily and avoid a nasty incident.

Traugott looked at his watch to see if he might stop by Höss' office and essentially beg for his suspension to be lifted early. Only then did he notice that the timepiece had been damaged during his brief encounter with the Polish partisans. The dial was smashed and the leather strap torn in half. He ripped if off his wrist with a curse and threw it away.

It didn't matter. Höss wasn't expecting him back for a few days. He wasn't supposed to be here and it wasn't like he had an appointment to keep. He had all the time in the world. A couple of hours spent showering, changing into a clean uniform and getting his ribs bandaged in the infirmary could only improve the odds in his favor.

The obersturmbannführer could wait, he decided.

Traugott stopped to catch his breath. Not letting go of the stolen rifle, he rested one hand against a building and placed the other over the burning pain in his side. He was having difficulty breathing and for the first time he wondered whether the broken rib might have damaged, or even perforated, a lung. The thought worried him and he grimaced.

All the more reason to swing by the infirmary first chance he got.

Traugott let his gaze sweep the camp, taking in the sights and sounds and smells around him.

Four dour-faced guards were force-marching two dozen inmates to an unknown task. Progress was slow and the guards were clearly growing impatient. One kept hitting his open palm with a truncheon and shouting at the shuffling zombies to walk faster. Someone would be in for a beating if they didn't pick up the pace, Traugott knew. It was only a matter of time.

The kommando charged with collecting dead inmates from the barracks every morning had completed its macabre rounds and was on its way to the ovens, where the sonderkommando would make sure the hellish furnaces never ran cold.

He then heard a familiar voice and looked to his left. Josef Mengele was explaining something in a loud and animated voice. Gesturing wildly, the mad doctor was clearly in a hurry and the short man next to him was having a hard time keeping pace. They were headed for the ramp, which meant a transport was expected shortly. Traugott caught but a few words of their conversation, just enough to know that they were discussing twins. Again.

Feeling slightly dizzy, Traugott headed for Kanada. He found it easier to make progress if he held the rifle by the muzzle and used it as an improvised walking stick. It was still a long trek, since the warehouses were situated at the far end of the camp.

To his right was sector BIII, known as "Mexico", where were temporarily housed those workers destined for other Nazi work camps. It owed its name to the fact that these workers were often clothed in multicolored blankets, some of which had come from Kanada itself.

To his left was sector BII, which held a succession of camps. First came the quarantine camp, where hundreds of newly arrived inmates were temporarily sent to reduce the risk of an epidemic decimating Auschwitz's fragile population. But this camp, instead of limiting the spread of disease, seemed to encourage it. Conditions were so horrific that many inmates who weren't sick upon arriving soon fell ill. The roofs leaked so badly puddles often formed on the floor and cold wind blew through the cracks. Upwards of one thousand coughing, feverish and diarrhetic prisoners could be crammed into barracks meant for 700 or 800 people.

It was a wonder any of them survived at all.

Next to the quarantine camp came the Theresienstadt camp, followed by the Hungarian Jews camp, the Men's camp and then, finally, the Gypsy camp. Thousands upon thousands of people fought conditions not fit for cattle, but Traugott paid them no mind. His gaze was fixed on his beloved warehouses, which he could now see in the distance.

He almost shoved aside the guard manning the last checkpoint. He had only been gone for a few days, but he felt as if he'd been away for weeks so eager was he to return. He hobbled quickly to the front door, still using the stolen rifle as a crutch, and pushed it open.

All the women, all of "his" women, were hard at work and his arrival went completely unnoticed. He was bone-tired so he just stood there, watching them, basking in the comfort of the familiar scene before his eyes.

The mountain of shoes was higher than he remembered it. A dozen women were crawling over it fearlessly, like ants over the carcass of a dead animal, searching for matching pairs. Next to them other women were yanking items out of a pile of dresses. There was also a pile of men's pants, a pile of winter clothing, a pile of underwear, a pile of socks, a pile of children's clothes. To some they looked like so many giant burial mounds - which, in a certain sense, they were.

The work went on endlessly. Some inmates spent their days tipping out suitcases and adding whatever they found to the appropriate mound. Theirs were some of the most prized jobs in this small haven of safety, since those who held them were the first to find whatever food the bags might contain. If they didn't eat it themselves, they could smuggle it out to pass on to others or even barter with the guards.

A Chinese tale tells of a bird who, every morning, flies to a mountaintop to sharpen its beak on the branch of a tree. Once the bird has whittled the entire mountain down to nothing, the tale continues, the first second of eternity will have elapsed.

Like the bird, no matter how hard the women worked, no matter how hard they tried, they couldn't so much as dent the mounds. As long as the trains kept coming, the piles would remain.

Traugott watched as a woman found an object in the pocket of a jacket. He couldn't tell what it was, but she examined it for a moment before dropping it in a locked box at the center of the room. The object landed with a soft *thunk!* and Traugott smiled. More loot for him.

Then his gaze sought her and he couldn't find her. His heartbeat quickened.

He looked again, certain she would emerge from behind a pile at any moment, but still he didn't see her. It didn't matter there were hundreds of women in this one warehouse. He knew *exactly* where *she* worked, *exactly* where *she* was supposed to be, he could have found her had the room been filled with ten thousand workers, but still... there was no sign of her.

His blood turned cold and he forced himself to remain calm. He'd give it another five or ten minutes, then he'd investigate further. She couldn't be anywhere but here. He just had to find her. He had been gone for less than two days. What could have possibly happened during that time? Had she fallen ill? Or worse... had there been an accident?

His pain and his earlier resolve to be patient disintegrated.

"Where the hell is she?" he asked as he grabbed Magrita by the arm.

The young woman almost screamed in fright. She'd been concentrating on her task and he'd caught her completely by surprise. A guard noticed the scene and walked rapidly in their direction. Traugott saw him coming.

"As you were. I'll handle this", he barked at him.

The man hesitated for an instant. He, too, was a bit thrown by the officer's appearance, but the voice was unmistakable, especially here. He stopped, saluted and turned away.

"Damn you, I asked you a question. Where the hell is she?" Traugott demanded again.

Magrita had also recognized the voice. She shook her head. "I'm sorry, herr untersturmführer, I don't know. A man came for her and took her away", she said.

Traugott was both stunned and, suddenly, terribly frightened. "A man? What man? Tell me before I kill you!" he howled, shaking her like a rag. A jolt of pain from his broken rib made him grimace.

He was hurting her terribly but Magrita dared not pull her arm out of his grip. Such an act of resistance and defiance could earn her a bullet in the head. Traugott was clearly out of his mind and she had to remain as calm as possible. "The man... the man with the dog, herr untersturmführer. He came and..."

Traugott suddenly dropped her arm and took a step back as if she'd burned him. *A man,* she'd said. *The man with the dog.* He stared at her, speechless, his mind reeling. "Where... where did he take her?" he finally managed to ask.

"She doesn't know, but I do", someone said from behind him.

He turned around. "I followed them when he took her away. He took her to a building, but I don't know why", Rita said.

"You followed them? You could have been shot", Traugott said weakly. He seemed on the verge of thanking her, but he caught himself. "Show me where they went."

Rita just nodded.

"This had better work", Robert Mulka growled. "This was your idea. If she doesn't break and if Morgen gets wind of this..."

Mockël swallowed. Already the hauptsturmführer was having second thoughts about their plan. He was already trying to distance himself by claiming, hypocritically, that it had all been Mockël's idea. And yet if it worked, if *neunzehnhunderteinundsiebzig* gave them what they needed to bring down Traugott and countless others after him, Mulka would certainly be on the first train to Berlin to claim all the glory for himself.

The two men were standing outside the brothel. It was just after seven and Mockël had gone to get some breakfast after visiting Adriana in her cell earlier. He had then unexpectedly bumped into his superior, Höss' adjutant, and Mulka had demanded an update.

"She'll break, herr hauptsturmführer", he promised. "Maybe not today, maybe not tomorrow, but she'll break. I'm sure of it. After a few days on her back with one stinking Jew after another squeezed between her thighs, she'll *beg* us to listen to her."

Mulka nodded curtly. "If anyone knows where Traugott is hiding his loot, it's her", he said. "Make sure she talks."

Mockël heard an unspoken threat in the last sentence. What if, against all odds, she didn't talk? What if she, in fact, knew nothing? What if she lost her mind before revealing anything useful? Would Mulka then turn on him to save his own skin? Of course he would. Mockël was absolutely sure of it. Mulka would do anything to ensure his own survival - lie to anyone, betray anyone and kill anyone.

But so would Mockël. He petted Achtzehn, thinking how easily an accident might occur. A misspoken command, a leash held a bit too nonchalantly...

He saluted the hauptsturmführer. "She'll talk", he assured him. "Leave her to me." Mulka pressed his lips together into a thin, pale line and nodded before leaving, looking as tenebrous as ever.

Mockël entered the brothel and went directly to Adriana's room.

Traugott was stuck on the wrong side of the last checkpoint when he heard her shriek.

Auschwitz was a place of screams and shouts and moans and howls, but this particular shriek cut through all the others and struck him like a bullet. He heard it as sharply as if they had been the only two people left alive in the world.

He elbowed aside the guard checking Rita's papers and ran straight for the building the old kapo had indicated. Unlike her, he knew *exactly* what this building was, and the knowledge terrified him. His broken rib was like a white-hot poker stuck in his side as he ran.

He was less than a hundred feet away when she shrieked again. How he heard her through the ambient noise, how he heard her while she was still inside the brothel, on the other side of doors and walls, he never knew, but heard her he did. And run he did, his eyes watering with pain.

Hang on, mein geliebter, I'm coming. Hang on.

A soldier guarded the entrance to the brothel. His job was to keep any and all unauthorized visitors out of the building. The man was immediately alarmed by this dirty, unkempt and disheveled officer who limped toward him on a cane that looked suspiciously like a rifle.

"Out of my way", Traugott thundered.

"I'm sorry, herr untersturmführer, but my orders are to..."

Traugott was in no mood to listen or argue. The butt of his rifle struck the guard in the groin and the man doubled over as his knees buckled. Traugott could have hit him again, but there was no need. He simply grabbed him by the back of his uniform and pulled, and the man toppled face first into the dirt with both hands clutched between his thighs.

The way was clear.

A single corridor stretched in front of him. There were five doors on each side and all were closed, except for the last one on the left. And in that doorway stood a man in a gray uniform.

"Mockël!" he shouted.

Otto Mockël had specifically ordered the soldier guarding the entrance not to let anyone in until he'd left. He had then turned his attention to the business at hand and hadn't heard the door open. So he was caught completely by surprise when someone called his name. He was even more surprised to see Traugott limping in his direction.

He snarled.

"Achtzehn! *Hier!*" he said without taking his eyes off Traugott. The dog appeared at his feet as if by magic. Mockël then pointed to Traugott. "*Fass!*" he ordered with a sick smile.

The monstrous hound immediately bounded down the corridor with hackles raised and fangs bared. Its evil yellow eyes zeroed in on its prey and it bounded again, swallowing half the distance that still separated it from this man its master had ordered it to kill.

The dog had been well trained. Dozens of prisoners had taught it with their lives, hapless men and women and even children who had suffered horribly as it bit and clawed them maladroitly, until they finally bled to death. Some of the first had been tied up to make it easier for it to learn, but the last? The last, Achtzehn had learned that it could simply knock down with its massive weight before clamping its iron jaws around their windpipes. The same thing was now about to happen to this puny man.

Achtzehn crouched on its haunches to launch itself at its prey.

Traugott leveled the stolen rifle at the beast.

Was the thing even loaded?

The dog leaped.

Traugott pulled the trigger. The rifle fired.

Achtzehn slammed into an invisible wall. It stopped in mid-air and fell to Earth, Icarus-like, and the impact made the ground tremble. There was a moment when time stood still and then Achtzehn growled one last time, as though to scare Death away, before it breathed its last. The bullet had struck it in the chest and burst its heart.

A few doors opened and heads cautiously poked out. If screams were nothing out of the ordinary in this place, a gunshot was something else entirely. But curiosity could also get you killed at Auschwitz, and one look at the dead hound told the whole story. No one would mourn the monster.

The heads disappeared and the doors shut.

"Achtzehn?" Mockël screamed as he rushed to his dead pet. "Achtzehn!"

The two men passed one another in the narrow corridor, each now completely oblivious to the other's presence.

Traugott hobbled to the open door, unsure what he would find on the other side.

Adriana sat on the floor, entirely naked and trying to cover herself up with the remnants of her tattered robe. She was sobbing and her body sported several long, bleeding scratches, mostly on the back of her thighs.

She didn't notice that anyone was watching her. Traugott had never seen her naked body before and he was ashamed to find that, despite the circumstances, he was enjoying the sight. He summoned his willpower and turned his back. To his right, Mockël was lying on top of his dog and whispering softly while stroking its fur.

He heard Adriana gasp when she finally saw him standing there.

"You", she simply said.

He turned back around and saw she had wrapped herself in a dirty sheet. "What are you doing here?" she demanded defiantly.

He stared at her, slightly hurt and angered by her attitude. If not for him, God only knows what would have happened to her – *what would be happening to her right now*. But then again, he knew who he was dealing with and he should have known better than to expect any gratitude.

"Tell me what happened here", he simply said, though the scene was rather self-explanatory. Her torn clothing and the scratches he'd seen on her body likely explained the two shrieks he'd heard from outside.

She was about to say something when her eyes grew wide at the same time he heard and felt movement behind him. He tried to spin around but his broken rib stabbed him and he froze when Mockël pressed the muzzle of his sidearm into the back of his neck. The obersturmführer then snatched the rifle out of his hand.

"Say goodbye to your whore", Mockël said angrily. "Or maybe you'll get lucky and my bullet will kill her as well and you two can burn in Hell together forever."

Mockël cocked his weapon.

Traugott knew he was doomed. Injured as he was, there was no way he could fight back. There was nothing he could do except perhaps try to save her, if she'd just take a step to the side.

Standing where she was, when Mockël fired, there was indeed an excellent chance that Adriana would be hit as well. He was gesturing at her, with his eyes, to move out of the line of fire, but she just stood there, staring back at him, and for a moment he wondered whether, perhaps, she didn't *want* to be killed.

Mockël pressed harder with his gun.

This was it. It was all over.

"Put your weapon down immediately!" someone roared down the corridor.

Neither man moved.

"Obersturmführer", the voice thundered, "I gave you a direct order. Put your weapon down or I'll have you shot where you stand."

Still Mockël refused to comply. Someone fired a shot and Traugott thought that perhaps he had just been killed, but the bullet splintered the wood a few inches from his head and still he lived.

That got Mockël's attention. The crazed man finally, reluctantly, removed his sidearm from the back of Traugott's neck.

Traugott couldn't see what was happening in the corridor, but he immediately heard the sound of rapid footsteps, hands grabbed him, and he stifled a cry of agony when he found himself shoved face first into the wall next to Mockël.

His face now turned to the side, Traugott saw he owed his life to the timely intervention of Robert Mulka. The gun in the adjutant's right hand still smoked and he looked eager to use it again.

Traugott also saw that the guard holding him by the back of his uniform and pushing him into the wall was the same one he'd hit in the groin earlier, which probably went a long way toward explaining the rough treatment he was now receiving.

"Herr hauptsturmführer...", Mockël began, most unwisely. His eyes were red and his nose still ran from crying earlier.

"Silence!" Mulka roared. "You will only speak if I address you!" Only then did he seem to recognize Traugott. "Ah, untersturmführer Traugott", he said with mock friendliness. "I wasn't expecting you back so soon. But of course, I should have guessed you'd somehow be involved in this."

The guard posted at the door had fetched Mulka after being attacked by an officer and then, shortly thereafter, hearing a gun fired inside the brothel. They had returned just in time to witness the final scene.

Mulka then caught sight of Adriana watching him. The woman was just standing there silently, her chin raised high, still wrapped in her dirty sheet, arrogantly observing him through the doorway. And suddenly, Mulka found he'd rather be anywhere but here.

"Take them away", he abruptly ordered the two guards. "I'll deal with them later."

The soldiers spun the officers around and marched them out of the brothel. They stepped carefully around Achtzehn's inert body, but the beast had terrorized its last victim.

Traugott glanced quickly at Adriana as he was being led away. He saw her for less than a second, but it was enough to read the word she mouthed.

Danke.

PART THREE

1

April 1944

The F-7 Liberator leveled off at just over 25 000 feet over southern Poland.

Captain Tyrone Andrews let out a relaxed sigh and began whistling *Bésame Mucho*. Jimmy Dorsey's latest hit, though but another cover of Consuelo Velázquez' creation, was getting heavy rotation on GI Jive, his favorite show on the Armed Forces Radio Service. He was pretty sure he was in love with the host, GI Jane.

His copilot smiled.

"Never took you for a jazz kind of a guy, cap'n", Lieutenant Matt Clarke kidded him.

It was Andrews' turn to smile.

"Do you even know what *Bésame Mucho* means, Clarke?" he asked with a twinkle in his eye.

Clarke shrugged. "Sure doesn't sound like English to me", he said.

"It's Spanish for 'kiss me much'", Andrews explained. "And it's what I'm going to do when I get back home to the States. I got a little honey just waiting for me and when I see her, I'm gonna go, 'Kiss me much, baby, kiss me much'!"

Clarke grinned. He had flown dozens of missions with Captain Andrews and he'd rarely seen him this relaxed. The fact that they controlled the skies probably had a lot to do with his state of mind. The Allies were clearly winning the war and he couldn't remember the last time they'd been strafed by a *kraut* aircraft. Still, he found it comforting to look out the cockpit window and see two P-51 Mustangs opening the way for them, one at 10 o'clock and the other at 2. Two others followed behind, one at 4 and one at 8, watching their rear.

If some crazy Red Baron wannabe came looking for trouble, he'd find it in a hurry – and then some.

"What about you, Clarke?" Andrews demanded. "What kind of music you into?"

"You know I'm from Chicago, cap'n", the lieutenant replied. He pronounced it *Chee-kaw-go*. "And in Chicago, ain't but one kind of music: the blues, brother, the blues!"

"The blues? Really?" Andrews demanded, even though this was a conversation they'd already had half-a-dozen times.

"I'm tellin' you, cap'n", Clarke said animatedly. "Last time I was on leave I went to this dive and I heard a guy... Name of John Lee Hooker, little skinny black dude... Just remember that name, cap'n. John... Lee... Hooker. There was somethin' about him... Never heard anything like it. I get goosebumps just thinkin' about it."

Andrews dropped his eyes and routinely checked the constellation of dials in front of him. Everything looked fine. Speed just above 185 knots and airspeed good and fuel plenty and compass NNW and blah blah blah. It was all so tedious, really.

Their flyboy uniforms might drive the girls wild whenever they went out on the town, but the truth of it was so mundane. At first, at least, there had been the thrill of outflying the German pilots or of baring his ass at the Devil by barreling right through a barrage of *8.8cm FlaK 37*... But now? More and more often Andrews thought of himself as little more than a glorified cab driver whose sole mission it was to get his plane from point A to point B and then back to point A safely.

"How long 'til we get there?" he asked his navigator, a new guy whose name he kept forgetting.

"A little over an hour", the man sitting behind him said after doing a few calculations.

Andrews nodded. "And what's the name of that godforsaken place again?"

"Monowitz", the navigator said dully. He was a math whiz who only cared about the numbers that got them to where they were going, not about the actual name of the place.

Names could and did change without any reason; coordinates remained forever. Names meant nothing; coordinates meant everything.

"There's a synthetic oil plant there we need to photograph to see if it's worth bombing."

"Hard to find?" Andrews asked.

"It could have been, 'cause it's kinda small, but it won't be 'cause it's right next to something much bigger, some sort of camp called Auschwitz."

Andrews shrugged. He had just turned 23 and he'd never been outside Missouri before enlisting a year ago. These foreign names all sounded alike to him. "So we find the big camp and then we find the little plant?"

"Pretty much, yeah", the navigator said.

Andrews smiled and began whistling again. The sky was bright blue, the sun was warm, his four Pratt & Whitney R-1830-35 engines roared like dragons and the war was essentially over. Life was good and he was a happy man.

His F-7 flew on.

Adriana looked up, intrigued by the sound. Airplanes overflew Auschwitz all the time, but this one sounded... different.

There were in fact five planes, she saw. Four smaller ones drew an imaginary square around a much larger aircraft. And even though the planes were thousands of feet in the air, her sharp eyes made out the symbols under their wings: not swastikas or the Luftwaffe's *Balkenkreuz*, but rather... a star, a large silver star against a blue circle with white lines on each side.

Her heart began to beat faster and she looked at Magrita standing next to her.

"Magrita", she whispered excitedly. "Those aren't German planes. They're American."

Magrita had also been looking up. When she returned her gaze to Adriana, her expression confirmed she'd seen the same thing.

"Do you think that means they know we're here?" Magrita asked in a low voice.

If they know we're here, why aren't they bombing us?, she wanted to reply. *Destroy the ovens and blast the railways and stop the trains from coming and...*

But no bombs rained from the heavens, and that could mean only two things: either the Allies didn't know about them, or they did know but didn't care. She wasn't sure which one was worst.

Traugott was watching her. Again. She could feel his eyes on her. Again. When she looked at him, she saw that he, too, had seen the airplanes and known what they were. But where she felt a glimmer of hope, he clearly felt terror. He knew he had lost and that it was only a matter of time before he and thousands of others like him were asked to account for what they'd done.

She might have asked him why he kept fighting for a cause he knew to be lost. Why go on?

Why not just throw the gates open and let everyone go? Wouldn't such an act of mercy, perhaps, earn him some of the same from the justice he'd one day face? Why this stubbornness that could only find him twitching at the end of a rope? Why even stay? Surely it must be easy for someone like him to vanish. Just burn that evil uniform and run!

But she didn't need to ask him any of these questions, to which there was but a single, ridiculously obvious answer: Traugott knew it was simply too late to alter his fate. The war would be over in less than a year, and nothing he did now could possibly erase what he'd done in the past. He had no other choice but to see it through to the end, like the proverbial captain who goes down with his ship because he can think of nothing else to do.

A small part of her also wondered if, perhaps, he wasn't staying because of her. Maybe he hoped to protect her in some way when the end – The End - came. Maybe he somehow saw it as his duty to be here for her when King Alaric and the Visigoths finally surged over the last of Rome's seven hills. But at the same time, he must have seen that his presence would only endanger her further. Not that she had any intention of going anywhere with him, but an SS officer fleeing with a Jewish inmate?

They'd be dead before the end of the first day.

"Stop daydreaming", Magrita whispered to her urgently.

The line was moving again. Every morning they were served a suspicious, brownish liquid that might have been coffee or tea, but most likely was something else. On the best days it was lukewarm, certainly never hot, and it had absolutely no taste. It did, however, leave a strange, chemical aftertaste in the back of the throat, and Adriana had heard it said that it contained a drug called "bromine" that kept the inmates apathetic.

She had no trouble believing this might be true.

She counted herself lucky not to need to drink it. As one of the *weißköpfchen*, she had access to sufficient food that she could disregard the regular fare every now and then. But since most prisoners existed in a state of perpetual hunger, they gulped the mixture down eagerly every morning, not caring what it might be. They probably wouldn't have noticed had it been a cup of that fat sycophant Goering's own piss, so hungry were they.

This was one of the few occasions on which Adriana exploited Traugott's affection to her own benefit. Rather than drink the mysterious beverage, she made sure the untersturmführer was watching before exchanging her cup with whoever happened to be in line in front of her, receiving an empty cup in return for her full one. The other prisoner was only too happy to get a double portion and always went along unquestioningly.

She had become quite skillful at this and most of the time, the exchange went completely unnoticed. Hundreds and thousands of inmates lined up every morning and there weren't nearly enough guards to see everything that went on. Still, she could have been harshly punished for giving her food away; doing another inmate a favor was absolutely against the rules and she knew she was playing a dangerous game. So Adriana always waited until she was around Traugott to act, figuring the other guards would be busy looking elsewhere. This usually worked, but on the couple of occasions when someone did had notice, Traugott had rapidly intervened and promised to punish her personally – which he obviously never did.

"Are you going to go through with it?" Magrita asked softly.

The line was moving again. At the next table they were handed a slice of moldy, grayish bread. Some inmates wolfed it down on the spot while others, despite the hunger gnawing at their stomachs, stuffed the bread down a pocket to be enjoyed later, knowing they would get no other food before well after nightfall.

Adriana nodded and bit her lower lip. "I'm the only one who can. If I get caught, maybe it won't be so bad."

The two women were the last of the *weißköpfchen* to receive their portion. Their conversation was interrupted when Rita then led them to the warehouses, where they got to work.

"It's still dangerous", Magrita needlessly reminded her almost an hour later, while they stood at the folding table.

Adriana snorted. "Don't talk to me about dangerous. Look at where we are."

A woman had come to her the week before and demanded a word away from all the others.

Adriana had expected another one of those requests with which she was continually bombarded, but this one had taken her breath away.

The woman's husband, Dolfi, was also at Auschwitz. A former accountant who, like many of that profession, had been enlisted by the Nazis to keep records, Dolfi and a dozen others were tasked with noting who arrived at Auschwitz, who left, who was assigned to which *kommando* - who lived and who died.

In other words, in a perfect example of rabid German efficiency, the Nazis were having them compile endless records that, in a few years, would be presented as proof of their own atrocities.

Dolfi and the other accountants worked in a building whose outer courtyard abutted the washrooms located at the end of Adriana's warehouse. Anyone daring, or crazy, enough could open a window and throw something over a fence and into that courtyard.

And this is what the woman had requested: that Adriana, next Tuesday morning, meaning today, throw at her husband enough clothes for four men. Dolfi, she had promised, would be waiting below the window, ready to receive the package.

The woman had stubbornly declined to say more. She had refused to divulge how she communicated with her husband, what the clothes were for or anything else. She had simply hinted that if whatever was afoot succeeded, Auschwitz would be rocked to its very core.

It was far from unusual for the *weißköpfchen* to smuggle goods out of Kanada. It even occurred on a somewhat regular and almost organized basis. But this... this was something else entirely. The woman was asking her to involve herself in a mysterious plot about which she knew next to nothing. The consequences could be immense.

Adriana doubted that even Traugott would be able to protect her if she got caught. He might not even want to, if she pushed him too far.

Adriana had thought about it for a couple of days and even discussed the matter with Magrita before finally agreeing to help the woman and her husband. As she'd told Magrita, she was the only one who could. Anyone else, if caught, would be immediately dispatched to the gas chambers. She was the only one who stood a remote chance of escaping with her life if things went wrong.

"I think you're crazy", Magrita whispered again. "You don't even know what they're up to!"

Magrita was dead set against the idea. Her main argument revolved around the risk-reward equation: as far as she was concerned, Adriana was being asked to run a huge risk in return for little or no reward.

Adriana didn't quite see it that way.

"I'm tired of just going along passively, like a sheep", she replied, trying to keep her voice as low as possible. "I want to fight back. I *need* to fight back. You saw those planes earlier: the Americans aren't coming anymore. *They're already here*. The Nazis have lost the war. It's just a matter of time before this is all over. I want to do my part to make that happen."

"All the more reason to keep your bloody head down", Magrita argued angrily while folding a pair of men's pants. "Let the Americans end the war while you stay alive."

Adriana sighed. "It's not just about me", she explained. "What if they've found a way to let a hundred people out? A thousand? What if they kill Höss? What if they blow up the gas chambers? And what if it all comes to nothing because I wouldn't help them?"

"They need an old shirt to kill Höss? Please. You don't know that what they're planning can even work", Magrita said stubbornly.

"And you don't know it can't", Adriana shot right back.

Magrita paused. "And what about *Krumme*? What if he gets caught up in it and somehow ends up dead?"

Adriana leveled a black, angry stare at her friend. Did she honestly hope to dissuade her with such an argument? Did she really believe that she cared that much about Traugott? "Then he dies", she stated flatly.

But her cold-heartedness rang hollow even to her own ears and she unconsciously sought him out with her eyes. He was standing a few hundred feet away, deep in conversation with another officer, unaware that she was looking in his direction. She stared at him for a moment and for the briefest of instants, to her shock and dismay, his uniform vanished, leaving behind nothing but a simple, imperfect and fallible man playing the hand he'd been dealt to the best of his ability. Had she met him anywhere but here, could she have guessed him to be what he was? No, of course not. He was just a being of flesh and bones, much like her. But what did she really know of his life, of the joys and sorrows he'd experienced, of the trials and tribulations he'd endured, of the choices he'd made – or been *forced* to make – that had led him here?

And what if he hadn't made those choices and not ended up at Auschwitz after all? What would that have meant for her? She knew she owed him her life many times over, not to mention what Mockël's dog would have done to her the previous fall had it not been for his timely intervention. That was also the time when she'd seen him injured, he'd moved gingerly with a hand often pressed against his side, and though she didn't know any of the details, seeing him thusly reduced had troubled her somewhat. It would be a gross exaggeration to say it had 'worried' her, but at the very least it had planted in her a seed of re-humanization - or of de-demonization – that now threatened to bloom.

So today, here and now, could she honestly claim not to care whether he lived or died? She could not. As much as she hated to admit it, Magrita had shaken her resolve. At the same time, the odds that Traugott might be injured, physically or otherwise, were beyond infinitesimal, but whoever knew? Did the risk even matter? Adriana instantly decided it did not.

If the plot did indeed have the potential of striking a major blow against Auschwitz, as the woman had said, then one man, and especially a Nazi, could not stand in the way of such a thing.

"You ladies really need to keep quiet", Rita chastised them gently from behind. "If you keep this up, it won't be just me overhearing what you're discussing."

Her warning broke the tension that had been building between the two of them. Apparently, they weren't being as discrete as they thought and hoped.

"I've made up my mind", Adriana said, snatching the pants from Magrita's hands and adding them to the small pile in front of her. "I'll be back in ten minutes if all goes well."

She headed for the washrooms without another word.

If all goes well, Magrita thought as she stared after her.

Otto Mockël sneered with despair and disgust at the empty bottle that lay on its side on the table in front of him.

He gave it a spin, as though playing a solitary game of bottle, and almost knocked it to the ground. He then shook it with an unsteady hand, hoping for one last drop his unfocused eyes might have missed, but it was empty.

He groaned and threw it angrily against the far wall of his room. It exploded in a shower of glass and he collapsed back into a bed that reeked of sweat and vomit. He pressed both hands against his face to keep his head from exploding.

If only he could sleep. Just for an hour, maybe two. Not the drunken quicksand that swallowed him every night and from which he always emerged even more angry and confused than before but real, restful sleep of the kind that had eluded him for the past several weeks.

How he missed his dog. Achtzehn's murder – for that was how he thought of its death - had affected him the way the loss of a soulmate might have affected another. He cried for a few days, until he noticed the smirks and snide remarks. Then he began drinking.

He hadn't even been able to give his friend a proper burial: by the time he returned to the brothel, the animal's corpse was gone and nobody seemed to know what had become of it. He suspected it'd been incinerated along with the bodies of dead inmates, and how he hated to think of the magnificent beast's ashes mixing with those of such impure and inferior creatures! It was enough to make him cry even harder.

Mockël simply counted himself lucky the fallout hadn't been as bad as he'd feared.

He reported to Robert Mulka's office with Traugott the next day as ordered, and on his way there they passed the two guards who had witnessed the altercation. They had just emerged from their own meeting with Mulka and had the look of men who've come face to face with the Devil. No doubt the inmates who had seen, or simply *might* have seen, something were already dead – with one notable exception, of course.

It rapidly became clear that the moody hauptsturmführer was in quite a hurry to bury the whole messy affair. He asked a few perfunctory questions before dismissing Traugott and Mockël curtly, with a stern warning to stay the hell away from one another.

Traugott had been mystified by the adjutant's attitude, while Mockël had understood perfectly the man's burning desire to keep the matter as quiet as possible to prevent it reaching indiscreet ears – such as those of Maximilian Grabner, the Gestapo chief at Auschwitz, who'd only be too happy to learn of two SS officers almost murdering one another over a Jewish whore. And it was better not to think what might happen if the news should climb the grapevine all the way up to Konrad Morgen.

Mockël sat up and almost passed out when his head buzzed like a wasps' nest. Bile rose in the back of his throat and he fought an irresistible urge to puke. His body desperately wanted to purge itself of the poison he'd been pouring into it, but he wouldn't let it. He could no longer stand to be completely sober and clear-minded. He needed to keep reality at arm's length lest it overwhelm and drown him.

Mulka had reassigned him to a new position and he needed to report for duty in less than an hour. It had certainly not escaped his notice that the hauptsturmführer had removed him from his immediate entourage, banishing him to the outer reaches of his inner circle – where, presumably, it was hoped he would do less damage and cause less trouble.

Just thinking about it made him want to hang himself. Not only had he completely fallen out of favor with one of the most powerful men at Auschwitz, but he'd also been handed one of the most boring jobs one could possibly imagine.

But what choice did he have?

His accountants were waiting.

Dolfi had never considered himself a particularly courageous man.

He wasn't a coward, not exactly, but neither was he the type to throw himself on top of a hand grenade to die a hero.

That whole flight or fight thing? Flight suited him just fine, thank you very much, and to hell with those who thought him a weakling.

To hell, also, with those empty-headed cretins who'd solve their problems with fists and hurtful words. He was all in favor of a reasonable, level-headed discussion. But the minute voices were raised, he dropped his eyes and slunk away. May the bullies bask in their empty victories; he knew better.

If Dolfi understood himself not to be the bravest of men, he also knew, beyond the shadow of a doubt, that his sense of duty formed the very bedrock of his existence. There was no point asking whether you felt like doing something that needed doing. If it had to be done, then you just did it. Or, as Leonardo da Vinci once put it, *Being willing is not enough; we must do*. In other words, shut up about it already and move your ass.

It was with such thoughts swirling through his mind that he quietly shut the ledger into which he'd been entering the names of prisoners who'd arrived the previous day from the Netherlands. Or were they Romanian? Hungarian, perhaps? He was so distracted by the task at hand that he couldn't concentrate properly. He'd have to check his work later for any mistakes.

At least he didn't have to worry about the new obersturmführer.

He glanced discretely in his direction and saw that, as usual, the man was barely sober. He was leaning lazily against a wall, with his head down and the bridge of his nose pinched between two fingers. He appeared hardly aware of his surroundings and a gentle breeze might be enough to topple him over, by the looks of him.

No, Dolfi wasn't a warrior of the usual kind, the type that attacked fortified bunkers with an icepick clenched between their teeth. But what he lacked in physical courage, he liked to think that he more than made up for in intellectual fortitude. So when a man had come to him with that mad plan, the danger involved had immediately tied his stomach into knots – while his mind had instantly set about examining how, exactly, this might be accomplished.

He got up from his desk and just stood there, waiting to see if the obersturmführer noticed him. Nothing happened.

In fact, it wasn't really Dolfi's help the man needed, but rather his wife's. The woman was one of the *weißköpfchen*, and it was common knowledge these ladies of the white handkerchiefs could procure just about anything. Dolfi hesitated before agreeing – putting himself in harm's way was one thing, putting his wife another entirely – but in the end he accepted...

Don't just talk about fighting the Nazis, do something about it!

...and ultimately he was glad he did. It had taken a few days, but his wife had apparently found a way to get him what he needed without endangering herself too much.

He took a few steps but his head began to spin slightly. He stopped to steady himself and catch his breath. Perhaps it'd be better to postpone the whole thing? The officer was definitely half-drunk, but he might not be drunk *enough*. And if he noticed that something was amiss, then the entire plan could fall apart. Yes, the more he thought about it, the more sense it made to...

Stop procrastinating, he chastised himself. *The others have done their part, now do yours. It's your duty. Get to it.*

This obersturmführer was always here on Tuesday mornings. That's why Dolfi had asked for the package to be delivered on a Tuesday morning. He had counted on the man being both here and essentially incapacitated, and he hadn't been disappointed.

He was still very nervous. He took one last deep breath.

"Begging the obersturmführer's pardon", he began.

Mockël winced as if the man had screamed at the top of his lungs. "Shut the hell up and get back to work", he growled.

Dolfi swallowed hard. This was the point where, normally, he would nod and obey – except that wasn't an option just now. He had to stand his ground and find a way to be allowed outside. "I need to use the latrines, herr obersturmführer", he insisted. The excuse sounded incredibly lame, but it had the advantage of being entirely plausible since most inmates frequently suffered from uncontrollable diarrhea.

Mockël made a face. "Of course you do, *du verdammter Arschficker*", he sighed disgustedly, sounding as though he was suffering tremendously. He wasn't supposed to let the inmates out of his sight, but feeling the way he felt this morning, going anywhere near those putrid latrines might be enough to kill him – something else Dolfi had relied on.

Mockël waved Dolfi away, and for an instant the man feared he was being dismissed and that his plan had failed.

"If you shit on my floor, I'll drown you in it. You've got one minute", Mockël finally said, looking at his watch.

Dolfi's mouth had gone completely dry and he had to lick his lips before replying. "*Danke,* herr obersturmführer".

He then exited the building as calmly as he could. Now, all he could do was hope for the package to be delivered on schedule.

Adriana didn't dare glance back over her shoulder to see if she was being followed.

She had to appear as confident as possible to avoid detection. She had to maintain the illusion of the industrious worker going about her legitimate business. So she squared her shoulders, stared straight ahead and tried very hard not to think about the way she walked. Was she going too fast? Too slow? Would anyone even notice? Was she attracting attention to herself by attempting to appear inconspicuous?

The more she worried about it, the more she tried to correct her gait, the more awkward it became, the less natural it felt and the more she worried about it. There were hundreds of inmates in the warehouse, but she might as well have been alone so sure was she that all the guards were staring at her. It was driving her crazy, as though every last ounce of concentration she possessed was being monopolized by the control of those two unwieldy appendages at the end of her legs.

She strolled by a couple of guards who didn't spare her a second glance. She then narrowly avoided colliding with a woman carrying a gigantic armload of handbags destined for Germany. No doubt some *fräulein* would be quite pleased to obtain one, never suspecting, or never caring, where it had come from.

The two women deftly danced around one another, like two moons that each orbit the other, and Adriana was about to relax when, perhaps unavoidably, her feet betrayed her. She tripped and fell to one knee, dropping the clothes she was holding.

"*Vorsichtig, faul Hure!*" the guard nearest her shouted. She simply nodded, quickly picked herself up and walked away.

Adriana was petrified.

She made sure not to look at the guard and tried to conceal her face from him. She was a bit too well-known in these parts and with any luck, the man hadn't taken a good look at her. If he had, he'd have absolutely no trouble identifying her later on.

Of course I recognized her. We all know who she is.

It was Traugott's whore.

Adriana finally reached the washrooms. There were a couple of women in there and she washed her hands and face while willing them to go away. The first one left after just a few seconds, but the second one lingered in front of the mirror for about seventeen hours. What she was looking at, Adriana had no idea, but she could only wash her hands so many times before beginning to attract attention. If the other prisoner didn't go soon, then she'd have a problem.

The two women finally looked at one another in the mirror, and after a quick and polite smile, the other inmate, perhaps sensing she was being importunate, left.

Adriana breathed a sigh of relief and counted to ten. When no one else arrived, she rapidly checked the stalls to make sure they were empty and then went to the window.

She groaned in despair.

The window was two feet higher than she remembered. She could barely reach it, even standing on tiptoes. There was no way she could throw anything into the neighboring courtyard.

She fought down a brief surge of panic. She couldn't stay here forever and she had to think clearly. Either she found a solution in the next few seconds or she'd have to get back to work.

She glanced quickly about the room, looking for anything she might stand on, but the Nazis were nothing if not paranoid: they knew that any object was a potential weapon, so everything had either been removed or solidly bolted down.

Time was running out. Adriana knew she risked being discovered at any moment. She took a few steps back from the window, wondering if she might, with a running start, leap high enough to grab the ledge and hoist herself up. Instead, she noticed that one of the tiles on the wall had been damaged and cracked.

Thank you Aaron.

The tile was about 18 inches off the floor. She dropped the clothes and began prying at it, but it was hopeless. She only managed to lacerate the tip of a finger, covering the white tile with her blood as she worked.

The tile refused to budge but she couldn't give up. Not now.

She turned her back to the wall and began hammering the tile with the heel of her left shoe. Nothing happened. Adriana kicked the tile again and again, cursing and swearing at it, almost crying, until she was rewarded by a cracking sound.

She smashed through the wall the next time she struck. Adriana almost cried out in relief. She rapidly cleared out the remaining debris and stared at the hole she had created in the wall.

It was small, but it was enough. She had her toehold.

The latrines were on the right. The courtyard was on the left. If the obersturmführer noticed him going the wrong way, Dolfi would probably be shot dead on the spot.

He paused outside the door with his hands clasped over his lower abdomen, feigning a bad cramp. He glanced to his left, hoping to see if there was any activity in the courtyard, but it was around the corner and mostly hidden from view. He wouldn't know until he got there.

His nerves failed him and he made a beeline for the latrines. He willed his body to reverse course and head for the courtyard, without any success. As though suddenly endowed of their own will, his legs took him to the latrines where, for lack of anything else he could do, he dropped his pants and sat over one of the stinking holes. The stench was worst than anything he could have ever described and he covered his nose and mouth with a hand.

He sat there for much too long, pondering his next move and cursing himself for a cowardly idiot. The mad obersturmführer had warned him to return in less than a minute and yet here he was, sitting in a sticky soup of someone else's feces, wasting what precious little time he had.

A column of prisoners was being marched behind the latrines. The column came to a halt and there were shouts and screams. Dolfi couldn't see what was happening, but he didn't need to; he'd already seen it a million times, and he knew what would happen next. There came the sound of leather against flesh, more shouts and screams, threats and menaces, soul-rendering pleas of mercy and whimpers of despair, and then, unavoidably, a gunshot. The column resumed its march.

That broke through his paralysis. His instinct had been to flee to the latrines, lured there by a mirage of safety. Unlike Ulysses, he'd had no men to tie him to his mast to prevent him from jumping into the sea when he heard the Sirens' song. He'd forgotten that no place was truly safe at Auschwitz. Any guard fancying some target practice could shoot him between the eyes, right here, right now, for not shitting correctly. He wasn't any safer here than standing in the courtyard.

Dolfi decided that if he were to die, he'd die like the Vikings did, with a sword in his hand, not cowering in the latrines while others found the courage to do what needed to be done.

Being willing is not enough; we must do.

He stood up, pulled his pants up and tied the rope around his waist. He'd have to walk by the building's entrance to reach the courtyard, and thus risk being seen by the obersturmführer, but he suddenly found that he didn't care.

Let the SS see him. Dolfi had never once been in a fight in all his life, but if it came to that, at least he'd go out with a bang.

The tip of the shoe wouldn't fit in the toehold, so Adriana kicked it off and shoved her bare toes into the opening, slashing them against the jagged tile.

She pushed herself up and bit her lower lip to keep from crying out when the ceramic tore into her flesh. Bright red blood ran down the grimy wall.

Adriana pushed the window open with one hand while hanging on to the bundle of clothes with the other. It was an impossible circus act of equilibrium made even more perilous by the atrocious pain now inflaming her left foot.

The courtyard lay directly below the window but that was the only part that, so far, was going according to plan. No one had apparently noticed, or at least no one had informed her, that a 10-foot high fence topped with barbed wire separated said courtyard from her building. The fence essentially reached to the bottom of the window out of which she now leaned. So instead of simply dropping the clothes down, Adriana would have to throw them a short distance and hope they cleared the barbed wire.

There was also the small difficulty that, as of right now, the courtyard was empty.

Adriana cursed and looked back over her shoulder to make sure she still had the washrooms to herself. She almost fell off her perch when she saw Magrita staring back at her with her mouth hanging open.

"What are you doing?" both women asked at the same time.

"Shut up and get out of here", Adriana hissed at her friend. "You'll get killed."

"So will you!" the other woman retorted angrily. She then noticed the blood on the wall. "What...?"

"Shutupshutupshutup!" Adriana rattled. "I don't have time for this, Magrita. You need to leave. *Now*."

Magrita stared back at her defiantly and crossed her arms over her chest like a child refusing to eat her broccoli. "You don't tell me what to do", she said stubbornly. "Do your thing. I'll stand watch and let you know if anyone is coming. Just hurry up."

Magrita then retreated into a stall from which she could keep an eye on the warehouse, all the while pretending to be relieving herself, and Adriana knew she had lost the argument.

She looked out the window again and sighed loudly. The courtyard was still empty. She decided to count to fifty before giving up. She had already been gone for far too long and now that she was endangering Magrita as well as herself, this couldn't go on forever.

She had reached forty-eight when a man suddenly materialized from behind the building and hurried into the courtyard. He was so thin and frail he had to hold his pants up with one hand as he shuffled along.

Adriana didn't know who he was, but he was looking straight at her and so he had to be the one. Without waiting, she threw one shirt out the window, as hard as she could, and it sailed over the fence and landed in the dirt in front of him. He immediately picked it up and motioned for her to throw him the rest. How he would conceal it or what he would do with it later wasn't her concern.

Three other shirts and three pairs of pants followed without any problem and Adriana began to think they were actually going to pull it off. The insanity that was Auschwitz was working in their favor. There was so much going on at any given moment, so much noise, so much movement, that they were much like the proverbial tree hidden in the forest.

Adriana threw the last pair of pants out the window and prepared to climb down. But either she overconfidently hurried her throw, or the demon that claimed Auschwitz as its playground decided to have some fun, or their luck just plain ran out, whatever happened, a breeze sprung up in an otherwise completely still day and blew the pants into the barbed wire.

Adriana and Dolfi both froze and stared at the pants, each apparently waiting for the other to save the day.

Adriana was the first to react. She reached out the window as far as she could, pushing the broken tile even deeper into her foot, but she would have needed arms six feet long to reach the pants. There was nothing she could do.

The pants were there, in plain view for all to see, fluttering in the wind like the world's ugliest flag, just waiting for the alarm to be raised.

Dolfi shook his head, as though emerging from a daze, and dropped the clothes he was holding. As Adriana watched, the small man began to climb the fence, perhaps the most suicidal thing anyone could do at Auschwitz. Any guard spying him would shoot without a single moment of hesitation.

He reached the top of the fence and began to tug at the pants, but they were completely tangled in the barbed wire. He tugged harder and Adriana heard a ripping sound...

...that melded with the sound of a gun being cocked behind her.

She froze.

"Get down from there", a voice she knew only too well ordered calmly.

She freed her foot from the broken tile and couldn't stifle a cry of pain. Blood began to flow freely from her wound. Standing on one foot, she slowly spun around and came face to face with Mattias Traugott, whose sidearm was trained not on her, but on a petrified Magrita.

"I'm sorry, Adriana", the woman whimpered. "I was watching you and he..."

Adriana wasn't listening to her. She was watching Traugott, trying to gauge his mood. He, too, was essentially ignoring Magrita and looking at her. He appeared angry, obviously, but underneath his outer layer of anger Adriana thought she could detect... what? Disappointment? Hurt? Betrayal? Something of the kind.

She let out a loud sigh. She could feel blood pooling around her foot.

"You can leave, Magrita", she said confidently. "This doesn't concern you. It's between him and me."

Magrita hesitated. She was staring down the barrel of Traugott's gun and didn't dare move. "But...", she simply said.

"Magrita, for the love of whatever god you believe in, just go", Adriana repeated a bit more forcefully. Her eyes never left Traugott's. "He won't shoot you. You were never here. Was she, herr untersturmführer?"

Traugott didn't immediately respond. But after a moment, as if to acquiesce, he slowly lowered and holstered his gun. Magrita quickly slipped away.

"I have every right to kill you where you stand", Traugott said after she'd gone.

"You have every right to kill me where I stand whenever you want", Adriana replied, her tone bordering on insolence. Traugott winced.

"What are you doing here?" he asked.

"Look around you. I came to take a crap."

He narrowed his eyes at her, a bit destabilized by her apparent insouciance at being caught red-handed. Any other inmate would have been quaking in fear, and that would in turn have dictated his own behavior. Their respective roles would have been etched in stone, clearly defined by Auschwitz's evil. But now... She almost seemed to be mocking him, as if she had not a care in the world and he had no power over her. The way she looked at him made him feel as though *he* was in the wrong and *he* should be apologizing to *her*.

Yes, any other inmate would have been groveling at his feet by now, begging him to spare their life. But *neunzehnhunderteinundsiebzig* wasn't any other inmate and that was the problem, now, wasn't it?

"You cut your foot", he said, pointing at it as though she might not have noticed.

She crossed her arms over her abdomen, under her breasts, and sighed again. "I most sincerely thank the untersturmführer for his concern. I'll go see Doctor Ada later on." There was no point lying about how she'd injured herself, since he'd seen everything.

"Why were you looking out the window?"

"I needed some fresh air. It stinks in here."

Her double-entendre was impossible to miss.

Traugott had had enough. He wouldn't stand here and be ridiculed by anyone, not even by her. "You're lying", he snarled as he pushed her aside.

Adriana slipped in her own blood and fell. She could only watch as Traugott placed the tip of his boot in the hole, grabbed the ledge with both hands and hoisted himself up.

He looked out the window. At first nothing happened as he oriented himself and took in the scene before his eyes, but then his face hardened and Adriana felt an icy dagger of fear plunge into her heart.

This time, she feared, she'd gone too far.

Mockël wanted to take an ax and split his head open. That, perhaps, would alleviate his pain.

Every heartbeat reverberated painfully against the inside of his skull, threatening to blow it apart. His eyes refused to focus and everything was a blur. His skin tingled painfully and his dry tongue seemed glued to the roof of his mouth. He'd tried eating something earlier on, but his stomach had violently rebelled and ejected his offering. Even a sip of water made him sick.

All he could think of was going back to his room and having a drink. A half-bottle of scotch or vodka would take care of everything that ailed him, he knew. Oh, the relief would be temporary, he also knew, but at least he'd be liberated from his misery for a few hours.

He looked as his watch and groaned when he saw it had only been ten minutes since... well, since... *since the last time he'd looked at his watch* was all he could conjure up. He'd looked at it a bit earlier on, but now he couldn't quite remember why. To see how much longer before his shift ended, probably.

No, that wasn't it.

His head hurt too much to concentrate. Everything in his brain was jumbled together. Yesterday and today and tomorrow and night and day and right and wrong and black and white and love and hate and life and death had all been melded into one by the furnace of his deepening insanity. Nothing made sense anymore. He tried focusing on simple, basic facts, hoping to restore some order to his mind, but even that failed. When he tried recalling his own birth date, his brain instead conjured up Adolf Hitler's, 20 April 1889, and from there his mind leaped to his dead dog, whom he'd secretly given the Führer's initials, and then he wanted a drink even more badly.

An image came to him, the ghost of a memory, a shape glimpsed through the fog in a dark forest... There had been a man. No, not a man, an inmate. Some thin, frail man, who... who...

Mockël suddenly looked up and almost passed out when a wave of pain struck him like a sledgehammer. He fought an irresistible urge to vomit and closed his eyes, pressing himself against the wall to keep from falling. The dizziness receded after a few moments and he looked to his left.

There was an empty desk at the back of the room. A man should have been working at that desk. A man who'd claimed to need to use the latrines.

That was when and why he'd looked at his watch. To make sure the man wouldn't be gone for too long. And now an inmate in his charge had been missing for over ten minutes and Mockël hadn't even noticed.

Just when you thought things couldn't get any worse.

Brutally half-sobered, Otto Mockël rushed out of the building.

The window overlooked a small courtyard behind a building where, to the best of Traugott's knowledge, a couple dozen clerks did whatever it was that clerks did – meaning nothing of great consequence.

A 10-foot-high fence topped with barbed wire separated the warehouse from the courtyard. A small piece of white linen fluttered in the wind, caught in the barbed wire like a flag of truce, but he paid it no mind.

He was getting ready to climb down when a man hurriedly emerged from the building. His uniform marked him as an SS officer.

The man looked first to his right, away from Traugott, and then to his left, as though he were looking for something or someone, and then their eyes met and the Earth stopped spinning on its axis.

Traugott. What the fuck was he doing there, looking at him, out that window?

Spying on him, of course. The jealous bastard was watching him, reporting to Mulka and Höss and Grabner and even the goddamn Bloodhound Judge his-own-almighty-self everything that he said and did. That explained his recent fall from grace. Traugott and his bloody whore had poisoned them all against him with their lies and falsehoods.

He was going to kill them.

The latrines were on the right, and that's where he should have gone to look for his missing inmate, but instead, driven by his paranoia, Mockël entered the courtyard, his eyes never leaving

Traugott's.

No words were needed as the two enemies stared at one another.

Mockël was about to say something when he heard and felt movement behind him. He spun around a bit too rapidly and his eyes swam for a moment before he could see clearly again.

"...for being gone so long", Mockël heard a man say when his mind finally reconnected with reality.

He shook his head. His missing inmate was standing in front of him, contritely staring at his bare feet. He seemed to be apologizing for... oh, who the hell cared what he was apologizing for?

"Get back to work", Mockël ordered summarily. "I'll deal with you later." Dolfi nodded and left.

Mockël dropped his head and exhaled noisily through his nostrils. He knew he should be relieved the inmate had returned, that no harm would apparently come from his drunken carelessness, but the rage that burned at the core of his soul blacked out everything else.

Now he understood why he had fallen so low so fast. He knew who had stuck all these daggers into his back.

Mattias Traugott had engineered everything. Mattias Traugott had plotted his downfall. Mattias Traugott had connived and cheated and lied. And ultimately, Mattias Traugott had orchestrated this inmate's momentary disappearance to deal Mockël a *coup de grace*.

The logic of Mockël's delirious reasoning would have completely escaped anyone else, but to him, it all suddenly appeared so very clear and obvious.

Yes, Traugott was responsible for everything that had gone wrong in his life, and he'd make him pay.

Three days later

The powerful Steyr 220 slowed as it approached the camp's main entrance.

The guard manning the gate was instantly alarmed. This was Rudolf Höss' official car, the one the camp commander used to travel to Berlin in a hurry. The mighty Austrian machine could outrace just about anything else on wheels, and no one used it but Höss himself.

The guard hesitated. He was under strict orders to inspect every single vehicle leaving Auschwitz, but no one had told him if the rule also applied to the dreadful obersturmbannführer. Should he follow his instructions to the letter and stop the car, or should he use some common sense and respectfully wave it through?

He shielded his eyes from the sun and tried to peer through the car's narrow windshield. He could make out four men, four SS officers, but their faces were obscured. But since Höss was the Steyr's sole user, who should be inside but the man himself?

The car was now less than 50 feet away, and while it had slowed, it showed no sign of stopping. The driver clearly expected the gate to be opened without further delay.

The guard swallowed hard and, in a split second, decided he'd rather be disciplined for excessive zeal than lack of it.

He raised his left hand and motioned for the car to halt.

The driver swore.

Stanislaw Gustaw Jaster gripped the steering wheel with all his strength to keep from shaking. His stolen uniform was drenched with sweat and his heart was pounding.

"He wants us to stop", he muttered through teeth clenched so hard they might shatter. "What do we do?"

"We can't stop", the man riding in the passenger seat immediately said, stating the obvious. Józef Lempart was a priest whose cool head and even temper had earned him the respect of the other inmates. "We'll die if we stop. Just keep going."

"I can't drive through the gate!" Jaster snarled.

"Slow down as much as you can, maybe he'll change his mind", Lempart counseled calmly.

The Steyr had slowed almost to a crawl. They were now less than 20 feet from the guard, who was still motioning for them to stop. A few more seconds and he'd be able to peer inside the car, and then it'd all be over.

"Some divine intervention would be timely, *ojcze*", Jaster said humorlessly.

Two other inmates sat in the back. Eugeniusz Bendera and Kazimierz Piechowski glanced at one another nervously. The four of them had already agreed on a course of action should such a situation arise and Bendera, who had masterminded the escape, did not intend to leave the outcome up to God.

"Hold the brake and rev up the engine", he ordered Jaster. "Make it roar. The more we slow down, the more suspicious the guard will become. Show him we're not afraid of him."

Jaster took a deep breath and obeyed. The powerful engine's growl made the whole car shake. If Jaster's foot slipped off the brake, the Steyr would certainly bolt uncontrollably and crash.

Bendera then punched Piechowski's shoulder. "Do it, Kazik", he said.

Piechowski, a 21-year-old Pole who had spent weeks removing the bodies of those executed along the death wall between Blocks 10 and 11, lowered his window. He pointed his sidearm directly at the guard.

"Wake up, you buggers!" he screamed in German, all the while carefully keeping his head concealed inside the car. "Open up or I'll open you up!"

The guard, already a bit unsettled by the engine's roar, just about jumped out of his boots when a gun emerged from the car's left rear window and he glimpsed the uniform of the untersturmführer holding it – the uniform of the SS-Totenkopfverbände, the dreaded unit that ran the death camps.

He took a terrified step back and almost tumbled backward before running to the main gate and scrambling to get it open.

The Steyr sped past him and disappeared in a cloud of dust.

"In my own car?" Rudolf Höss hissed for the umpteenth time. "They got away in my own fucking car! *Jemand mir bitte sagen, wie das passiert ist!*"

Maximilian Grabner crushed his cigarette in an ashtray on the table in front of him while Robert Mulka stared fixedly at an object only he could discern on the ceiling. Neither man could provide the camp commander with the answers he was demanding.

"Herr obersturmbannführer", the Gestapo chief began as calmly as he could. "The investigation has just begun. We'll know more in a few hours, perhaps tomorrow. My men are interrogating inmates as we speak."

Höss nodded. He knew what a Gestapo interrogation implied. If nothing else, it would at the very least discourage others from entertaining any notion of imitating the four jailbirds.

The daring escape had been discovered a few hours earlier and a search of nearby roads and towns had so far turned up nothing. Both Grabner and Mulka knew that finding the men would be exceedingly difficult, if not impossible. The four escapees were all Polish and since Auschwitz was in Poland, they wouldn't lack for sympathizers willing to hide them in an attic or a barn.

"I, too, have launched an investigation", Robert Mulka added. "All officers have been ordered to immediately report to me any information regarding this matter."

Höss' adjutant doubted very much that his order would yield any concrete leads. The camp commander needed names to save his own skin, he needed if not the actual culprits than at least plausible scapegoats, and any officer declaring any knowledge of anything even remotely related to the escape risked finding himself accused, sooner or later, rightly or wrongly, of incompetence and laxness. The officers were thus much more likely to simply keep their mouths shut.

Höss got up and, muttering to himself with his head bowed and his hands linked behind his back, began pacing back and forth at the head of the table around which he'd convened a dozen men for an emergency meeting. Then, in a sudden fit of rage, he picked up the chair in which he'd sat a moment earlier, lifted it above his head and smashed it against the floor. A three-inch-long shard of wood flew directly at Mulka, straight as an arrow, and the hauptsturmführer ducked out of the way just in time to keep from losing his right eye.

Höss never even noticed, so engulfed was he by his anger. It was completely inconceivable to an SS like him that they'd all been duped by four Jews, a people he regarded as being devoid of all intelligence and cunning. That such a thing could have happened went against absolutely everything he believed in.

"I want answers!" he howled. "I *demand* answers!"

Grabner sighed silently. All he had were fragmentary pieces of evidence he didn't feel comfortable sharing just yet, but perhaps that would placate the camp commander for the time being.

"We don't know much, herr obersturmbannführer", he warned. "Those who escaped are Stanislaw Gustaw Jaster, Józef Lempart, Kazimierz Piechowski and Eugeniusz Bendera." Grabner struggled with the pronunciation of the foreign names. "Bendera is said to have been a very gifted mechanic. That's apparently how he gained access to... the vehicle." He'd been about to say "to your car", but he changed his formulation at the last second for fear of provoking the commander's ire anew.

"You mean, that's apparently how he managed to steal it", Höss growled.

"Yes, herr obersturmbannführer", was all the Gestapo chief could reply. "It also seems Piechowski worked in the store block, where the guards' uniforms and ammunition are kept. From what we can tell, the other two, Jaster and Lempart, were simply recruited as accomplices, nothing more."

Höss was shaking his head in disbelief. That four inmates, *four putrid Jews*, could thumb their noses at hundreds of guards, that they could so easily evade one of the tightest security systems ever devised by man, was simply incomprehensible to him. There'd be hell to pay when Berlin learned of the escape, he knew, and he needed answers to fend off the calls that were sure to come for his head.

"They sneaked into the block through the trap doors that cover the chutes to the coal cellars", Grabner continued. "We think Piechowski had sabotaged them earlier so they could get inside. And since the block is deserted on Saturday afternoons, they knew they'd have the place to themselves."

"How did they manage to return to the block unnoticed?" Höss demanded angrily. "Someone should have checked if they were registered before allowing them to leave the main camp!"

"That we don't know", Grabner admitted. "But once inside the block, it was just a matter of breaking down the door to the storeroom, dressing themselves in uniforms and, well..."

Grabner left the conclusion unsaid and an uneasy silence descended upon the room. They were all waiting for Höss to say something when a discrete knock came at the door. A very young member of Mulka's staff walked in, saluted Höss and, claiming to have just received crucial information, respectfully requested a minute of his boss' time. The adjutant excused himself and returned shortly after conferring with the young officer.

The tension inside the room was palpable and Mulka allowed himself a rare smile before speaking.

"I have some good news, herr obersturmbannführer", he said before shooting Grabner a vicious look. "It seems the SS have succeeded where the Gestapo failed. My men have found your car abandoned about 35 miles from here, outside the original search perimeter."

He didn't need to point out that this perimeter had been determined by Grabner; they all knew it. Höss looked at his adjutant with the unconcealed eagerness of a child on Christmas morning. "And the inmates?" he asked.

Mulka pursed his lips. "I'm afraid there's still no sign of them, herr obersturmbannführer", he admitted. "But the stolen uniforms were found abandoned inside the car."

Höss frowned. "What? They fled naked or in their underwear? That makes no sense."

Mulka was a bit flabbergasted by his boss' apparent stupidity, so he took a moment to compose himself before replying.

"Of course it doesn't", he finally said. "A more plausible hypothesis is that they procured some civilian clothing, either before or after escaping, into which they changed to blend into the population. Four Polish *primitivlinge* would be much harder to find than four SS officers who don't speak much German."

Mulka despaired to see that Höss was still mystified, even though he suddenly wasn't. He knew exactly who he next needed to question.

Traugott stormed through the warehouse, indiscriminately shoving inmates and guards out of his way as he went.

He was looking for one of three women, and misfortune had it that the first one upon whom he should lay eyes was Rita, the elderly kapo.

He grabbed her by the arm like a teacher admonishing an impertinent child, making her wince. "Find her and send her to me now. If she's not in my office in five minutes...", he growled next to her ear.

He let the threat hang as he walked away. He obviously didn't need to specify who he was talking about.

A fearful Adriana arrived a few minutes later. Rita had come to her, as frazzled as Adriana had ever seen the usually placid old lady, to tell her Traugott was urgently looking for her – but mostly to warn her it had been at least a year since she'd last seen him in such a fury.

Adriana was under no illusion as to what to expect. She knew exactly what this was about. News of the daring escape, a few days earlier, had spread through Auschwitz like the plague and Adriana had connected the dots. She now understood what the clothes had been for, what she'd involved herself in. It was bigger than anything she could have possibly ever imagined.

But now that Traugott had also somehow connected the dots, she'd die.

So Adriana wiped the tears from her eyes, she raised her chin defiantly and she steeled herself to go toe-to-toe with him one last time.

The door to his office was open, so she just stood there silently. He knew she was there, just as she knew that he knew. The contest between them was engaged, the battle of wills begun. Would she cough discreetly to announce her presence, or would he look up and feign surprise to find her standing there, perhaps even offer up an insincere apology for keeping her waiting?

Traugott was bent over his desk, working on some document. His pen scratching dryly against the paper was the only sound. It went on for several minutes and Adriana was just about ready to yield when he finally put the pen down and began reading what he'd written.

Apparently satisfied, he sat back in his chair, closed his eyes and pinched the bridge of his nose.

"Do you know what this is, *neunzehnhunderteinundsiebzig*?" he asked without preamble, waving the sheet in the air but never opening his eyes to look at her.

Adriana swallowed. "No, herr untersturmführer", she simply answered.

Her mind was reeling. Who was this tired old man before her? She had expected a blood-thirsty ogre, she had expected to be yelled at and threatened and ultimately sent to die, she had expected a final battle to eclipse all others... What she hadn't expected was this shadow of a man, apparently completely exhausted, who was now addressing her as though nothing untoward had occurred, and she didn't yet know quite how to handle him.

Traugott smiled and even laughed softly at her reply. His laugh reverberated with an insanity that made Adriana shiver. "No, of course you don't. How could you?" Then his eyes flew open and the anger in his stare nailed her to the floor. "Because of this sheet of paper, because of *you*, someone died today."

Adriana frowned. What game was he playing? "I... I don't... I mean..." Then she fell silent, more destabilized than ever. This was supposed to be about *her*, about what *she*'d done... Why in the world was he talking about someone else?

"I've just come from a meeting with hauptsturmführer Mulka", he explained, as though she hadn't spoken or he hadn't heard her. "A very *unpleasant* meeting, but then there is no other kind with him. He's convinced himself that the four inmates who escaped procured civilian clothing before fleeing. I'm not entirely sure he's wrong."

He remained silent for a few seconds before continuing. "He wanted to see me because there is only one place where one can obtain civilian clothing inside Auschwitz, *neunzehnhunderteinundsiebzig*. Here. In my warehouse."

She began to calm down. Traugott was fishing for information, attempting to elicit some reaction from her, trying to get her to incriminate herself by prematurely repudiating accusations he had yet to formulate.

"I wish I knew what the untersturmführer is talking about", she said. "I know nothing of any escape."

It would have been more truthful to say she *had known* nothing of any escape when she'd thrown the clothes out the window and over the fence. But now her decision to fight back had come back to haunt her, as she had always known it might, and she'd have to pay the price.

Well, at least I helped save four men, she thought.

"I'm not expecting you to confess to anything", Traugott said. "But I know what I saw. I saw you in a position to pass contraband to another inmate, and that's all I need. Nobody cares about who actually did what. Guilt or innocence are beyond any relevance. Mulka is expecting me to find and punish someone, and that's what I've done."

Here then came her sentence. She resolved not to give him the satisfaction of pleading for his mercy. She had never fancied herself a martyr of any kind, but she would die with all the dignity she could muster. He was about to snuff out her existence with a single word; at least she'd go to her death knowing she had helped fight him and his like.

"I know it's pointless to try to argue with the untersturmführer", she said. "I'll accept whatever punishment he sees fit even though I did nothing wrong."

His eyes actually widened and he burst out laughing, as though this was the most absurd thing he'd ever heard. "You?" he asked. There was that echo of insanity again. "No, no, no... you must have misheard me before. I said that *someone* would die today, not that *you* would die today. Nothing's going to happen to you, my sweet *neunzehnhunderteinundsiebzig*. Absolutely. Nothing. I couldn't bear the thought of any harm coming to you, you know that. And yet I can't let what you did remain unpunished. So you shall be disciplined, but certainly not harmed."

Then and only then did she understand what was happening.

"You monster", she whispered. "You horrible, horrible monster. You can't do that. I won't let you."

"I can't? You won't let me?" he shouted, suddenly exploding in anger. He stood up, toppling his chair, and began pounding his desk to punctuate each sentence. "Again you forget who's in charge around here. If I decide to save your life and kill someone else, then that's what happens. And besides, you're too late. *It's already done.*"

She took a step back, as if she'd been shoved. "No, you can't...", she repeated.

"I save your life and this is the thanks I get? You ungrateful bitch. After what you've done I should have you skinned alive", he snarled.

"Then skin me alive. What kind of human being are you to make someone you know to be innocent pay for someone else's crime?"

His smile chilled her. "There is no human being, *neunzehnhunderteinundsiebzig*. Remember? No man, just a uniform."

Her own words left her speechless. "And besides, whoever said anything about an innocent being punished? You were not alone in this, were you?" Traugott added.

She took another step back. "Who...?"

"I've had enough of this, enough of you. You're dismissed, *neunzehnhunderteinundsiebzig*", he stated coldly. "Get back to work immediately!"

The cruelty of her punishment was like a weight pressing down on her chest, making it difficult for her to breathe. She could feel her heart pounding in her temples and her vision had narrowed to a single point directly ahead of her. Because of what she'd done, because of her acts and her decisions, one person, one innocent human being, was being sent – no, *had been* sent - to the gas chambers, and the guilt would haunt her for the rest of her life.

That was her sentence.

Adriana was in a daze. She began walking back toward the noise of the warehouse, but then she was struck by an even more terrifying thought and she began running as hard as she could.

You were not alone in this, were you?

She kicked off her shoes and the stitches under her wounded foot came apart. She began leaving bloody footprints as she went and almost fell when she slipped in her own blood.

This isn't happening, she kept thinking. *He didn't... he wouldn't... he can't...*

She entered the warehouse at a dead run and only stopped when Rita, who already knew and had been waiting for her to return, grabbed her in her arms.

"You're too late, little one, you're too late", the old woman said as Adriana howled and screamed. "There was nothing you could have done."

Adriana fought her for a moment, trying to get away, but Rita wouldn't release her. After a moment Adriana's strength and anger drained away and she simply collapsed against her kapo, crying softly on her shoulder. Rita began stroking her short hair to comfort her.

"Hush, Adriana", she said. "She went peacefully. She didn't fight them. She wanted to be gone before you got back."

Adriana didn't, couldn't, reply anything.

"There is much evil in this place", the kapo added, "but Magrita wasn't part of it. Never forget that, little one. Never forget it."

July 1944

Otto Mockël watched as two sonderkommando grabbed a cadaver, one holding the wrists and the other the ankles, and loaded it onto a slate on rollers.

The corpse was that of a girl who had been gassed just a few hours earlier. Her skin had turned a sickly, grayish blue and her tongue had swollen to almost twice its normal size, so that it now protruded grotesquely between lips that had cracked and bled. Her arms stuck out stiffly in front of her, as if she were offering one final embrace, and Mockël guessed she had been holding on to her mother upon the moment of her death.

The two sonderkommando tried to roll the slate into the oven but the child's arms hit the top of the narrow opening, as though she was still resisting, even in death. One inmate needed surprising strength to push them down and allow his partner to finally shove the slate into the oven. The door was shut. The sonderkommando had loaded two other bodies into the muffle prior to the child's, and they would return in about 30 minutes to remove the incinerated remains and repeat the whole process.

Mockël was disgusted by the smell – the oil of eucalyptus he dabbed under his nostrils did nothing to block it out - but impressed by the efficiency. The ovens had been designed and built by the firm of Topf and Sons to operate continually for days at a time with essentially no maintenance. They were fired up with coke when cold but after that, the heat generated by the burning of bodies kept them hot enough to burn the next batch, which meant there was practically no down time. The operation was repeated over and over, without interruption, and the ovens were fed thousands of bodies each day.

Mockël stepped out of the crematorium for a moment, but the summer heat was even more oppressive than that generated by the ovens. There was no wind and his uniform was soaked with sweat. He found a spot in the shade that was slightly cooler and lit a cigarette.

He really ought to know better by now than to leave his inmates unattended, even if only for a few seconds, but he was beyond caring. His career was in tatters and he was left with nothing but a load of anger and resentment that was too much for a single man to bear. What else could they possibly do to him? His previous posting with the accountants had seemed to him the ultimate humiliation, and yet he'd managed to sink even deeper.

And now here he was, living among the dead.

The investigation launched after the spectacular escape in the spring left dozens of bodies in its wake, including his. Heads rolled and Mulka washed his hands of him once and for all when it was established that one of his inmates had played a role in that humiliating debacle. Mockël shortly found himself reassigned to the sonderkommando, the least desirable of all positions at Auschwitz for reasons that certainly need not be explained.

How Traugott managed to escape any sanction, he didn't know, but that only made his anger burn even hotter and his thirst for vengeance more intense.

He dropped his cigarette and crushed it under his boot. He was about to return to his duties when a whistle sounded, announcing yet another transport. A second rail line leading to a new *Judenrampe* had been inaugurated in May and since then, it wasn't rare for thousands of new inmates to arrive daily, mainly from Hungary these days. They were so numerous that it was no longer feasible to sort those apt to work from the others - even the crazed Josef Mengele now showed less interest - so the newcomers were sent directly to the gas chambers and killed, which in turn meant ever more work for Mockël and his sonderkommando.

Mockël cursed and decided he couldn't face the hellish heat of the crematorium. Instead, he went to check out the new arrivals, a spectacle that never failed to cheer him up.

"I have some great news", Rita whispered.

Adriana didn't respond. She kept her eyes down and finished folding the shirt on the table in front of her. She then added it to a small pile on her left and went to fetch another one.

Rita patiently waited for her to return.

"Did you hear? I have some tremendous news", the elderly lady repeated.

Adriana sighed. "I heard you, Rita. But unless you mean to tell me that I'm about to wake up from this nightmare, safe in my own bed, that none of this ever really happened, then I don't really care." Adriana knew her tone sounded harsher than she meant, but she didn't say anything.

It was Rita's turn to sigh. "Alright, then. I'll come back some other time."

The old kapo had only taken a couple of steps before Adriana called her back. "Rita, I'm sorry. I truly am. I apologize. What's your news?"

Adriana had never known Rita to gossip, but now she seemed as excited as a schoolgirl on her way to her first dance. "The Allies landed in northern France last month", she said. "I just heard this morning. The guards obviously don't want us to know, but I overheard them talking. They're completely devastated."

Adriana didn't react so Rita went on, thinking her friend perhaps didn't grasp the magnitude of what had happened. "Don't you see what that means? There's now a second front in Europe. The Germans are squeezed between the Allies in the West and the Russians in the East. They're done. It's only a matter of time."

Adriana shook her head in both disbelief and anger. "The bloody Allies are a few weeks too late to save Magrita", she said. "They could have bombed this place to pieces months ago. We all saw the planes."

"You've been blaming yourself for Magrita's death for weeks now", Rita chastised her with a touch of impatience. "How much longer will you continue? You had nothing to do with her death. This has to stop!"

Adriana slammed down the shirt she was holding and stared at Rita with blazing eyes. "He killed *her* to punish *me*", she snarled. "I might as well have put a gun to her head and pulled the trigger myself."

Rita held back her reply while a guard walked by. The man glanced at them but didn't stop. Rita's age and reputation had earned her the guards' begrudging respect while Adriana... well, Adriana was Adriana and nobody messed with Adriana.

"That's ridiculous and you know it", Rita snapped after the guard had left. "He killed her, not you."

The whistle announcing the arrival of a new transport sounded before Adriana could say anything. Rita threw up her hands. "*Another* one?" she asked. "At this rate, soon there'll be more people inside Auschwitz than outside. Well, what can you do. Help me round up our ladies and let's return to the barracks. We can continue this some other time."

The woman awoke when the train slowed down.

Though dazed by heat and hunger, her thoughts immediately went to the baby clutched to her breast. The infant was less than a year old and it felt limp and lifeless against her, but the feeble rise and fall of the tiny chest showed that still it lived. It hadn't cried in days and, had it not stubbornly refused to suckle, it would have found her breasts dry.

The woman heard the shrill cry of a whistle in the distance, but the sound meant nothing to her.

The woman was accompanied by another child, a daughter who had recently turned eight. The girl was snuggled against her shoulder and seemed to be still asleep. Their hands were linked in the woman's lap and had been since they'd all been herded on board the train, countless days ago. The child had shown astonishing strength and resilience and only admitted to being scared once, when an old man sitting next to her began stroking her hair and calling her by a strange name. He seemed to think her his long lost granddaughter and only after the woman raked his face with the demented fury of a mother defending her offspring did he leave the girl alone, though he kept mumbling and never entirely reconnected with reality.

The woman looked at the man. She saw that he had slipped to the floor and that another deportee was actually sitting on his dead body. She felt nothing, not even relief.

The train came to a sudden halt, jostling the child awake. She rubbed her eyes and yawned, as if she were just awakening from a good night's sleep.

"Where are we, Mommy?" little Tatiyana, who shared a first name with her mother, asked.

Big Tatiyana shook her head in the darkness. "I don't know my love, but anywhere will be better than here, that's for certain."

Then the doors were thrown open, dogs began to bark and men to shout, and the woman was proven wrong when hundreds more Jews were delivered onto Hell's doorstep.

Otto Mockël was standing slightly apart, trying to remain out of sight. He wasn't supposed to be here and he'd get into even more trouble if he were seen, but the attraction was too powerful for him to resist.

No matter how low he may have fallen, at least here were people who were lower still, people whose lives counted for absolutely nothing – people whose lives weighed so little, in fact, that they'd be dead in just a few hours while he'd still be alive.

Mockël smiled as the doors of the boxcars were slid open. A few dead bodies tumbled out, as usual, and then the living dead began to show themselves, tentatively poking their heads into the sunlight.

Mockël thought back, with some amusement, to those golden days when no one had yet heard of places such as Auschwitz and Birkenau and Treblinka and Mauthausen. Back then the Jews had been so much easier to handle, so much more docile; they wanted nothing more than to believe themselves safely sent to a internment camp for the remainder of the war. Reality could be kept hidden from them until the very last moment.

No longer.

Word had spread and these new prisoners mostly knew exactly where they were and what fate awaited them. Nowadays it wasn't unusual for the guards to be attacked as soon as the doors opened. Some prisoners assaulted them with their bare hands or with makeshift knives or clubs, others threw feces or other objects, but always the result was the same: the attackers were shot dead or beaten to a bloody pulp or torn to pieces by the dogs, and once the brief revolt had been crushed, the others went to their fate resignedly, having done all they could to fight back.

Mockël discretely pulled out his gun. He wanted to be ready, just in case something happened. Maybe, if he were lucky, the Jews would riot and he'd get to shoot a couple of them, so his day wouldn't have been completely wasted. He was actually shaking with eagerness and excitement. His entire being felt electrified and his senses enhanced. It was as though he could see and hear everything, and it was that superhuman sight that allowed him to spot a face, a single face, in a sea of hundreds.

The woman was standing at the door, waiting for those in front of her to disperse so she could jump out. She had two children with her, a baby she clutched against herself with one arm and a little girl she held by the hand.

Mockël couldn't take his eyes off her. It was as though all the others had disappeared. He was sure he'd seen her somewhere, though he couldn't quite remember where.

He suddenly, inexplicably found himself sexually aroused. But his arousal was unhealthy, as it was mixed with anger and resentment of such intensity that it surprised him.

Who was this woman, and why was she the source of such feelings?

She said something to the girl. Then she sat on the floor and let herself slip to the ground before helping the child do the same. The guards rounded them up with the others and then the woman looked directly at Mockël.

And then he knew her. And he snarled.

He began shoving prisoners out of his way as he headed straight for the woman.

Vengeance, long denied, was finally at hand.

Adriana was lying in her bunk with her eyes closed, trying her best to ignore the excitement around her.

She'd been at Auschwitz for years and she'd lived through hundreds of these arrivals. And while she quite understood why some, most, rushed to view the newcomers, she had personally lost all interest a long time ago. Part of it stemmed from the knowledge that all those she'd known were already dead; the war had gone on for so long, there was no one left for her to find. Part of it also stemmed from her understanding and acceptance of her complete helplessness. Even if she were to spot some distant relatives she barely remembered, what, exactly, could she do about it?

Nothing, that was what. She hadn't been able to save Bea's grandparents two years ago, and she wouldn't be able to save those relatives either. She'd rather not even know they were here.

Adriana had almost dozed off when an eerie murmur rippled through the *weißköpfchen*, a single word, like wavelets pushed by the breeze across the surface of a pond on a chilly summer day.

It began with the woman whom the others had propped up to look out the window at the top of the wall, and then the name jumped from one to the next, as contagious and deadly as the plague.

Mengele.

A goose walked over Adriana's grave and she shivered. Her eyes snapped open and she sat up. She looked at Rita, who had also heard, and the two women exchanged a knowing, somber stare. While the others also knew of Mengele, only the two of them had been at Auschwitz long enough to truly grasp what the man was capable of. The stories they'd heard and the things they'd seen would haunt them for the rest of their days.

The other women mostly saw Mengele as a mystical creature, a being of legend akin to the monster under the bed or the bogeyman who snatches unruly children away; some doubted he even existed at all, few had ever seen him in the flesh, and fewer still believed him to be as evil and as monstrous as they'd heard.

Adriana and Rita, on the other hand, did not have the luxury of such delusions; they knew Mengele to be the Devil incarnate, and they feared him like they feared no other.

And now here he was, standing right outside their door, just a few feet away, and while it had once been routine for him to come examine the newcomers, it had been weeks since he'd bothered to do so. The murderous doctor didn't see the need to trouble himself anymore, since he'd given the guards standing orders to bring him all the twins that arrived at Auschwitz. His guinea pigs would be delivered straight to his door, and then the lucky ones would be sent to the gas chambers.

And yet here he was.

Adriana leaped off her bed. "Let me see", she said.

Some of the women grumbled. They all wanted to look out the window, on the off-chance that they might find someone they knew. The opportunity to do so, when it came, didn't last for very long and it didn't sit well with several of them for Adriana to simply demand to be hoisted up onto their shoulders.

The woman at the top stared at Adriana but gave no indication that she intended to yield her prized spot. If some among the *weißköpfchen* respected Adriana for the time she'd survived Auschwitz, for the knowledge and expertise she had accumulated, there were also those who immensely resented her relationship – more perceived than real - with Traugott.

In the end the two evened themselves out and Adriana found herself neither liked nor disliked. She was simply... tolerated.

"The high and mighty Queen Esther will have to wait her turn", Beatrijs spat. She had never forgiven Adriana for not saving her grandparents and to this day she refused to believe Adriana had been helpless to do anything about it. And now she stood in front of her enemy with her arms crossed over her chest, as though daring her to press her case.

"It may not even be him", Rita intervened. "But I'm too old to climb up there. Adriana is the only other person here who actually knows what he looks like. Get out of the way, Bea. If Mengele is here, *and if he means to come in here*, then don't you think we need to know about it?"

Beatrijs remained immobile for almost 30 seconds. Then she spat on the floor and stepped aside just enough to let Adriana through.

"Mommy, you're hurting me", little Tatiyana mumbled softly.

She had stuck her thumb in her mouth and was gnawing on it gently, something she did when she was worried. Her mother usually made her stop, but today she chose to let it go. She really couldn't blame the child for being scared.

Tatiyana smiled at her daughter, hoping to hide the primordial fear gnawing at her stomach, and relaxed her grip on the small hand. "I'm sorry, my love", she apologized. "I just don't want us to get separated."

Tatiyana was teetering on the edge of an abyss of despair into which she couldn't afford to topple. She'd hoped against hope for the stories to have been false, but now she knew she'd been wrong.

Even when her friends and neighbors began disappearing one after the other, mysteriously taken from their homes during the night or boldly snatched from the streets in broad daylight, she didn't, couldn't, wouldn't believe.

Even when the Nazis finally came for her and her children and loaded them on board that filthy train with hundreds of other lost souls and left them there for days until they were hundreds of miles from their home, she refused to believe.

And even when the train stopped and the doors slammed open and shouts and barks and cries assaulted them like so many blows, surely it was to let others on board or to provide them with a bit of food and water or to clean out the car before continuing the endless journey or to... she had come up with a thousand different scenarios to remain blind to the undeniable reality.

All in vain. This was as real as real got. The noise was real and the stench was real and the dogs and the guards and the barbed wire and the fences were all real, and most of all the fear was real. Not only her own fear, but the fear that radiated from those around her, the fear into which this whole place, wherever this was, seemed permeated - a fear that seeped into every last molecule of her being, until her very soul quivered in terror.

A man was standing next to her, staring at her.

The man had cold, vacant eyes, as though he were no more than flesh and bones, a Frankensteinish monster somehow living and yet not entirely alive. Whatever it was that elevated Man above the rank of simple animal, this man – with a small 'm' – certainly didn't possess. If not for the fact that he obviously moved and breathed and even perspired in the heat, one might have thought him a corpse returned to life.

Tatiyana looked at the man and tried to smile, while her daughter hid in the folds of her skirts. The look on the man's face aborted her smile before it ever truly formed.

"You're coming with me", the man said.

Tatiyana's knees almost buckled. She clutched her infant tighter to her breast and placed a hand on little Tatiyana's head.

"Certainly", she finally said, even though she knew she didn't have a choice in the matter. "May I ask where you are taking us?"

The look that then came over the man's face made her wish she hadn't asked.

"To take a shower", the man simply replied.

Those were the four most terrifying words Tatiyana had ever heard.

Adriana's breath caught in her throat when she saw the man standing less than one hundred feet from her barracks.

"Yes, it's Mengele", she whispered, knowing the others were awaiting her confirmation. The women began chattering excitedly until Rita told them to hush.

"What is he doing?" the elderly kapo asked.

"I don't know", Adriana said. "He's probably waiting for the new people."

She didn't have to say more. They all knew what this implied.

"Let me down, I've seen enough", Adriana demanded.

But then she caught sight of a lone SS officer escorting a single woman in the courtyard, and the scene froze her where she was.

"Wait, something's happening", she said.

"What?" someone asked.

"Wait", Adriana replied absentmindedly.

All her senses, those senses that had allowed her to survive Auschwitz for so long, were on high alert and warning her that something frighteningly odd and peculiar was happening. Something she needed to pay close attention to, something of tremendous importance.

The SS officer and the woman were coming closer. They were heading roughly in Mengele's direction, but first they'd have to walk directly by Adriana's barracks, less than twenty feet from where she was standing.

Adriana almost tumbled down the human pyramid when she finally recognized the SS officer, and only the quick reflexes of the women holding her up saved her from cracking her skull. The man was Otto Mockël, the officer who had tried to rape her and whom she'd almost strangled to death. This probably explained why all her alarm systems had gone off simultaneously.

She hadn't seen him in a while and she was shocked by the metamorphosis he had undergone. With his sunken eyes and cadaverous cheeks, he now resembled an inmate more than he did a guard.

Adriana then saw that the woman was accompanied by two little children, one whom she held by the hand and the other whom she clutched to her breast. They looked remotely familiar, but she was too distracted and scared by Mockël's presence to pay them more attention. The woman's head was bent and her falling dirty, gray hair hid her features.

And then, for no apparent reason, they stopped directly across from her window.

"Stop", Mockël ordered.

Tatiyana obeyed. She had no idea what this man wanted with her, but disobedience was the furthest thing from her mind. As long as he didn't hurt her children, she'd do anything he wished.

"Now face that building, and look up", he growled.

Tatiyana spun 90 degrees to her left, but she kept her head down so that her hair still hid her face. Mockël's reaction was as instantaneous as it was brutal.

"It told you to *look up*, bitch", he shouted. He grabbed her by the hair and tilted her head back so far she feared her neck might snap. Tatiyana let out a strangled cry and little Tatiyana began to cry.

Tatiyana repressed an urge to grab Mockël's wrist with both hands, since that would have meant letting go of her babies. He pulled her head back even further and her knees relentlessly began to buckle, until she found herself kneeling in the mud at his feet.

"Let go of my Mommy, you're hurting her!" little Tatiyana cried. She tried to tear herself from her mother's grasp, presumably to assault the SS, but Tatiyana quickly snaked her left arm around the tiny waist and pulled the child to her.

"Just close your eyes, baby", she whispered in her daughter's ear. "It's just a bad dream and you'll soon wake up."

Little Tatiyana wrapped her arms around her mother's neck. She buried her face in the dirty hair and began sobbing.

"Why are you doing this to me? What do you want?" Tatiyana desperately asked Mockël.

His twisted his fingers into her hair even tighter, making her cry out in pain. "I want her to see you die", he snarled next to her face.

Had Mockël's free hand held a knife, he would have appeared ready to slash her throat, like an ancient Druid about to offer sacrifice. He held her in that pose, entirely vulnerable and defenseless, until a soul-rending shriek flew from the barracks.

Then, satisfied, he smiled and released Tatiyana's hair.

"Come with me", he said. "The doctor will see you now."

Adriana leaped to the ground and almost broke an ankle. She landed awkwardly, her right leg buckled and she tumbled, knocking down a few women like so many bowling pins.

She instantly picked herself up and ran for the door.

"Adriana, no!" Rita shouted. "We're on lockdown. You'll be shot on sight if you go out there!"

But Adriana was lost to the world and Rita's words registered no more than the buzzing of an insect. She had almost reached the door when an outstretched leg sent her flying again.

Adriana landed flat on her stomach, and the wind was knocked out of her. She looked up, shaken.

"Going somewhere, my Queen?" Bea sneered.

Adriana didn't reply. She didn't care about Bea; hell, at this point, she didn't even know who Bea *was*. All she knew was that she had to reach the courtyard before it was too late. So she picked herself up again but this time, Rita was standing between her and the door.

The elderly kapo took a step back. Never before had she seen such a ferocious battle between despair and madness on any one person's face.

"Adriana, stop!" she repeated, trying to make her voice sound forceful and authoritative. She was desperate to keep Adriana from exiting the barracks and getting killed. "Tell me what's going on. Who did you see? Was it Mengele? What's happening to you, child?"

Adriana was momentarily frozen. She shook her head to say, *no, it's not Mengele*, and then she opened her mouth to explain who and what she'd seen, but the words wouldn't form. So she just stood there like an imbecile, incapable of coherent thought, unable to utter a single sentence, as though she'd suddenly been struck dumb.

Rita approached her as one would a wild animal and tentatively took her hands in hers. Adriana was shaking like a leaf despite the stifling heat inside the barracks. Rita stared at her friend with all the love and compassion she could muster, but the empty, vacant glare that she received in return scared her. She had seen more than her share of people go mad at Auschwitz, and once their sanity gone, they appeared much as Adriana did right now.

"Adriana, listen to my voice", Rita said gently. She was close to tears. She had known and lost so many people in all her years here that she could hardly bear the thought of losing Adriana as well. "You must come back to us or your soul will wander forever. Please, I'm begging you. You must return before it's too late."

The two women stayed there, holding one another, and for a moment Rita feared Adriana might be too far gone. Perhaps her mind had finally snapped, and if it had, after years of Hell on Earth, who could blame her? Perhaps there was no reaching her, not anymore.

But then a tiny spark flickered in Adriana's eyes and Rita smiled.

"Welcome back", she whispered. Adriana tightened her grasp on the wizened old hands, as though to anchor herself in the moment, as though she feared she might again be carried away by a riptide of madness. And then her eyes filled with tears and she began shaking even harder.

"Rita, it's...", she began, but then she stopped, unable to finish.

"Take your time", Rita said. "Tell me."

But Adriana couldn't say it. If she uttered the words, she'd be giving an illusion flesh and bones, she'd be dragging a nightmare into the realm of reality, and then she'd have to slay it.

"Adriana, please", Rita insisted gently.

Adriana let go of Rita's hands and collapsed to her knees. She buried her face in her hands and began crying uncontrollably, like a penitent begging for forgiveness after confessing a mortal sin. Rita knelt in front of her and removed her hands from her face, but this time she didn't say a word.

It was Adriana who spoke.

"I saw my sister", she finally sobbed. "I saw Tatiyana."

There was a moment of stunned silence. Then Bea clapped her hands and cackled with mad delight.

"Heil Hitler!"

Mockël fired a razor-sharp salute, clicked his heels together and stared straight ahead while eagerly waiting for Mengele to give him leave to speak. His revenge was finally at hand and he was almost shaking with anticipation. The whore's sister would die, maybe the whore would too, and in any event Traugott would lose his slut and he'd be avenged.

At long last.

"What do you want, obersturmführer?" Mengele demanded impatiently.

Mockël licked his lips. "Herr hauptsturmführer, this piece of filth just arrived from Hungary and..."

Mockël froze. He wanted to continue but found that he couldn't.

"And what?" Mengele barked. "Stop wasting my time."

Something was stirring in the deepest recesses of Mockël's mind, a presence felt but not seen in the darkness, a cold, slimy creature that brushes against your leg in murky water. Whatever was left of his sanity, whatever hadn't yet been consumed by his madness, was awakening and loudly clamoring for his attention.

No, it was saying, *you are handling this all wrong. This woman is much more useful to you alive than dead. Use her to...*

I'm already using her. I'm getting my revenge. That's all that matters.

Use her as leverage to get the whore to talk. Her sister lives if she tells you all she knows about Traugott. You know Traugott is corrupt, everybody knows. She's your last chance to take him down. You'll be a hero. You'll be redeemed.

Mockël was tempted and his determination wavered. Perhaps he *was* wrong. Perhaps he *should* be seeking redemption and not vengeance. Perhaps he *could* still emerge a hero. Perhaps there was *still*... but no; in the end, he couldn't bring himself to once again risk hoping, and so the temptation vanished.

It's too late. Mulka doesn't care anymore. Neither does Morgen. They all abandoned me. They all betrayed me. They should have listened to me. Now it's my turn to fuck them over.

No, you're wrong, you...

No. YOU'RE wrong and you need to...

"Obersturmführer", Mengele was growling. "I strongly suggest you close..."

"My apologies, herr hauptsturmführer, a momentary distraction, it will not happen again", Mockël quickly said. His prophesy would prove more prescient than he knew: the remnants of his sanity had just been snuffed out, never to be heard from again.

"This Jew just arrived from Hungary", he repeated. "She has a sister here and I thought they might be of interest to you."

That piqued Mengele's curiosity.

"A sister, you say?" he said slowly. "Are they twins?"

Mengele looked at Tatiyana and, had Mockël not still been holding her, she would have fled for her life. This man's eyes conveyed so much hatred, so much evil, that she would have picked up little Tatiyana and run. There was nowhere for her to go, she knew, but anything was better than just standing here, being scorched alive by this man's gaze.

Mockël wanted to lie. He knew Mengele only sought twins. He wanted to say, *Yes, they are the most perfect, most identical twins you have ever seen*, but that would be pointless. There was no way this woman and the whore could ever be mistaken for twins. He'd be found out in less than five minutes.

He still had to give it a shot since, at Auschwitz, the only fate worse than being sent to the gas chambers was being given to Mengele. Gas killed you in just a few minutes; Mengele could make death last for days and weeks. And for this woman, he wanted the worst fate imaginable.

"I'm afraid not, herr hauptsturmführer", he admitted. "But they are quite similar and this one has two little children with her, so I thought that..."

Mengele immediately raised a hand to silence him.

"Herein lies the problem, obersturmführer", the doctor said with mock indulgence. "The Reich is on the verge of losing the war because of stupendous imbeciles like you. Our ranks overflow with idiots such as yourself who choose to *think* when all that's required of them is to *obey*. How could you possibly be expected to *think* when you've just demonstrated that you don't even have the mental capacity to follow the simplest orders? Obey, obersturmführer. Do not *think*. *Obey*."

Möckel reddened under the stinging rebuke.

"If I wanted subjects who *look alike*, who are *similar*, that's the order I would have given", Mengele snarled. "But that's not what I said, is it? I specifically requested children...". He raised one finger in the air. "Twins...". He raised another finger. "And identical when possible". He raised a third and final finger.

"And you, spawn of a lice-infested peasant that you are, what do you bring me? You bring me two adult women who are not twins. Now, why did you *think* I might be interested?"

There was nothing Möckel could reply, so he remained silent.

"That's what happens when people like you *think*, obersturmführer", Mengele said. "Now get rid of this trash before I get rid of you."

Möckel saluted. He then dragged Tatiyana and her children toward the gas chambers, madder than ever.

"Of course I'm sure", Adriana replied angrily. "If you saw your own sister, wouldn't you know her?"

Rita knew she had to tread lightly, so she chose to avoid answering her directly. "I simply remember you saying you haven't seen her in years, that's all."

Adriana gingerly got back to her feet and winced when she put some weight on her injured leg. She then brushed the dirt from her clothes and wiped both eyes with the back of her sleeve.

"Tatiyana moved away to Hungary with her husband just a few months after they married", she conceded. "She was already pregnant by then. It's true I haven't seen her in maybe six or seven years, but I have no doubt, Rita. It's my sister and I have to save her."

Bea snickered. "Oh, that's so sad, but there's nothing you can do, remember?"

A few women, mostly those jealous of Traugott's interest in Adriana, laughed quietly, until they were shamed by others around them.

"You know what might – nay, what *will* - happen to you if you walk out that door during lockdown", Rita reminded her somberly.

Adriana nodded. "I do, but I can't just let her die. I have to try. If I get shot, then I get shot. I'd rather die trying than live with the knowledge that I might have saved her. I want to close the circle with her."

Rita was still standing between Adriana and the door. There was no way she could physically prevent her younger, stronger friend from leaving if that's what she wanted. At the same time, she knew Adriana would never lay a hand on her. All she had to do to keep Adriana safe from harm was remain standing where she was.

So she stood her ground, and Adriana played her trump card.

"What ever happened to your daughter, Rita?" Adriana suddenly asked her.

Rita was momentarily thrown off balance. "What... why do you ask?"

"Because you never told me", Adriana said firmly. "The villagers came for you at the police station, and then the police chief condemned you to appease them, and then you were sent here... But your daughter, Rita? What happened to her?"

Rita couldn't speak. She felt as though she'd been kicked in the gut. "I... I don't know", she finally said, in a voice that was barely above a whisper. "They took her away and I never saw her again."

Adriana pinched her lips. She felt guilty for dredging up such painful memories, for hurting a woman who had never shown her anything but kindness, but she was fighting for her sister's life and she wasn't about to pull any punches. Those who stood in her way would get trampled.

"And if she were to come back from the dead, as my sister has, and suddenly appear outside this door, you would just let her... die again?" Adriana asked.

Rita stared at her for a moment before slowly stepping aside.

"Thank you", Adriana said softly.

Rita simply nodded. She might as well have just handed her own child a noose. "I'll say a prayer for you", she whispered, but Adriana didn't hear her.

Adriana took the last few steps that still separated her from the door and calmly placed a hand on the handle.

Then she took a deep breath, opened the door and stepped into the unknown.

Adriana expected the fatal shot to ring out almost instantly, so she just stood there, frozen, waiting for the bullet that would end it all.

Nobody paid her any attention. Mengele was standing less than fifty feet away from her, but he seemed strangely distracted, defeated almost.

He wasn't alone. The Nazis were beaten and they knew it. The Allied landing in Normandy had crushed whatever was left of their morale. Theirs was now a lost cause and the end was unavoidable; whether it occurred in days or weeks or months mattered little - it was coming. If any further proof of the Nazis' growing panic was needed, in just a few days obersleutnant Claus von Staffenberg would fail in his attempt to assassinate Hitler.

The Nazis' earlier fanaticism had been replaced by a dark, somber rage. Whatever they now did, they did out of frustration and vengeance, not out of any belief in any mystical dogma of superiority. They were simply out to cause as much damage as possible while they still could. Perhaps this explained why some of them now didn't seem to care as much; they were just going through the motions and no longer fighting for their 1000-year Reich.

Still no shot. Adriana realized she was holding her breath. She had never thought to live this long after emerging from the barracks. She began to breathe normally again, and now found herself unsure what she should do next.

Where had Mockël even taken Tatiyana?

Then, miraculously, she spotted him emerging from the gas chambers, all the way across the courtyard from her, and she knew – not only where Tatiyana was, but also how little time she now had.

She could hesitate no longer. If she really meant to save Tatiyana, and she did, then now was the time to do it, now was the time to act, now was the time to roll the dice and pray for a seven. She took a first step, and then another, and then another, and then she was almost running, her entire attention focused on reaching the gas chambers alive. She willed herself to be invisible, she willed the guards to not see her and not fire, she willed herself to live and she did.

She was running, recklessly, carelessly running, with each step calling out Death and daring It to come for her.

And Death answered her challenge.

A mad, demented shriek came from behind her. Adriana stopped and spun around slowly, as if in a dream.

Bea... except not Bea, but rather a ghoulish, hellish reincarnation of Bea... was rushing at her with hands outstretched like talons, preparing to tear her to shreds. Adriana stared at this thing coming for her, with eyes bulging out of its head and spittle flying from its lips, and she didn't move. Her mind couldn't really comprehend what it was seeing, so while she knew her life to be in danger and while she understood the need to defend herself, she remained standing where she was, almost until it was too late.

She stepped aside at the last possible second and the Bea-creature ran right past her. It skidded in the dirt, spun around and rushed at her once again. Adriana prepared to fight and die.

A shot rang out. A small, black circle appeared almost directly in the center of Bea's forehead, and the back of her skull exploded in a shower of brains and blood and bones.

Bea remained standing for a moment, as if refusing to acknowledge her own death. Then, as Adriana watched, life vacated the body and it fell forward.

Guards were now rushing in their direction, but Adriana was barely aware of them. Instinct took over. She let herself fall to her knees and placed her hands behind her neck.

"Don't shoot, don't shoot!" she shouted. "I'm on duty in the crematorium, they need me there."

Adriana found herself surrounded by five guards who clearly itched but hesitated to use the weapons they had drawn. A couple of them knew her to be the famed *neunzehnhunderteinundsiebzig* whom untersturmführer Traugott had placed under his protection, while others were destabilized by her temerity. Prisoners had obviously been caught outside and shot during lockdown before, but those had usually been running *toward* the safety of their barracks, not *away* from it. And none had certainly ever been daring enough to sprint through the courtyard, let alone in Mengele's presence.

So while their orders in such a situation were clear, the guards held their fire and glanced at one another, each man seeking guidance from those around him, each man unwilling to pull the trigger first.

"What are you *schweine* waiting for, shoot her!" Mengele roared.

He had been observing the scene and was disgusted by the guards' lack of resolve.

Adriana didn't wait for them to comply. She quickly got off her knees and stood at attention. One of the guards actually took a startled step back and blushed under his comrades' stares.

"Herr hauptsturmführer!" she called out in a loud voice.

This was audacity beyond imagination. For an inmate to address a guard, or even worse an officer, without first being addressed was an offense of the worst kind, subject to the harshest punishment.

Adriana was staring straight ahead, but out of the corner of her eye she saw Mengele react as if he'd been struck. The man spun around slowly, pulled his sidearm from his holster and walked in her direction with the muzzle pointed directly at her head. Two guards hurriedly stepped out of his way.

"What did you say, *hure*?" he demanded in a tone where fury mixed with disbelief and outrage to form a lethal cocktail. His hatred was like heat radiating from a furnace. He pressed his gun against her temple and pushed, forcing her to tilt her head until her right ear almost touched her shoulder.

Adriana was as good as dead, which also meant she had nothing to lose. She rolled up her sleeve and showed him her number.

"*Bitte,* herr hauptsturmführer", she repeated. "I've been here for many years, almost since the very first day..."

Mengele glanced at her arm and couldn't quite conceal his surprise. Prisoners with such low numbers were all assumed to have been eliminated a long time ago. The strongest ones survived Auschwitz for a few months, a year at the most, but certainly no longer than that.

How was it that such a woman remained alive after almost three years?

Adriana knew she was desperately running out of time. Tatiyana was perhaps already dead by now. If she were to have any chance at all to save her, she had to trick Mengele into sending her to the gas chambers. She'd figure something out once there, if Tatiyana still lived.

Adriana knew that pleading for her sister's life would be a complete waste of time, so she took advantage of Mengele's momentary silence to ask him for the exact opposite.

"Herr hauptsturmführer", she said. "My sister has just arrived, so I ask you one thing... I wish to die with her and her children. Please send me to the gas chambers so I can kiss them one last time before we go together."

Mengele narrowed his eyes at her. It certainly wasn't the first time a prisoner had begged him for death, though such prayers usually came after days and weeks of unspeakable suffering at his hands.

This inmate, on the other hand, appeared reasonably healthy, but his attention was immediately drawn by something else she'd just said.

"Children? How many? Are they twins?" he asked angrily, unaware they were discussing the same woman Otto Mockël had offered him mere minutes earlier.

Mengele pressed down on his gun even harder. Adriana could feel the muzzle boring a painful hole into her flesh.

"No, herr hauptsturmführer", Adriana said. "They are not twins. But..."

"Then I don't need them and neither do I need her nor do I need you", he yelled.

Mengele took a step back – cleaning blood from a uniform was *such* a hassle - and aimed his gun at Adriana's head.

She never even saw him coming.

One second she was waiting helplessly for Mengele to fire the bullet that would shatter her skull and splatter her brains, quickly offering a silent apology to Tatiyana for her failure to save her and the children, praying Aaron to come escort them all to wherever it was they were going, the next there was movement, violent and sudden, on her right, a couple of guards collapsed, and then she was shoved with such force she thought her bones must surely break, and she went flying for almost ten feet, landing in the dirt and skidding on her stomach and stopping inches from Bea's dead body.

"What the hell is going on?" two men shouted almost simultaneously.

Adriana shook the cobwebs from her mind. Her ribs hurt from the blow and she'd scraped her palms and knees raw against the dirt. Still, she quickly sat up, wiped her hands against her clothes and spun around.

"This is my prisoner, what is she doing here?" Mattias Traugott demanded angrily.

Mengele roared. "I don't care who she is and I don't answer to you, *untersturmführer*", he said, making the rank sound like the dirtiest insult.

Traugott refused to back down. The two men were standing less than three inches apart, their noses almost touching, like two enraged dogs about to tear one another apart over a female in heat – which, in a sense, they were.

"She belongs to me. No one lays a hand on her but me", Traugott growled.

Mengele was infuriated by such insubordination. Even omitting the fact that he outranked this impertinent worm, his reputation alone should suffice to have the man cowering in fear. But the war was lost, the system was breaking down and hierarchy didn't mean much anymore.

As for Mengele's reputation, Traugott pissed on it and trusted his own to be more than a match for the mad doctor's.

"Go back to your *twins*, Mengele", he said with as much contempt as he felt. "I'll take care of this filthy Jewess."

The two men stared at each other for a long time. Mengele trembled with rage and Adriana saw that he still gripped his gun with white knuckles. All he had to do was raise it quickly and fire point-blank into Traugott's stomach. Then she noticed that Traugott was unarmed, barely dressed and completely out of uniform, as if he'd been roused from his sleep.

Mengele finally took a step back and Traugott seized the moment. He spun around, walked quickly toward Adriana, who was still sitting on the ground, and grabbed her by the back of her clothes.

"Crazy bitch, I'll kill you, I swear I'll kill you", he said as he dragged her over a short distance, away from Mengele and toward the barracks she had exited earlier.

"Mattias, wait, I need...", Adriana began, not realizing she had used his given name for the very first time.

He let go of her clothes and slapped her face. The blow stung but didn't really hurt, as if he hadn't put any force into it. Then Traugott began kicking her toward the barracks, but again these were glancing blows that lacked any conviction.

Adriana was puzzled. If anyone knew how to beat an inmate to a bloody pulp, in a place that had refined such things to an art form, it was Mattias Traugott. So why was he now faking it?

She played along and screamed in pain.

"Stop hitting me, stop, please!" she cried.

Each blow took them further away from Mengele and closer to the barracks, and only then did she catch on to what he was doing. When she felt they had gone a safe distance, she tried again.

"Wait, you need to listen to me, my sister..."

"Shut up", he growled as he bent down to mock-punch her head. "I know all about your fucking sister. What's her name?"

Adriana thought she must have misheard him. Tatiyana had only arrived at Auschwitz a few minutes ago. How could he possibly already know she was here?

"What's her name?" he demanded again as he delivered another feeble blow.

"Her name is Tatiyana", she finally replied.

They had reached the door to the barracks. Traugott picked her up by her clothes, stood her up and slammed her against the wall.

"You should have come to me yourself. I'll take care of your sister", he said in a voice so low only she could hear it. Then he backhanded her savagely across the face, a real blow this time, a blow meant to teach her a lesson and show her his anger, a blow to rattle her teeth and scramble her brains, a blow that left her stunned and dizzy and bloodied.

Then he yanked the door open, shoved her back inside the barracks, and left at a run.

Several hands caught Adriana and pulled her inside.

"Come, little one, come sit down", a voice she knew only too well said.

She fought them. "No, I have to go back, I have to..."

But she was exhausted and lacked the strength to get away. Her legs had turned to rubber and her head throbbed from Traugott's punishment. She had bitten her tongue and reddish saliva ran from the corner of her mouth.

The hands pulled her deeper inside the barracks, against her will, and sat her down on a bunk.

"It's out of your control", Rita said. "You've done all you can. Now it's up to him. We just..."

Adriana didn't hear the rest. A strange buzzing like that of an angry beehive suddenly filled her head, blocking out the entire universe, her eyes rolled up into the back of her head and she tumbled backward into a dark pool.

She awoke to cold water being splashed over her face.

"How long was I gone?" she asked weakly as she tried to sit up.

"Not long", Rita answered softly.

Not long - and yet probably long enough, probably too long. How long since Mockël had taken Tatiyana to the gas chambers? How long had she argued with Mengele? How long since Traugott had brought her back here? She didn't know, and in truth it didn't matter. Auschwitz's killing machine was functioning at peak efficiency, the furnaces never went cold, the Devil's fiery talons shot out of the chimneys day and night, covering the camp with a gray, greasy ash, and hundreds of prisoners were killed daily in less time than it takes most people to drink a cup of coffee.

Tatiyana was dead, and so were her children. She had failed.

"I need to see", Adriana said feebly. Rita tried to keep her from standing but Adriana gently pushed her aside.

The women had formed their usual pyramid and propped someone up to look out their only window. "Let me up", Adriana demanded.

The *weißköpfch* standing at the top of the pyramid, a young woman here mere weeks whose innate cheerfulness Auschwitz had yet to squash, smiled down at her with a twinkle in her eye. "You're too weak to come up here", she said benevolently. "You'll fall and break your neck, and then you won't be here to kiss your sister when *Krumme* brings her out. Trust me, if anything happens, I'll let you know."

Not *if* Krumme brings her out, she'd said, but *when* Krumme brings her out.

This complete stranger's faith that Traugott would save Tatiyana moved Adriana to tears for reasons she couldn't have put into words. Now that Bea was gone, the atmosphere inside the barracks had undergone a sea change and she really felt the other women pulling for her, rooting for her sister to be saved from a place whence no one had ever emerged alive.

She sat on a bunk next to Rita and the two friends linked hands. Rita was praying so fervently Adriana could actually feel the current running through the elderly kapo's body, but she couldn't bring herself to join her. If God wanted Tatiyana to live, then why had the Holy Bastard brought her here in the first place?

The wait lasted for an eternity. They were suspended between life and death, waiting to see which way the balance would tip, waiting to hear Fate's verdict, and the more time went by, the more Adriana began to lose hope, the more convinced she became that Tatiyana had died. No one could survive the gas chambers for so long.

But what had she expected, exactly? You couldn't think to fight Auschwitz and win. The evil in this place was simply too powerful; love and hope were outgunned every step of the way. It was a hopeless struggle and in the end the camp always won. She ought to know that by now.

She closed her eyes and began to cry silent tears, tears of rage, tears of despair, tears of defeat. It was all over. She'd tried her best, but her best hadn't been good enough.

Rita tightened her grip on her hand and Adriana rested her head against the kapo's shoulder.

And then the young woman let out a howl of triumph and everything changed.

"He's coming! He's got her! Oh dear Lord, thank You, I can see them", she shouted.

Adriana leaped off the bed and rushed to the door. She pulled it open and Rita caught her just in time to keep her from running out again.

"Don't, or it'll all be for nothing", the old woman ordered sternly.

A half-dressed man had just emerged from the gas chambers. His face was covered in filth and grime, his clothes were soiled and in disarray, but in his arms he held a naked, unconscious woman whose long gray hair now fell away from her face instead of over it, as before.

"Tatiyana", Adriana breathed.

Traugott crossed the courtyard slowly. He struggled to put one foot in front of the other and, as he came closer, Adriana saw that he was coughing uncontrollably. His eyes were red and bloodshot, snot ran from his nose and the front of his undershirt was stained yellow with vomit – his own or someone else's.

Tatiyana was so thin her ribs poked through her skin, yet Traugott struggled to carry her as if she weighed 400 pounds. Adriana ached to rush to him and take her sister in her own arms but Rita, sensing something, grabbed her by the back of her clothes.

"Don't", she repeated, and Adriana obeyed.

Traugott finally reached the barracks. He stared at Adriana for a moment, and she at him.

"She got some gas but she's alive", he said. "Take her to your doctor Ada the first chance you get."

He began coughing again. Adriana caught her sister's body just in time to keep him from dropping her.

Traugott bent over and coughed and retched for a long moment before the fit finally subsided. He wiped his mouth with the back of his hand.

"I couldn't save the children", he then added. His voice croaked but the sorrow it still conveyed almost broke her heart. "The little girl had the baby in her arms when I saw them, so they died together. Maybe that's a consolation. Maybe it's not. I couldn't do anything for them. I'm... I'm sorry."

Traugott glanced at Rita, who was standing behind Adriana's right shoulder. "You were right to fetch me. Mengele would have killed her."

Then he left without waiting for the thanks he knew would never come.

5 October 1944

The men of the 12th sonderkommando had no doubt their days were numbered.

"Israel, we must strike before it's too late", the young man pleaded urgently. "They'll come for us any day."

Israel Gutman looked at his companion and felt a surge of compassion. No one so young should spend so much time thinking about death. The boy should have been planning the next forty years of his life; instead, he worried about surviving the next four days. And whether he survived those four days or not greatly depended on Gutman's decisions.

Lajb Panub was only 16 years old but the deep lines that now creased his face made him look decades older. They had both arrived at Auschwitz a few weeks ago, on board the same train, and been immediately sent to replace the men of the 11th sonderkommando.

A pile of thin, emaciated bodies some demented SS had ordered them to burn had initiated them to Auschwitz. Gutman, Panub and the others had quickly realized these were their predecessors - and it was now only a matter of days before they, too, would be incinerated by the men who would then form the 13th sonderkommando. They had been at this for too long, they had seen and heard too much, and the Nazis would be replacing them shortly. Dead men tell no tales.

Gutman smiled.

"If we strike too early, Lajb, we'll ruin everything", the resistance leader said.

"And if we wait too long, won't that also ruin everything?" the young hothead replied impatiently.

Gutman looked away and spat. He knew Panub was right. The young man wasn't the only one pressuring him to put their plan into action. Each day that he delayed gave the SS one more day to discover everything. And yet he was loathe to move, loathe to risk all they had accomplished so far, before he could be assured of success.

They were so close to being ready. So close.

"You think too much", Panub reproached him with a sigh.

"And perhaps you don't think enough", Gutman immediately replied.

Now he knew how the leaders of the Warsaw ghetto must have felt the night before the uprising, the year before. He had fought alongside them, been wounded even, but he had never felt them to be timid or hesitant. They had always been self-assured and decisive – or at the very least appeared so. Only today, now that the mantle of leadership had been wrapped around his own shoulders, did he realize that they, too, must have been haunted by doubts that gnawed at their insides, that their facade of confidence had been nothing more than a thin charade.

And yet their apparent strength had still given him strength. Could he do any less for the men he now led?

"You're right, Lajb", he finally said. "We've waited long enough. I'll take delivery of one last parcel tomorrow. We strike the day after that. Spread the word, but be careful."

Panub's eyes lit up with excitement and he sauntered away, honored to be entrusted with such tremendous news.

Gutman shook his head and buried his face in his hands.

He had just turned 21, and he was about to send men to their deaths.

6 October 1944

Tatiyana found that, if she concentrated hard on her task, she could almost block from her mind the image of her children lying dead at her feet.

Almost, but not completely.

The SS had made them strip naked, and then a thick, noxious gas had shot out of the fake shower heads. Screams of surprise and terror immediately filled the room, only to be replaced by coughs, and then by the sounds of people suffocating and retching and vomiting. An indescribable stench rose all around them as bowels were voided.

The will to survive, that most basic of instincts, took over. People panicked and tried to escape. Fights broke out as people flailed blindly at those around them. Mild-mannered grocers and teachers and accountants were suddenly as ferocious as Roman gladiators. Those who fell were trampled. Somewhere, someone was banging on a door, thinking those outside might open it.

Tatiyana was shoved from behind and dropped her baby.

She howled and immediately dropped to her knees to pick up the child, but the gas made it all but impossible to see. She blindly felt all around her until her fingers closed around a small ankle. She instinctively pulled toward her and the air momentarily, cruelly, cleared just enough for her to see little Tatiyana with the baby clutched in her arms.

They were both dead.

That was the last thing she saw before passing out.

Tatiyana tried to scream but the Zyklon B seared her airways. She brought her hands to her throat, a warm liquid flowed down her thighs, she wanted to rip her own tongue out of her mouth to breathe, and then -

- and then she awoke, days later, in a place she didn't know, being cared for by a kind woman she didn't recognize, scared and lost and distraught until, of all people, her sister Adriana appeared to explain all that had happened.

No, Adriana said, *I am not a spirit and you have not died, but...*

But. Always that word. *But.*

Their brother Aaron, dead. Their parents, dead. Her own two children, dead. Countless others, also dead.

No, Adriana said, *I am not a spirit and you have not died, but... but you'll soon wish that you had,* is how she should have completed her sentence.

Tatiyana closed her eyes and fought the memory of the pain and despair that had then filled her. Never again would she let them overwhelm her.

All around her the *Weichsel-Union-Metallwerke* buzzed with activity. She glanced to her left. The two guards were busy talking and smoking, as they always were. Nobody was paying her any attention.

Good.

She poured a small quantity of powder in a square of paper that she quickly folded and hid in her clothes.

Her children would be avenged.

The day of reckoning was almost at hand.

Robert Mulka again read the note he had received an hour earlier. The enormity of its content was so staggering it left him incredulous, uncertain how much credibility it actually deserved.

A rumor, nothing more, in all likelihood.

Surely nothing so stupendous could have been in the works for so long without him learning of it sooner.

Surely the new security measures he had put in place following the theft of Höss' car and the subsequent, humiliating escape would have been enough to circumvent any such endeavors.

A dream, a wishful fantasy conjured up by desperate people. It had to be. His time would certainly be better spent solving real problems, rather than wasted chasing the phantasmagoric swirls of some guard's overactive imagination.

And yet, if he was wrong...

He couldn't afford to be wrong. Not again. Not after last time.

The good thing was he didn't need to risk it. Change was long overdue over there anyway.

He sneered as he picked up his phone.

He'd teach those subhuman creatures to even *dream* of such things.

7 October 1944

The men of the 12th sonderkommando shivered in the cold morning air.

They had been standing in neatly aligned rows since before dawn, all 300 or so of them. The sun had risen an hour ago, but that didn't make much difference. The sky was cloudy and gray and a fine drizzle dampened their clothes and added to their misery.

Lajb Panub was shivering through jaws he had clenched to keep his teeth from chattering.

"They know, Israel, I'm telling you... they know", he whispered to Israel Gutman.

Gutman heard him but stared straight ahead. He didn't want to take his eyes off the two guards who had machine guns trained on them. He was hoping for a sign before they opened fire. A twitch, a look, a smile... anything.

Maybe that'd be enough for him to dive to the ground and pull Panub down with him, and maybe he could prolong their lives by a few seconds.

"Do something", Panub urged him. "*They know.*"

The teenager seemed so sure, and yet... How *could* they have known? His men knew their success and survival depended on the most complete discretion. Could someone still have let something slip? Worse... could they have been simply betrayed? It certainly wasn't unheard of for some Jews to collaborate with the Nazis to save their own skins, even temporarily. Had one of their own sold out?

He was about to tell Panub to be quiet when two officers arrived, along with a dozen SS. Gutman knew them. Scharführer Busch and his acolyte unterscharführer Gorges. Two splendid henchmen devoid of all intelligence and initiative. Their mission, this morning, thus had to be very simple and straightforward, which could be either very good or very bad.

Scharführer Busch took a step forward. A gust of wind almost whipped the sheets of paper out of his hands. He frowned and licked his lips as he reordered them, his mental abilities strained to their breaking point.

He opened his mouth to speak.

Gutman held his breath. He tensed and got ready to dive on top of Panub at the slightest indication.

Now they'd know whether his young friend was right or not.

Adriana could sense Tatiyana was hiding something from her, and she was worried.

Her sister had quickly recovered from her terrible ordeal, in large part thanks to Doctor Ada's magic. She had been back on her feet in a matter of days, though she seemed to have aged 20 years in a matter of hours. Her short-cropped hair showed more white and gray than it did black, and lines now creased her face so deeply that she could easily have passed for Adriana's mother.

Traugott dispatched her to work at a small armaments factory adjacent to Auschwitz. But her recovery, as miraculous as it might appear, had only been superficial. While Tatiyana's body might have healed, at the very core of her soul, where it mattered most, a purulent wound still festered, spewing a steady stream of toxins that poisoned her entire being.

Adriana had always known her sister to be a calm, even-tempered woman who had probably never experienced a single day of anger in her entire life. No matter what the world threw at her, Tatiyana's attitude was always the same: let's see what happens, I'm sure things will turn out for the best.

But no more.

Tatiyana was devastated by the death of her children and she cried almost incessantly for an entire day, before collapsing into the sleep of exhaustion. She awoke the next morning a completely different person. Something had snapped inside her during the night, or perhaps something had hardened, and she hadn't shed a single tear since that day. She had sloughed off her old self, like a molting snake, and slipped on an armor of ferocious anger that nothing could dent, let alone penetrate, and woe betide anyone who even tried.

Adriana had also seen her, more than once, in the company of some she knew to be troublemakers – inasmuch as anyone could be termed a 'troublemaker' at Auschwitz. No matter how tight the security, no matter how harsh the punishment, there were always those who would rebel and refuse to be cowed.

She tried to warn Tatiyana, only to be rebuffed rudely and told to mind her own business. Tatiyana also reminded her, in a sneering tone, of the role that she, Adriana, had played in the escape of four men more than two years prior.

Adriana didn't know how Tatiyana found out, but she was left with nothing to say and her sister stumped away angrily.

Adriana had long ago stopped waiting for her sister's mood to improve. No longer did she believe the Tatiyana of old might one day return. A change she at first attributed to all her sister had gone through, and which she hoped to be temporary, showed no sign of abating. If anything, it had become even more ingrained and pronounced.

Tatiyana awoke every dawn with a dark scowl and went to sleep, 18 hours later, with the scowl intact. Her only conversations were held in low voices, always with the same small group of prisoners, with her back turned and with a wary eye constantly kept looking back over her shoulder.

Tatiyana never even asked about their parents' final moments or how they had all come to be here. And there was that time, once, when in a flare of rage she furiously reproached Adriana for her own survival and her children's deaths. *Why did you not let me die with them?*, she screamed. Devastated by such venomous words, Adriana was again left with nothing to reply.

And so it was that today, several weeks after Tatiyana's arrival at Auschwitz, the two sisters were barely on speaking terms.

The door to the warehouse opened and Rita entered. The elderly kapo struggled to shut it against the cold wind and then shook the rain from her clothes before coming to stand next to Adriana.

"It's the strangest thing", she said pensively, snapping her friend out of her reverie. "The sonderkommando are all lined up in the courtyard, not doing any work. I wonder what's going on."

Then a deafening roar echoed throughout Auschwitz, like a thunderous wave that crashes onto the craggy shore of a remote Viking cove, and their world changed forever.

Scharführer Busch glanced at the men assembled before him and grinned.

He remained silent a moment longer than was necessary, just to make them suffer a little bit more – just because he could. How he relished in this power of life and death that he, an uneducated oaf from the backwoods of Thuringia, had been granted over these wretches. Let them shiver in the cold a moment longer. Let them wonder a moment longer what he would say. Let them worry a moment longer whether he might kill them or allow them to live for a few more minutes. What did he care about their sufferings and doubts? He was a god, *their* god, and his will was the only one that truly mattered.

As his gaze swept over them and he felt their terror, he realized these were no longer human beings. These were hollow shells, helpless lifeforms robbed of their right to self-determination, creatures of flesh and bone reduced to their simplest expression. Auschwitz had enslaved them to him by a malevolent spell, and to him this feeling of absolute power was almost sexual in its intensity.

Reading from his list, Busch called out a number in a thunderous voice and, after a moment, a man hesitantly shuffled forward. The SS then called out another number, and another, and another, until twenty inmates had been selected to stand apart from the rest. The little group was then led away at gunpoint and, judging by the direction they went, it became obvious they were being taken to the death wall between blocks 10 and 11, where they would be summarily executed.

Israel Gutman's stomach dropped. He glanced furtively at Panub next to him, who happened to be glancing at him at the same time. Their eyes locked and a single thought, traveling at the speed of light, passed between them.

They know. The bastards know.

And in that instant a cold, steely resolve descended upon Gutman, dissolving his fears and doubts. The time to strike back had come, and the thought filled him with a clarity of mind, an almost surreal serenity, a peace that he'd only encountered once before in his life - on the eve of battle, in Warsaw.

He remembered hiding in some dank, smoke-filled basement with a score of other men he barely knew as the Nazis hunted them, as bomb after bomb exploded outside, rattling their hideout and showering them with dust in the darkness. A single grenade thrown through the right window would have killed them all. A single shell would have buried them alive. The glow of a single cigarette, a single sneeze, a single sob would have spelled their doom.

This second you lived, the next you died. Life was no longer measured in months and years and decades, but solely in minutes and hours – or perhaps days, for the most fortunate among them.

Men no longer cared to discuss what they wanted out of their lives. Their dreams and hopes, if they had not been vaporized, had certainly been plunged into deep hibernation, perhaps to reawaken if this nightmare ever ended. What purpose would it serve to fantasize about what might happen a year from now when you were not even guaranteed one more day? Better to wish for a few extra hours with these strangers who were now your blood brothers.

Not that the next day would be any better. For if they survived until then, when dawn rose he and his companions would file out of the basement to engage in close combat with the crazed *SS-Sturmbrigade Dirlewanger* of convicted child rapist Oskar Dirlewanger – an abomination of a man who would one day be considered by some as the worst sadist ever spawned by that regime of sadists - armed with little more than their courage and their willingness to fight evil.

And yet, even faced with imminent and certain death, these men spent their last hours on Earth joking and praying and telling stories in hushed voices. Some laughed, while others slept or just sat there, staring ahead silently, alone with their thoughts and regrets. There were no howls of despair or cries of anguish or tearful pleas sent up to an uncaring God; just men determined to do what needed to be done, men at peace with lives they knew were about to end.

This was it, then. Gutman didn't harbor any illusions that they might emerge victorious, or even that they might live for more than a few minutes; the best he could hope for was for their sacrifice to save thousands of others. All men are born to fulfill one overriding destiny, Gutman believed, all lives revolve around one single, defining moment, and today his destiny would be fulfilled and his life would be defined. Nothing that happened later in his existence, should he live to be 105, would be of greater significance than the next few minutes.

It was too late to turn back. All he could now do was charge ahead and cause as much damage as possible before it all came to its inevitable conclusion.

Panub was trying to tell him something, Gutman knew, but he wasn't listening. He needed to find one man among hundreds, one man to set in motion events that would never be forgotten, and he couldn't see him anywhere.

A wind of panic was beginning to sweep through the assembled inmates. Gutman and Panub weren't the only ones who now understood what was going on; they all did, and even in a place of death such as Auschwitz, no man ever willingly sees his time on Earth come to an abrupt end. The guards could sense the inmates' growing panic, which in turn made them fidgety and, Gutman feared, even more trigger-happy than normal.

He only had seconds to act before it was too late. But still he couldn't find the man who held the key to their destiny.

Scharführer Busch was still bellowing out numbers and men were still stepping forward, though a bit more reluctantly now that they knew they were being called to their deaths. Another group was led away; some prisoners went with resignation, while others kept looking back at their friends in anguish, somehow hoping to be saved.

And then they were.

The man Gutman had been searching for in the crowd, Chaim Neuhof, stepped forward of his own accord before Busch could resume his cull. Busch looked at him and sneered.

"Get back and wait to be called, worm", the Nazi growled.

Neuhof swallowed. "What does it matter to you, to kill one Jew or another? Kill me and let another live", he said.

"I'll not tell you again", Busch barked. He shoved Neuhof with both hands. "Get back where you belong and wait to be called."

Busch was a fat, massive man, and his sudden shove almost upended Neuhof, which might have ruined everything. But not only did the Jew remain standing, he also took a few courageous steps forward and came to stand less than a foot from Busch.

This sole act of defiance should have alerted the SS that trouble was brewing. But his obtuse brain couldn't adapt to new situations – all it knew was "yell, punch, kick and kill", in that order - and in the end that spelled his demise.

Neuhof looked back over his shoulder and, somehow, his eyes went directly to Gutman's, who nodded.

Neuhof smiled.

He released the head of the hammer he had hidden up his sleeve and the tool slid into his hand. He wrapped his fingers tightly around the wooden handle and turned back to face Busch.

"You fucking piece of...", the SS began.

He got no further.

"Hurrah!" Neuhof shouted, for no apparent reason.

He then swung his arm over his head in a wide arc and struck Busch in the forehead. Metal met bone with a sickening, meaty thud and the SS' eyes rolled up into his head. He collapsed like a puppet.

As though possessed of a single mind, the other prisoners roared and howled as they rushed the remaining guards. A few shots were fired and a few men fell, but it was too little, too late.

The revolt had begun.

Mattias Traugott dropped his pen and looked up from his work.

What the hell was that noise?

Auschwitz was a realm of chaos, its very fabric a tight weave of barking dogs and roaring guards and moaning inmates, but after a while that soundtrack faded away behind a thick curtain until you no longer took notice of it. And yet, as used as Traugott had gotten to it over the years, something had now reached out from behind that curtain to sink its claws into his flesh and claim his attention.

He pushed his chair away from his desk and stood up, his heart racing. He listened hard for the strange noise and... yes, he could still hear it. It was still there, like thunder rolling across a narrow valley.

What in the...?

The unmistakable sound of gunshots pierced the din and he instinctively pulled out his sidearm.

A siren began to howl, swelling in volume and rising in pitch. It was soon reinforced by another, and another, and another, until a dozen formed an infernal choir to serenade the Devil.

Traugott exited his office at a run.

"DOWN!"

Israel Gutman launched himself at Lajb Panub, tackling him down hard. The two men tumbled together as shots rang out around them. Gutman pressed a forearm against Panub's neck to keep him down while he raised his head to quickly take stock of the situation.

The guards who had accompanied Busch and Gorges were dead, as were the two officers. Each body was being torn apart by swarms of vengeful inmates. Gutman caught sight of a man, his shirt drenched in blood, who raised high above his head what looked suspiciously like a handful of human hair attached to a slice of scalp. Even more disturbing were the man's mouth and teeth, which were stained blood-red. The man howled like a werewolf, threw his trophy away and plunged back into the fray, viciously elbowing his comrades aside to get at the carcass.

But a dozen dead guards mattered not, Gutman knew, not when a hundred more were right this instant rushing to join the fight and crush the uprising. The advantage of surprise was already starting to wane.

The courtyard, by its very design, provided no cover whatsoever and the inmates were completely exposed. And now, having recovered from their shock, the guards manning the watchtowers were mercilessly gunning down the sonderkommando one after the other. They were essentially firing at point-blank range and some inmates were lifted clear off the ground or completely spun around, so powerful was the impact of the bullets. At least twenty men died in the few seconds Gutman watched. The first to go were those who grabbed the dead guards' weapons and attempted to fire back. Most died while still fumbling clumsily with the unfamiliar guns.

The prisoners were so densely packed the guards couldn't miss. Even the shots that did miss didn't really, since the bullets often felled two or three men at a time after shattering and ricocheting off the ground.

This was turning into a massacre.

Gutman instantly made up his mind and jumped to his feet.

"RUN! RUN!" he shouted at the top of his lungs. To his relief, the men around him immediately began to scatter left and right, prompting others to do the same, and soon the guards were no longer shooting fish in a barrel. Their accuracy dropped just as dramatically as the inmates' chances of survival increased.

Gutman then grabbed Panub by the back of his shirt and roughly pulled him up to his feet.

"Come on, we need to get out of here before it's too late", he urged his young friend, whose oft-expressed eagerness to fight the Nazis was about to be seriously tested. Gutman stopped short when Panub failed to follow him. He went back, grabbed him by a sleeve and pulled. "Let's go!" he urged him again.

But Panub now weighed a thousand pounds and Gutman couldn't move him, no matter how hard he tried. It was only then that Gutman noticed the look of horror on the teenager's face, whose feet were rooted to the ground as he stared at his two bloody hands.

Gutman swore and quickly checked his friend for wounds, but came up empty. Someone else's blood, then.

"Lajb, listen to me!" he screamed. "If we stay here, we're dead. We need to go, now!"

Gutman was ready to knock the young man out and carry him on his shoulders if need be. They simply couldn't stay put in this hailstorm of bullets.

And then, as if to forewarn them that the Angel of Death was about to swoop down on them, a bullet struck the ground directly between Panub's feet and exploded. A fragment sliced through Panub's pant leg and lightly scored his calf.

The pain finally snapped him out of his stupor. He looked down at his leg with complete disinterest, as if it were attached to another body, and then up at Gutman. "The bastards shot me", he said.

Not bothering to reply, Gutman grabbed him again and the two men began running toward the crematorium.

They had one more thing to do.

Otto Mockël was late for his shift. Again.

He had spent the better part of the previous night drinking - nothing new to report on that front -

and he'd awakened so late this morning that he'd had time to neither shower nor shave. His smell was so offensive he could detect it even above the nauseating stench that always permeated Auschwitz.

He stumbled out of his quarters and cursed the chilly weather. He stopped to light a cigarette with hands that wouldn't stop shaking and gave up after dropping his sixth match.

He lurched toward the crematorium on wobbly legs, hoping his tardiness might go unnoticed but knowing it likely wouldn't.

A strange, unfamiliar roar arose in the near distance. Then a siren sounded right above his head, threatening to shatter his skull. Poleaxed, Mockël instantly collapsed to his knees and clamped both hands over his ears to block out the deafening noise. A handful of guards ran past him at full speed, almost toppling him over and heading in the general direction of the crematorium.

This couldn't be good.

As soon as he removed his hands from his ears, a dozen more sirens came alive and their howl just about finished him off. More guards ran past him, followed by more and more guards, and a few shot him quizzical glances, wondering what an officer – even an unkempt, foul-smelling officer such as himself - was doing just kneeling there during such an emergency.

Having survived the sirens, though now afflicted by a headache so severe it almost blinded him, and not knowing what else to do, Mockël ambled after them as best he could.

He had only gone a short distance when the first gunshots rang out. He stopped again and reached for his sidearm.

His hand encountered nothing but supple, lukewarm leather, and his heart skipped a beat. The goddamn holster was empty. Cursing his ill-fated life, he double- and triple-checked it, as though the missing gun might have fallen at the very bottom, before finally accepting that it was gone. He then stupidly searched the ground beneath his feet, spinning around in circles like a dog chasing its tail, and even retraced his steps a bit, but obviously found nothing.

What the hell had he done with it? Had he simply left it back in his quarters? Had he gambled it away the night before? Had he traded it for a bottle of cheap sherry? Had someone stolen it? He had absolutely no idea and he knew it was futile to torture himself for an explanation that would never come.

More and more gunshots in the distance. Hundreds, thousand of them. Were the Allies or the Russianss here already, then?

Mockël was briefly tempted to return to his quarters, though he didn't really know that would achieve anything useful. It even rather risked making him look like a coward running *away* from a firefight. So instead, unarmed but suddenly quite a deal more sober, he began running *toward* the firefight.

He skidded to a halt when he finally reached the courtyard outside the crematorium. At first his brain couldn't make any sense of what his eyes were seeing. Hundreds of inmates running to and fro... dozens of bodies lying dead on the ground... some, uniformed, so mutilated as to hardly be recognizable as human... guards firing at anything that moved... It was all too much to take in and his mind recoiled.

Mockël reconnected with reality when three inmates suddenly ran at him with murder in their eyes. Those three knew they didn't have much longer to live, and they clearly intended to send this officer ahead of them down the road to Hell. One appeared completely demented, with his hands and the entire lower half of his face stained red with blood.

Reacting in a split second, he caught them by surprise by charging ahead and violently shouldering his way between two of them. He could have kept running and perhaps gotten away; instead, he stopped just as they did, and they all spun around at the same time.

Had Mockël been armed, this is when three well-placed bullets to the head would have resolved the situation. But he wasn't armed, and they were running at him again.

The odds were somewhat evened when two of them, the one on the left and the one on the right, were struck down. One was hit in the thigh and the other in the neck, and both collapsed with hands pressed against geysers of blood.

Mockël took a quick look around, trying to see who had saved him. The courtyard had turned into a killing field, with dozens of armed guards firing at hundreds of inmates bent on ripping them apart. He also saw several guards engaged in hand-to-hand, mortal combat with prisoners who, he noticed for the first time, were sometimes armed with tools or improvised knives. The mayhem made it impossible to tell who, for now, was winning, and Mockël would go to his grave not knowing to whom he owed his life.

He quickly returned his attention to his own immediate peril, because here came the red-faced, demented demon.

The man was several inches shorter and dozens of pounds lighter than Mockël, and while a year ago the fight would have lasted less than ten seconds, today the outcome was less than certain. The man was clearly insane, which probably rendered him impervious to pain and perhaps even granted him inhuman strength, while Mockël... well, Mockël had seen better days, both physically and mentally.

The demon reached for him with blood-stained claws and Mockël dodged out of the way just in time. He stuck out his foot and tripped his adversary as the man ran past him. The inmate stumbled and almost recovered his balance before finally tumbling into the dirt.

Again, the moment would have been perfect for Mockël to skedaddle out of here and lose himself in the confusion. The thought never even occurred to him.

Instead, feeling more alive than he had in months, Mockël seized the opportunity.

He jumped on the man's back and grabbed his head with both hands, thinking to smash it against the ground. As soon as the demon felt the weight on his back and the hands on his skull, he twisted his head to the side and sank his fangs into Mockël's flesh, drawing blood.

Mockël howled in pain.

Thinking rapidly, he reached for the small combat dagger all SS carried in one of their boots; if he could just get it, he'd plunge it into the man's neck and quickly end the fight.

Except the dagger was in his left boot. Since his left hand was trapped between the man's teeth, he had to reach over and behind his back with his right hand to grab it, which was next to impossible – even more so while straddling a wriggling human eel. Mockël brushed the hardwood handle with the tip of his fingers a couple of times without managing to pull the blade out of its sheath. He desperately gave it one more try, reaching further than before, blocking out the pain in his left hand, and was rewarded when he finally managed to wrap his fingers around the handle.

At that very moment the demon sank its fangs deeper into Mockël's flesh, and its teeth hit bone.

Mockël howled again and the dagger remained in its sheath. He tried to yank his hand out of the man's mouth, but it may as well have been caught in a bear trap. He began pummeling the man's face with his free hand, pulping the nose and shutting at least one eye. His sole concern, from now on, was freeing himself. He could think of nothing else. But either because his blows lacked real strength or because of the man's madness, he still couldn't break free. Worse, he could feel the man's teeth cutting ever deeper into his flesh. The pain was unbearable. A few more seconds and the man would take an actual bite out of his hand.

His hand still in the demon's mouth, Mockël repositioned himself to place a knee against the man's neck, crushing it with all his weight. He then reached down with his free hand and sank his fingers into an eye socket. He took no notice when the orb exploded wetly, covering his fingers with cold goo. His grip secure, he began pulling the man's head back, bending the neck against his knee.

The man finally opened his mouth to scream, releasing Mockël's hand. The SS let out a cry of intermingled relief and triumph, and immediately reached for his dagger with his mangled hand. He pulled it out and was about to sink it into the man's carotid artery when his hand suddenly went numb. His fingers opened of their own accord and the dagger dropped.

Sensing it might escape, the demon began to struggle even harder and Mockël had to use his injured hand to keep him from getting up, even though the outcome was now in little doubt. Mockël took a deep breath and yanked back hard with all his strength one last time; the spine snapped, the man shuddered and went limp, and Mockël collapsed next to him, completely spent.

Mockël just lay there for a few seconds, catching his breath and listening to the noise of the fight around him. Then, incredibly, he began laughing.

All around him men were killing and dying, and yet he was still alive.

Cradling his injured hand under his armpit, he scrambled back to his feet, retrieved his dagger and set out in search of his next victim.

The prisoners assigned to the *Aufräumungskommando*, the famed sector better known as Kanada, had been made to kneel down with their hands crossed behind their necks.

Their guards had then redeployed themselves so that they could both glance nervously out the window and keep a worried eye on the inmates.

However, lacking clear orders, that was as far as the guards' own initiative could take them, and now they hesitated. They were clearly torn between rushing to the aid of their comrades and their duties inside. They probably also feared themselves at risk of being attacked, just as those outside were being attacked. Their nervousness and tension were palpable, and the slightest incident might trigger a massacre.

"They're slaughtering them", Adriana whispered, trusting the sirens' wail and the noise of the fight to camouflage her voice.

She and Rita were both kneeling next to a mound of shirts that partly concealed them from the nearest guard.

"There's nothing we can do", the elderly kapo replied in a voice barely louder than a spring breeze. "The sonderkommando have risen up, and now they'll die."

Something in the way she said it tickled the back of Adriana's mind. "Did you know about this?" she asked.

Rita shrugged imperceptibly. "There are always rumors. Some are true, some aren't. Who's to know?"

Adriana remained pensive, with her head down, for a moment, but there was really only one thing she could ask next. "Is Tatiyana involved in this? Is my sister out there, dying?"

The sound of running footsteps came from behind them before Rita could reply. Mattias Traugott appeared at a run, slaloming between mounds of clothes, and stopped suddenly in the middle of the warehouse. He had drawn his gun and was slightly out of breath.

"What's going on out there?" he bellowed above the roar of the sirens.

"It's the sonderkommando, herr untersturmführer", a guard explained. "There seems to be a problem and..." The rest of his sentence was buried by a deadly thunderclap of shots.

"Rita, where are you?" Traugott shouted as he looked left and right for her.

"Over here, herr untersturmführer", Rita said, standing up slowly.

Traugott turned toward her voice and saw her. "There's a situation outside that we need to attend to", he understated. "You keep your ladies in line while we're gone. You know the consequences if you don't."

"Of course, herr untersturmführer", the elderly kapo simply replied.

Satisfied, Traugott turned his attention back to the guards. "All of you, you're with me. Let's go!"

He then rushed out the door, the guards right on his heels.

There was a moment of brief hesitation and uneasiness before the first inmate dared get off her knees. But once the ice was broken, all others also got up and began chattering excitedly.

"There'll be none of that, ladies", Rita announced in a voice of unchallenged authority. The chatter immediately died down. "Nothing has changed. I suggest you all stay down and away from the windows until whatever is going out there has been resolved."

As she finished her sentence, there was a flash of movement on her right. She called out, knowing what had just happened, but she was too late.

Adriana had already bolted out the door.

Gutman and Panub knew they had mere seconds to return to the relative safety of the crematorium, or it might all have been for nothing.

They ducked as they ran, zigging and zagging between small knots of guards and inmates viciously tearing each other apart, being careful not to trip over the bodies that now littered the courtyard and dodging more than one collision at the last possible second. Only once did their luck run out, when they bowled into a man neither of them ever saw coming. The man was launched into the air, landed hard, skidded over several feet and, as they watched, was riddled with bullets.

Gutman and Panub kept running. It was all they could do.

The crematorium was by now entirely deserted. They entered at a run and made straight for a small storage room in the back.

"Keep watch, I'll get it", Gutman shouted above the noise of the firefight.

Panub nodded and pressed his back against the wall, next to the door. He could see into the courtyard if he craned his neck, and he'd be able to raise the alarm quickly if a guard should return.

"Hurry, hurry", the teenager said nervously.

Gutman was already hard at work unstacking small crates of wood. There were dozens of them and the one he needed, obviously, was at the very bottom of the last stack, at the very back of the room. It took him a minute to reach it, but it might as well have taken him an hour.

"Got it", he finally said as he yanked it out with one last pull.

He set it down on the ground in front of him and, using a flat piece of metal that had been hidden in the room for that very purpose, began prying off the lid. That, on the other hand, took him only a couple of seconds, since the lid had been pried off and nailed back into place several times over the past few weeks.

Inside the crate were about a dozen homemade hand grenades fashioned out of sardines tins and gun powder stolen from the *Weichsel-Union-Metallwerke* by accomplices such as Tatiyana Zöbel.

"Now they're going to pay", Gutman whispered.

They planned to lob the grenades at the guards from the roof of the crematorium, in order to kill as many of them as possible. Gutman was to go first and, after he'd inevitably been shot, Panub would take over, until he too was killed. By then, hopefully, all the grenades would have been used and dozens of guards blown to pieces.

Panub almost ruined everything when he turned away from the door to admire their secret weapon. A guard entered the crematorium behind him less than a second later and by the time the sound of the man's footsteps registered above the noise of the fight, it was too late.

Otto Mockël grabbed Panub from behind and wrapped his injured arm around his neck in a strangle hold, while his other hand pressed the tip of his dagger under the teenager's left eye, drawing blood.

Panub let out an involuntary gasp of surprise and Gutman froze.

"Get up and step away from the crate", Mockël ordered with a growl.

Gutman obeyed. He stood up, slowly, and took a couple of steps back. Mockël looked down at the crate and frowned when he saw that it appeared filled with sardines tins.

He looked up at Gutman.

"You try anything funny, I'll shove the blade into his brain", he threatened. "Get down on your knees and face away from me."

"So you can slash his throat and then stab me in the back? No thanks", Gutman replied flatly, his eyes never leaving Mockël's.

The SS snarled. "I'm not *asking* you, I'm *telling* you", he said. He pressed down on the point of his dagger harder, Panub winced and a drop of blood – red and vibrant against his pale skin - ran down his left cheek.

"Go ahead, kill him. Then I'll kill you", Gutman said.

"Israel?" Panub immediately gasped. Gutman ignored him.

Mockël could have killed Panub a minute ago, and yet he hadn't. That decision puzzled Gutman until he noticed the mangled, essentially useless hand. The odds wouldn't favor a one-handed Nazi fighting a couple of prisoners with absolutely nothing to lose – especially a one-handed Nazi armed with nothing more than a glorified potato peeler. Both Gutman and Mockël knew that the guard's only strategy was to buy himself some time until reinforcements arrived, which was exactly what he was doing.

Gutman decided to press his advantage while he had it. "There's two of us and only one of you, herr obersturmführer", he stated in a mocking tone. "You better leave."

Mockël snarled again. "I can even those odds easily enough", he said. Quick as a striking cobra, he pulled his hand away from Panub's face and stabbed upwards, aiming to at least put out the eye.

Gutman and Panub screamed in unison. The teenager instinctively turned his face away and the razor-sharp blade, rather than plunging into his eye and perhaps his brain, scored into his left cheek a deep gash that began to bleed profusely.

Panub, seemingly unawares of how gravely he'd just been wounded, tried to take advantage of the confusion to free himself but Mockël, despite his wound, was surprisingly strong and wouldn't let go. Gutman grabbed Mockël's right wrist with both hands and slowly managed to raise it high above their heads, neutralizing the threat posed by the dagger. The SS was strangling Panub with one arm and fighting Gutman with the other, and while this was one fight he was bound to lose eventually, and while Gutman could feel him weakening slowly, every second they spent engaged in this struggle could be the one second that doomed their mission.

He needed to end the fight, and he needed to end it now.

There was a sudden thud and Mockël's knees buckled briefly when he was struck from behind. His grip on the dagger weakened and Gutman, sensing the opportunity, tried to pry it from his fingers. The two men fought over it until the weapon finally clattered to the floor. Gutman looked down and saw the blade at his feet. He was about to kick it behind him, where he might retrieve it more easily, but Mockël took advantage of his momentary distraction to heat-butt him viciously.

Gutman's ears rang and stars exploded in front of his eyes. He let go of Mockël's wrist and the Nazi immediately punched him in the face two or three times, sending him to his knees. Gutman shook his head and looked for the dagger, but the blade was gone.

Mockël's left arm was, somehow, still wrapped around Panub's throat, choking him. The young man was beginning to weaken and his face had gone a dark purple. Mockël was pulling on his left wrist with his suddenly liberated right hand, crushing Panub's windpipe even harder. The teenager began to kick out randomly, a sure sign of his desperation, and Gutman, who was still on his knees, turned away just in time to avoid being kicked in the mouth. The blow still struck him behind the ear and landed him on his ass, stunned.

Gutman knew he had mere seconds to regain his feet and save his friend. He made it back to his knees before losing his balance again, his mind spinning.

Mockël grunted with the effort of killing Panub. The young man's struggles were growing weaker and weaker, signaling that the fight was coming to its fatal conclusion. But then Mockël let out a different type of grunt. His whole body stiffened, as though shocked by a million volts, his eyes bulged and he released Panub to swat madly at something behind him.

Panub immediately collapsed to the floor and crawled away, retching and coughing, with one hand pressed to his throat and the other to his bleeding cheek.

Mockël was still trying to grab *something* behind his back. He spun to his left, then to his right, then to his left again, but whatever it was that had stung him seemed to be just out of his reach. His strength was draining away. He remained standing for a moment longer, incredulous and paralyzed, until he fell to his knees and toppled forward on top of the crate of improvised grenades, inches away from Gutman.

The handle of the dagger protruded between his ribs and bubbles of frothy blood formed around the wound, showing that he still lived.

A woman stood in the doorway behind him. In one hand she held one of the long metal rods the sonderkommando sometimes used to push the bodies into the ovens, and with which she had struck Mockël, to little effect.

Her other hand was empty. A second earlier, however, it had plunged the dagger into the Nazi's kidneys.

"Who... who are you?" Gutman asked.

"I'm looking for my sister", was her sole, urgent reply.

Before Gutman could make sense of her answer, there was movement behind her. The woman cried out in surprise and stumbled into the small room after being shoved.

A new SS, this one armed and obviously angry, appeared in the doorway and quickly took in the scene. It was only then that Gutman noticed the massacre outside seemed to have stopped, at least momentarily.

The SS' eyes came to rest on his fallen comrade, a dagger stuck in his back, and he paused.

"Mockël?" he finally asked.

The woman raised her head defiantly. "I killed him to keep him from killing them", she answered.

"How?" the man demanded.

"I came looking for Tatiyana", the woman explained. "I saw him run in here and I followed him. And I'm glad I did."

The man swore. "And I followed you when I saw you bolt out of the barracks. And now you've killed a guard. Are you completely insane? I won't be able to save you this time. You're done."

Gutman was having a hard time following their conversation, though it was amply clear that these two had some kind of history together. He also immediately saw how he might profit from it, and a plan began to form in his mind.

The SS was still staring at the body. Gutman dared not think what might happen if he noticed the crate underneath, and if he then saw what the crate contained.

Gutman willed himself to not look at the crate, to avoid attracting any unnecessary attention to it, and he began to breathe easier when the SS finally looked away.

"We can't stay here", the man continued. "They're setting up the MG42s outside. They're about to rip this place apart."

Gutman shuddered. The *Maschinengewerh 42* heavy machine gun would later indirectly inspire America's legendary M60 machine gun, and the carnage it could inflict was unimaginable. The gun spat out 1200 rounds per minute and Allied soldiers had quickly learned to flee from its fearsome growl.

Gutman had first encountered it in the streets of Warsaw and had hoped never to face it again, except in his darkest nightmares. The silence outside was now explained; the Nazis were waiting for the heavy weaponry to be ready. Those not already dead would soon be.

"I'm not going anywhere with you", the woman argued. "I'd rather stay here than end up in the gas chambers."

Gutman was finally able to regain his feet and the SS seemed to notice him for the first time. He immediately pointed his gun in his direction and Gutman docilely raised his hands. Time to put his plan into action.

"Take it easy. I'll stay behind and you can tell them I killed this piece of shit", he said, kicking Mockël's inert body, though no hard enough to risk toppling it off the crate. "I'll be dead in five minutes anyway. No one will ever know."

The SS seemed taken aback by the proposal and narrowed his eyes at him. "Why? Why would you do that? And why would *I* make a deal with *you*?"

Gutman held his stare. "You obviously want to save her and I want to save him", he said, pointing at Panub, who was still lying on the floor. "You take them both out of here and you give me your word that he'll be safe..."

"Israel, no...", Panub protested feebly, his voice no more than a croak.

Gutman ignored him. "...and I'll stay here to be shredded by your machine guns. When they find my body, they'll think I killed him and it'll end there. That way my friend lives and yours doesn't get gassed. Problem solved, no?"

Gutman could tell that the SS was tempted, but only because he didn't know about the grenades hidden underneath Mockël's body. If he saw the crate, the whole thing would instantly fall apart.

"Adriana, grab the boy and let's get out of here", the SS finally said.

"No, I'm not going to..."

The SS rounded on her so violently that she flinched. "And who'll take care of your goddamn sister if you die here?" he roared. "He's giving you a way out. Take it before it's too late!"

Adriana hesitated for a few more seconds before yielding to Traugott's implacable logic. She looked at Gutman. "What's your name?" she asked.

"Israel Gutman."

"Why are you doing this? You don't know us."

He smirked. "And that matters? There's no need to kill three Jews where only one must die."

Adriana looked at him pensively for an instant before nodding. "Well, Israel, at least you get to choose the manner of your death, and it will not be in vain. Thank you", she said.

Gutman half-grinned. "Just take care of my friend. He just turned sixteen."

"You have my word", she promised.

She helped Panub back to his feet. The young man tried to resist, but he was too weak to put up any kind of effective opposition.

The trio left and Gutman found himself alone with Mockël and the crate of grenades. The silence outside was both eerie and menacing. He grabbed Mockël by the back of his uniform and swung him off the crate. The Nazi gurgled and Gutman saw that he was not only still alive, but also conscious.

He grabbed him by the hair and pulled his head off the floor. "I got some good news, Nazi", he said, bringing his face to within an inch of the other man's. "I got you an express ticket straight to Hell."

Mockël somewhere found the strength to spit bloody, foamy saliva in his face. Gutman smiled and wiped it off with the back of his sleeve. He then reached under Mockël's body, found the dagger handle and twisted it viciously before yanking out the blade. Mockël let out a groan of pain and blood began gushing out of the wound.

Neither of them had much longer to live now.

Mockël was too seriously injured to resist as Gutman bound both his ankles and his wrists with twine. The young fighter then dragged him out of the storage room, toward the ovens.

Gutman didn't have to do this; he knew that. Worse, he knew that he *really* couldn't afford to do this; he was living on borrowed time as it was, and his luck could run out at any moment. The SS would be dead in less than five minutes anyway. He could just leave him to drain of his blood like a stuck pig.

But at the same time... how could he afford *not* to do it? The truth was he *wanted* to do this. The poetic justice of the act was simply too seductive to resist.

Mockël panicked and began to struggle. He tried crying out but the blade had sliced through the kidney and into the lung, and all he managed was a feeble mewling sound that would have shamed a wounded kitten. He tried again, harder, and this time choked on a mouthful of blood.

Desperation bloomed in his eyes and Gutman grinned as he picked him off the ground to lay him down on one of the rolling slates. He opened the oven door and cringed when the familiar blast of heat assaulted him from the bottom of Hell's deepest pit.

Mockël's eyes bulged out in terror and he tried to roll off the slate, but Gutman roughly shoved him back in place.

"Have a nice trip", the young Jew snarled before pushing him into the burning furnace. Mockël somehow managed to scream, once, before Gutman shut and barred the door.

And then there was complete silence, but just for an instant.

Gutman was about to return to the storage room to fetch the grenades when the Nazis opened up with the MG42s.

Gutman threw himself to the floor as the machine guns roared outside and bullets the length of his fist began flying overhead, piercing the brick walls as easily as if they were made of paper. Chunks of mortar and splinters of wood rained down on him as he crawled to the crate, grabbed it with one hand and dragged it back to the ovens.

One bullet found its mark and almost severed his right leg when it pulverized the knee. Gutman howled with pain and wrapped both hands around his injury as he writhed on the floor.

Outside, men were being mowed down, and he could hear them shouting and crying and begging for their lives. The thought that he might still save a few of them sent an additional surge of adrenaline coursing through his veins.

Climbing onto the roof was now out of the question. He needed a new plan, and he rapidly came up with one. He grabbed the crate again. He only had a few more feet to go. Inch by painful inch, he made his way to the second oven, next to the one where Mockël was now roasting, and, without getting off the ground, hoisted the crate onto the slate.

Bullets were still flying, shredding the crematorium, and now he'd have to risk it all. He couldn't open the oven door and push the crate in while lying on the ground, so he'd have to chance it before it was too late.

The MG42s fired endlessly. They never paused, as though they never needed reloading, and Gutman knew it was futile to wait for a lull. So he placed his good leg under him and, after taking a deep breath, launched himself up.

He was immediately struck by three bullets that spun him around. One hit him in the thigh, the other in the hip and the last in the right shoulder. He collapsed next to the crate, bleeding profusely, his entire body throbbing with pain and within seconds of death.

Gutman blinked tears of agony and rage out of his eyes. He wouldn't be defeated and he wouldn't be denied, not here and not now, not when he was so damn close.

He heaved himself onto his stomach, bringing his left arm to within inches of the oven, and fought off a wave of vertigo and nausea that almost doomed him. He then opened the door with fingers slick with blood and, with an ultimate effort, shoved the crate inside.

A bullet pinged loudly against the cast iron door just as he shut and locked it, taking three of his fingers, but Gutman didn't even notice. It no longer mattered.

He'd done it. He'd won.

He closed his eyes and waited.

Adriana, Traugott and young Lajb Panub emerged into the now-silent courtyard.

Adriana stopped suddenly and gawked.

The courtyard was littered with intertwined bodies - some alive, some not, some stuck in limbo between both worlds. All were covered in blood to some degree, sometimes theirs, often not, and it was essentially impossible to tell the living from the dead.

Those already gone were lying on the ground any which way. Some stared at the sky with vacant, lifeless eyes that sometimes still reflected their last instants of terror. Others seemed to be smiling and appeared relieved to have left this world. As they likely were.

Those still walking the tightrope that led from this world to the next sometimes moaned, sometimes tried to move, sometimes feebly called out for help. Many sought their mothers, as even the toughest of men are wont to do when all hope is lost. Adriana quickly looked away when one of the damned beckoned to her with an arm whose hand had been blown off. The limb ended in a stump from which hung ribbons of bloody, dripping flesh.

And then there were the mutterings of those who, for now, still lived. Their curses and supplications melded together into a low rumbling that, like thunder in the distance, forewarned of a dark future. Adriana wondered where some of them still found the strength to pray, after daring to rise up against evil and being so utterly annihilated. What further proof did they need that God had abandoned them? That God was toying with them? For the time being, they had been made to lie face down, hands crossed behind their heads, to await the mercy of their masters – as if their fate hadn't already been sealed.

The uprising had been crushed, of this there could possibly be no doubt. At least a hundred armed guards now kept watch over the prisoners in the courtyard. Traugott grabbed Adriana's arm and hurried her along. "Move faster, we can't stay here", he growled.

"Why? What are they going to do?"

Then, as if to answer her question, a command was barked and a man began counting backward from ten.

Zehn... Neun... Acht...

The guards withdrew at a run. A few inmates looked up in puzzlement and glanced worriedly around the courtyard, like moles peeking out of their dens, before lowering their heads again.

"*Hook up*", Panub mumbled. His slashed cheek was still bleeding and made it hard for him to enunciate clearly.

Adriana frowned. *Hook up?* Hook up with what?

It was only after a moment that she understood, when she noticed, atop the walls, a dozen pair of guards – each team composed of one gunner and one loader - setting up the dreaded MG42s.

So not *hook up*, then, but rather *look up*. Adriana felt her blood turn to ice.

She'd heard Traugott mention the machine guns earlier, but only now did she truly grasp what he'd meant: in mere seconds, the SS would open fire and all those still in the courtyard would be shredded.

Sieben... Sechs... Fünf...

"Oh no, this...", she said.

"Shut up", Traugott said at the same time, though he wasn't talking to her.

He grabbed Panub by the front of his shirt and roughly threw him to the ground. The young man tumbled and landed on top a small pile of corpses. Panub immediately made to get up, but froze when he found himself staring down the barrel of Traugott's sidearm.

"You lying pig", the young man managed to say.

"What are you doing? You promised!" Adriana protested.

"I promised nothing", Traugott replied loudly. "Now keep walking if you don't want to join him."

Vier... Drei... Zwei...

Adriana stared at him, stunned, until she noticed a dozen guards now observing them. And then it all became so blindingly clear that her mind spun: if Traugott could reasonably explain his decision to save one of his workers, especially one who had played no active part in the uprising, how could he explain his intent to also save a sonderkommando who had been one of the instigators? He couldn't, that's how. So young Panub had to die, and he had to die publicly, and Traugott had to make a great spectacle of it to extinguish any and all suspicion and protect his reputation.

His reputation, and her. From the very start, he'd only wanted to make sure no one would ever know she'd stabbed Mockël. His sole purpose was ensuring that she'd never be punished for the murder, nothing more. He'd never had the slightest intention of keeping his end of the deal he'd struck with Gutman. He'd only promised to save Panub so that Gutman would agree to remain behind and eventually be blamed for the murder.

Panub was the only one, apart from the two of them, who really knew what had happened, so he had to die.

"You bastard", Adriana whispered. "I'm not leaving him behind."

"Save the niceties for later", he replied in a low voice. "Now hurry."

She stumbled when he shoved her toward the warehouse.

Eins... ZERO!

The guards opened up with the MG42s.

Adriana cried out in fear and instinctively ducked. A dozen heavy machine guns firing simultaneously made a bone-rattling, soul-shattering thunder, and for a brief instant all she wanted to do was run back to the barracks and hide under her bunk, like a child frightened by a storm.

The courtyard behind her turned into a slaughterhouse. Those prisoners who still could tried to flee, only to be mowed down almost instantly. The SS had positioned the MG42s to cover the entire courtyard and it was impossible to escape the hail of bullets. Bodies hit multiple times erupted in geysers of flesh and blood. Adriana glanced behind her and saw two men run blindly into one another and get tangled up in their panic. A bullet struck the rear of the first one's head, completely obliterated his face when it exited through the nose, then entered his friend's mouth and exploded the back of the second man's skull.

"Hurry", Traugott shouted, shoving her again.

They were about 50 feet from the warehouse when, out of nowhere, a small, red-gray shape darted in front of them, also headed for the warehouse. Adriana immediately recognized him, and so did Traugott.

"Run! Run!" Adriana shouted as Lajb Panub darted left and right to dodge the rain of bullets.

Traugott calmly extended his right arm and aimed at Panub's back. There was no way he would miss at such short range. The bullet would strike the young man flush between the shoulder blades and he'd be dead before he hit the ground.

Time slowed down and everything seemed to happen in slow motion. Traugott tracked the boy for a few seconds, his arm moving impossibly slowly, and as Adriana watched helplessly, his finger began depressing the trigger.

"No", she screamed, sensing Panub's imminent death. The sound of her own distorted voice reach her ears as though it originated from very, very far away.

She wanted to shove Traugott, to make him miss, but her limbs had turned to lead and she could only look on. Each finger weighed a ton and lifting even the littlest one required superhuman strength. She knew what she wanted to do, what she *had* to do, and impotent tears filled her eyes as her mind raged against muscles and ligaments and tendons that were inexplicably failing her.

Then the crate of improvised grenades Gutman had shoved into the oven with the last of his strength ignited and the roar a thunderous explosion swept Auschwitz. A gigantic fist of air punched Adriana and Traugott from behind, blowing them off their feet and sending them flying through the air to sprawl in the mud.

Adriana tumbled head over heels until she slammed against the wall of the warehouse. The impact knocked the breath from her lungs and her world wavered when she tried to pick herself up. She collapsed again when a brick fell from the sky and struck her in the head. Bleeding and in pain, she remained lying on the ground for several seconds, protecting herself as best she could until the shower of debris ended.

Something was very wrong. The air was filled with dust that stung her eyes and made it hard to breathe. She sat up with her back against the wall and shook her head to clear her mind, before realizing she had gone essentially deaf. The world was coming to her as though her head was plunged in a pail of water. She pressed both hands over her throbbing eardrums, to no avail. Auschwitz's infernal soundtrack had been turned off almost completely, at least temporarily.

She couldn't see Traugott or Panub anywhere. All around her dozens of people who had also been thrown to the ground, like so many trees flattened by the explosion of a meteorite, were gingerly dusting themselves off and regaining their feet. Many, inmates and guards alike, just stood there, some with their mouths open, others clearly bleeding and injured, all appearing shocked and disoriented, as though the impossible had just occurred.

The ground was littered with chunks of bricks and mortar, and for a moment Adriana marveled at the thought that an Allied bomb might finally have fallen on Auschwitz.

And then the cloud of dust cleared somewhat and she saw it. Or rather, she *didn't* see it.

The crematorium no longer stood where it always had. In its place now rose a misshapen, darkened hulk from which rose a heavy plume of dense, black smoke. The sinister building had been eviscerated by a massive explosion, and the debris field clearly showed it had been blown apart from the inside. Several dislocated bodies lay all around the ruins.

It was Adriana's turn to stare, agape, when the enormity of what had just happened finally struck her.

Auschwitz had incinerated its last body.

The SS who had promised to keep him safe instead threw him to the ground.

Young Lajb Panub tumbled helplessly in the mud, unable to stop himself, and landed atop a dead body. This caused the corpse to release a torrent of thick liquid that immediately soaked through his thin clothes. Disgusted and revolted, Panub quickly tried to push himself up but his hand sank through a puddle of warm, squishy matter that clung to his skin when he tried to flick it off.

When he finally looked up, the SS had his sidearm pointed directly at him.

"You lying pig", he said. His slashed cheek was bleeding profusely and the blood he kept swallowing made him nauseous.

The woman with the SS said something he couldn't hear. She seemed to be protesting, but he paid her no heed as he pushed her roughly toward the Kanada warehouse. A man was counting down from ten and the SS was clearly in a hurry to find himself anywhere but here.

Panub could guess why. He'd spotted the MG42s as soon as they'd emerged from the crematorium and into the courtyard. While most people looked for danger right under their feet, Gutman had taught him to keep his head up to scan the horizon. That way, the young fighter had explained, maybe you'll spot danger before danger spots you.

The countdown reached *eins*. Panub crawled under a dead body and curled into the tightest ball he could, drawing up his legs against his chest, burying his face between his knees and wrapping his arms around his head. He knew he had to make himself the smallest target possible.

A second later, the MG42s began spewing out deadly mouthfuls of lead and people began dying.

The guns' thunder filled the courtyard and bullets buzzed over Panub's head like angry insects of doom. Many inmates panicked and ran for their lives, a strategy that proved fatal when they instead drew the guards' fire. Cries of terror and pain showed living targets were still being mowed down, which meant he'd be safe for a few seconds.

But only for a few seconds. Soon enough, the guards would begin raking the rows of dead and dying bodies, and the corpse he was hiding under would be shredded, and so would he. If he were to escape alive, he had to make a move now.

He risked poking his head up and spotted the SS and the woman quickly getting away. He saw where they were headed and figured that if the place was safe enough for them, it'd be safe enough for him.

He began crawling forward. Some bodies he slid under, others he shoved aside. Some were dead, others not yet. He pushed his way through a witch's brew of entrails and blood and torn flesh, and he might have lost his mind to the horror had he not been so focused on escaping alive.

Panub was nearing the edge of the field of bodies, and relative safety, when a hand suddenly closed around his ankle. His heart almost jumped out of his chest and he twisted onto his back. A crazed, almost toothless man was grinning at him, in his delirium thinking Panub his long-lost son come to rescue him. Panub shouted at the man to let him go, but the man only mumbled incoherently and pulled at him harder. Panub shouted again. The man shouted back, something about how a good son should not raise his voice to his father, and in the end, snarling, Panub had to kick him savagely enough to smash teeth and bones to get away.

He crawled a few more yards and stopped. There were no more bodies ahead and he could therefore crawl no further. Now he'd have to run, and when he ran, he'd draw the MG42s' fire just as surely as those who'd run before him had. And chances were, he'd die just as surely as they had.

Not that there was any safety to be found in just lying there, waiting for the inevitable.

The SS and the woman were less than twenty yards away, and he somehow felt they were the key to his survival. He took a deep breath, drew up his knees under his belly and launched himself ahead like a sprinter. His left foot slipped in a puddle of *something* and he almost fell, but he managed to keep his balance and he overtook the SS and the woman.

He went around them, then cut in front, expecting to be mowed down at any moment, and the woman shouted at him to run, run!

A massive blast suddenly swept him up from behind. He was lifted off the ground and flew through the air for several seconds, his arms windmilling uselessly as he rode the invisible wave. He tucked his head between his shoulders as he smashed through the door to the warehouse, tumbling on the other side.

Another body landed on top of him with a grunt. Panub glanced a gray uniform and immediately guessed to whom it belonged.

Knowing the fate that awaited him if he didn't keep running, he disentangled himself as quickly as he could and vanished into the cavernous building.

Rita was almost toppled off her feet when the blast rocked Kanada like a small quake.

The elderly kapo tottered and would have fallen had a woman standing behind her not reacted quickly and caught her. The two of them hung on to each other for a few seconds before becoming aware of the screams and wails that now filled the warehouse around them.

Many of the *weißköpfchen* had been thrown to the ground by the explosion and were being helped back to their feet by those who remained standing. Several had been slightly injured and seemed to be complaining of bruises or sprains. A few unfortunate others had stood near the windows and been killed outright by shards of flying glass plunged deep into their faces and necks and chests. Those who had been slashed but still lived lay where they had fallen, crying out as they bled. Many were already being helped by friends pressing handful of clothes against their wounds.

"What's happened?" the woman who'd caught her asked worriedly.

"I wish I knew", Rita answered softly. She patted the woman's hands both to thank and reassure her. "I'm fine. Go help someone else."

The woman nodded obediently and quickly walked away. Rita headed in the opposite direction, toward the door, but had to dodge out of the way of a running inmate after just a few steps. The man was covered in blood from head to toe and, though she merely caught a glimpse of it, the look of sheer panic and terror on his face told her he would have trampled her without any hesitation, had she not stepped out of his path.

She watched, puzzled, as the man ran past her and disappeared on the other side of a mound of clothes. This was most unusual; regular inmates were not to set foot inside Kanada for any reason, and the man must have been quite desperate – or completely mad – to break that rule. Leaving that mystery to be solved later, she again headed for the door, intending to see what had transpired outside, but her progress was once again blocked after just a few steps.

"Where did he go?" Mattias Traugott demanded angrily.

His uniform, hair and skin were coated in grayish dust. Behind him, through the ruins of the shattered door, she witnessed a scene of utter mayhem in the courtyard. She could only imagine what had happened. But judging by the alarms that now blared and by the number of people running around in all directions, it was clearly something... major, to say the very least.

She returned her attention to the man standing in front of her.

"Where is whom, herr untersturmführer?" she asked innocently, though she knew perfectly well he meant the mysterious blood-covered inmate.

Traugott growled and clenched his fists by his sides. "Don't play games with me, you old witch, or you'll pay for it", he said. "Tell me where he went."

Rita smiled. Traugott had never intimidated her, no Nazi ever had, and this one, more than any other, should really have known better than to try.

"I only wish I knew who the untersturmführer means," she said amicably. "I was thrown to the ground when the building shook and I must have passed out for a few seconds. I haven't seen anyone, only my fellow workers, several of whom now need urgent medical care. Shall I see to it or will you?"

Rita knew how jealously protective Traugott was of his workers. Though Auschwitz enjoyed an endless supply of free labor, it was simply too much of a hassle to replace one of the *weißköpfchen* if that could be avoided, since any newcomer was bound to be less efficient than an older, more experienced worker.

Traugott was also very wary about inserting new workers into his well-oiled operation, out of fear he might inherit a troublemaker or a thief even more brazen than the others. He much preferred retaining the workers he had, once he had trained and learned to trust them, and Rita knew he would therefore not let a single one of them die needlessly – especially now that several of them would need to be replaced at once.

Rita saw in his eyes that he knew he was being played. He still yielded to her. "See to it immediately", he finally ordered.

"As the untersturmführer wishes", she replied with a small bow that they both knew held more than a reasonable measure of defiance.

He hurried past her and Rita finally made it to the courtyard, where she found a bloody and dazed Adriana leaning against the wall by the door.

"Thank God you're safe, child! What's happening?" she asked rapidly. Adriana didn't reply. She just stared straight ahead with vacant eyes.

Rita frowned. "Adriana, why are you not...", she began before being silenced by the sight of the blasted crematorium. Her mouth dropped open and she slowly covered it with her hand, her power of speech momentarily gone. "Oh dear Lord", she eventually breathed, shocked. She jumped when Adriana finally noticed her presence and touched her shoulder.

"Where's Traugott?" Adriana yelled. Rita recoiled at the loudness of her voice.

"Why are you shouting?" she asked.

It was Adriana's turn to frown. "I can hardly hear you", she yelled again. "The explosion damaged my hearing. Have you seen Traugott?"

Rita wanted to ask about the explosion but she was struck by Adriana's urgency and knew her questions would need to wait until later. "Yes", she said a bit louder. "He ran into the building right on the heels of an inmate I'd never seen before."

Adriana's eyes widened and she pushed herself off the wall. Her knees almost buckled and, with her arms outstretched like a tightrope walker, she tottered for a few seconds before recovering. She then grabbed Rita's hands, as much to steady herself as to convey her concern. "A young man, maybe sixteen or eighteen years of age?" she asked when her world finally stopped swimming. "Is that who he was chasing?"

Rita nodded. "Yes. But why? Who is this man? Do you know him?"

"Where did they go?" Adriana shouted, ignoring her questions.

Rita pointed at the smashed door and Adriana immediately set off on wobbly legs that grew steadier as she first walked, and then ran. The wound on her head still bled, a trickle of blood ran down the side of her face and she was still a bit dizzy, but she was determined to keep that madman from murdering yet another innocent human being – especially one so young and whom he'd sworn to keep safe.

After the hellish carnage she'd just witnessed in the courtyard, the sight of a few injured women being tended to by friends inside the warehouse didn't faze her. Several guards had returned to keep an eye on the inmates in the wake of the explosion, but in Traugott's apparent absence, they seemed content to just stand by and let the prisoners take care of one another.

Nobody paid the slightest attention to another haggard, bleeding woman wandering aimlessly through the building.

Adriana had no idea where to look for Traugott and Panub. Kanada was immense and they could literally be anywhere. Her first instinct was to make for the very back of the building, toward the washrooms, figuring that's where Panub eventually ended up if he kept running and running and running.

She'd only gone a few dozen steps when a shout pierced her temporary deafness. On her left, between two mounds, she glimpsed Traugott holding a terrified *weißköpfchen* by the front of her clothes and berating her so vehemently that spittle flew from his lips. While she couldn't make out exactly what he was demanding, she could certainly guess. And then, as if to prove her right, the poor woman indicated a mound of coats with a trembling finger.

That's where the poor boy was hiding.

Adriana shuddered as Traugott's head whipped violently in that direction, like a wolf that catches the scent of its prey. He threw the woman to the ground and took a few steps back while firing blindly into the clothes. Wispy puffs of dust rose from the little holes that appeared where the bullets struck. He emptied the clip and then kept pulling the trigger, the gun clicking empty repeatedly before he finally threw it away. There was no way to tell if Panub had been hit or not.

"A gun! Someone bring me a bloody gun!" he bellowed.

A guard came running and handed him a loaded carbine. Traugott fired three more rounds, and that was enough to flush Panub out of his hiding place.

Knowing himself trapped and condemned, the young man did the only thing he could: he emerged from the mound of clothes directly in front of Traugott and attacked. The SS was caught completely by surprise and froze for half an instant before aiming the carbine straight at Panub's chest. The young man, on the other hand, never hesitated and bowled Traugott over just as the man fired. The round went into the ceiling and Panub kept running.

"This way", Adriana shouted. She doubted very much that she could save his life, but she would die trying.

Whether he heard her or not would never be known, but Panub made a beeline for Adriana. She stepped aside as he blew past her, never slowing. She watched him go for a second, covered in blood and a hand still pressed to his slashed face, until he vanished, and when she turned back around Traugott was less than ten feet from her. She crossed her arms across her chest and squared her shoulders, blocking his path.

"Move, now, *neunzehnhunderteinundsiebzig*", he growled. She read his lips more than she heard him.

"You'll have to speak up, herr untersturmführer", she still asked him to repeat. "The explosion damaged my hearing and I can barely understand what you're saying".

He took a menacing step closer. "First that old whore Rita, and now you", he said just loud enough for her to understand. "I'm done playing games with you two. Move out of my way. Now."

She raised her chin defiantly and stared at him. If he didn't want to play games, then neither would she. That was fine with her, though she felt that was a choice he might come to regret. "You promised to keep him safe", she reminded him coldly. "In exchange for my life, you guaranteed him his."

Traugott winced and took a worried glance around to see who might have overheard. He wasn't too keen for his fellow SS to learn he'd struck a deal with an inmate to save Adriana's life. "You better keep your mouth shut and mind your own business", he warned her.

She smiled tiredly at him. "You claim there's a man underneath that evil uniform you wear, not just a Nazi", she said, lowering her voice voluntarily. "You say 'For you, anything'. But those are just words, herr untersturmführer, empty words that mean absolutely nothing."

Her words seemed to puncture his anger and he appeared genuinely hurt. "I ran into the fucking gas chamber to save your sister, and yet you have the gall to say such things to me?" he demanded softly, forcing her once again to read his lips.

Adriana sighed inwardly. She knew her accusations were somewhat unfair, but she couldn't pull any punches if she hoped to win. Her aim was to keep him here, engaged with her, while Panub got away, and the best way for her to achieve that was to hammer the feelings he had for her. If she hurt him badly enough, if she made him suffer enough, she knew his pride would force him to stand his ground and do battle with her.

So far the strategy seemed to be working and if she could keep this up a bit longer, the young man might find his way to safety – for now.

"Why do you want to kill him?" she asked. "What has he ever done to you?"

Traugott opened his mouth to reply and then shut it. The answer that instantly sprang to his mind now refused to cross the threshold of his lips. So Adriana answered her own question. "You want to kill him because he's a Jew, nothing more", she shrugged. "That's the only reason you need, isn't it? He's a Jew, and that's cause enough to die. Period."

Traugott dropped his gaze. He looked back at her after a moment and seemed about to say something when a shot rang out somewhere in the warehouse. They both jumped when they heard it, and then a guard arrived at a run and saluted Traugott.

Adriana couldn't hear what the guard said, but the look that came across Traugott's face told her all she needed to know. Tears immediately filled her eyes and she angrily raised a hand to silence him.

"You may not have pulled the trigger yourself, but you're just as guilty as those who did", she snapped.

She then left him standing there, confused, and went to find Rita.

24 December 1944

"How do I look?" Rita demanded nervously.

Adriana looked her up and down for the umpteenth time and smiled. "Well, I doubt very much St. Nicholas was ever this short and thin, but the children certainly won't notice."

Rita nodded contentedly and went to fetch the bag of toys the *weißköpfchen* had sewn. Two lumps of sugar or a piece of candy were attached to each present, and in just a few minutes Rita would make a triumphant appearance at the camp hospital to distribute the loot to children under Doctor Ada's care.

Even Auschwitz's barbed wire and guard towers couldn't keep St. Nicholas out on Christmas Eve.

Adriana wished she could have played good old St. Nick, as did many other women, but the privilege had unquestioningly been Rita's. As much as the guards were feared and despised, the elderly kapo was beloved and respected, and more than one inmate owed her his or her life. Even guards had been known to treat her with inordinate respect and deference, a bit like children in awe of a stern – but kind - schoolmistress.

Rita returned with the bag of presents trailing behind her. "Lord, this is heavier than I thought", she breathed.

"I can go in your stead, if you're too old", Adriana joked. Rita shot her a stare that rendered words useless and Adriana smiled.

This was Adriana's third Christmas at Auschwitz, and also the one that thus far felt the most normal.

Her first year, in 1942, the SS put up a Christmas tree in the middle of the courtyard and placed the bodies of murdered men underneath. Then there was an additional roll call and hundreds of prisoners were made to stand in the cold for hours, causing dozens of them to collapse and die in the snow. On the stroke of midnight, the Nazis congratulated the survivors – this was their 'present', to have lived when so many others had either died or been killed - and wished them a Merry

Christmas, but not until they'd been made to listen to Pope Pius XII's infamous Christmas address.

Many returned to their barracks in tears. Christmas was already a time of impossible heartache and despair at Auschwitz, and to hear the pope's ambiguous words about race – understood by some to be an endorsement of the Nazis' policies - was too much to bear. What hope was there for them, when even God's vicar on Earth seemed to be siding with the Devil?

"We can go when you're ready", the young guard who would be escorting Rita to the hospital said. Then, seeing her struggle with the bag, he said: "Let me carry that for you, *Oma*". Adriana caught her breath upon hearing the young man use a term of endearment for one's grandmother.

Rita stared at him. He looked barely eighteen and his uniform was at least two sizes too big for him. She wondered how his few months of service at Auschwitz would impact the rest of his life. Would he be among the thousands who would be held accountable in the coming years? Had he already seen and done things that had forever altered the course of his existence? Would he be shown any mercy? Would he *deserve* any?

She began to feel some pity for this young man, to see him as much as a victim of the Nazis' madness as they all were, so she quickly put such thoughts from her mind. "It wouldn't do for St. Nicholas to be seen with someone like...", she began, before deciding she needn't be too harsh with him. "... with someone dressed as you are."

"Then I'll carry the bag all the way to the door and leave it there", he offered gently. "Then I'll remain out of sight."

Rita considered his proposal for a moment before accepting. The man swung the bag over his shoulder as if it weighed nothing and patiently waited for Rita to be ready.

In November 1943 Rudolf Höss was replaced as camp commandant by Arthur Liebehenschel, a Nazi cut from somewhat different cloth. On Christmas night the inmates were allowed to enjoy parcels sent by loved ones who had found refuge abroad, and the contents were shared joyously. But looming over these modest celebrations and dampening everybody's spirit was the knowledge that while the war was going badly for the Germans, it wasn't yet lost, and tomorrow this Night of Light would be nothing more than a painful dream, replaced by the Hell that was now their daily lives.

Not so this year. In December of 1944 the Reich was on its deathbed and wouldn't last another year. It had been months since a German plane had overflown Auschwitz; the only planes the inmates now saw were American or Russian or British. Some even claimed that, when the wind blew the right way, it carried before it the sound of artillery shells and bombs exploding far in the distance, the drumbeat to which Allied troops advanced – and to which German soldiers retreated.

Höss returned in May 1944 to supervise the extermination of hundreds of thousands of Hungarian Jews, the so-called *Aktion Höss*, but he encountered limited success. Then the crematorium was destroyed, and it was as though a pus-filled abscess had finally been lanced. Rather than rebuild, a couple of weeks ago Heinrich Himmler had ordered the crematoriums and gas chambers blown up and dismantled, in a futile attempt to conceal the horrors that had occurred here.

A stake had been driven through the evil that burned in Auschwitz's heart, dealing it a mortal blow from which it would never recover.

No, this year would be – *was* – different. This year, Christmas was as much a celebration of the birth of a God some still believed in as a celebration of the Nazis' unavoidable defeat.

When it became clear the inmates would be granted significant leeway to celebrate Christmas, the *weißköpfchen* mobilized to fabricate toys out of spare bits of clothing, sometimes forgoing all but one or two hours of sleep each night to work. The kitchen staff procured lumps of sugar and pieces of candy, a St. Nicholas costume was somehow assembled – the beard was nothing more than long thin strips of white cloth strung together - and Rita unanimously chosen to play the role.

The old woman had bowed her head and shed a single tear before thanking them all.

Adriana felt a presence behind her. When she turned around, her sister, Tatiyana, was standing there, staring at the ground with her hands linked in front of her.

The uprising, in October, led to the deaths of over 450 sonderkommando, including 200 who were forced to strip and lie on the ground before being shot in the back of the head. Three women – Ella Gartner, Ester Wajsblum and Ragina Safin – were charged with passing stolen gunpowder to the rebels. Why they hadn't already been executed was anyone's guess, but they were condemned to be, sooner or later.

Tatiyana, on the other hand, was never even questioned, even though she was at least as guilty as they were, and if this was in any way due to Traugott's intercession, he never said a word to anyone about it.

The two sisters had exchanged a few words since the uprising, but nothing of consequence. Tatiyana was quietly transferred to the *weißköpfchen* when the dust began to settle – here again Adriana saw Traugott's hand at play – but they were assigned to different sectors of the warehouse and didn't see much of each other during the day. Then, at night, like all others, they collapsed of exhaustion and waited for the next day to rise.

But Adriana sensed something different tonight. Tatiyana just stood there, staring at her feet, and after a moment Adriana noticed her sister was weeping softly.

Her heart broke. She went to her and took her gingerly in her arms. She didn't know what to expect – based on past experience, Tatiyana could very well try to claw her eyes out – but her sister immediately rested her head against her shoulder and began to sob harder, as though the weight of the world had finally been lifted off her shoulders.

Adriana couldn't believe how frail and old Tatiyana felt through her clothes, but she still hugged her a bit harder.

"I'm so sorry, Adriana", Tatiyana finally said, wrapping her arms around her only living relative. "I was so full of rage and pain. I... I... God I miss my children so much."

Adriana began to stroke her sister's short hair as her own tears flowed. She didn't say a word, for there was nothing she needed to say.

As Rita left the warehouse to go bring some joy to children on this night of forgiveness and renewal, a woman intoned a Polish carol and dozens of others soon joined in, their voices crashing over Auschwitz like the waves of a mighty ocean.

Bóg się rodzi, moc truchleje, the song went.

God is born, great powers tremble.

27 January 1945

Adriana awoke to the sound of champagne corks popping, and her heart leaped.

She sprang up and listened hard to the noise coming from outside. Was that what she thought it was? Could it be?

She dared not hope. Not yet.

Tatiyana stirred next to her. The two sisters had had a platform to themselves for the past couple of weeks, and they'd rediscovered how well they slept without someone else's feet in their face all night long. All around them, alerted by the same sound, women were waking and stretching and wondering.

"What's going on?" one whispered. "What the heck happened to roll call this morning?"

Prisoners always awoke well before dawn, in darkness so complete they couldn't see the hand in front of their face. Awakening in barracks bathed in soft gray light, and thus after the sun had risen, was unheard of – and more than a little unsettling.

More champagne corks popped outside and men began shouting.

"Adriana?" Tatiyana muttered, her voice rendered barely intelligible by the weight of sleep.

"Shhh... listen", Adriana replied softly. Her breath plumed in the cold.

There were voices, men's voices. The words were muffled and indistinct, but the emotions that carried them pierced the barracks' walls like bullets. Anger. Panic. Fear. Lots and lots of fear.

There was also the sound of footsteps. Not the footsteps of guards making their usual rounds, but the footsteps of men running for their lives. Hurried footsteps that crunched in the frost and snow, footsteps that told of danger and menace.

And then there were those champagne corks, hundreds upon hundreds of them, popping in the distance - the endless, chilling staccato of automatic weapons in their dozens.

Adriana would have known the rattle of German guns in her sleep – she'd certainly heard it often enough – but this... this was different. Yes, the Germans were firing at someone, but someone was also returning their fire. And judging by the size of the firefight, that *someone* hadn't come alone, which meant that...

Adriana shuddered and wondered where Rita was. The elderly kapo was always quick to reassure those she called *her* women, to bring them back under control in times of turmoil, to be the buoy they grabbed to keep from drowning, but this morning she was nowhere to be found and her absence made the wintry cold bite even deeper.

Adriana swung her legs off the bunk and Tatiyana grabbed her wrist to keep her from jumping.

"Where are you going?" she asked worriedly.

"To see what's happening, of course", Adriana explained, as though it were the most natural thing in the world to run toward a gunfight rather than away from it. "We can't just stay here like dunces waiting for *something* to happen."

But before she could move the door suddenly slammed open. A blast of cold air blew into the barracks, carrying before it hundreds of snowflakes that twirled madly around a small, dark figure. A few women cried out in fear and surprise before recognizing Rita, who shoved the door closed.

The elderly kapo dusted the snow from her clothes and blew some warmth into her cupped hands.

"Very well, ladies", she then announced as calmly as she could, though the tremor in her voice betrayed her trepidation. "Get your things together and get ready to march."

Get ready to *march?* What the hell did that mean? Where was she taking them?

A buzz of excitement rippled through the barracks, jumping from woman to woman like lice until Rita clapped her hands sharply.

"Not now", she snapped with unusual impatience. "You have two minutes to get ready. You'll need whatever warm clothes you have."

Adriana was both intrigued and slightly worried by Rita's attitude. She jumped off her platform and went to her old friend.

"What's going on?" she asked in a low voice while turning her back to the rest of the room. The floor was icy cold and she began to shuffle from one foot to the other. "Does this have anything to do with...?"

Rita silenced her with her eyes, and Adriana knew that it did. Her heart skipped a beat and she bit her lower lip.

Thousands upon thousands of prisoners had been evacuated out of Auschwitz these past couple of weeks. Each day, endless columns of inmates dressed in thin clothes, the vast majority of them barefoot, filed out the main gate and into the deadly cold under the escort of a handful of guards. They were apparently being marched to the town of Wodzislaw, in the western part of Upper Silesia, even though it was more than obvious that thousands would never make it.

But perhaps that was the whole point. Some claimed that the SS, now deprived of their gas chambers and crematoria, had decided to rely upon Mother Nature to do their dirty work for them. Walk malnourished, exhausted and under-dressed inmates in the brutal cold for long enough, and most will perish as surely as if you'd gassed them.

The handful that survived, well, you could just shoot in the back of the head.

There were also those who claimed – or perhaps *hoped* - that the Russian Army was growing closer by the day, and that the Germans had therefore begun to flee. While the sound of combat did echo in the distance daily, it still appeared to come from over the horizon, which meant that the Reds were still dozens, and probably hundreds, of miles away. And anyway... After so many years, Adriana could scarce imagine that Auschwitz would one day cease to exist. If God had meant to wipe this abomination off the face of the Earth, surely He would have done so a long time ago.

It also seemed completely absurd that He would make howling hordes of unbelieving bolsheviks His tool to eradicate it. The sanctimonious Americans? Yes, perhaps. But the Russians? Come on.

(Well, there *was* that persistent rumor that the demon Mengele had fled the previous week, but who could tell...?)

Whatever the truth of it may be, the departure of so many prisoners over so short a period of time, and the absence of any new transports in months, had left Auschwitz feeling strangely empty and deserted – haunted, almost.

Adriana began to wonder. Was this, then, what awaited the *weißköpfchen* on this day? Had their turn finally come to march out into the white emptiness, to meet whatever fate awaited them at the other end? Was this what Rita meant?

It wasn't, and her reply felt to Adriana like a punch in the stomach.

"The Germans are fleeing like rats off a sinking ship", she whispered. She almost sounded relieved to be sharing what she knew with someone else. "It's complete madness out there. Most of them slipped away during the night, but those who are still here..." The old woman paused and looked down, shaking her head as if to clear it of what she'd seen. "They're fighting, killing, stealing, raping... There must be fifty of them inside Kanada, grabbing whatever they can while they still have a chance."

Adriana's mind reeled and she stared at Rita for a moment. "Does this mean...?"

Rita nodded urgently. "Don't say it. *They* don't need to know. Not yet."

Adriana took a moment to collect her thoughts.

"What's your plan?" she asked.

"I honestly don't have a clue. I never expected this, and by the look on your face neither did you. For now all I know is there's safety in numbers, so we need to stay together for as long as possible", the elderly kapo said. "If they come for us, the more of us there is, the better."

Adriana shivered when she understood what Rita meant by *if they come for us*. At least twice already men had tried to rape her, and it wasn't an experience she cared to repeat any time soon.

"We'll file out just as quietly and discretely as possible", Rita continued. "From what I just saw outside, the Germans have much on their minds and we should be able to make it out the back gate and just... walk away."

The idea sounded ludicrous. After so long, to simply walk away from this place? Surely not.

"Go get your things", Rita ordered. "We're going and I'll need you."

A minute later the *weißköpfchen* were assembled in the center of the barracks, some clutching small bundles, most carrying nothing but the clothes on their backs, all of them eager to hear what Rita had to say. And once she'd said it, they stared at her in stunned, unbelieving silence.

"Why?" a voice asked in the back. "Why are the Germans in such a panic? Why are they fleeing?"

Of course someone would ask the one question she couldn't answer. That was the one bit of information she couldn't share with them, not yet anyway, for once they knew, there'd be no accounting for their reaction. And should they panic, should their tenuous cohesion dissolve, then their hopes of survival would go from slim to none. She needed to keep them together for as long as possible, even if that meant lying – or at least not telling the whole truth.

The *weißköpfchen* sensed her hesitation and turned suspicious. A nasty current ran through them and they became notably agitated, like sharks that catch the scent of blood in the water. But in the end it didn't matter, because the God Rita still so fervently believed in, the God she prayed to every night before going to sleep, the God she thanked for each new day, decided to reward her faith with an ultimate act of betrayal.

A blast of wind blew the door open. Before Rita could shut it, a woman pointed out and shrieked. Adriana glanced outside just in time see a gigantic tank, a green monster with a red star painted on its side, rumble outside the gate and disappear from view in a tempest of snow.

"The Russians are here! The Russians are here!" the same woman shrieked again, as though she'd spotted Beelzebub its-own-self urinating sulfurously in the snow.

Which, in her mind, she probably *had* seen.

These were the simplest of simple women, all of them uneducated peasants and workers and housewives who essentially knew nothing of the world around them. Only a handful could read and write, and it was doubtful that more than three of them had held a book in the past five years. Their world was made up of what they could see and touch and feel and hear. The rest was... was... well, the rest was foreign, and the rest was different, and the rest was strange, and more than anything else, the rest was so utterly *frightening*.

Weakened by their fear of the unknown, they had fallen easy prey to the juggernaut that was the German propaganda machine. It had been only too simple for Goebbels and his ilk to indoctrinate them – and millions of others - to think of Joseph Stalin and his Red Army as blood-thirsty monsters who killed and roasted little children for breakfast – and sometimes for their evening meal as well.

With such thoughts at the forefront of their minds, the *weißköpfchen* panicked and surged toward the door, intending to flee while they still could. Rita took a few steps back and raised her hands high to stop them.

"No, please, I'm begging you, we must stay together", she called out as loudly as she could. "Please, please!"

But in the face of their mindless terror, she was nothing more than a child's sandcastle assaulted by the raging tide. Those at the back began pushing and shoving, adding fuel to the fire of their infectious panic, and Rita had to take another step back to stay ahead of these women she cared so deeply about – a step she should never have taken, a step that proved one too many.

If only she'd stepped aside and let them go, Adriana would later reflect. *If only*.

The old woman tripped and fell with a small cry, and that was all the *weißköpfchen* needed.

Adriana was still on her platform collecting her things. She saw Rita go down, knew what was about to happen and tried to stop the unstoppable.

"No, stop!" she shouted, jumping off. "Stop!"

She tried to pry her way through the mass of women to reach her oldest, dearest friend, but the women were pressed against one another, front to back and back to front, so tightly she couldn't have slipped a sheet of paper between any two of them.

"Move!" Adriana shouted with tears in her eyes, knowing she was probably already too late. "Move, damn you! Let me through!"

No one paid her the slightest attention. In their terror, the *weißköpfchen* had lost all reason and become oblivious to the world around them. There was a hideous monster outside, and they needed to flee before it came for them. That was all that mattered.

Somehow the door had shut again, and the women at the front of the herd were being crushed against it by those behind. They panicked and began fighting one another, thus condemning themselves to a slow, suffocating death, until the door mercifully slammed open with a crack like a gunshot and they tumbled out into the snow. Their way now clear, the crazed *weißköpfchen* stampeded for safety like wilderbeest chased by fire on the African plains.

Through it all, Adriana thought she could hear bones snapping and perhaps someone calling out feebly for help. "Rita, no!" she shouted again.

Now blind with panic and furor, she struck the woman nearest her in the temple and the woman collapsed. Adriana desperately wanted to reach Rita but before she could rush into the void she'd opened, it was filled by the next woman, who simply stepped over the one who'd fallen.

Adriana reared back to strike another woman – she'd knock them all out if she had to – but Tatiyana seized her wrist from behind.

"You're too late, you'll get killed!" her sister cried.

"Let me go, let me go!" Adriana shouted. She fought with all her strength to free herself but Tatiyana wouldn't release her, and by now more than half the *weißköpfchen* had already escaped out the door and into the snow-covered courtyard, many of them leaving bloody footprints as they ran. A few more seconds and they were all gone, leaving behind only Adriana, Tatiyana, the body of the woman Adriana had knocked unconscious – and Rita.

Tatiyana gently released Adriana's wrist, but her sister remained where she was. After a moment, Adriana took a careful step forward, then another, as though she were walking on ice so thin it might give way at any moment.

She reached Rita's inert, bloodied body and slowly slunk to her knees. There was nothing she could do. She was too late. A silent tear slid down her cheek.

She reached out to caress her friend's forehead but recoiled when her fingers, instead of encountering solid bone, brushed against a mushy surface that couldn't possibly be human. Rita's entire face had a misshapen, slightly humanoid appearance that told of the trauma she'd suffered; she looked no longer like Rita, but rather like Rita's handicapped sister. Blood ran from both her mouth and her nose, and a single bloody, broken tooth had fallen from her mouth and lay next to her lips. Hundreds upon hundreds of feet had pummeled her fragile body, pulverizing every other bone and killing her just as surely as if she'd been run over by that Russian tank.

Adriana bent over her friend's body, shielding her in death as she'd failed to do in life, and she cried.

She cried not only for the loss of a woman who had been like a mother to her, but for the injustice of it all – to have survived for so long at Auschwitz, longer than anybody else, only to be killed when salvation and freedom were finally at hand. And to be killed not by the Nazis, but by those she had made her mission to keep not only alive, but as safe and healthy as one could be in such a place.

She cried for Rita who had been trampled by hundreds of feet, for Rita who had tried one last time to keep her women safe and paid for it with her life, for Rita who had been deserted and abandoned by her God in her time of greatest need, but who had nonetheless never stopped believing.

It was all too much to bear and Adriana would have howled, had she not felt so utterly drained. She didn't react when Tatiyana knelt next to her and began stroking her back to comfort her. And when Tatiyana, after a moment, tried to pull her to her feet, Adriana refused to move. She couldn't, wouldn't, leave Rita behind, not after all they'd been through together.

Let the Russians come and find her. Let them rape her on the floor like animals as often as they liked before slitting her throat. She no longer cared. At least it would then all be over. At least, when they were done, she'd go and join Rita and Aaron and her parents Simeon and Raanah... somewhere.

And that is precisely what might have happened, had the accursed door not suddenly swung open again, letting in another blast of frigid winter air.

Tatiyana instinctively sprang to her feet to stand between her prone sister and the intruder, fists bunched and ready to kill.

The intruder barely noticed her.

"You're still... What are you... How...", Traugott sputtered. The sight of Adriana prostrated on a blood-covered floor had seemingly robbed him of his ability to form complete sentences.

He harrumphed and coughed a few times to clear his throat. "When I saw them all run out I thought you'd be gone as well", he finally managed to say. "I feared I'd be too late."

Adriana finally raised herself off Rita's body, though she remained kneeling next to it. Traugott blanched visibly when he saw the kapo's broken and dislocated body. He'd seen the *weißköpfchen* rush out, and now he began to grasp what had transpired.

Adriana wiped the tears from her eyes. "You *are* too late", she said. "Had you arrived two minutes earlier, maybe..." She shrugged and shook her head sadly, as if she despaired of the futility of it all.

Adriana tore her gaze away from Rita to look at Traugott, and her mouth slowly dropped open. One of his eyes was quickly swelling shut and turning a yellowish tinge of purple. His nose, clearly broken, now lay crookedly across the middle of his face, and two rivulets of dried blood ran from his nostrils. His uniform was torn in several places and through one of the rips she glimpsed a thin red line that still oozed blood.

"Not the Russians", he immediately explained, reading her expression. "Three of my own. They wanted this. They should have known better."

He dropped a heavy burlap sack on the floor in front of her. Adriana frowned without touching the bag. "We haven't got much time", Traugott said urgently as more shots and cries came from outside. "You'll need this."

When Adriana still didn't move, Tatiyana grabbed the bag, quickly upended it and out tumbled boots and coats and sweaters and socks and mittens and hats... everything they'd need – and more - to flee into the cold and have a chance to make it. The bag also contained canned food and a couple of bottles of liquor.

Tatiyana sneered at him. "Your friends tried to kill you over a couple of ratty jackets?"

Traugott sneered right back at her and reached into one of his pockets. He pulled out a small leather purse that he threw at her. Tatiyana almost dropped it from the weight. "This is what they wanted. And now they're all dead."

Tatiyana hesitated only briefly before opening the purse. She gasped when she glimpsed its contents and handed it carefully to Adriana. Something metallic rattled.

Intrigued, Adriana peeked inside and let out a small cry. She dropped the purse as if it had bitten her. The purse at first remained upright, until one side finally collapsed to release a cascade of heavy coins – some silver, some gold – and a few shining stones of various colors. There was also a roll of paper bills almost as thick as her wrist.

Adriana slowly got to her feet and took a step back.

"You disgusting pig", she said in a low voice. "Take this filth and give it to the Russians. Maybe that'll buy you some mercy."

She kicked the purse with the tip of her foot and more coins and precious stones fell out.

A gold coin rolled hesitantly through Rita's blood and traced a thin red line on the floor before eventually losing its momentum and toppling over. On the exposed side was engraved a mythical winged beast with a thunderbolt clutched between its talons.

Tatiyana quickly dropped to her knees.

"Adriana, what are you doing?" she yelped as she put everything, including the coin stained with Rita's blood, back into the purse. She then gathered the scattered clothes and shoved them back into the burlap sack.

"No, what are *you* doing? You think this belongs to *him*? He stole everything from people like *us*", Adriana snapped. "It's covered with our parents' blood. It's got your *children's* blood all over it, and I want nothing to do with it."

That made Tatiyana pause for a moment, but in the end she dropped the purse into the larger sack, tied it shut and swung it over her shoulder. "Leaving it here for the Russians won't bring any of them back", she said, standing up. "I'd rather we have it than these red demons."

"He already almost got killed because of what's in that purse", Adriana reminded her stubbornly. "If people find out we have it, we'll be hunted down like rabid wolves."

"Then we'll have to keep it a secret, now, won't we?"

But Adriana wouldn't be deterred. "He's a murderer. Millions are dead because of him", she said angrily, not paying Traugott the least attention.

"And at least two are still alive *also* because of him", her sister replied. "As for those who died...". She paused and shrugged. "Maybe they died so we could have these things and live."

A weapon was fired nearby, almost right outside the door, and Traugott looked over his shoulder with more than a touch of alarm. There were angry shouts, a man cried out in pain, and then there were more gunshots. Then nothing.

"Listen to your sister", he urged Adriana. He reached out to touch her arm but she wouldn't let him. She jerked away from him, as though his hand had been replaced by a spitting cobra.

He sighed with exasperation. "Now both of you need to go. Make your way to Vienna and find my mother. Her name is Teresia Schlamelcher. Tell her I sent you and she'll keep you safe for as long as you need."

His mother had for weeks hidden Rosche Pflaumlocher, his old babysitter whom he'd called Mrs P, and her grandchildren; surely she'd do as much for Adriana and her sister.

Tatiyana grabbed Adriana's hand and pulled her toward the door. "Let's go, let's go", she said.

But before they could go anywhere, the godforsaken door was yanked open.

One final time.

Adriana and her sister cried out.

Standing before them were two of the strangest, ugliest creatures Adriana had ever come across in her entire life. Had the bowels of Hell loosened and discharged their contents, she thought, this is what would have flowed out.

The two men – for they seemed to be human, despite their appearance – had slanted eyes and yellowish skin. A thin stubble of dark beard covered their cheeks and chin, and they were at least a head shorter than Traugott. For a moment Adriana was reminded of the *drekavac* - a creature borne of the soul of a child who has died unbaptized and who can take the shape of a small, deformed infant - and she shivered in terror.

The two Russian soldiers – not demons in the least but rather Mongols from the endless steppes of Central Asia – were as startled as Adriana and the others. They recovered from their surprise first, raised their weapons and spouted orders in an alien tongue of guttural barks and whispers not one of them could understand, though their meaning was unmistakable.

Traugott almost tripped over Rita's body when he took a step back. Adriana and him put their hands up while Tatiyana gently lowered the bag to the ground. The soldiers shouted again, apparently repeating the same orders, and when their prisoners failed to comply, one of them made the mistake of stepping in front of his comrade to enter the barracks.

Traugott had been watching for the slightest chance to attack, and now he had it.

Despite his injuries, he charged the smaller man, grabbed his weapon with both hands and raised it to the ceiling. A round discharged harmlessly. Using his size and weight advantage, he shoved the soldier backward, into his friend and out the door, and all three of them tumbled into the snow, fighting. Another shot was fired.

Tatiyana reacted almost instantly. "Quick, let's go!" she said, picking up the bag and swinging it over her shoulder once more. She grabbed Adriana by the hand and the two sisters squeezed by the fighting men to emerge into the cold winter.

The courtyard was pure mayhem and it was hard to make sense of all they saw. Not ten yards from them an SS had stripped the shirt off an inmate whose head he'd pulverized with a bloody shovel that now lay discarded in the snow. He tried to slip it on over his uniform, which he'd kept on for a reason that made sense only to him, but it obviously would not fit. In his panic he pulled harder and the cheap garment simply ripped apart. The SS cursed loudly and began stomping the corpse, as if it were to blame for his idiocy.

His anger spent, he threw the shredded shirt away and set off in search of another. Luckily he didn't see the two sisters and their heavy bag.

Adriana and Tatiyana began running, but Adriana stopped when she heard someone shout out her name. When she looked back, Traugott and the two Mongols had regained their feet and one of them had Traugott in a bear hug from behind. The SS was struggling to free himself, but the small man seemed incredibly strong for someone his size.

Traugott saw Adriana looking at him.

"Adriana!" he shouted again. "Remember! Go to Vienna and find Teresia Schlamelcher...

Teresia Schla..."

But before he could finish his sentence, the second Russian soldier savagely plunged his bayonet into his lower abdomen. Traugott howled in pain as he finally broke free. He elbowed the Mongol behind him in the face with all the strength he could muster, smashing his jaw. The man brought his hands to his face and staggered back as a geyser of blood erupted through his fingers.

Then, astonishingly, Traugott grabbed the weapon that was still lodged in his flesh, pulled it out with both hands and, with a final superhuman effort, yanked it from of the hands of the startled soldier. He blindly pulled the trigger and somehow hit the injured Mongol behind him in the groin, completely incapacitating him and ensuring the man would never reproduce.

Then, in one fluid motion, he flipped the gun around and impaled the Mongol that still stood through the heart, killing him instantly.

The weapon slipped from Traugott's limp and bloody fingers. He looked up again at Adriana and seemed to want to say something, but then he clutched his stomach and slid to the ground, grimacing.

Adriana froze. For a moment, but only for a moment, she fought an urge to run to his help, to see if she could save him. Such wounds to the lower abdomen were almost always fatal, and those who didn't die right away very quickly wished they had, but perhaps if she put pressure on his bleeding, perhaps if she dragged him back inside the barracks, perhaps if she did all of these things and more, then perhaps he'd live and...

"Don't even think about it!," her sister shouted at her. "*He killed my babies!* And he would have killed you too, if not for his *dick*!"

Adriana barely heard her. She was still staring at Traugott; he had curled into a ball in the snow, with both arms wrapped around his middle section, and she couldn't tell if he was dead. "*He killed my babies!*," her sister screamed again.

Adriana knew this wasn't quite true. But then her senses returned and she lost all desire to rush to his rescue. Tatiyana was right. They had mere seconds to escape. The Russians seemed to be everywhere and would surely block all exits before long. If she ran back into the courtyard, in a futile attempt to save a condemned man, she'd be condemning not only herself, but also her sister. Any German they encountered would kill them, and who knew what they could expect from the Reds?

No. Traugott, if he wasn't already dead, would soon be, and it made no sense to risk everything for a dead man when freedom was less than fifty yards away. Yes, she owed him her life, and her sister's life, many times over, and yes his final act had been about her, his ultimate thought had been for her and her safety, but that wasn't a debt she could repay.

Not here, not now.

So she said one final, silent goodbye to Rita and began running again.

Adriana and Tatiyana never again encountered any of the *weißköpfchen*. It was as though the Earth had cracked beneath their feet and swallowed them up.

Which was precisely what they deserved after what they'd done to Rita, as far as Adriana was concerned.

She didn't care if she never saw them again, either in this life or the next, but Tatiyana argued vehemently that the elderly kapo had been right, that some safety might be found in numbers if they could catch up to them and that now wasn't the time for petty vengeance, and in the end she prevailed. So for the first fifty yards or so they followed the pinkish path the fleeing women had pounded into the snow, but the trail soon began to fade until it vanished completely.

They could still spot the odd bloody footprint here and there, but those too eventually disappeared and they found themselves blindly following a path of trampled snow without truly knowing who it was they might find at the other end.

Then, to make matters even worse, the tracks began to multiply and run in all directions, a sure sign the inmates who had fled before them had been just as lost as they now were.

The two sisters kept looking over their shoulder to check who might be following *them*, but all they saw was Auschwitz slowly receding into the distance until the wintry landscape swallowed it up completely.

"I think we made it out just in time", Adriana finally said. Tatiyana simply nodded and they plodded on.

In truth, the SS had evacuated out of Auschwitz – and then killed - most of the relatively healthy prisoners before the arrival of the Red Army. Those abandoned behind, even once free, had been too exhausted and diseased to go anywhere, and the Russians were just now discovering the horrors of the Final Solution engineered by the defeated Germans.

They'd be among the first to document it and, eventually, tell the world.

The bitter cold made short work of Adriana's earlier disgust and the sisters stopped for a few seconds to don several of the clothes Traugott had given them. Not only did the garments keep them warm, but they also covered their telltale camp uniforms. Dressed thusly, they looked like a couple of Polish peasants out about their business and therefore drew less unwanted attention.

Adriana still worried about the heavy bag they carried with them.

"It will get us nothing but trouble", she warned her sister. "Mark my words. Someone will ask questions, they'll want to see what's inside, and then what do we do? We need to get rid of it. Now."

They were still arguing over the matter – Tatiyana, who had made sure the leather purse went into the pocket of her own coat, wanted to keep everything to barter until they reached safety, wherever and whenever that might be – when it began to snow again.

When the first flakes floated lazily down from the heavens, Adriana stopped, spread out her arms, raised her face to the sky and stuck out her tongue. Tatiyana frowned at her.

"What are you doing?" she asked.

"Isn't it obvious? I want to melt a snowflake on my tongue", Adriana replied almost giddily.

Tatiyana frowned again. "But... why?"

"Because I can. Because there's no one to tell me I cannot. Not anymore. So be a dear and keep quiet for a moment, will you?"

Tatiyana swallowed her bitter retort about grown women playing like children while their lives were in jeopardy and dropped the bag next to her feet.

Adriana might have stayed that way, enjoying her newfound freedom, for several hours, had the wind not suddenly picked up and the snow begun to fall much more heavily, almost instantly obliterating the path they'd been following. The two sisters resumed their trek, but they now had to bend their backs and hold on to each other to fight the rising storm.

"We can't stay out here", Adriana shouted next to Tatiyana's ear. "Even dressed as we are, we'll die. We need to find shelter."

Then her foot struck something buried in the snow and she stumbled. She looked down, kicked the object again to investigate and, unable to tell what it was, bent down to clear the snow that covered it.

A human arm stuck out stiffly. Adriana's heart jumped and she jerked back, but she did not scream. The fingers had curled around an invisible object in their last moment of life and now seemed to be reaching for the two sisters, begging for their help. Urged on by a morbid curiosity, Adriana brushed a bit more snow off the limb and there they were, a row of numbers, dark against the frozen skin, that told of an inmate whose sudden freedom had cost him his life.

This was the first human being they'd encountered since fleeing Auschwitz.

And he was dead.

The Russian soldier didn't understand how the front of his body could be so cold and the rest so infernally hot.

He tried to move, but his muscles were strangely stiff and wouldn't respond to his commands. Only when he tried to raise his head and open his eyes did he realize he was buried under a few inches of snow.

How the hell had this happened?

He blinked the flakes out of his eyes and fought a surge of panic when tentacles of snow crawled into his nose and mouth. He shook his head again and managed to crane his neck enough to take a look at his surroundings.

Not that there was much to see. The blowing snow reduced visibility to mere inches and the stinging flakes made his eyes water, which really sucked since he hadn't a clue where he was – not in what city, not in what province, and certainly not in what country.

Being able to see something, anything, would have been most helpful just now.

He did remember his name, though. Vitali Anatoliyevich Grebenshchikov, son of Anatoliy Spartakovich Grebenshchikov, originally from Toguchin in Novosibirsk Oblast, on the Inya River, in the southernmost part of the Soviet Union.

His father, the assistant head of the local *partkom*, had delayed his only son's conscription for as long as possible. And when he'd done all he could and the war still hadn't ended, he'd got him a commission as a *старший лейтенант*, roughly the equivalent of a Junior Lieutenant in the

American army. Young Vitali had thus joined the mighty *Красная армия* in the dying days of the war by leapfrogging over men who'd been fighting the Nazis for years.

Which might explain why his comrades had now left him for dead in the snow, lying face down in several inches of deep, fluffy flakes. The snow had slithered into his uniform, melted and frozen his shirt to his chest.

That solved the first part of the riddle. Now, why did his butt feel so hot?

He lifted his left arm out of the snow, then the right, and then flexed his fingers one after the other, slowly at first, and then more and more rapidly, followed by his wrists and elbows and shoulders. His joints creaked and ached but blood flow was progressively restored, until he was able to move his arms almost normally.

His mind reeling, he plunged both hands through he snow all the way down to the frozen ground. He then raised himself out of the snow and flopped onto his back.

And when he did, he beheld Apocalypse, and his mouth dropped open.

Behind him, less than twenty yards away, brightly visible through the blowing storm, like a beacon in a stormy night, burned the charred hulk of a state of the art T-34-85 tank.

Scenes, flashes, memories half-remembered assail him. Charging exhilaratingly through a snow-covered field, feeling invulnerable... an explosion just ahead... a German tank on their left... not just any tank, but a bowel-loosening *Panzerkampfwagen Panther*... a mad rush to pivot the turret to return fire... their gunner, drunk as usual, a second too slow... the Panther fires first, the flash from its 75 mm gun almost six feet long...

Then the loudest noise the Universe has ever known... a direct hit... smoke and flames and shouts and screams... and blood, lots and lots of blood... the gunner, lying on the floor, his head ripped from his body, bright red blood spurting from the severed neck... then someone mercifully opens the hatch... a rush of frigid air...

Vitali wants to flee but keeps losing his balance. When he finally makes it to his feet, someone shoves him and climbs over him, stepping on his head to jump out of the burning tank. Vitali falls again. He's going to die here, burned alive.

Like hell he is.

He tries again. He slips in the gunner's sticky blood but remains standing. He reaches up, grabs both sides of the open hatch, pulls himself up, tumbles out...

Not that he remembered, but he must have then crawled a short distance before passing out in the snow. Why didn't the Germans finish him off? Maybe the storm hid him from sight. Maybe they thought no one could have survived a direct hit at such point-blank range. Maybe they saw him but thought him already dead.

It didn't matter. He still lived, thanks in part to the heat from the burning tank that kept him from freezing to death.

Vitali got up slowly and brushed the snow from his clothes. His head still spun and his ears still rang, but at least he could stand.

He took one tentative step away from the tank, then another, and then another. He began to shiver uncontrollably as soon as he left the protective circle of heat around the burning behemoth.

He wanted to stay here, where it was warm, but knew he couldn't. He was barely dressed, completely unarmed, and the first German who came along would shoot him dead. He had to find other members of his unit if he were to survive.

So he pulled his collar up around his ears, stuck his hands under his armpits, lowered his head and plunged headlong into the storm.

Adriana clenched her jaws together to keep her teeth from chattering.

The howling wind knifed right through her thick clothes, freezing her all the way to the bone. The cold was so brutal her very heart felt to her to be shivering. Every single one of her muscles seemed to have contracted to the point of snapping and she was beginning to feel sleepy, which she knew could only mean that an already desperate situation was about to turn worse, much worse.

Tatiyana fared little better. Her eyebrows and eyelashes sported a layer of ice crystals so thick her eyes were almost welded shut. Every now and again the two sisters would turn their backs to the wind, which provided a little relief from its relentless assault, but eventually they had to turn back around and resume their aimless trek.

Walking in the opposite direction, with the wind constantly at their backs, would have meant returning to Auschwitz. The wind was so violent it almost seemed as though it wished them to go back. But neither one of them even raised the possibility, knowing full well the other's response.

Adriana spared a brief thought for the *weißköpfchen* who had fled before them, but without the protection of Mattias Traugott's generosity. How many of them had been caught out in the open by the storm? How many of them now lay dead, frozen, under the snow? But then she remembered how those women had purchased their freedom by mindlessly trampling Rita to death, and she wished them all the slowest, coldest, most agonizing death possible. Let her come across one that still lived and that one wouldn't even get pissed on for fear the warmth might allow her to live one second longer.

They were trudging through snow that now reached above their knees, each step further sapping their diminishing strength. The wind gusted suddenly, whipping snow across Adriana's face and into her coat. She twisted her head to the side to escape the onslaught and by doing so caught a sudden flash of light in the distance. She stopped dead in her tracks and grabbed Tatiyana's arm, who also stopped.

Had Adriana turned her head the other way, she would have missed it, and even now she could see nothing more than a solid wall of snow. She squinted as hard as she could, but the snow remained impenetrably opaque. Perhaps she had ima... no, wait, there it was again and her heart jumped. Whenever the howling wind lessened and the snow with it, even for half a second, she glimpsed a beacon of light in the distance.

"Look over there!" she shouted next to Tatiyana's ear.

Tatiyana shook her head in incomprehension. Adriana rubbed her hands across her sister's face a few times, roughly dislodging most of the ice that blinded her, and pointed again. At least twenty seconds elapsed before the wind momentarily died down again, allowing the mysterious light to flash through the storm.

This time Tatiyana saw it as well, and her eyes grew wide.

"What do you think it is?" she shouted. "Looks like the headlights on a truck."

"I don't know what it is and I don't really care", Adriana replied. "It's our only hope. Let's go."

The two sisters linked arms to keep from getting separated and headed in the general direction of what they'd seen. They'd count one hundred steps, stop and wait for the light to peek through the snow again, so as to adjust their course accordingly. In this weather, if they went a few steps too wide to the right or the left and lost sight of their beacon, they'd never find it again. Better to stop frequently and make sure they were headed in the correct direction than plunge ahead blindly and hope for the best.

Adriana figured they had covered perhaps two thirds of the distance when they stopped for the fourth time. The two sisters huddled closely, face to face, each sheltered by the other's body, while waiting for the wind to let up. Adriana was troubled to notice that Tatiyana's coat still bore a faint trace of its original owner's perfume. Why had the woman packed such a heavy winter coat upon being chased out of her home? Where had she thought she'd be going? And what had then become of her? Had she been gassed like millions of others, or was she now wandering helplessly, lost and cold, in the storm?

Adriana imagined for a moment how that woman might react upon recognizing her coat on another's back, were they to ever come face to face with her. At the very least, she'd probably demand to have it back. The thought, for some sick reason, made her smile.

Then her smile vanished, for the storm had spawned a creature that came right at them.

Adriana saw it coalesce over her sister's shoulder, at first nothing more than a dark shape barely glimpsed through billions of swirling snowflakes, as though the flakes had decided to take human form, and for one otherworldly moment she thought the shape perhaps to be the unknown woman come to claim her coat.

Except it wasn't.

The shape became more distinct as it drew near, its arms held rigidly before it, evil claws opening and closing endlessly, its hair and skin and eyes and lips and even teeth covered with countless crystals of ice, an unholy ghoul of ice and snow drawn to the warmth of their flesh and blood.

Adriana let out a terrified shriek just as the creature let out its own cry – a throaty growl that may have been human but probably wasn't. The ghoul was less than three feet away, its blind, unseeing eyes staring fixedly ahead, and it was reaching for Tatiyana, whose back was still turned to it.

Alarmed by her sister's shriek, Tatiyana began to spin around, and Adriana tried to shove her out of the creature's reach, but they were both of them too slow and both of them too late. Tatiyana instinctively raised an arm to fend off the creature, but the ghoul still wrapped its dark tentacles around her and dragged her down into the snow with it.

Tatiyana's scream was choked off when she vanished into the deep powder.

For a moment it seemed as though the Earth itself had swallowed them, and Adriana just stood there in the darkness of the storm, transfixed and paralyzed, thinking her sister had just been taken down to the Underworld before her very eyes.

But then Tatiyana's head emerged above the snow, she shouted "Help me!" through a mouthful of snow, and Adriana's paralysis broke. She dropped to her knees and shoveled armfuls of snow off her sister. She then helped Tatiyana back to her feet and the two sisters clung to one another.

"Are you injured? I thought I'd lost you", Adriana finally said.

"No, I'm fine", Tatiyana replied. "But what the hell...?"

"What kind of creature was that?" Adriana asked.

"Not a creature, just a man", Tatiyana said. "He tried to speak to me, but where did he go?"

Without another word the two sisters began searching the powder for any sign of the ghoul. Adriana found it when her hand accidentally struck what she at first thought to be a tree limb, but which turned out to be one of the creature's arms. She called Tatiyana over and they dug it out as best they could while the storm still raged around them.

"Look", Tatiyana said after a moment, pointing. She brushed snow off the creature's shoulder, revealing a red star sown onto a gray uniform.

"A Russian?" Adriana said, astonished.

"Looks that way", Tatiyana confirmed.

"Is he dead?"

Tatiyana removed her mittens and placed two fingers against the Russian's throat. "No, his heart beats still, but his skin is as cold and hard as ice", she said. "What should we do? Just leave him here?"

The soldier let out a feeble, inarticulate growl as though to protest being condemned to a second frozen grave after escaping the first one.

Adriana shook her head. "I want to know who he is first. He may prove useful", she said. "Let's get him up."

The two sisters struggled to pull the half-frozen body out of the snow and then dragged it toward the light they'd seen earlier. They stopped short when they saw it to be a burning tank.

"Well, at least we'll be warm", Adriana finally opined. "Let's go."

Mindful of unexploded shells still possibly inside the tank, they walked cautiously toward the fire and stopped as soon as they began to feel its heat. The fire tried to lure them closer with its promise of thawed out flesh and bones, but they knew it to be a siren's song and remained at a safe distance.

Tatiyana searched through Traugott's loot and found a few items with which to clothe the soldier: boots (too big), a coat (about the right size) and a hat (a woman's, but the man didn't seem to mind).

"Now what do we do?" Tatiyana asked.

"Now we just wait for him to wake up", Adriana said. "And we hope that fire doesn't go out, or we're dead."

The raging storm and the burning tank battled over the three human lives for the remainder of the day and throughout the following night.

In the end they dueled to a draw. By the time enough snow had fallen to put out the flames and reduce the tank to a charred, smoking ruin, the storm had spent itself out and the skies begun to clear.

Adriana and Tatiyana awoke with the unknown soldier squeezed between them. The snow had accumulated into small drifts against them as they sat with their backs to the wind, but neither could quite remember how they came to be in that position.

"What... where...", Tatiyana mumbled when the rays of the sun had warmed them up a bit.

"I don't know, but my butt is frozen solid", Adriana said.

"Mine too", her sister replied.

"Did he make it?"

Tatiyana had trained as a nurse before marrying and she again pressed her fingers to the soldier's throat. She counted to one hundred. "Yes. His pulse is much stronger and his skin feels warmer", she said after a moment. "He's probably frostbitten, but I'd have to undress him to be sure and that's simply not going to happen. In any case, he'll live."

Adriana nodded. The two sisters propped the still unconscious Russian up against the tank. They then brushed as much snow as they could off each other and jumped up and down for a few minutes to get their circulation going and raise their body temperature.

"I'd have thought an invading army would have more than one soldier", Adriana said later. She had climbed up onto the burned out tank to take a good look around, but all she could see was a wide expanse of unending whiteness.

"We're probably too far from the roads", Tatiyana explained. "I think we got lost in the storm and..." She shrugged.

A squadron of airplanes streaked across the sky. The two sisters looked up but couldn't make out any distinctive markings. The sound of droning engines echoed around them until the planes vanished into the distance.

"Где я", the Russian soldier muttered.

Adriana jumped off the tank and the snow swallowed her up almost to the hips. Tatiyana plowed through the powder and came to stand next to her.

"Где я", the soldier repeated.

"What is he saying?" Adriana demanded without truly expecting an answer.

"He wants to know where he is", Tatiyana immediately translated.

Adriana looked at her sister with puzzlement. "And how come you to speak Russian, dearest sister?"

Tatiyana shrugged again. "After I married and moved away, the family that lived next to us were Russian. They had eight children and I'd babysit for them on occasion. Then, after I had my own children, the kids would play together and... well, I picked up a bit of the language, that's all."

Adriana was remembered that she had been separated from her sister for almost ten years. There was much about her that she now didn't know, that she would have to learn and discover. Sisters they may be in name and blood, but complete strangers would have better described their relationship today – it wasn't like Auschwitz had afforded them tons of quality time to catch up. It would take a while for the two of them to become reacquainted.

Adriana also saw a wave of conflicting emotions swirl across Tatiyana's face at the mention of her children – pain, sadness, resignation, rage... She squeezed her arm in comfort.

The soldier had now opened his eyes and was looking up at them with curiosity.

"Ask him his name", Adriana said. "Ask him where the rest of his army is."

"I'm not going to interrogate him", Tatiyana protested.

Adriana sighed. "I'm sorry, I didn't mean to order you around", she apologized. "Find out what you can."

Tatiyana crouched down to look the Russian in the eyes. The two of them conversed as best they could for a few minutes – Tatiyana's mastery of Russian was less than perfect and the soldier was hesitant to reveal too much to these strangers – until Tatiyana stood up again.

"Well?" Adriana demanded impatiently.

"He's harmless", Tatiyana said. "He's just a kid. His name is Vitali Anatoliyevich Grebenshchikov and he's only been in the army for a few months. He says the Germans were fleeing before them like rats and the front is probably miles away by now, which perhaps explains why we're hardly seeing anybody."

Tatiyana was about to add something when the soldier interrupted her. Tatiyana laughed out loud.

"What?" Adriana demanded.

"He says he's very grateful we saved his life but if his friends see him wearing that hat, they'll shoot him dead".

They shared a single tin of canned food in silence, each pondering what the wisest course might now be. Vitali eyed their bulging burlap sack with a mixture of surprise and interest, but didn't say a word. Tatiyana made sure the leather purse remained safely out of sight.

The tank still generated enough heat to melt a bit of snow, which they drank before setting out. They couldn't stay where they were, and their only viable option, in the end, was to try and catch up to the tail of the Russian army.

Adriana at first argued against such a plan. She had no problem sharing their meager provisions with Vitali and letting him keep the clothes but after that, she said, they should just shake hands and each go their own way.

And then what?, Tatiyana asked. Hope they encountered some partisans who gave them shelter? Trust in God the next humans they met weren't Nazis? Pray another storm didn't blow in and kill them?

That was entrusting much to their good fortune, wasn't it?

They argued back and forth for almost an hour, with Vitali intervening every now and again through Tatiyana, and Adriana demanding why she should again place her safety and well-being in someone else's hands. They had just escaped Mattias Traugott's self-serving "benevolence", she reminded her sister, and she had no desire to submit to anyone else's any time soon. Who knew what the Russians might demand in exchange for their protection? She'd rather chance it alone.

Tatiyana felt herself becoming more and more angered by Adriana's stubbornness.

"We can't survive out here alone", she finally stated. "It's either the Germans or the Russians, and we sure know what to expect from the Germans. How much worse can the Russians be?"

"I don't care to find out", Adriana said.

Tatiyana shook her head and threw up her hands. "Fine, then. I yield. If you think we're better off alone, then so be it. Let's go."

Her sister's abrupt abdication caught Adriana off guard. "Thank... thank you for trusting me, Tatiyana. I really think this is for the best."

Tatiyana looked at her with an air of such sadness Adriana's heart almost broke. "It isn't a matter of trust, sister. I've already lost my parents and my two children", she said. "You're all I've got left. I'll not lose you as well. Where you lead, I follow, and that's pretty much all there is to it."

Vitali asked what was going on, Tatiyana told him and the Russian's face fell. He then placed his right hand over his heart and spoke for almost a full minute. The emotion in his voice crescendoed until he appeared on the verge of tears.

"What was that all about?" Adriana asked with a frown, after he'd fallen silent.

"Wait, let me think", Tatiyana said. She gathered her thoughts and then explained: "He swears he won't let any harm come to us. He swears on his life, which we saved. He says he's seen the... the... I can't think of the right word..."

"The propaganda?" Adriana suggested.

"Yes, that's it. He says he's seen the Nazi propaganda about the Russians, so he gets why we might be afraid of him and his people, but he promises we'll be safe."

"Some promise", Adriana muttered. Tatiyana feigned not to have heard as she continued: "The Nazis might make them out to be monsters, but that's not necessarily a bad thing since it often takes a monster to slay another monster. And so far, he says, the Russians have slaughtered more monsters than anyone else. He'd rather die than let anyone hurt us. He says his father raised him to be an honest and courageous man, and that we can trust him."

Adriana sighed deeply. Something about her sister's blind fate in this stranger troubled her. They'd only known him for a few hours and yet Tatiyana was already willing to place their hard-won freedom in his hands. Was her sister being too trusting or was she, herself, being needlessly suspicious?

She kicked the snow around her feet and silently asked Rita for some guidance. *What would you do?* She waited for an answer, but none came. She was on her own.

"And you do? I mean, you do trust him?" she finally asked.

"Yes, I do", Tatiyana replied without any hesitation.

"Very well. If you trust him, then so do I. We'll have to trust someone again some day anyway, so it might as well be him. Ask him to lead us to his army."

The two sisters hugged and Tatiyana filled Vitali in. They then set out into the snow, in search of the liberating Red Army.

They found it less than three miles away. A half-dozen Russian soldiers had surrounded and seemed to be guarding a house.

A house from which emanated the shrill cries of those whose caged up rage has finally snapped its chains.

They heard the cries before they came within sight of the house. At first it sounded like birds, and Vitali surmised it was perhaps a murder of crows bickering over a carcass. But as they followed the sound and it drew nearer, it also grew clearer and human voices began to take shape in the frozen stillness.

They glimpsed the house and the soldiers through snow-covered trees and stopped prudently to observe the scene. The soldiers were milling around, smoking and chatting and laughing, and seemed not the least concerned. Two of them were examining a German helmet and one wiggled a finger through a hole in the metal. He said something and his friend threw back his head and roared, perhaps amused by a joke about the helmet's former owner having lost his mind.

The soldiers had about them an air of supreme confidence that bordered on arrogance, an air of near insolence the Roman legions had likely displayed after conquering yet one more barbarian land, an air that only comes from routinely routing one's enemy – an air Tatiyana found somewhat unsettling.

"Do you know them?" she asked Vitali. She spoke softly, even though the soldiers were unlikely to hear her above the din coming from the house.

The Russian shook his head.

"This could be dangerous", Adriana said.

"I'll go find out who they are", Vitali offered through Tatiyana. He took off his silly woman's hat, which he'd kept on for warmth, and, without waiting for the sisters' assent, emerged from the forest with his hands raised high above his head.

The Russian soldiers tensed and immediately trained their weapons on him. The clicking sound of rounds being chambered perforated the unholy cacophony behind them. The soldier who'd struck his finger through the helmet found that his flesh had frozen to the metal and couldn't pull it out in time. He ended up awkwardly holding his rifle with one hand, all the while attempting to conceal his other, trapped hand behind his back. Luckily for him, his comrades were too preoccupied by Vitali's arrival to notice.

Vitali stopped and called out to them in Russian. His voice sounded loud and clear in the cold.

"What is he saying?" Adriana whispered.

"He just identified himself", Tatiyana explained. "Vitali Anatoliyevich Grebenshchikov, of the Red Army's 322nd Rifle Division. They're asking him questions, but they don't seem too suspicious since he speaks Russian like them. Sounds like they're mostly curious about where he came from."

As if to confirm Tatiyana's impression, the Russian soldiers lowered their weapons and motioned for Vitali to come closer. The one trapped in the helmet took that opportunity to quickly turn his back and urinate on his hand, which allowed him to wrench his finger free without sacrificing a chunk of his flesh. He threw the helmet away with a curse and rejoined his comrades.

"Let's get ready", Tatiyana said.

"What do you mean?"

"You want to go over there dressed like this, dragging this bag behind you?"

Adriana immediately saw her sister's point. They took off their warm clothes and shoved them back into the burlap sack. Tatiyana then shook two precious stones out of the leather purse and handed one to Adriana.

"What...?" Adriana asked when Tatiyana placed her stone in her mouth.

"Swallow it", her sister explained. "That way, if we don't get to come back for the rest of it, at least in a couple of days we won't be completely destitute."

Adriana couldn't help but be amazed by her sister's survival instincts and made a note to trust her more readily. Tatiyana tied the purse shut with a double knot, dropped it in the sack and they buried everything deep in the snow.

"Try to remember where we put it", she said. "We may only have a few seconds to retrieve it later. It may even be night. Now swallow."

Adriana put a handful of snow in her mouth and downed the stone with the spoonful of water she got.

"Just in time", Tatiyana said. "Look."

Vitali was returning at a run. He stopped at the edge of the forest and called out, bidding them to show themselves.

The Russian soldiers watched with interest as the two sisters appeared tentatively through the trees. Vitali smiled and waved enthusiastically at them, as though he were greeting old friends he hadn't seen in ages.

"Come, come", he shouted with genuine enthusiasm. "Your friends are here. We've found them."

Our friends?, Tatiyana wondered.

The cold was bitter and the two women were shivering hard as Vitali quickly revealed what he'd learned. If he wondered where their coats and bag had gone, he didn't ask.

Tatiyana could hardly believe her ears.

"What?" Adriana asked impatiently.

More cries came from inside the house, along with what sounded like dishes and furniture being smashed. The three of them looked in that direction until the noise died down a bit.

"He says the house is full of people like us", Tatiyana explained.

"People like us?"

Tatiyana nodded. "Dressed as we are. The house is full of former Auschwitz inmates."

They carefully pushed the door open and entered an asylum taken over by its patients. So absolute was the mayhem that their arrival went completely unnoticed.

Vitali's comrades had encountered a dozen inmates on a nearby road and, seeing their sorry state, led them here. "Help yourselves to whatever you want while we stand guard outside", the soldiers told them.

This was the best offer the inmates had received in years, and they hadn't needed be told twice.

Adriana and Tatiyana shut the door behind them. On their right was a small living room that had been thoroughly trashed. A man was sprawled on a couch, one hand wrapped loosely around the neck of an empty bottle of whiskey, the other shoved down the front of his pants and presumably wrapped around something else. The man appeared sound asleep and Tatiyana was about to look away when she noticed that he was completely immobile. His eyes were half-lidded, his chest didn't rise and fall, and a sliver of sticky drool ran from the corner of his mouth.

She sighed. She didn't need extensive medical training to know the man was dead, killed by a massive overdose of alcohol after just a few short hours of freedom. Hopefully he'd died happy after years of hell.

A short hallway led to a kitchen where a half-dozen inmates, like locusts descended upon a field of wheat, were busy devouring everything in sight. A severely emaciated woman sat on the floor to their left, cracking one egg after another into her mouth. A gooey slime covered the lower half of her face and her clothes. She noticed the two sisters observing her, opened her mouth with deliberate slowness, popped in one whole egg, shell and all, and began chewing noisily, immensely proud that there was now one less egg for them to have.

A puddle next to her showed she'd already vomited at least once, but still she kept gobbling up the eggs. A carton was clutched protectively to her chest and she seemed determined to exterminate it as well.

Likely she'd soon be dead as well.

Adriana looked at her sister and the two women instinctively joined hands.

Four men had gathered around a rickety metal table on which stood a tall cooking pot. Each had a spoon that they dipped into the pot and brought to their mouths as rapidly as they could manage. Their faces and clothes were covered with orange splotches of soup that made them appear afflicted with some exotic plague.

Two of the men collided in their desperation to feed after eons of hunger. One dropped his spoon into the pot and, irate, instantly elbowed the other in the face, knocking him to the floor. He then plunged his arm into the hot liquid up to the shoulder to retrieve his spoon while his comrades kept eating as though nothing had happened.

They looked for all the world to Adriana like a pack of snarling wolves fighting over a dead deer.

A small nugget of fear began to burn at the pit of her stomach, so evil was the atmosphere inside the house. She spied a serrated, dirty knife on the counter. She reached for it carefully and, when no one reacted, wrapped her fingers around the sticky handle. She slid the blade up her sleeve, next to her arm and out of view. Tatiyana saw her do it and nodded her approval.

There was another room to their left, next to the kitchen. They went around the egg-eating woman, stepped over a fresh puddle of her vomit and entered a small sitting room.

"Have you come to rob me as well?" someone asked bitterly as soon as they appeared. "Take whatever you want. Not that there is much left."

A woman, presumably the owner of the house, sat in a rocking chair in the corner of the room. At her feet lay another woman, this one a former inmate whose hands seemed covered in blood. After a few seconds Adriana saw that the woman was actually crouched protectively over a crock of blood-red preserves that she was hungrily licking off her fingers.

Adriana and Tatiyana didn't reply. A stairway next to the wall on their left led up to a small landing around which stood three darkened doors - sentinels guarding the house's inner sanctum. But the sentinels had failed and the sanctum been violated. They could hear people up there, angry people, savage people bent on revenge and destruction, and the whole house shook when a large object – possibly a mirror – shattered thunderously against the floor.

The woman made to get up, the inmate at her feet growled like an animal and the woman sank back in her rocker.

"Did you know?" Tatiyana asked her.

The woman's clothes were torn and soiled. The side of her face was swollen, as if she'd been struck, and her salt and pepper hair fell in cascades of disheveled strands. It was impossible to tell whether she was closer to forty or seventy, but most striking was her complete absence of fear. The woman displayed a calm preternatural in one whose house was being ransacked and pillaged under her very nose.

Tatiyana sensed in her a cold hardness, like tempered steel in winter, that made her nervous. Adriana sensed it too and tightened her grip on the knife handle.

The woman snickered. "Did I know what? That you folks would be visiting? No, of course not. I'd have put on my nice dress if I'd known to expect company. Certainly I'd have made enough soup to feed you all."

Tatiyana felt her anger rising. This woman, incredibly, still found the courage to mock them. "Did you know?" she repeated.

The woman never got to reply. A horrendous shriek came from upstairs and two former prisoners, a man and a woman, flew down the stairs.

"Explain that, you witch", the man said, completely ignoring Adriana and Tatiyana.

"We found this in a closet", his companion explained to no one in particular. She then threw two uniforms at the woman.

Adriana caught her breath and so did Tatiyana.

The woman remained completely unperturbed. She smiled and picked up the first Nazi jacket, straightening out the sleeves and folding the lapels neatly, before doing the same to the second. She smoothed them over her thighs with a loving hand, as though she were caressing her child's head, and then looked at Tatiyana.

"Of course I knew. How could I not?" she spat with such venom that Tatiyana felt bile rise in the back of her throat. "When the wind blew the right way, I'd sit outside and just enjoy that delicious smell. I had many a pleasant evening out on my porch, with a cigarette in one hand, a coffee in the other and in my nose the smell of your filthy flesh burning. I could almost... taste it."

The woman closed her eyes and licked her lips lasciviously, as though she were recalling the scent of freshly baked cookies and not that of incinerated human flesh.

Tatiyana's mind began to reel and she grabbed her sister's hand for support.

She had known what the woman would say before hearing the words. Her children had burned in those ovens, and the smell had given this woman pleasure. This woman had known all along what was happening at Auschwitz, and yet she'd done nothing to stop it. Quite the opposite, in fact.

There was sudden movement. Adriana now stood with her back to the woman, and she was keeping the two former inmates at bay with her knife.

"There's been enough killing", she announced. "We are better than them."

"What are you doing, sister?" Tatiyana asked.

"They went to attack her, but I'll not stand for it", Adriana explained. "There's been enough blood shed."

The man and the woman looked at one another, unsure what to make of this Jewess who chose to protect a Nazi sympathizer. Behind Adriana, the woman in the rocking chair snickered again. "Let them do it", she said. "Let them show their true nature. Let them tear me apart with their teeth and their claws, like the animals they are. What do I care? I've already lost everything."

The man lunged at the woman but was stopped short by Adriana's knife an inch from his throat. "I said no", Adriana repeated. The man raised his hands in surrender and took a step back.

A strange noise came from the kitchen and the woman began to laugh hysterically. The noise came again, this time followed by a loud crashing sound that made them jump.

"Stay here", Tatiyana told Adriana.

She returned to the kitchen and froze. Three of the four men who had been eating soup were now convulsing on the floor. All their muscles seemed to have seized up, their tongues protruded from their mouths and they were gasping for breath. They had overturned the table and now writhed in agony in an ocean of squash soup.

The fourth man still stood. He was staring at the other three with an air of utter stupefaction. He then turned his head, saw Tatiyana looking at him and a thunderbolt of terror flashed across his eyes. He coughed a few times, dropped his now useless spoon, clasped both hands to his neck and began to choke. The man staggered to his left, slammed into the wall hard, tried to remain upright, but then his entire body was traversed by a million volts of electricity. He spun left and right and left and right, apparently completely at random, before finally collapsing.

He almost fell on the egg-eating woman, who hurriedly gathered her loot and bolted out the door.

Tatiyana tried to go to his help but retreated hastily when the man suddenly spun in her direction and began to kick out uncontrollably. All four men made horrible rasping sounds as they struggled to breathe and an inhuman stench arose when they voided their bowels almost as one.

Tatiyana then understood and knew they were beyond help. Their convulsions began to grow weaker and their muscles to relax as Death slowly claimed them. Strangely, the man who had fallen last died first, or at least he was the first to fall silent and become motionless. His companions followed, one after the other, until all simply appeared to have fallen asleep on the kitchen floor with bellies full of warm, delicious soup.

Tatiyana returned to the sitting room. "She poisoned the soup", she told Adriana, who was still holding the inmate at bay with her knife. "It's strychnine. She probably dumped rat poison in it when she heard them coming."

Certainly I'd have made enough soup to feed you all, the woman had said.

The woman was still laughing.

Adriana stared at her sister for a moment. Then she closed her eyes, unclenched her fist and allowed the inmate to take the knife from her.

They didn't turn around when the woman's laughter was replaced by bloody gurgling.

***

"Should we go to his mother in Vienna?" Tatiyana asked.

Adriana didn't reply. She kept her head down and stared hypnotically at the tips of her boots as she and her sister walked toward some unknown fate.

Vitali and the other Red soldiers had vanished when they exited the mad woman's house, which they found a bit odd. For a moment they feared their things might be gone as well, but Vitali hadn't repaid their trust with betrayal and they easily found their bag buried in the snow.

They dressed warmly and, for lack of any viable alternative, followed the only road available to them, the one that linked the woman's house to the rest of the world. After a brief moment they began to smell something burning. Looking back over their shoulders, they saw tendrils of smoke rising above the trees. The tendrils thickened into tentacles, and the tentacles interwove to form a towering column of dark smoke that rose almost straight up into the winter sky.

The two sisters didn't stop and eventually came to a larger road thronged with hordes of former prisoners, advancing Russian soldiers and fleeing Polish peasants. For the latter to take to the road and leave everything behind at the very moment of their country's liberation probably bore eloquent witness to their behavior during the Nazi occupation.

Most traveled on foot, but there were also some overladen carts pulled by donkeys, horses or oxen. The only motorized vehicles were those of the Red Army, but no matter the means of transport, it was slow going through this mass of humanity.

They had no idea how far they were from Auschwitz, but it had to be some distance since most prisoners had procured clothing against the cold – indicating that some looting had occurred along the way.

There had been a sign by the side of the road a little while back, and what had probably been the name of a town and a distance, but since neither of them could read Polish, they learned nothing from it. They tried asking a man – like them, a former inmate – how long he'd been walking and where they were all going, but the man just shrugged silently, as if to say, *What does it matter?*

As if to ask, *Isn't it enough to be walking* away *from that accursed place?*

At least the two sisters no longer stuck out like sore thumbs, and their fear that someone might prove overly curious as to the provenance of their attire began to subside somewhat.

The road meandered through dense woods. Those ahead began to slow down and almost stopped. There seemed to be something off to the side that was creating a distraction, clogging the road. Adriana and Tatiyana were having a hard time making progress through the mass of people. They were being pushed from behind but unable to advance, and the deep snow that lined the road on both sides made it impossible to just walk around the blockage.

For a moment Adriana was reminded of a scene from a lifetime ago, when she and her parents had been loaded on board the train in Spišská Nová Ves. Then, too, she had been shoved from behind, with nowhere to go. Her father's friend, the merry Sándor Pfircsik, had given his life to save hers a short time later. She made a mental note to tell Tatiyana about him.

Those behind began to shout for those in front to move and horns began to blare in the far distance. The two sisters could tell, by the dense knot ahead, that they were nearing whatever there was to be seen. Gasps were heard and people could be seen covering their mouths and eyes with their hands. Some began to weep, others to pray, others to curse.

A body was strung from a tree, perhaps a hundred feet from the road. It was that of a man, neither young nor old, and he was naked. He'd been hung by the neck, and his head now lolled unnaturally to one side as he spun and swung slowly in the wind. A red swastika had been carved into his abdomen and he'd been crudely castrated, so that the lower half of his body was covered in blood. It was hard to tell from this distance, but from the way his cheeks and lips bulged, it looked as though his testicles had been shoved into his mouth. His nose had been sliced off, as had his ears and eyelids, which gave him an air of perpetual stupefaction.

A sign placed around his neck read, in German, "*Zu spät, Joe. Dieser Jude ist unser.*"

Too late, Joe. This Jew is ours.

Adriana and Tatiyana could but stare. What was to be done against men who killed just because they could, in the name of some crazed ideology? They would have liked to feel disgust, some sense of revolt and injustice, but in truth their time in Auschwitz had rendered them almost immune to the Nazis' evil. They knew it knew no boundaries, and it had lost even its power to horrify them.

Not so for some around them.

A trio of men began to mutter angrily, until one said: "We can't leave him there. Let's cut him down and bury him, at least."

He and his two friends argued the matter for a few seconds, but in the end the man who had spoken prevailed. One produced a small pocket knife and a thousand curious stares followed them as they left the road and plowed a narrow path through the deep snow.

The leader of the three stepped on the mine less than twenty feet from the body.

The mine, a German *Schrapnellmine SMi-44*, was nicknamed the Bouncing Betty. It leaped about three feet in the air, as per its design, before detonating. Adriana saw it erupt suddenly from the snow, almost in slow motion, and threw herself on top of Tatiyana.

"Get down", she shouted at the top of her lungs.

Few were those who reacted quickly enough. The mine exploded, spewing a lethal spray of shrapnel in all directions. The three men were essentially sliced in half and died where they stood, their blood tinting the snow red. A piece of shrapnel somehow severed the rope, releasing the hanged man.

Shrapnel flew in all directions over hundreds of feet, striking dozens of people in the road. Many suffered only light flesh wounds, but others were struck in the face or throat or stomach and collapsed in cries of agony.

The road erupted into mayhem as those who still lived panicked and ran, creating ripples of fear that extended as far as the eye could see.

Adriana was still lying on top of her sister. "Are you injured?" she asked.

A heavy machine gun hidden somewhere in the woods opened up before Tatiyana could respond. Adriana recognized the jerky growl of the dreaded *Maschinengewerh 42* – the same weapon that had crushed the sonderkommando revolt the previous autumn - and shoved her sister deeper down to shield her with her own body.

Most people had already fled or dived for cover after the explosion of the mine, so few bullets found their mark. Dozens of tiny snow geysers erupted and a handful of refugees were mowed down, but the carnage would have been much worse had the concealed gunner opened fire just one minute earlier, when the road was still packed tight with people gawking at the hanged man.

Three Red soldiers arrived at a run. One quickly lobbed an RG-42 fragmentation grenade deep into the woods while his two comrades blindly returned fire in the general direction of the German machine gun. The grenade detonated with a loud roar, the explosion magnified a hundredfold by the tons of snow that cascaded down from the trees.

The machine gun fell silent.

A disembodied voice called out in German. The words were muffled by the snow, indistinct, but not their meaning: don't shoot, we're coming out, we give up, you win. There was movement through the branches and the Russian soldiers tensed. Two bloodied Germans stumbled out of the woods with their hands raised high above their heads. Neither appeared seriously injured, though how they had survived the Russians' brutal counter-assault was hard to fathom. One was weeping and appeared to be barely fifteen. His comrade, older by perhaps twenty years, defiantly spat a stream of bloody saliva into the snow when he saw the refugees staring at him.

The Germans knelt down in the road and crossed their hands behind their necks in a clear show of surrender. They were defeated and had no fight left in them. Two Russian soldiers approached warily, fearing another ambush, and positioned themselves behind the captives, with guns trained on their heads.

The third Russian soldier appeared to be in charge, though his coat lacked any insignia of rank. He silently removed his backpack, fished out a bottle of alcohol and took a large swig from it. He then walked slowly to the older German and, unexpectedly, handed him the bottle. The soldier hesitated but the Russian motioned for him to take it. When the prisoner still hesitated, the soldier standing behind him roughly pressed the muzzle of his rifle into the back of his neck. The man finally complied and, guessing what was expected of him, drank from the bottle before handing it back.

The Russian winked benevolently at the 15-year-old and passed him the bottle. Clearly not used to strong liquor, the teenager grimaced and coughed as the burning liquid slid down his throat. Like spectators much entertained by the show being put on for their amusement, some refugees laughed and hooted and the young man smiled timidly.

Their laughter might have been of a different sort altogether had they known how this show would end.

"What is he doing?" Tatiyana muttered to no one in particular. Next to her, Adriana shrugged and tried to dispel the cold ball of apprehension that had coalesced in the pit of her stomach.

The Red soldier produced a pack of cigarettes and a lighter that glinted as if it were made of solid silver. The two other soldiers eyed the heavy object with unusual alarm. It was as though they'd seen it before and its very sight now terrified them. The ball in Adriana's stomach exploded when they exchanged worried glances.

What the hell...?

The man lit one cigarette for himself and one for each prisoner. The Germans accepted eagerly. They seemed slightly amazed by such kind treatment, and indeed some refugees began to mutter that this had gone on long enough, that they only deserved to be shot like dogs, and certainly not treated like honored guests.

The Russian soldier, if he heard their discontent, gave no sign of it.

He took one last swig of the liquor. Then, without a single moment of hesitation, he doused the two soldiers with the rest.

"Oh no...", Adriana said. She took a step forward but Tatiyana caught her and pulled her back. Adriana struggled for a moment before finally turning her back to the scene unfolding before them and burying her face in the crook of her sister's shoulder. She could not bear to watch.

The soldier had perhaps expected the lit cigarettes to ignite the alcohol. When they didn't, he sadistically flipped his lighter open again and clicked it a few times, producing a strong yellow flame that barely wavered in the wind.

The two Germans had been temporarily blinded by the alcohol. They regained their sight just in time to see the Russian put the flame to them. The alcohol ignited with a characteristic *whoosh!* and the two prisoners transformed into human torches.

The 15-year-old's eyes grew wide and his mouth opened with shock. He began frantically beating at the flames consuming him. Had he rolled around in the snow to put them out, he might have made it. Instead, he did exactly the opposite; he panicked and ran, which only fanned the fire and made it burn hotter. After a few seconds he stopped and began to spin in place uselessly like a top. He seemed to be trying to remove his burning coat, but he was engulfed in so much flames it was hard to tell exactly what he was doing.

Tatiyana placed a hand over the back of Adriana's head, like a mother comforting her child, as some around them had the decency to gasp in horror and turn their heads.

The other German, also set alight but having perhaps fought longer, kept his wits about him for a few precious seconds. He knew he was done for, but he also knew he had an opportunity to take at least one of the Russians with him.

He sprang to his feet as soon as the flames engulfed him and threw himself at the nearest Red soldier – who happened to be the one who had set him ablaze. He moved so stunningly quickly the Russian couldn't react in time. The German wrapped his arms around the man and pulled him in, and the flames jumped from one to the other. The Russian tried and failed to disentangle himself, and the two men waltzed in the snow for several seconds as the flames grew in intensity.

Eventually they fell, the German's howls of pain mingling with the Russian's screams of terror.

More Red soldiers arrived. Faced with a scene straight out of Dante's Inferno, they instinctively fired at everything that moved, killing not only the two entangled men, including their own comrade, but also putting the 15-year-old finally out of his misery.

There was a moment of complete silence. The three bodies still smoldered in the snow and the smell of burnt human flesh, so sickeningly familiar to Auschwitz survivors, hung heavily in the air.

A Russian officer barked an order and his men quickly shoveled snow over the bodies.

Then someone said something the sisters' didn't hear, people laughed and, incredibly, several refugees began to cheer and clap.

The further they got from Auschwitz, the thinner the train of refugees grew.

It was hard to discern the wisest course of action. There seemed to be as many strategies as there were refugees. Many seemed determined to keep walking until they could walk no further.

Others had dropped off after finding refuge along the way. Others still had veered south toward Czechoslovakia, where the Russians were said to be also trouncing the Germans. Many hoped to then cross into Hungary, from where they'd been deported. The journey would last weeks and be fraught with peril, but they were like birds that migrate south every winter and wouldn't be deterred.

The sisters briefly entertained the notion of also heading for Czechoslovakia, of returning to their home in Rimavská Sobota, but what was there waiting for them?

Adriana vividly remembered how utterly alone, how completely abandoned and deserted she felt on the night the Hlinka Guards broke down their door. Surely their neighbors, their erstwhile friends, must have seen and heard what was going on? And yet had a single one of them raised the littlest of fingers to help them? Of course not, don't be ridiculous. So how could she now possibly bring herself to face these people, to act as if nothing had happened, to shake their hands and smile and say how-have-you-been-how-do-you-do-it's-so-very-nice-see-you-again-oh-my-how-the-kids-have-grown-so-what's-new-with-you?

She recalled the story Sándor Pfircsik had told of the young pregnant woman whom he'd given a crib and who, to show her gratitude, had led the Nazis to his door so that she could then plunder his empty apartment for gold that didn't exist.

Had the Zöbel's neighbors done the same? Why wouldn't they?

I'll burn in Hell before I ever set eyes on them again, Adriana vowed silently.

She'd been gone for nearly three years, Tatiyana for even longer, and no doubt all they'd known was by now long gone. Assuming the building still stood after years of war, they'd find their former apartment occupied by strangers, their possessions stolen, their very existence erased from the village's collective memory. There was no point in going back.

The Red Army was advancing relentlessly, and for now the sisters figured themselves to be relatively safe as long as they advanced with it. The last thing they wanted was to be left behind, to find themselves at the mercy of remnants of the defeated Wehrmacht, like those they'd already encountered, or of resentful Poles.

But this advance was a double-eged sword, since the Allies were closing in on Berlin from every possible direction. With each mile they covered, the Russians drew nearer to the very heart of the imploding Reich, and Adriana and Tatiyana were going with them – not exactly the choicest destination for two Jewesses.

There was also the matter of the front never being very far removed. Explosions boomed in the near distance daily, showing that war still raged mere miles from where they stood. Should the Germans launch a counter-offensive and the Russians suffer a setback, the Wehrmacht could be on top of them before they knew it.

"We need to find somewhere to lay low for a while", Tatiyana suggested after they'd discussed it. "Maybe go to ground for a month, let things settle down for a few weeks. Then we can figure out what we want to do."

Adriana immediately thought back to the crazy woman they'd encountered a few days ago. "I agree. But if they're all like *her*, we'll have fun finding someone who'll take us in."

Tatiyana tapped the leather purse hidden next to her body, under her clothes. "Leave that to me", she said.

So the sisters got off the main road the first chance they got, leaving the dwindling train of refugees behind them.

Lechoslaw Napierkowski loved chopping firewood when it was this cold. It made the work so much easier.

He raised the ax high above his head and let it drop with nary an effort. The edge of the blade was insanely sharp, the wood frozen solid, and the weight and downward momentum of the axhead enough to split the log into almost perfect halves. *Tchak!* He grabbed another log from the endless pile, stood it up on the stump in front of him, raised the ax and let it fall again. *Tchak!*

After a while he fell into a sort of rhythmic trance and lost all notion of time. His wife would eventually come get him, snapping him back to reality with a hand placed gently on his back, preferably when the axhead was not hovering above them, and he'd be pleased to see he'd split hundreds of logs without ever being truly aware of it.

But no matter how hard he worked, in the end it really didn't amount to much. They burned so much wood to keep warm and cook this time of year he'd have to do it all over again in just a few days. Hopefully they'd have enough to last until spring. If not... well, if not there'd be some damn cold nights in the Napierkowskis' future, that's for sure.

At least the bloody war seemed to be just about over.

His family had farmed this land since the rule of Stanisław August Poniatowski, who landed on the Polish throne in 1764 after being hand-picked by Empress Catherine II of Russia. It lay several miles from the nearest road of any significance – and thus away from most of the trouble. The only visitors they got were either completely lost or seriously determined.

Oh sure, they'd seen their share of German soldiers since 1939, but nothing of any consequence. What was there here to steal? A few scrawny chickens? A lame goat? They didn't even have a single attractive daughter to whet the soldiers' lust. Mrs Napierkowski, to her eternal shame, was barren and Lechoslaw would be the last of his line. Upon his death the land would go to his ne'er-do-well brother Bronimir whose drinking, he was sure, would promptly ruin the farm and end 300 years of history.

He placed another log on the stump, raised the axhead, the razor-sharp steel began its lethal descent – and then something went terribly wrong.

Was old Lechoslaw holding the ax handle too loosely? Had his gloves become moist with perspiration? Did the axhead strike a wood knot at just the right - or the wrong - angle needed for everything to suddenly go astray? Should he have been paying closer attention to a task that, while routine, clearly remained quite dangerous?

Whatever the case may be, the end result was catastrophic. The axhead struck the frozen log and it was as though it hit stone. Instead of splitting the wood neatly and easily, as it should have, it sent the log flying to the right and bounced off the massive stump. The jarring impact pulled Lechoslaw off balance, he slipped and lost control of the ax and...

… and a few seconds or several hours later he came to lying on his back in the snow, stunned and dizzy and with the aftertaste of vomit sour in the back of his throat.

He blinked a few times rapidly and rubbed his hands over his face to clear his mind.

Wow, he thought. *Another near miss*. Life on the farm was hard and hazardous and there'd been dozens of near and not-so-near accidents over the years, but St. Casimir be praised he'd never been seriously injured.

Better get up before the wife sees me or I'll never hear the end of it.

A thunderbolt of pain shot up from his left ankle all the way to his hip as soon as he tried to move his leg – a pain worse than any he'd ever felt before in his life, a pain that blinded him and stole his breath away, a pain that made him gasp for air and threatened to still his heart. He clenched his jaws and balled his fists to keep from howling as he fell back. Tears streamed down both sides of his face and he wiped them away before propping himself up on his elbows – gently, carefully – to take a look.

The first thing he saw, lying in the snow a few feet to his left, was the ax. There was some blood – his own, obviously – on the steel head, but really not that much. At least the blade hadn't embedded itself into his shin bone.

Then he took a look at his leg.

Blood had soaked into his pant leg up to the knee. There was a huge gash right above his ankle, where the blade had slashed through both fabric and flesh, and blood was still pouring from the wound.

Lechoslaw knew he'd bleed to death before anyone found him. His poor wife was increasingly growing deaf in her golden days and the nearest neighbor was three miles away, so there was no point shouting for help. If he couldn't save himself, that drunkard Bronimir would inherit the farm sooner than planned.

The ground sloped toward the road and, St. Casimir being apparently busy somewhere else just now, his injured leg now lay a few inches below the rest of his body, which only made the bleeding worse. He had to raise it, and he had to raise it now, to slow the hemorrhage.

He clenched his teeth and twisted the fingers of both hands into the fabric of his pant leg. He breathed in deeply three times and prepared to swing his leg onto the massive stump, which would raise it about a foot above the rest of his body.

On the third breath he lifted and pulled at the same time. Excruciating pain suffocated him, but he might still have made it had the blood-soaked fabric not slipped from his fingers. But slip it did and he lost his grip a fraction of a second too soon, his injured muscles couldn't hold the weight of the leg on their own, and the wound struck the rough edge of the stump.

A wave of pain washed over him, rising from his toes to erupt through the top of his skull. A bright, burning light filled his world and he prepared to die, for surely nothing short of death could possibly liberate him from such suffering.

He began to pray out loud, begging the Virgin Mary to come fetch him to Heaven.

The Holy Mother must have heard him, for that's when the angels appeared.

And She wasn't the only One.

"Did you hear that?" Adriana demanded. Tatiyana nodded that she had.

The two sisters had left the main road behind the day before. Numerous forks – some nothing but faint hunting trails merely wide enough for a single man, others paths with deep ruts that attested to their frequent use - plunged into the dark woods on either side, and once they'd made up their minds to go, they followed the 11th one they encountered (their brother Aaron's age when he was killed) and hoped it led them somewhere good.

They spent a cold night – Tatiyana refused to light a fire, to avoid attracting any unwanted attention – and set out again as soon as the sun peeked above the horizon. A few hours later they spotted a farmhouse in the distance, but it seemed so isolated and so remote that they were about to continue on their way when they heard a man's voice calling out loudly.

"It must have come from over there. Let's take a look", Adriana said.

"We don't know who lives there. Could be sympathizers", Tatiyana cautioned. For some reason she said it in a very low voice, as though she feared being overheard by the trees or perhaps the snowflakes that were their only companions.

Adriana sighed. As much as she appreciated her sister's caution, and as much as she often relied on it, she also sometimes found it a bit excessive. The Nazis were getting their asses handed to them by the Allies from sunup to sundown, and it seemed to Adriana that those who had placed a losing bet on Hitler's thousand-year Reich would be busy trying to save their hides – not exacting petty revenge on two lonely travelers.

"The man sounded in pain", she said, neatly sidestepping Tatiyana's objection. "He can't be too dangerous."

They began trudging up the small road that climbed up to the farmhouse. At first the man's voice grew louder as they approached, but then it became progressively fainter and weaker and the two sisters, seized by a sudden sense of urgency, quickened their step.

They were slightly out of breath when they finally entered the tiny courtyard where old Lechoslaw had been chopping his firewood.

"Oh dear Lord", Tatiyana muttered when they found him. But then her training took over and she sprung into action. "Quickly", she said.

She grabbed the bloody leg and placed it on the stump. Then she pulled a scarf from their bag, wrapped it around Lechoslaw's leg just above the gaping wound, and used the ax handle to twist it into a tight tourniquet.

She knew the procedure to be horrendously painful, and yet the man barely flinched. It was obvious he had already lost a lot of blood and Tatiyana hoped they weren't too late. She frantically felt for a pulse in his neck. It took her almost a full minute to find it, only to discover that the man's heart had gone into severe fibrillation. His pulse felt like a butterfly fluttering under the skin, and her own heart skipped a beat.

She bit her lower lip and tried to keep the worry from showing on her face, as she'd been trained to do. This didn't bode well at all.

"Go see if he lives alone", she ordered Adriana.

Her sister returned less than a minute later with a stout elderly woman who couldn't possibly have weighed less than 225 pounds. Tatiyana, ever suspicious, immediately wondered how she had managed to remain so corpulent through the war. Adriana led her gently by the hand, like one might lead a skittish horse, since, despite her size, the woman seemed positively terrified. She kept glancing from one to the other, as though she expected to be attacked and slain at any moment.

But then she saw her husband lying in a pool of blood. She froze for a moment, the scene not quite making sense to her, before finally letting out a mighty shriek and dropping to her knees next to him. She began screaming incoherently at him and, when that failed to resuscitate him, grabbed his coat and shook him violently.

Lechoslaw briefly groaned and opened his eyes under this sudden assault. Seeing him still alive, the woman collapsed on top of him and began sobbing against his chest.

"His wife?" Tatiyana asked Adriana, who simply shrugged.

"Perhaps", she said. "A relative of some kind, that's for sure. I tried talking to her, but she clearly couldn't understand me. She almost ran out the back door when she saw me."

Fearing her patient might suffocate to death, Tatiyana placed her hands on the woman's massive shoulders and gently but firmly pushed her off Lechoslaw.

"Are you his wife?" she asked the woman, who simply stared blankly back at her.

"Are you his wife?" Tatiyana repeated in Russian. This time she spoke more slowly and louder. This finally elicited a reaction from the woman, who nodded through her tears. She then placed both hands over her ears and shook her head from left to right a few times.

Tatiyana nodded her understanding.

"She's his wife but there's something wrong with her hearing", she told Adriana. "We must speak very loudly for her to hear, or very slowly so she can read our lips. But now we have to get him inside or he'll freeze to death."

Tatiyana checked the man's wound and was relieved to see that the bleeding had essentially stopped. She'd have to remove the tourniquet eventually, but for now it was all that was keeping him alive. Some color even seemed to have returned to his lips and cheeks.

"You two grab his arms and I'll take his legs", she instructed Adriana. "We'll have to be very gentle or the bleeding may start again."

She touched Lechoslaw's wife's hand to get her attention. Then she pointed at all three of them, then at the body and then at the house, trying to convey her intention to carry him inside.

Tatiyana made herself clearer than she wished.

The woman acquiesced vigorously. Then, before anyone could stop her, she slipped one meaty forearm under her husband's knees, the other under his shoulders, and picked him up as easily as if he were a newborn. She then set off at a thunderous run, forcing Adriana to quickly step out of her way to keep from being trampled.

Tatiyana could only stare, aghast, as the woman carried her helpless husband through the door and into the farmhouse. The man's limbs flailed every which way as she ran, the injured leg leaving a trail of blood droplets in the snow.

"Are you sure you know the Russian word for 'gently'?" Adriana asked.

Footsteps crunched in the snow outside, and Adriana bit her lower lip.

Tatiyana was lying right next to her and she felt her sister's body stiffen at the sound. She desperately wanted to turn her head in her direction, to find comfort and reassurance by making make eye-contact with her only living relative, but she dared not move, for fear the slightest noise might give them away and cost them their lives.

Whoever was on the other side of the thin wall was being very methodical, searching, probing, exploring, seeking, scrutinizing...

Adriana was reminded of a fox she'd once seen hunting in winter. Having heard a field mouse scurrying under the snow, the predator had listened and listened and listened, patiently plotting its prey's exact location, until the fatal moment. It had then launched itself in the air as high as it could and plunged head-first through the snow, to re-emerge a second later with the tiny, unfortunate mammal firmly clamped between its jaws.

Adriana knew they had to remain as quiet as Death itself, otherwise the fox would certainly hear them and punch through the flimsy wall to capture and devour them.

The man sneezed explosively, startling them, and Adriana bit her lower lip harder and tasted blood. He may as well have been in here with them, so close did he sound. Then he fumbled with his clothes and, a second later, sighed deeply as he released a powerful stream of pungent urine that made a sound like thunder as it pounded the side of the barn.

Tatiyana began shaking uncontrollably and Adriana grabbed her hand to steady her. The origin of her sister's distress became obvious when a sudden, wet warmth reached her right buttock. Tatiyana didn't utter a word, but Adriana still heard her.

He's pissing on me. The pig is pissing on me.

Adriana felt a sickening gag rise in the back of her throat. She closed her eyes and her mind, forcing herself to count backward from ten... nine... eight... seven...

The man farted loudly once, twice, and then, mercifully, he was done. He rearranged his clothes, belched for good measure and mumbled incoherently.

The footsteps then went away, but they'd return.

The hunt had just begun.

Old Lechoslaw's injured leg healed after a few weeks.

His wife, Vanda, endlessly told all those who'd listen (meaning Adriana and Tatiyana) this was thanks to her unending prayers and the votive candles - many devoted to Saint Rita of Casca, an Italian nun believed by some to be the patron saint of wound healing - she kept burning next to her husband.

Tatiyana smiled and nodded politely at this, all the while knowing she had saved the man's leg, if not his life.

Taking advantage of Lechoslaw's momentary unconsciousness, she immediately cleansed the wound as thoroughly as possible, rinsing out dozens of pieces of debris and probably preventing the leg from becoming too badly infected. She then sutured it close with what material she had at hand – Vanda's sewing thread and needles, sterilized in boiling water – and bandaged it tight with strips of clean cloth she replaced every few hours.

The first few days were nerve-wracking as the man burned with a low fever and slipped in and out of consciousness. This puzzled Tatiyana since the wound, while unavoidably red and puffy, did not appear to be that seriously infected. The flesh around it was neither inflamed nor unusually firm, the wound itself didn't suppurate or smell, and she eventually concluded the fever was either due to Lechoslaw having lost so much blood (somewhat unlikely, but not entirely impossible) or to some other unknown infection unrelated to his injury.

In any case the fever broke after a few days and the man began to regain his senses. His first thought was that he had died and gone to Heaven – he kept thanking the Holy Mother for sending these women he called "the two angels" to his rescue - but then, seeing his wife there in the room with them and fussing over him like a baby, he understood himself to still be very much alive, so he closed his eyes, sighed resignedly and slept.

"He's not completely out of the woods yet", Tatiyana warned Adriana. "He's still very weak. He'll need food to replace the blood he's lost."

Adriana took a look around and then back at her sister. "That might be a problem", she stated grimly.

Tatiyana nodded. It was amply clear Lechoslaw and his wife were barely surviving as it were. There was a small bushel of potatoes on the kitchen counter, another of turnips, but the cupboards were mostly bare and whatever meager provisions they may have had in the fall were now essentially gone.

Now with him incapacitated, two or three more months of winter still to come, and two more mouths to feed at least temporarily, the situation was nothing short of catastrophic.

Lechoslaw's wife was staring at the two sisters intently and seemed to guess what they were discussing. She touched Tatiyana's shoulder and then spoke for a couple of minutes, pointing first at their backyard, then at the barn, and then at a point somewhere to the west. Her voice was unusually high-pitched for such a large woman.

"What did she say?" Adriana asked.

"Well", Tatiyana began after a moment spent collecting her thoughts, "There's good news and there's bad news. First they have some meat buried in the snow out back, there's a goat in the barn we can slaughter as a last resort and there's a market about three miles from here where food can be purchased."

"I'm guessing that's the good news", Adriana said. "What about the bad?"

Tatiyana sighed deeply. "They were counting on that meat to make it through the rest of winter, but wolves stole most of it a couple of weeks ago. She says there's less than ten pounds left."

"So the goat...", Adriana began.

"So that goat is all they have left; if we eat it, they'll have nothing to sell in the spring to buy seeds to plant their crops."

Tatiyana paused before concluding. "And they have absolutely no money to buy anything at the market. Unless we offer the goat for trade, which we can't do."

The two sisters exchanged a long stare. "So there's no food left, we can't eat the goat and we can't barter it away", Adriana finally summed up. "That leaves only one option."

Tatiyana nodded before looking at Vanda. "Tomorrow we'll go to the market to get some food", she announced slowly and loudly.

Vanda's eyebrows shot up and her voice rose by a couple of octaves. She was gesturing wildly, repeating that the two of them were completely destitute, and grew so agitated Tatiyana couldn't get a word in edgewise.

In the end, Tatiyana pulled from her pocket the small leather purse Mattias Traugott had given them. And when, from that purse, she extracted as if by magic a gold coin, Vanda was silenced as effectively as if she'd been struck between the eyes by a sledgehammer.

The fat woman stared at the coin with eyes the size of saucepans and her mouth kept opening and closing, though she emitted no sound.

Tatiyana immediately regretted her imprudence. It was quite reckless to divulge so much to a woman they knew nothing about. A few crumpled paper bills would have sufficed, and would have had the added advantage of keeping their secret fortune... well, secret.

But now the cat was out of the bag and it was too late to shove it back inside. In the end, her decision would indeed prove a grievous mistake, but not for reasons she could have possibly imagined at that time.

Night had fallen and the temperature was plummeting.

Adriana slipped her hands under her armpits and clamped her jaws shut to keep her teeth from chattering. Her woolen hat had ridden up, exposing ears that now felt painfully frozen, but she did not dare yank it back down since the slightest noise could get them killed. She kept wiggling frozen toes vigorously inside her boots, to little avail. She took only the shallowest of breaths, exhaling through her nose as slowly as she could, to keep her pluming breath from seeping through the planks and possibly betraying their presence.

Tatiyana, next to her, might as well have been dead, so little did she move. No doubt was she as cold as she was, perhaps even more so since she lay next to the outer wall. What little warmth their bodies produced instantly bled away into the frigid night, leaving them to shiver until their bones might shatter. Only the rise and fall of Tatiyana's ribcage proved she still lived. Adriana matched the rhythm of her sister's breathing, this elementary complicity bringing them both a small measure of comfort.

There was a noise and the goat bleated in alarm before falling silent. Adriana's eyes snapped open. Had she really fallen asleep? How long had they been hiding here? She blinked a few times, rapidly, and tried to remember. It had been mid-morning when... and now it was dark... so... what? When did it get dark this time of year? Soon after dinner? Maybe a bit later? So again... how long? Eight, maybe nine hours?

Was that all? Her cramping and aching muscles, not to mention her bursting bladder, screamed it had to have been much, much longer.

That noise again. But not outside like earlier that day, not a predator prowling in the snow, but inside this time. Inside the goddamn barn.

A mouse perhaps?

Like hell.

Her heartbeat quickened instantly and sweat beaded on her forehead despite the freezing cold.

She felt Tatiyana jump in surprise. Had she too fallen asleep and just awakened? She slowly reached for her sister and they clasped hands. Her other hand she wrapped around a small stone, more of a pebble really, she had found. How effective a weapon this would prove against a potential enemy remained to be seen but maybe, if she threw it hard enough and accurately enough, and if with a bit of luck she punctured an eye or broke a tooth, it would buy them a few seconds of surprise to get away.

There was definitely someone inside the barn. And most certainly not a mouse, unless that mouse happened to weigh a few hundred pounds.

The goat bleated again and the stranger hushed it rudely.

Whoever was there now stood on the other side of the thin wall, mere inches away from them. She could hear the intruder breathing heavily. He stank of garlic but not, thankfully, of alcohol.

Unless the stench of garlic camouflaged that of cheap booze, of course.

The stranger seemed undecided. He was just standing there, catching his breath, as though trying to figure out his next move. After a moment Adriana heard him put something on the ground, and then there was a muffled thump when he dropped to one knee in the dirt, and then to the other.

All hope that they might yet remain safe vanished when the intruder began removing the empty crates that concealed the secret entrance to their lair. He definitely knew they were there, and he was coming for them.

Wood grated against wood, the false wall rattled and Adriana almost screamed when the stranger finally yanked away the narrow panel the two of them had hurriedly crawled through a few hours earlier.

Adriana's entire body was as taut as a bowstring. She struck first, not giving the intruder any chance to harm them.

She threw the pebble as hard as she could through the opening, there was a satisfying scream of pain and she prepared to fight.

Adriana, it was decided, would go to the market alone the next day.

The sisters hated to separate, especially in a foreign land in such perilous times, but in truth they had little choice in the matter. Tatiyana needed to remain at the farm in case Lechoslaw took a turn for the worse, and Vanda's size precluded her walking any further than the barn. So either Adriana went, or they slowly starved to death. And while Adriana, unlike her sister, neither spoke nor understood any language that others might readily use around here, she trusted that a bit of cold hard cash would earn her a fair amount of sympathy, patience and goodwill.

Then ensued a brief discussion regarding how much she should take with her. Traugott had given them a small fortune – perhaps enough to feed a family of ten ogres for five years. Still, the sisters needn't be told how unwise it would be for a stranger to suddenly appear and begin flashing such riches around. So the gold and silver coins would be left behind, as would the precious stones. To keep from attracting undue attention, Adriana would only take a handful of Polish *złotys*, the currency most people were likely to have stashed away in these parts.

Adriana's expedition was delayed when the next morning dawned overcast and windy. The skies soon unleashed a mixture of wet snow and freezing rain unto the world, draping a heavy blanket of misery over the land. So they all huddled around the small stove and tried to keep warm while the storm raged outside. The sisters hated to think what might have become of them in such weather, had they not left the main road, fortuitously come upon the injured Lechoslaw and then found shelter here.

They took turns fetching firewood and Tatiyana checked Lechoslaw's bandages every now and then, more to relieve the oppressing boredom than because this was really needed. Conversation was quite limited, if not impossible, what with Vanda being essentially deaf and only able to communicate with Tatiyana, and in the end they settled into a companionable silence that was only perturbed by Lechoslaw's occasional moans, the howling wind and the wood crackling in the stove.

Around midday Vanda melted snow into which she threw some vegetables and a few pieces of frozen meat she had fetched from their dwindling reserves outside. About an hour later they had a stew that, if far from tasty, at least kept them warm and full. The meat was quite stringy and Adriana wondered if the goat might not have had, in the not too distant past, a companion. They spooned a bit of broth into Lechoslaw's mouth, who thankfully was still too out of it to fully realize what they were feeding him.

The two sisters went to bed that night hoping the inclement weather would not endure. While they might stand one more day cooped up with Vanda, with nothing to do but feed the stove and eat bland stew and check bandages that need not be checked, any prolonged confinement would be intolerable.

Vanda and Lechoslaw certainly appeared to be decent and hard-working and trustworthy people, but in truth Adriana and Tatiyana knew absolutely nothing about them – and they therefore had no way of knowing just how safe they were, exactly. What they did know, on the other hand, was that they had fought too long and too hard for their freedom and survival to blindly place everything in the hands of the first people they encountered. They might stay here a few days, perhaps longer, but they might also feel the urge to move on sooner rather than later.

The next day rose sunny but cold as hell, which at least froze the previous day's slush into a hard surface that would support Adriana's weight. She took with her an old sled she found in the barn, on which to carry back whatever she might purchase, and she set out on her mission.

Sometimes the temptation to sin is just too strong. And sometimes, truth be told, it just feels too bloody damn good to sin to even bother resisting.

So Vanda let out a string of soul-scorching curses for which a couple dozen rosaries would atone the next day.

She brought her hand to her mouth, where the stone had struck her, and the blood gleamed darkly against her fingers in the dim light of the barn. She held back more curses; no need to pile *Ave Marias* and *Pater Nosters* on top of her already considerable, though self-imposed, chastisement.

"What is wrong with your *zwariowany* sister?" she whispered angrily in the dark.

Adriana and Tatiyana slowly emerged from their hideout, a secret compartment old Lechoslaw had built between the barn's inner and outer walls to conceal... well, things that, for whatever reason, needed to remain concealed. It was about six feet long by two feet wide, and thus barely large enough for two grown women.

The two sisters could hardly move after such prolonged and enforced confinement in the cold. Their muscles were stiff and their movements awkward, and Vanda had to pull them out through the narrow opening, somewhat like a farmer helping a calf into the world. They then spent the next five minutes stretching muscles that wouldn't stretch and loosening creaky joints and massaging blood back into limbs as rigid as oak trunks.

Just how exhausted they actually were was revealed when they attempted to rise. The world immediately began to swim and they would have fallen, had Vanda not propped them both up. Not only had they been immobile for almost ten hours, but they'd also had nothing to eat or drink since forever, and their reserves of energy were beyond depleted.

"What's that smell?" Vanda suddenly asked.

"He pissed on us", Tatiyana replied harshly, after translating the question for Adriana's benefit.

The fat woman took a moment processing the answer and, to her credit, managed to suppress the laughter that bubbled up deep inside her.

"Good thing I brought fresh clothes, then", she said instead. "And food, of course."

Adriana was slightly annoyed by the idle chatter. "Is he gone?" she asked.

Vanda shook her head after Tatiyana had translated. "No, he's still in the kitchen, but he's so drunk he cannot stand", she said. "You're safe for now. Lech is with him."

From a bag she had brought with her she handed each woman strips of cold beef, some bread and a bottle of water. The sisters were famished and the food vanished in the blink of an eye. Tatiyana burped softly after gulping down the last of her water. "I need to change", she then announced to nobody's surprise.

"So do I", Adriana said.

The two sisters grabbed an armful of clothes from Vanda and retreated to the goat's pen to change out of their urine-soaked garments. The animal bleated in protest at this intrusion but was ignored. They returned a minute later feeling considerably drier and more comfortable, even though their heavy winter coats were now unwearable. Vanda promised to return with blankets to keep them warm until they could safely reemerge back into the world.

"How long will he stay, do you think?" Adriana demanded.

Vanda shrugged. "Hard to say", she said. "The man likes his drink. I've seen him like this before. Sometimes he goes to sleep, and when he wakes he immediately starts drinking again, until he passes out again. Sometimes this goes on for days."

Adriana groaned with despair.

"And he's very suspicious", Vanda added. "He thinks he's subtle but he's not. He asks too many questions. Never before has he cared so much about us. He's an ass."

"So...?"

"So I continue to come see you when I can. But for now..."

She pointed at the opening and shrugged helplessly. Adriana groaned again.

Even in freedom we find ourselves prisoners, she reflected with a touch of anger.

The two sisters hugged for a moment before crawling back into their hideout. Vanda replaced the panel and the crates, sealing them alive in their tomb, and left. At the last moment she remembered to take the soiled clothes with her.

If the man decided to take his next piss *inside* the barn, it wouldn't do for him to stumble across a pile of discarded women's clothing.

Adriana was happier than she'd been in a long while and, had it not been for the bitter cold, she might even have considered this an essentially perfect day.

The sled was overloaded with her purchases, and pulling it across the frozen snow was back-breaking work that made her sweat profusely, but a wide grin still split her face from ear to ear. This time her efforts would profit *her* and not someone else. The food she'd procured at the market – slabs of meat and jars of preserves and bags of dried apples and loaves of bread and even modest quantities of honey, flour, sugar and salt – would keep them not only alive, but well-fed for a few weeks.

Lechoslaw and Vanda's farm indeed lay just a few miles from the village, just as the farmer's wife had indicated. Adriana followed the narrow road and came upon the market almost by accident, in the cobblestone courtyard of the village's medieval church. The few farmers present on such a cold day at first eyed her suspiciously, but the roll of *złotys* she produced rapidly allayed their worries – to such an extent that the vendors, desperate for any advantage that might earn them a sale, began coming to her instead of hoping she'd eventually make it to their stall.

Some even materialized out of thin air with their wares, as if my magic, when word of her presence spread. Adriana began to fear for her safety when she found herself surrounded by all manners of individuals shouting and gesticulating to get her attention, even more so when a fistfight broke out between two farmers who had both been trying to sell her hogs' heads. The two men fell to the ground, where they proceeded to roll around in the snow and pummel each other with more determination than actual efficiency.

Taking advantage of the diversion, a stray dog darted in, seized a snow-covered head in its jaws and was gone in the blink of an eye.

Adriana just stood there for almost an hour, nodding her interest or lack thereof, using her fingers to show how many of each product she might buy, then negotiating the price as best she could.

This proved the hardest, since she had not the slightest notion of the value of the currency she was using and since she could only communicate with hand signals. As a rule of thumb her opening offer was usually no more than a third or a quarter of what the vendor was asking; if a farmer showed her ten fingers, for example, she countered with no more than three or four. A few farmers feigned to be so insulted by her stinginess that they threw up their hands and stomped away, only to return a few moments later to agree to her price – all the while making a great show of their displeasure, as though they were selling their firstborn to the Devil.

But the farmers caught on soon enough and Adriana understood her shopping to have ended

·

when prices suddenly skyrocketed. She tried to keep it going for a while, but despite all her precautions, on a couple of occasions a gleam in the eye of the man with whom she had just closed a deal told her she'd been gouged, and she fumed. She decided to walk away when even a fifth of the asking price became too much.

Adriana eventually managed to extirpate herself from the melee, though she was briefly pursued by a man trying to interest her in bottles of a clear liquid she presumed to be homemade alcohol. The man only gave up when she turned her pockets inside out to show him they were empty, a sign universally understood to mean *I'm-broke-I-don't-have-any-more-money-so-leave-me-alone-you-idiot*.

The sun had passed its highest point in the sky and begun to sink again toward the horizon when she was finally able to head home with her purchases. She hadn't given much thought to this part of her journey beforehand and now began to worry just how wise and safe it was for a lone woman to travel, even briefly, through a country blighted by war for so many years – especially a woman in possession of so much food.

Luckily the road was mostly empty and she didn't have very far to go. So she lowered her head and bent her back, knowing her only recourse was to get home as rapidly as she possibly could.

She had been walking for almost an hour and the temperature had plunged noticeably when she heard a motor vehicle coming up behind her. This in itself was unusual; this road seemed to be used mostly by locals traveling between the village and the nearby farms, and indeed she'd only encountered local residents going about their business.

The main road, the one crowded with soldiers and refugees, the one Tatiyana and her had walked earlier, lay a couple of miles to the north. There was therefore little reason for a motor vehicle to be here – and yet there it was, coming up rapidly and throwing up an arc of snow.

It sped by her, pelting her with ice and snow, and for a moment she hoped it might keep going, but it obviously didn't and instead swerved to a sudden stop about fifty feet in front of her, blocking the road.

Adriana's heart sank.

The road beyond was completely deserted. She looked back over her shoulder, praying for someone to be coming, but there was no one. It was getting late and those who'd been out had already returned home by now. She was the tardy one, she now realized.

Four young men tumbled out of the GAZ-67 4x4 command car – the Soviet equivalent of America's famed Willys Jeep. They were all laughing and drinking, and Adriana had been around enough drunken soldiers to know this did not bode well for her.

Not well at all.

Her heart in her mouth, she quickened her pace and lowered her head, hoping to simply squeeze between the back of the vehicle and the edge of the road. The sled was heavy and slowed her down considerably, but in the end it made no difference. As soon as she came abreast of the vehicle, one of the soldiers stood directly in her path, blocking her way.

Adriana stopped and kept her head down. She glanced discretely to her right and briefly considered making a dash for the forest that lined the road, but she would have to plow through twenty feet of deep snow before reaching the relative safety of the trees. Assuming she even made it to the woods without being caught or shot, her chances of escaping would then be extremely slim – tracking her would be child's play - and she only risked making things even worse.

All she could see were the soldier's pants and boots. She desperately wished she'd taken a knife or some sort of weapon with her. When the man didn't move, she had no choice but to look up at him, and when she did her fear turned to elation.

"Vitali?" she cried out.

Vitali Anatoliyevich Grebenshchikov, of the Red Army's 322nd Rifle Division, whom she and Tatiyana had saved from freezing to death soon after escaping from Auschwitz, stared at her with all the intelligence of an ox harnessed to a cart. Adriana watched his eyes for any sign of recognition, but there was none. He didn't even seem to recognize his own name.

The lights were on but there was nobody home.

She peered at him more closely, hoping to jog his memory, but Vitali's eyes were unfocused and he seemed to have trouble keeping his balance.

"Vitali?" she repeated. "Adriana? Tatiyana?"

Adriana smiled gratefully at him. While she didn't speak Russian, as Tatiyana did, surely Vitali would still remember her?

Vitali took a long swig from a bottle of vodka. When the glassiness finally cleared from his eyes, it yielded to something that made Adriana want to scream with terror.

Two other soldiers suddenly grabbed her arms and twisted them behind her back, almost wrenching her shoulders out of their sockets. This happened so quickly she had no time to react, let alone fight back.

"Vitali, please", she begged with tears in her eyes. "You must remember me. We... we saved your life."

Vitali's sole answer was to empty his bottle and throw it away. It sank into the deep snow and disappeared. He then began rifling through her pockets methodically, as though he were looking for something.

"деньги", he mumbled. "где деньги?"

She knew he was asking her something, but she didn't know what. She tried smiling at him.

"I'm sorry Vitali, but I don't know what you want", she said as calmly as she could. "I don't speak Russian, remember? But Tatiyana does. You know Tatiyana? Ta... Ti... Ya... Na? If you'll just follow me it's not..."

He was paying her no attention whatsoever so she fell quiet. She might as well have been speaking to a dim-witted child.

"деньги?" he asked again, but this time with a touch of impatience that bordered on anger.

Vitali finished going through her pockets. When he came up empty, his interest in her seemed to evaporate and he returned to his vehicle, where he found another bottle. He sat in the snow with his back against a rear wheel to drink it.

The two soldiers still holding her seemed at a loss what to do, now that their leader had walked away.

The fourth soldier, Adriana now realized, had been going through the contents of her sled.

When she managed to glance back over her shoulder, she was horrified to see half her purchases now scattered around in the snow.

That made her inexplicably angry.

"Hey you stop that right now!" she shouted at the man.

That got his attention and he came to stand directly in front of her.

"деньги?" he said. That word again, but this time two fingers rubbed together finally told Adriana what they were after.

They wanted her money. Her spending spree at the market hadn't gone unnoticed, and now these men wanted to steal the rest of her presumed fortune.

Adriana didn't know whether to be worried or relieved. Was this all this was about? A handful of crumpled bills? If only she had any money left, they'd be welcome to it. She immediately wished she hadn't spent it all, or perhaps that she'd taken a precious stone with her after all, if only to now buy her freedom and safety.

But she had absolutely nothing left, and that placed her entirely at the mercy of these drunken, unpredictable men.

She tried to put a brave face on it.

"I'm very sorry", she said, though the man certainly didn't understand her. "I don't have any money left. But please help yourself to any of the food I have. It's yours."

A few pounds of salted ham would be a small price to pay to walk away from here unscathed.

But the men didn't want salted ham or honey or flour. They wanted money, lots of it preferably, and the man was now once again going through her pockets, and growing angrier by the instant as he too found nothing.

Then a look Adriana knew only too well came across his face and he barked a command at the two holding her.

"Vitali! Vitali!" she shouted hysterically as they pulled her toward the sled and slammed her down onto her back.

The third man sneered as he came to stand before her. He then unbuttoned both his coat and pants and lay down on top of her. He smelled of sweat and stale cigarette smoke and alcohol, and the scent made her heart rise in her throat. He began kissing her face and neck and she could feel his hands pawing her body through her thick winter clothing.

She could also feel *his* body and the sensation sent a jolt of anger and revulsion coursing through her entire being. This again? Now that the war was essentially over? How many men had tried to rape her? Three? Four? She'd lost count. All she knew was they'd all failed, and this one would too.

She began twisting violently left and right, fighting him the only way she could. She looked for any opportunity to sink her teeth into his flesh, but the man was being careful to stay well out of reach of her teeth – perhaps he'd been bit before.

The man was drunkenly trying to push her skirt up to her waist when, miraculously, Adriana's left arm came free.

Knowing she had mere seconds to save herself, she punched the soldier who'd been holding her on that side twice in the face, breaking his nose and shuttering one eye. The man brought both hands up to his bloodied face and collapsed in the snow.

Adriana then began pummeling her would-be rapist. Her blows had little effect – the man's lust rendered him almost impervious to pain – until she grabbed one ear and twisted it viciously. The man howled in pain.

He reared up, tearing himself away from her, and grabbed her left wrist with his right hand. He reared back with his free left hand to knock her unconscious, but then his eyes went to her left arm, the one he was holding, and he froze.

Adriana had flinched and closed her eyes in anticipation of the blow she feared was coming. When it didn't, she looked at the man and saw him staring at her arm with a mixture of horror and fascination.

The sleeve of her coat had ridden up, exposing her Auschwitz number.

1971.

Neunzehnhunderteinundsiebzig, the SS had called her.

She gasped and the man looked at her.

"Yes, I was at Auschwitz!" she shouted as loudly as she could. "Auschwitz! You know the name, you bastard? Auschwitz! Auschwitz! Auschwitz!"

The man stood up and stumbled back like a vampire sprinkled with holy water.

She tore her arm free of the remaining soldier and got to her feet. She began advancing on the Red soldier, and for each step forward she took, he took two backward.

"I survived Auschwitz!" she shouted again, waving her tattoo at him like a crucifix. "And I didn't make it out of Auschwitz just so you could rape me here! Auschwitz!"

The soldier could not get away from her quickly enough. His progress was slowed by his still-unfastened pants – they kept dropping and he kept having to pull them back up – but he dared not stop to fasten them again.

He shouted something at the two other men, who came running, the injured one dripping red blood on the white snow and using his comrade as a crutch.

They picked Vitali up by his clothes and dumped him head first into the vehicle. The rapist jumped behind the wheel and drove off so brutally fast that his injured comrade was caught off-balance and almost tumbled out; luckily for him the man managed to catch himself just in time, or he'd surely have been left behind to die in the cold.

It all happened so suddenly that Adriana was left to wonder what had just occurred.

She stared at her tattoo, the numbers dark on her pale skin, and wondered about the soldier's reaction. Perhaps he'd liberated Auschwitz, seen the horror, tasted the madness, and decided she'd already suffered enough.

Or, more likely, perhaps he feared she'd been tainted by the evil of the place. Perhaps he feared becoming himself some demon's plaything if he violated her.

But in the end what did it matter why he ran? He was gone. She was safe. She'd escaped again... somehow.

Adriana dropped to her knees for a moment, breathing deeply.

She rearranged her clothes, brushed the snow off her coat and returned to her sled. It took her less than ten minutes to put it back in order and then she resumed her trek home.

The others were waiting.

The goat was bleating furiously.

Adriana awoke choking and gagging.

She shook her head. Her lungs were scorched and her throat was on fire.

A violent coughing fit racked her entire body. Every muscle spasmed 'til she thought her bones might shatter and her tendons snap.

Her hands rose to her neck as she began to suffocate. Smoke stung her eyes and she sat up to escape, in her panic forgetting that the ceiling was barely two feet high. She banged her head painfully, saw stars and collapsed back.

She forced herself to remain calm. Perhaps someone was simply burning trash out in the yard and the wind was blowing smoke their way.

That would account for the smoke... but not for the heat. The crackling of dry wood burning came to her from far, far away, and panic submerged her.

Oh God. Someone had set the goddamn barn ablaze.

Adriana tried to call out but her lungs filled with acrid smoke and she began to retch, her tongue protruding like a hanged man's and saliva drooling onto her chin.

Tatiyana.

She reached over with her right hand and found her sister next to her. She shook her as hard as she could.

"Tatiyana?" she croaked feebly. "Tatiyana!"

Her sister didn't respond. She shook her again, trying to wake her up before it was too late, but her body felt as limp as a sleeping baby's.

Perhaps it was already too late.

The goat was bucking madly, its tiny hooves striking the walls of its pen angrily.

Adriana began to pound the panel that was their only salvation, but lying there as she was, on her back with barely enough room to move, her blows lacked any strength. And without strength she had no hope of dislodging the crates and bags piled on the other side.

They were trapped. They would either burn to death or asphyxiate.

They had escaped Auschwitz's ovens and gas chambers only to suffer the same fate here, as free women. How stupefyingly ridiculous.

"Vanda!" she called out with what breath she could muster. "Vanda!"

But the fat woman was deaf, and even had she possessed hearing as sharp as an owl's, Adriana's voice was so weak she'd never have heard her.

Adriana grabbed one of Tatiyana's hands and the other she placed over her mouth and nose, trying to keep out as much of the smoke as she could.

Her last thought before passing out was for Aaron, their parents and Rita. Hopefully they'd be waiting on the other side to guide them to wherever it was they were going.

Perhaps she shouldn't have taken old Lechoslaw with her that morning. Perhaps it would have all turned out differently if she hadn't.

But it had been over two months since the valiant old farmer had almost lopped his leg off with an ax, the wound had healed cleanly, he was growing restless – and they were running out of excuses as to why he should stay abed. He wasn't the type to contentedly whittle his days away just lying around, not when he could be doing something productive. Spring was just around the corner and he was itching to be let out of the house.

Farmers never take a day off, he kept repeating; when they do, people starve.

So, in the end, they gave up. Short of having Vanda sit on top of him, which might have been ill-advised, there was nothing more they could do. Never before in his life had Lechoslaw been coerced into such a lengthy period of inactivity. He now claimed to feel as strong as a man half his age, which he probably did. He also argued, not without reason, that he needed to strengthen his leg before sowing season, otherwise he'd never be able to get the job done.

Tatiyana however refused to allow him to resume his duties unhindered. While she worried that keeping him confined against his will for too long might have a deleterious effect on his health, she worried even more about what might happen if he injured himself again. Might her sister and her then remain stranded here even longer?

So far their stay at the Napierkowskis' had been one of both convenience and charity. While it suited them to have a warm place where to hide while winter, and the remainder of the war, ran their course outside the front door, it had also become quite rapidly clear that Lechoslaw was the workhorse in this marriage. With him injured and out of action, it would have been a death sentence for the old couple for the two sisters to have moved on before he'd fully recovered.

Having said that, they had no intention of staying put forever. Spring was almost here, the days were growing longer and warmer, and Adriana and Tatiyana more and more felt the unspoken urge to move on. But first they needed to get Lechoslaw solidly back on his own two feet.

And that's how the old man came to accompany Adriana that morning on one of her trips to the village market.

Adriana had honestly not foreseen that she might one day need to go back. She had returned from her first excursion with enough food, she had believed, to last until Lechoslaw had fully healed, and then they'd leave him and his wife to their own devices. But Vanda, perhaps not surprisingly, turned out to have an appetite of gargantuan proportions. On any given day the fat woman consumed without any apparent effort twice as much as food as the three of them combined. At times it seemed as though only sleep could interrupt her feeding frenzy. She ate almost without cease from the moment she opened her eyes in the morning to the moment she shut them at night.

They'd even known her to fall asleep with a half-eaten piece of *something* clutched protectively in a massive fist. She'd rouse immediately and finish devouring her prize if anyone tried to pry it out of her grasp.

So Adriana, despite her misgivings considering how her first expedition had almost ended, made a second, then a third, and then a fourth trip to the market. The farmers began to know her by name and to anticipate her visits. They knew what she purchased and what she did not, and that she had money, but really nothing more. Who was she? Where had she come from? Where did she live? Why did she need so much food so frequently? The lack of a common language left those questions and several others unanswered and maintained a certain aura of mystery about her.

She was Adriana, no longer of the luxuriously long hair but now of the unending appetite and apparently bottomless purse. And that's probably how it would have remained, had old Lechoslaw not tagged along that sunny March morning.

"*Braciszek?*" someone roared behind them as Adriana completed her final purchase.

Lechoslaw had been chatting with a friend, reenacting yet again the accident that had almost cost him his leg, when they were interrupted. He froze in mid-sentence before slowly dropping his head. His shoulders slumped and he looked like a man who has just learned of a tragic death. He then looked up again, back at the villager, who shrugged apologetically as if to say, *What can I do?*

Of what ensued Adriana obviously understood nothing. But when they returned to the farm later on, Lechoslaw explained what had occurred to Tatiyana, who then warned her sister that trouble was now more than likely.

Lechoslaw slowly spun around to face the man behind him.

"Bronimir," he said coldly. "It's been a long time. But not yet long enough."

Lechoslaw's brother, the inveterate drunkard who was one heartbeat away from inheriting the family farm, burst out laughing uncontrollably as drunkards are wont to do, as if this insult were the funniest thing he'd ever heard. His long winter coat, once of indifferent color, was now a quilt of suspicious stains, and out of one pocket he pulled a handkerchief with which he wiped his nose.

"It's good to see you too, dearest brother," he said with a complete lack of sincerity. Then his features hardened dangerously and he asked: "Who's this?"

Adriana almost recoiled when the man suddenly whipped an arm in her direction. She looked at Lechoslaw, whose eyes never left his brother's.

"Someone you need not concern yourself with," the old farmer replied. His tone was as sharp as the ax that had almost taken his leg.

That evasive answer only piqued Bronimir's curiosity further and he squinted at his older brother. "Does Vanda know about her?," he asked, malevolently implying that Lechoslaw might be having an affair with a woman a third his age and further be foolish enough to brazenly show himself in public with her.

Strong as an oak despite his age and injury, Lechoslaw towered over his sibling by at least three inches. He took one step toward his brother and Bronimir almost fell when he reflexively took one back. He needed a moment to regain his balance and his arrogance.

"I'll take that as a no," he then said with a taunting smile.

"She's the grand-daughter of our great-aunt Konstancja," Lechoslaw growled, randomly plucking a name out of their family tree. Konstancja had been sister to their maternal grandfather. Neither of them had ever met the woman and knew nothing of her family, so there was no way Bronimir would know he was lying.

Bronimir was momentarily thrown off balance, but only for a moment. "Then why has she no Polish, or even no Russian?," he inquired, demonstrating surprising perspicacity for a man who'd spent the better part of his adult life staring down the neck of an empty bottle, wondering where all the drink had gone and willing it to return immediately.

It was Lechoslaw's turn to be caught off-guards. He side-stepped the question. "She showed up at *my* farm a couple of months ago with a letter from a woman named Walentyna," Lechoslaw said. He hammered the word 'my' to try to regain the upper hand, but the effect on Bronimir was less than decisive.

"This Walentyna claimed to be Konstancja's daughter and this lady's mother, and she begged us kindly to take her in," Lechoslaw went on. "We did. You'd have met her before if you visited more often. Your concern over my injury really warmed my heart."

Bronimir ignored the last barb. His smirk showed he was far from convinced. "That's quite a tall tale, brother," he said tenaciously. "A pretty young woman like her, arriving alone from God-knows-where, in the middle of the war... What *ever* possessed her mother to send her on such a perilous journey and to believe she'd be safer here than wherever she came from?"

To this Lechoslaw had no answer, and Bronimir took advantage of his brother's silence to land one more devastating blow. "And I hear she's quite wealthy, too," he added. "Perhaps that convinced you to open your home to her."

All activity had now ceased in the market as both vendors and sellers listened interestedly to the exchange. Perhaps the riddle of the mystery woman would now be solved?

Lechoslaw noticed the silence and knew it was time to put an end to the show. Fortunately for him, Bronimir was too much of an imbecile to quit while he was ahead and he decided to press his advantage ever further.

"Perhaps that's also why Vanda turns a blind eye while you and her...," he began.

Lechoslaw's massive, work-hardened fist caught him right under the left eye, almost knocking him out of his boots. Bronimir landed on his rump with a thud and then collapsed to the cobblestones with two hands pressed against his face, moaning.

Lechoslaw came to stand over him.

"Next time you stop by the farm, I'll pour you a drink and answer all your questions, *brother*," he said.

He then grabbed Adriana by the elbow and they left without paying him or anyone else any more attention.

They had already gone a distance when Bronimir muttered: "Oh don't worry, *brother*. I'll be visiting soon. Very soon."

In the end, it was decided that the dead body would be best concealed in the partially-charred barn. With the goat.

The goat's feelings regarding this uninvited, and quite deceased, guest in its pen were of very little concern.

"The nights are still cold enough," Lechoslaw opined. "It shouldn't begin to smell for a little while."

"And when it does?," Tatiyana asked. The old farmer simply shrugged. "We've been at war for five years," he said without taking his eyes off the corpse. "The woods are littered with dead bodies."

"Won't anyone miss him?" Tatiyana insisted.

This time Lechoslaw glanced at her sideways and snorted. "That's most unlikely. He had very few friends."

Translation: *Perhaps on the third day after Hell freezes over for the second time.*

Vanda entered the barn and came to stand with them. She, too, stared at the dead body for a moment before speaking.

"Your sister has awakened," she then announced, with as much enthusiasm and emotion as one informing guests that dinner was being served.

Tatiyana smiled. She had never doubted that Adriana would get better, but she was still relieved to know she had regained consciousness. "Thanks to both of you," she told Vanda. "If you hadn't come when you did..."

Vanda shrugged. She had smelled the fire, warned her husband and both had rushed outside. Lechoslaw shoveled snow onto the nascent flames, extinguishing them and saving the barn, while Vanda, knowing where the sisters were trapped, used her prodigious strength to smash and rip out enough of the outer wall to pull them out just in time.

Both women had been rendered unresponsive by the smoke, but at least they still lived.

Tatiyana came to after just a few minutes and immediately inquired about her sister. Told that Adriana was still unconscious, she rushed to her and was relieved to find her pulse strong and her breathing deep and steady. It had then only been a matter of keeping Adriana warm and fed as her body healed.

Still, that had been almost three days ago and Tatiyana, in all honesty, had felt a few pangs of concern. Why had she recovered in mere minutes while Adriana was taking so much longer? She could only surmise that having been positioned next to the barn's outer wall had somehow protected her from the worst of the smoke while Adriana, having lain closer to the fire, had inhaled more of the noxious gases.

But it was all of no concern now. Adriana was awake and she'd go check on her in a few minutes.

Tatiyana looked at Vanda, who was still staring at the dead body, and tried to imagine what was going through the fat woman's mind. Yes, she had saved two lives, perhaps three, but she had also taken one. While that put her ahead by at least one, that was likely to be of very little comfort to someone so deeply religious.

Thou shalt not kill came in at number six on the list of commandments imposed upon good Christians, right between honoring your parents and not committing adultery (which, in Vanda's case, appeared laughably improbable to earn her eternal damnation).

Lechoslaw wrapped his arm around his wife's massive shoulders and gave her a gentle squeeze. The gesture conveyed both understanding and forgiveness for what she had done. Tatiyana still saw a single, solitary tear roll down the woman's left jowl, and could only guess at the torment gnawing at her.

It had all happened very fast.

Tatiyana came to in the courtyard, coughing and sputtering, and the first thing she saw were the stars in the night sky. She rolled onto her side and retched for several long minutes as her lungs cleared of soot and grime. Only then did she begin to feel somewhat better and to get a vague sense of what had happened.

"It's really not very nice to keep secrets from your own blood, *brother*," someone said with a sarcastic laugh. "And there's *two* of them. And me there thinking there was only one goose laying the golden egg."

Tatiyana sat up and her head immediately began to spin. The dizziness passed after a moment and she was able to look over her shoulder at the man who had spoken.

Bronimir had arrived unexpectedly two days earlier, shortly after his confrontation with his brother at the market. Luckily, Adriana and Tatiyana had both been in the barn at the time, which had allowed Vanda to come hurriedly shove them into the secret space that would become their home for the foreseeable future.

Vanda and Lechoslaw tried to get rid of him, telling him Adriana had left the day before, and while he feigned to have no interest in her, he kept asking questions, subtle or otherwise, until it became very clear he would only leave once he had made absolutely certain she had indeed gone – and taken her money with her.

"Did you set the fire, you drunken sot?" Lechoslaw snarled.

Bronimir tried to dismiss him with a wave of the hand. "I did you a favor," he said indignantly. "With all the money these two have, we'll build ourselves a fucking palace."

Bronimir then wrung his hands expectantly as he stared at the two sisters. "Now which one of them has it on her? Let's start with this one."

He was almost salivating as he knelt next to an unconscious Adriana and began rifling through her pockets. Tatiyana moved to defend her helpless sister but Lechoslaw beat her to it.

"Leave her alone!" the old farmer shouted.

He grabbed his brother by the shoulders and tried to pull him off Adriana. But his injured leg betrayed him, his ankle twisted and he fell back with a cry. Bronimir immediately rounded on him.

"You think you can have it all," he said coldly as he stood over his brother with fists clenched by his sides. "The farm, the land... And now their money? Well *I* want it and *I'll* have it. Why should *you* have everything and *me* live like a pauper?"

"You live like a pauper because you're a dirty *pijak* who hasn't worked a single day in his entire life," Lechoslaw retorted angrily. His brother recoiled as if he'd been struck.

"I still owed you for this," Bronimir growled while gingerly fingering his puffy eye. "But now I owe you double for calling me that. And now I'm going to pay you back."

He was about to crush Lechoslaw's crotch under his boot when two meaty tentacles slithered around him from behind. The tentacles grabbed him in a bear hug and lifted him several inches off the ground.

"Let me go, you fat cow!" he howled.

Vanda squeezed harder. Bronimir tried to fight back, to somehow slip out of the woman's grasp, but to no avail. He was no match for an angry Vanda defending her mate. His eyes and tongue bulged out of his head as he began to suffocate.

Tatiyana wanted to tell Vanda to release him, knew she *had* to, but her mouth wouldn't open. All she could do was watch – mesmerized, transfixed, horrified - as Vanda slowly squeezed the life out of her brother-in-law.

Death was nothing new to her. She had seen the SS take countless lives, but somehow this felt... different. The Germans had killed out of malice and evil, nothing more. Here, tonight, Vanda killed because it had come to rest upon her shoulders to save them all. If she didn't silence Bronimir forever, he'd return the next day at the head of a drunken posse to claim the sisters' gold, and then there would be many dead instead of just one.

And then there was a loud, sinister crack – a whip cracking against bone, a rifle shot in the quiet of the forest, a thunderclap in the dark of the night - that seemed to echo endlessly through the silence. Bronimir's whole body shuddered before going as limp as a rag doll, and he died, his spine snapped like a twig.

When Vanda finally released him, he simply collapsed in place, like a puppet whose strings have been cut, and a deep, almost religious silence descended upon the courtyard.

Tatiyana crawled to him and pressed her fingers against his neck. She removed them after a few seconds and dropped her head.

Words were not necessary.

Three months later
Vienna, Austria

"Is this it, do you think?" Tatiyana demanded.

Adriana took another look around and sighed. All these cookie-cutter houses looked more or less identical, so it was near impossible to determine if they'd at long last found the right one. The last man they'd stopped had pointed in this general direction and muttered something about yellow flower boxes – well, if she wasn't exactly sure about the flower boxes, she'd definitely caught *gelb*, the German word for yellow.

"Have we finally found her?" Tatiyana asked again.

Adriana had known from the start it would be pointless to simply ask random strangers where they might find one Teresia Schlamelcher: the odds of encountering someone, anyone, who might know her were infinitesimal, and they'd be at it for weeks without any guarantee of success.

No. A more promising strategy might be to inquire where one might find the former home of one Mattias Traugott, formerly of the Hitler Youth. While there was absolutely nothing remarkable about him having joined the *Hitler Jugend* – it had been just about compulsory for young men to do so - , Adriana had gleaned from their various conversations that Traugott had been a somewhat prominent member of the organization in Vienna, so there had to be someone, somewhere, who would remember him.

But even that tactic did not at first yield the expected success.

"I give up. We'll never find her," a dispirited Tatiyana said at the end of the third day. "The city is immense and we don't even know if she's still alive. Hell, *we don't even know if we're looking for the right person!*"

The sisters had stopped to rest on a park bench after walking all day; they were tired and sweaty and hungry, and Adriana didn't respond. She couldn't fault Tatiyana for being cranky. Looking at the devastation around them, it seemed more than likely that Teresia Schlamelcher – if that was even her name – had been pulverized by an Allied bomb years ago.

They had only two clues, two names, one of which was totally unreliable. If they were sure of the first, Mattias Traugott, the second was a foreign name heard but twice – the last time shouted from a distance by a dying man in the midst of a furious firefight. Had Adriana heard it right?

They went first to City Hall but the building, like countless others, had been heavily damaged, and helping the sisters find "Mattias Traugott, son of Teresia Schlamelcher" wasn't exactly a top priority for the handful of bureaucrats who still bothered to show up for work.

"Look around you," one of them replied angrily. "The streets are gorged with refugees. One half of Vienna is looking for the other half. You think you're alone? Now that the war is over everybody is looking for their uncle or their cousin or their bloody kindergarten teacher, so please, I beg of you... *Just... go... away!*"

The city had been deeply traumatized by the war: its infrastructure was shattered, chaos reigned, and it would have rapidly imploded into an insane asylum without Allied and Russian troops to prop it up. What had once been the normal, logical way of doing things no longer applied, and everywhere they turned it was the same story: we have much bigger fish to fry, so expect no help here.

"We just need to rethink this," Adriana said after a moment. "We know he was in the Hitler Youth, so we need to start from there. We need to find someone who was also in the Hitler Youth and who might have known him back then."

"Every other teenage boy and his brother were in the Hitler Youth, so there has to be tens of thousands, millions, of them," Tatiyana said sarcastically. "That's no help."

Adriana ignored her tone.

"No, on the contrary," she went on. "I'm talking about those like Traugott who were really into the whole Hitler Youth thing, the fanatics, not those who joined because they had to or because it was expected of them. That has to narrow it down tremendously. What happened to those hard-core bastards once they outgrew the Hitler Youth?"

Tatiyana thought for a moment. "I guess they joined the Wehrmacht or the SS or some other thing," she said.

"Some other thing... like the police."

"Like the police", Tatiyana conceded after mulling it over for a moment.

Military police from the United States, France, the UK and the Soviet Union patrolled the streets of Vienna – they wore an armband showing the flags of all four countries - and maintained law and order as best they could. Adriana and Tatiyana had fruitlessly talked to many of them, but there were still "native" Viennese policemen around, and that was an avenue they had yet to explore.

The sisters headed for the nearest police station. The policeman on duty looked at them dubiously: he was clearly suspicious of these two disheveled women, with their hesitant German, who claimed to be seeking a "friend", a former member of the Hitler Youth who had later joined the SS.

"I know nothing of the Hitler Youth or the SS," the man lied.

Something new then dawned on Adriana: the war in Europe had ended in May - they'd been on the road after leaving the Napierkowskis and had celebrated Berlin's fall by drinking the last of Traugott's alcohol -, Germany and the Axis had been bombed back a hundred years, and now all those on the losing side would be at their wits' end to distance themselves from the atrocities of the war.

Me? No, I don't know anything about that. I was never part of anything. I don't recall anything. No one told me of any such thing. I was just doing my job. I was just following orders. You know how it is.

"I'll return in a moment," Adriana announced.

They exited the police station and Adriana re-entered a few minutes later, alone. She discretely placed a silver dollar from their hoard on the counter and slid it over to the policeman.

"Now, where might I find someone who, unlike you, might have once been a member of the Hitler Youth?"

The man looked at her with greed. "Don't even think about it, you pig," Adriana snarled in the rudimentary German she had picked up at Auschwitz. "My sister has the rest and she's gone. You'll never find her. So tell me."

The man thought about it for a moment, and then gave her the name of "someone he vaguely knew" at an other station, about two miles away.

Adriana had no way of knowing if the information was accurate, and there was nothing to stop the policeman following her until she rejoined Tatiyana to get his hands on the money he now knew they had, but she had to risk it; it was her only possible move.

The sun had almost set when Adriana and Tatiyana finally reached the second police station. Adriana looked over her shoulder one last time to check if the cop had followed them, but he was nowhere to be seen. She then feared he might have phoned ahead to warn his colleague of their imminent arrival, and to suggest that they be promptly arrested and searched, so she again went in alone. She left Tatiyana a few street corners away, after sternly warning her not to come looking for her if she failed to return.

She asked for the policeman by name and he was called, but he too seemed to be suffering from complete amnesia. His condition was however cured by the sight of another silver dollar, and he suddenly remembered having once known one Mattias Traugott who had lived not so very far from here.

Adriana once again went to find Tatiyana, making numerous detours and stops to make sure she wasn't being followed; by this time night had fallen and they decided to wait until the next morning before making their way to the street mentioned by the second policeman. Their chances of a decent welcome would probably be greater early in the day than in the middle of the night.

And now here they were, standing on this strange doorstep, as hesitant and timid as the world's oldest lost children.

"I mean is this even a good idea?" Tatiyana protested. "She's his *mother*, for the love of God. What are we supposed to tell her? What if she doesn't know anything of what he's done?"

Adriana didn't reply. While her mind might agree with her sister, her heart told her he wouldn't have sent them – her – here if it weren't safe for them to come. She couldn't imagine him seeking to entrap them from beyond the grave.

The sisters had taken their leave from Vanda and Lechoslaw some three months earlier, after helping them dispose of Bronimir's body. They dropped the corpse in a bomb crater somewhere in the forest, covered it with a thin layer of earth and leaves, and just left it there to rot.

As Lechoslaw had said, the woods were littered with dead bodies, and one more would make absolutely no difference.

They gave Vanda and her husband enough money to see them through at least until fall, in the event Lechoslaw wasn't as strong as he both felt and claimed. If Vanda would have none of it – she drew a cross in midair and said something about the money being cursed by its provenance, which the sisters were hard-pressed to dispute – in the end common sense prevailed; in other words, Lechoslaw took the money without telling his wife and placed it in a metal container he buried in the backyard... you know, just in case.

Then they hit the road again. Lechoslaw suggested they first head north to the city of Łódź, and from there north again to Płock on the Vistula River. He had a cousin in Płock, he said, who would help them catch a boat all the way to Gdańsk on the Baltic coast. And once in Gdańsk they would board a ship across the Baltic Sea to Sweden, a country that had remained neutral during the war and would presumably prove a safe haven.

It was a very interesting and exciting proposal – the prospect of finding shelter in a friendly country where no one would seek to harm them was quite enticing – but one that was also fraught with peril since it entailed traversing hundreds and hundreds of miles of foreign land, alone and, if not entirely helpless, then at least somewhat vulnerable.

They thanked Lechoslaw for his idea and then rejoined the dwindling train of refugees for a few days while they pondered their next destination. It eventually became clear that, as much as they might dislike it, they really had but one viable option open to them.

Adriana was about to remark that knocking on this door could do no harm – if they had the wrong house, perhaps the occupant could point them to the correct one – when she saw it: *T. Schlamelcher* painted in faded white letters across the middle of the small wooden door, and it all clicked into place. She shivered.

She grabbed Tatiyana's forearm and pointed at the barely legible name.

"We've found her," she simply stated.

This was the moment of truth: either they went for broke or they walked away. But walk away to go where?

Adriana took a deep breath and rang the doorbell but, anticlimactically, nothing happened. She pressed the button again, this time a bit more forcefully, and listened more closely for a chime, but still heard nothing. It was clearly defective, so she gave three sharp raps with the door knocker. Again, nothing. She counted to sixty, slowly, before knocking again.

Still no one came to the door, but the curtain behind the window to her right twitched slightly. Was it just a draft or was someone fearfully observing them?

An armored personnel carrier overloaded with Red soldiers rumbled behind them and slowed when the driver spotted two lonely women standing on the sidewalk. Adriana shuddered and tried to ignore them. The war might officially be over in Europe, but Vienna was still far from a safe city.

The Soviet 3rd Ukrainian Front entered Vienna on April 13th, 1945, after losing almost 20 000 men over a span of nearly two weeks. The soldiers immediately embarked upon a vengeful orgy of sexual violence and it would be weeks before Moscow, having finally had enough, decided – with very little success – to crack down on its soldiers' atrocities. Data compiled by the Austrian police later attributed over 90 percent of violent crime committed in 1946 to men in Soviet uniforms.

The personnel carrier came to a complete stop and the soldiers began shouting obscenities at the two sisters. A few grabbed their crotches or wiggled their tongues suggestively.

Adriana knocked again, this time with quite a bit more urgency. They had to get off the street.

"Please, fräulein Schlamelcher, open the door," she called out.

The door remained firmly shut. Perhaps the woman had moved? The house did appear somewhat decrepit, as though no one had maintained it in quite a while. Or perhaps she was home but didn't wish to involve herself in whatever was about to unfurl on the street. If she opened the door, the sex-crazed soldiers might just decide to take her as well, and not just these two strangers.

Two soldiers clumsily slid off the personnel carrier and stumbled toward Adriana and Tatiyana. They were completely drunk and had to lean on one another to remain upright. One of them shouted something the two sisters couldn't understand but that needed no translation.

"Please, fräulein Schlamelcher, your son Mattias sent us," Adriana pleaded. This time she pounded the door with her open hand, and the silent house echoed hollowly like a bass drum.

More soldiers jumped off the carrier to join their comrades. The men were laughing and back-slapping each other. The two women were trapped with nowhere to go and the soldiers were clearly enjoying the sport. If Teresia Schlamelcher didn't open the door in the next few seconds, they would be gang raped. There would be no miracle to save them this time.

"Please, fräulein Schlamelcher!" Adriana repeated desperately.

The soldiers were now less than twenty feet away.

Tatiyana turned to face them.

"Have your mothers taught you nothing?" she shouted in Russian at the advancing soldiers. The men froze, perplexed. "This is my daughter and you'll not touch her if I have anything to say about it."

Adriana sometimes forgot her sister looked at least twenty years older than her actual age; the past few years had not been kind to her and she'd aged prematurely. Once before, after they'd left the farm, she'd passed herself off as her mother to repulse would-be attackers. While the tactic had succeeded then, it was far from certain it would again today.

"Your mothers would curse the day they spread their thighs for your fathers if they knew the свинья their sons have become," Tatiyana shrieked. A few of the soldiers actually dropped their gazes shamefully, but several others seemed angered by her words.

Tatiyana's strategy might yet backfire.

Adriana had given up all hope Teresia Schlamelcher might open the door. Either the old woman wasn't home, or she was content to watch them get raped to death on her doorstep.

She pressed her back against the door and cast about for something, anything, she might use as a weapon. There was nothing, just an empty flower pot with which she might brain a single soldier, which would leave ten of them to contend with.

A man arriving from the opposite direction, on the other side of the street, stopped to watch the unfolding confrontation between Tatiyana and the soldiers. When Adriana caught his eye and silently begged him for help, the stranger first appeared startled, then ashamed; he quickly looked away and almost began to run.

Adriana cursed him and his cowardice to Hell.

"You lay one finger on my daughter and I'll rip your balls off one at a time," Tatiyana threatened. Her sister sounded genuinely angry but Adriana, who had known her forever, could also hear in her voice the echo of a bottomless terror that, hopefully, the soldiers could not.

A few of the soldiers threw up their hands and returned to the personnel carrier, having concluded there was no need to battle a banshee who looked fit to claw out their eyes, not in a city that was chock-full of easier prey. But several of their comrades refused to back down and stared defiantly at Tatiyana. One of them whispered something to the man next to him and they both grinned, their teeth stained black and brown with tobacco. Another snarled, wolf-like, and there was an evil glint in his eyes.

"*Wer ist da?*"

Adriana almost jumped out of her skin. A voice – disembodied and ethereal, the ghostly whimpering of a lost soul, the howling wind in a stormy night – demanding to know who goes there.

She spun around and slapped the door with her palm, a single, urgent stroke that conveyed both a desperate fear of imminent death and a desperate urge to live.

"Please, fräulein Schlamelcher!" she screamed, not caring who might hear. "Your son Mattias sent us. Mattias! Mattias! I beg you! Open the door before they kill us!"

Silence. She banged on the door again, with the same result as before. She pressed her ear against the door and listened closely, hoping for a sound, any sound, a sob, a breath, a hiccup, but heard nothing.

Perhaps there had been no voice. Perhaps her mind, derailed by fear, was playing tricks on her.

There was no one here, just her sister and the soldiers.

"Not one more step," Tatiyana growled in Russian. Adriana looked over her shoulder and her knees weakened when she saw the soldiers now less than twelve feet away and closing. Whatever apprehension had previously kept them at bay had now melted away and they were coming for their prize. The game was up, and there was nothing Tatiyana could say or do to stop them.

"*Hat Mattias noch leben?*" the voice demanded.

Oh Lord.

"*N... Nein,*" Adriana said after taking a deep breath. "*Es tut mir leid.* I'm very sorry, fräulein Schlamelcher. He died saving our lives, but before he did he sent us to find you. He promised you'd keep us safe."

That does it, Adriana thought. *There's no reason for her to open the door now that she knows he's dead. Perhaps if I had lied and told her we had a message from him...*

Then, miraculously, bolts were pulled, locks snapped and the door opened. But before Adriana could react and find refuge inside, a tiny woman, barely taller than Rita had been, rushed out of the house and came to stand between Tatiyana and the nearest soldier.

"Marshal Tolbukhin left this at my house last time he visited," she told the man in perfect Russian, her blazing sea-blue eyes boring holes through his skull. She then threw a richly-adorned cap at him. "Would you be so kind as to return it to him?"

The soldier fumbled the cap as though it were a red-hot coal and almost dropped it. Then he got a good look at it, his eyes grew wide and he looked up at Teresia Schlamelcher with a mixture of awe and terror. Half a minute later he and his comrades had vanished around the corner, leaving behind them nothing but the sour aftertaste of fear.

The three women just stood there, catching their breaths and not knowing what to say.

"What...? How...?" Adriana finally begun somewhat clumsily.

"She claimed to be a friend of marshal Tolbukhin," Tatiyana told her sister in German, since her Russian had allowed her to understand Teresia Schlamelcher's veiled threat.

"And who is marshal Tolbukhin?" Adriana asked, also in German.

Teresia Schlamelcher sighed. "Fyodor Ivanovich Tolbukhin is the supreme commander of the 3rd Ukrainian Front, to which these men belong," she said. "They might not fear God, and they might not fear us, but they most certainly live in mortal terror of Fyodor. And yet he's such a sweet man, so considerate. Not at all a brute like them."

Adriana was left momentarily speechless. "And you truly know him?"

Teresia smiled thinly without looking at her. "He left his hat at my house, did he not? Now tell me about my son."

Teresia Schlamelcher had fallen on hard times since Traugott's visit, almost two years earlier.

Her troubles began when Rosche Pflaumlocher, the famed Mrs P she'd hidden in her attic, caught a nasty cough and died after just a few days, leaving behind her two very distraught grandchildren, Renata and Benjamin.

Things might have turned out differently had Mrs P been considerate enough to expire on the first floor, preferably near the door. But as it were, she breathed her last up in the attic, as far removed from the street as one could possibly get.

Teresia Schlamelcher was in a bind. She had never envisioned that one of her guests might die and thus found herself completely unprepared now that it had happened. She could neither leave the body to rot where it was, nor ask anyone's help in getting rid of it. She'd need to get it at least down to the ground floor before figuring out her next step.

She somehow managed to get it down the narrow staircase that led down from the attic and, as the horrified children watched, dragged it toward the staircase that led downstairs.

And that's when everything went tragically wrong.

Mrs P was no longer the big-boned, jowly woman of her youth, but she still weighed a lot more than Teresia did – just about everyone did. So when Teresia tried holding the body by the wrists to slide it down the stairs, the laws of physics dictated but one possible outcome. Gravity suddenly asserted itself, Teresia lost her balance, and the momentum of the sliding body essentially catapulted her head over heels, over the body and down a dozen hardwood steps.

She hit her head on the way down, saw stars, and barely felt it when some 200 pounds of Rosche Pflaumlocher landed on top of her, knocking the wind out of her lungs. A second or an eternity later she became aware of crying children trying to disentangle two interlocked old ladies, one dead and their grandmother, the other alive but a stranger they barely knew.

Teresia regained some of her senses and tried to stand, but a sharp stab in her back made her cry out and she fell again. She could hardly breathe, her eyes filled with tears and her mind spun. She gasped a few times, trying to speak but paralyzed by pain.

The little boy, Benjamin, was crouched over his grandmother's body. He was slapping her cheeks, begging her to wake up in a voice heavy enough with sorrow and despair to pulverize granite. His sister, Renata, was standing just a few inches from Teresia's face, staring into her eyes and...

… and Teresia knew what the child would do before the child herself knew it, and she was helpless to stop it from happening.

"No... no.. don't...," she croaked feebly.

Renata bolted for the front door, unlocked it and ran into the street screaming as if all of Hell's demons were on her heels. The police were called, an investigation was launched and, because no one could disprove Teresia's claim to have met the deceased woman mere moments before her death, but mostly because someone somewhere somehow remembered that her son was an SS officer, the whole matter was covered up. The body was removed, the children taken away, and Teresia issued a stern warning to be more careful whom she let into her house – and to clean up that pigsty of an attic, before anyone began to wonder what was really going on up there.

The immediate impact was to deprive Teresia of the source of income that had allowed her, until then, to live a somewhat comfortable life by purchasing whatever she needed on the black market, usually at extortionate prices. Previously a man had come at the start of each month, asked to see Rosche Pflaumlocher and, upon finding her whole and healthy, left an envelope of cash behind before leaving silently.

The man didn't show up the next month, as if he'd somehow learned of the woman's death. He never returned.

"I heard him call out my name and when I looked back..."

Adriana paused and sighed as her eyes dropped to the china cup of hot water on the table in front of her. A meager slice of lemon (a luxury fit for a king!) they'd shared among the three of them floated in the yellowish water. Teresia apologized for not being able to offer them anything fancier, to which the sisters demurely replied that after three years of almost endless starvation at Auschwitz...

Teresia's eyebrows immediately shot up like rockets. "You came from Auschwitz?" she demanded, her interest as sudden as it was unexpected.

Adriana and Tatiyana exchanged a quick glance. "Not directly, no, but... Yes, we were there for many years," Adriana explained. "You... How... I mean, you know of it?"

Teresia pinched her lips before replying, as though she regretted her outburst of curiosity. "Well, I've heard rumors, nothing more," she explained. "Ty... I mean Mattias... That's where he was posted? At Auschwitz? That's how you came to know him?"

Teresia had blanched visibly, and it was clear she knew more about the death camp than she was letting on. This in itself was surprising, since the existence of such camps was by no means common knowledge at the time. Whatever the case may be, her interest was certainly not as innocuous or innocent as she might wish it to seem.

"When's the last time you saw Mat... your son?" Adriana asked. She still found uttering his first name nearly impossible. Human beings deserved names, SS monsters did not. They were just... monsters.

"He was here maybe two years ago," Teresia immediately replied. "I'm afraid we parted on less than cordial terms."

"And... did he tell you anything of what he did?" Tatiyana intervened.

Teresia thought for a moment before answering. "He told me he worked in a camp for prisoners of war," she said carefully. "He also referred to criminals who posed a threat to the Reich."

This last was welcomed with a silence of lead. "But you ladies are clearly neither prisoners of war nor criminals dangerous enough to topple the Reich," Teresia noted sharply.

When neither sister spoke, she looked straight at Adriana and said: "But I interrupted you earlier. Forgive me. Please continue."

Adriana stirred the water in her cup absentmindedly, trying to find the right words to describe what she'd seen.

"There's something you must absolutely know," she went on, side-stepping the hardest part. "He saved both our lives, and countless others as well. The two of us would not be here if not for him. My sister was in the... well, my sister was literally seconds away from death when he rescued her. And that's the brutal truth."

Adriana almost blurted out that Traugott had run into the gas chambers to save Tatiyana, but then she decided to hold back a bit.

Teresia sighed. "I know my son was no angel," she said. "His heart hardened after his father left us. He filled with a burning anger the Nazis exploited greedily."

Adriana could not deny her assessment, only temper it a bit. "Yes, there was a dark side to him," she conceded. "A dark, violent side. But he also risked his own life countless times to save me... to save us and others."

Another silence. "But for every one of you that he saved, how many did he kill?" Teresia asked without restraint. "Can you answer me that?"

"No, I cannot. But it must have been hundreds, thousands," Adriana finally said.

"And now he's dead?"

There was no avoiding the question this time.

"Yes," Adriana breathed. "He called out my name and when I looked back... I saw a Russian soldier plant his bayonet into his belly... Here..."

She pressed a hand against her own abdomen, just above the hip, to show where the blade had entered.

"But then... then he... I mean your son... yanked it out... I've never seen anything of the kind..." Adriana closed her eyes, reliving the scene in all its gory details. "He pulled the bayonet out, then he used that weapon to shoot the soldier holding him from behind, and then he shot the one in front of him... Then he stood for a second or two, and then he collapsed in the snow... And..."

Adriana fell silent. She couldn't go on. And what was there left to say anyway? She'd told Teresia all she could.

The silent stretched on for several long, uncomfortable moments.

"So he basically died with your name on his lips," Teresia finally said.

Adriana was gobsmacked. She'd never thought of it in this manner. In fact, with all that had happened over the last few months, she'd hardly had time to think of anything at all, except her immediate survival.

"Well, yes, I guess he did," she finally said. "But why would he send us to you? Do you know?"

Teresia nodded, as if this confirmed something that had, until then, remained in doubt. "Let me show you to the attic," she said. "You may stay as long as you need."

It would really have been a lot simpler if Teresia had lived just a little bit further west, on the other bank of the mighty Danube. Even a few blocks to the southwest would have done just fine.

No such luck.

In the waning days of the war, the Allied powers divided Vienna into five sectors – somewhat like what would later occur in Berlin, but without the massive historical repercussions that ensued. The Soviet Union, the United States, France and the United Kingdom would each govern a sector, while the fifth – the *Innere Stadt*, the heart of the city – would be occupied jointly by all four armies.

A document signed on 9 July 1945 thus granted the Soviet Union jurisdiction over five Viennese districts: Leopoldstadt, Floridsdorf, Wieden and Favoriten. The fifth, Brigittenau, was obviously where Teresia had her house.

Less than a mile to the west, on the other side of the *Donaukanal*, the United States ruled over the sector of Döbling, while further to the southwest was Alsergrund, also American territory. Everything else in the neighborhood – Leopoldstadt directly to the south and Floridsdorf to the east – belonged to the frigging Reds.

So, in other words, for lack of just a few streets Adriana and Tatiyana once again found themselves virtual prisoners, though this time of Teresia's home. Unable to go out neither during the day nor at night for fear of the roaming Russian soldiers they'd already encountered once, the sisters passed the time as best they could, playing cards or exchanging stories with their hostess, but mostly planning their next move.

"Where do you mean to go?" Teresia asked them one day, perhaps a month after their arrival.

Adriana exchanged a glance with her sister and shrugged. "We've discussed this many times," she said. "All we know is we can't go home. There's nothing left for us there. All we knew and had is certainly gone."

"After we left Auschwitz we just kept walking and walking and walking," Tatiyana went on. "We just followed the others, just followed the army, but we never gave much thought exactly to *where* we were going. Every step took us a bit further away from that *place*, and that was all that really mattered to us."

Teresia sighed. "Well you can't stay here forever, that's for sure," she said. "And I certainly don't mean to imply you've overstayed your welcome. I mean the future here is much too uncertain for you to bet your future on. The Red soldiers, now *they've* already overstayed their welcome, but will they ever go away? I have a feeling they could be around forever."

"They fought the Germans, in fact they bloody *annihilated* them," Tatiyana objected. "They can't be that bad. You know that old saying, the enemy of my enemy is my friend?"

Teresia stared at her gravely for a moment. "History will remember Josef Stalin as having been as bad, if not worse, as Adolf Hitler," she prophesied. "You mark my words. As long as his dogs are around..."

"We're stuck here," Adriana completed. Teresia nodded gravely.

"Then, if what you say is true, we need to get to an American sector," Tatiyana said. "From there we could probably go wherever we wanted in the West. Perhaps even to America itself."

Adriana narrowed her eyes at Teresia. "How easy, or difficult, is it to cross from one district to another?"

"I don't really know," the woman admitted. "This is all still quite new to me, to us, and I wouldn't be surprised if the rules changed daily. We'll have to go find out."

The damage inflicted upon the city by the Allied bombers, the retreating Germans and the advancing Soviets was hard to fathom. One couldn't go fifty paces without having to step over broken glass or shattered masonry. Every other building seemed to have sustained damage of some magnitude, but there was no pattern to it and that only testified to the capricious nature of war. One three-story building had been eviscerated by a bomb and its innards now lay exposed immodestly to gawkers; the one next door, for reasons known only to the gods, merely showed broken windows, like so many eyes blinded by the tip of a sword.

Three women walking the streets of such a wasteland should by no means have felt safe, and yet they did. Adriana and her sister had hardly been out of Teresia's house since their terrifying encounter with the Red soldiers about a month earlier, but today they were struck by how much things seemed to have changed over such a short span.

It wasn't anything specific they could have named, but a different feeling had definitely descended upon the city, as soothing as a cold cloth draped over a burn. The war was over and the people they met on the streets, while still mostly grim-faced and worried-looking, would also on occasion look up and smile and nod in greeting. A young man still dressed in his dirty, dusty work clothes even winked flirtatiously at Tatiyana, making her blush – something that would have been unthinkable just a few weeks ago.

Even the Russian soldiers they encountered seemed somehow... *saner*, was really the only word that came to mind. These were now clearly regular troops, professional soldiers blessed with more discipline and self-control and better officers to keep them in check. Would Adriana have felt safe coming across them in a remote alley after dark? Of course not. But at least now the demented, unwashed beasts that had formed the vanguard of the Red Army seemed to have gone off, probably in pursuit of the fleeing Germans.

Next to her the woman who had given birth to Mattias Traugott walked with her back straight and her head held high, as though the streets belonged to her, as though challenging any and all to come tell her to her face they did not. Whether that self-confidence was genuine or made-up, whether it came from something that glowed at the core of her soul or from her mysterious relationship with that fearsome marshal Tolbukhin, mattered not. All that mattered was the woman had about her an aura of defiance that was a bit contagious and Adriana caught herself returning the lusting stares of a few soldiers and actually making them look away in shame.

The feeling of power, of *fearlessness*, that gave her was somewhat intoxicating.

Thinking back over the past few years, Adriana was struck by the number of people Fate seemed to have placed in her path for the sole apparent purpose of keeping her safe: there had been Traugott, of course, but also Rita and Magrita and that saintly Doctor Ada and Sándor Pfircsik and Lechoslaw and Vanda and... and now this woman, Teresia Schlamelcher, the mother of the man who should have been her worst nightmare but whose love for her, instead, had made him keep her alive to see this day.

Oh sure, she had also encountered more than her share of monsters... Otto Möckel and fat Hiltrude and Mengele and even those women of the *weißköpfchen* who had looked out first and foremost for themselves... but over all there seemed to be far more names in the "Good" column than there were in the "Bad", and that probably spoke something to humanity as a whole.

They walked the streets for a couple of hours. Several churches, including the *Brigittakirche* and the *Allerheiligenkirche Zwischenbrücken*, had sustained heavy damage. Fleeing German troops had also blown up the Floridsdorf Bridge, but this was of little concern since it only meant Brigittenau was partly cut off from Floridsdorf, another Russian-controlled sector on the other bank of the mighty Danube.

No. Their salvation, if such a thing could be hoped for in this day and age, lay across the *Donaukanal* and into the heart of the American-controlled sector of Döbling. So they followed *Adalbert-Stiffer-Straße*, a major artery that slashed across the length of Brigittenau from the northeast to the southwest, all the way down to a small bridge that leaped over the narrow canal...

... only to discover that even this modest piece of real estate was guarded by a couple of hard-faced soldiers who seemed as likely to allow them across freely as they were to begin waltzing with one another.

The three women observed the scene for a few minutes, trying to get a sense of the situation, but the only person the soldiers interacted with was a 10-year-old boy on his bicycle whom they shooed away when the child tried to sell them a bottle of homemade liquor. Adriana thought the boy was lucky to get away with both his bike *and* his bottle, and she was about to suggest they turn back and try somewhere else when Teresia said: "I'll go talk to them. You stay here."

Before the sisters could react and protest, Teresia was across the street and walking determinedly toward the two soldiers, who reacted with visible alarm to her sudden approach. Adriana's heart skipped a beat when one of them swiftly leveled his weapon at Teresia, until his comrade just as swiftly pushed it down and barked something unintelligible at him. The first soldier grunted and lowered his rifle, reluctantly, but never took his eyes off Traugott's mother.

Teresia wisely chose to address the one who seemed the most sensible of the two – which meant the conversation lasted perhaps two minutes instead of being cut short after only thirty seconds. Teresia bowed respectfully, said a few words the sisters couldn't hear and pointed toward the other end of the bridge, where other soldiers, presumably American, also stood guard.

The Red soldier listened to her politely, but then shook his head and slashed the air with his open hand, in an unmistakable gesture of refusal. Teresia tried a different tack, the soldier's eyebrows shot up in surprise – Adriana suspected she had just played her hidden ace by invoking marshal Tolbukhin – but the effect was short-lived; the soldier shrugged, crossed his arm nonchalantly over his chest and again shook his head.

Then he said something that made his comrade laugh. Defeated, Teresia bowed again, thanked him for his time and walked back to the two sisters.

"You don't need me to tell you that didn't go well", she immediately announced.

"There's no way we're getting across that bridge?", Tatiyana asked.

Teresia shook his head. "No, you're not crossing the bridge", she said. "Only those with a special permit are allowed through. Fyodor would certainly get me one if I asked him, but..."

"But nothing", Adriana interrupted her. "You've already done more than enough. You may need more of his favors in the future, so let's save his help for when it's really needed. We'll just have to find some other way of reaching the American sector. Let's go check out the next bridge. We may have better luck."

"You won't", Teresia stated firmly.

Adriana had already begun to walk away, but now she stopped and turned around to look at the woman. "What are you saying?", she asked with a touch of irritation. "That we're stuck here forever?"

Teresia smiled thinly. "No, of course not, that's not what I'm saying at all", she said.

Adriana glanced at Tatiyana, who simply shrugged to indicate that she, too, wasn't quite following. It was only then that Adriana noticed the impish twinkle in Teresia's eye, and she recalled what the woman had said.

"You said we wouldn't have any luck crossing any of the *bridges*", Adriana repeated slowly. "You never said anything about the canal itself."

"No, I didn't", Teresia confirmed, and the twinkle gained new intensity.

"What are you two talking about?", Tatiyana demanded, still confused.

Adriana turned slightly to look at her sister. "All the bridges are heavily guarded and there's no getting across any of them", she began. "That leaves us with only one option, assuming we don't wish to spend the rest of our lives in Vienna with a Red boot pressed against our throat."

"Which we don't", Tatiyana said.

"Which we don't", Adriana repeated. "So how do we get to the other side if we can't use any of the bridges? We fly?"

Tatiyana made a face. "Of course not", she said. "All we could do is..." She stopped as the answer came to her. "You want us to bloody *swim*?"

"In fact it was his suggestion", Teresia intervened. She jerked her head slightly in the soldier's direction. "He told me if I wanted to go over to the other side, I'd have to swim. His friend seemed to think this was quite funny."

***

The water was bone-chillingly cold and their frozen fingers kept slipping off the improvised raft.

Behind them, on the Russian bank of the *Donaukanal* watching them go, Adriana could just about make out the ghost of Teresia Schlamelcher outlined darkly against the city lights. She had begged her to come with them but the woman had stubbornly refused, saying she was too old and would only slow them down. Adriana suspected she had simply not wanted to leave behind her home and all she knew.

The wind kicked up a small wave that splashed her face, momentarily blinding her. She wiped the water from her eyes and peered straight ahead, trying to pierce the darkness. Somewhere ahead of them, she knew, lay the American sector of Döbling, the starting point of what they hoped would be a new life – if they ever got there. The crossing had seemed relatively short with both feet safely planted on solid ground, but Adriana estimated they had now been in the water for some fifteen minutes and still she couldn't make out the other bank.

She began to shiver, both from the cold and from a sudden surge of worry.

Adriana kicked her legs harder, all the while being careful to avoid breaking the surface and remain as silent as possible. She could hear Tatiyana breathing hard next to her and placed her frozen hand over her sister's. Tatiyana had been secretly terrified by the prospect of spending so much time in the water, but she had concealed her fear behind a mask of iron determination and Adriana had pretended not to notice.

Tatiyana squeezed her hand back and they swam on.

For the thousandth time Adriana futilely wished they'd found another spot from which to launch their attempt. It was nearly suicidal to cross less than five hundred feet from the bridge the Red soldiers had refused to let them cross a month earlier, but the canal was much wider upriver, while downriver the current grew dangerously stronger. Adriana could guess the bridge's dark outline to her left, but nothing else. She couldn't tell if tonight the soldiers walked its length or remained stationary at their post. They'd seen them do both during the weeks they'd spent preparing their flight.

They'd also seen them occasionally and randomly sweep the canal with bright spotlights. For now the Cyclops slept, but the slightest noise risked awakening them. Adriana clenched her jaws shut to keep the filthy water out, but that made it hard to breathe and after a while she relented and cracked her lips open.

She pressed down gently on their raft and was relieved to find it hadn't much deflated. Assembling it from old rain suits held together with homemade glue and sealed with candle wax had been quite the challenge. Their first two prototypes had been unmitigated disasters, and only on the third try did they succeed in putting together some misshapen thing that would presumably keep them afloat during their crossing.

They'd hoped to be ready to go within a week, but reality obliterated that utopia and in the end it took them four times longer. They had first thought to buy whatever they needed on the black market with the rest of Traugott's loot, but eventually fear of attracting unwanted attention blocked that avenue; it was one thing to buy shriveled turnips at a farmer's market in the countryside, but quite another to source a rubber raft in a major city carved up by canals and a large river.

So in the end they spent over three weeks merely putting the raft together, and then they lost an additional week waiting for the first moonless night - which meant it was now early October, almost two months after their arrival in Vienna, and already there was an autumn chill in the air. Still, once the decision to flee had been made, there had been no turning back. As cold as the water was tonight, it would have been even colder another week from now, let alone a month.

Their clothes and what coins and precious stones they still had had been sealed in a pouch. The paper money they had given Teresia, knowing it risked being soaked and destroyed during their crossing. Tatiyana had looped around her chest a length of rope tied to the pouch, so that it now trailed about twelve feet behind her.

The pouch held all they possessed. If the rope broke, if the pouch floated away, they would lose everything – and whoever eventually found it would be in for one stroke of life-changing luck.

Adriana peered ahead again. Had they made any progress? Were they any closer to the American bank? How long had they been in the water? Twenty minutes? Twenty-five perhaps? It should not have taken them this long to cross to the other side. Perhaps they had underestimated the force of the current. Perhaps it was sweeping them sideways and perhaps they were traveling diagonally and not so much in a straight line.

She was getting tired and her muscles were beginning to cramp. The cold was also making it hard for her to concentrate and she kept losing her focus.

This could mean trouble.

She tried to imagine what their lives would be like a month or even a year from now. Tatiyana seemed determined to start afresh in the U.S. while she, personally, felt nothing but a deep, bitter resentment toward America. To Adriana that faraway land was the land of those shiny, mighty bombers blissfully overflying Auschwitz without dropping a single bomb. How many lives might have been spared if they had only obliterated the railway that led to the camp? How much suffering avoided if they had blasted the gas chambers to kingdom come?

But they had done nothing and so Adriana wasn't at all sure she wished for a future in selfish, cold-hearted America. She felt no compunction about swimming to Döbling and using the Americans to escape to a new life; as far as she was concerned, they *owed* her at least that much and probably a million times more too. But actually moving to the U.S. and living there? Yes, a quiet farmhouse somewhere in the Midwest with naughty kids and a loving husband and a dog and chickens scrabbling in the yard sounded very appealing - just not appealing enough. Could she then bear to part from her sister after so much time spent together? After all they'd been through? She might have to. Adriana felt as though she'd been on the run forever and she simply wanted to find somewhere to settle and just... rest, for a thousand years.

There was a sudden tug and Tatiyana's hand slipped from hers. Her sister's small yelp of shocked surprise turned into a sputtering choke when she immediately went under. Adriana had the presence of mind to hold on to their raft as she caught her sister with her other hand, pulling her head above the water.

Tatiyana was on the verge of panic. She grabbed Adriana as soon as she surfaced, threatening to submerge them both, but then one of her hands accidentally found the raft and she hung on to that instead, saving them both from drowning.

"What happened?" Adriana whispered.

"I... I don't know," Tatiyana replied after a moment. She was completely out of breath and

Adriana could hear the terror in her voice through her chattering teeth. "I'm stuck and I can't go anywhere. Something's holding me."

"Stuck?" Adriana repeated. She saw her sister nod nervously in the darkness.

How could she be stuck when there was nothing but water all around them? How could she be hung up on water?

"Try swimming with me," she whispered again.

Tatiyana kicked her legs but made no progress. Adriana then saw, gleaming above the waterline and stretched taut, the rope tied to the pouch.

She swore under her breath.

"What is it?" Tatiyana asked.

"Stay here and no matter what you do, don't let go of the bloody raft," was Adriana's sole reply.

Stay here? Where the hell was she supposed to go, exactly?

Adriana forced her numb fingers around the rope and followed it all the way back to the pouch. She found it had tangled around a jagged piece of metal that protruded perhaps four inches above the surface. She had no idea what it was – probably a sunken ship or a crashed aircraft - but their raft must have missed it by inches just seconds earlier. Had it instead impaled itself on the metal, it would have been all over for them in a matter of seconds.

She tried releasing the rope but it was a hopeless task. Her fingers were frozen, her muscles cramped, her entire body shook with cold, her brain was slowly shutting down and there was so much tension on the rope that she now began to fear the metal might slice through it and then their precious pouch would just float away and be lost forever.

She thought of swimming to Tatiyana and returning with both her sister and the raft, so as to lessen the tension on the rope, but bringing the only thing currently keeping them both afloat and alive nearer this razor-sharp, metal iceberg would have been suicidal. One wrong move, one sudden gust of wind, one treacherous wave, and that would be it.

Their idea to keep the raft and pouch separate, so as not to automatically lose one if they lost the other, had seemed very prudent at the time. Now it might cause their doom, and she cursed it.

She tried reeling Tatiyana in just enough to get the job done. It was much harder than she anticipated. Something very powerful was pulling Tatiyana and the raft *away* from her, keeping the rope stretched taut no matter what she did.

She yanked on the rope a bit harder, and then all Hell broke loose.

She heard a cry and immediately knew what had happened.

"Tatiyana!" she shouted as frantic splashing sounds erupted somewhere in the darkness ahead of her.

Her sister, surprised by the tug, had slipped off the raft and was now drowning. Never letting go of what was now her sister's lifeline, Adriana, a clumsy swimmer at best, raced in her direction as fast as she could, knowing she had mere seconds to save her.

She had almost reached Tatiyana when shouts of alarm arose from the bridge. Blinding daggers of light pierced the night and began sweeping back and forth across the water, seeking the source of the disturbance. Adriana finally grabbed a handful of Tatiyana's hair. She pulled her to the surface, choking and crying, and her sister began flailing wildly, once again threatening to drown them both.

A spotlight found them and there were more shouts from the bridge. The soldiers, had the sisters heard them, were ordering them to stay where they were – of all things – and threatening to shoot if they didn't comply.

Adriana somehow managed to spin her sister around, pressing her back to her chest. Their raft was gone and there was only one thing they could do if they wanted to live.

"Kick Tatiyana! Kick!" she shouted in her sister's ear. "Kick, kick, kick!"

Adriana grabbed the rope and, not minding the Red soldiers' orders, they began swimming back toward the piece of metal that was now the only thing keeping them from freedom. The spotlight followed them, more orders were shouted, but the sisters kept swimming.

The first shot rang out ten seconds later. Adriana actually saw the bullet plunge into the water not twenty feet from them, where a tiny watery geyser erupted. By now they had returned to the tangle and she was busy trying to undo it, though she could only use one hand since the other was needed to keep Tatiyana from sinking again.

There was a second shot, and then a third. That one struck much too close and the next one might prove lethal.

Adriana knew they were sitting ducks. If she could just get the rope untangled, then they'd just float away on the current, away from the shooting soldiers, and let Fate take them where it may.

A shriek pierced the night, followed by dozens upon dozens of small explosions and flashes of light in rapid succession. The Red soldiers, momentarily distracted, stopped firing at the sisters and turned their attention elsewhere.

"What... what was that?" Tatiyana gasped. "Are the Americans shooting at the Russians?"

"No. My guess would be mama Traugott," her sister said curtly.

So that's what was in the bloody bag, she then thought.

Teresia Schlamelcher had brought along a mysterious paper bag whose content she had refused to divulge. Having foreseen that a diversion might be needed to allow her friends to get away safely, she had secretly contacted her friend the marshal. Now, seeing the sisters about to be shot and killed, she put a match to the bag and with a shriek threw it at the Red soldiers. The firecrackers inside ignited, distracting the soldiers long enough for her to get away unscathed.

Hopefully Adriana and Tatiyana would now be able to do the same, for as of right now they were on their own and there was nothing more she could do for them.

"For the love of your God, Rita help me before we die here," Adriana grunted while yanking mightily at the stubborn rope.

And then, as if she had just recited some magical incantation, they were floating away, carried by the current out of the circle of light and back into the safety of the darkness. A few more bullets, fired in anger and frustration, whizzed by harmlessly, and then the night was quiet again.

They both hung on to the pouch for buoyancy and began kicking their legs again. Adriana got the feeling they were picking up speed but she was completely disoriented, beyond exhausted, and she had no idea where they were. She had to fight an overwhelming urge to sleep and every ounce of strength she had left she needed to keep Tatiyana clasped to her. If she gave in and dozed off, they would both drown.

But it was a losing battle. The cold sapped all her energy and she could swim no longer. Already she tottered between consciousness and unconsciousness and her head kept going half-under, the water rudely jolting her awake every time – until such time when, inevitably, she would not awaken and they would simply sink like stones to the bottom of the canal, at long last to rejoin all those who had gone before them.

"Gotcha!" a gruff voice suddenly barked behind them, and two strong hands grabbed her by the shoulders.

The two sisters let out simultaneous screams of surprise and terror.

"Come help me! There's two of 'em mermaids!" the gruff voice shouted with some alarm.

Feet splashed in the water, more hands grabbed them, and the women were yanked out of their watery grave and onto dry land. Blankets of warm wool were wrapped around them, someone clicked on a flashlight and the sisters found themselves surrounded by grinning American soldiers.

One of them thrust a metal flask at them.

"Welcome to freedom," the man said. "You ladies want a drink?"

PART FOUR

1

Vienna, May 1974

"Gee, where's my tie? The new one?," the man shouted from the upstairs bedroom.

The woman dropped her head and in mock exasperation winked at the child standing next to her.

"I swear my sweet one", she whispered conspiratorially, "if your father's head wasn't bolted onto his shoulders, some mornings he'd wake up and think to himself, 'Now, where did I leave that thing last night?'"

The child clasped her hands to her mouth and giggled silently, her eyes alive and sparkling in that manner that melted her mother's heart.

Gundula wiped her hands on her apron, leaving wide streaks of flour, and called in a loud voice: "It's where all your other ties are, Ty. Top middle drawer of your dresser."

There was a moment of silence as the man rummaged around for the wayward piece of clothing. "No, I don't see it. It's not... Oh wait there it is, I got it, never mind, thanks."

Gundula sighed again, rolled her eyes comically and the child giggled once more.

They had been married almost fifteen years now, and it was a good marriage – as good as any marriage could be, anyway.

The first few years after the war were hard on everyone, even more so since she found herself on the losing side of a fight she'd neither picked nor wanted, but she was lucky enough to somehow keep her job at the *biergarten*. The Germans went, but then the Americans and the Russians and the French and the Brits came, so the place did brisk business and she kept paying the rent.

And then a few years later, about twenty years ago, *he* returned.

Emaciated and weak as he was, freshly released from a Russian POW camp as he later explained it, she still immediately knew him. He collapsed more than he sat on a wooden bench, almost exactly in the same spot as ten years earlier, and she placed a large cool glass of foaming beer on the table in front of him.

His head appeared too large for his body and his muscles not nearly powerful enough to hold it up. Still, he looked up at her and the spark of life that flashed in his eyes the instant he saw her, slaying the deadness that had resided there a second earlier, sent shivers coursing through her own body, and she knew her life had just been flipped upside down.

"I didn't order this", he protested feebly.

She smiled at him. "No, but you would have sooner or later. I just saved you some time."

He looked around. "Where's my buddy Hermann?"

She sat down across from him. "A bomb fell on his house about a week before the war ended," she said. "Some say it was the last bomb to hit Vienna."

"Tough luck," he replied coldly, without looking at her. He took a sip of his cold beer and closed his eyes blissfully. Nothing had ever tasted this good before in the history of mankind.

"Speaking of tough luck, looks like you've seen your share," she went on.

He shrugged. "Nothing I didn't have coming," he simply stated. "We picked this fight, we lost, we had to pay. But some had it way, way worse, believe me. You don't want to know what I've seen."

"No, I probably don't".

They married five years later, the time it took him to return to what he considered reasonable health and find a job to support the two of them. It then took her a long, long time to become pregnant – a delay they attributed to his nasty wound and to the beatings and starvation he endured during his captivity. He still had nightmares about one drunken Russian guard who day after day, week after week, month after month, year after year stomped his testicles while two others held him down, his legs apart, defenseless and terrified. The guard, his deed done, would then laughingly gloat to his friends this was one German pig who would never again reproduce.

But in the end they proved the guard wrong. Just as the Soviets and the Americans were threatening to blow one another back into the Stone Age over a handful of missiles in Cuba, their daughter - their *wunderkind*, as they called her - was born. And while the world around them always felt to be teetering on the edge of a nuclear precipice (would the war in Vietnam ever end?), she became their refuge, their oasis; nothing could possibly harm the three of them, cuddling as they were on their tattered old couch, reading and re-reading the tales of *die Brüder Grimm* (*Cinderella* was her favorite, of course, though *Rumpelstiltskin* had recently climbed the charts) until she fell asleep and he carried her up to bed.

The war – the War - might have been officially over for almost thirty years, it certainly didn't *feel* over. You still had the Americans and the British and the French on one side, and someone else on the other – no longer the Germans, but the Russians and the Chinese; Brezhnev and Mao and bland old Gerald Ford might not be Hitlers, but what bloody difference did it make? They were still sons of bitches and still crazy enough to blow up the planet. Instead of fighting one huge, all-encompassing war, the world now fought dozens of smaller ones, and in each one burned a potential nuclear Armageddon.

Her husband came bounding down the stairs and she heard him stop and gasp at the bottom. When she turned her head to look at him, his hand was pressed against his lower abdomen and he was grimacing in pain.

She knew better than to say anything; there was nothing to say anyway. He had his good days and he had his bad days, and today was clearly a bad one. Still, he saw her – them – looking at him and he tried to smile, and she loved him for it.

"Just pulled a muscle," he told his daughter with a wink. She knew nothing of what he'd done *before*, let alone of what had been done to him, and they saw no need to tell her anything. He'd been a different man then, they both agreed, and that man had nothing to do with the husband and father he was today.

She was almost twelve now, and thus probably old enough to sense they were keeping something from her, but as long as she didn't challenge them, the lie survived and served as truth.

"Would you like some breakfast before you go?," Gundula offered.

He shook his head. "No, thank you. I don't have time. I'm already late."

He kissed them both and was out the door, limping slightly, before she could protest.

He took no notice of the two men who sat waiting for the bus across the street from his house. There was no reason why he should notice them; they were just two men reading a paper while waiting for the bus that would take them to work.

The men, however, took notice of him. They waited a few seconds, folded their papers neatly and calmly began following him.

Vienna, three weeks earlier

The rhythm of his soles pounding the pavement had a hypnotic, almost psychedelic quality that tended to make his mind go blank.

Well, no, *blank* isn't quite the right word. Rather, he would forget where he was, sometimes even *when* he was, and then his mind, set free of the chains that bound it to the here and the now, would fly away toward lands unknown, and he would go along for the ride, never quite knowing where the journey would take him.

These days he was but an anonymous salesman, walking mile upon mile in his itchy suit and cheap shoes, knocking on door after door to peddle his wares to silly housewives who smelled of home cooking, and while he was quite good at it, it really was nothing when compared to what he'd been *before*... In those days, yesterday and thirty years ago, Lord have mercy he'd been *someone*, someone of stature and standing, someone of might, someone with the power to order death or grant life with a simple nod... His uniform had made women swoon with desire and men shiver with terror, his word had been as the Word of God Himself, and he'd been part of a thousand-year plan to make the world a better place.

Yesterday and thirty years ago, that had been his life.

But then yesterday and thirty years ago, something went wrong. The Messiah turned into a Madman and the dream imploded into a nightmare. The Russians came on one side, the Americans came on the other, and the most powerful army the world had ever seen, the invincible Wehrmacht, was vanquished. It took mere months to erase what had taken ten years to accomplish, and just like that... it was over.

Then some half-breed Russian stuck his bayonet into him and almost a month later he awoke in a POW camp run by the cheerful men of the NKVD, weak and in pain and helpless but alive. And alive he somehow remained.

Sometimes, as he walked, his mind returned to those hellish days when pain and hunger had been the only constant, but mostly it returned to what he liked to think of as his glory days, those days when he'd been nothing short of a minor deity walking the Earth. And when it did a face always emerged from the darkness, the face of a woman he'd known, a woman with the voice of an angel and hair like a raven's wing, a woman who'd hated him as much as he'd loved her – a woman who troubled him still, all these years later, even though she was certainly dead by now.

And what cause did he have to be troubled anyhow? Gundula was an absolutely irreproachable wife and mother, loving and kind and caring and everything a man could possibly want, and then some. She had welcomed with open arms and an open heart that walking cadaver who'd stumbled into the *biergarten* and then waited patiently while he rebuilt his health. Then their daughter came along, the joy of his life, the very core of his existence, and now he was pushing fifty and it was for her that he got out of bed every morning.

So what cause indeed did he have to be troubled? Why this ghost from his past that had long overstayed its welcome? Why did he find himself at its mercy, unable to exorcise it out of his life once and for all? It was the only cloud over what was an otherwise sunny and enviable existence.

He shook such thoughts from his mind and smoothed his thinning hair with his hand. It was slick with sweat and perspiration made his shirt cling annoyingly to his back. He hated when this happened. Much of his success, and by the same token of his livelihood, depended on the first impression he made when the door opened. Things went much smoother when he looked spiffy and clean than when he looked like a disheveled hobo – in other words, when he looked like the man he'd once been... proud and magnetic and strong... rather than the feeble, stooped old man he'd become.

He fished a sheet of paper out of his pocket and read the first address. Forty houses today, eight hours minus a thirty-minute lunch... An average of eleven minutes per house to close the deal – hello-my-name-is-would-you-be-interested, no-thank-you-for-your-time, yes-please-sign-here-thank-you-someone-will-be-in-touch. Next house.

He'd been demoted from Lord of Life to Lord of Life Insurance and the fall from Mount Olympus had been savage. It was enough to make him want to blow his brains out. If only the Russian had stuck him an inch or two higher... *If the Russian had stuck me an inch or two higher, I wouldn't have Gundula and my daughter and I'd be a poorer man for it, so stop feeling sorry for yourself and just shut the fuck up about it already.*

He took a deep breath, smoothed his hair again and climbed three short steps to the front door. He rang the doorbell and fired his most radiant smile at the housewife who answered.

"*Guten Tag, mein Fräulein!,*" he began. "My name is Mattias Traugott. Would you be in need of some life insurance?"

Her hand shook so badly that she dropped the receiver on the cradle. Startled by the loud noise, her cat hissed menacingly and darted under the couch.

She paid it no attention.

Dare she make the call? What if she was wrong? What if she was right?

Maybe she should wait a bit, maybe a few days, to make up her mind about it. You know, just to be sure.

Like there was anything to be sure *of*. She *was* sure. She'd know that monster anywhere. He had, after all, saved her life. Her babies he'd killed, but her life he'd saved for the sake of winning her sister's heart.

She had simply not expected to ever see him again. Certainly not here, certainly not today, certainly not on her doorstep, offering – all of things – to sell her life insurance. *Life insurance! Him, who'd been in the business of dealing death on a daily basis!* How perfectly schizophrenic.

So why the hesitation? Did she feel, somewhere deep down, that she owed him something, that she had a debt to repay? Like hell she did. She wasn't her sister. That would certainly have been her attitude, but it wasn't hers. Her bleeding heart of a sister would have run back to try and save him all those years earlier, if she'd let her. Good thing she hadn't.

He'd been a Nazi and he had to pay. No, not *had been* a Nazi, *was* a Nazi. The cheap suit he wore nowadays mattered none; all that mattered was his soul, and his soul was dark and evil. She knew that for a fact. She'd seen it.

So what then? Fear. That's what it was. Fear - but not fear, not quite; more like a residue of fear, an echo, a shadow... a memory. She vividly remembered fearing him, so much so that the memory of that fear was in itself enough to scare her. Yes, as absurd as it might sound, she still feared him. A bear, even defanged and declawed, remains a powerful beast capable of killing with a single swipe of a massive paw. You fear such an animal not so much for what it is than for what it once was – what you fear is not the beast itself, but its very nature.

She went to the living room and poured herself an inch of dark rum. She added a couple of ice cubes, let it cool for a moment, and then downed it. That steadied her nerves, but the effect would be short-lived and she'd need another one before too long.

She picked up the receiver again and this time managed to dial the number she'd found. It rang and rang and rang and she was just about ready to hang up when someone finally picked up.

"Hello?," a man said.

She found that she couldn't speak.

"Hello?," the man said again.

Still she couldn't speak and a lengthy, heavy silence descended. At any moment, she knew, the man would hang up and she'd have to do it all over again – if she found the courage. But the *click* never came and the man remained on the line.

"It's alright to be afraid," he finally said. "It's even *normal* be afraid. Most people who contact us are so scared they're barely coherent."

That somehow gave her her voice.

"They are?," Tatiyana finally asked.

"They are," the man replied patiently. "It's not unusual to hear them vomit on the phone. I've had some walk into our offices and piss themselves. They're terrified, and with good reason. Monsters never die. They never lose their power to scare us shitless. But that doesn't mean we can't fight back, that we *shouldn't* fight back."

She didn't not say anything.

"So I'm guessing you've stumbled across one of *them*?," the man prompted her gently.

She began sobbing softly. "Yes," she said. "*He killed my babies!*"

"Tell me about it. I've got all day," he went on, and there was a note of eagerness in his voice Tatiyana found strangely thrilling.

So she told him about the life insurance salesman who'd rung her doorbell that morning.

Vienna, May 1974

"Mommy, why is Daddy not home yet?"

Gundula looked up from her plate at the child sitting across the table from her. The child stared back uncertainly, a mixture of fear and worry draped over her angelic features. Feeling her lower lip begin to quiver treacherously, Gundula quickly dropped her eyes before the tears flowed.

"Daddy's just running late," she lied. "He'll be home soon."

Then she blinked the tears away and forced herself to look up at her daughter again and smile. No matter the rat gnawing at her stomach, she had to be strong for both their sakes.

"Now eat your dinner," she said gently.

She dropped her eyes again and looked at the dismembered chicken that littered her plate. It looked as though someone had shoved a grenade up its feathery backside and pulled the pin. Breathing deeply, she reluctantly brought a small bite to her mouth, but it tasted and felt like rubber and she almost gagged. She downed it with a large swallow of beer.

Her daughter didn't seem to have much of an appetite tonight either. She couldn't blame her. The atmosphere inside the house was heavy and oppressive, and her stomach clenched at the mere thought of food. On the stove behind her was the skillet in which her husband's meal was keeping warm – a husband who should have been home two hours ago.

She got up and emptied her plate into the bin. She glimpsed outside the window, hoping to finally see him come walking down the street, but the street was empty.

The cuckoo clock chimed thirty minutes past seven. Gundula watched the colorful little bird do its dance before it retreated inside the clock, and that somehow made up her mind.

When the cuckoo returned to announce the arrival of the new day many hours from now, she'd phone the police to report her husband missing.

And if by chance the man returned before then, well good for him; she'd greet him with a smile and a hug and she'd take his coat and she'd ask him how his day went and she'd serve him his dinner like a good housewife, that's what she'd do.

But hopefully their daughter would have gone to bed by then, because she'd also brain him with the skillet.

Adriana sometimes wondered what had become of her sister.

She also wondered what would have become of the two of them, had it not been for that American soldier. Would things have turned out so very differently? She believed they might very well have.

It began less than 72 hours after they'd been plucked from the canal. That's when she first spotted Tatiyana on the arm of a massive, hulking black soldier. The man was by far the tallest, biggest human being Adriana had ever seen, and she wondered what kind of food they had in America to breed such giants.

No wonder the Americans had kicked Hitler's scrawny ass all the way back to Berlin if they had such monsters fighting for them.

In any case, the way Tatiyana stared up at this specific monster left no doubt as to her feelings.

They were a strange couple. Tatiyana, frail and thin and prematurely gray-haired, her bird-like hands incapable of encircling one massive bicep on a man who appeared strong enough to lift up a tank, neither one speaking the other's language. But Adriana was happy for her. Her sister had made clear her desire to start a new life in the United States, and if that man could help her reach that goal, well all the more power to her.

Her happiness soured the next day when she visited the nurse for her daily checkup.

"You may want to tell your sister to be wary of Big Abe," the nurse told her through an interpreter.

"Big Abe?"

"The soldier. Abraham. His parents named him after the President who abolished slavery. He's known as Big Abe for reasons that are surely obvious – and for others that are... *concealed*, shall we say," the nurse explained.

"Why should she be wary?"

The nurse shot her a look of pity that said, *Really? Are you seriously that naive?*

"You mean...?" Adriana asked after a moment.

The nurse nodded. "I should know," she said bitterly. "I was one of them."

Them?

"And so was I," the interpreter offered. The two women exchanged a look of feminine solidarity – and betrayal – that chilled Adriana's blood.

"Very... very well," Adriana thanked them. "I'll talk to Tatiyana."

She attempted to do so that very night. The conversation, if one should care to so qualify what passed between them, lasted about thirty seconds.

It also completely incinerated a relationship that, over the past few years, had withstood some of the worst of what mankind had to offer. In the face of apparent jealousy and betrayal, it was reduced to ashes to be dispersed by the coming storm.

There would be no phoenix-like rebirth this time.

"I don't believe a word of it," Tatiyana snapped angrily. "He's been nothing but kind and generous to me. He's even teaching me English. *Abe, you so big*. See? That means, Abe I love you."

Adriana sighed. "And why would he do that, do you think?"

That only intensified her sister's fury tenfold. "Oh, of course, how silly of me," she roared. "What could a man possibly see in me, right? I'm just a dried up old hag, a bag of bones really, a walking corpse, next to my gorgeous sister. How could a man possibly prefer *me* over *her*!"

"Oh God, Tatiyana, that's not what I meant and you know it. I'm just trying to..."

"I know *exactly* what you're trying to do," Tatiyana howled. "You're just jealous, and so are those two bitches who said all those nasty things about him. If I break up with him, maybe you all could have him, right? At Auschwitz, *you* had a protector, a benefactor, but now it's *my turn* and it's just driving you crazy, isn't it? Your precious Krumme is dead, I've got Abe, and now I'm in charge. The roles have been reversed and you just can't stand it, can you? Well, you know what, my beloved sister? I'm not giving Abe up, not for you, not for them, not for anyone, not for anything, and if you can't accept that, well you can just go fuck yourself."

Stunned speechless by such absurdity, Adriana could only stare agape at her sister, who mistook her silence for an admission of guilt.

Tatiyana didn't speak to her for almost a week. To make matters worse, by that time Abe, having presumably obtained what he desired, had lost all interest in Tatiyana, a situation the poor woman laid entirely at her sister's door.

One night soon thereafter Adriana returned to the tiny room they shared to discover her sister had left the American camp.

She never knew what became of her.

6

The men sneaked up behind him and almost caught him by surprise.

Almost.

He had the setting sun to his back and an elongated shadow stretched in front of him, monkeying his every move. Then he heard a small noise, no more than the quiet cough of a shoe scuffing against the pavement, and then there appeared on his right another shadow, and then one materialized on his left.

Traugott didn't know whose shadows these were, but that mattered not much at all. Those who mean you no harm hardly ever sneak up silently behind you.

Traugott's heartbeat quickened and his breath shortened. He flexed and unflexed the fingers of his free hand to loosen the joints, and a familiar surge of adrenaline made him grin. He had been in more fights than these strangers, whoever they were, could possibly imagine, and he'd always come out on top. More often than not battered and bruised and bloodied, but always alive, and today would be no different. Yes, he was older, and yes, he was a bit slower, but on this day losing likely meant not going home to his wife and daughter tonight – and that would more than make up for whatever that old bastard Father Time had taken from him.

So the fight was on. These guys just didn't know it yet.

The first shadow had appeared on his right, so logically the stranger closest to him had to be on that side. Traugott counted to three to lure the men in even closer before spinning suddenly in that direction, raising his suitcase as he did. Caught by surprise, the man instinctively raised his arm and tried to duck out of the way, but to no avail. The edge of the briefcase struck him square on the temple, filling his head with fireworks and knocking him into his companion.

The briefcase's handle snapped under the force of the impact and it flew out of Traugott's hand. It spun through the air a few times, like a flying saucer, and then exploded violently against the ground, vomiting its contents of contracts and receipts and forms into the wind.

The other man stumbled without falling. He recovered quickly and charged Traugott, who side-stepped the attack with admirable agility for a man his age. The former *untersturmführer* slammed his left fist into the side of the man's head, aiming for the jaw in the hope of scoring a knockout blow but instead striking the skull.

It was enough to shove the man sideways, but not nearly enough to put him out of action.

Traugott felt the bones of his hand explode into a million pieces and the pain reverberated all the way up his arm, through his shoulder and down his spine. He let out a roar of agony and fell to his knees, cradling his shattered hand against his body, but he immediately regained his feet. If he stayed down, he was dead.

His vision had blurred with tears of pain and his knees felt rubbery, but he began running. And he might have got away despite it all, had he not looked back over his shoulder to see if the man was giving chase.

He went three steps before a truck – or at least what felt like a truck - slammed into him sideways. He went flying and was catapulted into a flowering rosebush. The thorns lacerated his clothes and his skin as he fought to disentangle himself from its grasp, and he emerged bloody and disoriented.

The first man, the one he'd struck with his briefcase, had regained just enough of his senses to rejoin the fight. He'd blindsided Traugott, tackling him sideways like a rugby player to keep him from fleeing. But the man was still dazed and he was now down on one knee, perhaps ten feet away from Traugott, and shaking his head.

Traugott saw he had one ultimate chance to make his escape, but it wasn't to be. Just as he turned to flee, his shirt caught in one last thorn, and the second it took to rip it free changed his life forever. The second man grabbed him from behind in a bear hug, lifted him off his feet and slammed him to the ground. Traugott's broken hand howled in pain, the breath was knocked from his lungs, and he knew it was over.

He knew he had to keep fighting, he wanted to keep fighting, if he didn't he might never see his wife and child again, but he simply couldn't. They, whoever *they* were, had him.

Nothing happened for several seconds. The only sound was that of heavy breathing as all three of them fought for a second wind. Then the man who now lay on top of him got up on his knees - one on the ground, the other pressed against the small of his back - and handcuffed him, ignoring his hiss of pain when he twisted his arms behind his back

"Untersturmführer Mattias Traugott," the man breathed heavily. "You are under arrest for war crimes."

7

Georg Konrad Morgen narrowed his eyes at the picture on the desk in front of him and frowned.

Was this the same man? Was this the *right* man? Could it be, after all these years?

He propelled his mind back through time, he plowed aside thirty years of memories, and tried to conjure up the face of the man he'd then known as *untersturmführer* Mattias Traugott – a crook and bandit if there ever was one, but a crook and bandit who'd been clever enough to slip through his fingers back then.

He wouldn't let him slip away again.

This man denied being Mattias Traugott, but that was only to be expected. The identity he'd given, that of one Bruno Schmidt, was being verified and was certain to come up bogus. His fingerprints, if nothing else, would give him away sooner rather than later. The Nazis had been meticulous record keepers and much of their paperwork had survived the war. It was only a matter of tracking down the correct file.

The man in the picture resembled the Traugott Morgen remembered, but mostly in the way a father might resemble his son. This was a fatter, older, balder, grayer and more seasoned version of Mattias Traugott – and that, too, was only to be expected. Gone were the chiseled Aryan features and piercing eyes that had once radiated with fearsome intelligence. The outline of the jaw was softer, the jowls drooped a bit, and the hair had receded significantly, leaving behind a wide expanse of forehead.

The man staring back at him had suffered tremendously - it was etched all over his face, each line and wrinkle the echo of a different torture, rivulets carved in rock by a millennia of thunderstorms – but he wasn't defeated. There was still something in those eyes, something hard, something defiant, something untamed and reminiscent of a madness that had burned half of Europe to the ground thirty years earlier.

These were not the eyes of a man who would go willingly to the gallows. Rather, these were eyes that said, *Come after me, I dare you; I'll fight back with everything I've got. So come on fat man, let's waltz one last time.*

This man still had, somewhere in his life, something worth fighting for, even something worth dying for.

He pushed the picture away, removed his glasses and rubbed the bridge of his nose. If this man was indeed Mattias Traugott, as he suspected and as at least one semi-credible witness claimed, he'd know within a few days. Hunting down Nazis was as tiring work today as it had been back then. Well technically back then he'd hunted *corrupt* Nazis, not Nazis *per se*, but who cared about such minute distinctions three decades later.

His new bosses certainly didn't. He was good at what he did, and in the end that was all that really mattered.

The man formerly known as the Bloodhound Judge wisely surrendered to the Allies just as Berlin fell. He was briefly incarcerated, until it came to light that he'd prosecuted for murder not only Auschwitz commandant Rudolf Höss and Auschwitz Gestapo chief Maximilian Grabner, but also the commandants of several other concentration camps, including Dachau, Buchenwald and Majdanek. That earned him a certain begrudging respect from his captors, even more so when he forcefully argued – with some credibility, it turned out – that these prosecutions had really been launched to impede the mass exterminations ordered by Hitler. He was released after a few months and allowed to resume his legal career.

And there might have ended his path through History, some anonymous attorney in a second-rate Berlin law firm, had the Federal Prosecutor's Office not phoned a couple of years ago to inquire whether he'd have any interest in joining a new bureau tasked with tracking down fugitive Nazis. When at first he politely demurred and replied that those days were behind him, it was suggested to him – nicely, yet firmly – that he should consider the proposal very seriously for a few days, after which time he was certain to discover that he did *indeed* have a very great interest in joining this bureau.

So join it Konrad Morgen did, and two years on he still wasn't entirely sure how he felt about the work. He was being asked, after all, to send some of his former comrades to hang. But at the same time, thirty years later, he no longer burned with the Nazi fanaticism that had once prompted him to cull the flock of its most diseased members. He'd always thought that the thousand-year Reich need not be erected on a foundation of blood and suffering, and he'd frequently wondered whether the dream might not have become reality had it not been for the psychopathic brutality exhibited by some – including its founder.

Crimes he'd found at best repugnant at the time now appeared to him, once dissected under the microscope of history, completely appalling. And so in his mind there was a certain poetic justice to tracking down men like Mattias Traugott: if not for their corruption and barbarity perhaps, just perhaps, things might have turned out differently. He was using today's laws to repay them for their role in the abject failure of what might conceivably have been mankind's greatest achievement.

But these men were tenacious, and finding them – let alone punishing them – was exhausting work. Bruno Schmidt? Please. Was that really the best he could come up with? Why lie? Why delay the inevitable? How could they possibly hope to get away once caught? Who might save them now?

Problem was, the Nazis were not gone. Not even after thirty years, not really. After accepting, though reluctantly, his new position, Morgen had been stunned to come across dozens of his former colleagues now working and living openly, as if nothing had ever happened. The Interior Ministry teemed with former Nazi storm troopers or members of the SS, including many in positions of leadership. Countless others were employed by the Justice Ministry, and thus in a perfect position to obstruct any investigation.

And these were but the Nazis he knew of. There were also persistent rumors of shadowy, underground networks of former Nazis. Did they really exist? Possibly. Probably. And if they did not exist, how could one account for the fact that monsters such as Josef Mengele remained at large, or that Adolf Eichmann evaded justice for years after the war? Someone, somewhere, had to be helping them, protecting them, hiding them.

If such networks were not real, why had Konrad Morgen's wife found a rat hung by the neck on a tree in their yard just a few months after he'd taken up his new position? The message had been clear: rats would be exterminated today just as the Jews had been back then. So he purchased a small handgun the next day and constantly kept it in his pocket, ready to fire.

Would anyone now intervene to save Mattias Traugott? Time would tell.

One thing he already knew for certain: if a small handgun might suffice to stop an assailant in a darkened alley, a much, much bigger gun would be needed to send Mattias Traugott to his fate. In fact, he'd need a cannon.

And he knew just which cannon he needed.

Except the cannon he had in mind wouldn't fire.

"With all due respect, herr Morgen, you can just *go... to... hell*," Adriana snarled. She hammered the last three words as hard as she could, like so many punches thrown at his fat stomach.

Konrad Morgen winced as if she'd slapped him.

Adriana was too distracted to notice his reaction. She was torn between fear and rage, between panic and stupefaction. How did this ghost from her past come to be here, in her living room, propelling her 30 years back to a life she'd believed and hoped dead and buried?

This could not be happening. This was not her life, not any longer, not anymore. Once already she'd found herself enmeshed in the web of these men's intrigues, at a time when she'd had no say in the matter. But today she did have a say.

"Fräulein Zobël, please hear me out," Konrad Morgen said with all the patience he could muster. "I do not think you fully appreciate the complexity and the gravity of..."

She raised a hand to silence him.

"On the contrary, herr Morgen," she said coldly. "I appreciate only too well the complexity and the gravity of the situation, as you were about to say, and that it precisely why I want absolutely no part of it whatsoever."

The light that then flashed in her eyes reminded him of lightning jumping through black storm clouds on the horizon. It forewarned him of more vicious blows to come, and Morgen braced himself.

"And before you add anything else, tell me," she went on, her voice dripping with frost. "Does it burn your tongue like acid to address me as *fräulein Zobël*? Not so very long ago, in your eyes and those of your ilk, I was merely a number... nay, I was *barely* a number... and certainly not a human being deserving of a name!"

Morgen could only drop his eyes and stare at the tip of his shoes. What purpose would it serve to argue with this woman? To try and convince her that he had never fully endorsed the Nazi ideology? That he had always been, at best, a reluctant actor in the Führer's insane play? She'd seen him at the height of his power and she knew better. Such lies and half-truths would only lead to more futile discussions.

"And how in the hell did you even find me?" she demanded angrily.

Morgen just shrugged, as if her question wasn't even worthy of a response.

Adriana spent six weeks searching fruitlessly for Tatiyana, but it was as though her sister had fallen off the edge of the world. And she would have kept searching had the Americans not-so-subtly nudged her off their base to make room for newer refugees.

She used the last of Traugott's money to rent a small flat in Vienna, not really because she intended to settle there permanently, but because she had nowhere else to go – and because she was loath to leave the city where she'd lost her last known relative, figuring this was still the place where she had the best chance of eventually picking up her trail.

But then Traugott's money began to ran out and life took over. She found a job at a Jewish bookstore, unavoidably ended up marrying the Jewish bookseller, and they had two children together, now both grown and living their own lives, her son in America and her daughter in Israel. She often thought of moving to be closer to at least one of them, especially since the premature death of her husband two years earlier, but rather than risk hurting one by choosing the other's country, she stayed put.

Having said that, her daughter's engagement and the distinct possibility of grandchildren on that front in the near future had recently rendered moving to Israel very attractive, even more so considering that her son rarely mentioned the same girlfriend twice when they spoke on the phone.

She now wondered whether Morgen would have been able to track her down if she'd packed her bags six months ago.

"But I'll tell you what, herr Morgen," Adriana went on in a tone that chilled his blood. "I'll make you a deal. Tell me what that number was, the number you Nazi monsters gave me, and I'll agree to help you out."

The silence that followed lasted perhaps ten seconds, but to Konrad Morgen it felt like an entire ice age. He glanced involuntarily at Adriana's left forearm, where he knew the number to be tattooed, but she had covered it with her right hand.

Adriana sighed and removed her hand. She thrust her forearm at him, the dark numbers clearly legible against her pale flesh. "That number was *neunzehnhunderteinundsiebzig*. I did not expect you to remember it, but as you can see, you made sure I'd never forget it."

Morgen was being trounced and he could feel his anger rising. Who did she think she was, to oppose him in such a fashion? Either she bent to his will, or he'd flatten her under the weight of the law he represented.

Or perhaps he better not. This woman, he knew from past experience, was intelligent and fearsome, neither easily cowed nor intimidated, and he'd not win her to his side through threats and brute force. If he hadn't succeeded into scaring her into collaborating back then, he'd certainly not do so today.

He needed to find a different strategy, and quickly.

"There is really nothing useful I can say about those events that transpired thirty years ago," he began slowly. "Having said that, apologies are clearly owed and explanations, if you feel are needed, I will gladly and sincerely offer."

He paused to wait for her reaction, to see if she did indeed demand an apology or an explanation. When she remained silent, staring at him – or rather *through* him – with eyes that could have melted steel, Morgen fished an envelope out of his pocket and handed it to her.

"Very well, then," he said. "Would you at the very least please tell me if this is the man you once knew as untersturmführer Mattias Traugott?"

At first Adriana didn't, couldn't move. She just stared at the proffered envelope, seeing it suspended in midair between the two of them like a magic carpet, and she wouldn't touch it. If she took it, if she opened it, she knew there would be no turning back. She'd become part of this whole thing again, whatever *it* was, and it would certainly take her somewhere she did not wish to go.

Still, she took the envelope and opened it with trembling fingers. She pulled out a black and white picture and...

... and when she next opened her eyes, Morgen was staring at her with a very worried expression, shaking her knee and asking if she was quite alright.

"Yes... yes, I'm fine," she said after a few seconds. "What... what happened?"

He frowned. "I'm not certain," he said. "You pulled out the picture, you took a look at it, and then your eyes rolled up into your skull and you went limp and you seemed to slump in your seat. But it only lasted a few seconds and you came to almost immediately."

Adriana realized she was still holding the picture in one hand and the envelope in the other.

"Should I deduce from your reaction that this is indeed untersturmführer Mattias Traugott?," Morgen asked gently.

Was it?

Adriana took a deep breath and looked at the picture again.

Blood instantly roared in her ears and her vision dimmed. Her stomach clenched and bile rose in the back of her throat. She felt as if she were falling backward, and she risked toppling over into a bottomless abyss unless she quickly fastened herself to reality. So she slapped a hand on her knee and dug her fingernails into the flesh, the sharp pain anchoring her into the here and the now.

She handed him back the picture.

"It's him," she said curtly. Were it not for Morgen being here with her, she'd run into the bathroom to cleanse her hands with bleach and a steel brush. Or perhaps scorch the skin off with a blowtorch.

"Are you certain?"

She stared at him with undisguised contempt and the sneer in her voice was unmistakable as she replied: "I am. You're not?"

Morgen sighed. "We are certain *enough*," he admitted. "He gave us a false identity and it's proving somewhat more complicated than I anticipated to unravel everything. Every thread we pull seems only to tighten the knot."

Adriana did not miss a beat before kicking him in the balls. "It's almost as though someone is protecting him, isn't it?"

Morgen was stunned. "How would you know...," he began, before stopping and starting again. "I mean, if you know anything about anyone interfering with the due course of justice by protecting criminals, perhaps it would be wise to..."

"Herr Morgen, you can't even begin to fathom how many of *your* people exited the war obscenely rich at *my* people's expense," she snickered. "And some of these leeches can trace their fortunes directly back to Mattias Traugott, and they're still out there, dining freely on champagne and caviar every night, and the last thing they want is for him to be questioned by the likes of you, just in case he should decide to name names."

"And do you know who these people are? Because, if you do, I would..."

"You've had all the help you'll get from me," she interrupted him. She wasn't about to share anything more with this man. If he knew nothing of the vast Jewish networks that had coalesced after the war, of the intelligence they gathered and the files they compiled and the men they tracked, then all the better. Let him sort the rest out for himself, if he could.

Morgen feigned to not have heard her last comment.

"Fräulein Zobël, please realize that, as strange as it may sound, you and I find ourselves on the same side today," he said. "I want nothing more than to bring this individual, *these individuals*, to justice. And while I would never presume to know what lies in your heart or your mind, I am sure you yearn for the same. I am not motivated by vengeance or by decades-old grudges, solely by justice."

That struck home and gave Adriana pause. Did she wish to see Mattias Traugott brought to justice? Truth was, she did not know. But then again she was not being asked whether he deserved to answer for his crimes – for he most certainly did - , but whether she wished to play any part in it. Perhaps it wasn't up to her to decide whether he ever ended up before a judge.

She glanced at the painting hanging on the wall above Morgen's head. It showed Pontius Pilate washing his hands of Jesus' fate. It was a very bad painting by an unknown artist of extremely limited talent, but she'd purchased it a flea market a few years ago as a constant reminder that God had washed His hands of the Jews' fate during the war.

Now the scene it depicted took on a different meaning.

"How did you find him?," she asked.

Morgen stared at her for an instant, visibly ill at ease. "Well, that's a bit problematic," he began tentatively. "Someone recognized him and phoned Simon Wiesenthal's organization and they passed the information on to us and..."

She immediately sensed that he wasn't being entirely truthful and transparent.

"Why would it be problematic for *someone* to recognize him and phone Simon?"

She secretly hoped he'd notice that she was on a first-name basis with Simon Wiesenthal. Let him take a quick peek behind the curtains and see that she was no longer alone.

"We are not entirely certain that this person is trustworthy," Morgen said, still trying to skirt around the issue. "We need someone to corroborate what she says."

Adriana snorted impatiently. "Who is this person that you are so desperately trying to avoid naming, herr Morgen?"

Morgen stared at her flatly for a moment longer than was necessary. It was his turn to kick her in the nether regions, and he relished the opportunity.

"When did you last speak to your sister Tatiyana, fräulein Zobël?"

And to think all these years they'd lived less than two miles apart.

Two stupid, silly miles. They'd walked five, six, seven times that distance, day after day after day, when the flow of refugees had carried them to their destiny thirty years ago.

Two miles. And yet, not once had they crossed on the street, or bumped into one another on the bus, or encountered by chance at the grocer or the dentist or the florist. One might as well have lived on the other side of the Moon and the other at the bottom of the Mariana Trench.

Adriana's heart was pounding and she was sweating despite the chilly weather.

She had walked out into a fine drizzle earlier that morning, as determined and eager as she was nervous and scared. She glanced down at herself and hoped she didn't look overly silly just standing there in her yellow raincoat and matching rubber boots. Perhaps she should have waited for nicer weather.

Right. Nicer weather. That had to be the key to the success of her endeavor this morning. If only she'd worn leather shoes! That would have assured her of success, while these rubber boots guaranteed failure. How very likely that was.

She still wondered why Morgen had shared the address with her. Surely that type of information had to be confidential or something.

But she'd asked, and he'd told her, so here she was.

Perhaps he was manipulating her. Perhaps he'd always intended to tell her. Perhaps that had been the true purpose of his visit the day before. Perhaps he'd dangled his mysterious *informer* before her nose willfully, hoping she'd rise to the bait, which she had. Perhaps her being here this morning somehow served his purpose. But if it did, she couldn't figure the how or the why of it, so the hell with that train of thought. She had better things to do than decipher Konrad Morgen's machinations.

She took a deep breath and rang the doorbell.

Rita, Aaron, Margrita, wherever you are, please, please help me, she prayed under her breath.

She jumped when the door opened almost immediately, almost as if whoever lived here had been watching her – and waiting for a chance to pounce.

"I wasn't sure you'd ever work up the courage to ring," Tatiyana said.

Adriana was left momentarily speechless. She hadn't seen her sister in thirty years, but this woman – this hag of a witch - now staring her down, daring her to look away, looked one hundred years older than she recalled.

In her mind Adriana relived Tatiyana's arrival at Auschwitz three decades ago. She couldn't believe how much her sister had aged then, and she could even less believe how much she'd aged now.

Perhaps they'd sat next to one another on the bus after all. She'd never have known.

"I wasn't sure I would either," Adriana finally said. "How long have you been observing me?"

"Long enough."

Long enough? Long enough for what? To decide whether or not you'd answer if I rang? Does that mean you're willing to talk? Or long enough to make up your mind to tell me to go to hell one more time?

Tatiyana stood in the doorway with arms folded across a very flat chest, the passage of time having robbed her of what little breasts she'd once had. She didn't invite her sister in, but neither did she shoo her away. Adriana was undeterred by this frigid reception. She had things to say, questions to ask, and unless Tatiyana slammed the door in her face, that's exactly what she meant to do.

So there they stood like two gunslingers in a windblown town, each impassively waiting for the other to draw first.

A gust of wind broke the stalemate. Adriana winced when thousands of tiny droplets suddenly stung her face and Tatiyana took a step back. Then her sister turned her back to her and disappeared into her apartment, leaving the door ajar - neither opened nor closed, neither welcoming nor threatening, neither a hand extended in friendship nor a fist closed in menace.

As if to say, *So what will it be, sweet sister? Will you dare enter and face whatever dangers may lurk inside?*

Adriana hesitated for less than a second before following her in.

The chill in her flesh yielded to a chill in her soul.

Adriana slowly and reluctantly closed the door behind her. It clicked softly, the lid of a coffin slamming shut, and she shivered. What if it locked and she remained trapped here, forever sealed inside this ancient tomb?

Entering made the soul shrivel and the flesh recoil. Raiders desecrating the final resting place of some long-dead barbarian king surely felt the same dread and the same sense of foreboding that now assailed Adriana. A vestigial part of the primal reptilian brain, one that has evolved solely to warn of imminent mortal danger – a saber-tooth tiger lurking in a tree, a gust of wind before the funnel forms, a man on the subway wearing a heavy coat despite the heat - now began to howl and scream, unreasoned and uncontrolled, the urge to flee all but impossible to resist.

Tatiyana's flat didn't feel of death as much as it felt of... lack of life. Her sister lived here, that much couldn't be denied, but the apartment might otherwise have been deserted ten years ago.

There were no pictures on the walls. Not a single one. In many places the old, faded wallpaper had begun to peel away like a leper's skin, exposing the pale flesh underneath.

All along the baseboard, unavoidably in such a place, were what looked suspiciously like rodent droppings.

On a small table in a corner of the hallway rested an empty bird cage – except that it was not so much empty as it was currently vacant. Looking more closely, Adriana spotted the abandoned, dessicated remains of what must have been its last tenant amid the yellowed newspaper shreds that covered the bottom.

It was doubtful her sister had taken notice of her pet's death.

Or of the fact that the tiny carcass had been gnawed on, presumably by the source of the aforementioned droppings.

From that point the hallway angled to the left and disappeared into darkness, presumably toward the kitchen. The air, stale and ancient and dusty, also smelled of something slightly spicy – spicy and rotten.

Adriana cared not one whit to track down the source of the odor. She had seen enough. She wanted to speak to her sister and then be on her way as soon as possible.

"I'm in here, don't be afraid," Tatiyana called from a room to the right, in a tone meant to be either mocking or taunting.

A faint, wavering glow framed the doorway that opened onto that room. Intrigued, Adriana took a few careful steps, the feeling of being somewhere she didn't belong and the need to flee stronger than ever, and the scene she witnessed on the other side soon made her wish she had heeded the urge.

Her sister knelt on a large cushion in the center of the floor, hands resting on bent knees and head slightly tilted up. She wore a dress so faded and threadbare as to be almost translucent. Her eyes were half-closed and she seemed to be swaying slightly, as though she were in a trance.

Up the wall across from Tatiyana rose two massive candle-holders, each supporting a towering candle at least four feet tall, bathing the room in a soft, yellowish light.

The candles flanked a gigantic painting, and it was that painting that made Adriana's mind reel.

It showed a massively muscled black man with a tiny, gray-haired woman on his arm. The man also had a girl who seemed to be about eight by the hand, while the woman clutched a baby to her breast.

"Oh my God, Tatiyana...," Adriana murmured.

"We make a nice family, don't we?," her sister replied. "Now look closely behind him. On that hill, over his right shoulder."

Adriana narrowed her eyes and grabbed the wall for support when her knees weakened: there were three crosses atop that hill, an instantly recognizable biblical scene of murder and torture, and she didn't need to step any closer to know who had been crucified onto the middle one. She could see the SS uniform from where she stood.

"I know why you're here, sweet sister, and you'll not talk me out of it," Tatiyana said in a voice that came from a thousand miles away. "Your beloved *Krumme* will burn in hell, of that you can rest assured."

Adriana wanted to stay and argue, knew she *had* to, but this time her reptilian brain wouldn't be denied: she spun around and fled down the hallway.

She fought the doorknob for a second, her sweaty hands slippery against the metal, and for the briefest instant she feared she might indeed remain trapped here until the end of times.

But then the doorknob turned, the door mercifully opened and she escaped running into the rain.

Behind her, unheard and unheeded, her sister began to cackle like the madwoman she'd become.

10

Mattias Traugott lay on his bunk with his right hand behind his head, staring drowsily at the ceiling of his cell, his throbbing left hand in its cast his only distraction, wondering why no one else had seemingly noticed that time now stood still.

He'd sometimes heard, during his previous sojourn on Earth as a minor deity, those in his charge affirm that time had lost all meaning. Seconds and minutes and hours and days and weeks and months, nights and days, mornings and evenings, even summers and winters, if they were to be believed, had all melded into one gray, shapeless blob of indistinguishable features. Today might as well have been yesterday and yesterday might as well have been tomorrow, for all the difference it made in their lives.

Time, it had been revealed to them, is an invention of Man, an artificial construct meant to give shape and structure to something that, by its very nature, is devoid of both.

If he'd not quite understood what they meant back then, he most certainly did now. His last visit had been five days earlier. Or at least he thought it had been five days ago. Perhaps it had only been yesterday. Or the day before. But it had most definitely been Gundula, without their daughter, and she'd not been happy.

"You've not been truthful," she immediately accused him.

Not *I'm glad to see you* or *I was so worried* or *How are they treating you?* or *How's your broken hand?* or even *Do you know when you might get out?* No. Just plain, *You lied, asshole.*

"You knew I did bad things during the war," he shot back. "You've *always* known."

She fired a double-barrel shotgun blast of air from her nostrils, as she always did when she was most upset and getting ready to rip his head from his shoulders, and suddenly he was grateful for the steel bars that kept him out of her reach.

"Hardly anybody survived the war without doing *bad things*," she said.

He wanted to ask whether this statement applied to her as well, but then thought better of it and instead sucked in his cheeks. But she still read his mind and the flames of anger that already burned in her eyes flared even hotter.

"If all those who did *bad things* during the war were in jail today, then you'd have five new friends keeping you warm at night in there", she snarled. "But since you're all alone, it looks to me like those who are in jail are solely those who did *really, really bad things*."

And what was there to reply to such a thing? On a couple of occasions she'd asked about his role in the war, and he'd answered as truthfully but also as vaguely as possible, until there emerged between them an unspoken agreement that he didn't want to say anymore than she wanted to know, so the topic died and they buried it in an unmarked grave in their backyard.

And there it lay, undisturbed and forgotten, until a very large rodent named Konrad Morgen trotted along and dug up the putrefying corpse.

"Has Morgen been to see you?," he asked.

She nodded. "He has. Who is he? Who *was* he?"

Again, he answered both truthfully and vaguely. "Who he *is* I'm not entirely certain. Who he *was* is someone I'd hoped to never hear from again."

She snorted at his sibylline explanation. "And what does he want with you?"

He chose to ignore the question. "What did you tell him?"

"Nothing. I didn't like the looks of him, so I sent him on his way. He had no power to compel me to tell him anything, so I told him to bugger off."

That both comforted and distressed him, as did the fact that he had languished here for how-many-days-had-it-been-now without anything happening.

He need not be told some people, the same people who had provided him with his new identity, were working very hard behind the scenes to yank him out of Morgen's claws. Since he remained in jail still, perhaps these people were not encountering the hoped-for success; on the other hand, perhaps they were, since he also had yet to face any charges.

Had she answered Morgen's questions, Gundula might have unwittingly torpedoed their efforts – if only by telling him that she had most certainly not married anyone named *Bruno Schmidt*. On the other hand, sparring with the man might also have allowed her to find out, exactly, what he both knew and didn't know, and most importantly what he still wanted with him after thirty years.

"You have a visitor, herr Schmidt," a guard announced loudly, snapping him out of his reverie.

As though summoned from the darkest recesses of his past by his very thoughts, a fat man waddled in, grabbed a wooden chair and sat in front of his cell, well out of harm's way.

Traugott glanced at the newcomer out of the corner of his eye and then fought to keep all emotion and reactions from his face. He forced himself to keep staring at the ceiling, but inside he groaned and his heartbeat quickened.

"Do you know who I am, herr Traugott?," the fat man asked.

Traugott waited a full thirty seconds before answering. "You have the wrong man. My name is Bruno Schmidt."

"Please drop the charade, herr Traugott", the fat man said. He threw up his hands and slapped them down on his meaty thighs. "It is all quite futile, I assure you. Those papers you have, well... they'll only shield you for so long."

"And beside, we have confirmation of your identity. Your true identity, I mean."

That struck home, hard, but Traugott kept staring at the ceiling. Maybe, surely, the man was bluffing.

"So again, I ask you: do you remember me? Do you know who I am?"

Traugott recognized that question for the trap that it was. If he admitted to remembering his visitor, he might as well confess to everything they suspected, for how else would he know who this man was if he himself wasn't who they claimed him to be?

He glanced sideways at his visitor for a few seconds and then smirked when he returned his eyes to the ceiling.

"I don't remember you, but I still know you who you are," he said.

"I'm not sure I quite follow," the fat man said.

Traugott smirked again. "You're the motherless turd who put me in here for no good reason."

"Excuse me?"

Traugott swung his legs off to the floor and sat on his bunk across from his visitor, this time staring him full in the face.

"See, this is the story I heard about you," he began. "I'm told your mother was so ugly that your father couldn't fuck her face to face since that made his tiny wiener shrivel in fear. So all he could do was spin her around and fuck her up the ass."

The fat man instantly turned a deep red, but Traugott went on before he could say anything.

"And then one day your mother was suffering from one hell of a bellyache so she went outside in the woods behind your house to relieve herself. She raised her skirts - something I'm told she did all the time, but for other reasons - and she pushed and pushed and pushed until one huge, smelly turd shot out of her ass and landed between her feet. *Splat!* And when she looked down to see what she had done, there you were, staring up at her and crying, so she picked you up and made you her son."

That left the fat man speechless.

"So you see, you *are* a motherless turd," Traugott concluded before lying back down on his bunk and closing his eyes, his left arm in a cast across his chest.

The fat man got up, ran a hand over his ruffled clothes to give himself time to regain some of his composure, and replaced the chair in the corner of the room. Traugott thought he would then leave, but the man had other plans.

"How low you have fallen, herr Traugott, how utterly powerless you must feel to resort to such childish insults," the man said calmly. "Thirty years ago you were nothing but a common thief, but like the eel that you are you managed to slip through my fingers. But you see, no one ever gets away from me. Not really. Had I caught you then, I would have no cause to be here today. You'd have served maybe two years in jail, the war would have ended... In any case. As I say, it would really have been much preferable for you to have been caught then than to find yourself in that cage today."

There was a pause as both men waited for the other to make a move.

"I know who you are, herr Traugott," the fat man repeated. "If you're relying on your *friends*, whoever they are, to rescue you, please stop hoping. Oh they tried, believe me, but they failed. I'm afraid you're not that important to them; you were not back then and you are not today. They quickly realized it'd be more dangerous – for them, I mean – to keep fighting for you than to abandon you to your fate, so consider yourself abandoned."

Morgen paused, but only briefly.

"Tomorrow you will be formally charged with war crimes and, if I have my way, before too long you'll be sentenced to hang. A thief goes to jail. A war criminal hangs."

Another pause, this time for dramatic effect.

"Oh, before I forget. *Neunzehnhunderteinundsiebzig* sends her love. Well, maybe not her love, but you are most definitely in her thoughts these days, just perhaps not for the reason you'd hope."

Konrad Morgen then waddled out as he'd waddled in minutes earlier, leaving Traugott feeling as though he had just been launched off the roof of a thirty-story building.

"I don't think they have much of a case."

Gundula narrowed her eyes at the young lawyer and snorted angrily, which immediately alarmed Traugott. The last thing he needed was for his wife to rip the man's head off.

"What do you mean?," he asked in order to preempt anything she might say.

To be honest, he couldn't really fault Gundula for being suspicious. Defending former Nazis wasn't the most sought-after job in town and Rolf Lüdwig, their lawyer, while he seemed eager enough, also appeared to have graduated from law school that very morning and shaved perhaps twice in the past month.

Young Lüdwig had been assigned to them by the public defender's office after a dozen others had refused to represent them. Traugott could only hope that his enthusiasm didn't melt away when he inevitably crossed swords with the fearsome, battle-hardened Konrad Morgen.

"Have either of you ever heard of Bohdan Stashynsky?"

Traugott and Gundula exchanged a quick, puzzled glance. "No," they answered at the same time.

"Stashynsky was a KGB assassin who committed several murders in the Federal Republic in the 1950s," Lüdwig explained. "But at his trial in 1963, the tribunal only found him guilty of having been an accomplice to those murders, since they were ordered by his superiors in Moscow."

Traugott and Gundula exchanged another puzzled glance. "And this is relevant to our case how, exactly?," Gundula asked.

Lüdwig grinned somewhat foolishly and Traugott realized that the young man was somewhat smitten with his wife who, despite the years, had lost nothing of her magnetic charm. While her blond hair had paled and grayed, it still shone like gold when the sun struck it just right. Her teeth were as white and straight as ever, her skin was as supple and soft as kid leather and her bosom jutted out proudly, like the dragon masthead on a Viking ship.

This wasn't the first time he'd witnessed the spell Gundula cast on men, but it had been a while, and as always she remained completely oblivious to what was happening.

"Well the implication is that, under a totalitarian system, only those called the *executive decision-makers* can be convicted of murder," Lüdwig finally managed to explain. "Those who were merely following orders, their underlings and henchmen and whatever else you may wish to call them, can only be convicted of having been accomplices to those murders."

Gundula began to see where he was going with this and a brief ray of hope pierced her soul, like sunshine poking through the dark, heavy clouds of a thunderstorm.

"A totalitarian regime... You mean like the USSR or..."

Lüdwig smiled again, this time with more confidence. "Like the USSR. Or like Nazi Germany."

There was a moment of silence as Gundula and Traugott digested this rare piece of good news.

"But surely Morgen is also aware of this," Traugott eventually said.

Lüdwig nodded. "Oh I'm sure herr Morgen is well aware of this. But he has no say in the matter. The precedent is clear, and he is as bound by it as we are. Whether that pleases him or not is of no relevance whatsoever. In fact, to be truthful, I'm even surprised he's decided to pursue the matter altogether. Surely he has bigger fish to fry."

Lüdwig was fishing for information and the question, though unasked, was clear: is there anything that I don't know, but that I should know, about this case, that might explain why the bloodhound is coming after you thirty years later? Traugott wanted to change the subject, but Gundula had also picked up on Lüdwig's silent question and he could feel her eyes boring into him.

Him he might throw off the scent; her, never.

"I don't know why either," Traugott lied. "We crossed paths briefly during the war when he came to Auschwitz to investigate some petty thefts, but that was it. I'd forgotten all about it, and him, until I landed here."

"Some petty thefts?," Gundula repeated.

Traugott wished, and not for the first time, that he'd taken as his wife a blond with huge breasts and the brains of a bird, instead of a blond with huge breasts and a mind as sharp as a dagger.

"Yes," he said. "Some soldiers had taken to pilfering the Jews' luggage. Alcohol, money, jewelry... I informed Morgen as soon as I became aware of the situation, those responsible were apprehended and that was the end of it."

If only.

"And did you, yourself, ever steal anything?," she asked, as Lüdwig watched with great interest.

Millions. I stole fucking millions. But I have none of it left. It's all gone. Some I gave to her *when Auschwitz fell, and the rest...*

"No."

"But Morgen has charged you with war crimes, not theft," Lüdwig observed. "So it seems unlikely those events are the reason you're here today."

"War crimes is very vague," Gundula said. "To me it sounds like *we're not sure what you did, but we're sure you did something, and we're sure it was bad, so there you go...* You're accused of war crimes!"

There was another moment of silence, during which young Lüdwig thumbed through the thick file he had brought with him. Having found the sheet he was looking for, he pulled it out and placed it on the table for all to see.

"This is doctor Franz Lucas," he explained. "He was at Auschwitz in 1943 and 1944, before serving short stints at Mauthausen, Stutthof, Ravensbrück and Sachsenhausen. Do you know him?"

Traugott shook his head to show that he didn't.

"Well, the good doctor, an obersturmführer, was tried a few years ago. Several witnesses testified that he selected which prisoners would live and which would die, that he threw Zyklon-B into the gas chambers and that he personally oversaw the murders of dozens and dozens of inmates," Lüdwig said. "Lucas eventually confessed to four murders, but he also claimed to have acted against his conscience and to have only been following orders."

"And?," Gundula asked.

"And he was sentenced to three years and three months in jail," the young lawyer explained. "But he was released after just a few months, there was a new trial, and he was acquitted."

Gundula jumped out of her chair. "He confessed to four murders and he was *acquitted*?"

Lüdwig nodded. "Indeed he was. Several former inmates – I believe they were Norwegian women he encountered at Ravensbrück - came forward to testify very positively on his behalf during the second trial, and he walked free."

"Then what kind of a game is Morgen playing?," Gundula almost screamed. "This doctor Lucas confesses to four murders, for God's sake, and walks free, but my husband is..."

She stopped when Traugott reached out and grabbed the pen from between Lüdwig's fingers. He flipped the sheet over and on the back wrote:

Adriana Zöbel. Neunzehnhunderteinundsiebzig.

He then pushed the sheet back to Lüdwig.

"Ask Morgen where you can find her," he said. "We're going to need her."

Adriana asked herself what might happen if she just got up and left.

Let's say she just gathered up her things and nonchalantly walked out the door... would someone try to stop her? Probably not. No one paid her any attention. Well, there *was* a security guard at the end of the hallway, but he kept nodding off on his crosswords puzzle and looked like he couldn't stop a 6-year-old from robbing a candy store. She would just walk right by him and be gone.

Besides, he had no reason to care. He didn't know who she was. And even if he had known... What of it? She'd done nothing wrong, she hadn't been arrested. Still, guards of any type made her nervous, for reasons that probably need not be explained.

Yes, she could just get up and leave. But that would only delay the inevitable. There was no escaping it: one day, if not today then next week or next month, she'd find herself back here, in this same spot, with the notable difference that she'd then very likely be under arrest and in handcuffs.

A tiny alarm bell, the same as always, rang furiously at the back of her skull. *What are you doing here?*, it kept asking her. *This is not your fight, it wasn't then and it isn't now*, it kept reminding her. *Just get up and walk away*, it kept urging her.

Why do they keep dragging me back into this?, she asked herself.

Because you let them, the tiny alarm bell retorted.

There was nowhere she could go, it seemed, nothing she could do, to place herself beyond their reach once and for all. No matter what life she made for herself, they always found her, and her past always came charging out of the night to blindside her and knock her flat onto her back.

She was seated on a polished wooden bench in an endless corridor that stretched from one end of the courthouse to the other. She glanced at her watch and saw she'd already been waiting for an hour – the only problem being that she didn't know what, exactly, she was waiting for.

She had an inkling, of course, but nothing more.

First Konrad Morgen had asked her to identify Traugott, which she had. But he'd also wanted her to come testify under oath, which she'd flatly refused to do.

A couple of weeks later a young man showed up on her doorstep and introduced himself as "Rolf Lüdwig, legal counsel to Mattias Traugott". At first Adriana could only stare at him in disbelief; there she found herself again, once more caught in the crossfire of the men who circled Traugott: Morgen on one side, this Lüdwig on the other.

Would this never, ever end?

"Go away," she managed to say, but her voice lacked conviction, so he stayed.

"Do you know herr Traugott?"

Tears of despair and frustration filled her eyes. She wanted so desperately to tell him to leave her alone, to return quietly to the life she had built since escaping Auschwitz, to be allowed to forget and move on once and for all - if only they'd let her.

So instead of telling him to bugger off, she said: "You wouldn't be here if you didn't already know that I do."

He smiled. "I know it must be difficult for you to keep revisiting those memories."

You don't know anything, she thought. *You weren't* there. *You didn't* see. *You didn't* hear. *You didn't* smell.

"Morgen and you are *making* me revisit them," she corrected him angrily as tears flowed down her cheeks. He handed her a clean handkerchief and she found him slightly more sympathetic.

"If I may, I have but three quick questions, fräulein Zöbel," he went on. She sighed and nodded reluctantly.

He took out a notepad and a pencil to jot down her answers.

"Would it be fair to say you wouldn't have survived Auschwitz without herr Traugott?," he demanded.

That was so ludicrous that she laughed despite herself. "Many people survived Auschwitz without him," she said. Then she hardened her tone and hammered every word: "And many, many, many more died there *because* of him."

"I am asking you personally."

She stared at him and in his eyes she read so much innocence, so much eagerness that it broke her heart. *Wait 'til the world has slapped you around some, my young one*, she thought. *Then we'll talk.*

"I am a very tough woman, herr Lüdwig," she stated. "Would I have survived without him? We'll never know, now, will we?"

"That could be interpreted as admitting that he *did* play a role in your survival."

She refused to yield. "What's your next question herr Lüdwig?"

Seemingly satisfied, he nodded and took a few notes before continuing.

"Did you ever witness him also save the lives of others?"

She understood what he was after and snickered. "If you're looking for someone to portray him as a saint, you've got the wrong person", she warned him. "That man is a monster."

He dropped his eyes and distractedly tapped the tip of his pencil against his notepad a few times before looking back at her. "I am under no illusion as to the type of man herr Traugott is. Or *was*," he said. "My sole purpose is to grant him the justice he denied so many others. And to attain that goal I need facts – all the facts. So my question to you, fräulein Zöbel, is quite simple: are you aware of lives herr Traugott saved at Auschwitz, in addition to your own?"

A vision of Traugott emerging from the gas chamber, half-naked and coughing and retching, the lifeless body of Tatiyana in his arms, popped unbidden in her mind, and bile rose at the back of her throat.

"Yes." She handed him back his handkerchief and he pocketed it.

"And may I ask who it was that he saved?"

"Is that your third, and final, question?"

The sharpness of her mind made him grin. This one was not to be trifled with. "It is not. Would you be willing to repeat all you've just told me under oath?"

It was her turn to smile. "The answer to that one is easy, and it's the same I gave that swine Morgen: you've had all the help you'll get from me. Goodbye."

She hoped that would be the end of it, but then about a month ago a bailiff came to her door with a summons. She immediately tried to shut the door in his face, but he blocked it with his foot in a practiced move and offered to return in an hour with the police. There was a moment of hesitation, then she snaked her hand through the narrow opening, he handed her the summons, informed her that she'd been served, bid her a good day and left.

The summons was brief and uninformative: she was to report to the Vienna courthouse a week from that day, at 8 am sharp. If she did not, it warned, "appropriate measures" would be taken to ensure her compliance.

A door creaked open across the hall, a bit to her left, and through the opening Lüdwig's head emerged almost comically, appearing to Adriana very much like a groundhog peeping out of its burrow after hibernating through another endless winter.

He at first seemed as bewildered as said groundhog in the light of the spring sun, but then his eyes alighted on her and he smiled.

"Fräulein Zöbel, you are here," he stated. He shut the door and came to sit next to her.

"Was there ever any doubt that I would be?" she asked, turning away from him and staring fixedly at the opposite wall. "At least if it had been Morgen's doing!"

He knew she was referring to the bailiff he'd sent to her home. He crossed his arms across his midriff and stared at the wall as well. She could feel his unease, but she didn't care. She didn't doubt that, deep down, he was an earnest and decent young man, but would this never end? When would she finally be allowed to live her own life without the past continually interfering?

"Is he here?" she finally asked, when the silence between them began to stretch a bit too long.

"Herr Morgen?"

She sighed with impatience. "No, *not* Morgen."

"Ah." He hesitated. "Hum... yes, he is. Of course. I was with herr Traugott and his wife a bit earlier. They are waiting in a room adjacent to the courtroom. They'll be let in at the last moment, when everybody else has been seated."

His wife? He's married??

Another door opened to their right and a young couple emerged. The woman began sobbing and the man – her boyfriend or husband, presumably – cradled her in his arms. It looked as though the weight of the whole world had just crashed down on her. She buried her face against his chest as wave after wave of grief washed over her body.

Adriana returned her eyes to the wall in front of her.

"What is my role here today? What do you want from me?" she demanded.

Before he could reply, a gray, ethereal shape flew in from the right, passed right before them without stopping, appearing to float above the ground like a ghost, and entered the room from which Lüdwig had emerged moments ago.

They never saw the shape's face, but Adriana didn't need to. Her breath caught in her throat and she coughed.

"Is that...?" the young lawyer asked.

She nodded. "Yes. That's my sister Tatiyana. Is she also here to testify?"

Lüdwig seemed flabbergasted. "I... I honestly do not know," he admitted. "Well, she *is* listed among the witnesses herr Morgen might call, otherwise she wouldn't be allowed on this floor, but..."

"Morgen can't possibly be that desperate," Adriana opined. "She's endured enough grief to last her several lifetimes and her mind is completely gone."

"I agree. Calling her as a witness would be most unwise. It would completely undermine his credibility."

"Then what is she doing here?"

He shrugged. "She is a free woman, so far as I know, and the proceedings are open to anyone who wishes to attend. On that topic I must say that the public gallery is quite full, for a hearing that is otherwise quite unremarkable."

"Apart from the fact that the fate of a Nazi is to be decided."

"A *former* Nazi," he corrected her.

"There is no such thing," she fired back immediately.

"Do you really believe that?"

She laughed softly and finally looked at him. "With every single fiber of my body," she said. "You are so very young, herr Lüdwig, and you interpret the world with the idealism of those your age.

There is no doubt in your mind that he deserves justice, and that you are making the world a better place by helping him get it."

She paused and he remained silent. "I, too, was once a young idealist, full of dreams and ambitions, and I too once believed that I could make the world a better place."

"And you no longer do?"

She laughed again, but her laugh was as arid as the desert in summertime. "Oh please," she said. "How could I? One day some men who believed themselves superior to me invaded our home, killed my brother and took my family and me to a place you can't even begin to fathom."

"Auschwitz."

"Yes, Auschwitz. And you know what I learned at Auschwitz? I learned that there is no God, herr Lüdwig. *There... is... no... God*. Auschwitz taught me that it's much better to believe in the absence of God, of any god, than to believe in the existence of a God who's perfectly content to sit idly by while some of the kindest, gentlest people you'll ever encounter are crushed to a bloody pulp by jackbooted thugs such as *your client*."

"People can change, fräulein Zöbel, if given the chance," Lüdwig said.

"Some, but not all, and most certainly not men like *him*," she snickered. "I really don't care what he claims to be today, what he's convinced you that he's become, because I know what he *is*, and such a man will not and cannot change."

Lüdwig was getting worried. She was the sole witness he had, but the depth of her hostility was causing him to reconsider his decision to call her to the stand.

"I disagree," he said. "I did not know him then, but I have spent much time with him these past few weeks. I saw the look in his eyes when he stares at his child. The man you knew and the man I know are not the same individual."

Adriana shook her head.

"And because of *him,* how many people stared at *their* child one last time as they were being dragged to the gas chambers by their hair?" She shook her head. "You think he would have become the *loving family man* you claim to know today if the Germans had won the war? Of course not. His hordes of demons and him would have ruled the world, so why would they have changed? One day your eyes will open, and the awakening will be brutal."

The young couple slowly walked by them. The woman appeared inconsolable and her companion propped her up by the elbow to keep her from collapsing. Adriana watched them go until they disappeared around the corner, and she wondered what tragedy had so befallen them on this day.

Lüdwig hesitated. "Be that as it may, herr Traugott did save your life at Auschwitz."

He was fishing for confirmation, defying her to refute his statement. When he'd asked her the very same question during their first encounter, she'd hedged her response and refused to admit that she owed her survival to Traugott. And yet that was the sole reason he'd called her here today: he needed her to declare, on the stand and under oath, that Traugott had saved her. That was perhaps his client's sole chance of escaping the gallows.

"What if he did?" Adriana said, this time edging closer to the response he needed.

He shrugged, trying to appear nonchalant. "That has to count for something. That *will* count for something."

"That's not for me to say. I am only here because you threatened to have me *dragged* here if I did not come of my own free will", she said. "What happens now?"

He took a moment to collect his thoughts and briefly considered sending her home. She was far more unreliable than he'd imagined; she was even borderline hostile. But in the end, he reasoned he had nothing to lose, since Morgen already had a slew of potentially damning witnesses lined up against Mattias Traugot. What would one more be, if she blew up on him on the stand? It wouldn't make the rope any shorter.

"Well, this isn't the actual trial," he explained. "The judge will hear the evidence from both sides and then decide if a trial is warranted."

Adriana saw red. "You mean to say that this is still not the end? *That I may have to return yet again?*"

There was no point lying to her. "Yes."

Adriana's mind was spinning furiously, and unbeknownst to Lüdwig, propelling her toward collaborating with him any way she could. Her reasoning was very simple: if the evidence against Traugott was too overwhelming, the judge would have no other choice but to order a trial, and then a year from now she'd be back here yet again, dragged back yet again into a past that refused to die.

On the other hand, if the judge decided there was no case and allowed Traugott to walk out of here a free man, here and now, then *perhaps*, just *perhaps* that would finally be the end of it.

She no longer cared about justice. She no longer *believed* in justice. All she wanted was to be allowed to move on with her life.

So she looked at young Rolf Lüdwig and flashed him her most radiant smile.

"Tell me what you need from me."

Adriana took a deep breath to slow her heart and quieten her mind, opened the door and entered the courtroom.

The smell inside was of things old and musty, like catacombs buried deep below a city. It almost felt as though she were entering a church; she stepped as lightly as she could, almost reverently, but the ancient floorboards creaked under her weight and many heads turned to glimpse this noisy newcomer.

She made her way to the front of the room, where she scooted down a long wooden bench worn smooth by thousands of behinds over the decades.

Walking down the center aisle she glimpsed Tatiyana sitting at the back of the room, in the very last row. She stopped a moment to observe her sister: Tatiyana wore the same faded, translucent dress as during their last encounter, her hands were clasped anxiously between her knees and she rocked back and forth slowly, all the while muttering to herself unintelligibly.

Adriana walked on. There was nothing she could do for her. Not anymore.

There was still no sign of Traugott. And yet, the simple knowledge that she would find herself in his presence in a matter of minutes made her heart race.

Rolf Lüdwig sat at a table at the front of the courthouse, engrossed in some documents. Konrad Morgen sat at another table, to the left of Lüdwig's, and seemed deep in thought. His forehead rested against his steepled fingers and his eyes were closed, and he almost appeared to be praying. But then, as Adriana observed him, he looked directly at her. She averted her stare almost immediately, but not quickly enough to miss the enigmatic smile he shot her.

She was a fly trapped in the web of the world's fattest spider, and she had just caught it licking its lips.

Two policemen guarded the inside of the door through which she had entered a a minute earlier and two flanked another at the far end of the room, presumably the one through which Traugott and other participants in today's hearing would eventually appear.

There were fifteen or twenty people in the courthouse, a mixture of men and women, on top of

Tatiyana. They all appeared to be in their fifties, as she was, and her best guess was that they, too, were Auschwitz survivors.

She scanned their faces rapidly but didn't recognize any of them. There had been thousands of people at Auschwitz, and even if there happened to be here today someone she had known back then, she'd never know it; time had passed, and with it, hair had grown, cheeks filled out, skin sagged and wrinkles formed.

Still, there was a flash of recognition in the eyes of a man who glanced in her direction as she examined him. That made her uneasy and she quickly looked away. She had no idea who he was, but the nasty scar that ran the length of his left cheek tickled the back of her mind.

Another man – well-dressed and distinguished-looking - sat in the very front row, on Morgen's side of the room. One leg was draped over the other and his hands were clasped around his knee. He seemed utterly unconcerned and aloof, if not for one foot that fidgeted up and down incessantly.

At the very front of the room on Lüdwig's side, two rows ahead of Adriana, sat a woman whose thick, luxurious blond hair cascaded down her shoulders to the middle of her back, spilling over the top of the bench like a waterfall of gold. Adriana couldn't see her face, but she radiated a certain magnetism, a certain aura that all could sense.

She became aware of a low buzzing sound behind her, similar to that of an angry beehive. She looked over her left shoulder and saw that the public gallery was indeed almost full, as Lüdwig had mentioned earlier. It hung above the main door, and thus could only be accessed from the next floor. It held three rows of a dozen seats and most of the spectators, Adriana noticed, were young men in their teens and twenties, and they were chatting animatedly.

Then, to her utter dismay and disgust, one of them shot a sloppy Nazi salute to the two policemen guarding the far door. Her head snapped back around quickly enough for her to catch one policeman wink at the young man.

What the hell was going on here?

"Well imagine that, meeting you here," someone said next to her.

Startled, Adriana stared for a moment at the elderly lady who had sidled up next to her, unnoticed, before she could reply.

"Teresia," she breathed. "I mean... Mrs Schlamelcher."

Traugott's mother grabbed her hand and grinned without looking at her.

"It's good to see you as well, child. Although I wish it were under different circumstances, as I'm sure you do."

Adriana couldn't tear her eyes away from her. Teresia had aged, they all had, but she looked healthy, her eyes shone brightly and her grip was strong; still, she'd last seen her some thirty years ago, so Teresia had to be in her seventies today, and was perhaps even nearing her eighties.

Her hair was now a majestic snowy white and she had it tied in a ponytail that fell to her shoulders.

"Have you also been called to testify?" Adriana finally managed to ask.

Teresia's grin faded away and a veil of sorrow clouded her eyes. She gave Adriana's hand one last squeeze and released it.

"I've spoken to my son perhaps five times since the end of the war," she said. "I know he has a wife and daughter, but I've only seen them in pictures. So no, I'm not here to testify; there's really hardly anything I could tell them about him."

"That's quite sad," Adriana said. "Heartbreaking, really."

Teresia shrugged. "His choice, not mine. But as you may know, nobody holds a grudge like Mattias Traugott."

Adriana knew very little of the dispute between them, and now was certainly not the time to fish for details. Still, that last remark puzzled her.

"He still sent us, my sister and me, to you, in spite of everything", she said.

Teresia shook her head. "No child, not in spite of everything. *Because* of everything. That's how he knew I'd take care of you. And I did."

How did he know? Adriana wanted to ask. *How did he know you wouldn't just turn us away?* The answer to that question, she felt, probably lay at the heart of whatever had happened between them. But that question was destined to remain unanswered today and perhaps forever.

"And you did", Adriana echoed, bringing that part of the conversation to a close.

There was a brief silence as they each collected their thoughts.

"But if you won't be testifying..." Adriana began. "His lawyer told me this floor is solely for witnesses and such."

Teresia shrugged. "I'm sure the guard would have stopped me, had he not been fast asleep", she explained. "And you? I assume that means you're here to testify on his behalf? They want you to save him from the rope?"

It was Adriana's turn to shrug. "I'm so tired of all this", she said, not really answering the question. "*So* tired. At this point I'm not really sure what they expect from me, but the thing is, I don't much care anymore. I'll do just about anything they want if that means then being left in peace to live my life."

Teresia grabbed her hand and squeezed it again. "No one could blame you. Now I wish they'd get on with it. My butt isn't as comfortable as it once was."

Almost as if on cue the door opened and a court official entered. He announced in a ringing voice that Doctor Edgar Reisenleitner would preside over today's proceedings. He then demanded that all those in attendance rise and stand in silence, which they did – except for Tatiyana, who was hopelessly lost in the labyrinth of her insanity.

The man then stepped aside to allow the magistrate to enter. Doctor Reisenleitner didn't cut much of a figure: a small mousy man who stood a hair taller than five feet five inches, he didn't walk as much as he scurried about, which only further enhanced his resemblance to a rodent. His head was entirely bald except for a crown of bushy hair that circled his cranium from ear to ear; round glasses were perched on the tip of an elongated nose and his jaw narrowed to a point that jutted forward like the prow of a ship.

Some in the public gallery actually snickered at his appearance, but he seemingly didn't hear them – or if he did, he chose to ignore them.

He took his seat on the bench, shuffled a few sheets of paper, and then simply nodded at the two policemen.

Adriana's heart froze and time slowed to an icy crawl.

One of the two knocked on the door three times. A few seconds later, the door opened for a third – and final – time and a new policeman appeared. The man took a quick look around and, apparently satisfied, gestured for someone behind him to enter.

And then, for the first time in almost thirty years, Adriana Zöbel, daughter of Simeon and Raanah, sister to Tatiyana and Aaron, Auschwitz survivor, came face to face with Mattias Traugott, the avowed Nazi who had once taken a vow to eradicate all Jews from the face of the planet and the man who had long ago professed his love for her.

His eyes first found the blond woman, but then a fraction of a second later they jumped to her and he just stared without moving.

Adriana wanted to look away but couldn't. She was paralyzed, as though his gaze had turned her to stone. There was suddenly no one else in the room but him, and had a bomb exploded under her bench at that very moment, it was doubtful she'd have heard it. He was all she could see, and the only sound was that of blood roaring loudly in her ears.

"What the heck happened to his arm?" Teresia whispered, but Adriana didn't hear her.

He was older and grayer and heavier, softer and gentler and perhaps even tamer, but looking at him now, she did not see a fifty-something insurance salesman with a slight paunch and an arm in a cast and wrinkles that crinkled at the corner of his eyes: she saw the dashing young SS officer who, in May 1943, changed the course of countless existences when he asked her to sing for him – for with a single song she sowed such trouble in his soul, such uncertainty and such fear that he was moved to save her life, thus toppling the first domino in a chain reaction whose shockwaves would spread through eternity.

Adriana knew the blond woman had turned to stare at her. She could see her, *feel* her, staring at her, but she couldn't stare back. She wanted to pry her eyes away from Traugott, to break the spell, but it was 1943 and she was barely 22 years old and he was the only human being who truly mattered in her life for he alone kept her alive, for he alone decided if she would live to see the next morning, and so she couldn't look away until he did, for that would constitute grave disrespect and she might then...

But no, that wasn't it, that wasn't how it happened. Yes, it might be 1943 and she might barely be 22, but a frail young woman living in constant fear of displeasing her lord and master? Hell no. Absolutely not. She'd fought a thousand battles with him and won nine hundred and ninety-nine of them. Not once, no matter how hard he'd tried, had she allowed him to shed his uniform to reveal the man he claimed existed underneath. Yes, a few of his arrows had found their mark, piercing her armor and providing her with a measure of joy and comfort at a time when she'd craved both, but that counted for nothing. In a time of great famine, even moldy bread becomes a feast.

The trance began to break and she became aware of several things at once.

Reisenleitner, the judge, was shouting in a surprisingly loud voice for someone his size.

Somewhere in the distance people were chanting.

Somewhere else, someone else was howling.

And Teresia seemed to be arguing with someone.

Reality crashed back into focus.

There was no question as to the source of the howling. Adriana glanced in Tatiyana's direction and saw her sister kneeling on her bench, both hands clasped over her ears, eyes closed and head tilted back like a wolf paying homage to the full Moon.

In the public gallery, the young men had bounded to their feet and were enthusiastically singing *Es zittern die morschen Knochen* - "The rotten bones are trembling", the official song of the Hitler Youth. Most of them were saluting Traugott.

Wir werden weiter marschieren

Wenn alles in Scherben fällt

Denn heute da gehört uns Deutschland

Und morgen die ganze Welt

Today, these young Austrians were chanting, *Germany is ours, and tomorrow the whole world shall be*.

Adriana's looked back at Traugott, who seemed as bewildered as she was by the turn of events.

He, too, was staring at the spectacle in the gallery, but then he looked at her and seemed to shrug helplessly, as if to dissociate himself from the young hooligans' actions.

"You're her, aren't you? The Zöbel woman? That's you?"

The blond woman was shouting at her, making herself heard above the cacophony. Adriana looked at her, but couldn't respond; her brain was still reeling and her mouth wouldn't form the words, so she just stared blankly at the woman, as though struck dumb and suddenly deprived of the power of speech.

"She's the only chance my son has," Teresia replied immediately. So that's who she was arguing with. "Without her, my grand-daughter will grow up without her father, so you..."

The blond woman ignored her completely and kept adressing Adriana.

"If he hangs because of you", the blond woman growled, "don't bother running. There'll be nowhere you hide that I won't find you."

Before Adriana could say anything judge Reisenleitner managed to restore a semblanoc of order to his courtroom. The little man was actually standing on his chair and pounding madly on his desk with his gavel, all the while screaming at the top of his lungs that this wasn't a circus.

A very fragile, very superficial calm returned. Tatiyana had quietened down, as had the young men in the public gallery. Adriana looked back over her shoulder one more time: Tatiyana was rocking back and forth slowly, like the mad woman she now was, and the hooligans were still chatting animatedly, but this time in a very low voice so as to no longer interfere with the proceedings.

Had the blond woman actually threatened to kill her if Traugott was convicted? At the very least she had threatened to track her down and hurt her badly. Should she report her to someone? To young Rolf Lüdwig, perhaps? That would be pointless, of course. No one had heard or seen anything in the mayhem, except perhaps for Teresia. It would be her word against hers, and that would lead nowhere.

The blond woman had again turned her back to her. Traugott had taken a seat next to Lüdwig, who was conferring with Konrad Morgen. After a moment the two men nodded and Morgen returned to his own side of the room.

"Herr doktor", the fast man said without sitting down. "If it pleases the court, my colleague and I are in agreement to forge ahead with the proceedings, despite the recent... disturbance."

Morgen then sat down while the judge pondered the situation.

"Very well", the little man said. "I'll agree. But let me reiterate that I shall clear the courthouse without hesitation if I hear so much as a mouse fart."

Someone in the back, assuredly one of the young men, chuckled, but was quickly shushed by his friends.

"Call your first witness", he told Morgen.

Adriana was once again struck by the power of his voice, which seemed to fill the room and come from all directions at once.

Morgen stood up. "I will demonstrate that the accused, Mattias Traugott, committed war crimes and crimes against humanity when he served as a guard at the Auschwitz concentration camp and that he should be made to answer for those crimes", he announced. "To that end I call my first witness, Lajb Panub."

Adriana gasped.

Lajb Panub was the young man who had helped obliterate the crematorium. Traugott had agreed to save him in order to also save her, before reneging on his promise.

And Lajb Panub was also supposed to be very much dead. Traugott had first abandoned him to the heavy machine guns and the killing field outside the crematorium. Then she had, with her very eyes, seen Traugott empty one gun, then another, into the mound of coats where the then-teenager hid after the attack.

Panub had bolted out, and there had been one last, final shot – which, she now realized, she hadn't witnessed.

The man who'd caught her eye a moment earlier, the one whose cheek had been scarred by Otto Möckel's dagger, stood up and walked to the front of the room, where he swore to tell the truth and nothing but the truth.

Adriana glanced at Traugott, but her old nemesis was using a pencil to scratch under his cast and appeared unperturbed. He didn't seem to recall Lajb Panub, or if he did, was unconcerned by what he might have to say.

Morgen and Panub had clearly rehearsed his testimony. Panub had ready answers for every question, and it was more than obvious that Morgen had told him what he'd be asked and what in turn he needed to answer.

Panub first recounted how he came to Auschwitz, how he was assigned to the 12th sonderkommando, how his first task was to dispose of the bodies of the 11th sonderkommando, and then how he and others, under the leadership of Israel Gutman, planned to strike back.

"Now please tell the court of the events of 7 October 1944", Morgen asked gently.

Panub took a deep breath. "The uprising began when my very courageous friend Chaim Neuhof brained scharführer Busch with a hammer", he said.

A few of the young men in the public gallery actually booed softly, but Adriana didn't hear them. In her mind she was reliving that fateful day, when she had slipped a blade between Otto Möckel's ribs and deep into his lungs. Traugott had arrived shortly thereafter, struck a deal with Gutman to save both her and Panub, and then...

"I was led out of the crematorium by untersturmführer Traugott", Panub said. "There was someone else with us, the woman who killed the other guard, as I described a moment ago, but I do not know what became of her."

Adriana was trembling. He clearly knew who that woman was, what had happened to her, and where she was today. Why, then, not identify her? And then it came to her: he knew she'd killed Otto Möckel, he'd seen her plunge the dagger into his back. While it was highly unlikely she'd ever get in trouble over that murder, who could say for sure, given the climate evidenced by those in the public gallery? Safer to let all believe that the murderess was now lost to history.

Besides, Panub was Morgen's witness, and it was entirely possible that Morgen had asked him to avoid incriminating her in any way. Perhaps Morgen needed her testimony to be as credible and as untainted as possible later on.

Adriana felt Traugott's eyes on her and looked in his direction. He was staring directly at her, the itch under his cast forgotten. He seemed to be trying to tell her something with his eyes, but she looked away.

"But once outside the crematorium untersturmführer Traugott betrayed me and left me to die", Panub continued. "He shoved me to the ground, where I guess he expected me to be killed by the machine guns. But I ran for the barracks, past him and the woman, and hid inside."

"And that is how you survived?" Morgen asked.

Panub shook his head. "Oh no, not at all. The untersturmführer chased me inside, so I fled. Eventually I plunged into a mound of clothes, where I hoped to remain hidden until... until... I don't know. That was all I could think to do."

Morgen nodded pensively. "But he found you. How?"

"Someone gave me up", Panub explained. "Someone told him where I was. One second I am hidden, the next there are bullets shredding the coats around me, so I ran again."

"And what did you see then?"

"I saw untersturmführer Traugott holding a carbine. There was a look of absolute rage on his face. But I didn't stay to chat. I was running for my life."

Morgen nodded again and motioned for his witness to continue.

"I reached the door and opened it. I heard a shot, it felt like someone had hit me with a sledgehammer... and later I woke up in the infirmary."

Adriana was fascinated. She clearly remembered hearing that final shot, the one she'd assumed had ended Lajb Panub's valiant life.

It had not.

"I owe my life to Doctor Ada", Panub said.

Adriana shivered. *Doctor Ada. Where was she today?*

"After a few days she bandaged both my arms up to the elbow, to hide the tattoo on my left forearm, she bandaged my face almost completely, and she gave me something that put me to sleep. I woke up on board an ambulance, dressed in a bloody uniform. We were outside

Auschwitz."

Adriana realized she was holding her breath and forced herself to relax.

"I had no idea what was going on. They took me to a hospital. Whenever someone spoke to me, I just placed my hands over my ears and shrugged, to show I couldn't hear. It was very plausible, with those bandages around my head. I also kept my eyes shut as much as possible, as if I'd passed out or fallen asleep. In any case, that very first night someone came to see me."

"Who came to see you?" Morgen asked.

Panub shrugged. "To this day I do not know, but it was a young woman. But I remember what she said. *Ada sent me*. Then she cut my bandages, gave me some clothes, and she led me outside the hospital in the dead of night. She took me to a house nearby, where I stayed for a few days, then I was taken to another house, and another, and so on until I found myself in Sweden about three months later."

Adriana remembered old Lechoslaw suggesting that Tatiyana and her make their way north all the way to Gdańsk, where they would board a ship across the Baltic Sea to Sweden. Panub had apparently taken that trip.

Morgen sat down, apparently satisfied, and Rolf Lüdwig stood up.

"I have but a single question", he announced. "Mr Panub, how can you be certain that it was my client who fired into the hiding place you described? A mound of clothes I believe you said it was?"

Panub appeared flummoxed by the question. "When I emerged he was standing there with a carbine, so I..."

"But you never actually witnessed him firing in your direction?"

"No", Panub was forced to admit.

"And when you ran, you had your back to him?"

"Obviously."

"So how can you be certain that you were shot by my client?"

To this Panub had no reply.

"Are you assuming that you were shot by herr Traugott?"

Again Panub remained silent. There was but one answer he could give to that question.

"Surely my client wasn't the only armed guard at Auschwitz at the time."

Panub shook his head feebly. "No."

"So you could have been shot by any one of them, is that not correct?"

Panub simply nodded.

"Someone shot you just as you were exiting the warehouse. Correct?"

Panub nodded again. "Yes. That's what I said two minutes ago."

"And were you shot from the front or from behind?"

Panub's face fell. "I... I don't know. No one ever told me. I never asked."

Lüdwig sighed impatiently. "Mr Panub, did anyone, anyone at all, ever witness my client firing in your direction, trying to kill you?"

Panub's eyes flicked to Adriana for a nanosecond. She had seen him. She was the sole witness.

"No, not to my knowledge", Panub said.

Some in the public gallery cheered and applauded.

Morgen asked for a short recess, during which he reviewed several documents.

When the court reconvened, he announced he was forgoing calling his next six witnesses – presumably because he now saw that they, as had just happened with Panub, would also be incapable of implicating Traugott directly in any crime, and it would therefore be pointless, and perhaps even perilous, to hear from them. Better send them home rather than risk weakening his case even further.

Reisenleitner called out five names and five men Adriana didn't know, but who all bore faded tattoos on their left forearms, stood up and exited the courtroom under a thunder of jeers and whistles.

Juden Raus!, someone shouted above the cacophony.

And then the madness continued.

"I would now like to call herr doktor Friedrich Lasch", Morgen said after calm had been precariously restored.

The well-dressed and distinguished-looking gentleman in the very front row got up, buttoned his jacket, approached the bench with confidence and swore that he, too, would tell the truth and nothing but the truth.

His voice had a forceful sonority Adriana found quite soothing. When this man spoke, paying attention was mandatory.

"Please state your name and occupation", Morgen demanded.

"I am herr doktor Friedrich Lasch", the man began. "I teach chemical engineering at the University of Hamburg. My specialty is the safety assessment of pesticides."

"Chemical engineering? Pesticides?" Teresia whispered, but Adriana could only purse her lips; she was as puzzled as she was.

Morgen nodded almost comically, as though this momentous revelation at long last confirmed something he'd always suspected. He returned to his desk to retrieve a small cardboard box Adriana hadn't noticed until then. He placed it on his desk, opened it and pulled out an object Adriana couldn't see, since the fat man had his back turned to her.

But others did see it, and jolt of a million volts of electricity coursed through the room.

Morgen placed the object theatrically before doctor Lasch, almost as if he feared dropping it, and only when he returned to his desk did Adriana finally see what it was.

Her head began to spin and she wanted to vomit.

"Please tell the court what that is, herr doktor", Morgen asked.

Lasch appeared unfazed. "This is a canister of Zyklon B poison gas", he announced after glancing at the object.

It might as well have been a chocolate shake, for all it seemed to worry him.

Slightly too large to wrap two hands around, the canister was a sickly beige that made two words pop out menacingly: *Giftgas!* in the middle and, at the very top, against a black background, *Zyklon B.*

Adriana had seen thousands of them at Auschwitz, but she couldn't tear her eyes away from this one.

"What is Zyklon B?" Morgen demanded.

"Zyklon B is commonly known as hydrogen cyanide. It is a prussic acid", Lasch stated. "Inside this canister are pellets that turn into a poisonous gas when exposed to air. It was originally produced as a pesticide to cleanse large buildings like warehouses and barracks. It has the smell of bitter almonds and marzipan."

Morgen paused to let that information sink in.

"Could you please detail its action?" he then asked.

Lasch stared at the canister before him for a moment before responding.

"In layman's terms, Zyklon B attacks the brain. It causes extremely violent pain and kills anyone who inhales it from cardiac arrest within seconds."

The silence in the courtroom was thick enough to hear a fly fart.

Morgen waited for Lasch to go on. "I'm afraid I'm going to have to ask you to be even more precise", he said testily when the man remained silent.

Morgen appeared cross. Perhaps his witness wasn't following the game plan?

Lasch shrugged, as if it were of no concern to him to detail the action of such a nightmarish substance.

"Zyklon B is lighter than air and penetrates by inhalation into the smallest branches of the lungs", he said. "There it blocks cellular respiration. The brain and the heart are first attacked. It begins with a stinging feeling in the chest, then it causes spasmodic pain – similar to epileptic seizures. Death by cardiac circulatory arrest occurs usually within seconds."

"Within seconds, you say. Doctor, it is well documented that the Nazis used Zyklon B to exterminate those they deemed 'undesirable' in camps such as Auschwitz", Morgen stated. "Are we then to conclude that all those exposed to Zyklon B died relatively quickly? That their agony, though intense, was brief?"

It was Lasch's turn to appear cross. He sighed deeply before answering.

"Not at all", he said. "Cyanide is one of the fastest acting poisons. Having said that, it is unlikely the gas worked at the same speed in all areas given the size of the gas chamber. The unfortunate people who were breathing lower concentrations would suffer much more. A lower intoxication leads to a blockage of blood in the lungs and thereby causes shortness of breath. Commonly one speaks of water in the lungs. Breathing will then always be deeper and stronger, because the body craves oxygen."

He paused, and then added: "The agony could last more than half an hour."

Adriana closed her eyes and tried to shut from her mind the cries of endless agony she still heard in her nightmares. But how could she forget that her sister's own children had succumbed to such torture?

"Thank you", Morgen said. "I have no further questions."

Young Rolf Lüdwig got up and declined to cross-examine him. He, however, reminded the court that not a shred of evidence implicated his client in the use of Zyklon B.

"We do not dispute that atrocities occurred at Auschwitz", he stated very calmly. "We do however dispute that my client played any role whatsoever in these atrocities. And that is the sole purpose of today's hearing, to determine whether herr Traugott's alleged actions while he was stationed at Auschwitz might constitute war crimes or crimes against humanity, and thus warrant a full trial."

Lasch was excused and Morgen announced he had no further witnesses to call.

Rolf Lüdwig stood up again and paused before continuing.

"I now call fraulein Adriana Zöbel", he said.

Adriana got up very slowly and made her way to the witness stand, from where she faced the courtroom for the first time.

Directly across the room from her, above the entrance door, was the public gallery. Some three dozen young men were assembled there, one of whom was staring at her with undisguised hatred. When she stared back he snarled and grabbed his crotch with one hand, making both his feelings and his intentions amply clear.

She quickly looked away.

At the very back of the room sat her sister Tatiyana, whom she'd seen earlier. Tatiyana wasn't paying her - or anyone else for that matter - any attention and seemed lost in her own world; her arms were crossed tightly across her flat chest, her hands stuck under her armpits, and she seemed to be swaying to the rhythm of a melody only she could hear.

In the front row, maybe thirty feet from her and a bit to her left, was the blond woman – Traugott's wife, apparently - who'd earlier threatened her under cover of the young men's song. She, too, stared at her with a hatred so intense it was almost incandescent. Her eyes were like flamethrowers roasting her alive.

Two rows behind her sat Teresia Schlamelcher. Traugott's mother mouthed something she couldn't decipher, but her eyes conveyed nothing but courage and benevolence.

And then there was untersturmführer Mattias Traugott himself, also a bit to her left, sitting next to his lawyer. He appeared strangely detached from all of this, even though he clearly had the most to lose. He was staring at his fingertips and seemed almost bored, although to him this was nothing but an endless formality whose issue in his favor was a foregone conclusion.

The shock of seeing him for the first time in thirty years had dissipated and the sight of him no longer turned her into a pillar of salt. Observing him, Adriana saw with even more clarity than before the added weight and the gray and the lines he now carried.

Time had inflicted much damage upon the mighty SS officer, depriving him of his former glory. His power to intimidate and frighten had melted like the wax in Icarus' wings. He was now a mortal, no longer a minor deity, like Icarus fallen to Earth after invincibly soaring through the heavens.

Feeling the weight of her eyes on him, he looked up after a moment and gave her a thin smile which he probably meant to be complicit – *Well look at us now, my old friend! Look what's become of us! Here we are, after all these years! Can you believe it?* - but she simply ignored him and shifted her body slightly to the right, away from him.

Lüdwig was asking her to identify herself.

"My name is Adriana Zöbel, daughter of Simeon and Raanah, sister to Tatiyana and Aaron, and Auschwitz survivor", she stated as calmly as she could. "That is who I am."

"Fraulein Zöbel, for the record, please explain how you came to be at Auschwitz", Lüdwig asked.

Adriana's mind catapulted her back to that day of October 1942 when the Hlinka Guard bounded up the stairs to their apartment and threatened to break down the door unless her father opened it *immediately*. Simeon Zöbel offered them their most precious possessions to go away, but the men just sneered and dragged him to his death by his beard.

Then two of them tried to rape her, and they might have succeeded had Aaron not miraculously returned to save her at the cost of his own life.

"We were then loaded onto a train like cattle and shipped to Auschwitz", she said.

"Is this when you first encountered herr Traugott?", Lüdwig demanded. "Upon your arrival at Auschwitz?"

Adriana sighed and against her will her eyes went to Traugott, who was staring at her fixedly. She could tell that he, too, was reliving their first meeting in his mind.

"It is not", she replied flatly.

Lüdwig waited to see if she would volunteer anything else, and prompted her when she did not. "Could you then please detail your first encounter with my client?"

Adriana shook her head in disbelief and sniffed. "I first met untersturmführer Traugott when he asked me to bloody sing for him", she said, and some in the public gallery laughed. She made it a point to use his Nazi rank, to illustrate to those listening that this was how she still saw him. She gave the word all the weight she could, and willed it to crush him like a bug.

Lüdwig stared at her and, sensing his growing impatience, she raised a hand to quieten him. "For some unknown reason upon my arrival at Auschwitz I was recruited to sing at obersturmbannführer Höss' birthday party", she said. "That has to be when your client first noticed me. When I next encountered him, he asked me to sing for him, and then he assigned me to his weißköpfchen.*"

After making her explain who and what the weißköpfchen had been, Lüdwig asked: "He recruited you because of your singing voice? That seems a bit far-fetched. Surely there were dozens of inmates with lovely singing voices, even in a place such as Auschwitz. Why did he single you out?"

Adriana immediately saw where he was going with this and she had no desire to follow him, but what other choice did she have?

"You'd have to ask him."

"He's not on the stand. You are."

She knew perfectly well what answer he was fishing for, but she was still torn between her hatred for the Nazis and what they'd done to her family and her desire to perhaps, just perhaps, finally be allowed to close this chapter of her life once and for all by helping Traugott walk out of here a free man.

"My personal belief is that untersturmführer Traugott became infatuated with me", she said after a moment. "I believe that's why he recruited me."

The blond woman in the front row turned a glowing red, as though she was boiling with either anger or shame.

Konrad Morgen, also sensing where this was going, tried to object that this was nothing but conjecture, that only Mattias Traugott would know his feelings for the witness, but judge Reisenleitner waved him off – although he clearly did so reluctantly.

"Would it be fair to say that your assignment to the weißköpfchen saved your life?", Lüdwig persisted.

Oh no, it won't be that easy, you prick. No way in hell. I'll at least make you work for it. You'll not get it on a silver platter.

"It would be fair to say that many, many people who were not assigned to the weißköpfchen also survived Auschwitz", Adriana replied, paraphrasing what she'd told him in private a few days earlier.

"But still..."

"But still nothing", she snapped. "Many people survived Auschwitz, but many, many, *many* more did not - including members of my very own family."

Lüdwig's eyes lit up and she immediately regretted her last comment.

"Members of your family, fraulein Zöbel?", the lawyer repeated.

I hate you, she told him mentally. He probably heard her, but he didn't care. His sole mission, here today, was ensuring the freedom and survival of his client, and he would stop at nothing to attain that goal.

"My mother and my father died at Auschwitz", she said with as little emotion as she could. "And so did my nephew and my niece. And there may be others I never knew about."

She dared not look at the public gallery to see how this was being received. Instead she looked at Teresia, but the old woman had closed her eyes and her lips moved imperceptibly, as though she were praying.

"Did herr Traugott play a role in their deaths?", Lüdwig asked.

I hate you I hate you I hate you oh God I fucking hate you.

"Not to my knowledge, no", she admitted.

"Did he personally witness their deaths? Did he inform you of their deaths?"

Adriana remained silent, her mind churning like the sea during a hurricane.

"Fraulein Zöbel?"

Adriana was on the verge of tears. She took a deep breath and explained how she lost track of her parents just as they were being loaded onto the train. And how later, while working in Kanada, she came across her father's shirt, how she knew it from the smell and the small tear her mother had mended, and how this could only mean her parents had been exterminated at Auschwitz.

"I am sorry for your loss", Lüdwig said insincerely, "but there is nothing in your story that even remotely implicates my client in their deaths. I might even argue that, had my client not assigned you to the weißköpfchen, you would never have found out what became of your parents."

You pig, Adriana thought. *You hypocritical, devious, twisted, scheming pig.*

Before she could say anything, he asked: "You also mentioned a niece and a nephew? They died as well?"

In the back of the courtroom, Tatiyana suddenly stopped swaying.

"They did."

"Please explain."

"They died in the gas chambers. A newborn and a little girl."

"Oh. And did their mother die as well? Was she with them?"

Tatiyana became unnaturally still. Adriana wanted to vomit.

There was absolutely no doubt in Adriana's mind that Lüdwig had already heard the story from Traugott – if not, why else would he specifically ask if their *mother* had died with them, and not their *parents*?

And that was precisely why he also needed the court to hear it.

"She was with them, but she lived."

"You mean to say that some survived the gas chambers?"

Adriana wanted to rip out his tongue and claw out his eyes.

"No one ever survived the gas chambers", she said.

"Then I'm afraid I don't understand."

Adriana stared at Traugott for the longest time, and he stared right back. This was it. The time had come to decide. After all these years, his fate now probably depended on the next few words out of her mouth.

Tell them he saved Tatiyana, and he might live.

Claim to not remember who pulled her out, and he might hang.

Tell the truth, and he might live.

Lie, and he might hang.

But before she could make up her mind, icy tentacles of betrayal slithered around her heart and she understood everything. She stared at Lüdwig who, when he saw that she had figured it out, at least had the decency to appear uncomfortable.

Morgen hadn't planned on making Tatiyana testify. He had. He'd lied earlier about not knowing why she might be here. She wasn't Morgen's witness. She was his. She was his trump card, his ace up the sleeve.

If Adriana didn't relate how Traugott had saved Tatiyana, then Lüdwig would take his chances with her. He'd call Tatiyana to the stand and pray for a testimony that was at least half coherent.

Tatiyana had clearly been tricked; even lost in her insanity she would never have agreed to testify on Traugott's behalf. Lüdwig had probably lured her here by offering her the chance to tell the whole world "how that monster killed your babies". He knew perfectly well that such an accusation held no water and would thus not harm his client in the least; all he needed was for her to take the stand and recount how Traugott had pulled her out of the gas chambers.

But he killed my babies! Yes fraülein, we are so sorry for your loss. But please tell us, who saved you? *He did, but he killed my babies!* Yes fraülein, but for the record, who's "he"? *That man over there, Traugott! But he killed my babies!* Yes fraülein, that is terrible. So my client entered the gas chamber at unbelievable personal risk to rescue you? *Yes, but he killed my babies!* Yes fraülein, thank you.

Even such an imperfect testimony from such an imperfect witness would probably, in this day and age, be enough to set Traugott free.

But like the rest, that mattered not in the least. The game was over. Lüdwig had won.

"Untersturmführer Traugott saved my sister", she breathed. She could barely hear herself, but others clearly could. The blond woman grabbed her head with both hands in relief and the young men in the public gallery began to hoot and holler.

"Why did he do that? Why would he do such a thing?", Lüdwig asked when calm had returned.

"Because I asked him. He ran into the gas chamber and saved Tatiyana because I asked him. He also tried to save the children, but he was too late. He did it for me", Adriana said, this time without any hesitation.

There was no point in holding anything back any longer. Let the chips fall where they may, and the hell with all of this.

More hooting and more hollering in the public gallery. Konrad Morgen had turned ghastly white;

clearly he'd known nothing of this, and once again he could feel Mattias Traugott slipping through his pudgy fingers.

Adriana answered the rest of Lüdwig's questions mechanically. All the fight had gone out of her; she'd made her bed and now she'd lie in it.

When he asked if Traugott had indeed saved her when she provided clothes to the four men who escaped behind the wheel of Höss' very own Steyr 220, she admitted that he had, that he'd known everything and could thus have had her killed.

When he asked whether Traugott had indeed saved her from the brothel, she admitted that he had.

When he asked whether Traugott had indeed saved her from Josef Mengele's claws, whom she was begging to kill her instead of her sister, she admitted that he had.

When he asked whether her relationship with Traugott had indeed led the other inmates to nickname her Queen Esther, as a testament to the power she wielded over – or perhaps, through – him, she admitted that it had.

And then, for good measure, she volunteered that she used this power to help as many of her fellow inmates as she could, including her friend Magrita who might have died of a fever had Traugott not sent her to Doctor Ada at her request.

But then later he had her killed to punish me. She kept the thought to herself, since she had no way of proving definitively that Traugott had ordered her death.

So in other words, yes, Traugott did save countless inmates, either directly himself or indirectly through her.

No, Traugott hardly ever refused her a favor. *For you, anything.*

But this was all icing on the cake. She'd testified that Traugott had run into a gas chamber to save a Jew, for the love of God!

By the time she ended her testimony, the hooligans in the public gallery were on their feet, chanting and saluting, and the blond woman in the front row was crying tears of joy and relief.

Teresia, her expression unreadable, simply nodded at her, as if to say that everything was going to be alright.

At the back of the room, forgotten in the mayhem, Tatiyana moaned mournfully and reached under her skirt.

Konrad Morgen, his face the color of wet ash, did not even reply when the judge asked him whether he wanted to cross-examine her. After what she'd said, what would be the point?

Traugott was home free. Of this there could be no doubt.

And that should have been the end of it, and that could have been the end of it, and that probably would have been the end of it had not Konrad Morgen, figuring he had nothing left to lose, called Traugott to the stand.

Of the three witnesses heard so far today, two had essentially cleared Traugott of any wrongdoing, and the third had mostly served as a material witness. What could possibly be risked by hearing from Traugott?

Lüdwig tried to object, out of fear his client might let slip something damaging, but he was quickly overruled.

"I understand your reluctance. But if I am to decide whether a trial is warranted, I will most certainly hear from the man whose trial it would be", Reisenleitner growled at Lüdwig, who nodded his surrender and sat down.

"We are, after all, confronted with events that push the limits of human imagination", the judge added almost as an afterthought.

He then motioned for Traugott to take the stand.

"You belonged to the SS?", was Morgen's first question.

Traugott swallowed hard. He, too, understood the jeopardy he now faced.

"I did."

The fat lawyer stared at him. "Did you join the SS of your own accord?"

"I did."

"You were not conscripted or forced to join in any way? It was your own decision?"

"I was not, and it was."

"And did you, at the time, know what the SS represented? What they stood for?"

"Only to a certain extent."

"What do you mean?"

"Exactly what I just said. Certain things I knew, others I did not."

"Please explain."

Morgen was being relentless. Beads of sweat had formed on Traugott forehead. He wiped them away with the back of his sleeve.

"It is hard to describe to someone who was not there. It is simply inexplicable."

"That is not an answer."

"It's the only one I can provide."

Morgen sensed thaty Traugott was treading very carefully. He tried to keep him off balance by launching an offensive on another front.

"What were your duties at Auschwitz?"

Traugott almost seemed relieved by such an apparently harmless question, as if there were such a thing. He related how obersturmbannführer Rudolf Höss has tasked him with ensuring that no valuables would be lost, that anything of potential value or use to the Reichsführer, and brought to Auschwitz by the prisoners, would be appropriated.

"Valuables?" Morgen asked innocently. "You mean money, gold, precious stones... such things?"

Traugott nodded. "Of course. But also clothes for our troops or food for our widows. *Anything* could be of use."

Morgen smiled at Traugott's cleverness. His foe had managed to masquerade an act of outright pillaging into an act of noble patriotism.

"So you were nothing more than an accountant, is that right?", Morgen asked. "Inventorying, making lists, balancing... correct?"

Lüdwig immediately saw that Morgen was setting him up. He tried to warn his client of the impending danger with his eyes, but Traugott never saw him. "Yes, that's about right", he agreed before Lüdwig could rise and object.

Morgen sighed with mock exasperation. "Herr Traugott, you must really think us all complete fools. But you will not get away so easily."

He paused as if to gather his thoughts. Then he came as close to Traugott as he possibly could and jabbed his finger at him to punctuate his words as he shouted: "You were no little cog! *You were part of the mass murder of millions in an inconceivable crime!*"

The unexpected ferocity of this attack elicited gasps in the courtroom and boos from the public gallery. Lüdwig immediately got up to object, but Reisenleitner just as quickly motioned for him to sit down and be quiet.

"I don't know anyone, at that time, who didn't think like me – that Jews were the enemy of Germany. That was simply the atmosphere of the time", Traugott tried to explain. His voice was thin and he was clearly shaken.

Morgen was encouraged. Who knew what Traugott might volunteer if he kept hammering him in such a fashion?

There might be hope after all.

"And that makes everything right in your eyes?"

Traugott shook his head. "There was a self-denial in me that today I find impossible to explain", he said. "Perhaps it was also the convenience of obedience with which we were brought up, which allowed no contradiction. This indoctrinated obedience prevented registering daily atrocities as such and rebelling against them."

And there it was. That one word. *Atrocities*. Traugott had just tripped and confessed. Konrad Morgen could barely contain himself and Rolf Lüdwig could feel his victory slipping slowly away.

"An interesting choice of words. Atrocities."

Traugott seemed oblivious to what had just happened. What was wrong with admitting that he'd witnessed daily *atrocities*? That wasn't the same as confessing that he'd committed any of them, was it? No it wasn't.

Further, by describing what he'd seen in such a manner, wasn't he helping his cause by making his disapproval amply clear? In his mind he was, so on he went.

"And yet it's the only one that's appropriate. Those on board the trains hadn't a clue what was about to happen to them. It was the gates of Hell", Traugott said. "It was unimaginable to think that the Jews would leave the camp alive."

"You keep dodging my questions, herr Traugott", the lawyer chastised him. "You are very clever, but not clever enough. So let's stop playing games, you and me, shall we? I am asking you quite clearly about your actions at Auschwitz."

Traugott took a moment to compose himself. He looked first at Gundula, then at Adriana who had resumed her seat in the courtroom, next to Teresia, before answering. He never looked at his lawyer, who could not save him at this time.

"I knew Auschwitz was a place I didn't want to be", he began. "It scared me, but I didn't know why. On my first evening, myself and other SS newcomers were plied with alcohol by our superiors. It was revealed to us that Jews arriving at Auschwitz who were considered unsuitable for slave labor were *disposed of*. Exactly what this meant I wasn't sure, but the words still completely shook me. I had had five glasses of vodka and continued to think about it when I woke up the next morning."

He paused.

"The answer came a few days later when I was awakened to chase down inmates who were attempting to escape", he said. "In the process, I saw prisoners herded into a building and gas poured into an opening on the side of the building. Then I heard screams from those inside. The cries grew louder and more desperate, until they fell silent..."

Traugott was being very careful to always describe himself as a *witness* and never as an *active participant*. This was far removed from the truth, but there was no one here today to contradict him – well, that wasn't true either. There had been one woman with the power to send him to the gallows, one woman who could at the very least have testified to one death for which she knew him to be responsible, but she'd chosen to remain silent.

Sensing he might be on to something, Traugott continued along the same lines.

"I had a breakthrough moment when my enthusiasm for Hitler began to wane: a crying baby was discovered hidden in one of the suitcases, most likely left by a mother who had hoped to save it", he said. "I witnessed an SS guard pick the baby up by the ankles and smash the back of its skull against a wall. It was the worst moment of any I had experienced."

But again, solely a witness and certainly not an actor.

Morgen sighed. This was leading him nowhere. "What, exactly, were your duties at Auschwitz? I know I have already asked you, but I need a more detailed answer on your part."

Morgen certainly did not need Traugott to explain how he'd been in charge of Kanada and what had gone on there. This line of questioning would simply give him a few minutes to think. It might also trick Traugott into lowering his guard a bit, and then who knew what might happen?

"You would be surprised to know with how many valuables the Jews arrived at Auschwitz", Traugott said. "They had brought as much of their wealth as they could in the deluded hope they might thus save their lives."

He paused to collect his thoughts while Morgen was reminded of the years he'd spent futilely trying to prove Traugott's corruption.

"There were people who made themselves comfortable with silk sheets to sleep in... Whatever the Jews brought with them. With the traveling Poles there was nothing to be found. But the Hungarians, we knew, had big bacon", Traugott said.

"Why did you take it?"

"It belonged to the State. The Jews had to hand it in."

"Were there any grounds for that?"

"The Jews didn't need it anymore", Traugott stated matter-of-factly.

And then it came to Morgen. There was one final line of attack that remained available to him.

"What was your relationship with Adriana Zöbel?"

Traugott hadn't expected that and remained silent.

"The woman I believe you called *neunzehnhunderteinundsiebzig*?" Morgen prompted him unhelpfully.

"I know who she is", Traugott replied angrily. Morgen smiled. Good. That blow had scored a hit. "There isn't much to say."

Morgen smiled again, but this time in mockery. "I beg to differ", he said. "Just a few moments ago fraülein Zöbel testified that she entertained a very special relationship with you. I wish to hear your side of the story."

Traugott was staring at Gundula, who was staring back at him: if he confirmed what Adriana had said, he might well save his own life, but in the process lose his wife and daughter; on the other hand, if he contradicted her and denied everything, he'd annihilate her credibility as a witness and then he might hang.

Morgen was clearly baiting Traugott. Sensing the peril, Rolf Lüdwig demanded what reason anyone had to doubt Adriana's testimony, but his feeble objection was quickly batted aside.

"The witness will answer the question", judge Rcisenleitner said.

So Traugott closed his eyes and found himself standing on the platform at Auschwitz, alone with a train that should have been completely empty was wasn't.

"I heard a sound", he said. "At first I wasn't sure what to make of it. It sounded like... like the wind whistling in the silence. I tried to ignore it, since I thought for sure I was alone. But then it came again. A moaning, like ghouls and ghosts. And..."

He paused before continuing. "And I was afraid."

Morgen snickered. "You were *afraid*? You? A mighty SS... *afraid*?"

Traugott nodded. "Auschwitz was a very sinister place", he said coldly. "But the sturmbannführer already knows this. He graced us with his presence often enough."

Traugott was gratified to see Morgen drop his gaze for a second, as though he'd taken a punch to the gut.

He grinned.

Had the judge known of Morgen's Nazi past? Maybe. Probably. And if he hadn't, well, let him find out now. Hell, let it be revealed to the whole world that Morgen had been fully aware of what was going on at Auschwitz. Let it learn that the man now trying to send him to the gallows was former SS judge and lawyer Georg Konrad Morgen, *sturmbannführer* Georg Konrad Morgen for the love of God, and then let it wonder why this man so conveniently now found himself on the right side of the law.

"Continue", judge Reisenleitner ordered.

Traugott took a deep breath. His eyes left Gundula and went to Adriana, who placidly stared back at him.

"So I pulled out my sidearm and investigated, and that's when I found her", he explained, lifting his chin slightly toward Adriana. "She was so covered in filth from head to toe I could barely see her in the darkness of the boxcar. But then she spoke."

"What did she say?" Morgen asked, having regained most of his composure after being publicly exposed.

"She kept repeating the same name", Traugott said. "Aaron. She kept calling out for Aaron."

Adriana's mask of cold indifference immediately imploded. Her eyes filled with tears, her lower lip began to tremble and her hands to shake.

She hadn't known.

"Who's Aaron?" Morgen demanded.

"I believe Aaron was her brother", he said. "Her *late* brother."

"And you know this... how?"

"She told me."

Morgen smiled. Traugott had just confirmed, indirectly, that he'd entertained a relationship of some intimacy with Adriana; otherwise, how might he be privy to such knowledge?

"Then what did you do?"

Traugott smirked. "I tried to kill her", he said, as if it were the most natural thing in the world. Adriana's eyes grew wide and her mouth opened slightly. That, too, she hadn't know. "I fired a round at her head."

He paused again. "I really meant to kill her. I was that angry, that hateful. But I missed, even though I never miss. Maybe that's what fate is all about. Had I killed her, would we all be here today?"

"How much longer do you think he'll be?"

Rolf Lüdwig had just returned from conferring with Traugott and his wife, who had politely, but firmly, requested to be left alone while they awaited the judge's decision.

He glanced at his watch and grimaced. It had been almost three hours since Traugott's testimony had ended and judge Reisenleitner had retired to his chambers to consider the evidence before him. He should have ruled by now. After all, they were only here to decide whether grounds were sufficient for the actual trial to be held, not to seal Traugott's fate.

She scooted over reluctantly and he sat on the bench next to her. After all that had just transpired inside the courtroom, she simply could not bring herself to liking this naive young man who still believed in the ideal of justice.

"I have known judge Reisenleitner for a while now and he's a great believer in the expediency of justice", he said. "I'm sure he'll summon us soon."

They'd been here all day and over the past few hours Adriana had ridden a roller-coaster of emotions through a long-ago time that fought with every ounce of strength it possessed to keep from being forgotten.

In her mind, its voice as clear as the sound of a chiming bell slicing through the morning mist, she could hear its taunts.

You are me and I am you.

Without you I am nothing and without me you are nothing.

I will never be forgotten for I will never allow you to forget me.

Shut your eyes at night and I will be there to bid you sweet dreams.

Open them when the sun rises and there I shall still be to bid you good day.

I am the nightmare that doesn't dissipate with the new day.

I am the darkness that kills the light.

I am the howling wind that snuffs out the candle of hope.

I am the...

She shook herself out of her reverie. This was it. This was the final chapter, the last verse, the ultimate song... whatever you wanted to call it. Before the end of today it would be all over, once and for all. She'd told them everything, and then some, and Morgen, despite his best efforts, had barely made a dent. Her testimony was all that really mattered, and she'd provided Reisenleitner with all the reasons in the world to set Traugott free.

"You lied to me", she accused him.

Lüdwig sighed, leaned back and stretched his crossed legs out in front of him. He took his time before answering.

"I did, but keep in mind that I have but a single purpose here today", he finally said.

"To see Traugott go free?"

"Not in the least", he replied wearily. "As I told you before, my sole intention is to make sure he is treated justly and fairly. What happens beyond that is not up to me. Or to you, for that matter."

"Justly and fairly", she repeated slowly. "So the end justifies the means? Even if that means tricking and exploiting a poor woman who's clearly lost her mind?"

He seemed hurt by her words.

"Your sister was a willing participant", he said. "She came here of her own accord. Rest assured she was not coerced."

"Oh please, I'm sure you didn't have to twist her arm", Adriana snickered. "But how could she possibly pass up the chance to speak at the trial of the man who, the way she sees it, killed her children?"

Lüdwig remained silent and just stared blankly ahead.

"You took advantage of her, and that's something you can't deny", Adriana went on angrily. "You tricked her, pure and simple. So do what all lawyers do and play with words all you like. We both know what you did, and that will forever lie between you and your conscience. Traugott and you really make a fine pair."

The hallway was crowded with people hurriedly coming and going. She watched them as they walked by, young and old, men and women, and tried to read their faces. Was this one happy? This one preoccupied? That other one angry? Who could tell? People only show what they want others to see; the essence of what they are remains safely hidden behind locked doors and drawn curtains.

We are all of us nothing but actors faking our way through this gigantic, galactic play that we call life.

Still she tried to imagine what their lives were like, away from this place. You, young lady, have you children yet? Do you want some? How many? And you, young man, you look like the type that secretly prefers men over women... am I right? Come on, you can tell me, no one will ever know. And you, do your parents still live? Have you someone special in your life? What is your greatest dream, and have you the courage to chase it? Your greatest fear, and have you the courage to fight it?

Each human on the face of the planet, Adriana had learned, was a book whose contents you could barely guess, and each had a life that was just as rich and complex as your own.

Someone snickered far to her left, at the very end of the hallway. A few of the young men from the public gallery had come down one floor and, to their unending amusement, found her. They were watching her and pointing at her, and as soon as they saw that she had noticed them, one bent over and his friend mimicked a sex act on him, reproducing what they imagined Traugott had done to her. Then the first one got down on his knees, turned around and began tugging at his friend's pants, clearly begging him to do it to him some more.

Adriana watched them coldly, but Rolf Lüdwig was of a different mind.

"They shouldn't be here", he said angrily. "The public is to remain on the floor above. This floor is exclusively for court personnel and witnesses. I'll have the security guard expel them."

"You should go talk to them", she ironized. "Maybe they too would like to testify on Traugott's behalf. They could tell the judge what an inspiration and a role model he is to them."

"That is entirely unfair and uncalled for", he retorted immediately.

He got up, really meaning to have the young hooligans expelled, but she caught his sleeve and forced him to sit back down.

"Don't be an even bigger idiot than you already are", she said. "The guard is probably the one who told them I was here. They're but young fools who know nothing of the world. They think they know everything, but in truth their ignorance is so vast that it gives rise to bottomless stupidity. They wouldn't have survived a single day at Auschwitz. I find them utterly..."

She stopped in mid-sentence when the door to the courtroom finally opened and the clerk announced that judge Reisenleitner was requesting their presence – which could only mean that he'd made up his mind and was ready to announce his decision.

Despite herself, Adriana needed a moment to catch her breath and settle her mind before she could stand up. Lüdwig chivalrously offered her his hand, but she almost rudely waved it away and entered the courtroom right on his heels.

All the main actors, except for the judge, were already in place

Traugott was seated in his previous spot and Lüdwig went to join him. Morgen was on the other side of the room from them. The blond woman, whose name Adriana still did not know, was also seated in her previous spot, in the front row, still with her back turned to her.

And at the back of the room, having apparently not moved a single inch in the past three hours, still sat poor, mad, deranged Tatiyana, who seemed barely aware of her surroundings. She had both hands stuck deep under her armpits and seemed to be hugging herself as she rocked slowly back and forth with her eyes closed.

Adriana rejoined Teresia, who immediately grabbed her hand and wouldn't let go.

Same as before, a court official demanded in a ringing voice that they stand in silence while Doctor Edgar Reisenleitner took his seat on the bench. The little man entered and scurried to his chair, more mouse-like than ever. Adriana tried to read his face, his body language, but he gave nothing away. Only when he spoke would they find out what was to be Traugott's fate.

But Reisenleitner was not to be hurried. The next ten minutes he spent shuffling papers, occasionally pulling a sheet from the lot and reading it before putting it back. He almost seemed to have forgotten their presence and only when the young men in the public gallery grew noisy and agitated did he finally glance up and signal that he was ready to render his decision.

"This matter is not an easy one to arbitrate", he said. "Many years have passed and the events in question took place under extraordinary circumstances. The world was a much different place then and that, crucially, must be taken into account. It would be unfair to pass judgment after examining those events through our modern eyes."

Which meant what, exactly?

"Having said that, on the basis of what this tribunal heard today, it seems possible, and perhaps even likely, that crimes were committed - crimes that defy the passage of time, acts that were criminal then and would still be criminal today."

He paused again.

"But this tribunal was not tasked today with determining the culpability or the innocence of herr Mattias Traugott with regards to those acts. It was tasked with determining whether herr Traugott should be made to answer for them at a later date."

"So let us review briefly all that we've heard today."

First there had been the testimony of one Lajb Panub, who had told a harrowing tale of running for his life through Auschwitz and of seeking desperate refuge in a mound of coats inside the Kanada warehouse, where someone had shot at him, and where he'd later been shot and almost killed.

No one knew for sure, however, who had fired any of those shots.

A few young men in the public gallery cheered.

Then had come the testimony of herr doktor Friedrich Lasch, the chemical engineer who had made it amply clear that no one should ever, under any circumstances, inhale Zyklon-B gas and who had explained in excruciating and blood-chilling detail the atrocious fate that befell those who did. It was also a well-known and undisputed fact that Zyklon-B had been used at Auschwitz to exterminate prisoners.

But where was the link between the suspect and the use of Zyklon-B? No one had testified to seeing him use it. Had herr Traugott known that Zyklon-B was used at Auschwitz? How could he have not? Had he not confessed as much during his testimony?, the judge reminded them. He had admitted, for all to hear, that he had witnessed inmates be gassed to death at Auschwitz.

But did that make him complicit? Should he be held responsible, let alone punished, for the actions of others? Had he not proclaimed himself revolted by what he'd seen, and had he not repeatedly requested a transfer out of Auschwitz?

More cheers, this time more vigorous and numerous, from the public gallery.

And then, of course, there had been the riveting testimony of Adriana Zöbel, who had held them spellbound with her tale of improbable survival in large parts thanks to the intercession of one Mattias Traugott.

Fraulein Zöbel, the judge reminded them, had not implicated the suspect in any crime of any nature. Quite to the contrary, according to her testimony, untersturmführer Traugott, at immense personal risk, had run without hesitation into the hell of a gas chamber to save the witness' sister, thus coming within an inch of losing his own life.

At that was but the beginning of it. The suspect had also saved the witness' life on numerous occasions, including when she'd willingly helped four inmates escape and when she'd found herself gripped by Josef Mengele's talons, not to mention when he'd rescued her from a brothel where, had it not been for his intervention, she'd certainly have suffered a fate perhaps worse than death.

It was all over. Adriana closed her eyes and tried to wall off the outside world as judge Reisenleitner repeated the rest of her testimony, how she'd been nicknamed Queen Esther by the other women, how Traugott had sent Magrita to Doctor Ada at her request, how...

The magistrate went on for several more minutes, but all Adriana heard was a droning sound.

When judge Reisenleitner's voice finally came back into focus, he was saying, "... so this tribunal is left with no other possible conclusion..."

This was it. A moment 30-plus years in the making had finally come. With the next few words Traugott's fate would be sealed and he'd walk out of here a free man, hand in hand with that blond woman, and they'd go celebrate together and then live long and happy lives and have many children before finally dying in each other's arms fifty years frow now.

And all of it, *all of it*, because of what she'd said.

"I hereby declare..."

The soul-scorching wail of a banshee arose from the back of the room. Low and tenuous at first, almost imperceptible, but then louder and louder, until it seemed to fill the whole room. It seemed to go on endlessly, as though the being from which it emanated need not take a breath, and when it peaked, its intensity was such that the two policemen guarding the door through which Traugott had entered whipped out their sidearms and swept the room, looking to identify its source and terminate it.

The gray, ethereal shape of the banshee entered the far reaches of Adriana's field of vision and she stood to bar its way - but she did so instinctively, without a single conscious thought, as though *something* or *someone* had taken control of her limbs and was moving them for her.

"Tatiyana, no, stop!"

But the banshee wouldn't be deterred. Not here, not on this day. No, it wouldn't be denied its destiny.

Tatiyana, perhaps aided by the fact that her sister was still slightly off-balance after standing so suddenly, or perhaps imbued of the mysterious might of the mad, shoved her out of the way with a power that belied her size. She placed a hand squarely in the center of her sister's chest, between the breasts, cocked her elbow back and, without even stopping, just... *pushed*. Adriana fell over backward, tripping over her own feet and almost crushing Teresia who moved out of the way just in time, and got the wind knocked out of her when she landed in the narrow space between her bench and the one in front.

Then came three screams.

The first, strangely wet and garbled, lasted but a fraction of a second.

It was followed by several gunshots that echoed in the empty courtroom.

The second scream, this one of pain and shock, came immediately after.

And then the third and final scream, like that of a tormented soul being plunged into Hell's deepest lake of fire.

"NOOOOOOOOOOOOOOOOOOOOOOOO!"

Still dizzy and short of breath, Adriana somehow regained her feet with Teresia's help and beheld the scene in front of her.

Immediately to her right, in the middle of the center aisle, lay the inert body of her sister Tatiyana. Dead. She had been shot at least twice; one bullet had pierced her left shoulder, but another had entered under her right eye and exited through the back of her skull, killing her instantly.

Next to Tatiyana, drenched in blood, lay the body of the blond woman. She was bleeding profusely from the neck and at first Adriana thought that she, too, had been shot. She still lived, barely, and was desperately trying to breathe. Her hands were wrapped around her neck and blood poured endlessly through her fingers as she gasped for air.

Traugott ran to her and cradled her in his arms, slipping in her blood and almost falling.

"Nonononononononononono!", he cried.

The blond woman's hands fell limply away from her neck and she closed her eyes.

And Adriana saw, protruding from her flesh, the handle of a pair of scissors.

"Gundula! Gundula!", Traugott shouted as he rocked her body. "Stay with me my love, please stay with me!"

Gundula had seen Tatiyana hurtling down the aisle, rushing at her defenseless husband's back with a sharp metallic object raised high above her head, and she had sacrificed her life to save his – the scissors, which Tatiyana had meant to plunge between Traugott's shoulder blades, had instead severed her carotid artery and pierced her trachea.

The wound was fatal, and after a few seconds, she died in her husband's arms.

Traugott felt the life flow out of his wife's body and knew he'd lost her forever. He began sobbing uncontrollably and held her against him with all the strength he could muster, as though trying to inject some of his lifeforce into her to bring her back.

The courtroom was eerily silent, and only his sobs could be heard. Teresia knelt next to him and placed her arm around his shoulders, but he was completely oblivious to her presence.

After a moment he raised his head and looked at Adriana.

"Tell me what you see", he implored her through his tears, his voice strangled by grief.

But she could only stare back at him, speechless and helpless, as the blood that had spurted from Gundula's neck slowed to a trickle.

The circle was complete. It had all began with a death, that of Aaron, and it all ended with another, that of Gundula. Adriana has never forgotten the sight of Aaron's tiny soul rising from his body after his death, but on this day, she didn't see anything.

"Tell me what you see", he said again when she didn't reply. But this time she heard a voice from thirty years ago, a voice from Auschwitz, a voice that sometimes echoed dangerously with a low growl that warned to thread carefully.

But still she remained defiantly silent.

"TELL ME WHAT YOU SEE", he roared at her "FOR THE LOVE OF GOD TELL ME WHAT YOU SEE."

She met his stare, one on one, equal to equal, one last time.

And standing there, her eyes locked on his, she plunged down those two bottomless pits of sorrow. They sucked her deep inside him, past the confines of his soul to the very core of his being, and inside the furnace of pain that burned there the past three decades were incinerated and turned into ashes that were then blown away by the wind.

So finally she spoke.

"I see a man", she whispered.

Then Adriana took a few steps back, away from him, turned around and walked out of the courtroom.

EPILOGUE

Thirty years later, maybe more

Somewhere in Israel

The ground rumbled, and the boy froze.

His grandmother tightened her grip on his hand softly and looked down at him with a benevolent smile. His fascination with trucks never ceased to amuse her. The bigger the better, and this one was *huge*! It roared by them in a cloud of dust, creating a small earthquake, and was gone.

The boy looked at it go even after it had disappeared, and he might have stayed there for a few eons - rooted to the pavement, mouth hanging open, eyes the size of saucers - had his grandmother not gently tugged him along.

"Come on, Aaron," she said. "You're friends are waiting."

The boy snapped out of his vehicular reverie, smiled up at his beloved grandmother, and began skipping along merrily next to her. Yes, he *absolutely* loved trucks, but he loved it almost as much when she took him to the park – where his friends and him would usually hijack the sandbox from the girls to play at being truck drivers and heavy machinery operators, obviously.

"Go, play nice," she said a minute later. She let go of his hand and he took off like a rocket to join a group of little boys who hailed him like a returning Roman conqueror.

That made her heart swell with love and joy.

Her grandson was the sweetest, nicest, most considerate boy you could imagine. He always found a way to make those around him happy, and already his friends trusted him to arbitrate their disputes with Solomonic wisdom – even though he would only turn five in a couple of months.

It was almost enough to restore her belief in God that such a human being could exist, that she could feel so much love both for him and from him.

Almost.

She had been moved to tears when Rita, the youngest of her six daughters, had decided to name her first-born after an uncle she'd never known, but whom she knew to still occupy a large place in her mother's heart.

How could this Aaron have turned out any differently, considering who is namesake had been?

"Excuse me, but are you Adriana Zöbel?" someone asked gently behind her.

She jumped a bit and turned around. She came face to face with a bespectacled young man of about 30. He had the curliest, thickest brown hair permitted by law, beautiful hazel eyes and the lean, muscular build of a swimmer, but was otherwise entirely unremarkable.

He looked harmless enough, but being approached by strangers asking her to identify herself still made her wary, even after all these years.

"I don't know you," she said.

"My name is Thomas M. Williams," he immediately replied. "The 'M' stands for Marianne, my mother's name. And I've come all the way from America to find you."

"I still don't know you," she repeated.

Williams could tell, no pun intended, that this would be no walk in the park. He had expected her to be wary, for that he had been prepared, but she was almost hostile, and that threw him somewhat off balance.

Recovering, he gestured at a vacant bench nearby, from where he knew she could keep an eye on her grandson.

"Please, could we sit? I'll but take a moment of your time."

She hesitated, before nodding curtly and allowing him to take her elbow as they made their way to the bench. Her pride resented the gentlemanly gesture, but her arthritic knees welcomed it.

"So you've told me your name and where you're from, Mr Williams," she said immediately. "But you've not said why you've come all this way to find *me*."

"I have not, but I'll explain if you bear with me for a moment. You see, Mrs Zöbel, I am a writer, and I earn a living telling the best stories I can find," he began.

"Do you now."

"I do. And I recently found myself on assignment in Vienna for an American magazine, boring through tons of documents and files hunting for something in which *this* instantly made me lose all interest."

He handed her a sheaf of papers. She looked at him, grabbed the papers and began to read. She stopped after the first few lines.

It was a transcript of her testimony at Traugott's trial.

She handed him back the papers and clasped her hands in her lap to keep them from shaking. She was having trouble breathing.

"You are *that* Adriana Zöbel, aren't you?" he asked needlessly. She didn't respond, nor did she need to.

"I must say... It left me completely breathless," Williams said. "But this was only the starting point. I have spent the past two months researching this story, and I became addicted. I have never, ever heard of anything so amazing. For a Nazi to fall in love with..."

"You really don't need to tell me about my life, Mr Williams. I was there. I lived it. Or rather, I lived *through* it," she said with more anger than she truly felt. She fixed her gaze on Aaron in the distance and tried to regain control of her emotions.

"Yes, of course," he said, seeming a bit flustered. "As I've just said, I spent the past few weeks completely immersing myself in your story and that of herr Traugott. I read all I could find and spoke to as many people as I could locate. Since I was in Austria I tracked herr Traugott down, but..."

She caught her breath. So the old bastard still lived!

"I almost convinced him to speak with me, but in the end his wife intervened and chased me out of their house and told me never to return again," he explained.

"So that's why you're here," she said. "Because *he* wouldn't talk to you."

"No, of course not," Williams defended himself. "Since I was already in Vienna, when I discovered that herr Traugott lived nearby, it was only logical for me to go to him first."

"Of course, I apologize," Adriana said. "You must appreciate, Mr Williams, how difficult this is for me. I sometimes feel as though I'll never be allowed to forget those awful years, no matter how much time passes."

She looked at him directly in the eyes.

"You think my story is wonderful and romantic?" she asked with a touch of irony. "Let met correct you, it was nothing of the kind, Mr Williams. My story is a story of survival and deceit, nothing more. I did what I had to do to survive, and more than anything that meant deceiving untersturmführer Traugott."

She paused again and he waited for her to go on.

"You think he helped me because he suddenly felt guilty?" she snickered. "Or because he suddenly realized that *this... was... all... so... wrong*?"

She raised her hands, palms up, and drew circles that encompassed the park around them as she spoke, but what she was really showing him was Auschwitz and the ovens and thousands of the living dead.

"*Please.* I saw him commit some of the worst atrocities you can imagine, and I testified as much. You think I don't know what he wanted from me? Oh I knew, believe me: he wanted what all men want from all women. But he never got it. *Never.*"

Another pause. In the distance, Aaron was busy directing his friends in the sandbox. They ran left and right, obeying his every order, but what exactly it was that they were doing was known only to them.

"I never led him on, not for one second, I never promised him anything," Adriana resumed. "But despite everything I said and did, he wouldn't be deterred. He kept hoping, and I never had the courage to extinguish his hope once and for all. I never had the courage to trust that I could survive that awful place without him, on my own. I took all I could take from him – my life, my sister's life, the lives of so many others – and in return he got *nothing*. *Nothing*, you hear? So you see, there really is nothing romantic about this, this is not the Auschwitz version of Romeo and Juliet. He wanted to bed me and I wanted to survive. In the end, I got what I wanted, but he didn't. Period."

Williams waited to see if she would go on.

"I'm not sure that's entirely true, Mrs Zöbel, at least from his point of view," he said when she didn't. "From what I've learned, I believe herr Traugott's feelings for you went beyond a simple carnal desire. I believe that he truly cared for you, that perhaps he even loved you."

That struck home. This young man was right, no matter how hard she denied it – and no matter how hard she'd tried to forget it over the years.

Yes, Traugott had loved her, deeply and sincerely. But how does one reconcile having been loved by a monster? Even worse, how does one reconcile having once entertained feelings, though certainly not love, for this self-same monster? For that was what had truly happened back then: Traugott had loved her, and in the end his love had sown deep within her soul... *something*... something that had kept her alive through the worst days, a glowing coal buried under cold ashes, a treasure chest to which only she possessed the key.

But that had been then, and this was today. And these days, that coal no longer glowed and the treasure chest had rotted away. These days, words spoken sixty years earlier and distorted by the passage of time sounded like the words of a man telling her what she'd needed to hear to spread her thighs willingly.

So she puffed angrily, as if she had never heard anything so ridiculous in her entire life.

"Here I was, having a perfectly fine day at the park with my grandson, and then you come along, and all of a sudden I'm no longer Grannie Addie, all of a sudden I'm once again *neunzehnhunderteinundsiebzig*."

"Your Auschwitz number," he said.

She resisted the urge to cover her left forearm with her right hand, as she always did, and glanced at him sideways. "You've done your homework," she conceded. "What do you want from me, Mr Williams?"

"It's very simple, Mrs Zöbel: I wish to tell your story."

"The answer is no, Mr Williams," she replied immediately. "I've absolutely no wish to relive those years yet again. Twice, once for real and once during *his* trial, is already two times too many for a single lifetime."

He opened his mouth to argue his point, but she cut him off. "My answer is no, Mr Williams," she repeated. "I'm terribly sorry you came all this way for nothing, but I'll not change my mind. So I'll ask you to kindly be on your way and leave me to my grandson."

Williams sat there in silence for a few seconds before getting up. He bowed respectfully to her, thanked her for her time and began to walk away, wondering where he was supposed to go from here.

"Why?" she called after him, after he'd gone a dozen steps.

He stopped, smiled and turned around slowly. "Why what, Mrs Zöbel?"

She stared at him for a moment, still unsure she could trust him, still unsure she *wanted* to trust him.

"Why do you care?" she explained. "All these things... these events... happened such a long time ago, before you were even born. They mean absolutely nothing to you. So why do you care about my life, Mr Williams? Why do you wish to tell my story?"

He walked back toward her slowly, treading as carefully as if he were approaching a spitting cobra about to strike. His choice of words, he knew, would probably seal his fate.

"Because your story is the story of mankind," he began. "The story of mankind is a tapestry of countless individual stories, of lives lived, of births and deaths and triumphant victories and crushing defeats and obstacles overcome and enemies vanquished. And each time one of these stories is lost to the darkness of time, we lose a thread in that tapestry, and it becomes that much less complete, that much less vibrant."

He paused and looked around at the playing children. He pointed at them. "Each one of these children is weaving its own infinitesimal part of that tapestry. They've only just begun, and who's to say how long it'll take them to finish? Who's to say what image they'll contribute to the mosaic of humanity? You are one of the lucky ones, Mrs Zöbel. You've been weaving yours for almost 80 years, and I daresay your work is... different, shall we say? I don't want it to be lost when you go. That is why I care."

Adriana stared ahead without blinking for such a long time that Williams began to worry. Was she having a seizure of some kind? In truth, Adriana was replaying in her mind the movie of her life, revisiting each scene and asking herself whether he might be right. Was this something the world needed to know? Was this something that needed to be preserved for eternity?

Finally, she blinked and trained on him a gaze that burned with such intensity that it felt like a physical blow and he took a step back.

"If I am to tell you my story, Mr Williams, I must start in the beginning," she said. "And my story begins with my little brother Aaron, who had gone to find our lost cat."

THE END

"And no matter how much I relate, and how much my friends will relate - it will never be enough, there is no such thing, no paper, and no words that could describe what we went through, that we're still alive, and passing this on, to our dismay, to generations that are living this to this day. And it's still not enough, and it will never be enough, but when we are no longer here, so that something will remain - we owe it to those saints that went through such a hell as that and are no longer here with us."

— Helena Citrónová

NOTES
(HISTORICAL AND OTHERWISE)

This novel was inspired by the mind-boggling relationship – if one can call it that – that developed between Helena Citrƒnovƒ (also known as Zipora Tehori and Adriana Tzitron; Adriana Zƒbel in the novel) and *SS-Unterscharführer* Franz Wunsch (or Wunch; *SS-Untersturmführer* Mattias Traugott), from the time of Helena's arrival at Auschwitz in 1942 until the camp was liberated by the Russian Army in January 1945.

Most of the events it relates – such as Adriana's terrifying encounter with the murderous doctor Josef Mengele – are rooted in fact, while others are pure fiction. For instance, Adriana never served in Auschwitz's brothel and Otto Mƒckel – Traugott's archenemy – never existed (but someone just like him certainly did). A guard (though obviously not Mƒckel) was indeed burned alive in the ovens by the sonderkommando who later destroyed the crematorium with homemade grenades.

Traugott's trial was freely inspired by that of Oskar Groenig, the actual "accountant of Auschwitz". Many testimonies included in this novel are in fact excerpts from testimonies heard during Groenig's trial.

Helena eventually settled in Israel, where she died well past the age of 80 after raising a numerous and loving family. Anyone wishing to read her firsthand account of her time at Auschwitz should email Leah at Yad Vashem, at leah.teichthal@yadvashem.org.il.

In this regard, I must absolutely acknowledge the invaluable contribution of Gili Loftus, who translated a 60-page document from Hebrew into English – all for a batch of homemade brownies. I can only wish that all those whose assistance I sought in bringing this tale to the world – including those individuals and organizations whose mission it allegedly is to make sure the Holocaust is never forgotten – had been as selfless, as generous and as friendly as she was.

Thanks to my buddy Klaus, who remembered me more 25 years later. Without him, this story would have been radically different – and not in a good way. Thanks also to Mrs Marilyn Barlow for entrusting with me a veritable treasure trove of information amassed by her late father, Auschwitz survivor Dennis Urstein.

As for Franz Wunsch, he essentially vanished after his trial for war crimes in the 1970s. It is simply known that he settled in Austria, where he married and worked as a salesman. He passed away in 2009, one month shy of his 87th birthday, without having ever spoken publicly about his past – or about the woman who, by at least one account, allowed him to reclaim part of his humanity.

Printed in Poland
by Amazon Fulfillment
Poland Sp. z o.o., Wrocław